mept

"A clever plot coupled with a first-rate husband-and-wife detective team make for a sweet, sweet combination that's hard to beat."

—*Monterey Herald* on *Sweet, Sweet Poison*

"Wilhelm's *Sweet, Sweet Poison* is both a contemporary and graceful tale, woven as much around the weld of modern marriage as around the warp of heinous crime."

—Austin *American-Statesman*

"Get very comfortable before you start Kate Wilhelm's new novel, because you won't be able to put it down."

—Roanoke *Times & World News* on *The Dark Door*

"Charlie and Constance are something special: middle-aged, decidedly unglamorous, and sharing the kind of subtly conveyed emotional intimacy that is the antithesis of hard-boiled."

—*Booklist*

"Author Wilhelm is considered a grand dame of science fiction, but, as she proves with this latest Meiklejohn mystery, she is also a shining star when writing murder in the present."

—Charleston *News and Courier*

"Kate Wilhelm always knows how to make the world symbolize the inner self, how to suggest psychological conditions from narrative events. [Kate Wilhelm] brings delight both through fine feeling and fine writing."

—*Los Angeles Times*

"Wilhelm is a master. . . . Her plots are taut, compelling, and insightful."

—*Library Journal*

"One of the masters of psychological fiction in America."

—*San Francisco Chronicle*

"An outstandingly fluent, sensitive writer, Kate Wilhelm is able to really get inside her characters' heads; she makes those small observations of behavior and emotion that go further toward defining human psychology than all the poetry and virtuosity in the world."

—*Minneapolis Star-Tribune*

THE CASEBOOK OF

Constance and Charlie

VOLUME 2

The Deepest Water
(forthcoming)
No Defense (2000)
*The Casebook of Constance
and Charlie, Volume I*
(1999)
Defense for the Devil (1999)
The Good Children (1998)
Malice Prepense (1996)
A Flush of Shadows (1995)
The Best Defense (1994)
Justice for Some (1993)
Seven Kinds of Death (1992)
Naming the Flowers (1992)
And the Angels Sing (1992)
Death Qualified (1991)
State of Grace (1991)
Sweet, Sweet Poison (1990)
Cambio Bay (1990)
Children of the Wind (1989)
Smart House (1989)
The Dark Door (1988)
Crazy Time (1988)
The Hamlet Trap (1987)
The Hills Are Dancing (with
Richard Wilhelm) (1986)
Huysman's Pets (1986)
Welcome, Chaos (1983)
Oh, Susannah! (1982)

A Sense of Shadow (1981)
Listen, Listen (1981)
Better than One (with Damon
Knight) (1980)
Juniper Time (1979)
*Somerset Dreams and Other
Fictions* (1978)
Fault Lines (1977)
*Where Late the Sweet Birds
Sang* (1976)
The Clewiston Test (1976)
The Infinity Box (1975)
City of Cain (1974)
Margaret and I (1971)
Abyss (1971)
Year of the Cloud (with
Theodore L. Thomas)
(1970)
Let the Fire Fall (1969)
*The Downstairs Room and
Other Speculative Fiction*
(1968)
The Killer Thing (1967)
The Nevermore Affair (1966)
The Clone (with Theodore L.
Thomas) (1965)
The Mile-Long Spaceship
(1963)
More Bitter than Death (1963)

THE CASEBOOK OF
Constance and Charlie

VOLUME 2

Kate Wilhelm

ST. MARTIN'S MINOTAUR
NEW YORK

"Torch Song" first appeared in *A Flush of Shadows: Five Novellas*.
"Christ's Tears" first appeared in *Ellery Queen's Mystery Magazine*, April 1996.
"An Imperfect Gift" first appeared in *Ellery Queen's Mystery Magazine*, August 1999.

Design by Nancy Resnick

ISBN 0-312-25378-8

First Edition: January 2000

10 9 8 7 6 5 4 3 2 1

Contents

THE CASEBOOK OF

Constance and Charlie

VOLUME 2

The Dark Door

1

June 1979. Carson Danvers knew he was being overly cautious, getting insurance quotes for all four places he was considering, but he had time, and it was better to be cautious before the fact than have cause for regrets afterward. Although River House was fourth on his list, he and Elinor had already decided this was the one they really wanted. Half an hour out of Washington, D.C., through lush countryside with gentle hills and woods, a tiny village a few miles past the inn, it was perfect. He would keep the name, he had already decided. River House, a fine gourmet restaurant for the discriminating. He glanced at Elinor's profile, caught the suggestion of a smile on her lips, and felt his own grin broaden. In the backseat his son, Gary, chatted easily with John Loesser. Gary was seventeen, ready for Yale in the fall; it was time to make the change if they were ever to do it. He suppressed the urge to laugh and sing; John Loesser would never understand.

Carson pulled off the Virginia state road onto a winding blacktop driveway and slowed down to navigate the curves, several of them before the old inn came into sight. The grounds were neglected, of course—rhododendrons thirty feet high, blackberry brambles, sumac—and the building had the windows boarded up. But even so, its air of regal affluence was unmistakable. Three stories high, with a wide antebellum porch and beautifully carved pillars that reached to the third level, it bespoke the graciousness of the century past.

"We'd keep the upper levels for our own living quarters," he said over his shoulder to John Loesser. "A main dining room downstairs, several smaller rooms for private dinners, a lounge, that sort of thing. I'll have to do a lot of remodeling, of course, but cheaper than trying to build at today's prices."

"If it's structurally sound," John Loesser said in his precise way.

He did not have stars in his eyes, and that was all to the good, Carson thought. One of them should stay practical, add up the pennies, add in insurance costs. That was John Loesser's department, assessing the insurability of the place. He stopped his Buick at the front entrance. As soon as they left the air-conditioned car, the heat of late June in Virginia assailed them. Carson pulled off his coat, and after a moment John Loesser did also. Elinor was sensibly dressed in a cotton shift and sandals, her legs bare, and Gary had on shorts and a tank top. Only the businessmen, Carson thought with some amusement, went through the motions of suits and ties. And after he bought River House, made it the restaurant he had long dreamed of owning, he promised himself never to wear a necktie again in his life, or a coat in the summer.

"I have flashlights," he said, opening the trunk of the Buick. "I loosened some of the boards on the windows last week, but the basement's like a cave." He handed John Loesser a large flashlight, took another for himself, and saw that the other man was staring at two rifles also in the trunk. "Gary's going to get in some practice while we're going over the building." He closed the trunk and tossed the keys to his son.

Elinor watched the three men remove some of the window boards, then go on to the next bunch and take them down. How alike they were, she thought, surprised, all three over six feet, all blond. Of course, Gary was still somewhat frail-looking, having shot upward over twelve inches in the past year; it might take him three or four years to fill in the frame he was constructing for himself. Seventeen, she found herself marveling. A sharp image superimposed itself before her eyes, eclipsing for a second the three men: an image of herself walking with Carson, with Gary in the middle swinging from their hands, laughing. Yesterday. Ten years, twelve years ago. She shook her head and turned to the front door of the inn, put the key in the padlock, and opened it. When she entered, she left the door wide open to admit air and more light.

On one side was a wide sculpted staircase sweeping up in a graceful curve. They would have a women's lounge up there; permit the customers to fantasize briefly of being the lady of the house, making a grand entrance to a crowded, suddenly hushed ballroom, glittering with the wealth of the Virginia aristocracy. Elinor smiled to herself. That was her fantasy. The area to the right had held the registration desk; nothing was there now. A closed door led to a narrow hallway and small offices. To the left of the entrance stretched a very large room with a centered fireplace built with meticulously matched river stones. She could visualize the palm trees, the velvet-covered lounges and chairs, low, ornately carved tables, brass lamps. . . . Only faded, rose-colored flocked wallpaper remained. She moved through the large open space toward the back of the building. Suddenly she stopped, blinded by a stabbing headache; she groped for the doorway to steady herself.

An overwhelming feeling of disorientation, of dizziness, swept her, made her catch her breath and hold on to the doorframe; her eyes closed hard. The moment passed and she could feel a vein throbbing in her temple, a knife blade of pain behind her right eye. Not now, she moaned to herself, not a migraine now. She opened her eyes cautiously; when the pain did not increase, she began to move again, through a corridor to the rear of the inn. She unlocked another door and threw it wide open, went out to another porch to lean against a railing. She took one very deep breath after another, forcing relaxation on her neck muscles, which had become like iron. Gradually the headache eased, and by the time Carson and John Loesser moved into sight, it was a steady throb, no longer all-demanding.

Carson saw her leaning on the rail and felt a familiar twinge of pleasure. Standing like that, in profile, as trim and as slender as she had been twenty years ago, she looked posed. She looked lovely. "Are you married?" he asked John Loesser.

"My wife died five years ago," Loesser said without expression.

"Oh, sorry." Loesser was already moving on. Carson caught up again. "Here's the back entrance. We'll have a terrace down there, and tables on the porch overlooking the river. The property extends to the bank of the river. I want it to be like a garden, invite strolling, relaxing."

They went through the open back door, on to the kitchen, which would need a complete remodeling, walls to come out, a dumbwaiter to go in. Carson was indicating his plans when John Loesser suddenly grunted and seemed about to fall. He

reached out and caught a cabinet, steadied himself, stood swaying with his eyes shut. By the time Carson got to him, he was
pushing himself away from the cabinet. A film of perspiration
covered his face; he looked waxy and pale. Carson's first
thought was *heart attack*, and with that thought came the fear
men his age, mid-forties, always suffered. Loesser was that age,
too, he knew. He took Loesser's arm.

"Let's go outside, get some air. Are you okay?"

"I'm all right," John Loesser said, pulling free. His voice was
faint; he sounded puzzled, not afraid. "A dizzy spell. Could
there be some gas in here? Bad air?"

Carson looked at him doubtfully. "How? I've been all over
this building three times already. Elinor, Gary, we've been in
every room, and that was with the boards on the windows,
before we were allowed to open it up at all."

Loesser drew in a deep breath, his color back to normal, a
look of irritation the only expression Carson could read. "Whatever it was, it's gone now. I have a bit of a headache, maybe
that's to blame. You understand any figure I come up with is a
ballpark figure, contingent on many other reports. A termite
inspection, for example."

Carson nodded and they wandered slowly throughout the
other rooms on the main floor. Something was different, he
thought suddenly. It was true that he and Elinor and Gary had
prowled through the building three times, but now something
was changed. He felt almost as if something or someone lurked
just out of sight, that if he could swivel his head fast enough,
without warning, he might catch a glimpse of an intruder. He
had had a violent headache ever since their arrival. Pain
throbbed behind his eyes. It was the damn heat, he decided;
maybe a storm was building, the air pressure was low. Or high;
it felt as if the air was compacted, pressing against his head. He
and Loesser went up the wide, curving staircase to the second
floor, where he began to outline the plans for a women's
lounge.

Suddenly he heard Elinor scream, a piercing shriek of terror,
cut off by a gunshot. He turned and raced through the upstairs
hallway to the rear stairs. John Loesser ran toward the stairs
they had just ascended. Before Carson reached the first floor

there was another gunshot that sounded even louder than the first. He tore out to the porch, pounded to the far end of it, and saw Elinor crumpled on the floor.

One of her sandals was gone, he thought distantly. How could that have happened? He touched her face. One eye was open, as blue as the dress twisted about her thighs. The other side of her face was gone. He touched her cheek, whispering her name. He started to gather her up, to lift her, carry her inside, straighten out her dress. . . . From a long way away he heard a man's anguished wail. Angered by the noise, he jerked up, snapped around, and saw his son, Gary, leveling the rifle at him. He was still moving when the gun fired, and fired again. He was flung backward by the momentum, stopped briefly by the porch rail. Then he toppled over it to fall to the thick underbrush below.

He came awake slowly and did not know where he was, why he was sleeping in the shrubbery. He tried to rise and fell back to the ground. Someone sobbed; he listened to hear if the other person would say something. An insect chorus crescendoed. He tried to roll to one side and prop himself up, but found that one of his arms had turned to lead. There was no pain. Something was wrong with his vision; he wiped his eyes with the hand that worked. Sticky. Suddenly he really looked at his hand and saw blood; memory returned, and pain swamped him. He heard the distant sob again and knew this time that he was making the noise. Elinor! Gary! He began to work at pulling himself up, rising first to his knees. Then, fighting dizziness and nausea, he got to his feet. He staggered, fell, and rested before starting again.

Falling, crawling, staggering, pulling himself along with his good hand grasping the brambles and scrub trees, he hauled himself to the building, then up the stairs to the porch, where he collapsed again. After many minutes he started to inch his way to Elinor. The entire end of the porch was awash in blood. Elinor was not there.

A wave of pain took his breath away; he pitched forward and lay still. When he could open his eyes again, he saw her footprints, one shod, one bare. She must have gone for help, he thought clearly, and in his mind the vision of her destroyed face and head swelled, dwindled, and swelled again like a pulse. He forced himself to his feet.

For the next hour he followed the bloody footprints, sometimes on his knees, sometimes staggering on his feet. At the bottom of the curved stairs there was a bigger pool of blood, more prints. He picked up a wallet. Loesser must have dropped it, he thought distantly, the way Elinor lost her sandal. He put the wallet in his pocket and pulled himself up the stairs, resting more and more often now; sometimes he slept a little, woke to hear his own groans. Slowly, he moved on upwards.

They were all around him, he realized during one of his rests. The intruders he had sensed before were still here, everywhere, watching him, surrounding him, pressing against his head, waiting. He came to the rifle and rested by it, moved on. Then the prints stopped. He lay with his cheek on the floor and knew one of the bloody trails was his own. Straight ahead was a closet with an open door; the bloody path ended there. He sighed tiredly and lifted his head, tried to see past a blackness that filled the doorway from top to bottom. Inky blackness, nothing else.

He rested. They were here, everywhere, he thought again, from a great distance. Waiting. Suddenly he jerked awake. Waiting for him to bleed to death. Waiting for him to die! Slowly he began to retrace his trail. He rolled most of the way down the stairs. He found himself at the Buick and fell onto the front seat and rested a long time. It was getting dark. Key, he thought. He had tossed his keys to Gary. Without any thought or plan, he found Elinor's keys in her purse on the passenger seat. He got the car started, and aimed at the state road. When he reached it, he slumped forward and slept.

He heard a soothing voice, felt hands on him, tried to return to the drifting state that was not sleep, but pleasanter because it was dreamless oblivion. The voice persisted.

"Can you hear me? Come on, Mr. Loesser, wake up. You're safe now. You'll be all right. Wake up, Mr. Loesser."

He was being pulled back in spite of himself.

"A little more, Mr. Loesser, then you can sleep again." The

voice changed slightly. "He can hear you and answer if he wants to."

A different voice spoke. "Who shot you, Mr. Loesser?"

He opened his eyes, realized that only one seemed to work, and reached up to feel a bandage that covered most of his face. He remembered being awake earlier, remembered wanting, being denied, a sip of water, being allowed to sleep again.

"Who shot you, Mr. Loesser?" The speaker was out of focus, thin-faced, sad-looking.

"Gary," Carson said and heard it as a croak.

"Did you say Gary? You mean Gary Danvers?"

"Gary," he said again and closed his eye. "My wife—"

"Yes. Your wife? What about your wife?"

"Dead," he said in his strange croaking voice.

The other voice came back, the soothing one. "Go back to sleep now, Mr. Loesser. Your wife died a long time ago. Remember? That was a long time ago."

"What's that all about?" the sad man asked.

"He's confused. Shock, trauma, loss of blood. His wife died in an airplane accident more than five years ago. Let him rest now. You won't get much out of him until the Demerol wears off, anyway."

"Okay. Okay. I'll drop in tomorrow."

Carson Danvers drifted and thought that if he were John Loesser, he would have grieved for his dead wife a long time ago. He slept.

2

Mr. Loesser," Dr. McChesney said, "go back home. Don't hang around here. I can recommend a doctor to oversee your convalescence now. You need to be with friends, relatives, people who know you and care for you. All this brooding about what you might have done is pointless, Mr. Loesser. I've talked to the detectives, and they all agree that there was nothing more. In fact, it was very brave, perhaps even foolhardy, for you to try to help at all."

Carson Danvers sat on the side of his bed. His face was swathed in bandages. A bullet had grazed his cheekbone, had torn away most of the flesh on one side. He would need plastic surgery. His right arm was in a cast. A bullet had gone through his shoulder. His torso was bandaged. They had gone in and removed part of a rib shattered by the third bullet. The rib had deflected it, sent it back outward through a second hole. Except for the plastic surgery, he was repaired, healing, ready to be discharged from the hospital.

Dr. McChesney stood up. "If you decide to stay around here, I can recommend a rooming house where they'll take care of you, and I'll have my nurse set up an appointment in my office next week."

"That's what I'll do," Carson said. Talking hurt; he kept it at a minimum.

"Okay, I'll make the arrangements. Your company will pick up the bill, they said. You're on sick leave for the next three months and we'll evaluate your situation then. Nothing to worry about on that score." He regarded his patient for a moment, then put his hand on Carson's shoulder. "I don't know how the hell you dragged yourself up those stairs, either. God knows, John, you did more than was human as it was. Don't torture yourself. I'll send in the nurse for you."

Carson knew he had to tell them the truth about who he was, but not yet, he thought. Not yet. Elly's parents, her sister, his parents . . . How could he tell them Gary had gone crazy and killed his mother? Even trying to form the words it would take to tell them brought a long shudder and made his eyes sting with tears. Not yet.

The strange thing was the ease with which he was getting away with being John Loesser. They had found a wallet—Loesser's wallet—in his pocket; Carson's things were in his coat left in the Buick that day. Even the man the company sent out had accepted him. Of course, he had not known Loesser personally, but he had seen him a time or two. Carson had not been expected to talk then, and the bandages had concealed his identity further, but even so, he mused, even so. The few times he had started to explain, he had gone dumb, started to shake, lost control. Twice they had given him an injection to put him to sleep again, and the last time they had sent in a new doctor whose name had already escaped him. A shrink, he had realized after a short time. Guilt, the shrink had stated ponderously, was the most debilitating emotion of all. He had talked on, but Carson had stopped listening. Guilt of the survivor, he realized, was what the shrink assumed he was suffering from. And he was, he was. Guilt over doing something so horrible to Gary that he had turned on his own parents with a gun. Guilt over not being able to help his dead wife. Guilt over not being able to help his child. Guilt, guilt, guilt. But as John Loesser the guilt was abstract, distant. He would tell them later, he had decided that day. Much later.

Two weeks after leaving the hospital he flew to Richmond and let himself into Loesser's apartment. He still had bandages on his face, would have them until plastic surgery did its magic. People he met averted their gaze, and that was fine with him. The apartment was scrupulously neat—almost obsessively so— with good paintings, good books, good furniture, good stereo and television. Money, he thought bleakly. Loesser had had money. He had not given it any consideration until then. He went through the apartment carefully, getting to know his host, not liking him, but reassured because it became more and more apparent that Loesser had had no friends or relatives. Had he become a recluse after his wife's death, or had the trait always been there? There were names in an address book; he recognized a few from cards he had received—impersonal, duty cards—while he was still hospitalized. He found the financial statements. There was real money. Mrs. Loesser's insurance had been half a million dollars, a traveler's policy that anticipated the worst scenarios, and now and then paid handsomely. He found her picture, a pretty woman with a small mouth, upturned nose, blue eyes. A forgettable face. The picture had been put away in a closet in a box of mementos, along with her college diploma, and medical records dating from childhood up to the time over five years ago when they had ceased to matter.

He spent the weekend there, learning about Loesser, learning about money, about stock holdings, bonds, certificates of deposit. No one challenged him. The building superintendent knocked on the door, and when Carson opened it on the chain, the man hardly glanced at him. He had heard, he said; what a hell of a thing. If there was anything he could do . . . He went away.

Carson sat in the darkening room on Sunday and suddenly was overwhelmed with grief that shook his frame, made his cheek hurt with a stabbing pain, made his chest tighten until he feared—and would have welcomed—a heart attack. He had to call her parents, he knew, but not yet. Not until they found her, found Gary. No bodies had been recovered. Not yet.

He drove Loesser's Malibu back to Washington, and collapsed into bed as soon as he arrived at his rooming house. He could get an apartment, he thought, staring at the ceiling, a good apartment with a view, and there he would wait until they found her, found Gary, and then he would call her parents. The next day he drove out to the inn.

Someone had come and boarded it all up again, exactly the same as it had been the first time he had seen it. He walked around the building and stopped at the back porch where he had found her. Although it had been scrubbed clean, in his mind the blood was there, her body was there, one sandal missing. Where had it gone? He almost went down the stairs to the tangle of briars to search for it. He clutched the rail with his good hand and rubbed his eyes with the other. He remembered rising, seeing his son with the rifle. Suddenly, cutting through the memories, there was the other thing again, just as it had been the last time. Something present but out of sight. Carson did not move, held his breath listening. No sound. But something was there, he knew without doubt. Something. Slowly he turned, and now he closed his eyes, concentrating on that something. He felt as if he had moved into an electrical field vibrating on a level that did not affect muscles and skin, but was active deep inside his head, making it ache. For a moment he swayed, but the dizziness passed quickly and all he felt now was a headache that was growing in intensity. Like a hangover, he thought from a distance, spacing himself away from it, the way he had learned twenty years ago in college. Pretend it isn't there, think yourself away from it, and let the damn thing ache all it wants. Cholly's advice. Cholly, his college roommate whom he had not thought of in years. The headache became manageable and he opened his eyes with caution, as if afraid of startling away that something that was there with him. He could still feel it; he felt surrounded by it, pressed from all sides. Moving very slowly, he started to back away, backed down the steps to the overgrown path, walked deliberately around the building to get inside his car, Loesser's car. It was still there with him. He turned on the ignition, and then it was gone.

That night he stood naked before his mirror and regarded the long ugly scar that started somewhere on his back out of sight, curved under his arm, and went up to just under his nipple. The scars on his shoulder were uglier, bigger. The skin and bone grafts would blend in, the doctors had said, but it would take time. His face was the worst of all. Hideously mutilated, inflamed, monstrous. Plastic surgery would hide it all, they assured him. He was an excellent candidate for the kind of reconstruction they were capable of now. His gaze traveled down his body and he was mildly surprised to see how thin he had become. He had lost nearly forty pounds. The doctors had been amazed that he had lived through his attack, that his recovery was going along so uneventfully, so quickly. He had been amazed at the same things, but now he knew why he had been spared, knew what he had to do. He had been spared because he had to kill the thing in the inn.

He moved the next day to a bright, airy apartment with a view of the Potomac that looked lovely, inviting. He thought of the river below the inn; was that where the bodies had been hidden? He knew even as he wondered that that was wrong; they had been taken behind that darkness of the doorway. This time no tears came. He began to think of what he would need. Crowbar. Flashlight. Gasoline. He already had decided he had to burn it out, let fire consume and purify the house. Matches. How terrible it would be to have everything ready and no matches. After a thunderstorm, he decided, when the woods would be wet. He did not want a conflagration in the woods, did not want to hurt anyone, or chance having the fire put out before its work was done. An interior fire that would be out of control before it could be spotted from outside, at a time when no one would be on the road to call a fire department. He made his plans and the next day began to provision himself. There were thunderstorms almost every afternoon; he was able to pick his night.

He felt *it* as soon as he stopped the car at the inn. It was three-thirty in the morning, an inky black night, the air heavy with leaf mold and forest humus, earthy smells of the cycle of life and death repeated endlessly. He could smell the river, and the grass. He circled the inn to the back, where he forced open the boards on several windows. He climbed in and opened the door, then went back to the porch. Carefully, he poured gasoline where her body had been, followed her invisible tracks through the house, one foot shod, one bare, both bloody; no traces remained, but he knew. He covered the trail with gasoline. Up the curving stairs, through the hallway, to the door where the bloody prints had stopped, where the abyss still yawned. That was where Elinor and Gary were, he knew. They had been taken into the abyss. He sprayed the walls with gas, soaked the floor with it, then finished emptying the can as he retraced his own trail from that day, down the back stairs, to the porch. It was done. A distant rumble of thunder shook the air. The things all around him, pressing against him, vanished momentarily, then returned as the thunder subsided. Now and then he found himself brushing his hand before his face, as if to clear away cobwebs; his hand passed through emptiness, and they were still there, pressing against him. The dizziness did not come this time, but his head was aching mildly. He struck a match and tossed it to the gleaming wet gasoline where she had lain. The porch erupted into flames that raced through the building, following the trail he had made, through rooms and halls, up the stairs. There was a whoosh of flame from the upper floor. He had not closed the back door; belatedly he wondered if he should have knocked boards off in the front to admit a cross draft. He stood watching the flames blaze up the kitchen wall, and he knew he had done enough. Slowly he turned and walked to the car, taking the *something* with him, oblivious of the death he had planned for it. He got in and turned on the ignition; as before, it fled. He drove away without looking back.

————

Over the six months he had more surgery on his shoulder, plastic surgery on his face. A scar gleamed along his cheekbone. They could fix that, they told him. Give it a few months first. He did not go back. He learned to use his right arm all over again; the bank, lawyers, no one questioned the changed signature. They all knew the trauma he had suffered, the difficult recovery he was making. He took from Carson Danvers very little. Carson had been a master chef, and the new person emerging equipped his kitchen with the best cookware available and bought good spices and herbs, but he used them very little. John Loesser had been obsessively neat; the new man liked neatness more than he had realized, but not to such an extreme. Carson had been outgoing, friendly, talkative. He had liked people, liked to entertain people, kid around with them. The new man knew no one; there was no one he wanted to talk to, no jokes, no stories worth repeating anymore.

He spent many hours in his darkened apartment in Washington watching the lights on the river, watching the patterns of light in the city, thinking nothing. He spent many hours reliving his past, going over scenes again and again until he knew he had recaptured every detail, then going on to other scenes. At first the pain was nearly intolerable, but over time it lessened and he could even smile at the memories. Their first date, how awkward he had been, how afraid he would offend her, bore her, even frighten her. He had loved her from the very first, and had declared his love much too soon, long before she was ready to consider him seriously. He had been so dumb, tongue-tied with her, and adoring. The pain diminished, but the emptiness grew.

The company sent someone out to see him again, and for the first time he suggested that he might never return to work. He talked to the man—Tony Martinelli—in a shadowed living room, making certain he was hidden by shadows. Martinelli did not press him, was probably relieved. They would wait, he had said; there was no rush, no quick decision to be made. But no one had urged him to mend quickly and return. Loesser had had no real friends in the company; no one would miss him. In time they sent papers; he hired a law firm to represent his interests, and paid no more attention to any of that until one day when he received a letter asking politely if he would mind sending back certain records, certain computer information. He went to the study, where he had John Loesser's computer, records, files, books—all boxed. He had not looked at any of it. That afternoon he unloaded one box after another and examined the contents. He got out the computer manual and connected parts to other parts as directed, but he did not know what to do with it. There were books on the insurance industry, on computers, on statistics and rates and liability schedules; there were actuarial tables. At last he had something to do, something he could not ask for help with; Loesser was supposed to know all this. It had been weeks since he had called the police to inquire about the missing bodies, weeks since he had thought about revealing his own identity. That night he realized that Carson Danvers was as dead as Elinor and Gary Danvers.

He learned how to use the computer, learned how to copy the disks, use the modem. He took a large folder to a Xerox machine and copied everything in it, then reboxed the originals. He sent the company the information and was finally done with them. He could not have said why he wanted copies; there was no real reason other than it was something to do. Without pondering further, he gradually learned the business through John Loesser's accumulation of records and notes and his modem connections.

He had been startled one day when, following John Loesser's directions, written in the man's precise, minute handwriting, he had found himself accessing a mainframe computer that apparently held data from the entire insurance industry. Fascinated by the information available, he had scrolled through categories. Liability claims: flood damage in Florida, starved cattle in Montana, wind damage in Texas . . . accidents in supermarkets, on city buses, in neighbors' yards and houses . . . medical claims for hernias, broken bones, hysterectomies, bypasses . . . He was appalled by the automobile claims, then bored by them. He learned how to ask for specific groupings: shark attacks, bee stings, food poisonings. . . .

His fingers were shaking when he keyed in the request for hotel fires. There it was, his River House, followed by *Arson— unsolved*. He was shaking too hard to continue. What if they had a way of tracing who looked up information like that? What if they came back to him? The next day he registered as a public insurance adjuster, making his use of the computer data appear more legitimate. Why? he asked himself, but he did not pursue it. He looked for a list of closed hotels and marveled at the number. Carson Danvers would have liked seeing what all was available, he thought.

Some days later it occurred to him to look up instances of sudden madness and homicides, and again he was appalled. He scrolled the list and went on to something else, then stopped. Camden, he thought. He had seen something about Camden, Ohio, in the papers recently, and there was one of the abandoned hotels in Camden. He went back to that list and found it. Dwyer House, built 1897, closed 1936. Forty-two rooms. Used as an office building from 1938 to 1944. In litigation from 1944 to 1954. Owned by Gerstein and Winters Realty Company. Insured for forty thousand. It sounded almost exactly like the inn that Carson Danvers had been looking for. Wrong place, but right building.

In his mind's eye he saw the wide back porch, Elly's body sprawled, the bloody prints that led up the handsome, curved staircase. And he felt again the unseen presence that had swarmed all around him. Saw again the vacant, mad look on Gary's face, the look of homicidal insanity. . . . He turned off the computer and went out for a long walk in the city.

The next day he looked up Camden in the library newspaper files. He was no longer shaking, but instead felt as cold and hard and brittle as an icicle. He found the story that had caught his eye, the match his mind had made. Mildred Hewlitt had gone mad and slaughtered several patients in a nursing home on Hanover Street, where she worked. She had vanished, and so had one of the victims. The hotel, Dwyer House, was also on Hanover Street. That was what had stopped him. He walked home and looked up the computer listing for the claim that had first sent the hairs rising on his arms and neck. Two weeks earlier, a college boy had gone mad and run his car through a pedestrian mall; he had fled on foot and vanished. One of the victims had filed a claim; the mainframe had recorded it. That day Carson Danvers packed a suitcase and left for Camden.

He stole an Ohio license plate from a parked car in a shopping mall, and put it on his car the morning he reached Camden. He checked into a motel outside town, read the local paper from the past two days, walked downtown. He chatted with a waiter, the motel desk clerk, several others. He did not go to the real estate office. He went to the shopping mall, where the clerks were all ready to talk about the terrible accident.

"He came in over there," a woman said, standing outside a Hallmark shop, pointing to a stretch of pavement that was barricaded now. A row of wooden planters had been smashed, store windows were boarded up. "He revved up and came in doing maybe fifty, sixty miles an hour, screaming like a banshee. My God, people were flying this way and that! Everyone screaming! Blood everywhere! And he got out and ran. No one tried to stop him. No one had time to do anything, what with all the screaming and the blood. He got clean away."

Carson shook his head in disbelief and walked on to a Sears store, where he bought a crowbar and heard the same story, embellished a little because this time the salesman relating it had not actually seen what happened. He put the crowbar in his car and went to a Kmart, where he bought a gas can and flashlight. Then he found his way to Hanover Street. It started in town, went straight through a subdivision, and then became a country road very quickly. The nursing home where Mildred Hewlitt had worked was a few blocks from the subdivision; after that there was a small store and gas station combined, and then farmland and sparse woods. A four-lane highway had been built three miles to the south; business had followed, and Hanover Street was left to the truck farmers. The same as River House.

He drove slowly until he reached the driveway to Dwyer House. There was a chain across it. The hotel was not visible from the road. The woods had invaded the grounds, deciduous trees with new April leaves not yet fully developed—ash trees, maples, oaks, all scrawny and untended. High grasses and weeds and hedge gone wild filled in the understory. There was a path through it, well trod, evidently in daily use. He drove another hundred yards and came to a turn on the side of the road of the hotel and drove onto it. It was dirt, rutted and unkempt, but passable. A service entrance? Why no chain, if so? And why would Mildred Hewlitt have come back here, and the boy, and the four or five others he had read about? Mystified, he kept driving slowly until he came to a clearing, an old parking lot maybe. He could see the hotel from here: three stories, a frame building ornately decorated with cupolas, balconies, porches with handsome rails and fancy posts. It was boarded up, but he could imagine the stained-glass windows it must have boasted. Inside there would be the paneling, the carefully dovetailed joints, the elaborate patterns in the walnut floors. He felt as if he knew this building intimately; it was so like the ones he had investigated a long time ago, looking for a place to create a fine restaurant. So like them. He stopped and turned off his engine, and he felt *it* again, and that too was the same. A pressure, a presence, like cobwebs with an electrical charge. This time the headache was slight, a distant throbbing. He got out and stood by his car door, looking around, and now he understood why people came here. Lovers' lane, a place to park out of sight of the road, beyond the sound of passing cars or the inquisitive eyes of anyone. That explained the ages, he thought, not moving away from the cobwebs, brushing at his face now and then. One girl of eighteen, a suicide. The college boy, twenty-one. Mildred Hewlitt, twenty-five. Another young man of twenty who had been apprehended smashing windows at the elementary school. When seized, he had collapsed in a catatonic state from which he had not recovered. Others, mentioned in whispers, with puzzlement, just weird things, the desk clerk had said in a low voice. Weird, you know? Carson Danvers stood brushing away electric cobwebs that were not webs at all, and he nodded. He knew. He got in the car again and turned on the ignition, and was alone again. He drove out.

A fine rain had started to fall, soft, promising spring growth, smelling of newly sprouted seedlings and fragrant earth. Spring, Carson thought, warmer nights, couples in cars with engines turned off, mayhem. Back in his motel, he set his clock for three-thirty and lay down, but did not sleep. When it was time, he drove to the hotel parking lot and turned around, so that his car faced out. He ignored the webs that found him instantly, and unloaded his equipment methodically. He pried open a door in the rear of the building, dropped the crowbar on the porch, and entered cautiously, flashlight in one hand, gas can in the other. This time there was no need to make a trail, to obliterate the past with fire. He made his way through the blackness, following his narrow beam of light, moving with great care, not wanting to fall through a rotten floorboard, or trip over an abandoned two-by-four. He found the stairs and climbed them, testing each step. The building was solid, filled with real cobwebs and dust and mold. He was disoriented momentarily at the landing on the second floor, but closed his eyes and drew a mental map, then continued down a hallway to where he judged the center of the hotel was. Many of the doors were open; none was locked. He opened more of them and then began to splash the gasoline around the walls, through the hall. He brushed away webs and shone his light around to make certain he had soaked the place thoroughly, and then went back downstairs, dribbling out gas as he moved. He tried to find a spot roughly under the gas-soaked area, and emptied the can, spilling the last drops on a handkerchief he had knotted around a rock. He looked about with the flashlight one more time, then went to the back door he had forced open. There he lighted a match, touched it to the handkerchief, which blazed instantly, and heaved the handkerchief to the bottom of the stairs to ignite a trail of fire. He could feel the webs all around him, pressing as he picked up the crowbar and returned to his car. He put the empty gas can in the trunk, brushed away webs, got in his car, and turned the key. It fled. He drove out carefully. No sign of fire was visible when he drove past the main entrance. The rain was falling, more like a mist now, settling gently with great persistence, as if a mammoth cloud were being lowered to earth. He got back to his motel, back to his room, and fell into bed—and sleep—without undressing.

It was one of the very few nights of the past nine months that he was untroubled by dreams, that he awakened feeling refreshed and vital.

3

October 1985. Constance Leidl drove home happily that October afternoon. The two-year-old Volvo still smelled of apples; a stack of books from the university library added its own peculiar, comforting odor, but the dominant fragrance was of fall, of wood stoves, frosts to come, and burning leaves. "The world is draped in the glory of autumn," one of the patients in the hospital had murmured to her. A hopeless schizophrenic, wandering in a world of poetry and surrealism. Constance shook her head, then smiled, remembering Charlie's complaint as they had picked apples over the past three days.

"Honey, I don't get it. Why do we tend all these damn trees and then just give away the apples?"

"Do you want strangers in here picking them?"

"Come on!"

"Well then . . ."

"It's not one or the other," he had said indignantly.

"We could sell off the hillside."

He garumphed at her grin. "Okay. But tell me why we are doing this." A cold breeze had colored his cheeks as red as the apples they were picking. He had stopped working and was regarding her with a mutinous expression.

"Well," she had said with what she considered great practicality, "because."

"Ah," he had said, illuminated, and they had returned to the chore of picking apples.

Today she had delivered three bushels of them to the hospital. There were twenty bushels on the back porch, some to be called for, some to be delivered. She hummed under her breath. Just because. She loved this section of the drive home from the hospital she had visited. On one side of the blacktop county road stretched a pasture graced by three sorrel horses that struck poses whenever traffic was present. A white fence completed that picture. On the other side, the side she lived on, a two-hundred-year-old farmhouse marked what she thought of as her stretch. The old house was of stone and wood and bricks, with a slate roof; the Dorsetts lived there. They said Dorsetts had always lived there, would always live there. She believed that. Next was a tall, cedar-sided house with a southern face constructed mostly of glass. The Mitchums lived there. They had four sons, all husky football types. Two of the boys had come over to complete the apple-picking, and had taken away two bushels of apples for their labors. Sometimes Constance fried the special Swedish cookies that Charlie loved more than any other sweet, and gave most of them to the Mitchum boys. She had explained that, also. If she kept them in the house, Charlie ate them, and at his age—fifty plus—he did not need all those calories. The boys did. When he asked if she couldn't simply make fewer, she had said no.

Everywhere maple trees blazed and cast red light on the world. Autumn had been benign so far. Its progress had been gentle, with a few early hard frosts, then a mellow Indian summer, and now more frosts. There had not been a tree-stripping windstorm, or slashing rain. A long expanse of pasture—the Mitchums kept goats—and finally her own house appeared. The lowering sun turned the maples in her front yard into welcoming torches. It fired the chrysanthemums that edged the driveway with a carpet runner of red, rust, glowing yellow, and white. There was a silver Mercedes parked in the center of the driveway in front of the garage door.

Constance scowled at the other car. The drive was wide enough for two cars, but not if one that size took the center. And, she thought with irritation, she'd be damned if she would run over the chrysanthemums. She stopped behind the Mercedes and got out. As she walked toward the house, she saw that Charlie and an unknown man were in the garage. From the roof of the garage the gray tiger cat Brutus glared at her with slitted yellow eyes.

Charlie came out to meet her. He was wearing jeans and a plaid shirt that emphasized his huskiness. His hair was crinkly black with enough gray to look distinguished, and, since moving out in the country, he had turned a rich mahogany color.

She thought he was extraordinarily handsome and often told
him so. He liked that. Now he kissed her and murmured, "The
mountain has come to Mohamet."

Where he was dark, she was fair, her hair pale to nearly
white, her eyes light blue—some thought gray—her skin a
creamy ivory, touched so lightly with color it was as if she seldom spent time outdoors. Yet she was out even more than he
was. She was tall and lean; she would be a stick of an old
woman, she sometimes said, almost regretfully. They walked
together to the garage, where the visitor waited, looking ill at
ease. A gray man with a tight mouth, she thought coolly, a city
man who should stay there alone, where he belonged.

"Honey, Mr. Thoreson," Charlie said. "My wife, Constance
Leidl."

"Oh, ah, Mrs. Meiklejohn, or is it Ms. Leidl? How do you do?"

She had known his handshake would be limp, she thought,
still very distant and cool, if proper. "Either, or both at times,"
she said. "Shall we go inside?" She watched with clinical interest
to see if he would unconsciously wipe his hand on his trouser
leg. He did. A gray man, with a gray, fearful soul. Sixty, sixty-
two. Gray hair, sallow complexion, gray suit, discreet maroon
tie. She started for the front door.

"Honey," Charlie said, "we can talk here."

"I apologize for parking like that," Thoreson said almost simultaneously. "Cats were running everywhere. I thought it best
simply to stop."

Just then Candy, the orange cat with butterscotch eyes, approached Constance with a melting-legs walk, meowing. Constance started to pick her up, but she slunk away, looking
nervously at Thoreson and Charlie, complaining.

"Charlie, what's been going on?" Constance demanded.

"Nothing, not really. I opened the door and the cats all ran
out just when Mr. Thoreson pulled in, and I came out to meet
him, and then you got home."

She watched him, wondering what he was hiding, and then
turned to enter the house. The front door stood wide open.

"We'll just wait here," Charlie called after her.

When she glanced back, he grinned his most engaging smile,
and Mr. Thoreson looked more uncomfortable than ever. Cau-

tious now, she entered the house and immediately choked on the thick, sharp smell of burning chili peppers. Her eyes teared, and she groped for the door and backed out again, coughing.

"Charlie," she cried, "why didn't you warn me?" She continued to cough, fumbling in her purse for a tissue.

"You would have wanted to find out for yourself," he said reasonably. "I was going to make Hunan chicken. It starts with frying ten chili peppers."

Thoreson looked from him to Constance, back to Charlie. He examined the garage with disdain, then said, "Mr. Meiklejohn, is there some place we can talk? Phil Stern assured me that you would at least listen."

"I suppose it gets worse on in the house?" Constance asked.

"Sure does," Charlie agreed. "Kitchen's uninhabitable. I turned on the exhaust fan and opened windows."

"Mr. Meiklejohn! Damn it, I drove all the way out from New York to see you! I apologized for not calling ahead of time. Stern promised he would call and explain the situation to you."

"He didn't call," Charlie said. He looked at Constance. "Benny's?" At her nod, he turned to Thoreson. "There's a roadhouse down the road, four, five miles. Let's go have a drink there. And you can talk. I'll listen."

Thoreson's lips had drawn into a thin line.

"You'll have to follow us," Constance said and started back to the Volvo. She did not look to see if Thoreson was dismayed by the lack of hospitality she and Charlie were showing. City man, go home, she thought, and take your problems with you.

"Who is he?" Constance asked, in the car with Charlie driving now.

"Hal Thoreson. He said he was supposed to come with Phil's recommendation, but Phil never got around to it. Actually Thoreson called a week or so ago, wanted me to meet him in New York, but I knew you'd think I was trying to duck out of picking apples." What Thoreson had done, although Charlie did not say this, was order him to a meeting.

"I don't like him," she said.

"Uh-huh."

"He's an *insurance* man!"

Charlie laughed. "So's Phil."

"That's different, and you know it."

"Not where business is concerned." He had known Phil Stern in college, and they had remained friends over the many years since then. When Charlie took an early retirement from the New York City police force, Phil had turned to him for a private investigation, then another, then several more. What Phil had bought was not so much Charlie's expertise as a detective, although that had been important, but rather his unmatched knowledge of arson. Charlie had been a fire department investigator for years before becoming a city detective. It was Thoreson's fault, he thought aggrievedly, that he had burned the peppers. The damn cookbook said you could do the preliminaries early and in less than ten minutes turn out the dish. Hah! He had wanted to surprise Constance, had heard a car and had gone to look out the front window; the chili peppers burned, and he ended up with the sourpuss Thoreson. It had not been a good day, he brooded, parking at Benny's. Thoreson's silver Mercedes was right behind him. He caught up with them before they entered the roadhouse.

Benny's was virtually empty that afternoon. It was not yet six. A man in a leather jacket sat at the bar talking to Ron, the spindly bartender who would leave as soon as Benny arrived. Two women were talking in low voices in a booth at the rear of the room. Charlie and Constance waved at Ron and took another booth; they sat side by side, Thoreson opposite them. Ron slouched over, took their order, and slouched away again. No one spoke as they waited for the drinks to arrive, but the moment the drinks came, Thoreson began, as if the service were his cue.

"Two weeks ago there was a conference of underwriters in Dallas. I attended, as did Phil Stern. I have known him for many years, of course. During one of the informal meetings a startling fact was unearthed. When I mentioned the matter to Stern, he suggested that I might discuss it with you. I have been trying to do so," he said with some bitterness. "I know that I am not an engaging man, Mr. Meiklejohn, Mrs. Meiklejohn."

He had rehearsed it in his silver Mercedes, Constance realized with interest. First the teaser, then his abject self-abasement, and now he would reveal the startling fact. She glanced at Charlie; he appeared engrossed in spearing an onion in his Gibson.

"I seldom have to deal with the public, and never have had to deal with a matter of this delicacy, and, frankly, the thought of hiring a private investigator for such a . . . a discreet matter is abhorrent to me."

"You have your own investigators," Charlie suggested.

"Of course. However, we feel that there may be a leak somewhere. Phil thought, and I agreed ultimately, a private investigation would be more to the point."

Charlie got the onion and ate it with evident satisfaction. He smiled at Thoreson. "Why don't you cut the bullshit and get to the point."

"That is precisely why Phil was supposed to talk to you," Thoreson said in a plaintive voice. "He knew I would bungle it alone."

He actually sighed. Constance felt Charlie nudge her leg, and she looked away to keep from smiling.

"It came to our attention that there has been a series of hotel fires," Thoreson said. "So far, three insurance companies have paid out a million dollars in claims. That's one of the reasons we thought an independent investigation would be wise."

"It just came to your attention," Charlie murmured.

"Yes. They are widely separated geographically, and span a period of five years."

"How widely spread?" Although he still sounded lazy and not very interested, Constance knew from his voice that Thoreson had finally said something that worked.

"Vermont, Ohio, North Carolina, California, Idaho, and Washington State."

Charlie shook his head in disbelief. "A serial arsonist working from coast to coast? I don't believe it."

"Were there casualties?" Constance asked, almost in spite of herself.

"None. In fact, each hotel was closed down, out of use when it burned."

Charlie looked blank, rather dull. "You need the ATF or a national organization to investigate something like that. Spread over five years? There won't be anything to see anyway. It's probably coincidence."

"Phil said he would tell you the modus operandi—is that the phrase? It's the same in each case. We know there have been at least six deliberate fires, probably three more that we aren't so certain about. In each case, the fire started in an interior room and burned outward, and by the time the fire departments arrived, the buildings were practically gutted already. Always between two and five in the morning. Almost always when it was either raining or snowing, the exceptions being during a dense fog in one instance, and following a week of rain in the other. Every one was considered arson at the time."

Charlie was shaking his head. "And you think someone in one of your companies must be in on it? Why?"

"Not in on it, not that way. But maybe feeding information to someone else. Information about where abandoned hotels are, what the coverage is for them."

Very kindly Charlie said, "Mr. Thoreson, go home. If you suspect a conspiracy to commit a crime, tell the FBI. If you suspect arson, notify the ATF. Let them take care of it." He glanced at Constance, who nodded. ATF, the Bureau of Alcohol, Tobacco and Firearms, had a national arson investigative team.

Thoreson's lips had tightened again. He had not yet touched his scotch and water. Now he put it to his mouth, then set it down sharply. "That's about the last thing we want to do. There certainly would be a leak then, maybe publicity. Do you know what it would mean to have this publicized?"

"Copycat fires," Charlie said. "But the ATF can be very quiet about what they're up to. Very discreet."

"And they solve three percent of all arson cases they investigate!" Thoreson snapped. "We decided to keep it private. One person, you, asking questions, looking into this matter, would not attract undue attention. A flock of men asking questions? How long would that remain concealed? Mr. Meiklejohn, the insurance industry depends on discretion. Without discretion there would be no insurance industry." He picked up his drink again, and this time he downed it all. "We are prepared to be very generous, sir. What we are most afraid of is the possibility that someone has started a new service, a syndicate, if you will, that has a task force composed of people knowledgeable in the business of arson. With inside information about where the old buildings are, if they're insured, they could approach the owners, make a deal, and light the fires. Mr. Meiklejohn, this matter has already cost three of our companies over a million dollars!"

"And what if I look into it and decide that it was all coincidence, after all?"

"That would be the absolutely finest report any of us could hope for."

Charlie was gazing at him fixedly, his eyes narrowed. "There's something else, isn't there, Thoreson? What is it?"

Thoreson drained a few drops of melted ice into his mouth, then, keeping his gaze on the glass, he said, "In those firm cases I mentioned, each time, the fire department—volunteer departments in every case—seemed to delay fighting the fires. Almost as if they deliberately let them burn past saving before they went into action."

Regarding Thoreson with near indifference, Charlie lazily held up his hand to catch Ron's attention. In a moment Ron appeared with a tray of new drinks. Only then did Charlie speak. "So you think the various volunteer fire departments are in on the conspiracy, too?"

"I don't know what to think," Thoreson admitted. "A million in claims, Mr. Meiklejohn, that's what I really think about. Old abandoned buildings, good for nothing in most cases. And there must be hundreds more just like them scattered around the country. Hundreds!" He rubbed his eyes. "With your experience, you could go to some of those places and talk to the people in the fire departments, find out what they know, if they know anything. Find out if they really did delay taking action, and if so, why. Stern showed me the manual you wrote, the bible for volunteer fire fighters, he said. Those people would talk to you. You could say you're gathering data for a new book or something. They'd talk to you."

Constance wanted to shout, No! He won't work for you! Go away! She wanted to hold Charlie and whisper, Not this one. Not this time. No more fires. No more arson. No more burned-out buildings with rotten timbers ready to fall on you, floors ready to cave in, walls ready to crumble down. "Charlie," she said, touching his arm. He turned his face toward her, but she knew he was not seeing her, not now. His eyes had gone flat, like chips of coal, ready to flare, ready to burn. "Charlie," she said again, more insistently. The light came back to his eyes. "We have to go to San Francisco in ten days, remember? And then a couple of weeks in Mexico. Remember?"

He blinked, looked back to Thoreson, and shrugged.

"Let me leave the reports with you," Thoreson said, in near desperation. "I have them all here in my briefcase. Don't decide right now. Look over what we've managed to get together first. We wouldn't expect you to drop everything and concentrate on just this matter. After all, it stretches out over five years as it is. But if you can look into it in the next few weeks, the next few months . . ."

He means he'll be sure to have Phil call, Constance wanted to say, and drank her Irish coffee. Charlie thought the same thing, but he said mildly that he would read the reports, study the claims, and be in touch. Thoreson was so relieved, he would have signed a blank check, Constance thought.

"We asked Phil Stern to handle the details," he said. "Since you've worked with him in the past, it seemed appropriate. His company is one of a consortium, as is mine. We're equally responsible, but he will be the liaison, if that is agreeable." He tasted his second drink and stood up. He did not offer to shake hands with either of them.

"If you can let me know in the next day or two . . ."

"By Friday," Charlie said, also not offering to shake hands. He did not rise. Thoreson looked from him to Constance, his lips a tight line; then he nodded and left.

"Charlie, this is insane," she said as soon as Thoreson was out the door of the roadhouse. A few new people had drifted in; voices and music were rising to a routine volume. "What can you possibly do five years after the fact? Do you really intend to spend the next few years traveling from Vermont to California to Ohio, and wherever else he mentioned? Alone?"

He grinned at the threat. "Nope. I'd hire Tom Hoagley to do some preliminary research for me while I stay home and pick apples, and then go to San Francisco and listen to you on your panels."

She felt a chill. Was that the reason he had not tossed Thoreson out? She had written a series of articles on xenophobia and its impact on everything from the behavior of elementary school children to national foreign policy, and as a consequence had been invited to participate in a national psychology symposium. She had assumed he was looking forward to going to San Francisco for a week with the same enthusiasm she felt.

Although in theory she was retired, in practice she was as busy as she ever had been, giving papers, writing books, doing research, consulting. The only thing she had dropped was teaching. Also in theory Charlie was supposed to be using his time in writing a definitive book on fire investigative methods; the manual Thoreson had mentioned was the only product to come out of his efforts.

"An assistant," Charlie said with a nod. "Tom Hoagley. Let someone else find out things, like were there unusual strangers in the areas before the fires? Any repetition of any unusual behavior? Developers casing the places? Offers to buy the properties? Unusual newspaper subscriptions before the fires? Owners showing signs of unusual wanderlust in the past few years?" He was gazing thoughtfully at the room, filling now with the usual weeknight customers. "If a stranger showed up in our little community and did anything weird, how long before everyone in this place would know, do you suppose?"

"The next day," she said. "Charlie, are you going to take this case?"

"Not sure yet. Like I told him, I'll go over the reports, then decide. See who investigated, for instance. Some pretty good guys out there prowling about, you know. What really gets me is that he said the fire departments let the places burn. Not that I believe him. He's an asshole. But there are some pretty good people out there poking about in the ashes. I wonder if that's what they're saying."

She looked shocked. "You don't believe that!"

He had been thinking out loud and now regarded her soberly. "I don't believe or not believe it. But if it turns out to be true, I sure as hell want to know why. Let's have dinner here. Hungry?"

They made their way to the dining room a few minutes later and he looked at her with horror when she ordered sweetbreads. A shudder passed over him.

When they got home that night the acrid smell of burned

chilies was nearly gone, but the cats acted as if an invading army had moved through the house. They went from room to room sniffing warily and jumped when Charlie dropped Thoreson's briefcase.

During the night Constance came awake to hear a howling wind savaging the trees in the yard. The long mellow autumn had come to an end.

4

You look like hell," Charlie said to Phil Stern, who was in bed in his Manhattan apartment. "Why'd you send Thoreson out cold like that? Is it serious? Should I keep my distance?"

"It is serious," Phil said darkly. "If it wasn't serious, I wouldn't have to be in bed, right? Since I am here, it must be serious." He grunted when he shifted his position. "Keep your distance. Flu. What are you doing here?"

"Helping Constance deliver apples." He shook his head. "It's a long story."

"So you met Sore Thumb."

Charlie felt blank. "Sore thumb? I give."

"Thoreson. Halbert Thoreson. Those of us who know and love him call him Sore Thumb. If he made it, you know why."

Ah, Charlie thought, the man in pain, with the tight lips. He nodded. "You up to talking? Shouldn't you be quiet? Rest, or something?"

"I'm resting. I'm resting. Up to my gills in dope, swimming in dope and resting. Sore Thumb's a pain in the ass, but he's probably onto something. I'm surprised he showed up. The thought of scandal scares him more than the bogeyman."

Phil repeated much of the story Thoreson had told. He thought the number of arson fires was probably closer to ten, or even twelve, but some of them were doubtful. "Look," he said a few minutes later, "Thoreson's company has been hit harder than anyone else in this mess—one reason they abhor publicity. Thoreson's name's not even linked to any of this, that's how cautious he is, how careful about his company's reputation. I'm fronting. Me and the company," he added. "Not that old man Boyle's happy about it, but that's how it is. So you decide, and we send out the contract, except I'm taking off for Bermuda as soon as they unlock my door here. Sick leave," he added, too smugly. "I have good insurance."

Charlie spread his hands and said, "Then there's no case at this time, not until you're back in harness."

Phil started to shake his head and grunted again. "That's one of the things I shouldn't do yet," he said after a moment. "You're on, Charlie. If you'll look into it. God, we've got more than forty of those white elephants on our books! We haven't been hit yet, but I'm afraid we will be."

"Usual terms?" Charlie asked.

"Whatever you say. Sore Thumb complained about the amount, but I said you don't work cheap. We'll have a check mailed tomorrow. Give yourself a raise. I'll initial it. A reasonable raise, that is."

Charlie leaned back and surveyed his friend critically. "Must be a hidden head injury, brain fever. Okay. Meanwhile, Bermuda's a good idea."

"Yeah, I know." Phil closed his eyes. "I'm tired. You talk. What's this bullshit about apples?"

Over on Houston Street Constance was regarding her old friend Patrick Morley with affection. "It really is about ten bushels," she said. "But we couldn't pack bushels very well, so we scrounged up the liquor boxes instead. "You'll just have to explain the best you can how you came by ten liquor boxes, my friend."

Father Patrick Morley, executive director of the children's home that occupied most of the block, laughed with delight. "And you say there is no independent good or evil! Come along inside and let me give you a cup of coffee. Where is Charlie?"

Two adolescent boys appeared and started to unload the boxes of apples. One of them kept looking at Constance with a shy smile. Patrick led the way inside the massively built school. A few more children peered at them from a doorway; the door closed softly when they drew near. A faint grin played on Patrick's face, the only indication of his awareness of his charges' interest in the visitor. Everywhere the building needed repairs—paint, new woodwork, a window. . . . It was scrupulously clean. They went into his study and sat down near a low table that held a few mugs and a thermos. He righted two of the mugs and opened the thermos, inspected the contents, then poured. "I probably could find some sugar and cream," he said without conviction.

She shook her head. "Charlie's visiting an old friend. We'll meet for lunch. How are you?"

"Well," he said, dismissing the subject. He looked dreadful, too thin, pale. He was dying of leukemia. Looking at him, aching for him, Constance could almost admit to the evil that he believed had an independent existence.

Somewhere a bell rang, and the quiet beyond his study door was broken by young voices, footsteps, doors opening, closing. Patrick's smile widened. Constance sipped her coffee. It was very bad coffee. Why are you sacrificing your life? she had wanted to ask him many times, though she never had, and never would.

He was regarding her again, his eyes calm, serene. "Do you remember the game we played in school?" he asked suddenly. "Someone in the back row tapped the person in front of him and whispered, 'Pass it on.' "

She nodded, grinning now. "By the time it got to me it was more than just a tap."

He laughed. "Exactly. The multiplier effect. Good is like that. A good thing happens to you, you pass it on, bigger, better than you received. It multiplies." The smile left his face, and with its absence he seemed suddenly very old, very aware. "Evil's like that, too, Constance. People like you, so basically good, call the good you do reasonable. You call the evil you see irrational, evil behavior done by people who need help. In that context even evil becomes reasonable. Your own rationality is dangerous, Constance. It can be a trap more deadly than you can conceive."

"What a terrifying world you live in," she said softly, chilled by his death that seemed too close now, too imminent.

"For me there is no terror," he said, and she believed him. His personal serenity was unshakable, his faith beyond question. "You see my world as terror-filled because I admit to absolutes—absolute good and evil, absolute faith and belief. I see your world as even more terrible, Constance. You can't measure good and evil with a relative yardstick. When you see absolute good you have to search for hidden motives, puzzle out a compensation system, even if the good is your own. I'm afraid that when you are confronted with absolute evil, you will find your rationality gone, and without reason or faith, you are truly lost. Then you become a tool of evil, no more than that; or you die."

"I'm not afraid of death," she whispered. "That isn't evil. Death is part of all life. You know that."

"We pass on our knowledge of death, our fear if it's present. Some feel it as a tap, others as a blow. But when that death is brought about by a confrontation with evil, what we pass on can be a fatal blow and those we leave behind feel it that way. Some recover. Many don't, and they in turn pass it on, ever harder, ever more insistent, ever stronger with the force of evil behind it. It multiplies its effects until someone is strong enough to deny it again, to quell it for the time being. It doesn't die, it waits for a new victim to start the game again."

Constance stood up abruptly. "I have to go. I'll be late."

Patrick rose also. "Remember when our paths crossed over twenty years ago? How outraged you were that I had become a priest. You told me very firmly that if I ever tried to convert you, our friendship would end. I never did, did I?"

"Of course not," she said coolly. "Nor I you."

He laughed and took her hands. "Good-bye, Constance. Thank you for the apples. For all your goodnesses." He did not immediately release her; his hands were hot.

"Why did you talk to me like this now?" she asked, making no motion to draw away.

"I don't know. Ever since you called, I've had a darkness in my mind about you. My dreams are . . . troubled these days, dreams of old friends, people I have loved, people I must speak to, people I must ask to forgive me for injuries so old they seem to belong to someone else. People I must warn. At least one person I felt I must warn. You." He studied her face, then kissed her on the forehead. "I feel that you're in grave danger. I'm sorry."

Whenever Charlie and Constance got to town together they had lunch at Wanda Loren's restaurant on Amsterdam, half a dozen blocks from the apartment they had lived in for so many years. The neighborhood never changed yet was always different, Charlie thought as he strode briskly, half an hour late. One shop vanished, was replaced with another not very different. Fondue was out, yogurt in. Sushi houses had appeared; the Italian restaurant that used to serve the world's best veal in marsala was gone. An Indian restaurant was there instead. The crowds were exactly the same people, he felt convinced, just wearing different clothes. Suits for men and women were in; casual jeans and T-shirts out. The air smelled the same, a poisonous mix of exhaust fumes and metal and people. The noise level was the same, five decibels above tolerable. He ducked into Wanda's.

"Hey, Charlie, how are you, for Chrissake! She's here already."

Wanda greeted him with a hug. She was four feet ten inches, weighed too much to talk about, she always said, and had a beautiful face, a cameo face with perfect lines, almond-shaped eyes, and not a blemish or touch of makeup.

"Wanda, if I weren't such an old man, I'd sweep you off your feet," Charlie said and kissed her on the mouth. "You've lost a couple hundred pounds."

"Twenty, Charlie. Just twenty so far. But thanks."

He joined Constance and saw with surprise that she had a bottle of wine in an ice bucket and was already drinking it. Before he could comment, she asked, "You're taking the case? Tell me what you've been up to. Okay?"

His put his hand over hers for a second, then poured wine for himself and started to recount his morning's activities. He knew about Patrick, knew it must have been bad. Later she would talk about it, he also knew, but now he would fill in the silence.

Afterward, he thought that if it had not been for Patrick's approaching death and his warning that had so disturbed Constance, everything would have been different. She would have been sharper with her questions; he probably would have turned over more of the investigation to Tom Hoagley. Aware that the very fine food Wanda served them was being wasted on Constance, that she was deeply abstracted, he found himself including her in his plans, assuming a partnership, taking it for granted that she would allow herself to become involved. Anything, he thought, to wipe that blank look from her face, to make her refocus her eyes on the here and now, not on some vision Patrick had implanted. He would need her help in reading the newspapers, he said, and she blinked finally and looked at him.

"Tom is going to get newspapers together from the communities where the fires broke out," he explained again. "It's going to make quite a stack, I'm afraid. I'll need help in going through them, searching for anything that might link one area to another. Okay?"

He had intended to have Tom Hoagley do that, but saying it this way made him aware that he wanted to do it himself, with Constance helping him. Together they might spot relationships that someone like Hoagley might not see, although he was quite clever.

"You really think all those fires are related, make a pattern?"

"Yes," he said without hesitation; until that moment he had reserved judgment. Even then it might not have been too late if she had pressed him for a reason, pressed him to defend his position. He could not have done it then, but it might have made a difference.

5

Charlie paused outside the partly open door to Constance's study. She was talking: ". . . and the children who remained in the environment until adolescence never did develop a recognizable form of xenophobia. Instead, what they manifested throughout their adult lives was an attitude of acceptance, empathy, and curiosity about other people. God damn it to hell!"

Something slammed onto a table. He glanced inside. She had banged her notebook down. She glared at him.

"Sorry," he said. "Lunch. If you want some."

She got up, carefully pushed her chair under her desk, her motions exaggerated, the way she moved when she was mad, then left her room. "That idiot! That damn thick-headed idiot!"

"Waldman?"

"You know what he told me on the phone? Ten minutes! Because Isaacson wants on the panel, they're cutting our presentation time to ten minutes each!"

They went to the dining area in the kitchen and he ladled soup for her, then himself. "You have to condense your presentation?"

She tasted her soup, nodded, then nodded more vigorously. "Good soup. Let me try it on you. First I'll start with definitions. Derivations. Xeno from *xenos,* an old Greek word that was derived from an even older word, *xenwos,* of unknown origin. The word means *strange, stranger, foreign, alien.* That sort of thing. As far back as language has existed and been recorded, there has always been a word for the others. Okay. Phobia from *phobos,* Greek again, meaning *fear, flight, panic.* That derives from *bhegw,* and *phebesthai,* and means again, *panic, to flee in terror.* So that gives us *xenophobia*—a panic reaction to flee from the stranger. Now Isaacson and his gang are claiming that xenophobia is innate, and they use animal studies to prove it. You know, the chicken is born with an innate reaction to a chicken hawk, or any outline that vaguely resembles the real thing. I say we're not chickens and the world isn't made up of chicken hawks. And there is this study of a group of children who were collected as infants in England during World War II. A real mixed bag of kids. The study that was done on them was looking for neuroses. You know, kids taken from parents, that sort of thing, but it works beautifully to prove that no one taught them to fear each other, or strangers in general, and they didn't, then or later. Non-xenophobic. They don't see the same world that other people do, where every skin variation means a threat. That's the point I want to make in my initial presentation, and I simply can't do it and make the other points I need to make in ten minutes."

He listened to her, served himself more soup, and watched the changing expression of her face, the way the light from the late afternoon sun caught her hair. Even he could not tell where it had started to turn white and where it was simply the very pale blond hair that he had loved for more than twenty-five years. When she paused, he said, "Honey, what would happen if you ran over your allotted time? What if you talked for thirteen minutes instead of ten? Would they turn off the lights? Pull the plug on your microphone? Stage a walkout?"

She looked at him in speculation and suddenly grinned. Presently she chuckled.

When they were finished with lunch she went with him to his study and looked at the map he had taped to the wall. It was the United States, and there were pushpins here and there.

"Red for the hotels that were stripped first, then burned," he said. "Blue for those intact. White for the two without collectible insurance."

"Stripped?"

"Yeah. Sometimes, before an unexpected and unfortunate fire breaks out, it happens that the owners sell off paneling, or fixtures, or flooring, stained glass, that sort of thing." His voice was dry, noncommittal. "The builders included features that were the ordinary affluence then and are nearly priceless now. Sometimes they get sold before the fire."

"Did they start in the Northeast, move west?" she asked, studying the map.

"Nope. The first one, in this series, anyway, was in Ohio, then North Carolina, Vermont, on over to California, Idaho, then Washington."

"This series," she murmured. "If Phil was right and there were twice this many, there may well be others that no one suspects, so many that you probably won't be able to find a pattern, even if there is one."

He conceded the point; the phone rang and she drifted back to her work while he went to answer it. It was Stan Kraskey, one of the investigators who had inspected the ruins of the hotel near Longview, Washington. Stan had been a rookie under Charlie's tutelage fifteen years ago in New York City.

After the pleasantries, Stan said, "Jesus, Charlie, you know you can't prove anything like that, but twice in a row? No way.

It was the same down in California, the Orick fire. Look, the Longview fire was twelve miles from the station house. Those guys are pretty good up there, lots of practice during the dry season running to forest fires, and for them twelve miles should have been a snap. It had been raining a couple of months steady, the way it does up there in the winter. Supersaturated everything. And the joint burned to the ground. They knew it was set, and I knew it was set, but that's not the point. The point is they could have put it out, everything in their favor, and they didn't. They were late in getting there, trouble with a hose, trouble with a pump, low pressure, not enough water in the tank. Jesus! The guy I talked to looked me straight in the eye and lied in his teeth and knew, by God, that I knew he was lying."

"Why?" Charlie muttered. "What was in it for them?"

"Not a damn thing I could figure out. If I'd had a clue about why, I would have nabbed them for it. Not a clue."

"Local stories about the place? Bad reputation?"

"Charlie," Stan said aggrievedly. "Come on."

"Yeah." There were always stories about an abandoned building, especially a big one that had been famous to any degree at all. "But was it more than usual there, or down at Orick?"

"If it was, I couldn't dig it out of anyone. I had to give up on both of them."

"Any sign of usage on either of them? You know, drugs, transients, anything of that sort?"

"Nope. One of the reasons the fire crews gave for their delay was the state of the access roads in both cases. And they had a little bit of a point, not enough, but a little. They weren't in use."

Charlie asked a few more questions and finally hung up, more dissatisfied than ever. "Firefighters don't just let buildings burn to the ground, damn it," he muttered.

The next day they flew to San Francisco. On Sunday they had a dim sum brunch, and Indian *tandoori* chicken for dinner and Charlie began looking forward to the week ahead with more enthusiasm than he had been feeling. He planned to attend only the two panels that Constance would participate in, eat very good food at frequent intervals, go out on a fishing expedition, visit a couple of his old friends, and in general relax.

Instead, on Monday he decided to drive up the coast and visit the scene of the Orick fire.

He decided at the Embarcadero, where the symposium was to open in a few minutes; he was watching Constance mingle with people he did not know and had no desire to meet. There was a long spread of coffee and pastries, fruits, juices, even a champagne–orange juice punch. A man standing at his elbow was saying: "Of course, considering the many ramifications of the overt behavioral systems manifested by the inner-city inhabitants, it is necessary to concede that without proper psychological evaluations starting at birth and continuing throughout childhood, those children are simply enacting the predetermined roles that have been designated—"

"Excuse me," Charlie said and put his glass of punch down carefully on a railing and walked away. The man seemed oblivious; he continued to talk.

Charlie started to wend his way to Constance and overheard snatches of different conversations. "First we have to provide an environment which will permit the actualization of the potential—"

"You see, there was this parcel of land—seven acres, for heaven's sake!—and I got this idea. Most of the patients really need physical activity in addition to psychological counseling. Don't you agree?"

Charlie looked at that woman with awe. Farm labor bringing in a hundred plus an hour? He moved on. Another couple was talking about the impossibility of landing a teaching job anywhere. "The old fogies just hang on and on," a handsome young man said mournfully.

"Hi," Constance said close to his ear. "You look lost."

He turned to greet her. "I thought I was tougher," he said, "tough enough to stand it for a few days. Wrong. I want a gun and a high spot already and the meetings haven't even started yet. It's still get-acquainted-and-share-a-sweet-roll time and I'm going berserk."

Laughing, Constance took his arm. "I know. You'd rather talk about water pressure per square inch and hose material and if the new chemicals released in today's fires are really worse, or do you just know more about them."

"Damn right," he said fervently. A man standing at her other side was watching with amusement. He had a light brown beard neatly trimmed and short, and brown eyes and hair; he was dressed casually in a sweater and slacks.

"Okay," Constance said. "Before you stage a spectacular break, I want you to meet Byron Weston." She made the introduction.

"We met before, didn't we?" Charlie asked as they shook hands, then followed it with a denial. "No, television. I saw you on television."

Byron Weston nodded, still amused. "Do you mind if I use you to demonstrate something, Mr. Meiklejohn? Would you cooperate?"

Charlie glanced at Constance, who looked too innocent. "Sure," he said.

"What I want you to do is close your eyes, and then answer some questions for us. That's all." Charlie closed his eyes. "How high is the ceiling of this room?"

"Thirty feet."

"How many people are in here?"

"Two hundred forty, including seven hotel service people, three plainclothes detectives, and one hotel detective."

Constance felt more than a little awe as Charlie answered a few more questions of the same sort, each time without hesitation. When Byron thanked him, she squeezed his arm.

"That was the demonstration?" Charlie asked. "It only proves how effective thorough training is. It becomes second nature to notice the things important to your line of work."

"That is exactly my point, Mr. Meiklejohn. Your wife and I were talking about the team I'm training to handle postcrisis effects. Sometimes people appear fine immediately after a crisis, only to have their own crises months later, even years later. Hostages, victims of gunmen on towers, innocent people threatened by bank robbers, even survivors of natural catastrophes. There is some resistance to prophylactic therapy, but we're trying to win converts."

Charlie nodded thoughtfully. "We see it with fire victims," he said. "At first you think it's just the immediate shock of nearly dying in a fire, but sometimes I think it's more like guilt. The guilt of the survivor. If a firefighter enters a building without being suited up, and sometimes you have to, the guilt increases for some reason. As if the protective gear, the helmet, the equipment reassures them that they really couldn't have done anything, after all."

A discreet chime sounded and people began to return to the long table to get rid of cups, napkins. Byron Weston glanced toward the doors with annoyance. "Mr. Meiklejohn, that's exactly the sort of thing I've been looking into. Could we have dinner, tonight maybe?"

"Sorry, don't think I'm going to be around." He turned to Constance. "I thought I'd go up to Orick and get a firsthand account, spend a day or two there."

Byron laughed. "How about tomorrow night? It just happens that I'll be in Orick tomorrow night."

Charlie shrugged. "Why not?"

"I'll be at the Seaview Motel, a few miles south of town. Leave a message where you are and we'll get together. Wonderful, Mr.—Charlie. Thanks." The chimes echoed again and somehow managed to sound a bit impatient. He made a face and said, "Gotta go. See you tomorrow night, Charlie." He nearly ran as he left.

"Well," Charlie said, watching him move out of sight. "He must not want to miss opening ceremonies."

Constance smiled ruefully. "Darling, he is the opening ceremony. He's the keynote speaker. I have to go too."

He kissed her. "I'll call tonight." He watched her walk away quickly, and then wandered through the emptying room that he had described accurately to Byron Weston, although he could not remember making any particular effort to notice any of those details.

That evening Charlie watched the sunset from the broad windows of Sam's Fish House, ten miles south of Orick, California. Sharing his table was J. C. Crandle, thirty-five, ex-FBI, and currently the chief of police of Orick. J.C. was heavy-set and very tanned. His hair was thinning, pale brown, sun-bleached nearly blond in front. His eyes were dark blue, without warmth.

"You can ask all the questions you want," J.C. was saying. "It just won't do you any good. It's in the report, exactly the way it happened, and there's nothing more to add. That's how it is."

"You weren't on the police force then, were you? How can you be so sure it's all in the report?"

J.C. drank his beer and waved his hand for another. A young woman in red slacks who doubled as server and bartender sauntered over, winked at them both, and took away the empty bottles.

"It's there," J.C. said, scowling not so much at Charlie as at the rest of the dining room, the other half-dozen people in it, the gaudy sunset beyond the windows. "I know it's all there because no one gave a shit about that goddamn fire."

Charlie ordered a bucket of steamer clams and they went to work on them and a loaf of hot bread that was included. Neither spoke for several minutes.

"Look, Charlie," J.C. said then, "the insurance guy who came down after the fire, he was a jerk, you know?"

Charlie shrugged. "Actually he's pretty good. He's got a nose for arson."

"Maybe so, but he's a jerk. That was too soon after all the trouble here. People who could talk just wanted to talk about the trouble. People who couldn't talk about that just plain couldn't talk about anything. He thought they were being evasive. Evasive, hell! They just didn't give a shit."

"What trouble was that?" Charlie asked and knew immediately that this was what J.C. wanted to talk about, *all* he wanted to talk about.

"See? That's how you're different from that other one. People'd bring it up and he'd close his notebook, say thanks, and go away. It was in the papers. You probably saw it and forgot already. They haven't forgotten here."

His voice had become low, almost menacing. He looked up from his bowl of clam juice and bread, cast a quick, wary glance about the room, and lowered his voice even more. His story was interrupted repeatedly by the busboy removing shells, the woman in red slacks bringing more clams, other customers who greeted him, the arrival of more beer, his own long silences as he pondered what to say or stopped to eat again. It took him over an hour.

Two sisters, Beth and Louise Dworkin, had moved to the

coast ten years ago, he said. Beth was fifty-three, Louise forty-three. Neither had ever married. They had been schoolteachers in Sacramento until they moved to Orick to start their own boarding school for children up to the sixth grade. Some children were left with them for a week at a time only, some for a season, some a year.

"They hired a music teacher, another teacher to help out, a bus driver for field trips—just like any school. And they made out like bandits, that's for sure. Then the trouble started." J.C.'s dark blue eyes looked black and dull.

"Around Christmas most of the kids went home, but a bunch of them stayed on up there over the holidays. A week before Christmas, four years ago, one of the little girls, eleven years old, was found wandering in the woods stark naked and crazy as a bedbug. Gibbering, screaming. A bunch of college kids spotted her. Two of the guys took off after her. She was really crazy, fighting, screaming. Anyway, she got loose and ran to the cliff and went over the side."

The college kids had gone to the police, and about the same time the Dworkin sisters had called to report the little girl's disappearance. Their shock at hearing about the death was complete, and they talked about sending the rest of the children home and closing down the school for a while, or maybe even forever, but people talked them out of it. Other children were acting strangely, but the doctor called it hysteria. Beth had developed severe headaches, and he said that was stress-related. With Christmas at hand, sick kids, a sick teacher, it was more than the doctor could cope with, and he was due for a couple of weeks in Hawaii, so he tended to dismiss all the symptoms as hysteria, effects of the unfortunate death that no one was responsible for. It would pass, he reassured Louise, as soon as the new term began and things got back to normal, and he left on his planned vacation. Another doctor in Orick was on call for the school, but no one knew him well, and somehow no one ever got around to calling him. Christmas came and went; the disturbances continued, maybe got worse. From then on the entire affair was too cloudy to make sense of, J.C. said.

The young teacher the sisters had hired returned, the music teacher came back, children began arriving for the new year, and to all appearances things were getting back to normal. Then the music teacher vanished. She went to the school on a Wednesday as usual, took a walk in the woods, and was never seen again. A groundskeeper vanished. A few days later a deliveryman went to the police to report that there had been terrible screams coming from the upper floor of the school, and that Louise had acted so crazy that he had been afraid of her. She had started to pull off her clothes, was talking obscenities, crazy.

J. C. Crandle sat up straighter when he neared the end of the story, as if telling it had relieved him of a great burden. "So," he said, "when they got up there, the sisters were both batty. One kid was dead, beaten to death. Two were missing and never did show up. The music teacher never turned up. The other young teacher was found smothered to death. Out of twenty-six kids who either had returned or hadn't gone away, eleven had locked themselves in one of the upper rooms for three days, the rest were all molested, beaten, tortured, missing, crazy, or dead. That was our trouble, Charlie. And two weeks later when the hotel burned, your guy thought it was funny that no one wanted to talk about *that!*"

"You weren't here then?" Charlie asked.

"No." He took a deep breath. "You'll find out about this, too. Tonight, tomorrow. As soon as I leave, if you're still here in the restaurant. The doctor who went on to Hawaii came home from his vacation and went up to the school and hanged himself. He was my father."

Charlie remained after J.C. left. He drank two cups of coffee and finally went back to the Seaview Motel. He had been able to get a room there, the same motel that Byron Weston would stay at the following night. Postcrisis therapy, he thought, parking at the motel. Postcrisis therapy. He was not ready for bed; it would be hours before he would be ready. He went to his room, placed a call to Constance, and was glad that she was not yet back from dinner. He left a message and went out to walk on the beach in the cold dark night.

6

The next afternoon Charlie walked to the highest reach of the point, the site of the burned-out hotel. He preferred to view the ocean, its vast expanse spread out before him. Actually, there was nothing to see of the hotel. The fire had been thorough in its destruction, and wrecking crews had bulldozed the debris and filled in the cavity that had been a basement and sub-basement. Now saplings were growing in the driveway, in gaps in the brickwork of a former winding path. He stood at the edge of the cliff, leaning on a chest-high stone wall capped with smooth limestone.

The hotel had boasted extensive formal gardens, paths, trails to the beach below—it must have been something in its day, he thought, offering as it had this view of the sun vanishing into what looked like a snowdrift on the horizon. Fog moving in. Dense fog the night it burned, he remembered. The whole point must have glowed like an aurora. And no one had come until it was too late. He scowled at the ocean, which was turning gray now, decorated with ruffles of white foam.

"Mr. Meiklejohn?"

He started, and turned to see an old man at the end of the driveway. At his nod the old man advanced. He wore a baseball cap, a heavy sweater, what looked like sailor pants, and boots. His hair was white and long, hanging out from under the cap, blowing in the wind. His face was deeply seamed and brown.

"Burry Barlow," the man said as he drew near, extending his hand.

His hand was as hard and dry as driftwood, his grasp firm. Charlie leaned against the wall and studied him. Barlow was studying him just as intently.

"Heard you were looking for me most of the day," he said finally and turned to gaze out at the ocean.

"That's right," Charlie said. "I'm investigating the hotel fire. Why'd they let it burn, Mr. Barlow?"

The old man glanced at him, then chuckled. "Don't beat around the bush, do you?"

"Might be the only one in the whole damn county who doesn't," Charlie admitted.

Barlow's chuckle sounded again and he nodded. "We use your little book down at the station, you know. The manual. Pretty good stuff in it. Good training manual."

Charlie waited.

"You talked to J.C.," Barlow said after a moment. "Course, he wasn't here until after his dad hanged himself, so he doesn't know what it was like. Bedlam, Mr. Meiklejohn. It was like Bedlam."

"The hotel didn't burn until a couple of weeks after the trouble," Charlie said bluntly. "No connection."

"Maybe, maybe not. But the trouble hadn't stopped yet, either. Mildred Searles ran her car off the cliff, and Carey Duke went for a walk in the ocean and never came out. That was after the sisters were put away. Maybe we still had trouble, Mr. Meiklejohn."

"Tell me about the night of the fire," Charlie said harshly.

"Right. I was dispatcher, as they must've told you around town. Haven't gone out myself for maybe ten years, but I keep a hand in. Know every road in the county like it was my backyard." He continued to study the ocean as if searching for whales. "Four in the morning got a call from Michael Chubb. Said the school was on fire. That's all. He could see it on his way down to the docks. No one knew if they'd be able to go out fishing—the fog, you know—but they went down to the docks to hang around, see if it lifted when the sun came up." He took a deep breath. "I went out with my glasses and looked over the point here, just a little glow, no more than that, and I thought it was the school, too. We all did. And we wanted it to burn, Mr. Meiklejohn. We surely did want it to burn. In fact, we took it for granted that one of us, someone hurt real bad by all the trouble, put the torch to it. Someone like Joe Eglin, maybe. Poor Mrs. Eglin screamed for three days. You hear about that? She stopped screaming finally and hasn't said a word or made a sound that anyone knows about ever since. If Joe had put the torch to it, there wasn't a one of us who'd blame him. That's how it was."

"When you found out it was the wrong building, you lied about it anyway," Charlie said bitterly. He felt tired, the way he used to feel in New York after prowling through ashes and ruins, even if only for a few minutes. The thought of fire made him weary.

Burry Barlow shrugged and looked over the site of the hotel. "Don't know that it was the wrong building," he said slowly. "The trouble stopped after it burned. Couple of people said they slept for the first time in weeks; we all felt like something heavy and bad had been taken off our backs. Besides, by the time the men got up here, it was too far gone. About all's they could do was watch."

" 'Trouble with a hose; electric outage silenced the alarm; you stumbled and were winded for another ten minutes, delaying the calls. . . .' You committed perjury, you know. All of you did. Why are you telling me now?"

"You're one of us, Mr. Meiklejohn, a firefighter just like us. Didn't seem right, when you knew anyway. But, of course, the record doesn't change, and I'm an old man with a senile mind, memory shot to hell and gone. But you should know."

Charlie grunted; he was one of them, all right. "See any strangers around that night?" Barlow shook his head. "Did you come up for the fire? What was it like when you got here?"

"I came," Barlow said. "It was set, all right, and a good job too. Started up on the second floor, interior room, burned up and down a long time before it reached the outer walls. Funny thing, Mr. Meiklejohn, you know how things sort of lean out with an explosion, point to the center by pointing away is how I think of it."

"An explosion?" Charlie said. "What was in there to explode?"

"Not an explosion," Barlow said meditatively. "I'd say an implosion. A vacuum formed and just sucked stuff into itself. Big beams, things like that pointed all right, leaned in toward the middle." He looked at Charlie shrewdly. "Any explanation for something like that?"

"No. What else? You might as well tell me all of it."

"Yep, there's more." He slouched against the wall, his back

to the sea. "I stood right here when it burned. No wind, no rain, just the fog and the fire. Pretty. You know how that is."

Charlie nodded. Fires were the most beautiful things in the world; every firefighter knew that.

"Yep. Pretty in the fog. Next day, when it cooled off, me and J—me and another guy came up and went in. Found most of two skeletons. Not all, just most."

Charlie felt a chill that could have come from the ocean; a steady wind was now blowing in hard, it was very cold. "Go on," he said harshly.

"Uh-huh. We talked, started to call the sheriff, talked some more, decided to call in the state police instead. Then the other guy got sick and we talked some more and finally we buried them again. They're in there. I said a few words, and that was that. No more trouble, we decided, no more trouble. They were good and dead. For all we could tell, they could've been dead for years. So we buried them."

"Males? Females? Children? Who were they?"

"A male, six-footer. A woman, five-five maybe."

"Could anyone have driven up here before the fire?"

"We had to cut the chain across the access road the night of the fire. Rusted together. Well, that's all I know, Mr. Meiklejohn. That's the whole story now. And I'll deny every word of it if it gets out. Thanks for listening." He hunched down against the wind and started to walk away.

"Barlow," Charlie called after him, "thanks."

The old man waved his hand, but did not look back.

In his motel room Charlie poured a drink, turned on the television news, and sat staring at it without seeing or hearing a thing. He had driven past the school on his way to the hotel site and had paid no attention to it; he reconstructed the trip. The school grounds and hotel grounds shared a common fence, the buildings a little over a mile apart. In the fog it probably *had* seemed as if the school were burning, especially to people in town who desperately wanted the school to burn. At least he understood now why the volunteers had been in no rush. He reviewed the various accounts of the "trouble." The music teacher had vanished, and a groundskeeper. The skeletons in the hotel? Why? He drank deeply and put the empty glass down. It was nearly seven and he knew he would get very drunk if he did not eat soon. He wanted to call Constance, but decided she probably had gone to dinner by now. He missed her.

He had left his window open a crack; the wind moaned as it entered. He got up and closed the window. The problem was, he decided, he had let them mix up his fire and their "trouble" in his mind, and he couldn't separate them again. And that was because he was too hungry. Abruptly he left his room for the motel dining room. If Byron got there before he finished, fine; if not, that was also fine. He stopped at the desk to leave a message, and at that moment Constance and Byron Weston entered.

His laughter was as spontaneous and unguarded as a child's when he saw her, ran to hug and kiss her. Ten minutes later the three of them were seated in the dining room.

"I finished by one and we were both ready to leave, so we left. This afternoon and tomorrow the feelies are in control of things," Constance said, holding his hand on the table.

"And touchies and yellers," Byron said gravely.

"And yowlers and pacers and leaders," Constance added, laughing. She and Byron had played a word game describing various therapies during the last hour of the trip. She gave Charlie's hand a squeeze and let go to pick up her menu. "Enough of this levity. I'm starved."

Eventually, they had their food and Charlie was content to listen to Byron talk about his postcrisis therapy.

"Are you treating J. C. Crandle?" Charlie asked.

"You know him?"

"Just met him."

"The answer is no. Actually he wasn't here, you see, until the crisis was over. His father might have been a candidate for our therapy, but not the son. He came home mad as hell, wanting to hit someone. Still does, I bet. But he's not the victim we're out to find and help."

"How about Burry Barlow?"

Byron shook his head. "I don't even know him. What was his connection?"

"Damned if I know. Just wondered." He ate in silence for a

moment, then asked, "What about the sisters who went wonko? And poor Mrs. Eglin?"

"You've been getting around, haven't you?" Byron asked. His gaze was a bit less friendly than it had been minutes ago. "Look, our whole purpose is to help those who were affected by the outburst, not those who committed the crimes. They're in a hospital, the state hospital I assume, although I don't know. They probably had electroshock therapy, drug therapy, God knows what all. Not my province, any of that. As for Mrs. Eglin, her condition has nothing to do with any of this affair. She must have been a prime candidate for a schizophrenic break for years. It just happened, the way it does sometimes for no reason that we can ever find. But it is unrelated to the matter we are concerned with."

That was when Charlie began to listen with his public face on, Constance realized. He looked bland—maybe even a little dull—made the right sort of comments at the right times, and was using the greater part of his mind on his own thoughts. And Byron did not suspect a thing, she also realized, with more than a little dismay.

Over coffee Byron asked her to meet with his group the next day, sit in on their discussion of the past month's achievements. She started to turn him down with regrets, when Charlie said, "Why don't you do it, honey? I'm going to be tied up most of the day. Maybe you'll even get an article out of it."

Byron looked flustered for a second. Disingenuously, Charlie asked, "Would you mind if she wrote something about your work here?"

"Not at all," Byron said then. "Of course, you understand that I have written about our work in some detail myself."

"No doubt, but her work does get published in the damnedest places. *Harper's, The New Yorker*, places like that." Constance kicked him under the table and he smiled sweetly at her. "Would you like a brandy?"

"Just what was all that about?" she demanded later in their room. "He's not a charlatan, for heaven's sake! The work they're doing is important and worthwhile!"

"I expect it is," he said, taking her into his arms. "I missed you. Your hair smells good. Anyway," he said when she pushed him away, still glaring at him, "I wanted him to let you ask questions, and if he thinks there's a chance of publicity, he'll welcome questions. Publicity is money, right? Grant money, state money, whatever. Otherwise, he might have wanted to steer by himself, the way he did at dinner. I just got out of the way and let him take over, and that's what he did. Right?"

She took a deep breath, then nodded. "Right. He does that."

"So he thinks I'm the dumb cop and you're the brains of the family. And he's right, of course. Get him to show you the records, if you can. Find out who's on his patient list, and what their connection was with the school, and if there was any connection with the hotel at all. Does anyone have nightmares about the hotel, the fire, anything to do with it, that sort of thing. Okay? What made him choose some people and not others for his list? Why not poor Mrs. Eglin or J.C., for example."

She was watching him closely. "Do you think there's a connection between the madness at the school and the hotel fire?"

He shook his head. "No. I don't think anything yet. Too early. I'm just damned curious. And your hair does smell good. Let's go to bed."

Joe Eglin was twenty-eight; his wife, Maria, was twenty-five. She had not spoken, had not made a sound, had not moved of her own volition in four years. This much Charlie had learned from various people in town that morning. He had driven up into the hills and down a steep road, and had come to the fifteen acres that Joe farmed. It was a pretty setting, with redwoods high on the surrounding hills, pine trees in the valleys, ocher-colored grasses, and a fast-running stream. It appeared that there were millions of chickens and turkeys, geese and ducks, all running loose, most of them on the narrow gravel road. Joe admitted Charlie to his living room with reluctance. The noise of the fowls outside made it impossible to speak and be heard until the men were in the house with the door closed. Charlie had called, had said he wanted to talk about an insurance claim. Apparently that was all Joe Eglin had needed to hear.

"What about insurance?" Joe demanded. He was a little too flabby, too paunchy, and there were dark hollows under his eyes.

"I'd like to see your wife," Charlie said pleasantly. He glanced

about the room, spartan in furnishings, very clean. Very dull.
The walls were painted light green, a tan rug was in front of a
tan sofa, a television and VCR in the middle of the room, two
wooden chairs with cushion seats, a coffee table with nothing
on it. A venetian blind covered a picture window that was almost the full width of the room.

"She's taking a nap," Joe Eglin said. "What's this all about?"

"I represent the insurance company trying to make sense out
of the affair at the Dworkin school," Charlie said easily, as if
not very interested in any of this. "We're reviewing claims as-
sociated with the Dworkin sisters and their school. We want to
get the matter behind us, and you and your wife's names came
up. You know, it all sounds insane to me, but I wasn't here.
There's a memo with your names, but we can't find a claim.
Did you file one?"

Joe Eglin moistened his lips. He nodded toward a chair. "You
want a beer, or something?"

"No, thanks."

"We haven't filed yet. I've been waiting to see if she snaps
out of it."

Charlie shook his head. "Mr. Eglin, I want to level with you.
I heard in town yesterday that your wife is dead, that there isn't
any Mrs. Eglin. No one's seen her in four years. You don't let
anyone in here. You see where that leaves me? I mean, if I go
away and next week you show up at the office with a woman,
what does that prove? Did your wife ever have fingerprints
made? Of course not. Why would she? I really do want to see
her today, Mr. Eglin."

Joe Eglin's fists balled and he took a step toward Charlie,
then another. "Get out!"

"Sure," Charlie said. "But, Mr. Eglin, consider. I have the
company backing me. If I say in my report that I agree that
there is no Mrs. Eglin, where will that leave you if ever you
want to collect her life insurance, for example? Five thousand,
isn't that it? Not a fortune, but on the other hand, if she does
die, you'll need it for the funeral and all." He went to the door
and stood with his hand on the knob. "I wonder what it would
take to get J. C. Crandle out here poking around. Is there a
death certificate anywhere on file?"

"Wait a minute," Joe Eglin said. He was sweating heavily. "Give me a minute. You know about her?"

"I heard something."

"Yeah, I bet. Wait a minute, for Chrissake!" He rubbed his hand over his face. "Okay, she's not right in the head. The doctor would have put her in a hospital and I wouldn't let him. I can take care of her. But now . . . It's been four years and she doesn't get any better. Did you come out here to offer a settlement? Is that it? How much?"

"I want to see her," Charlie said.

"A lawyer. I need a lawyer. A settlement, that's it, isn't it? I can sue the pants off you and your fucking company!"

Charlie shrugged and turned the knob. "I'll go have a chat with Crandle, let him get a warrant or whatever it takes."

"Wait a minute!" Joe Eglin yelled. "You can see her! She's sleeping. I have to get her up and dressed. Five minutes! Wait five minutes, damn you!"

Charlie waited thirty seconds, then followed him through the living room down a short hall and paused outside a door. He could hear Joe Eglin muttering on the other side. Silently he turned the doorknob and opened the door.

A naked woman was standing in a bedroom, her face toward the door where Charlie stood. Joe was trying to get a robe on her. She was totally without expression, neither resisting her husband nor helping, just standing like a flexible doll. Her hair was unkempt. There was a dark bruise on one side of her face, red marks on her breasts. She was pregnant, six months at least. Her stare was vacant, her face empty. Except for her swollen belly, she was desperately thin.

Charlie turned and walked away, no longer trying to be silent. Behind him he heard a hoarse oath, and then choking sobs. He left the house, drove carefully through the chickens and ducks that roamed onto and off the road, to the gate in the high fence, and let himself out.

"Christ!" J. C. Crandle muttered, regarding Charlie with hatred. "Let it rest, why don't you?"

"That girl belongs in a hospital where they can help her, if there's any help for someone like that. She doesn't need what she's got."

"Okay. Okay. When does it stop? When the hell does it all stop?"

Charlie shrugged. They were in Crandle's office. Maria's medical report was on the desk, the police report beside it. Joe and Maria had gone to the school to deliver two turkeys the day the eleven-year-old girl had dived off the cliff. Maria had waited in the car while Joe made the delivery. When he returned, she was holding her head, moaning. At his touch, she started to scream. Dr. Crandle had given her a shot to put her to sleep. He had reassured Joe; she was tense, hysterical, she needed to rest and she'd be fine. When she woke up, she started to scream again. Another shot, and by then the trouble had begun at the school. Maria screamed for three days, when she wasn't heavily sedated. Then she woke up and did not scream. An appointment had been made for the following week; Joe did not keep it. No one at the office had seen Maria again.

Charlie got up and rubbed his eyes. He simply wanted to collect Constance and drive away from here, away from the spiraling madness that seemed without end.

Constance looked alarmed when she saw him. "What happened?" she asked, and took his hand.

"Bad day. Tell you later. What did you come up with?"

"Not enough," she said regretfully. "Look, I told Byron we'd meet him for a drink, but not dinner. Okay with you?"

He kissed her. "My psychic wife."

"And if you'd rather not even have a drink with him, I sort of covered that in advance, too. I said I'd check and either we'd meet him in the bar at six-thirty, or he should not count on seeing us."

Charlie laughed. "What the hell. Let's go have that drink and then duck out for dinner. I'm curious about Wonder Boy and his methods that exclude the really interesting cases."

She looked as though she wanted to comment, then held back. "Okay." She started to go into the bathroom, and at the door she paused and said, "But I have to agree with Byron. I just don't see how any of that mess at the school has anything to do with the fire at the hotel weeks later. It just doesn't make any sense."

That was the problem, he thought grumpily. It made no

sense. And yet, he also thought, there was a link. They just hadn't been able to find it. There had to be a link. Someone had taken those bodies to the hotel; they didn't just get up and walk there by themselves. And they had to be the music teacher and the groundskeeper, who was also missing. Old man Barlow thought so, and so did he. There had to be a link. And most important, why had poor Mrs. Eglin screamed? And screamed and screamed.

7

The most interesting thing that came out of the social hour with Byron Weston, Constance decided, was his apology to Charlie. That had been completely unexpected. They had been chatting, the three of them, in the polite way people do when they are mildly antagonistic without obvious cause. Byron had been talking about his training efforts, what his team looked for, how they handled people who wanted to be left alone.

"You have to assume that the ones who need help most are often the last ones to look for it," he said, making rings on the tabletop with his dripping glass. "I thought you were needling me about my two worst failures here," he said, glancing from Charlie back to the intricate patterns he was making. "I'm sorry. I was snappish."

Charlie was surprised and wary. "J. C. Crandle and Maria Eglin?"

Byron nodded. "He's a murderous impulse looking for a place to happen. He gave me the bum's rush when I approached him. And I truly didn't know about Maria Eglin for almost a year. I never even saw her, just her husband." He grimaced and stopped playing with his glass. "I should have known about her. There were hints. He was said to be brutal; she's young, a newcomer to this area, friendless. But in spite of all that, I dismissed her. She just didn't fit the pattern. She didn't know anyone at the school, no friends, no children, no reason to feel guilt over not doing anything. My God, they live miles out in the country. I made a decision that her mental collapse was independent of the other events, a coincidence. Maybe I was wrong. I just don't know. But we have to make those decisions all the time. You draw the boundaries and work within them, or nothing can get done."

"She'd be the first case, inside my boundaries," Charlie said.

"But how? She never even got out of the car. He made the delivery, left her in the parked car, and came back in five minutes at the most." Byron shook his head.

"I didn't say I like having her inside instead of outside the boundaries," Charlie protested. "If it's your job to turn over rocks, you probably will find a hell of a lot of things you'd rather not, but you keep turning those rocks."

"But it's not your job anymore. Why are you still turning those rocks?"

"Because I'm the best there is," Charlie said, perhaps too bluntly. "And I learned a long time ago to let the facts determine the outline, not the other way around."

Byron glanced at his watch, finished his drink, and stood up. "I have to go," he said. "I wish I didn't. I assume Constance pumped me and the others today at your request. I hope you find whatever it is you're looking for, Charlie. I really do."

"He's all right," Charlie said after he and Constance were alone again.

"Of course," she said in the tone that meant, I told you so.

He laughed. "I know this little dive down the road a piece. Best steamer clams on the coast, good dark beer. How about it, kid?"

While they worked their way through two buckets of clams, she filled him in on the details she had gleaned from Byron and his group. None of the people they were treating connected the fire with the other troubles, or the hotel with the school. "Of course," she admitted, wiping her hands finally, "that isn't as meaningful as it might seem. Patients often follow where the therapist takes them, and if the therapist didn't make such a connection, that path was probably closed. It's all unconscious, on both sides."

He grunted, looked in the bucket, picked up another clam,

then put it back with a sigh. "It would sink me," he said. Over coffee he told her about Maria Eglin.

Furiously she cried, "What's the answer? People knew she needed help! They had to know it. They just butted out!"

"There isn't any," he said. "Answer. No complaints, no problems."

When he paid the bill, the waitress in the red pants said, "Hear about J.C.? He went out to Joe Eglin's place with his deputy and beat the daylights out of Joe. Put him in the hospital, so they say."

Charlie thanked her, complimented the food, and wondered: Would that be enough to placate J.C.'s murderous impulse? He doubted it. He took Constance back to the motel. The next day they drove down the coast, stopping here and there, wandering in the rain through the redwoods, beachcombing in drizzle, sunning themselves in Malibu. One week later at breakfast she said, "Let's go home." He was as ready as she.

Constance pushed newspapers to one side of the kitchen table. She propped up her chin in one hand, tapped the fingers of the other on the tabletop, staring off through the glass back door past Charlie, who sat opposite her. They had been home for two weeks. "No good," she said with finality. "Not a mention of the hotels that burned until after the fact. But, my heavens, one cryptic, noninformative story after another about strange happenings—suicides, murders, disappearances, madness, accidents . . . I keep wondering what the reality of those situations really was." She held up a few of the papers. "In Orick," she said, "the papers were full of the stories of the mad sisters, the insanity at the school, but not a word about Maria Eglin. The doctor's suicide is given a paragraph of non-news reportage; the woman who drove off the cliff is labeled a one-car accident victim; the guy who walked out to sea is called the victim of a freak wave. That's in a place where we know pretty much what was going on. Without more information than in the articles, anyone would take them all at face value. Why not? And there's nothing really strange there, if you take them at face value." Charlie started to speak and she held up her hand. "I know. I know. Thoreson's afraid of a leak if we start asking too many questions. I've been thinking about it, and it might get out if you nose around, but I can do it. There are state statistics, state agencies that keep track of insanity, admissions to hospitals, private doctors' new patients. I'm going to make some phone calls."

"I think we're putting together a pretty comprehensive list of mayhem and altogether weird happenings," he said, leaning back in his own chair across the table from her. But that was part of the problem; they had not been searching for mayhem and weird happenings. They had been looking for something to link the fires. The papers had been arriving for the past ten days; motel records had started a bit later, enough to keep them busy for the next month. But he felt her dissatisfaction. Too long. Too chancy. And worst of all, no paper had printed a line about the hotels until after the fires, but every community had had more than its share of madness and violence. That bothered him most of all.

"Two things are wrong with this method," she said. "First, we don't have a control group. We'd need sister towns, at the very least. Maybe things like these happen all the time everywhere. *Boys Hole Up in School and Set Off Explosives.* Boys have done things like that in a lot of places, when they saw a chance of getting away with it. And this one: *Farmer Kills Neighbor's Cattle.* How many other farmers have killed their neighbors' cattle? We don't know."

"And this one," he said dryly. *"Mother Throws Three Children Out of Seventh-floor Window, Leaps After Them."*

"Even that sort of thing happens. Anyway, we need controls. And the other reason is that too many things just won't make it to the newspapers. If the mayor's wife turns into a kleptomaniac, that won't get in the papers. They pay off the bills and quietly take her away for a rest. Or if Mrs. Croesus develops a phobia about dirt and germs and won't eat, you'll never see that in the news. A nice vacation in a beautiful hotel-like setting, that's how they'll take care of that. If a highly regarded man becomes a flasher overnight, or turns his house into a bordello, or does anything short of murder, chances are you'll never know about it. Accidents, disappearances, actual murders, they get reported, not the lesser things. And sometimes the people responsible for the lesser things are just as deranged, just as desperately in need of help, just as likely to commit mayhem eventually if they don't get help."

He shrugged. "You win. What bothers me is that there's no one pattern. People are going nuts in a hundred different ways. Nothing you can pin down, nothing to connect any of that with the hotels."

"No problem about the madness," she said, dismissing it. "That's how insanity works. There are some physical conditions that result in certain syndromes, but functional disorders take too many different forms to look for any one pattern. What I see a lot of in these stories is what my colleagues tend to call paranoid schizophrenia. That's to make sure they cover all bases."

"And you wouldn't call it that?"

"The term is too loose to mean much. Schizophrenia means cut off from reality, and paranoia, you know, feelings of persecution, deeply held feelings, but still. . . . See what I mean? Descriptive, but then what? Not very long ago the good family doctor would say something like, oh yes, you have the grippe, and he would describe the symptoms, what to expect in the days to follow, and everyone was reassured somehow. Descriptive. Now we say things like schizophrenia and use drugs, shock treatments where they're still allowed, and everyone's reassured somehow. It's mostly descriptive, and the treatments are elephant-gun mentality at work. Not many people get cured, although some get better. And no one can say for certain what the cause is. We have ruled out some things—demons, possession by spirits, original sin, an evil nature of the victim. We suspect diet, vitamin deficiencies, hormonal imbalances, a genetic accident. Too many things are suspect. And none of them would fit this pattern, if there is a pattern. Why acute onsets in places so widely separated? It just doesn't make any sense. I'm going to make some phone calls."

Even if there was no pattern in the nut cases, Charlie brooded after she left, there was in the arson fires. One person had started them all; even a rookie could have spotted that much if his attention had been directed to it. Upstairs room, gasoline, forced entrance, between one and three in the morning. One firebug, busy as a little bee.

When Constance returned to the kitchen an hour and a half later, she found Charlie on his hands and knees backing Brutus up into the corner under an antique maple hutch. Charlie was muttering: "John Daniels, Carl Larson, John Lucas, Carlton Johns, John Carolton—" He looked up at her and scowled. "That damn cat snitched my cheese for the last time. I'm going to catch him and rub his nose in the plate and then heave him into the next county. Brutus, you've had it." The gray cat Ashcan had come in to watch; he approached Charlie, sniffing at his hands, and started to lick one. "Out, damn it! This is our final showdown, you asshole!"

Ashcan rolled over and rubbed his cheek against Charlie's arm. Brutus gave a leap, cleared both Charlie's outstretched hands and Ashcan, and sauntered into the living room, flicking his tail disdainfully. Charlie sighed and began to haul himself up from the floor. He scowled harder at Constance, who had started to laugh; she quickly stifled it and turned her back. Her shoulders continued to shake.

"Well?" he snarled, taking the empty plate to the counter.

"I have spies at work. It'll be a couple of days. Who are the men on your roll call?"

"One man," he said. "Bet you five it's one man."

She shook her head. "Betting is against my moral principles. Besides, I always lose. Tell me."

"He's on the motel lists. Always checks in a day or two before the fire, always gone the day after. Drove a 'seventy-nine black Malibu until last year, when he had an 'eighty-four, black again. Always has the right state plates on the car, but that's easy enough to arrange. Pays cash for a room. Lists his business as real estate appraiser. People go nuts; he shows up and burns down a hotel. People stop going nuts. Enough?"

She nodded, then asked, "What's a Malibu?"

"Never mind. Just take my word for it—there's a zillion of them out there on the roads. Who's cooking tonight?" His expression had gone innocent suddenly.

"You are. Charlie, assuming you're right, how would he know where to go? That is, if the madness and arson are connected. Not from the newspapers. We can't do it."

"I was wondering that same thing," he said with a touch of smugness. "You have sources, state shrinks, and so on, but you know who else has sources, just as good, or better even? Insurance claims people. Who goes into a hospital without insurance these days? No one, let me tell you. So who pays? You and I and every other policyholder on earth. And who keeps the records? Health insurance companies. Sore Thumb thought he had a leak, and so do I. Someone has access to that information, you better believe."

"It would be in their computers," she said, looking past him, thinking.

"Yep. If you know how to go about it, if you have your own little handy-dandy computer at home, if you have a modem, you too can scan the lists, arranged in any order you call up, by area, dollar amounts, diseases, accidents, or illnesses, whatever you want." He went to the pantry and opened the freezer. "You remember those steaks we had over on the coast? Cajun style? Blackened steaks, they called them. Dijon mustard, garlic, and lots of cayenne, wouldn't you say? Anything else?" He came back with a butcher's package. She was walking out of the kitchen. "Hey, where are you going?"

"I'm going to close doors so smoke won't fill the house, and I'll bring the fan from the attic. Open the exhaust before you start this time, will you?"

While the steaks were thawing, he called Phil, who was back from Bermuda. He told Phil he wanted the computer printouts of claims and listened patiently to the many reasons why that was impossible, and then he said he also wanted the list Phil had mentioned of other hotels at risk. He moved the telephone away from his ear and winked at Constance.

When Phil subsided, Charlie said kindly, "And you just take it easy, old buddy, and get well."

"Charlie, about those claims, you know it's probably illegal to give that out. Unethical, for sure; illegal, probably. Sore Thumb will have a coronary. And speaking of Sore Thumb, he's driving me batty. Did you tell him to do something highly immoral and possibly illegal to himself?"

Charlie laughed. "I did, but he won't. One more thing, a list of people at the conference in Dallas when you talked about the hotel fires. A list of attendees."

"For God's sake, Charlie! I can't just snap my fingers and have lists appear! What else do you want? A list of registered voters? List of high school graduates for the years 1950 through 1980? Some other little thing on that order?"

"Now, Phil, don't get testy on me," Charlie said. "Tomorrow? The next day? Send them Express Mail, will you? Good talking to you, pal. Take care." Gently he hung up. He looked at his package of steaks and started to sing lustily—and not very well—bits and pieces of *The Marriage of Figaro* in no particular order.

Two days later Charlie sat upright at four in the morning. A window, he thought, wide awake, shivering. And gasoline. Constance woke up and said, "What was that?"

"I don't know. Get a robe on." He was already pulling on his robe on his way to the door. He touched the handle, the wood paneling, sniffed, and then opened it. The smell of gas was stronger. No heat, no smoke, no flickering light. Only then did he turn on the hall light and start downstairs. He followed the strong smell of gas to the living room, where a window had been broken. No fire. He went out on the porch and found that the front of the house had been drenched with gasoline. The can was on the porch. Constance was right behind him.

"It's okay," he said, his voice hard and flat. "It'll evaporate fast in this breeze." He picked the can up carefully, using the back of his finger under the handle. It was empty. He carried it inside, through the house to the back porch, where he put it down. Then he inspected the rest of the house, starting at the ground floor and continuing on to the basement, the garage, upstairs, even the attic. When he finished, Constance handed him a glass nearly full of bourbon. He took a long drink, and stopped shivering.

Constance drew him to the kitchen table, where she had a second glass. She pointed to a rock and a piece of crumpled paper. "I tried not to mess up any prints there might be," she said. Her voice sounded strained and unfamiliar. He put his arm around her shoulders and leaned over to read the note without picking it up.

Butt out or the next time I'll light it.

He took a deep breath, raised his glass, and drank again.

Constance had been seized with a fury so intense that it frightened her. Fury and fear, fear of the fury, fear for Charlie.

She had flashes of the year in New York, toward the end of his career with the fire department, a few years filled with nightmares, jerking from sleep to wakefulness just like tonight, but without cause. She saw again how he had felt doors before opening them, how his gaze had traveled over a new room, seeking the fire escape, searching for the fire trap, the piled-up clothes behind a door, the flammable curtains, the spilled combustible. She heard again his garble of words as he fought with dream demons who breathed fire, who were creatures of fire. His thrashing about, muttering, moaning, then the sudden jerk into full wakefulness that would remain the rest of the night, whether it was only an hour or two, or six or seven.

Dear God, she breathed, don't let it start again. Please.

The orange cat Candy slunk into the room, complaining bitterly, looking about with wild eyes. Brutus watched through slitted eyes from on top of the refrigerator. Ashcan had gone into hiding somewhere. What good were they? she thought sourly. Not a peep out of them, not a clue that the house was under attack. What the hell good were they?

"I'll make some breakfast," she said. "No point in going back to bed now."

"I'll put some cardboard over the window."

"I did it while you were looking around."

"I'll clean up the glass before a cat walks through it."

She started to say no, sit down and try to relax, but she knew he would not relax again that night. Nor would she.

"He knows we're closing in," Charlie said as he left the kitchen for the vacuum cleaner. "He's running scared."

And so was she, she admitted silently. So was she.

8

In his dreams tenements burned, high-rise condos burned, office buildings burned, factories, single-family houses, schools. He ran here and there futilely as screaming people, ablaze, leaped out of windows. Eventually he was always inside the burning building, running down one hallway after another, feeling doors, watching doorknobs glow red, burst into flames, watching walls start to smoke, char, burst into flames. He ran until he dropped in exhaustion, and the fire raced toward him from different directions. He buried his head in his arms and waited for it, and woke up, sweating, shaking, through with sleep for that night.

The reports came in, the lists arrived, microfiches, Xeroxes of Xeroxes of newspaper accounts, photocopies of insurance claims, police statements, statements from fire department heads. Thoreson called daily, demanding action; Charlie stopped returning his calls. Phil sent funny postcards but did not call.

Charlie was staring moodily at a photograph of John Loesser, who had left his last apartment without leaving a forwarding address. Outside, a guard dog padded quietly on her patrol of the yard. The cats were in a panic because of the dog, who simply ignored them all. He knew so much, Charlie thought bitterly, and not the important thing: why. Loesser had survived an attack, had quit his job with one of the biggest, most prestigious insurance companies in the world in order to become an independent adjuster who apparently never adjusted anything. Two weeks after his release from the hospital, the first hotel had burned, the one in which he had been attacked. He had access to computer data, knew how to use it, how to interpret it. People began to go mad here and there; Sir Galahad arrived and burned down a hotel; people stopped going mad. Probably he had enough now to make an arrest, Charlie thought; a formal investigation would cinch it, and yet . . . He had no intention of turning over a damn thing until he had a clue about the why. He scowled at the photograph, cursing John Loesser under his breath. You son of a bitch, he thought, why?

Constance entered his study and touched his shoulder. "Charlie, Byron Weston is on the phone. You should talk to him."

Her voice was strange, remote, her face set in the expression she had when she was controlling herself perhaps too much. Charlie moved the photograph of Loesser away from the telephone on his desk, and put it facedown. He lifted the extension. "Yeah," he said.

"Charlie, when you were in Orick, you were asking questions about the old hotel. Why? What did that have to do with the epidemic of madness?"

"I don't know," Charlie said softly. "Why do you ask?"

There was a pause; Charlie could hear other voices, then the slamming of a door. Byron returned. "Sorry," he said. "Charlie, did you watch the news tonight, national news?"

"No."

"Okay. There was a story. It'll be a bigger story tomorrow. We have a repeat of the Orick madness, and this time I didn't predetermine the boundaries. I've just been listening."

"Is there a hotel involved?"

"Two of them," Byron said harshly. "No fire, though. Look, you brought up the fact that people in Orick had been infected, affected, something—people I excluded in my study there. Well, this morning a sniper held a trainload of people hostage in a tourist attraction here. Nine people were killed before it ended. My office was called and I flew out and arrived within an hour of the end of the seige. I began to listen to people real early this time, and I let them direct the conversations. They say incidents began over a month ago in the town of Grayling in California, and they link the old hotel to the madness. What can you tell me about it, Charlie? I need help with this!"

"Why will it be a bigger story tomorrow?" Charlie asked easily. Constance, listening, shivered at the sound of his voice now.

"Because some of the survivors are telling reporters that a

dead man got up and walked. The press will have a field day with this one."

Charlie talked with Byron for another fifteen minutes; when he was finished, Constance took the phone to make airline reservations for the following morning. She used her name, Constance and Charlie Leidl, she said, spelling it out, and gave her credit card number. Charlie raised an eyebrow, then nodded. She expected Loesser to show up for this one every bit as much as he did.

Flying in to Las Vegas was always a shock, Constance thought, watching the view from her window. Miles and miles of arid wasteland, and then high-rise glitter and neon; barren mountains and straggly sage; and slot machines in the terminal. Then, the silence of the desert and the cacophony of heavy traffic on Interstate 15. Charlie drove, following Byron's directions, to the California border, where he left the interstate for a state road to Grayling. An hour out of Las Vegas, Byron had said, but it was only fifty minutes to the small dusty town.

The state road became Main Street where they passed an adobe building, Grayling High School, and then a feed store, a car dealer with half a dozen used cars on display, a few small shops, drugstore, a furniture store, a ten-cent store, a St. Vincent de Paul outlet . . . Everything looked tired, gray, dusty. A scattering of bare trees trembled in a high wind that was very cold. Charlie turned onto Mesquite Street and stopped in front of number 209. Two other cars were already there, one a sleek baby-blue Cadillac, Byron Weston's car.

Charlie stopped in the driveway, got out, and went to open the trunk. He hauled out the suitcases, and then stood surveying the dismal scene. The street was not long, eight or ten houses on each side, and then the desert started again. Most of the houses were wooden, paint cracked and peeling on many of them; no more than one or two appeared well maintained, with lawns and some shrubbery. There had been a little activity on Main Street, a few cars in motion, a few people bundled against the wind; here no one was in sight. At the end of the street a dust devil formed and raced away erratically.

"Well," he said, shivering. He regarded the house before

them glumly. Peeled paint, gray, a few misshapen sagebrush plants on the sides of the steps. "I don't think," he said, "I'd be tempted to relocate here. Let's do it."

Constance nodded, chilled through and through by the biting wind, just as dismayed and disheartened by the dreary town as he was.

The woman who admitted them to the house was tall, beautifully built, with straight black hair and black eyes. More Indian than Spanish, Constance thought, shaking her hand.

"Beatrice Montoya," the woman said. "I'm Byron's assistant. I'm to show you your room and give you a drink—coffee, whatever you want—and then let you start examining the reports, if you wish."

She led them through the house as she talked. The living room was furnished with heavy black Spanish furniture that looked uncomfortable. Very fine Indian blankets hung on the walls, relieving the darkness and heaviness. They went through the kitchen, sparsely equipped with a stove and ancient refrigerator and scant cabinets, and on the other side of it into a narrow hall painted white. There were several closed doors. Theirs was the last room. Here there was plenty of light, with east windows, white walls, and more of the lovely blankets, one of them on the bed, two on the walls.

"Not the Waldorf," Beatrice was saying as she motioned them to enter. "But not too bad. Byron said to let you decide. If you'd rather go to the motel, it's only a few blocks away. It's just that it's full of outsiders right now. You know, the curious, a few reporters, ghouls, that sort of thing."

She was too polite, Charlie decided, regarding her thoughtfully when she paused. Too reserved, hardly even trying to pretend she was interested in them. He and Constance were also outsiders, he realized, ghouls, curiosity-seekers. Beatrice started to turn away and he said, "Did you think we'd be better off in the motel?"

She looked startled for a second, then shrugged. "It's up to you. Byron and the others will be back in another half hour or so. I'll let you wash up, or unwrap, whatever, and go put on some coffee."

"I don't know about you," Constance said as soon as the

woman closed the door, "but I'm freezing. I intend to change clothes and then we'll see."

When they returned to the kitchen a few minutes later, Beatrice had a tray ready. She picked it up. "This way." She led them into the other side of the house, where they stopped at a comfortable room that probably had been intended as a den. There was a wood-burning stove, some beanbag chairs in a corner, an overstuffed sofa, also pushed out of the way, and two desks and several office chairs. A computer system was on one desk. An assortment of bottles and glasses was on an end table, and computer printouts, maps, rolled-up papers, notebooks, seemed to be everywhere.

A large topographical map had been thumbtacked to one wall. Three red circles made a triangle. Charlie walked to it.

"Here's Grayling," Beatrice said, pointing to one of the circles. "This one is the big resort hotel going up, not quite finished yet, and that one is Old West. That's where . . . where the incident occurred."

Charlie nodded. He had looked up the area at home, but this map was a superb USGS map that showed every rock, every dip and hollow. That's all that was out there, he thought: rises, dips, hollows, chasms, peaks, dry lakes, dry riverbeds, barren rocks, scrub desert brush. . . . Behind him Beatrice was pouring coffee.

"We started at seven this morning," she was saying to Constance, "and by this afternoon, Byron knew we all had to see the location for ourselves. The stories just weren't making any sense, and they vary so much about where things happened. We drew to see who'd go today, who'd wait until tomorrow. So Polly and Mike and Byron went out, oh, an hour ago, maybe. They'll be back any minute now."

Byron wished that Beatrice had come instead of Polly, and knew it was unfair, and even tried to force himself not to see the little byplays that always occurred when Polly and Mike were together. If only Mike weren't such an ass, he thought, and knew that was hopeless too. Mike was an ass, yearning so openly for Polly's attention that it was embarrassing for everyone around them. And Polly could be a bitch, he also knew, teasing just enough to make Mike even more an ass, but never enough to warrant a dressing-down. Mike was twenty-six, Polly a couple of years older and very attractive, with pale hair and blue eyes with incredible lashes. Mike was overweight, a wrestler who would make a damn good psychologist someday, but at the present time was simply a pain in the ass. At the last minute Byron had decided to let Mike drive his Land Rover in, more to keep him busy than because he feared for his Cadillac. After all, he had thought, the road was used every day by the workers at Old West; it had to be okay. Okay turned out to be an overstatement. It was just passable, with deep ruts and rocky places and precipitous hills. Mike loved driving it. He kept glancing in the rearview mirror to grin at Polly, who was being shaken like a malted milk.

He rounded a sharp curve and Old West came into view. Two buildings, the old hotel and another one halfway down the street, were the original structures, aged, weathered silvery, looking very much at home in the desert. Everything else was new. Dust swirled in the street, settled, swirled.

"See if you can drive all around the place," Byron said when they drew close. The road wound by an area with a portable toilet and a parked trailer, then behind the old hotel, and the new buildings, and finally behind the railroad station, where it ended. The last quarter mile there was no real road, just a bull-dozed surface. It was late enough for the shadows of the buildings to fill the street and made deep pockets of darkness. Wood that had not turned silver gleamed golden in the shafts of sunlight streaking in low between the buildings. As soon as the motor noise stopped, the whistle of the wind rose. The sign hanging over the entrance to the saloon swished as it was lifted, dropped, lifted again. Polly drew her shearling coat tighter, the collar halfway covering her head, and picked up her pad of graph paper. Mike checked his camera and started down the street, and Byron turned his attention to the train station platform.

In his mind he reconstructed the scene of the massacre as he had heard it described over and over that day. The train pulled in on the other side of the platform; people got off and milled about. A broad walkway went down both sides of the street in front of the buildings. Eight feet wide, ten feet, with two steps down here and there, lined with railings, hitching posts, big Mexican pots that were still empty, but would hold greenery one day. People started to move down both sides, looking into the shops, with shopkeepers, customers all in costume, going about life as it had been in 1880. Then the show started.

Byron gazed down the length of the street to the hotel at the far end, half a mile away. On the right from here, halfway down the street, was the saloon. The corral was off to one side of it, not visible from here. The cowboys had come from there, whooping and yelling, shooting blanks into the air. Down a few doors from the saloon, opposite it, was the jail; the sheriff had come out with his gun ready, and at the same time several men had run out from the saloon, also with guns. More shooting, more noise. And then the real shooting had started. Byron turned his attention to the saloon again, to the upper story with a narrow balcony where the madman had held the entire town at bay for three hours.

He scowled at the scene, seeing it the way he had heard it described half a dozen times already. Workers had come from the far end, puzzled by the screams, which had not been in the scenario. They had been shot at too, and several of them had been hit, fatally, according to the stories. The ones who could run away had done so. Some of them had not yet been located.

Someone had tried to drive out in a truck and had been shot. From the balcony the killer could see the entire area, and he had been a good shot. Two men finally had crawled behind the saloon building, out the back way on foot, and they had summoned help. And one of the dead men had got up and walked to the hotel. Byron's scowl deepened as he stared broodingly down the wide street of Old West to the hotel. Obviously the man had not been dead. He had wandered inside, out the back door, out on the desert where he had died, and had not been found. But he had not been dead when he got up and walked. He had not.

Most of the mess had been cleared away, windows boarded up; here and there glass shards gleamed in the golden afternoon sunlight where it streamed in between the buildings. The wind whistled maniacally, and the sign swung up and down with a whooshing, creaking noise. There was nothing else to be gained here, Byron decided, and now looked for Polly. He realized almost absently that he had been noticing Mike for the past several minutes. Mike had stopped snapping pictures, had stopped moving at all, in fact, and was facing away, toward the hotel. Byron had assumed that Mike was waiting for the right light, for a shadow to move or something, in order to get a shot of the hotel. Then Mike dropped his camera. Still he did not move. Polly walked through one of the rays of sunlight, into the next shadow. Slowly, almost ponderously, Mike turned and started to walk toward her. She was concentrating on her feet, avoiding the broken glass. Byron felt his throat go dry when suddenly Mike lunged for Polly.

Byron vaulted the rail of the boardwalk and raced toward them. Polly screamed and tried to run, but Mike caught her and dragged her off the boardwalk, onto the street. She rolled away and struggled to get up, he knocked her down, and this time went for her throat. Byron reached them and grabbed Mike's arm, tried to pull him off. Mike swept him away effortlessly. Byron's hand closed on the heavy camera. He raised it, swung as hard as he could, and hit Mike in the temple. Mike grunted and pitched forward on top of Polly. She was sobbing hysterically.

Byron heaved at Mike's inert body and finally rolled him off Polly and pulled her clear, helped her to her feet. Then he looked at Mike and his stomach churned. Mike's eyes were wide open, unseeing, the stench of death on him.

"Oh, my God!" Byron said, and then again, and found he could not stop saying it. He was half dragging Polly away, toward the station platform, toward the Land Rover, and she was sobbing and choking, and he was repeating, "Oh, my God!" over and over. She staggered and he held her, then got her moving again, but she looked back and screamed piercingly, and crumpled at his side. He turned to see Mike on his feet, his eyes wide open and blind, coming toward them. He felt frozen, paralyzed. Mike took another step, halting and slow. Byron tugged at Polly; he stooped, keeping his gaze on Mike, who was advancing slowly but steadily. Byron lifted Polly by one arm and slung her over his shoulder and began to back up toward the platform, unable to take his eyes off Mike. He backed up the three steps to the boardwalk, crossed to the other side, and only then turned and ran to the Land Rover.

Mike had left the keys on the dashboard. He fumbled with them until he found the right one and turned on the ignition. Mike stopped then, on the boardwalk, twenty feet away; he turned around and started to walk in the opposite direction. Byron killed the engine trying to start it, and saw with horror that Mike had turned his way again. He got the engine going and backed up with a roar, turned, squealing the tires, and raced back over the leveled ground to the road. When he looked one more time, Mike was walking toward the hotel.

9

When they got back to the house Polly was conscious. She was shaking and weeping, but able to sit up and, Byron hoped, able to hear him with comprehension.

"We have to call the sheriff," he repeated. "Mike went berserk and attacked you. I hit him and we got out of there, left him behind. Do you understand?"

She nodded.

The sun had gone behind the mountains and now the shadows filled the countryside: inky pools, black pits, unfathomable chasms. The wind had let up marginally, and although it was very cold, Byron knew that neither his nor Polly's shivering was due to the temperature. At the house he brought the Land Rover to a jerking stop and got out, helped her out, walked with his arm around her shoulder to the door.

Byron was vastly relieved when he saw Charlie and Constance. He told them briefly what had happened and asked Beatrice to call the sheriff. Polly was too shocked to speak yet. Constance took her to the bathroom to examine her injuries, wash the dirt from her face. She was certain the young woman was totally unaware of her.

By the time Sheriff Logan Maschi arrived, Byron had cleaned himself up a bit, and no longer was visibly shaking, but he was pale and had the staring eyes of someone still in shock. Polly was in worse shape, ghastly pale, trembling.

"Holy Christ!" Maschi muttered when Byron finished telling the story. He had condensed it, said no more than that Mike had gone crazy and attacked Polly. Maschi was a heavy man in his sixties, tanned like old mahogany. He wore cowboy clothes: hat, boots, and all, even a silver buckle on his belt.

Charlie watched as the sheriff asked questions, made notes, and got up to leave. Charlie walked out to the porch with him.

"The man on the balcony the other day, did you know him?"

"Yep."

"I take it there was no reason for him to break like that, no medical problems, financial, whatever?"

"Trevor Jackson was the most decentest man I've known," the sheriff said heavily. "Hell, one of the guys he shot dead was his own brother-in-law! And now this." He drew a deep breath. "I just wish to God old man Lorrimer had kept his money in the casinos over in Vegas. Nothing but trouble since he got that goddamn wild hair up his ass about rebuilding that ghost town. Ghost town! Hah! Tell you this, that town might never get finished. That's for sure. Ain't nobody wanting to go back in, and now this."

"You won't do any searching tonight, will you?"

"Hell no! No point to it. You been out there? Guy with a head injury, falls in a hole, who's to know? Especially by night. We'll look for him tomorrow."

Charlie went back inside; chilled to the bone, he thought gloomily. And the house was not a hell of a lot warmer than out on the porch. He rejoined the others in the den and rubbed his hands together hard.

"Okay," he said. "Several questions. What do you do for heat in this place? What do you do about food? And what happened out there today? First the heat."

Beatrice was staring at him as if he had suggested an orgy. He lifted an eyebrow. "Heat," he said again.

"Sorry. There's a thermostat in the living room. It was so warm early, I didn't think of it." She left.

Charlie turned to Byron. "Food?"

Byron looked blank.

"There's nothing like dinner stuff in the fridge," Charlie said patiently. "I looked. You must have planned on something to eat for dinner. What?"

Byron moistened his lips. "We hoped to get someone to come in and cook, but no luck so far. We've been eating at the restaurant next to the motel. Jodie's. We have breakfast and lunch materials."

"Jodie's," Charlie repeated in satisfaction. He went to the phone, found the telephone book, and riffled through it. Then he dialed, waited a few seconds, and said, "I want to order five steaks, rare to medium rare, baked potatoes, salads for five, all the works. When will it be ready?" He listened, then said, "Of course, to go. When can I pick it up?" He listened again. "Look, you cook, I deliver. When?" He examined the ceiling while he waited, then said, "Gotcha. The name's Leidl." He spelled it. "Okay." He hung up. "Forty-five minutes. Now the last question."

Beatrice had returned. She went to the makeshift bar and poured a drink, then sat down next to Polly on the sofa. Polly was huddled under a blanket, staring at Charlie with wide eyes, very frightened. She shook her head when he glanced at her. He turned to Byron. "What really happened out there?"

This time Byron told it the way he remembered, all of it. Charlie listened intently, and noticed at the same time with interest that the drink Beatrice had poured was really for Polly. She put it in the girl's hands and even helped her get it to her lips. She'd do, he decided.

"You see why I couldn't tell the sheriff?" Byron said helplessly. "Who's going to believe us? And, in fact, I don't believe it myself any longer. I must have just injured him."

"Maybe," Charlie said. He looked at Polly. "You were supposed to be sketching the layout, weren't you? How far down the street did you get? Did you see anything strange, feel anything, hear anything?"

What little color had returned to her face drained away again. Beatrice glared at Charlie. He made his voice harder, flatter. "Polly, I asked you a question."

She drank a little, then said, "I got a headache. I remember that. I was drawing and I felt dizzy for a second or two, and then I had a headache. That's when I decided I had enough in the notebook. That's when I started back. That's when Mike . . ."

"How far had you gone?"

"Past the saloon, not all the way to the end, a few doors from the end maybe."

"And you dropped your sketch pad there, didn't you?"

She looked around guiltily.

"That's all right, but I want you to sketch the place for me now, before you forget the details. Okay? Will you do that?"

She took another sip of her drink and got up, as if relieved that she could do something. Byron nodded, and Constance felt almost smug about Charlie's handling of the girl. Exactly right, and he had no training whatsoever.

Charlie glanced at Beatrice. "Is there someplace where she can draw and not be disturbed by our voices?"

"Of course. Come on, Polly. Let's go to the kitchen table." They left.

Charlie poured a drink for Constance and another for himself, and sat down near Byron. "Now, fill me in on what the hell's been going on at Old West. Okay? And here at Grayling. I take it that it's involved too."

Byron pulled a notebook from his coat pocket. He remembered and dismissed the memory of how he had dominated the conversation when he had had dinner with Charlie and Constance at Orick, how he had thought then that Charlie was too phlegmatic to be interesting.

"I have a timetable here," he said. "Incomplete, of course, but an indication. The first incident was nearly five weeks ago. Nellie Alvarez had a breakdown and ran out on the desert and vanished. They found her body a week later. That's when I think it all started."

Charlie took the notebook and started to glance through it. Constance asked, "Did you feel anything out there? See anything?"

"No, nothing for me. Polly didn't mention her dizziness before, or the headache, but of course the wind was pretty fierce. That could account for it."

Without looking up from the notebook Charlie asked, "Were all these people at Old West before they went bonkers?"

Byron gave Constance a look of reflexive protest. She rolled her eyes and shrugged.

"I don't know," Byron said.

"Find out, will you?" Charlie said absently, turning a page.

"You tell me something," Byron said then. "What are you investigating? Fire? Or something else? You thought the trouble at Orick was connected with the hotel there, didn't you? And now another old hotel. What's going on? And why aren't you using your own name?"

Charlie had introduced Constance to the sheriff as Dr. Leidl, and himself as her husband without adding another name. He shrugged and stood up. "Wish to hell I knew. Time to go collect dinner. Point us in the direction of the restaurant, okay?"

The town was small enough to crisscross on foot several times in under half an hour, but the wind was cold enough to make them glad they weren't walking. All the businesses were closed now, Main Street bleak-looking. They went up the two blocks, turned left, and before them the street became state highway again; the black desert, empty and barren, seemed ready to invade the town. Jodie's was a welcoming oasis of flashing neon signs and a crowd of parked cars. Next to it a motel sign said No Vacancy. The motel was far back from the street, its parking lot also filled.

Charlie drove through both parking lots slowly, scanning the cars, satisfying himself that no late-model black Malibu was among them. Then he stopped near the entrance to the restaurant. "I'm going to bribe the desk clerk while you hunt and gather food. Division of labor, all that." He grinned at her fleetingly and ambled away.

Constance had to wait ten minutes for the order to be completed, and during the delay she talked to the woman behind the cash register. That woman turned out to be Jodie, Lorraine Jodrell, middle-aged, gray-haired, with shrewd dark eyes; she was on a first-name basis with her customers.

"We got wind of the tourist attraction three years ago," she said confidentially. "This place"—she indicated the restaurant with a sweeping gesture—"was a pigpen. Beer and hamburgers, that was what it offered, and loud country rock. We borrowed money from Homer's father and bought it, and turned it into a good restaurant. Figured workers deserved decent food, and then, of course, the tourists, when they began to come. Took over a year to get it the way we wanted it." She looked past Constance with troubled eyes. The restaurant was attractive, with many lush green plants in ocher-colored clay pots, a relief from the harsh landscape beyond the windows. "Food's good too," Jodie said.

Constance listened to her, asked a question now and again, and watched the clientele. The restaurant business was good, if quiet. It appeared that every table was filled; the booths that lined the walls were packed. Most of the customers were in Western clothes, local people, with only half a dozen obvious tourists among them. The tourists stood out by the way they were dressed—designer jeans, silk shirts, cashmere sweaters, glossy boots—and the way they stared at the local people. Occasionally someone got up from a table full of people talking in low voices to go join a different table where they were talking in low voices. Many of the tables had only men, and altogether the men outnumbered women two to one. The prevailing emotion was fear, Constance realized. These people were desperately afraid.

". . . be wiped out, of course. Poor Homer, poor old Dad."

"You shouldn't think that," Constance protested. "This will all blow over, the way things do."

"Not this thing. Four, five men vanished, and today rumor has it another one disappeared. People going crazy, doing crazy things. And then the shooting. No one's going back over there. Wait and see. Oh, they'll try to bring in a lot of outsiders to finish up, but when things start to happen to them, they'll take off, too. Wait and see."

"Have you been out there?"

"Once, early on. Took the lay of the land, you see. We send out a lunch truck, hot soup, sandwiches, stuff like that. We have a boy who drives out, sells lunches, and comes back. I went out to see if he could get in and out again. Not sending him anymore. That's over with."

They chatted a few more minutes and then the food arrived, packed in a large cardboard carton, and Constance left. It wasn't as if she had learned anything factual, she told Charlie as they drove back to the house. But she had a feeling now for what the people here were going through. They were scared to death.

"They attribute it to everything from an old Indian curse to radiation leaks from the nuclear tests in Nevada. From faulty government nerve gas storage to the work of the devil."

He nodded. "They don't single out the old hotel, far's I could learn. In fact, they're saying they might even go finish the new one, maybe. But it's the old town reconstruction thing as a whole that scares them. Talk's about bad vibes, being blasted with rays from invisible machines, maybe even in orbit somewhere." He sounded morose. Then he said, "You know what time it really is? After ten!"

Constance realized that he sounded so low because he was hungry. They had not eaten since breakfast and that seemed days ago. Something had been served on the airplane that had looked vaguely like fish, but neither of them had tried it. Now good food smells were filling the rented car, and she felt stomach pangs. She patted Charlie's leg, offering sympathy; he covered her hand with his, accepting it.

That night, after they had eaten the excellent steaks and enough accompaniments to feed three additional people, Byron practically forced Polly to take a sleeping pill and go to bed. She acceded only when Beatrice promised to sleep in her room that night, and added that she was a very light sleeper.

"She's afraid Mike will come for her," Beatrice said flatly after the younger woman had gone to sleep. "I think she crosses the line from therapist to patient starting tomorrow."

She looked at Byron levelly but did not add the rest of the statement that hung in the air. He did not refute or acknowledge the implication that perhaps tomorrow he also would change roles.

"Let's see what tomorrow brings," Charlie said in the lengthening silence. "And tonight I'll level with you both about my own investigation. Afterward you tell me if you want to opt out, or to cooperate. Okay?"

He summarized the incidences of fires that had spread out over a period of six years and ranged from coast to coast. "In each case where we've been able to dig out details, the events are the same generally. People start going mad, terrible things happen, then the hotels burn and it all stops. That was the pattern at Orick, and so far it's the same here."

Byron looked blank. "That's all you have?"

"That's it," Charlie said almost cheerfully. "The way I see it, you two, and anyone else you bring in as part of your team, have the perfect chance to ask questions that the police won't be bothering with. They wouldn't know what to do with answers anyway. First, we need to know just who was in that hotel, or even near it at any given time. Some went mad and some didn't. Why? The people from town here who went crazy over the last few weeks, what was their connection? Who vanished? The story is that four or five men have disappeared, but what does that mean? It's one thing if a settled family man doesn't show up again, and something else if a transient moves on. Presumably the sheriff's men, or state troopers, or *someone* searched the entire reconstructed town for the men who vanished the day of the shooting. Why weren't any of *them* affected? You see what I mean? You can ask questions of that sort and get answers that no one else is in a position to get. I sure as hell couldn't."

Beatrice looked disbelieving. She shook her head. "It doesn't make any sense. Why the hotel? Why not the town as a whole? Why now? They've been working on the place for two years. People have been in and out of every building there hundreds of times without seeing anything out of the ordinary."

Charlie nodded approvingly at her. She'd do, he told himself again. "All good points. Points I have no answers for. But in every case I've mentioned there is a old hotel that's been closed for many years. And in every case troubles ended when it burned. Sorry, that's all I have to go on, but that's how it is." He turned to Byron, whose eyes were narrowed in concentration, all traces of shock gone now. "Is there electricity over there?"

"No. That's one of the things they argued about in the beginning. They decided to keep it the way it was back in 1880 hereabouts. There's a generator unit in a truck for power equipment they're using for construction."

"Another similarity. None of the places was wired, or else the electricity was turned off and had been off for years." He grinned at Beatrice. "You can see how I'm clutching at any straws I can find. You want to think about it awhile?"

She looked at Byron and stiffened at the expression on his face, the intense look of concentration that furrowed his forehead, tightened his mouth. "We can't turn our work into an investigation for an insurance company!" she said sharply.

Byron started and opened his mouth to respond, but Charlie stood up and beckoned Constance. "Let's go for a walk," he said. "Cold or not, there's a bright moon, and they say the desert in moonlight is a rare treat. Game?"

She nodded, as troubled now as Beatrice was. They got into warm coats and started to leave. At the door they were stopped by Byron's voice.

"If we don't help, what then? What will you do?"

"Oh," Charlie said, "talk to the sheriff, the state police, whoever's in charge. See if they'll have a go at it. I think they might."

"That's despicable," Beatrice said. "You don't know what shape those people are in. They need help, not harassment."

Charlie shrugged. "Maybe I know, maybe not. I do know there'll be more just like them if we don't get to the bottom of it. See you in a little bit."

They walked on a dirt road that led away from town. The wind was light now, and the air was fragrant with strange smells, not of leaf mold, but more primitive odors of exposed earth and rocks and the most primeval of plants. Behind them a dog howled, another barked sharply, and in the distance a creature answered, or taunted—a fox or a coyote. The desert glowed in the moonlight. The shadows were the black of the abyss and the light was silver, cold, and alien.

"You're upset with me," Charlie said after they had walked several minutes in silence.

"A little. She's right, you know. Therapist-patient—that's a relationship that should not be subverted for any reason. But you're right too. That's the dilemma."

He grunted, his hand on her arm warm and full of strength.

"As soon as you catch the arsonist, you're through with the job you were hired to do."

This time he didn't bother to grunt. He knew.

"And what difference will it make just to confirm what you

already suspect, or even know? That the hotel has something in it that does that to people? An invisible, untraceable, portable something that makes people crazy? I mean, you already have accepted that much."

"Yep. But why not everyone? Why just some people?" His hand tightened on her arm, but his voice was light and easy when he continued. "You haven't said the other thing. I'm out of my depth here. I have to go to the police eventually—why not now?"

She was relieved that he had brought it up. And it was true, that was the other thing that had to be discussed. "Charlie, what if it's a gas? You can't sample it or analyze it. What if it's a ray of some sort? What if it's a mad scientist's escaped discovery? People have searched those buildings and found nothing. What can you do alone?"

"Don't know," he admitted. "But picture the scene. I go into the police station and say: by the way, there's something weird in that hotel. And the kind captain says, I've been over every inch of it, pal. So have the FBI, or the ATF people. Nothing's there. I say, yeah, but look at how those poor people go nuts. And he says, you look at my statistics, pal. Thousands of people go nuts every month. And I take my hat in hand and go home."

"You were convinced," she pointed out.

"I know. But I don't have to state my case to a police captain, or a commissioner, or a mayor, or anyone in a position to tell me I need a rest leave. That helps. Talking to people in Orick, reading all those papers, seeing Polly, it all helps. But, honey, I've had over a month to think about it. Unless and until I get John Loesser with the gas can, all I've got is a theory that I don't even believe in yet. So I'm playing it alone for now. But you're right. Eventually we get help. Eventually."

They had been walking downhill for several minutes, a gentle slope that was hardly apparent, but suddenly they both realized that the lights of town had been eclipsed by rocks. Now there was only the silver moonlight, and an uncanny silence. Constance shivered.

"Right," Charlie said briskly. "Back to the house, hot coffee, people."

It was amazing how fast that had happened, he thought with gloom. He had wanted to investigate, see if his idea had any possibility of success. He now doubted that it did, doubted that he could catch his guy with the gas can out on the desert on the way to the hotel. The damn land was just too treacherous.

"You know what makes it so hard, why you'll have trouble convincing anyone else?" Constance said. "Fear. You're touching on two such basic fears. First, fear of insanity. Everyone's afraid of it even if they don't admit it. And fear of the walking dead. Our myths and nightmares, our horror movies are full of that one. Accepting that such a terrible thing could happen shatters every belief system we hang on to. If that's possible, anything is, and that's too frightening to deal with."

The lights of the town returned to view. A dog howled, another barked, and from a vast distance a more primitive creature answered. Its voice sounded mocking.

10

Things were happening, Charlie thought the next afternoon, just not the right things. A helicopter flew in circles for a time, searching for the missing people; officially four in all, he had learned, including Mike. None of them had been found. A parade of automobiles, jeeps, trucks wound out onto the desert, into Old West, and wound out again. The sheriff returned to ask Byron questions, the same questions, eliciting the same answers, and they were of no help. Byron and Beatrice went to Doctor Sagimore's office, where they were interviewing people. Polly begged off. The sun came out and the day was too warm. The dogs did not bark.

Constance had started listening to the tapes made over the past two days by Byron and his team. In real time, she said with an eloquent shrug. Beatrice returned for lunch, glanced at Polly, and insisted on taking her to Las Vegas, where she put her on a plane headed for home. Polly had become a patient overnight; she had wept in her room all morning.

Most of the day Charlie wandered around the town talking,

listening, asking a few questions. He drove over to the new hotel nearing completion—an opulent high-rise that looked incongruous on the desert just across the Nevada state line. It was luxurious, with gaming rooms on the first floor, a mammoth swimming pool, playground. Welcome to Nevada, he thought, surveying it. He wandered out back and saw where the train loaded passengers, climbed aboard and walked the length of the train, as richly finished as the hotel, with red plush seats, and gleaming brass fixtures. He chatted with some of the men who had returned to work here. No one was working down at Old West. And finally he returned to the house, where Constance was at the kitchen table, still listening to tapes and making notes now and then.

"Package from Hoagley," she said, pointing to a manila envelope. She rubbed her ears.

He had ordered a complete rundown on John Loesser, and here it was. His school days through college, the death of his wife in an airplane accident, the attack that put Loesser in the hospital and evidently killed the Danvers family. Charlie sat down heavily as he read.

"I've got the son of a bitch," he muttered after a moment. He stared past Constance. "Today, tomorrow, he'll show up. Soon now."

After another second or two, she said, "Charlie, it's time to bring in the local authorities. You've done your job."

He looked up. His eyes were just like the little pieces of obsidian she had seen for sale at the airport. Apache tears, they were called. He grinned, but it was meaningless; he wasn't even seeing her, she knew.

Constance caught his arm. "Listen," she said quietly. "All day I've been hearing these people talk about the horror down at that place." She picked up a tape and put it down again hard. "Charlie, there are degrees of madness, different manifestations, varying levels of homicidal impulses, or suicidal impulses. The ones affected by whatever is down there are extreme examples. It's as if every repressed murderous thought is activated, set loose. Do you understand what I'm saying?"

They heard the front door open and close; Byron and Beatrice walked into the kitchen. He looked haggard, very pale;

even his elegant beard had started to look unkempt. Beatrice was shaking.

"We just heard," Byron said. "One of the sheriff's men who was in the search party today went home and beat his wife senseless. She was five months pregnant, lost the baby. She'll recover, probably. Neighbors subdued the guy, and he curled up and started to cry and hasn't stopped."

"When will it end?" Beatrice cried.

"When the hotel burns," Charlie said.

"For God's sake! Let's tell the sheriff what you know and let them burn the thing down!"

"And then it will just start up somewhere else," Charlie said wearily. "Next month, in three months, next year, sometime."

Beatrice ran to the telephone near the back door. "I'm calling the sheriff. We have to warn people to stay out of there even if we don't do anything else."

Charlie shrugged. "I say we sit tight until we have the firebug and then decide."

"I don't give a damn about the fires and the insurance!"

"Neither do I," Charlie said in a low voice. "But this firebug has something we need. Two things. Information, and immunity. Apparently he can walk in there and set his fire and walk out again unscathed, or else he's so crazy he can't be driven any further. I say we need him before we do anything else. If the sheriff or his men close in on him, there's going to be shooting. Chances he'll survive are practically nil considering the state of everyone's nerves around here."

She stood with her hand on the telephone, meeting his gaze unblinkingly. Then she drew a deep breath and turned away. "One more day," she said. "Tomorrow at this time I won't let you talk me out of telling everything you've told us."

Byron went to make them all drinks and returned to the kitchen with a tray of glasses, which he handed out. "Charlie, have you considered that your man might register in a motel over in Vegas? It's just an hour away. You'd need an army to keep track of who goes in and out at night over there."

Charlie sipped bourbon hardly diluted at all with ice and water. Just right. "He's a city man," he said then. "Same as I am. I've been all over the area today, just trying to get a feel for it, where you can drive in it, how fast. He'll need to do much the same. That's his pattern; it never has varied. He goes in and scouts the area a day ahead of time, then lights his fire and vamooses. I don't think he'll change this time." If Loesser did change this time, lit his fire, made his getaway, it could be years before they got this close again. If Byron hadn't called, he wouldn't have known about Old West until too late, after it became another arson statistic.

Beatrice and Byron left for dinner in Las Vegas soon after this. "I want to get away from here for a few hours," he had said. "And I want to get you away with me."

Constance and Charlie walked to Jodie's. He dropped in at the motel for a chat with the desk clerk, came back, and shook his head. Nothing yet.

The restaurant was filled again, and more subdued than the night before. The conversations were lower, the expressions on the faces of the customers darker. Constance and Charlie sat in a booth near the rear of the restaurant, where he had a good view of the place. They would shoot first, he thought again glumly, and he knew he couldn't blame them a damn bit.

"Well, we might as well talk about it," Constance said after they had sat silently for several minutes. "You or me?"

He grinned, and this time meant it. "You."

"Right. The people on the tapes are all locals, construction workers, or people who were hired to run the shops. You know, the dry goods store, the saloon, all those people. They were out there one other time for an orientation, but it was noisy and filled with the construction crews that day, the saws going, and so on. Again and again they say it was very different on the day of the shooting. Apparently the generator makes a lot of noise, and when it was turned off that day, the quiet was eerie; the town seemed haunted. Many people mentioned that period of stillness, how strange it was. Something frightened them during that short time. Most of it you have to discount as after-the-fact rationalizing, but not all. At least four people complained of dizziness and headaches. The dizziness passed, but the headaches lasted for most of the time, at least until they were all so frightened that they simply forgot about them."

She took a deep breath, considering, remembering the terrified voices, the shrillness and incoherencies and babble. "Anyway, the train blew its whistle on the butte before it was actually in sight, and they turned off the generator, and the few construction people ducked back behind the hotel. They moved the truck that housed the generator so it wouldn't be in view and spoil the effects. That's when, they say, there was the eerie silence, when Trevor Jackson must have got his rifles from his truck. They all seem to have at least two rifles in their trucks."

She shook her head in wonder, then went on. "No one mentioned seeing him do it, but they don't know when else he could have done it. He went inside the saloon through the back door. The train pulled in making a lot of noise, blowing the whistle, and people began to spill out, all laughing, having a good time. The plan was for a few speeches, a welcoming ceremony or something like that. The guests were all shareholders and friends who had gathered in Las Vegas, had a party the night before, and were going to wrap it all up at Old West. Then Trevor began to shoot."

Charlie had listened intently. He relaxed a bit now. "Pretty much the same story I kept hearing from various people who aren't patients. Also, what I got is that the guests on the train have all scattered back to their various homes. If any of them are nuts, the family probably won't mention it."

She looked pained at the expression, but she did not protest. "Charlie, there are other implications here. In some cases the insanity and violence seem to come on together, but Trevor had time to get his weapons and ammunition. He must have looked normal to anyone who noticed him. And the sheriff's deputy who went home and beat his wife, he must have appeared normal. They aren't all like Mike, who reacted with instant violence. You don't know what to expect from John Loesser. He may appear to be as rational as . . . as an insurance agent, and be as homicidal as Mike."

"You think Loesser's crazy?"

"Well, of course. I mean, making a career of setting fires, giving up his profession, his entire life apparently, in order to do it. Why? You don't?"

"You're the expert," he said with a slight grin. Actually he thought John Loesser was behaving in a totally reasonable way: he searched for and found a nest of vipers and burned them out, then searched again, and again.

They had eaten their meal and were ready for coffee when a waiter dropped a tray with several glasses. Instantly half a dozen men were on their feet, their hands under their coats, or in pockets, in a way that made Charlie hold his breath until someone laughed and they all resumed their seats. The laughter was not picked up, and it had sounded artificial, more a sob than mirth. The waiter had frozen in place. Carefully he moved away from the mess at his feet when a busboy appeared and started to clean it up.

"Let's go home for coffee," Charlie said in a voice that had gone flat and tired.

The next morning Byron called from the doctor's office immediately on his arrival there. "Charlie, I thought you'd better know this. Some forensic people are coming in this morning to take air and dirt samples from Old West. The sheriff's escorting them out around nine."

Charlie felt relief mixed with regret. If Loesser turned up today, this might make him take off again, go to Vegas and wait out the official types, or leave the area altogether. On the other hand, if there was something that could be analyzed and countered, Loesser could wait. They'd find him. He gnawed his lip, frowning at the wall map of the triangle that was made out of the points Old West, Grayling, and the new hotel.

Slowly he narrowed his eyes and moved in closer to the map. He traced a ranch road that wound around rocks, up and down steep inclines, meandered on south. But it was within a mile of Old West at one place, accessible from a dirt road that left the state road there. Another four or five miles. It was possible, he thought.

"Let's go watch," he said to Constance.

She was startled. "I don't think that's a good idea at all."

"Not with them, over here." He pointed to the spot he had picked out, more than a hundred feet higher than Old West, separated from the site by a deep ravine. There was no way to reach the town from that road, he had decided, but that was fine with him. He had no desire to get close to the hotel yet. Not yet. Maybe never.

She studied the map and nodded with some reluctance. Was

a mile far enough away? She hoped so. "I'll get the binoculars. We should take the Land Rover, don't you think?"

He followed her to the bedroom and opened the suitcase, brought out his old Police Special, and loaded it. Then they were ready.

The first part of the drive was fast, on the state road. The next section was six miles long and it took nearly an hour. "It's not even a road," Constance cried out once when the Land Rover tilted precariously as the left wheels rode up and over a boulder. The land was gray; the sage was gray-green; the sparse grasses were gray. Boulders, dirt, vegetation were all camouflaged the same color, hiding from what? Rimrock was black here and there, and in a sheltered spot or two where winter runoff nourished more growth, straggly trees huddled close together. They were gray also.

The track curved sharply around outcrops, dived down slopes, climbed other slopes at a steep angle, turned back on itself around a deep gouge in the dirt. There were cacti here, dwarfed and thick, with wicked-looking needles. Finally Charlie stopped the car, shaking his head at the next turning place. It was pointless to pretend he could maneuver it. A goat track, maybe, he thought. He visualized the map again. That was supposed to be the road that would take them to the edge of the ravine where they could hide behind rocks and have a clear view of the Old West scene.

"How far do you suppose it is?" Constance asked.

"Maybe a mile. Walk?"

She nodded. "I sure don't want to drive on that."

They walked the last stretch, and came around a turn to see the tourist attraction off to the left. Through the clear air, the buildings were sharp, the railing on the boardwalk visible even without the binoculars. They looked around for a good spot to wait and observe. In the sun, they were too likely to be seen from over there, Charlie decided, but in the shade it was cold. Finally they walked around a boulder to sunlight, where they would wait until there was something to see.

"At least it's too cold for snakes," Constance said after they were settled.

Charlie shuddered. Snake country. Scorpions. Black widows.

What else had he read about it? Gila monsters? He thought so. In the summer it could reach well over a hundred degrees by this time in the morning, so arid you could dehydrate and die within a couple of hours. And yet, he marveled, it also had a beauty of its own. The air was so clear, the shadows had such sharp edges, were so deep and black, the sky so distant and blue, it was like being in country not yet used, not corrupted somehow.

Now that he was no longer moving, he could see that the gray was not uniform. The rocks had touches of color, streaks of green, flecks of a flashing mineral. Gold? Silver? Quartz? He tried to think of other minerals that would gleam in the sun like that, but he kept coming back to gold, and decided arbitrarily that what he was gazing at was gold. A contrail appeared, two parallel lines as sharp as a geometry problem. Two parallel lines didn't meet when he was in high school, but now they did, he mused. He watched the plane draw the perfect lines, and then stiffened, as he felt Constance draw a deep breath and hold it. A second later he heard it too, the sound of automobile engines.

They moved to the front of the boulder, keeping in shadows now, and watched three cars come into sight one by one on the dirt road behind the old hotel. That road was nearly as bad as the one they had driven, from all appearances; the caution the drivers were showing was apparent. The lead car stopped by the generator truck and a man got out and climbed into the truck as the car moved out of sight behind the hotel. The other two followed. Suddenly a blast of roiling smoke shot up from the truck, and its roar carried the mile to Constance and Charlie. She felt that she could almost smell the fumes.

"They'll need light in the basement of the hotel," Charlie murmured. "Maybe in the interiors of some of the buildings." The cars had reappeared at the end of the railroad station, and they stopped there; men got out. There were seven in all. Charlie recognized the sheriff, but none of the others, who went to work at once. He and Constance took turns with the binoculars, although there was little worth watching. They took scrapings of paint, samples of dust, parings of wood. They put the samples in vials or plastic bags, labeled everything, then moved on down the street to repeat the action at regular intervals. At the

far end several of them walked into view with an orange extension cord and a box. Other wires were plugged into the box,
and the men separated, carrying light with them into the hotel
and the first building by it. All the work was methodical and
precise and slow. None of the conversations carried this far,
only the noise of the generator truck; no smoke was showing
now.

When he had the binoculars again, Charlie swept the entire
town, then continued off to the corral, where the desert started
again, up a steep hill that ended in a rimrock. He continued to
study the surrounding terrain, back to the town, the railway
station. He followed the tracks until they vanished behind a
rocky hill, picked them up again only to lose them on another
curve. Then he stopped moving. A man was standing in a deep
shadow, hands in pockets, Western hat hiding his face; he was
also watching the scene in Old West, from that side of the ravine. "Loesser," Charlie said under his breath. "I'll be damned!"

11

Charlie watched the man he was certain was John Loesser, and
Constance continued to watch the activity in Old West. The
men had split up into groups; pairs on each side of the street
were making systematic searches of the buildings and shops,
vanishing into shadows, emerging, padlocking each in turn. In
the center of the street, midway between the hotel and train
station, three men stood in a tight cluster, talking; one of them
was the sheriff, who gesticulated now and then, pointed this
way and that, indicated the train tracks, the saloon, with wide-
arm motions. The other men were collecting samples of everything that could be scraped up, scooped up, or dug out of
wood. Now and then the searchers carried the electric line into
the buildings. They moved down the street slowly. Beside her,
Constance heard Charlie mutter. He lowered the binoculars
and squinted.

"He went behind those rocks," he said. At the same time two of the men approached the hotel, paused on the wide porch, then entered, carrying a light with them.

Constance did not realize she was holding her breath until her chest started to ache and she felt light-headed. She exhaled softly and felt Charlie's hand on her arm in a firm grip. He was still intent on the rocky slope where the other man had vanished.

Below, the collectors and scientists had finished their chores and were walking back toward the cars. The searchers finished the last building before the hotel and stood as if uncertain that they should enter. One started to walk toward the sheriff, who now left the other two men he had been talking with; they turned to go to the cars also. The sheriff spoke with the two who had finished their side, and they all looked toward the hotel. One must have called out, but his voice did not carry to where Constance was watching. He strode toward the hotel, then turned and went around the side of it to where the generator truck was parked. The two who had gone inside the old building appeared on the porch, one of them winding the electric cable as he walked, dangling the bulb protected by a wire cage. They had all dispersed by now, some of them possibly to the cars, hidden by the train station, when suddenly the man winding the cable dropped everything and fell to his knees, clutching his head. The sheriff ran toward him as another man ran from around the hotel; he threw himself at the sheriff and they rolled in the street. A car revved loud enough that Constance could hear; it plunged from behind the train station and roared across the desert picking up speed as it raced over rocks, over cactus and sagebrush, until it went out of control in a shallow dip and rolled over and over down a slight hill. It came to rest in a cloud of dust that only gradually settled over it. The sheriff had got his gun out by now and he swung it and hit his attacker in the head. Now all the men were running; dust clouds made it impossible to tell exactly what was happening. Men were dragging the injured, half carrying each other, stumbling until they were all out of sight around the saloon. A car sped away, behind the hotel, behind the workers' area, and back up the dirt road, the other car close behind it.

It had all happened so fast, so unexpectedly, that Constance had hardly been able to follow it. She felt drained, exhausted suddenly, and now she let out a long shuddering breath. Beside her Charlie had grabbed her arm hard. "Jesus Christ!" he breathed. "Jesus!"

Neither moved for several minutes. The dust settled down below, but in the street the electric cable looked like a snake, and out on the desert a short distance, the car was unmoving, on its back. No one had emerged from it.

"Let's get the hell out of here," Charlie said. Fear made his voice thick and almost unrecognizable. They backed away from the ridge, watching the old town until they were well away from the rim, and then he hurried her back the way they had come, to where they had left the Land Rover. His face was set in such rigid lines with a faint sheen of sweat that it looked metallic. And that was the worst of all, Constance thought, terrified. For Charlie to be afraid was the worst of all.

Charlie drove to the motel before returning to their house. Nothing yet. No John Loesser, no late-model black Malibu. But the son of a bitch was in the area, he knew. At the house, he eyed the phone grimly, then looked up the sheriff's number and dialed. His face was still set in rigid lines, his eyes hard and flat-looking.

"Charles Meiklejohn," he said to the phone. "Tell Sheriff Maschi I have to speak to him before he sends anyone in to Old West to collect that body. I'm staying at Dr. Weston's house in Grayling." He hung up.

Constance busied herself making coffee, anything to keep moving, she thought, anything to stop the scene from playing like a tape loop in her head. "How much are you going to tell him?"

Charlie was pacing in quick jerky strides. He did not stop. "I don't know yet. I hope the bastard hasn't already sent a bunch in there. God, I . . ." The phone rang and he snatched it up. "Meiklejohn," he said in a clipped voice. "I called, Sheriff," he said, "to give you some advice. Have you already sent people to Old West to collect the guy in the car that smashed?" He closed his eyes, then said, "Get on the radio, Sheriff, and tell them to keep the engine running all the time they're in there. Whatever it is won't go near them if a motor's running. Can you get the message to them?" He listened, then cut in sharply. "If you don't want some more homicidal maniacs on your hands, get through to them and warn them! I'll be here!" He slammed the receiver down.

Constance had stopped slicing bread, and now resumed. "Sandwiches," she said, "and coffee. Nourishment to see you through when they haul you off to the pokey. I'll visit every day, of course."

He came to her and put his arms around her, rested his cheek against her hair with his eyes closed. "What you'll do is go home and see if the damn cats are starving to death. Okay?"

"Not okay. Then who'll bring you cake and files and such?"

He backed off a bit and held her shoulders, looked directly at her. "I'm not giving them Loesser yet. He's mine."

"I know. Liverwurst and onions, or ham and cheese?"

"You know damn well that's not even a choice!"

"For me it is," she said. The phone rang and he left her to answer again, expecting the sheriff.

He listened, and very softly said thanks and faced her once more. "That was my tame desk clerk. Loesser just checked in." His voice was silky smooth.

Grayling was filled with more outsiders than it had been since their arrival, Charlie noted. More news specials? Probably. He was surprised that Loesser had been able to get a room. He was calling himself Jerry Lawes this time; sticking to his pattern. Charlie nodded when he drove through the motel parking lot and found a year-old black Malibu. Another part of the pattern. The desk clerk had given him the room number—147, first floor rear. The drapes were drawn over the window. Charlie pulled in at an empty slot and got out of the car. Constance came around to get in behind the wheel, and he walked away. At the black Malibu he paused briefly at the driver's side, slipped a flattened wire down the window opening, jiggled it, and opened the door. He pulled on the lights, then closed the door again. He went to room 147 and tapped on the door. When it opened on the chain, he said, "You left your lights on, mister."

The door closed; the drape moved a little, then fell back into place, and the door opened. The man came out and started for the Malibu. Charlie walked by his side and said pleasantly, "We'll take my car instead. But first we'll turn off the lights, just so no one will ask any questions." The man froze, then jerked around to look at Charlie, and Charlie had one more shock. This was not the man in the picture; he was not John Loesser.

"Who are you? What do you want? Get away from me!"

"Mr. Lawes, don't make a scene. Just go on to your car and turn off the lights. Then we'll go someplace and have a talk." Maybe he wasn't John Loesser, Charlie thought darkly, but he was the man he had seen out on the desert watching the mayhem at Old West. The man did not move for another second, and Charlie said even more softly, "I have a revolver in my pocket, Mr. Lawes, and if I shoot you now and say you were out there today when people were going mad and trying to kill each other, why, I think I'd be a hero." Lawes blanched, and they began to walk.

They went to the Malibu, where Lawes turned off the lights; they walked side by side to the car, where Constance was waiting, and they drove back to the house in silence. Charlie thought he could almost hear the machinery at work as Lawes stared ahead: gears shifting, toggles on, toggles off, switches thrown, everything erased to start over. Constance led the way into the house and waited until they were inside to close and lock the door. Charlie studied the man then. About six feet tall, slender, fair complexion, blond hair—all that fitted Loesser's description, but this man did not look like the picture Charlie had memorized. He was not Loesser.

"Who are you?" Lawes demanded.

"Uh-uh," Charlie murmured. "My question. We were just about to have a sandwich. Let's do it now."

Constance began to reassemble the sandwich material and Charlie pulled a chair away from the table. "Please empty your pockets, and then sit down," he said.

Lawes looked from him to Constance and back again. "You're both mad. This is kidnapping! I'm leaving!"

Charlie took his hand from his pocket, bringing out the .38; Lawes stared at it wide-eyed. "At this particular place and time," Charlie said soberly, hefting the gun, then pointing it at Lawes, "it's a little hard to say who is mad and who isn't. I believe most people around here would understand anyone who shot without proof right now. Your pockets."

Lawes continued to stare at the gun as he pulled things from his pockets, moving carefully. There was not much: car keys, motel key, change, cash in bills, a matchbook. No wallet. No identification. Charlie watched dispassionately. He shook his head when Lawes stopped. "Most people have ID, driver's license, registration. You just have cash. Strange."

Charlie made him turn around and put his hands on the wall and then patted him down; there wasn't anything else. He picked up the roll of bills, five or six hundred dollars, and put it back on the table.

"Take your stuff," he said, moving back a step. "And now let's all sit down and have lunch."

Constance came around the counter with a platter of sandwiches, smiled at Lawes, and went back for the coffee. He stuffed his belongings back inside his pockets. They all froze when the doorbell rang.

Charlie had put his gun away. He motioned to Lawes to move ahead of him. "Do you mind, honey?" he asked Constance. "I'll show our guest the Indian art in our room."

She waited until they had gone into the bedroom at the end of the hall, and then went to see who was at the door. Sheriff Maschi stood there glowering, his face dark red and angry. "I'm looking for Meiklejohn," he said.

"Oh, come in, Sheriff. He's around here somewhere. I'll go find him. Do you want a sandwich?"

He followed her to the kitchen and she hurried ahead to the hall to the bedrooms. The sheriff stopped to wait.

"Sheriff Maschi," she announced inside the bedroom. Lawes looked desperate. His eyes were examining the room as if seeking an exit.

Charlie glanced from him to Constance. "Mind waiting here until I get rid of him?"

He forced back a grin at the look that swiftly crossed Lawes's face. Constance shook her head, and Charlie walked out, closed the door. At the kitchen he reached for the platter of sandwiches. "Sheriff Maschi, you're just in time for lunch. Let's go to the den." There was a thump from the bedroom. Charlie picked up the platter.

"What was that?" the sheriff demanded, looking past him.

"Just Constance exercising. Come along." He led the way to the den.

Carson Danvers had not believed his luck when Charlie Meiklejohn left him with this woman. He had not even given her the gun, and a glance proved that she did not have pockets capable of hiding a weapon. He waited a few seconds, then moved to the bedroom window. No screen, of course. He unlocked the latch, and she came to his side.

"Charlie really wants to talk to you," she said politely. "Let's sit down and wait for him."

"Another time," Danvers said and shoved the window up all the way. He felt her hand on his arm and shrugged it away, and then found himself sitting on the floor. It happened so fast he wasn't even sure she had done something. She didn't look as if she had done anything. She pulled the window down partway and smiled at him. Gingerly he got to his feet.

"Let's wait for Charlie," she said in her nice low voice. Her smile was as pleasant as it had been earlier. Not a hair was ruffled. "A long time ago," she said easily, "Charlie decided that women should learn to defend themselves if they have to. I wasn't happy about it at first, but then I got pretty good. Our daughter practices, too. Sometimes we put on mother-daughter demonstrations, but I always feel self-conscious when we do. Please sit down. You take the chair; I'll sit on the bed here."

He eyed her silently and she stopped smiling.

"I don't want us to be enemies," she said softly, "but neither do I want you to try to leave. At worst, I'll call the sheriff and I think he'd shoot you, just as Charlie thinks. They are so very afraid right now."

He slumped down on the straight chair. "You don't know what you're getting mixed up in."

"Not as much as you do, I expect. What's down there? What's in the hotel?"

"The devil," he said. "It gets to people and turns them into monsters. And it laughs and looks for the next one to invade. They won't find it with their samples of dirt and paint. It hides until they're unprotected. It's pure evil down there, that's what's in the hotel. Pure evil."

The image of Father Patrick flashed before her eyes, his face grave and troubled; she heard his warning again. She blinked the memory away and shook her head. "Madness isn't evil. That's medieval superstition. Those people need help, not condemnation."

"You can't help them!" he cried. "They're tools of the devil, past help. All you can do is burn out the evil in the old building and wait for it to show up somewhere else and burn it out there." He hung his hands between his knees and bowed his head, as if exhausted. The scar on his cheekbone had turned bright red. "Once the devil claims them, they're his to do his bidding. You can't help them."

"That's what it means to be insane," Constance said. "It means being irrational, doing things that defy explanation. Turning on people without warning. Many of them simply withdraw, become empty, catatonic. They aren't evil. They're just very ill."

"You don't know," he said miserably. "I've seen them. One minute happy, loving, giving, trusting, then demonic. In a flash they're possessed and get the gun and shoot his mother and father. In the face. He shot her in the face, I saw him, possessed, demonic . . ."

He talked in an undertone, not looking at Constance. She had been as bewildered about who he was as Charlie. Not Loesser. She had studied that photograph, and he was not Loesser. As he talked, she remembered the report the police had filed about the attack on Loesser, the deaths of the Danvers family, their disappearance. She felt a stab of pity for this man.

"Mr. Danvers," she said gently, "the boy loved his parents, both of them. Everyone said so. Something affected his brain. He couldn't help himself; he didn't know what he was doing. He became extremely ill, not possessed, not invaded by evil. He was to be pitied, Mr. Danvers."

He raised his face, haggard and pale and very tired. "You know?"

She nodded. "We know."

He began to sob and somehow she got him to the side of the bed, where she put her arms around him and held him as he wept.

———————

"Why'd you lie about who you are?" the sheriff demanded as soon as Charlie led him into the den.

"Now, Sheriff, I didn't, if you'll recall. I introduced Constance and said I was her husband. God's truth. You want a liverwurst with onions?" He poked at the sandwich with a look of distaste. "She thinks organs are edible, God help her."

"I don't want no sandwich. Look, Meiklejohn, I want some answers. What are you doing here? Who hired you? To do what? How did you know about the motors down at the old town?"

He stood with his hands low on his hips, like a gunslinger, Charlie thought with interest. He wondered if they still practiced quick draws. He looked at the sheriff with candor and said, "I'm here for the ride. Constance is a psychologist, reviewing the records of the various problems here. I came along because I didn't have anything better to do. And I figured it out about the engines from reading the reports. Every single instance of madness came about only when things were all turned off over there. It seemed to add up. Worth a shot, anyway." He picked up a ham and cheese sandwich.

Sheriff Maschi drew in a deep breath and reached past him for a liverwurst. "We got our guy out of there without any more trouble. How'd you know about him?"

"No secrets hereabouts," Charlie said, chewing. "If I were you, I'd sure have some barricades put on every road going over there."

"Yeah, yeah. We are. And a guard on each one."

Charlie stopped chewing. "How far away from the town?"

"Far enough." He reached for another sandwich. "Goddamnit! I've been over everything down there half a dozen times! Nothing's in there!"

Charlie nodded with genuine sympathy.

"You really retired? Pretty young to be retired."

"From the New York Police Department? Never too young to retire."

"Yeah, I guess. I've been sheriff for twenty-nine years. Feuds, fights, brawls, shoot-outs, vandalism, survivalists and environmentalists mixing it up, you name it, we've had it here. But this! Last year it was wetbacks and airloads of dope being dropped. Bad news. I'd take back all of it in exchange for what we've got now. All of it, doubled. Wish to hell I was retired, reared back on my porch watching the paint peel on my house."

"You thought about calling in the Feds?"

"Yeah, more and more. Maybe I'll do that. After the reports come in, maybe I'll do that." He finished the last bite of his sandwich and nodded at the platter. "Good. Thanks. Look, Meiklejohn, you get any more ideas, give me a call. Right?"

Charlie walked out to the porch with the sheriff and watched him out of sight, then turned grimly back to the house. Now, he thought, he wanted some damn answers of his own. No more games, Lawes, or whoever the hell you are, he muttered to himself as he strode down the hall to the bedroom. He hoped Constance hadn't hurt him too much, not enough to keep him from talking anyway. He pushed the door open and stopped, completely nonplussed and helpless. The man who had splashed gas on their house, the man he wanted to sock was sitting on the bed in his wife's arms, crying like a baby.

Constance glanced up at him and raised an eyebrow. "We'll be out in a minute or two."

12

Charlie stalked to the kitchen, to the den, the living room, back to the kitchen. Constance finally appeared.

"He's in the bathroom, be right out."

"He'd better." She passed him, poured coffee and sipped it. When the man entered the kitchen, Charlie stood with his hand clenched.

"Charlie," Constance said from across the room, "this is Carson Danvers. My husband, Charles Meiklejohn."

Carson turned bewildered eyes toward her. "I thought you said you knew."

And Charlie found himself speechless. After a moment he muttered, "I'll be damned!" His anger flared again. "You son of a bitch, why'd you douse my place with gas? I'm going to beat the crap out of you for that!"

Carson Danvers spread his hands helplessly. "I don't know you, anything about you. She said you knew who I am, and even that's a lie. What's going on?"

Charlie turned to regard Constance with suspicion. She tilted her head and sent the message: he's telling the truth, and he felt his hands relax, his shoulders sag a little. "I wish to hell I knew," he snarled.

"You'll have to be John Loesser," Charlie decided two hours later; they had sat in the den talking all that time. Danvers, Loesser, whatever he chose to call himself, was still pale and red-eyed, but he was calm. He had been able to talk about that first attack, what he had done, what he had seen. He had not been able to eat anything. "We have to call you something," Charlie added aggrievedly.

The other man nodded. "I have identification in the glove compartment of my car. John Loesser."

"Okay. So I hired you to assist me in this investigation. That's covered. But damned if I know what you'll do, or what I'll do either, as far as that goes." Something about Loesser nagged at him, and suddenly he realized what it was: he had the glinty eyes of a fanatic. Religious fanatics, political fanatics, sports fanatics, they all seemed to share that one common trait; their eyes glittered. John Loesser's eyes glittered. And Charlie knew precisely what John Loesser would do as soon as he had the chance. The glittery eyes, the scar on his cheek that flamed now and then, even his gauntness added up to a picture of a man driven by forces he could not resist. He wondered if Loesser ate or slept when he knew the thing was loose in a hotel again.

John Loesser drank coffee and put the cup down. "The same pattern will hold as before. They'll look for radiation, chemicals, gas, anything. And they won't find a thing. Eventually they'll go away. I go in and burn the building down and everything stops. Pretty soon people don't remember much about it."

"To start somewhere else," Charlie muttered.

"Next week. A month. Three or four months. It starts again somewhere else." He shook his head. "I've tried to help them.

Two different times I sent letters, made calls, told them everything I could think of, and it was the same. They go in and get samples, or look around. If they turn off the lights, or engines, whatever, they go mad—many of them go mad—and they hurt each other. They go back with others, and try to find something again, more men, armed men, same thing. Over and over. I tell them to keep motors running, and if they do, they don't find anything. If they don't, they go mad. Same over and over." He grinned a crooked grimace. "One of them burned the hotel once. Beat me to it. They knew, and called it unsolved, another arson fire."

Constance had been writing. Now she looked up from the table. "Were all the buildings wooden—frame buildings?"

"Yes."

She made another note and frowned at the paper before her. "Why just here? Why not in Asia, Africa, Europe?"

"We don't know that it isn't happening in other places," John said. "No one but the three of us knows there's cause to link the incidents in this country."

"Well, we have to tell them that," she said almost absently, gazing again at the notes she had written. She did not see the way John Loesser's jaw became rigid, how the scar flared, the way his hands clenched. Charlie did and became more wary than before. "What I have," Constance said in her practical manner, "is a list of similarities. One, the hotels are always isolated, at least a mile from other buildings where there are activities going on. Two, they all were wooden. Three, they don't have electricity, or it isn't working. Four, not everyone is susceptible to whatever happens. Five, the madness has no particular pattern. Six, people who are affected seem to have a compulsion to return to the hotel. Seven, neither time, distance, nor treatment seems to alleviate the psychological condition. I'll have to look into that one to make sure," she murmured, and wrote.

"You forget a couple of things," John said savagely. "The dead people get up and walk through the doorway to hell. Their bones turn up later."

Constance turned her pencil over and over and shook her head. "We don't know that."

"You're just like the others," he said with great bitterness. "There's a line you can't cross, isn't there?"

Constance studied him and finally nodded. "Yes. Of course. That's true of everyone, including you. How hard did you try to get help? Did you go in person to the police? Of course not. You sent anonymous letters, made anonymous phone calls. You knew as well as I that you would be ignored; you would be free to carry on your own private vendetta, and when they did look into the situation, without the links between all the hotels, without your personal testimony, they would be stymied. You dealt with your own guilt by ignoring the implications, hiding behind superstition about the thing you burned out again and again. What drove you to that, Mr. Danvers? Fear? Afraid of crossing the line to examine what might really be in those hotels? This is much bigger than a personal vendetta, and you know it. It's going to break wide open, possibly right here in Old West, in Grayling, and then how will you manage your fear and guilt?"

He looked as if he were ready to leap from his chair and start running, perhaps never stop. Before he could move, Charlie murmured, "That's a funny thing about it always being a hotel. Why? Why not abandoned farmhouses, or barns, or warehouses, or anything else you can name? In this country most of them are made of wood, if that's the deciding factor."

John leaned back in his chair. "I couldn't find a reason."

"Me neither, not yet anyway. Let's brainstorm. What do hotels have in common besides many rooms?"

"Lobbies," Constance said.

"Long halls," John added after a moment.

"Did they all have more than one floor?" Charlie asked. John nodded. "More than two?"

John Loesser frowned, remembering. "The ones I had anything to do with all had at least three. Two of them had four floors."

Constance wrote: *three or more stories.*

"Why did you always start your fires on the second floor, near the center of the building?" Charlie asked.

"I wanted to get as near the door as I could."

"The door. You've mentioned it before, but why those particular doors, not just any door?"

"*His* door," John Loesser said. Constance snorted, and he

went on almost desperately, "The door the devil comes through."

Charlie remembered one of the rumors he had heard, that some footprints had gone to a door that connected two rooms and stopped there. "You said it was like a shadow that filled the doorway."

"Not really. Like a void. Emptiness. I turned my flashlight on it and the light just stopped there, not like shining a light into the dark of a room."

"Did you ever try to go through it?"

John looked as if Charlie had gone mad. "I tossed a rock in once. It just vanished. I went to the other side, out through the hall into the next room. No rock. Just the blackness, the void. All the way to the top, side to side, down to the floor. No doorway, just the void, the entrance to hell."

"How high are those doors in the old hotels? A standard door is six-eight."

"Higher. Eight feet, three and a half feet wide. Over my head a good bit. At least eight feet."

"Another similarity," Charlie muttered, wishing he knew what to do with the similar items.

Soon after that Byron and Beatrice came back. They were both showing the strain of interviewing shocked survivors all day. Beatrice looked near tears when she sat down with a large drink.

"The same thing over and over. How could it happen to Mary, or Ralph, or Tommy? What's wrong with Susan? Why did so-and-so turn on me that way? I loved him, her, whoever." She held up her glass in a mock salute. "Cheers."

"What do you tell them?" John asked, watching her.

She and Byron had accepted him as Charlie's assistant without question. Beatrice shrugged and said wearily, "There's not a lot to say, now, is there?"

Byron tossed a couple of tapes to the table. "We're mostly trying to keep them talking for now," he said. "We're encouraging people to say everything that comes to mind dealing with this . . . phenomenon, so that it won't sink below consciousness and return to cripple them at a future date. The therapy is a bit difficult." He was as tired as Beatrice, as frustrated and helpless as Charlie. He looked at John Loesser, then at Constance and Charlie. "We don't know what the hell we're doing, that's the problem. We don't know why those people went mad, why Carlos turned on Luisa, why Mike tried to kill Polly, why—" He stopped abruptly as his voice started to get shrill. "Sorry," he said and went to the bar to pour himself bourbon.

Constance had been listening distantly, thinking of the list of similarities she had jotted down. That was part of it, she thought, but all along they had been ignoring the other part, the people who actually went mad. "Byron," she said, "we need to look into those cases. Maria Eglin, the Dworkin sisters, the others. Who was it, Carlos? As many as we can."

"Not my field," he said.

"Mine neither, but we have to. Look, if there are lesions, physical damage of any sort from chemicals, from anything, that's one thing, but if the primary maladaptive functions are endogenic in nature without any immediate activating agent, it's a different avenue of approach. Have there been autopsies yet of any of the affected people? I want to know if there have been lesions found. Not in the cortex, or neocortex, obviously, but perhaps the hypothalamus? Who would know?"

Byron's look had changed from impatience to interest. "A hallucinogenic? Something like that? It could be. A chromosomal examination . . ."

Charlie turned to John Loesser. "Didn't you say you could cook? It's that or Jodie's restaurant, or my scrambled eggs. There they go." He watched Constance, Byron, and Beatrice seat themselves at the kitchen table and start to make sketches, diagrams, God alone knew what, he thought. "Lets go shopping."

John Loesser was watching Constance with near fascination. She was too many people, he decided, too complex to comprehend. He found his gaze moving on to Beatrice, so dark against the fairness of Constance, and for the first time in over six years, regarding this young woman who looked like an Indian, he felt the pangs of longing for a woman other than Elinor. When Charlie touched his arm, he was startled from a great distance away. "I'd like to cook," he said.

"We'll need to know if they've done CAT scans, EEGs, what drugs they've tried, what effects . . ."

Charlie and John left without drawing the attention of anyone at the table. And that was Constance in her working persona, Charlie thought happily. He admired her more than he could express.

Outside, Charlie said, "If I had a can of gas in my trunk, I'd be scared to death the sun on it would set it off. Gets cold as any pole here at night, but that old sum heats up real fast real early."

John Loesser stood without motion for a few seconds. "I won't bolt," he said. "Why didn't you turn me in when the sheriff was here?"

"I didn't think you would," Charlie said. "Let's walk. It's only a couple of blocks to the store they call a supermarket. Only a couple of blocks to the motel, too."

"Let's get my car then." He laughed shortly. "I'll move my spare gas into the shade somewhere. You didn't answer. Why didn't you turn me in?"

"You're the only person I know who can walk into that place and walk out again. Seemed a shame to lock you away somewhere."

John Loesser stopped again. His voice was strained now when he spoke. "I told you what I know. It's the devil in there. They won't find anything, and your wife won't." She would want to reason with it, he thought with bitterness. Devise tests for it, find out what made it work, how it operated, why. But no reasoning was possible with evil. It was its own excuse, and Constance did not, maybe could not, understand that one basic truth about it. "I'm going to torch it, Charlie. I have to."

"Maybe you will and maybe you won't. Maybe I'll help you when the time comes. I know a few tricks you haven't thought of. Let's get your car and shop before the store closes."

Jodie's parking lot was jammed full; two California state police cars were there, and an ABC television van. Charlie steered John across the street, and approached the motel from the opposite direction. When they drew near the small lobby, they could see a nattily dressed woman and a man in jeans with a camera slung over his shoulder, talking to the desk clerk.

"You want to move in with us?" Charlie asked.

"Yes. The damn fools will get into the hotel somehow. The

new thrill of the week in thirty seconds, after this little message."

"Right. Let's get your gear and your car and beat it before someone spots us and wants an eyewitness account of the strange happenings in that sleepy little town on the edge of the great California desert. Come on."

Carson Danvers had been a master chef; taking an alias did not change that. He had bought an ordinary piece of pork, Charlie knew, and common things like tarragon and cream and wine, potatoes, carrots, and salad makings. Yet he transformed them into a gourmet meal, and in under an hour. It just wasn't fair, Charlie thought, that he verged on gauntness.

Over coffee, Beatrice asked, "Have you been a detective very long, Mr. Loesser?"

He had flushed over the praise of the food, and now he said very gravely, "I'm not really a detective. I'm more an authority on old buildings." And that was the truth, he added silently. He probably knew more about old abandoned hotels in the United States than any other living person.

"Isn't there a television around here somewhere?" Charlie asked. "I think Grayling's made the big time with the news."

Beatrice remembered where it was and John went with her to get it from one of the bedrooms. They all watched the news at ten. As Charlie had said, the sleepy little town had made the big time.

"How do you account for those happenings?" a pert young woman asked a bearded man. Beatrice and Byron had groaned together when he was introduced.

"Mass hysteria, more likely than not. It has happened again and again through the ages, you see. One adolescent girl faints and sets off a pattern of fainting, that sort of thing. As soon as the focus swings away from the people caught up in a movement such as that, the occurrences stop. A year later no one wants to talk about it. Ashamed, you know; they feel foolish and can't account for their own behavior."

Byron switched channels twice. Grayling took thirty seconds on one newscast, an entire minute on another, and was not mentioned at all on a third.

In their room later, Constance asked Charlie, "Can we trust John Loesser to stay put?"

He grinned and held up car keys. "I picked his pocket. There was another key in a magnetic contraption under the fender. I found it too."

"That poor man," she said then with great compassion.

He nodded. "You know the best thing about this damn cold house?"

"What?"

"Bed. A warm bed, cold room, hot woman."

She groaned and bit his neck.

Late the next morning Constance hung up the telephone and went searching for Charlie. He and John Loesser were going over every case step by step. John knew about all of them that Charlie knew, and several others. Constance watched them from the doorway to the den for several seconds as she thought out her plan. Better to drive to Las Vegas and fly to Los Angeles, or just drive the two hundred miles and be done with it?

"Charlie," she said then, "you remember Jan Chulsky?"

He looked blank. "Nope."

"Of course you do. She came to our wedding. We exchange cards and even talk now and then, at least several times over the years. We went to school together."

A patient expression settled on his face as he waited.

"She's treated some of those people up in the state hospital, and she'll be in Los Angeles for the next few days. She commutes."

Charlie nodded and turned to say to John, "Now we'll see the old-boy network swing into operation."

"The question is," Constance said, ignoring the comment, "do I want to drive to Las Vegas and fly, or just drive over. I'd have to land at the L.A. airport. Ugh. I'll drive."

"And this is known as thinking on your feet," Charlie added to John. "Want me to tag along?" he asked Constance.

This time she looked blank. "What for?"

He followed her to the bedroom, where she packed enough for overnight. "Jan's going to have the records printed out for me by the time I get there. And I'll spend the night in her apartment and drive back tomorrow. I'll call and tell you when.

Oh, her number." She made a note of it for him. "And you'll keep away from that place, won't you?"

He embraced and kissed her. "There's no place on earth I want to visit less than Old West at this particular time. Be careful out on the desert."

Charlie and John continued to compile data until shortly after four, when Charlie stretched and yawned. Strange how empty the house felt, he thought for the third or fourth time. As soon as Constance was gone, a house felt like a simple building; when she was inside with him, her presence seemed to fill it. He was aware of her at all times then, moving about the kitchen, in her study, in the bedroom, out digging or planting in the garden—even that counted. But this house felt bleak and empty and cold. The coldest damn house he'd ever spent any real time in. It leaked air at every joint, every window, around the doors. Must be a bitch in the summer when the air leaking in would be superheated.

John leaned his head forward into his hands, propped up on the table. "We have to tell the police," he said dully, surprising himself with the realization.

"Yeah. I'm afraid so." So far they had amassed information that said forty-two people had died; an unknown number were in various mental institutions around the country; and a further unknown number were suffering the aftereffects of the attacks. Twelve people had vanished. And, as Constance had warned early on, they just knew about the ones who made it into the records. How many more were being treated privately? Unanswerable.

"Okay," John said. He was benumbed by the totality of the figures. He had managed not to think about the victims. That had not been his job, he had decided long ago; there was nothing he could do about any of them. His job was to track down the devil and burn it out when he found it. And it wasn't working. It just appeared somewhere else and started over again.

"They'll arrest me," he said, and found he did not care. That never had been a real consideration. Freedom had meant only that he could find it again and burn it again, and try to make it up to Elinor and Gary, the two people he had loved beyond expression, the two people he had failed.

"What for?" Charlie asked, and they both thought of Constance asking just that, with just that inflection a few hours ago, when he had asked if she wanted him to go with her. Charlie grinned. "They say that people who live together begin to look alike after a while. Not us, no sir. We just talk alike. But it's a valid question. You're a respectable independent public insurance adjuster, dragged into this because I needed your expertise since you've been following these arson fires for the past several years. It'll fly."

"There hasn't been any arson here."

"Right. I made the connection between the fires and the cases of people losing their marbles, unprovable at this point, but worth investigating. I called on you to help." He shrugged. "And besides, do you give a shit if they believe me? What can they do, thumbscrews?" He grinned again, this time enjoying the thought. "Sore Thumb will have a fit when he finds out I've blabbed his little secret."

Charlie had to leave a message for the sheriff again. He called back within a few minutes. "It's out of my hands, Charlie," Sheriff Maschi said with evident relief. "The governor turned the whole damn mess over to the state police. They're sending in their team first thing in the morning."

"That won't quite do," Charlie said. "It's bigger than the state police, I'm afraid."

There was a long pause, then the sheriff said, "You at the house still? Might drop in for a sandwich, cup of coffee, something."

"Bourbon?"

"Sounds good to me. Five minutes."

"What the hell," he said in less than five minutes when Charlie put a glass of bourbon, hardly touched by ice or water, into his hand. "It's after five, and I ain't got any duties to speak of right now."

Charlie introduced John Loesser, the insurance adjuster, and the sheriff didn't ask him a single question. He leaned back on the couch in the den, put his feet on the coffee table laden with papers, and savored his drink.

Charlie straddled one of the wooden chairs, just as relaxed as the sheriff, and started to talk. Only John couldn't be still. He moved around the room, touching this, straightening that, studying the map on the wall, and finally interrupted. "I'm going to make something to eat. You want some dinner, Sheriff?"

The old man nodded, keeping his steady gaze on Charlie, his face as unreadable as a piece of the desert. Beatrice and Byron arrived home; Beatrice went out to help John; Byron joined Charlie and the sheriff. Every day he and Beatrice looked more exhausted, more helpless.

Charlie did not reveal John Loesser's identity, or that he had set the arson fires; he told the rest of it. When he finished, the sheriff handed him his empty glass. Charlie got up and refilled it, refilled his own, and waited.

"You know it don't make a bit of sense," the sheriff said finally. "Why didn't you tell me yesterday?"

"Tell what? Like you said, it don't make a bit of sense."

"And there ain't been no fire here, neither. What brought you to this place if you're investigating fires?"

Charlie shrugged. "It's exactly like Orick, except for the fire. And Camden, and Longview, and Moscow, Idaho, and all the others, except for the fire. Guess I thought that would come, too."

"I called him about Old West," Byron said tiredly. He looked ten years older than he had appeared in San Francisco in October. "We were up at Orick at the same time; I knew he was looking into something that might have a bearing on my work. So I called him."

Sheriff Maschi was frowning at nothing in particular now. "Dick Delgado is taking charge," he said finally. "Young, forty maybe, ambitious. Lorrimer, the owner of Old West and the new hotel, is upset. He wants this all straightened out right now, wants his men back on the job over there, wants any shadow removed, superstitions put to rest, wants his grand opening. So he puts a bug in the governor's ear and the governor brings in the state investigators and they tell me to herd my cattle and let them get on with the business of clearing up a non-mystery. Suits me. Four months I'll have my thirty years, and I'll be sixty-five. Both together. Four months. Hate to think I could blow it, and I know damn well that if I tangle with Dick Delgado, I blow it real good. They want that attraction to open for the Christmas trade, you know. Jesus Christ, Charlie, I wish you'd stayed home."

"So do I, Logan," Charlie said softly.

The sheriff looked at his drink and set it down. He got to his feet and went to the wall map. He reached up and pointed to the wall above it. "Up there's Death Valley. And over here is the Devil's Playground." He touched the map in an area only a dozen miles or so from Grayling. "Devil's Playground," he repeated. "Only seems to me the devil ain't playing games. Seems he's playing for keeps."

"Sheriff," Byron asked then, "if you can accept this, why don't you think this other man will? Delgado? We can tell him exactly what Charlie's told you."

Sheriff Maschi waved his hand, as if waving away gnats. "Not what Charlie told me so much as what I saw for myself. I saw those men go crazy. Dick Delgado ain't seen anything like that yet. He'll have to see it for himself. And I figure he will tomorrow. He will."

"What do you mean?" Charlie asked, but he already knew the answer.

"He's getting a crew together in the morning, and they aim to go in there and prove there ain't nothing in there and never has been. First thing in the morning."

13

Sheriff," John Loesser said, "they won't listen to you. That captain won't believe he can't just walk in and take charge and put an end to it. That's what they always think. Would it help if you could get some outsiders to tell them what happened in other places? I mean cops, even army officers."

"You got names like that?" Sheriff Maschi regarded him with more interest than he had shown before.

"I'll give you some names," John said, and sat down on the couch, started to write. His hand was shaking so much his script looked like that of an old man.

Charlie watched him also for a moment. John's scar was vivid, his face pale; a line of sweat was on his upper lip. "Our resident expert," he said to the sheriff in a light tone. "He's been watching this thing happen for several years." The sheriff made a noncommittal sound.

There were five names on the list John handed over after a minute or two. Names and towns, no phone numbers. "They shouldn't be too hard to reach. The towns are pretty small, like Grayling."

The first name was Foster Lee Murphy. John remembered him quite well. He had marched eight men into a plantation mansion that had been turned into an inn and finally abandoned altogether. He remembered the live oak trees shrouded with pale Spanish moss, the wraithlike fog that drifted head-high and was warm. He never had felt warm fog before that night. He had watched from behind an oak tree that spread its arms out over a hundred feet, arms as thick as an average tree trunk, also warm. Earth, trees, fog, all warm that night. It had been a noisy night, with insects, a whippoorwill, tree frogs in full voice. And then the shooting. Screams. Foster Lee Murphy had taken eight men in; six ran and stumbled out. At three in the morning of the next day, John had gone in.

He had heard nothing of what the sheriff said on the telephone, but when Maschi hung up, his face was bleak. "Noxious swamp gas," he said. "Murphy says the official report lists toxic fumes from an upwelling of swamp gas as the cause of the illness there." He put his finger on the next name. "Luke Hanrahan."

The hotel had been on a bluff overlooking the Mississippi River. One man had walked over the edge; one had vanished. John had watched from across the river the fumbling attempts to find the evil by surrounding it first and advancing in a solid line. A great tugboat pushing a long river train of cargo had saved the men. John had felt precisely when *it* turned off, when it turned on again after everyone had left, but first one man had walked off the bluff; one had gone into the hotel and had not returned, ever.

Maschi said without inflection, "One guy went AWOL; one tripped and fell off a cliff while under the influence of alcohol.

Case closed." He tried one more name, and this time was told that a few men on an investigation of drug dealers had got hold of and tried some bad dope.

Silently John went to him and took the piece of paper from his hands, tore it in half, and let the pieces fall to the floor. "Forget it," he said. He walked from the room.

Sheriff Maschi made a few more calls, an FBI agent he knew in the area, a captain in the state investigation office, others. Tomorrow, they all said; they would look into the matter tomorrow. He put in a call to Delgado; it would be returned, the answering sergeant said. He put in a call to the lieutenant governor; that one also would be returned. He tried to call the local representative in Congress and got an answering machine. Finally he walked away from the telephone, his face expressionless.

"You mean no one will listen?" Beatrice asked incredulously. "That's insane!"

"Not really," Sheriff Maschi said. "It's the chain of command. Probably the lines are hot with calls going in for Delgado. And probably he's telling them all there's nothing to be worried about, the sheriff's a senile fool who got kicked off a case and is expressing his discontent."

In spite of the distractions, John had prepared another superb dinner. He was incapable of cooking anything but excellent food. He ate very little of it, and no one talked during dinner except for comments on the meal. Shortly after that Sheriff Maschi took Charlie's arm and they went back to the den.

"I'll be watching in the morning," the sheriff said. "Want a ride?"

"To where?"

The sheriff went to the map and put his finger on a spot. "I figure about here, about a mile away, safe distance, I'd say."

"No road," Charlie murmured, looking at the spot.

The sheriff snorted. "People's been traveling that desert a good many years without worrying overmuch about roads. Around seven?"

Charlie nodded and soon after that the sheriff left. Charlie returned to the map and studied the terrain carefully. He was startled by John's voice at his side.

"Forty-two dead. How many more tomorrow morning? I'm going in, Charlie. Tonight."

Beatrice and Byron were at the kitchen table talking in low voices. Charlie glanced at his watch. Twenty minutes before nine. The supermarket closed at nine.

"Let's take a walk," he said.

John couldn't do it alone, he was thinking as they walked in the clear, cold air. That was the problem, the only problem. Men were staked out on the road leading into Old West, and that meant he would have to go cross-country, and that meant not alone. The sheriff might be able to do it, but not John Loesser, not Charlie, at least not at night. He visualized some of the crevices he had steered around carefully, some of the boulders that had almost upended the Land Rover, and that was in broad daylight. And the Land Rover was high; it could clear rocks that John's car would not clear. The sheriff's deputy had come to collect all of Mike's belongings, including his car; they would have to use John's Malibu. Charlie grinned bleakly at the thought. This was what he had set out to do: find the son of a bitch and his black Malibu. And he had. He had.

In the grocery he bought a quart of orange juice in a waxed carton, a box of cereal, a package of waxed paper, a gallon jug of milk, and a package of candles. There were six twelve-inch tapers in the box. John watched, mystified. He had expected them to buy lighter fluid, or kerosene, or something flammable.

"It's a multipart problem," Charlie said as they walked back to the house. "We can't get closer than half a mile, maybe more like a mile, with the car. And the men staked out will be looking down there from time to time. As soon as they see a blaze, they'll be down there, and they will have trucks or cars. Two, three minutes at the most, not enough time to get out before they get in. You've had a clear shot at it before, but not this time. So we prepare our little time bombs and get the hell out before there's a blaze to see. If we do it right, the building will go up like a torch, no problem there, and we'll be well away from it."

"You can't go in there, Charlie. Not half a mile, not even a mile. My God, you should know that by now."

"I don't intend to," Charlie agreed. "I stay with the car, with the motor running, the getaway car, as we call it in the trade."

At the house Charlie paused to gaze at the moon rising over the rocky hills. It was large, not quite full. Good news and bad news, he thought. They would be more visible in moonlight, but without it he doubted they could find their way in at all. He had counted on the moon, and at the same time knew it could add shadows and distort sage, turn it into lurking monsters or boulders. Well, he thought, you do what you can. No more, no less. He turned to enter the house.

"I know why I'm doing this," John said then in a low voice. "But why are you? You could sit back like the sheriff and just let it happen."

Charlie shrugged. "Damned if I know," he said lightly. "Keep thinking we need time, need real plans, need deliberation. We don't need to charge in and hope for the best. We're buying time, that's all." But it was more than that. He thought of the snappily dressed young woman he had glimpsed in the motel lobby, and her cameraman; thought of the bright young men in the state police force, the other reporters in the area, the innocent, ignorant bystanders. All hell would break loose, he knew, if they didn't do this tonight. Delgado and his men, armed men, going mad, others rushing in for the story, the thrill—all going mad. He thought of Maria Eglin, standing like a stony-faced doll, mad. And Polly, who had witnessed the madness firsthand, and might not be good for anything for a long time because of it. He shrugged again. "You play cards? Got any cards?" John shook his head, and it was just as well.

Actually Charlie had his own deck of cards that he always traveled with. He did not offer to play with anyone, but started laying out solitaire. He lost and gathered them up, shuffled, and started over. Beatrice and John talked in the den. Byron read through reports until nearly eleven and went to bed. Beatrice went to bed soon after that. Without looking up from his cards, Charlie said, "Why don't you rest? I'll call you."

John hesitated, then went to his room and lay on his bed, staring at the ceiling. He knew he would not sleep. He never slept before he faced the devil again.

Charlie dealt the cards over and over for the next hour, then he put them away and retrieved his bag of groceries, which he had left on the porch. He retrieved John's can of gasoline from the side of the house and took it in. He poured the milk out in the sink, rinsed the jug and set it to drain. He started to pour out the juice, but filled two glasses first, and emptied the rest. As he worked, he sipped the orange juice. He emptied the cereal into the garbage, prodded it down out of sight and covered it with crumpled newspaper. Then he got out the candles and measured one against the cereal box, trimmed it to size, and put it down, and repeated this with the juice carton, cutting a second candle to fit inside with about an inch and a half to spare. He trimmed the wick ends of the candles to expose nearly an inch, and dropped all the shavings and the extra pieces into the cereal box. He pushed the waxed-paper lining down the sides of the box, and began to tear more waxed paper from the supply he had bought. He crumpled each piece and pushed it down in the box until the mass was several inches high; then he worked one of the candles down through it so that it was upright, supported by the paper nest he had made. He added more paper until the box was two-thirds filled. He cut through the juice carton, making a hinged lid, and wiped out the interior, and then made a second paper nest for a second candle. He surveyed them both and nodded. He closed the carton and the cereal box and put them both on the table; they looked perfect, he decided. Now he went to the bedroom and looked at the Indian blanket on the bed, but found he did not want to destroy that. It was too beautiful. He removed it and took the second blanket instead, an old brown one that looked like Army issue. He started back to the den, paused at the bathroom and added two towels to his bundle, and continued. John came from his room and followed him silently. Charlie put his finger to his lips and took his supplies to the den, returned to the kitchen and got the bottle of salad oil and took it back to the den. He closed the door this time. Moving without haste, he spread the blanket on the floor, laid the two towels on it, and then sprinkled them with the oil. It pooled and puddled, as he had known it would. He left it to soak in and went out to pour gasoline into the gallon milk jug. Finally he cut a strip from the edge of the blanket, put it aside, and then began to assemble his package. He folded the blanket in at both sides to cover the towels, then folded the entire package lengthwise and put the jug of gasoline and the cereal box and orange juice carton in a row on it. He wrapped them all neatly, used the strip he had cut to bind the whole thing, and had enough left over to form two loops. He stood up, lifted the bundle, and slipped his arms through the loops; it looked like an ungainly bedroll. It was ten after one.

At the same time Constance lifted her foot from the accelerator with a jerk. Automatically she glanced at the rearview mirror. She had hit eighty-five again, she realized, clutching the steering wheel in a death grip. She did the arithmetic again; she was about ninety miles from Grayling, eighty miles of which was Interstate 15 and the remaining ten miles state road. Less than two hours. And Charlie was probably asleep, sprawled on the bed, his arm flung out on her side, as if searching in his sleep for her.

At eleven she had realized that she would not sleep in her friend Jan's apartment that night. For several minutes she had resisted her impulse to leave, had got a drink of milk, nibbled on a cracker and cheese, settled down once more to read through the various reports Jan had gathered for her. Finally she had tossed her few things back in the overnight bag and left, taking the papers with her. Nothing had come with the feeling, only the intense need to go back, to make certain Charlie was all right. Go back, go back. It had come down to just that: Go back!

The first hundred miles had taken more than two hours. She had had to find a gas station, fill up, get out of the Los Angeles traffic, head north in the maze of freeways. The next ninety miles would take an hour and a half at the most, closer to an hour. On both sides of the interstate the land had yielded to desert, wrapped in the surreal light of the oversized moon. The landscape was grotesque with elaborate shadows that seemed to have nothing to do with the objects that cast them. The land was silver and black under the luminous sky, and on the highway eyes appeared behind her, came close enough to blind her, then turned into glaring devil eyes that dwindled and disappeared. Monstrous trucks with thousands of red eyes rushed on her, swerved, vanished, and the roar existed in her ears without the substance. Her car shuddered.

At two Charlie and John left the house quietly. Charlie drove the Malibu. He had memorized the map, knew exactly where he had to leave the state road, head out across the desert. He did not hum under his breath, although if John had not been with him, he would have.

They drove southwest, skirting a rocky hill north of the road. Charlie slowed at four and six-tenths miles, and turned off the highway shortly after that. They would follow the base of the hill to its northern extremity, then turn and zigzag up a slope until they were on the ridge overlooking Old West. On a road map it would seem a snap, but the topographical map had shown the route to be treacherous and deceptive. Old rivers had gouged the land here; there was a dry lake bed, with areas of quicksand remaining where the poison alkaline waters had gathered below the surface, trapped by hardpan, or an impenetrable rock ledge. The rocky hills had been shaken by earthquakes more times than history could record. Rocks had slipped and slid, piled up precariously only to be dislodged days or even minutes after the cartographers had gone, changing the topography, sometimes beyond recognition.

But Sheriff Maschi said he intended to drive in and would watch from that ridge, Charlie told himself firmly. That meant it was accessible. Period. As soon as he left the highway, he turned off his lights, and he and John sat silently waiting for their eyes to adjust.

Finally Charlie began to drive. Within two hundred yards, the car lurched and came to a grinding stop at an angle. Neither man spoke for several moments. "Not a shadow," Charlie said then. Carefully he opened his door and looked out over a dropoff on his side; five or six feet only, but enough to roll them. More carefully he backed up a few yards and stopped again. "Okay," he said. "One of us has to walk it first, guide the other one in. Take turns. You want to go first?"

John had not made a sound during this. Now he swallowed hard and nodded. "Sure."

It was excruciatingly slow. John walked in a back-and-forth pattern, making certain there was room for the car to move in. Once he and Charlie had to roll a boulder out of the way to avoid backing up hundreds of feet. The dry lake gleamed smooth and deadly off to the left. All around them the desert seemed frozen: no animal stirred, no night bird flew or rustled; everything was holding its breath, waiting for them to pass.

Then Charlie was the guide, walking back and forth, beckoning as he went. They turned at the edge of the hill and started the last part of the trip. It was three in the morning. The shadows had shrunken, hugged the sage and rocks, creating small black caves at the bases. Charlie was guiding when the Old West town came into view. He stopped and gazed at it in the moonlight. It was less than a mile away two hundred feet below them. The buildings were shadows looming above the land; the two old buildings with silvered wood caught the moonlight and reflected it eerily. The hotel looked bigger than Charlie remembered; he knew that was a trick of the light, nothing more. He moved on, waving to John to follow. This was not a good place to stop. They needed an area where they could turn the car, have it pointing out when the job was done. They would drive back around the hill, stop and wait for the fire to rout the thing in the hotel, and then return to watch it burn. By then there would be enough morning light to allow them to drive out faster than they had come in. By then the state police would have their hands full down there, not be watching for strays on the desert, they hoped. The only real danger in all this, Charlie told himself again, was in showing a light in the darkness. That would be visible for miles. He found a spot where John could turn the car around with half a dozen forward and backward maneuvers. Then they both stood and regarded the scene below. Less than a mile, Charlie thought with some uneasiness, but the car's engine noise was behind him, signaling safety.

Charlie returned to the car and pulled out the pack he had assembled, slipped his arms through the loops.

"I'm going down," John Loesser said at his elbow.

"Nope. There may be a guard down here. And he could be crazy as a bedbug, or sleeping, or listening to a radio. Point is we don't know. But John, keep the motor running, right?"

His voice was low and easy, revealing nothing of the fear he felt. John Loesser hesitated a moment, then nodded. They shook hands, and Charlie started down the slope cautiously. Fifteen minutes to get down there, he was thinking, checking his slide. Not a good time to start tumbling, take it easy, no rush. Fifteen minutes to get there, five to arrange things, ten to get back. Not bad, not bad. He dug in his heels and grabbed a boulder when loose dirt shifted beneath his feet. After a moment he started again. Half an hour.

Constance was aware that headlights had appeared behind her, but she ignored them as she sped through Grayling to the house. She ran inside, to the bedroom where the bed had been torn apart, and stood there for a second. She looked inside John's room, hurried back to the other one, and searched the bureau drawer for Charlie's gun. It was there, and it was loaded. She slipped it in her pocket, turned, and ran from the house. Sheriff Maschi caught her on the porch, and her hand tightened on the gun in her pocket. That was what it was for, to keep anyone from stopping her, she realized.

"That damn fool gone?" Sheriff Maschi demanded.

"Let me go," she said. "I have to leave."

"You can't get near that place," he said, holding her shoulders. "That goddamn fool." He shook her with anger. "They'll hold you until morning, then escort you back to the house. Come on. Come on. I know where that damn fool went." He nearly pushed her to the police car.

He slowed down at the spot where Charlie had turned off the highway, sweeping the area with his searchlight, then drove on to leave the road half a mile farther down. He drove with his lights on, bumping and jouncing, but making good time, swerving now and then, cursing steadily.

Constance did not speak; she stared ahead fixedly and now and then relaxed her grip on the gun, but she did not take her hand away from it.

The moonlight was tricky, Charlie thought, crouched behind the corral fence, examining the hotel and the street of Old West. Moonlight flattened everything, erased depth. No radio noise, no motor noise now, but he hoped that was simply because he had gone out of range. Nothing moved. He edged around the fence and onto the porch of the old silvery hotel. The boards creaked alarmingly, but there was no help for that. He stepped in closer to the building, hoping the boards would be tighter there. Twice he had seen a light on the ridge opposite where John Loesser was stationed; the state police, no doubt, on patrol, out of range. The fact that he had been able to see their light meant that he had to be careful with his, he knew, and did not use his small-beam flashlight yet. A tarp was over the double doors at the front entrance, the way the construction men had left it when they decided not to come back. The heavy plastic-coated material had been nailed down loosely. He pulled it away from the doorframe enough to permit him to enter; inside, the blackness was deep and hollow-sounding. He waited for his eyes and ears to adjust before he moved again.

No one had been out back, on the porch, or anywhere else in sight, and he was certain no one was in this building with him. Not yet. He flicked on his flashlight and looked around swiftly. He knew the renovation of the hotel had been started, just not how far it had gone. There were two-by-fours stacked up, other lumber here and there, but the floor and the outside walls were intact, as far as he could tell. As soon as he was away from the tarp-covered door, he turned on his light again, and this time kept it on and began to move fast.

In the upper hallway he removed his pack and began to arrange his materials. First the blanket, then, at both ends of it, the nests he had made for the candles. He poured the gasoline on the blanket carefully and let it soak in for a moment or two as he opened the bath towels he had soaked in cooking oil back at the house. He covered the blanket with them. He did not want fumes to ignite prematurely; and when they did ignite, he wanted an explosive reaction. He folded the sides of the blanket in over the edges of the towels and examined it all with his flashlight. Finally he went to the candles and lighted first one, then the other. He closed the top of the juice carton, then the cereal box top, counted to five, examined his candles again, and grunted with satisfaction. He left the hotel quickly. He was tempted to open a can or two of paint, but the heat would do it for him. Don't be greedy, he told himself, swiftly scanning the street, the other buildings. Then he was in the corral, out the other side, and on his way up the slope to where John Loesser was waiting. It had taken less than five minutes.

John Loesser's relief left him feeling weak when Charlie reappeared. Not a flicker had betrayed him, not a sound. Experience counts, he thought dryly. Charlie started up the slope.

Mike Dorrance and Larry Womack had pulled the dumb assignment, they both agreed. Sit on a barren ridge and guard a ghost town. They had grumbled at first, and then had frightened each other with stories of cougars and Sasquatch and flying saucers; they had shared a couple of joints, and for two hours had alternately dozed and jerked awake. "Guard it from what, for Christ's sake?" Womack had exclaimed when they first arrived in the jeep at midnight. The old town looked like a movie set down there. Delgado had not said from what. He had drawn a line on a map and said don't get any closer than that, and don't let anything or anyone in. That was all.

There were only three possible ways to get in: by the road on the other side of the valley that had been barricaded, over the narrow-gauge railroad tracks, or through the open desert and over the damn ridge they were to patrol. Now and then one of them left the jeep to walk a dozen or so feet and look around, but there wasn't anything to see. Womack emptied his thermos of coffee, stretched and yawned, and went to have a look around this time. It was getting colder; a chill breeze had started to blow in. He went the ten feet or so that they had decided was their patrol, and then he stopped and shook his head. Lights, for God's sake! Who the fuck would be wanting in at this hour? Delgado? A relief car? He hoped so.

He called Mike Dorrance and they watched the lights wobble over the rough ground. Then Mike heard another engine. He turned his head, listening hard. "Hear that?"

It took a bit longer for Womack to make out the noise. He nodded, more frightened than he had been at the talk of cougars. He reached into the back of the jeep and pulled out a semi-automatic rifle. The approaching lights went out. Nervously they waited. The car must have gone around rocks, behind a hill, something. Very slowly they accepted that it was coming the rest of the way without any lights, or that it had stopped and whoever was in it was coming on foot. Mike Dorrance drew his .45.

"You cover the guy coming in," Dorrance said. "I'll find the other one."

They separated, moving cautiously, very nervous.

"Two cars," Sheriff Maschi muttered at the spot where the

tracks he had been following suddenly became tracks of two separate vehicles, one set going off to the right, one to the left. The air was pungent with the fragrance of newly crushed sage, and that was as much a trail as the car tracks. He made his decision and turned to the right. He had his lights off, just in case someone was on the ridge opposite Old West; he had not considered that Delgado would have a patrol on this side. But that was what it looked like to him now.

He inched forward again, then stopped. "Hell and damnation," he muttered. "If that's Delgado's patrol, they'll blow us off the desert if we sneak up on them. I'm going to scout ahead. Can't be much farther, ain't much farther you can get."

"You keep the motor going," Constance said, opening her door. "I'll look."

"Stick close to the rocks there," he said. "It's got to be just on the other side of that outcrop."

She slipped out, did not let the door close all the way, and vanished into the shadows of the outcropping. A second or two later, Maschi heard, very close to his side of the car, "Old man, turn off that engine and toss the keys out! Pronto! Or I'll blow your head off!"

He jerked around to see a man with a rifle pointed at his face. "I'm Sheriff Maschi," he said. "Who are you?"

"I don't care if you're the king of Siam," the man said. Maschi heard the tremulous note of fear, the soft undercurrent of nervous excitement, and he knew this man would shoot him.

"I'm here on official business," he said, and pushed his door open. "Delgado knows I'm up here, goddamn it!" He swung his legs out the door and with every second he expected to hear the report, feel the impact. The man was moving in; suddenly he sprang and grabbed Maschi and twisted him around, slammed him face first onto the back door. He reached inside the car, yanked the keys out, and put them in his pocket while Maschi gasped, trying to get his breath.

Constance edged around the outcropping; there was the black Malibu. She let out a breath. The engine was running. Then she stopped again. A man had appeared; he reached into the car and pulled the keys out, and at the same time John Loesser stood up. She had not seen him until then. He had been squatting at the top of the hill, looking down, she realized.

The man who had taken the keys yelled, "Freeze! Police!" John froze.

She realized suddenly that the other engine had been turned off, and she pushed away from the rocks, shouted, and then felt disoriented, dizzy, out of control. She reached for the rocks to keep from falling; a stab of pain in her head made her close her eyes. When she could open them again, the dizziness fading, she saw the officer with the gun moving almost in slow motion in her direction, the gun raised. His face was blank; the moonlight intensified the mask of madness over it. Behind her someone was yelling. The madman turned from her and went that way, walking like a zombie. At that moment, Charlie appeared over the edge of the hill; when he saw her his expression became incredulous. And then he changed. He stopped advancing. He stood without moving. A strangely hurt look passed over his face; his eyes flickered but did not close.

Constance found the gun was in her hand; she did not know when she had taken it from her pocket. She raised it, aimed at Charlie, and fired.

14

Constance heard John Loesser yelling, heard other gunshots, and paid no attention. Charlie was sprawled on the rocky ground, not moving. She raced to him, pulled his jacket open, and located the wound, high on his right arm.

"Start the engine!" she screamed at John Loesser and began to search through Charlie's pocket for his knife. She found it and cut the jacket away from his arm, cut his shirt away, and rolled up the sleeve to make a pressure bandage. Another light came on, shining on Charlie; the sheriff stood over her cursing.

"How bad is he?"

"It isn't too bad. We need a hospital, a doctor. . . ." She looked up finally and he was shocked at the lack of color in her face. "He . . ."

"Yeah, I know. I'll get the other fellow to help carry him to my car. Just hold that bandage in place another minute or two."

John Loesser sat in the Malibu revving the motor, staring at Constance. Sheriff Maschi had to shake his arm before he was heard. "I need help," he said again. "Listen to me," he ordered when Loesser got out of the car. "Delgado's man killed his partner, tried like hell to kill me, and he shot Charlie. You understand?" Loesser stared without comprehension. Maschi repeated it roughly, and finally he nodded. Together they returned to Charlie near the top of the ridge. The hotel suddenly became a torch; flames exploded from half a dozen upper windows all at once. The light breeze scattered sparks and a second building erupted.

Sheriff Maschi and John Loesser got Charlie into the backseat of the sheriff's car, with Constance holding the pressure bandage. Her face looked like ivory, even her lips. Delgado's men would come collect the body of the officer, the sheriff said to John Loesser.

He looked at the man closely. "You okay? If you're not, sit tight. Delgado's going to be up here in no time." He glanced at Charlie and shifted gears. "We'll be at the clinic in Grayling." The glow from the fire was like a false sunrise, he thought distantly. Before he drove away, he added, "You know that if anyone went down that slope, there'll be a trail. People out here put stock in things like trails. Lots of loose boulders around, though, might've rolled down when they were disturbed. Never can tell." He left, driving fast.

John Loesser went back to the edge of the ridge and watched the fire that was leaping from the saloon to the dry goods store. Then he started to roll boulders over the edge of the hill. He did not stop until cars and trucks appeared on the road going to Old West on the other side of the valley.

"Mrs. Meiklejohn," Sheriff Maschi said, glancing over his shoulder at her. She wasn't going to faint, not yet anyway. "Listen a minute. Delgado's man went crazy, just like we all expected someone would. He shot Charlie, and then his partner. Case closed. Got that, ma'am?"

"Yes."

Thank God she didn't argue. He went on: "Now, listen, Constance. You mind if I call you that?" He didn't wait for her response. "We have to tell the doc what you think might have happened to Charlie. We can't let him be fixing up your husband when he wakes up, and not be prepared, just in case."

"Yes," she whispered. "I know."

When had she told him anything, she wondered. "John Loesser saw. He knows."

"Way I figure it, he knows more than he ought, considering how he just got here, but anyway, we agreed that Delgado's guy did it. I took you up there to meet Charlie and his associate. We all wanted to see the show when it started, and then Delgado's man started shooting. Delgado's not going to like it, but what the hell can he do?"

He was talking to fill in the black spot of doubt that was in the car with him. He had counted the shots, he knew when the shot had come in from the edge of the hill, and by the time he had got there, Loesser had been inside the car racing the motor, and she had been on the ground taking care of Charlie. That had been plain enough. And he knew the only thing that could have made her shoot Charlie was the awareness that *it*, whatever the hell it was, had tried to take him.

It was all Delgado's fault, sending two guys out without telling them anything. Two more men gone: one dead, one raving out on the desert. Charlie maybe infected, whatever the hell that meant. And if he was crazy, then Constance . . . He cursed under his breath. Goddamn Delgado, let him take the rap for it all, including Charlie.

John Loesser/Carson Danvers watched in awe as the whole town blazed. Abruptly he turned and left. "The whole damn town," he muttered. Had Charlie planned that? He knew better, but the police probably would assume it. And this time they might look harder for the arsonist. He wondered how much insurance would be involved this time, and he did not want to hang around long enough to find out. He knew, with regret, that it was time to kill off John Loesser.

He drove to the clinic to check on Charlie. He was sleeping, his arm bandaged up to his shoulder, restraints on his legs, on his good wrist. John hesitated in the doorway to the small makeshift hospital room.

"I'm leaving," he said softly to Constance, who was sitting by the bed. She still looked ghostly pale.

She started, then relaxed and stood up. "They'll want to ask you questions," she said. "They'll take fingerprints maybe, find out . . ."

"I'm leaving," he said again, and this time she nodded. "I don't know yet where I'll be, or when." He looked past her at Charlie. "I'd like to know . . ."

Almost in a whisper she said, "There's a place in New York. Father Patrick Morley. It's a home for boys, on Houston Street. Tell him . . ." She shook her head. "I don't know what you should tell him. I'll call him as soon as we know." Why was Charlie still unconscious, she wanted to ask, demand of him, of anyone who might know something about *it* and how it worked on people. She reached out, her hand was on his arm, but she withdrew it and shook her head. She didn't dare ask; the question implied her fear about Charlie, and she was desperately trying to refuse even the possibility that he had been affected.

The doctor came in to examine Charlie again; John Loesser was gone when he was finished. Constance sat in the chair by the bed once more, waiting.

At two-thirty in the afternoon, Charlie stirred, grunted when he tried to roll over, and finally opened his eyes. Constance pressed the call button, as she had promised to do, and watched Charlie. The doctor entered, holding a syringe. If Charlie woke up insane and violent, the restraints might not hold, he had warned Constance.

Charlie blinked at the ceiling and tried to lift his arm, then his torso. He turned his head and saw Constance. She watched the puzzlement, the pain, and finally anger that he could not move, and when he looked at her, she found that she was holding her breath.

"Charlie," she whispered in a long exhalation. The terror she had been holding back, the tears, the guilt, the uncertainty, all exploded together and she lowered her face onto his chest and wept.

———

They decided that Charlie would be as comfortable at the rented house as in the clinic, and Constance took him home just before dark. Sheriff Maschi had dropped by to help.

"No more dope," Charlie said firmly in the den, his feet up on the coffee table, his arm supported on the sofa arm. "A double bourbon, kissed by an ice cube, and forget the water." While Constance made drinks, he looked at the sheriff. "What's going on?"

Logan Maschi shrugged. "Too much. Your pal is gone, the insurance guy, John Loesser. Caught a plane out of Vegas to L.A., left his car in the lot. That whole town's burned to the ground, lock, stock, and barrel. Delgado's man is still out there wandering around on the desert, far's anyone knows. His partner's dead, of course. Thanks," he said to Constance and took a glass.

Charlie took his own and drank, less deeply than he had intended. He still had too much dope in him, he knew. Nothing that the sheriff had said so far seemed very important. The important thing was that Constance had shot him and saved his life. He watched her move about the den, watched Maschi watch her also, and knew that Maschi was aware that she had shot him. He was gazing at her with near reverence.

Sheriff Maschi drained his glass and stood up. "I'm going home. Charlie, Constance, take it easy tonight. Tomorrow you'll have Dick Delgado to deal with, and he's madder'n hell, but there's not a hell of a lot he can do, far's I can see."

"One question," Charlie murmured. "Why pin it on Delgado's guy? Not that I object, but why?"

Maschi shrugged. "Delgado's going to be looking for a way to get you, get me, all of us. Be careful with him. Like I said, he's mad. No point in having him put Constance through a lot of grief, though. No point at all. See you."

Charlie grinned at Constance after they were alone again. "Thanks, by the way."

"Think nothing of it," she said, just as airily. "Will that story hold?"

"Should. Who's going to refute it?" He yawned. "Christ, let's sleep. You haven't closed your eyes at all yet. Come on."

Delgado was as angry as Sheriff Maschi had said he would be. His face had been flushed, his eyes black and dangerous-looking, and he had been helpless. He had asked questions and left again. Now Byron leaned forward and regarded Charlie with a steady gaze.

"Look, you're the only one we know who was attacked and recovered. And you, Constance, you saw what was happening, recognized what was going on, and you were in the zone of its influence. This may be the breakthrough we've needed from the start. Charlie, can you remember how it felt, what you thought, anything?"

Charlie opened his good hand and flexed his fingers, then started to close them as if around an object. "Like that," he said, watching his hand. "Being squeezed, like a soft snowball that is going to crumble any second. Only not with anything phys-ical. Pressure, not electrical actually, but not physical either. That's as close as I can come."

"Was it painful? Hot? Cold? Steady? Intermittent?"

"Painful," Charlie said, sipping bourbon between words. "Steady."

Byron turned to Constance. "What did you feel and see?"

She described it exactly as she had lived through it, the dis-orientation, the blinding pain, dizziness. She looked startled, then added, "But I kept feeling something afterward. Like a charged area, like under a high-tension tower." She shook her head in quick denial. "Not like that, not really. I don't know what it was like. All around me."

Byron was making notes as they talked; now he put his note-book aside and picked up his drink, scowling darkly at it. "You're both sure it wasn't directional? Like a beam of energy, rays, something like that?"

"Already thought of that," Charlie said. "Just wasn't the way it was."

Constance was equally certain. Whatever she had felt had been all around her, not coming from any one direction. She described the state policeman and his look of madness, and then said, "I knew that whatever had hit me was attacking Char-lie, only the effects were different. I was doubled over with a stabbing pain in my head, but he looked hurt, erased somehow, blank."

"Can you put it in a time frame?" Byron asked. "Apparently the policeman was attacked at the same time, and you couldn't watch what happened to him. How long did it go on with Charlie before the shot?" He believed the mad deputy had shot Charlie, as everyone else did.

She reconstructed it in her mind, her distance from Charlie, taking the few steps she had taken, raising the gun, firing. Finally she said, "Ten seconds, fifteen at the most." She looked at Charlie and said softly, "I saw the moment it attacked you. One moment you were looking at me and I could read you, and then you were blank, hurt. I saw it happen."

And the shot had set off a rush of adrenaline, an electrochemical shock reaction in his brain that must have been explosive to the thing, whatever it was. As much as any motor was, any electrical activity. By then John Loesser had got the Malibu engine running again, and the danger was past. But if she had not shot him, if she had stopped to think, to take better aim, to do anything, he would be dead, he was certain. Dead at the hands of the sheriff, or Delgado, or the other madman, his own hands, hers. And if not dead, then brain-dead, living dead, maybe for twenty or thirty years or longer. He shuddered.

"When I get back to L.A. I'm going to see if I can't get some people from the physics department to investigate all this," Byron said, but he sounded doubtful.

"The problem," Charlie said, "is that there's nothing to investigate until it pops up again somewhere else. If you hear, let me know, will you?"

"And you, too."

Delgado returned once more to demand information about John Loesser. "We just met the man for the first time right here," Constance said calmly. "He's an independent adjuster."

Charlie shrugged, then winced.

"We'll find him," Delgado said. "And when we do, we get him for arson, and that, Meiklejohn, means we'll have you as accessory."

"Then arrest me already," Charlie said. "Because if you don't, I'm going home tomorrow. You know damn well your men were scrambling because of gunfire a long time before the blaze started. I was busy getting shot at personally, and John Loesser was busy trying to keep the car motor running. Shit or get off the pot, Delgado."

He left in a white fury.

"He's right," Constance said. "No jury will believe we all just happened to go up there to see the show. Not at three in the morning. Charlie, can they do something to you? As accessory?"

"I'm not a damn accessory," he grumbled.

She looked startled, then whispered, "Dear God."

15

Two weeks later Charlie and Constance were in Phil Stern's office with Phil, Thoreson, Sid Levy of the Bureau of Alcohol, Tobacco and Firearms, Arson Department, and Fredrick Foley of the FBI.

"Charlie," Sid Levy said, "this is a fairy tale, right? Look, we've known each other what, twenty years? Enough. With fires, we never played games before. Why now, Charlie? Why?" Sid's cheeks were pink, his hair white; over the years he had become heavy through the middle. It would take very little makeup for him to be a good Santa Claus. Charlie had often said he was the second-best arson snoop in the country.

Charlie looked slightly bored. "I've given you a champion arsonist, Sid. He's a real pro. That's hardly a game, old buddy."

"So? You give us a name. Where's the man? Dropped off the face of the earth, that's where. And you tell us a ghost story. What should we do with the ghost story, Charlie?"

"Set up a team, bring in scientists, people with equipment to deal with it, and the next time this thing shows up, be ready to finish it off for good."

Sid shook his head sadly. "Not my department."

Charlie turned to Fredrick Foley. Put him in a tux and stand him on a wedding cake, Charlie had once said of him. He'd look right at home there. He was a dapper man, almost delicate-looking, which was deceptive because he was a runner who entered marathons and usually finished very early, though never a winner, never attracting attention that way. Everything about him was meticulous—his stylish dark hair, his manicured nails, his custom-made suits. When he talked he revealed his origins, the Bronx. "Well?" Charlie asked mildly, watching him.

"How I read it is that this man, Loesser, turned the corner when he was first attacked by the kid. Did something to his head, and he's seeing the same thing happening everywhere he looks now. Happens, so I hear. So he lights a fire and moves on. I've read the reports, Charlie, all of them, and there's just nothing to latch onto. Nothing."

"Okay," Charlie said, and stood up. "I tried. I've given you all the dope. Do what you want with it."

"Look, Charlie," Foley said, "you admit no one knows where it might start up again, or when, or even if. What do you expect? Station someone at every abandoned hotel in the country? Wait for it to show? And this equipment you think we should dream up, for what? You don't even know what we should look for. Charlie, you really think they'd blast something like this, if they believed in it at all? Don't kid yourself, pal. They'd take it home to play with. But they won't because there's nothing to go on. Bring us something solid, Charlie, okay? Something we can get our teeth into."

"More than forty dead people. Not solid enough? Couple dozen nuts in institutions. Not solid? What would it take, Fred?"

"I don't know. But I'd know it if I saw it."

Constance had been watching silently throughout the meeting. Phil Stern was satisfied; he was not connected with any company that would be hit with a massive claim as soon as the legalities were settled. Thoreson was thinner-lipped than ever, furious with Charlie for letting the arsonist set the fire under his nose. His company had been the major insurer of Old West. He had said with unconcealed bitterness, even hatred, that he regretted making that drive out to engage Charlie in the first place. At least no entire town had burned previously. Sid was unconvinced of anything more than the arson fires. But Fred Foley, Constance thought, would take a few steps, would probe a little. She had risen when Charlie did, and they moved together toward the door. She glanced at Phil, then the others, and said, "If anyone does hear about madness in connection with an abandoned building, I hope you remember to keep a motor running, or set up some kind of electrical field. Come out to visit, Phil. Good evening," she said generally to the others.

Charlie picked up his coat from a chair. A paper bag was under it. "Almost forgot," he said, putting the coat on. He picked up the bag containing a large object and crossed the office, handed it to Thoreson. "You left it at our place," he said.

Thoreson's thin lips seemed to vanish; he glanced inside the bag and turned livid.

"Thought you might have a use for it," Charlie said. He went to Constance and took her arm as they left. In the hall outside the office they stopped and he said, "Pay up."

She dug a five-dollar bill from her pocket. The gas can was Sore Thumb's. "See why I don't bet ever?" she murmured, and they went to the elevator. She had disbelieved very briefly. Not a real threat, Charlie had said. Sore Thumb had just wanted action, pretty damn quick.

"Well, you tried," she said in the elevator.

"And we both knew where it would get us. Okay, dinner with Father Morley, prepared by his newest miracle chef." But he was troubled by what Foley had said, and he cursed himself for being a naive idiot. Obviously the FBI would want to study it if they got involved at all.

Constance did not think this arrangement was what she had been thinking of when she gave John Loesser Father Patrick Morley's name. She had meant for him to get in touch with Patrick, who could relay news about Charlie's condition. At least, she told herself once more, that was what she had told herself she meant back then. Now John Loesser was cooking for the boys' home. He had dinner with her, Charlie, and Patrick that night. The dinner, pork with rosemary, sautéed apples, potatoes Chantilly, green beans in vinaigrette . . . She sighed her satisfaction over coffee. John Loesser knew how to make coffee, too. She remembered the awful brew that Patrick had given her in October when she delivered apples. Another lifetime.

While two of the teenage boys cleared the table, John told about the son of a friend. "He went through the course right up to cakes and pastries, did really well on everything. Then they spent a week making tiered cakes, decorated them all beautifully, and had them all on display for the parents' day ceremonies. When the time came, the teacher and judges went down the tables, sampling icing, rubbing it between their fingers testing for graininess. They tasted it, and went to the next test. They cut the cakes. When they got to Bill's he burst into tears. The following week he dropped out of chef's school and enrolled as an architecture student."

One of the boys giggled and, shushing each other, the two hurried from the room. John watched them with a slight smile. "I'm starting cooking lessons here. They're both enrolled."

Patrick brought out a bottle of brandy and they leaned back savoring it and the very good coffee. "You know how the police track down people who try to hide?" Charlie said, watching the film of alcohol climb the inside surface of his glass. "Old habits. A stamp collector just can't resist a philately show. Readers haunt libraries and bookstores. Football fans, model airplanes, whatever the old pleasure, it still pleases, and the fugitive thinks, I'll go this time. There'll be so many others, no one will notice me. That's the first thing. Then there's the name. It's really funny about names, how attached to them we all become. The guy runs and hides and changes his name from Timothy Wells to Tommy Will. Or Ralph Warren to Robert Williams. They seem to go for the same initials every time, or the same sound, something to hold on to from the past. Sometimes they even mix up their own names with their mother's maiden name, or their wife's maiden name, but it's the same effect as soon as you know the variations available." He swirled his brandy and finally tasted it, then sighed. "All right!"

Patrick and John had both been listening intently. Now John nodded. He was calling himself Carl Lambert these days. He glanced at the door, and said in a low voice, "I told Patrick everything, Charlie. I thought it wasn't fair any other way."

"I tossed John Loesser to the wolves," Charlie said bluntly. "I hoped it would be enough to make them want some of the action. It wasn't. They think Loesser went nuts years ago and sees other nuts every place he looks."

John shrugged. "Did you really expect anything else?"

"Damned if I know," Charlie admitted. "I wanted something

else, but can't say I expected it. Foley, the FBI agent, probably will look into it, but without much enthusiasm or money. Only because he's thorough. You have your computer set up here?"

John Loesser nodded. "Charlie, I'm a simple cook now. With classes to teach. I'm out of that game."

"Right. And if you get wind of a new series of incidents, let me know real fast, okay? If I can get Foley involved alone when there's something to see, he'll make a good ally. But he's got to be persuaded that there is something first."

John was shaking his head with regret.

"Listen to me, pal," Charlie said, leaning across the table, closing the space between them. "If you go in alone and get yourself killed, we've lost our best shot at it. You have more experience than all the rest of us combined, and I want you alive and well. I'm going to get the son of a bitch, John, Carson, Carl, whatever you call yourself. With your help or alone, I'm going to get the son of a bitch."

"You don't dare get near it," John said. "You may be more susceptible than ever after your encounter."

Charlie nodded grimly. "With your help or without."

They left the private dining room, returned to Patrick's study, and agreed to keep in touch, tried to formulate a plan that had a chance of working. Constance listened, joining in only when asked a direct question. She felt her gaze resting on Charlie again and again, and tried to force herself not to look at him, not to study him, examine his features for a change, for a sign that something had happened and was still happening with him.

She had told Charlie about the brain damage the insane people had suffered. Their brains looked as if they had been riddled with tiny pellets, or perforated with acid, or electric wires had burned their way through. No salvation was possible after such massive destruction of brain tissue. It varied from brain to brain of those who had been autopsied, but in every case the damage had been irreversible. Whatever had done that to those other people had also attacked Charlie, forced its way into his brain enough to make him stop his movements, to freeze, to look hurt and blank. She watched him with fear that became terror now and again.

By nine Patrick was too tired to play host any longer, and

they got up to leave. No one knew what to do about the thing, Constance thought wearily. She had gone over it with Charlie, with Byron, with herself, and there seemed to be no answers to the question it posed.

Driving home, Charlie outlined his thoughts about it. "It's not directional, not like microwaves. It's not intelligent. It's inoperative in any sort of electric field, or where there are motors running. It needs space for its portal, if what John saw was a portal. But damn it, people have to go somewhere when they vanish. They have to come from somewhere when their bodies turn up again. We'll call it a portal, a black hole that fills a doorway, that takes time to start and turn off, that needs more space than ordinary doors have these days. I'm assuming the size is important, and the isolation, and the lack of anything mechanical in the area—peace and quiet."

"Charlie," she said when he paused, "if it's like the signal from a television transmitter, it doesn't matter where it comes out, only where it originates. You could keep blowing up television sets for the rest of your life."

"Even if Foley could get anyone interested," Charlie said, as if she had not spoken, "what would be the point? They would try to communicate with it, like an ant nest trying to communicate with the foot as it descends. How long have we had things like microwaves, radar, lasers?"

"I don't know."

"Me neither, but not very long. A hundred years ago we couldn't have traced a microwave to its source, no matter how hard we tried. Who knew about radon in houses fifty years ago, much less how to measure it?"

Constance drew in a deep breath, strangely reassured now. He had been so quiet for so many days, so distant, she had thought with rising fear. This was Charlie back, angry, arguing out loud, talking it through for his own benefit as much as hers.

"Why not intelligent?" she asked during the next pause.

They had left the city now, were on Highway 17, heading north. Snow was expected that night and it was very cold; the road had little traffic. About half an hour farther on they would stop at a roadhouse, where she would have coffee and Charlie a double bourbon; after that she would drive, another hour and a half at the most, if she dawdled.

Although she hated driving in the city, and usually chose to go by train, she had offered to drive both ways this trip, to spare Charlie's arm, but he had wanted to drive. He never had minded the traffic, had grown up with it, and sometimes complained it was too eerily silent in the country. She let the thoughts flow through without trying to stop any of them, patiently waiting for Charlie to answer her question.

"What are they after?" he said finally. "Those autopsies didn't show any damage except to the brain. Right? The liver, heart, lungs, all intact, and the brain riddled with holes. They're after the contents of the brain. They're doing brain scans on living tissue and killing it!" His voice grew harsher as he spoke, and suddenly the car swerved. He caught it and held it steady, both hands hard on the wheel.

"Charlie? What's wrong?"

"Don't know." He began to tap the brake, shifted down, and came to a stop on the side of the road. "Don't know," he said again in a strange remote voice. He leaned his forehead on the steering wheel.

"Charlie!" She heard the panic in her voice that could no longer be suppressed.

"It's okay," he said, in his usual voice. "It's okay. You'd better drive."

They got out and changed places and strapped themselves in. She touched his forehead, cool. He caught her hand and kissed her palm, but he looked frightened, as frightened as she was.

Without prompting, he began to talk about it. "I had a feeling of being in a small, dark place, pressed in. It was suffocating, no doors or windows, too tight." He had seen it, felt it, had been there, and at the same time had been driving, watching the road, talking to her. The two sets of sensations, of memories, occupied the same time, the same place. He shook his head.

"Has it happened before?" Constance asked, very calm now. Perhaps too calm, Charlie thought.

"A couple of times, less intense than this one, not as real or as long."

"What about the onset? What starts it?"

He reached over and rested his hand on her thigh, the way

she did with him when he drove. She covered his hand with hers for a moment, returned it to the steering wheel. She rarely drove with one hand on the wheel; he did most of the time. His hand on her leg now told her he did not want her to speak in her professional voice, not to him. She swallowed hard and glanced at him.

"Charlie, can you talk about it? How it starts, how it ends, anything?"

He patted her leg, but kept his hand there. "You've known," he said slowly. "I've caught you watching me."

"I knew something was wrong," she admitted. She was speeding and made herself slow down. The roadhouse was ahead, but she had no intention now of stopping anywhere. Home, she kept thinking, go home.

"Yeah, you knew. Okay. I'm doing something, it doesn't seem to matter what, like driving just now, talking. Then there's another feeling of being somewhere else, cramped, in a dark space. Both feelings are there together. One doesn't interfere with the other one. It just happens all at once. Nothing goes with the feeling. No need to do anything about it, go anywhere. It's almost like a memory of being there, wherever it is. Then it's gone. Again, no warning, no fading away, just not there."

He was facing straight ahead, no longer looking frightened, and that was right, Constance thought, because she had taken all the fear into herself. It lay coiled over her heart, squeezing.

She drove them home too fast, now and then remembering not to speed, then finding herself edging back up to seventy-five, eighty. It started to snow lightly during the last half hour, a fine dry snow that could accumulate to a depth of several inches before morning. She parked in the garage and they went inside their house, where Charlie went to the kitchen and mixed hot buttered rum. The cats stalked around him indignantly, as if to demand a stop to the nonsense, coming and going at all hours, making it snow. Charlie muttered as he danced around them to make drinks.

"When I come back, I want to be a cat," he said, pushing Brutus out of the way with his foot. Candy cuffed Ashcan on her way to weave infinity patterns around his feet. He pushed her away too, and she walked stiffly out of the room, grumbling. "Tomorrow," he went on, "they'll sit in the window and watch me shovel snow, use the snowblower, freeze my ass while they complain about not enough yeast on their food, or not enough chicken liver. What a life!"

"Well, I'll sit inside and let you play with snow, too," Constance said. "You know I want to hire one of the Mitchum boys to take care of it."

"Nope. My job. You don't complain about not enough chicken liver or yeast on your food, and that, my darling, makes all the difference."

"Charlie," she started, but he caught her in a tight embrace, buried his mouth and nose in her hair and drew in a breath.

"We'll talk about it," he said into her hair. "Tomorrow. Tonight we'll have our nice hot drinks and go to bed. Okay?"

She pulled back and shook her head vigorously. "Not tomorrow. We'll talk about it now. Charlie, you are not going mad. You have nothing to worry about as far as brain damage is concerned. You wouldn't function if you had the kind of brain injury the others showed."

"Good," he said. "So let's have our drinks and go to bed."

"Charlie, look at me! Stop this!"

His face was set in hard ridges and lines. She trailed her finger across his cheek, down his chin. "Charlie, please. I don't know what's happening to you, but it isn't like the others. You know it isn't."

His facial muscles relaxed a bit and he nodded. "I know."

Over the next two weeks they both pored over the accounts of insanity, the terrible effects the thing had had on others. Constance made her special Christmas cookies, and they both shopped, bought and decorated a tree, and welcomed their daughter home for a week during the holidays. And they waited. Charlie had another attack, no worse than before.

There was the damn cramped space, darkness, a feeling of being hemmed in, and during it he was perfectly aware of his actual surroundings.

He called John Loesser, invited him out.

"Can you come to dinner? Anytime. Or we can meet you in the city."

John would come out by train, he decided. Patrick was ill, probably would be admitted to the hospital again for treatment.

New people were due at the home, to relieve Patrick of his duties. It was time to move on, but first he would visit.

It snowed again the day John was due. The yard was like a postcard scene, with snow piled high on sweeping branches of the blue spruces, and banked against the front of the house up to the windowsills. Constance tended her bird feeders and looked at the lovely world with troubled eyes. Cardinals and chickadees waited for her to move on so they could eat; the cats watched them broodingly, too lazy and warm inside the house to be a serious threat, but wistful. Constance shivered and hugged her parka closer around her. It was her fault, she thought suddenly, remembering the day they had picked apples, remembering that Charlie had taken the arson case only because she had been so busy, going here and there, speaking, publishing. She shook her head and hurried back inside, denying the thought as hard as she could. She and Charlie both went to pick up John. Charlie did not do any driving now.

Her dinner was not up to John's standards, but he was too polite to mention that, and, in fact, was very complimentary. They had coffee and Cognac in the living room before the fire, each of them with a cat. Ashcan had been stuck with the stranger and for several seconds had hesitated, sniffing his shoes, then his trousers, finally a hand, before he eased himself onto John's lap, where he curled up and started to purr.

"Tell me about those doors," Charlie said then without preamble. No mention had been made until now of the strange happenings or fires.

John nodded. "Right. A blackness that filled the doorway. I walked around it in one of the buildings, looked at it from the other side, two connecting rooms with that . . . that void in between, exactly the same on both sides; just a void, an absence of light."

"Did you toss something in besides the rock you mentioned? Especially at Orick?"

Now John looked startled. "Yeah. Twice. Once was at Orick. The first time was at Moscow, Idaho. I made a Molotov cocktail—I thought that was appropriate—and threw it into the blackness. The fire burst out all around and I ran out. Period. I couldn't tell if it went all the way through, or got stuck, or bounced back into the room. So I tried again at Orick. This time I made a time bomb, sort of. Not as well as you would have done, I guess, but I tried. I rigged up a cardboard box, propped it up with newspapers, and put a wine bottle on top of it. I found one of those corks with a hole through it, the kind that wine makers use, and I put a cotton cord through it into the bottle, filled it with gas, and used the twine as a wick. When the fire reached the paper holding the box up, it was supposed to burn it, let the bottle roll down into the void, the blackness, taking the burning wick with it, and soon the whole thing should have caught. I didn't hang around to see if it worked."

"Something worked," Charlie murmured. "One of the firemen out there said there was an implosion. He was pretty sure of the word he used."

John shrugged. "It didn't work enough to slow them down."

"Maybe it didn't go in far enough," Charlie said absently. "Or it wasn't a big enough charge for the job. Or something else."

Charlie always knew when Constance was signaling him. It wasn't anything that he could demonstrate or prove; usually neither of them would even talk about it, but there was something. When he was feeling jovial about it, he said she scratched him between his shoulder blades with invisible fingers; when he was bothered by it, he said she turned her witch eye on him. Whatever it was, he knew. And she was signaling now. He glanced at her.

"You can't go near it again," she said. "Charlie, you know you can't go near it again."

He did know, but he also knew that it had touched him, that something was in him that had not been there last month. He regarded her soberly and did not agree, but did not dispute her either; in fact, he did not acknowledge her in any way. For a moment she looked foreign, alien, unknowable. He shook his head and turned back to John Loesser.

"Several people have gone through the doorway, haven't they? And returned? Some of the people who disappeared. Very thorough searches were made of the hotels, and yet their remains turned up in the ashes. Probably two in Orick."

"They turned up dead," John said bluntly. "No one's gone through and come back to talk about it."

"Let's hope that pattern is not invariable," Charlie said after a moment, and then he smiled, his usual warm, somewhat skeptical grin that took many years off his age and made him look vulnerable.

16

The fire burned low while they talked; the wind had started to howl outside, and now and then a gust blasted its way into the chimney, swirled the blaze strangely, and blew smoke into the room. More snow, Charlie thought with resignation. A real storm was due this time; John would be a houseguest for a couple of days at least.

John was explaining his problems to Constance now; until he had a new identity established, it would be difficult to get a car, a new driver's license, any ID at all.

Charlie grimaced and made a note on a scratch pad, handed the paper to John. "If you've got cash, you can get a car here, license, whatever you need. No questions will be asked. Any idea where you'll go?"

John shook his head. "Thanks for this. It didn't occur to me that you'd know." He leaned forward, upsetting Ashcan, who protested and stalked away. "Charlie, I think the FBI is interested, after all. I've talked to Beatrice a couple of times; she said they're asking questions. Some scientists from JPL are interested, too."

Charlie shrugged, but the thought of the scientists from the Jet Propulsion Lab getting involved made him distinctly uneasy. "I thought they'd ask around. Byron's keeping me posted with what they're up to. So far about all he can report is that there's no periodicity in the events, assuming, that is, that they have enough information to work with." He stared at the quiet flames, thinking fire was the prime example of how good and evil can coexist in the same place, same time. He said, "The people Byron's been in touch with are saying there can't be anything to it, but if there is, it's the find of the century. They've turned the big computers on to the problem of source, periodicity, probabilities of its happening again and where." He laughed without humor. "They have a new puzzle to solve, a new game to play along with their Star Wars problems."

"Christ," John muttered. "They'll be like all the others. No one believes until he sees what it can do, and then it's too late." He shook his head. "Maybe it's best. They can be in position within hours, no doubt, as soon as the reports start coming in about madness anywhere near one of the hotels. Let them do whatever they want. God knows, I don't want this to be my personal war any longer."

"What will they do?" Charlie asked, turning to Constance. She and Byron had discussed this part, he knew.

"First, they'll seal the area, we think," she said. "They probably will set up equipment to measure radiation, radio signals, whatever they can think of that they know how to measure."

John snorted. "The very instruments they use will stop whatever it is they want to find."

"Maybe. But they don't know it, or believe it if anyone tells them. They'll want the scientific data. They probably will use animals for experimentation in the beginning. Birds in cages, cats in cages, dogs, maybe even chimps. And then sacrifice them to examine their brains." Both men were gazing at her with unconcealed looks of distaste. She rolled her eyes. "I'm not making the rules, guys, just telling you the procedure if you want a scientific study. Eventually, if the thing is still contained, they'll have to use people, of course. The dilemma is that if you protect the people, there's nothing to find; eventually they'll decide volunteers are in order."

Charlie exhaled a long breath and turned his brooding gaze back to the fire. "There's a story I came across years ago," he said. "It's about this missionary in Africa back around the turn of the century. He'd been out for months before any mail caught up with him, and then he had a newspaper, the first he had seen since his arrival. He read it, then read it again, over and over until he had memorized it. Finally, he put it aside and his natives snatched it up and carried it away. Such powerful magic, they thought. It had to be powerful magic, or why would he have bathed his eyes with it for so many hours?"

Constance nodded. "Think of the implications of a newspaper," she said to John, who was looking confused. "Language, education, manufacture of paper and ink, invention of the printing press, delivery systems, systems of gathering news . . . It might well be considered magic."

"I always wondered what the natives actually did with the paper," Charlie said. "Stared at it? Rubbed it on themselves? The ink would have come off, of course; magic ink? Rubbed their eyes with it? Could put an eye out like that, I'd guess. What will our people do with the thing in the hotel?"

That night eight inches of snow fell, and during the next day six more inches. The next afternoon Constance watched Charlie and John Loesser drawing hotel plans at the kitchen table.

"Okay, this is the hall, the one up in Camden. And you think the door with the shadow must have been about here. Right?"

"I don't know. I wasn't looking for it then," he said. "I was acting from instinct, copying more or less the first layout. Later I began looking for it, not then. But if it was like the others, then yes, it probably was about there. I simply glanced in rooms and noticed that there were open doors that night."

Charlie shuffled through the pages of graph paper, then withdrew one. "This is the Moscow, Idaho, hotel. This is where you tried to toss a Molotov cocktail through?"

John moistened his lips. That was the first one he had actually tried to examine. He had groped his way through the echoing building, aware of rot and crumbling flooring, aware of the moan of the wind through cracks around every window that had long since been replaced by boards that had worked loose, hung crookedly. Talking about it now had brought back that night with chilling vividness. The corridor had stretched out before him, doors closed on both sides of it, like the entrance to a mine. The beam from his flashlight had been lost in the darkness. He remembered the webs, real cobwebs that had become burdened with dust, and the other webs that were not real, but were like an electrical charge that would not be brushed away, no matter how often he tried.

He became aware of Charlie's quiet patience. He moistened his lips again. "I went up the stairs and began trying doors, first one side of the hall, then the other. About midway I found it. Connecting doors, the door missing, and the abyss in its place."

He opened the door cautiously and the wind moaned as it forced its way through cracks in the boards at the windows, brushed him on its way to the corridor behind him. He swept his light from left to right, examining a wall, the windows, another wall, and then stopped. Where the beam of light landed on a wall, the surface appeared with faded wallpaper hanging off in long curling streamers, then the unpainted boards, the window frames with peeling paint, and then nothing. The light stopped when it touched the abyss. It reflected nothing.

"So you went out to the hall and into the next room?" Charlie prompted after a few seconds.

"Same thing. It filled the doorway, top to bottom, and it simply swallowed the light. I threw the rock from the second room and went back to the other one, but it wasn't there."

Constance rubbed her arms briskly; goose bumps gradually subsided.

Charlie found the plan of the Moscow, Idaho, hotel grounds, which showed the county road that wound up a hill to it and a fishing camp less than a mile away. He already had drawn a circle with the circumference of about a mile. Six people had wandered into the danger area and had gone mad; ten people had died before the hotel had burned down. Why there? Why for God's sake there?

Suddenly he said, "That's the wrong damn question!" Constance and John looked startled. "Why not there? That's the question. Look, there are a number of things we know, or can assume. It likes wooden buildings. It doesn't like electricity or mechanical things. It likes big doorways to set up shop in. It doesn't give a damn exactly where it is as long as the place meets those criteria."

"That's crazy," John said.

Charlie shook his head. "Remember the moon lander we sent up? I recall that there was a good bit of unhappiness about where it landed, not the best place for studying the lunar surface, not where the scientists wanted it, but a place where its chances of landing safely were best. And the Martian probe?

Again, not exactly where they wanted to have a look around, but a place that met other criteria. Sort of like that old one about the guy on his hands and knees under the streetlight. A cop comes along and asks what's up. Lost my watch, the guy says. And the cop asks where. Over there, he says pointing down the street. Then why the hell are you looking here? The light's better, he says."

"You don't think our people are doing this," Constance said in a low voice, her goose bumps back again.

"No. Think about the Martian probe, honey. We land a gizmo that is programmed to do certain things. It doesn't do anything else, just what it was told a long time ago. Let's pretend. Here's the probe." He pushed his coffee cup to the middle of the table and cleared an area around it. "First thing is turn on the light." He drew a large circle around the cup. "Next, you start collecting and analyzing everything within reach. Now here are some poor little blind Martians; they can't see the light, but they can feel something funny about the air, maybe it gives them a headache. If they wander too close, they get analyzed." He pushed a few crumbs into the area, then scooped them up and dropped them into the cup. "Poof, gone. Never knew what hit them."

"In time," John said bitterly, "they'll figure it out, but how many crumbs have to go first?" He held a roll over the cup and crumbled it.

"What scares me," Charlie said then, "is the possibility that they'll learn about that damn door and try to move it to a safe place where they can explore it at leisure. I wonder what kind of programming it has to protect itself from such an eventuality. Would we lead the savage headhunters home? Why assume they might?"

"It might not even be programmed," John said. "Maybe there's an intelligence guiding its every move."

"Don't think so," Charlie murmured. "Seems it would have caught on by now that you're hot on its tail with a gas can and changed its *modus operandi*."

Constance looked from one of them to the other as they spoke. The goose bumps had gone, but the chill had settled inside her, squeezing her hard and tight. "Stop it!" she cried in an unfamiliar voice, her speaking-to-an-asinine-bureaucrat voice. "You're both acting like children," she went on, dripping ice water with each word. "You make assumptions and then act as if each one is undisputed truth."

"You're absolutely right," Charlie said then in the same tone, with the same inflection she used when he was being unreasonable. She clenched her fists and drew in a deep breath. Charlie glanced at John and said judiciously, "She likes lists. We should make a list of possibilities. You want to go first?" he asked her, gazing at her with a blandness that made her want to hit him.

"Our own government could be testing something. A scientist could have a runaway experiment. A foreign government might be doing it. Mass hysteria might have magnified a simple effect. There could be gases in those buildings. We didn't know about radon twenty years ago. Who can predict what will be discovered next year? Mass hypnosis. Like the Indian rope trick." Charlie was not writing. He was regarding her with great warmth and sympathy, she realized, and she stopped talking. The silence held for several seconds. She said, "Charlie, what's wrong with you? Do you know?"

Her voice was almost inaudible, but he heard the question, knew what she meant, knew the reason for the pallor that had spread over her face, knew about the ice that had invaded her. It was within him too.

"I just have assumptions," he said gently. She opened her lips; when no sound emerged, she nodded. "Something sends a gateway, a doorway to a building where chances are good that it will not be disturbed. Maybe it could operate just as well out in the open, but we don't know that. Maybe it simply takes time to get things ready; we don't know that either. When it is operational, there is an area that it can influence, a field, a pattern of some sort of radiation, something. We don't know what it is, just that it seems to extend out for roughly a mile in all directions. Up? We don't know. Down, into the ground? We don't know. Some people seem to be unaffected by it, like John. About one out of four people who experience the effects of this field, radiation, whatever it is, go mad. They become murderous, or suicidal, or completely withdrawn—catatonic— or show other symptoms that we generally associate with insanity. They are incurable; their brains are destroyed by the radiation, or force. Let's suppose they are invaded by something that riddles the brain, then departs. But whatever it is, it can also activate the various systems that make people move. It can make dead people get up and walk. It forces them through the doorway, the portal to wherever the sending mechanism is, possibly. Maybe there is more elaborate testing equipment there. We don't know that, either. Until the building housing the doorway is destroyed, it continues to exert its influence on those it has invaded. They go back to it if they can. Dead people get up and go to it. Later, after the fires, their bones turn up in the ashes sometimes. Not always. Not all of them."

Constance started to speak and he regarded her with a gaze that was distant and strange. "We know it's true," he said. "That damn building in Old West was searched from top to bottom, and after the fire the remains of two men were found in the ashes. One of them was Weston's assistant, Mike, and he was dead before he went in. Probably the other one was too, but we don't know. They went through the portal and came back out. They went somewhere, stayed there for days, and then showed up again. The rock John threw in, the Molotov cocktail, they went somewhere, too."

"Why didn't the burning gasoline destroy that 'somewhere'?" she demanded. "You're guessing, just guessing about all this."

He shrugged. "All we can do is guess. Maybe there wasn't enough air to sustain a fire. Maybe there are protective devices. Maybe there's an interim space before you get to the actual source of the thing itself. Maybe it admits only people, not objects. But it admits people and everything they are wearing or carrying on their persons. Sheriff Maschi said one of the corpses in Old West was holding a wrench. That guy took it in and brought it back out."

He rushed on before she could speak again. "When the doorway senses a motor, electrical activity above a certain level, it turns off, just like that, and then turns on again as soon as quiet returns. The thing isn't gone during that period; it's just not working. The activity doesn't force it out, is what I'm saying. Nothing has forced it out of anywhere yet, except fire. And that doesn't seem to have any effect at all on the sender, the source, whatever it is. Maybe it doesn't even know a receiver, a doorway and its field have been destroyed. Maybe its programming doesn't allow for that. Maybe there is a time limit involved. After so long, it stops, the sending mechanism scans for a new location and sets up a new field there. We don't know. Maybe it can just attach itself to a carbon-based material, wood, and when the wood burns, it collapses."

Constance had not moved as he talked, almost too fast to follow. Suddenly he stood up and went to the counter, brought back the coffee carafe and poured for them all. He looked inside his cup, took it to the sink and put it down, and brought out a clean one from the cabinet. Outside, the silent snow continued to accumulate; birds streaked to the sheltered feeder, away again in flashes of red and black. She thought of a show she had seen, people talking about organic methods of pest control. "If you put these granules down," a bearded man had said, sprinkling tiny pellets on a table, spreading them with a pencil point, "the ants find them irresistible, don't you see. We have a film." She had watched the ants struggling with the grains that had assumed gigantic proportions among them. "They get them inside the colony and with the humidity and warmth, the pellets emit fungus spores," the bearded man had gone on. "Deadly to the ants, of course." Time bombs, she had thought, and switched channels. Time bombs. Would the doorways be like that? Time bombs? In her mind she could see men struggling to cut away a doorframe from the surrounding walls and floor, without warping it, without touching the opening at all. They could do it, she realized. They could haul it away and set it up in a laboratory somewhere, and when the laboratory power was turned off, it would go to work with its diameter of madness reaching out for a mile all around. Or would sensors tell it to increase its power? Or not to function at all? Or do something altogether different? What it had done to Charlie was different; no one else had exhibited his symptoms. Maybe it would emit fungus spores, deadly, of course. She knew she was on the verge of insane laughter, and forced herself to lift her cup, to sip the steaming coffee, to stop seeing ants and bearded men talking about death too nonchalantly.

She kept her gaze on her cup then, and said, "You didn't answer my question. What's wrong with you? Do you know?"

He shrugged and said almost lazily, "Nothing much. I think

we've got a tiger by the tail, the biggest damn tiger in the world, and it's taking us here and there as it wants."

She knew he was evading her again, and he knew she was well aware that he had not yet answered her, and by now she must know that he would not. Could not, he corrected. There had been few secrets over the twenty-five years of their marriage, but now and then there was a secret. Now there was a secret, he corrected again. The others had not lasted very long.

The snow was letting up slightly; the sky was lightening. When it stopped he would get out the snowblower and start working on the driveway, the walks around the house. He groused about clearing snow, but in fact there were times when he enjoyed the labor, enjoyed the still cold air and the pure beauty of a world under wraps. He would enjoy it that afternoon. The unanswered question hung over them heavily, silencing John, who did not know their many varied ways of communicating but seemed to understand that no new business should be raised right now. Constance continued to watch the cardinals at the feeder, but her gaze did not shift to follow their flight, to focus on newcomers. Charlie looked at the snow but he saw the cramped black space, smelled strange air, felt pressure against his head that grew and grew until he wanted to swipe at his hair, knock it away. And he saw the doorway that John had described with loathing and terror. But to Charlie it was not a thing to fear. It was velvety blackness that would be welcoming, that yearned for him even as he yearned for it. During the past few weeks he had dreamed of that doorway several times. In his dreams he walked toward it at first, then ran, and then, miraculously, the way it can happen in dreams, he flew unencumbered by his awkward body, and, flying, had gone to it joyously, only to come awake in a sweat.

He knew he would not get near an area where it operated. He knew he would resist the temptation to approach, to see it for himself. He knew it was insane to think anything else about it. And yet, he thought bleakly, he felt like a bee so loaded with pollen it could hardly fly, and was unable not to launch itself and return to the hive. Programmed to take home pollen, it could do nothing else. Something had invaded his head, he thought clearly, and it wanted to follow its programming and go home. Knowing this made all the other things he knew about the doorway and his need to stay away from it inoperable.

17

We fear others, Constance thought that afternoon at the front window, watching Charlie clear the driveway, because we don't understand their values. And even more because we suspect they have no regard for ours. John Loesser came into view with a shovel to attack the front walk and steps. Sometimes his scar from the plastic surgery seemed a bright red line of warning; other times it was invisible altogether. She wondered if he saw it every time he shaved, if he touched it now and then, remembering. And she wondered if he realized that she was immune also, if he had thought through what it meant for those who had had the wrenching headache, the assault of pain, and then looked up uninvaded. Polly had come away like that. And she had also.

It was inhuman; there was no defense, and she was deathly afraid of it, whatever it was. John was immune, she was, but Charlie had been affected. She no longer saw his red jacket, the snow plume, the emerging black driveway. Charlie had been affected, she said again, hearing the words in her head. How? She did not know and if he knew, he would not say. But she accepted that the only way he would be safe was if they found and destroyed whatever it was that operated the doorways and the fields of insanity that surrounded them. How many times had countless humans come to that same awareness? There is the foreigner, the alien, the enemy that must be killed.

She thought of the presentation she had prepared for the meeting of psychologists and psychiatrists in San Francisco, how vehemently she had denied that xenophobia was innate, how rigorous had been her arguments proving it was a learned response. In theory she might still take that position, but in practice, now that every cell in her body seemed sensitized to a threat, when she could see how Charlie had changed because of contact with the alien presence, now she knew that something more primitive than her reasonable mind was motivating her, dictating her every thought. And that more primitive part knew the strange other had to be destroyed.

Abruptly she turned from the window to go to the kitchen to make apple pie for dessert. Hot apple pie and cheese. John was a better cook than she was and he would make dinner, but she would make the pie. She almost wished she had a gingham dress and a starched apron with apples and strawberries appliquéd on it; she would be certain to rub flour on one cheek, have the house fragrant with spices—cinnamon and cloves— and the men coming in from their chores in the frozen wasteland would realize the American dream. She stifled a giggle that threatened to turn into a moan and went about her own chore of making pie.

"I hardly ever use the electric stove in the winter," she said later to John, who was studying the wood range with interest. "Even for pie," she added. "Of course, in the summer it's a different matter."

"It's a no-win situation," Charlie said, tired but feeling good from his exertions with the snow. His face was ruddy, his eyes bright. He and Constance were at the table, leaving the cooking area to John, who had never cooked on a wood stove. "I cut the wood for exercise, and she makes things like pies."

"Use the electric stove," Constance said. "That one takes getting used to—" The phone rang and she reached behind her and picked it up. "Yes?" She listened for moment, then said to Charlie, "It's Byron, for you."

Everything changed. They had been at ease, and now the air was thick with tension. Charlie's voice was charged, probably not noticeably to anyone but Constance, but she knew. He sounded more relaxed then ever, sleepy, but his eyes had lost their shine and now looked blank, blind even. He listened, then said, "How do you know that?" Listened again. "Can't," he said then. "In case you haven't heard, we're snowed in. Be a couple of days before anything moves around here." This time he listened longer and then drawled, "How are things, Fred?"

Foley, Constance thought, Fred Foley, the FBI agent. Now they made a tableau, John unmoving at the stove, Charlie looking asleep with the phone at his ear, she frozen at the table. The cat Brutus stalked into the room and glared at them, turned, and left again.

Finally Charlie said, "Sure, Fred. Sure. If I see him, I'll tell him." Very gently he hung up. "They want you," he said, glancing at John. "I said I'd tell you if I see you."

"They know I'm here?"

"They seem to think you're in New York somewhere, in the city. Byron said Beatrice told them."

John shook his head. "I didn't tell her where I was. She couldn't have told them."

"They really want you," Charlie said kindly. "If they think they can find you through her, well . . . Anyway, Byron and Foley will be in the city tomorrow, if they can get a flight in, or the next day. They said to tell you they'll wipe the slate clean, whatever you've done in the past, all forgiven, understandable."

"Dear God," Constance whispered. "It's started again, hasn't it?"

"Well, they didn't say that in just so many words," Charlie said. "But if they're looking for John to run point for them, I'd assume it has started again." He crossed the kitchen to stand at the wood stove with John. "Now, you tell me what kind of heat you want, and I'll tell you which wood will provide it. Quick and hot, the little sticks of applewood. Medium and sustained, the oak."

"They must have clamped down on information going into the mainframe," John said, looking past Charlie. "There wasn't anything yesterday."

"I suspect that's right," Charlie said. "And they do have resources, you know."

"I should go."

"Snowed in, remember? Snowplows hit our road out front after the interstates are clear, and the federal highways, and the state roads. We're way down on the list. Let's build up the fire now."

He built the fire while John started chopping onions and

carrots. He admired the way a master chef handled the knife and food he dealt with, seeming to pay no attention at all to what he was doing, but instead to be thinking out loud.

"Beatrice must have mentioned to Byron Weston that she had talked to me," John said, at the counter. "They're tapping her phone, the bastards. Flying in to New York. Must be within driving distance then. Probably have it sealed off already, if they can get to it. Might be snowed in. No leaks this time. No way to find out where it is." The knife stopped in midair, then resumed. The carrots had been reduced to the size of rice, the onions almost to a mush. He pushed everything to one side and started on garlic. The knife blade flashed with precision. "They don't need me if they just want to burn it out. They want to study it, have someone who can go in and out for them."

He stopped cutting and turned to look at Constance. "What do you want?" she asked.

"I want it utterly destroyed. To hell with their studies."

He resumed chopping.

Charlie stood out of the way, listening, watching, his arms crossed. So far he had found no fault with anything John said. Strange, he thought then, he had tried to interest Foley, Sid Levy, anyone, had told them everything—nearly everything, anyway. And now that they were involved he just wanted them all out again. He had wanted them to use their vast powers of destruction, and now . . . If you call on the gods to hurl thunderbolts, you'd better be pretty damn nimble. Byron Weston had been excited, unable to conceal his excitement over the phone. Chance of a lifetime, Charlie thought soberly, the find of the century, of the millennium. A bunch of kids playing with dynamite caps.

"I could get in touch with them," John said, cutting parsley now. "Find out where the damn thing is, then split."

Charlie snorted and turned to the table where Constance sat, very watchful, very still. "Martinis," he said. "We are asking this guest to cook without a martini at hand."

She set the table while he mixed drinks, and then they turned on the radio for news: it was all about the storm and road problems and school closings. When it became obvious that no one was listening, Charlie turned it off again.

"Sid Levy," he said suddenly. John Loesser was stuffing

chicken breasts with the vegetables he had sautéed. He glanced at Charlie with no understanding, and continued his work, frowning in abstraction. Charlie looked at Constance. "Sid might know where the thing is supposed to be."

He left the kitchen, and returned in a moment with his telephone directory, already open, his finger on one of the names. He made the call from the kitchen.

Neither Constance nor John spoke or moved as Charlie performed on the telephone. He had an index card that he shook before the mouthpiece; he scraped the phone with his finger; he blew long whistling breaths across it, all the time complaining that he could not hear, please speak up, slower, louder, they were having a blizzard, for God's sake! "I told you," he said, although he had not told Sid this before, "I can't hear you any more than I could hear Fred Foley. Where? Say it again! Where?" He crumpled the card and blew across the mouthpiece and listened intently. "I'll call you back tomorrow, or the next day. Are you there, Sid? Can you hear me? I'll call back when the lines are in order again."

He hung up. "Lake Pike, New Jersey," he said softly. "We're to meet at a hotel in Lake Pike and go on from there." Constance had already gone for the atlas. They pored over it together and located the small village at the edge of Kittatinny Mountain. "Deceptive," he murmured then, studying the surrounding countryside. "Summer houses, boys' camps, fishing camps on the lake, and the river, what, five miles from town? Skiing nearby. Deceptive. It looks empty and is probably crawling with people."

It was rugged, mountainous country, probably not plowed out all winter, and humming with traffic all summer. Their atlas did not show the topographic features of the area, but Charlie could remember it generally from past trips—steep hills, rotten-slate hills, fast mountain brooks dammed here and there to make brilliant blue lakes that came complete with A-frames and trailers, retreats for religious groups, Boy Scout and Girl Scout camps, and hunting and fishing resorts. Two hours from New York when the roads were passable. Two hours from home when the roads were passable. And now with the snowstorm in the area, it might as well be on the moon as far as accessibility was concerned. Of course, he thought then, the army had snowplows, too. National Guard plows? Foley would find a way to get in; there would be personnel to see to it if he had any priority at all.

They were at dinner when they heard the snowplow on the road in front of the house. Charlie had not completely finished the driveway. He had learned not to dig it all the way out until after the plow had gone by. Otherwise he had to do it twice. An hour of work, he thought distantly. Tomorrow, after one hour of work, he would be mobile again. Heading toward New Jersey.

"This is wonderful," Constance was saying to John. "Not quite chicken Kiev; better, I think. I'd like to keep you." She spoke to John Loesser, but her gaze was on Charlie, had returned to him again and again; she felt almost that she could follow his thoughts about the snow, the driveway. "Sit still, John," she said lightly, "I'll clear and bring coffee and pie. Charlie, ice cream or cheese?"

He nodded, caught himself, and said cheese. The cheese was pale sharp New York cheddar; the pie was spicy and fragrant and warm; the coffee excellent dark Colombian. Charlie brought in Cognac. So very civilized, Constance thought. So very civilized.

"You know," Charlie said then, "only three percent of arson fire cases are solved annually?" John shook his head in amazement. "Fact. We know who did it most of the time, but proof is hard. Very hard. The evidence goes up in smoke, you see. So this guy has a big insurance policy on his warehouse, say, and it burns while he's at dinner with a dozen other people. We know it's arson, and we know who is responsible, but so what? He collects and that's that." He sipped his coffee, touched the Cognac to his lips, and sighed in contentment. "Sometimes when we go in there's still a wall standing, maybe a lot of walls standing, and we know they won't stand very long, so we set a charge and tumble them ourselves. With proper precautions, of course. Lots of ways to tumble those walls, depending on what else is in the building. Chemicals, that's one thing; natural gas, something else. Wooden frame, concrete, lots of steel beams—they're all different, take different approaches."

"What are we going to do, Charlie?" Constance asked then in a low, steady voice.

He shook his head.

"It's us, or no one," she said. "Not you alone. Not you and John. Us."

"I should have finished the job years ago," John said. "I didn't know how. My little Molotov cocktail! Tell me what to do, Charlie. How to do it. That's all I want to know. How."

"Can you ski?" Constance asked him.

"Afraid not."

Constance said, "Look at the map." She got up and brought it to the dining room table. "Here's Lake Pike. Let's say what we're looking for is within a ten-mile radius." She consulted the scale and then measured off about an inch from the village, traced a rough circle with that diameter. "What we want is somewhere in there. Hills, mountains, brooks, the lake. And all snowed in, I bet. They'll plow the road, maybe even the driveway to the hotel we're after, but they'll also have people there to keep out intruders. We're intruders. So, if we go in at all, it has to be off the road, off the driveways, through woods, through snow that may be hip-deep, deeper even. Skis or snowshoes. Can you manage snowshoes?"

"I'm from Virginia, Constance. Not too much chance to learn skiing or snowshoes. If you can get in, so can I, if I have to wade through it up to my chin."

She brushed that aside. "Tomorrow morning while Charlie is finishing the driveway, I'll give you a lesson. You can practice when we go to town to get the charge. MacPeters will have the stuff you need, won't he?" she asked Charlie in the same breath. MacPeters was with the volunteer fire department.

He nodded, watching her with amusement as she turned back to John Loesser, whose look was not at all amused.

"Cross-country skiing isn't a thing like downhill," she said. "If you can balance at all, you can do it. And you don't go very fast or anything like that. It's rather like walking with funny shoes. You'll see in the morning." She added, generously, Charlie thought, "Don't worry about it. Maybe there won't be enough snow over there to worry about. More coffee?"

"I'll do it," Charlie said, waving her down. He left with the pot to make more.

"So we have a charge," John was saying as Charlie went out. "And you teach me to ski in a hour or so in the morning, and the roads are clear enough to drive over to New Jersey, and we manage to avoid Byron and Foley and their group—"

Abruptly Constance stood up and walked from the room. In the kitchen Charlie was at the sink unmoving, both hands clutching the edge of the counter. She hurried to him and took his arm. It was rigid. After a moment he shuddered, then looked at her. Again, she thought. She was certain she had known each and every time he had gone away like that. That was how she thought of it: he went away for a few moments, a minute or longer. Then he came back. And when he came back he did not at first recognize her, or anything else. His eyes were blank, his face expressionless. That changed and his expression was of fear, then he was Charlie again. Neither spoke. She squeezed his arm slightly, kissed him, and picked up the coffeepot.

"I'll do it. Do we need more logs inside tonight?"

Candy came in complaining about strangers cooking in their kitchen, and Ashcan followed, darting suspicious glances here and there. Charlie danced around them both, cursed them, and went to check on the fire, on the supply of logs, and now Constance stopped her coffee-making motions and shut her eyes hard for a moment. "You can't have him!" she said under her breath. "Leave him alone!" Her words were addressed to the thing behind the black door, the thing that lived in the abyss, the thing that had touched Charlie with evil. "We'll blow it to hell and gone," she added, still not moving, answering John's unfinished question. When they had the charge and did whatever they had to do to get it to the right place, inside the black doorway, they would blow the evil back to the hell it had come from.

She made the coffee and they all went to the living room before the fire that hissed and crackled now and then, but was mostly quiet and steady. Charlie made good fires.

"I'll—we'll need your moon suit," Constance said after a few moments of silence. Charlie regarded her with a cold, hard expression. John looked blank. "It's a protective suit, boots and all," she said. "Sometimes there are toxic fumes, things firemen wouldn't want to get on their skin, much less breathe. It might come in handy tomorrow." To Charlie she said patiently, "Isn't that what you were thinking?"

Sometimes when she pulled things out of his head he hated it; sometimes it amused him; sometimes it left him feeling chilled, as if in the presence of a strange creature he could not fathom at all while she turned on him a look of complete understanding and awareness. That was when he hated it, he thought, when she knew him so completely and was so opaque to him. He shrugged.

"All right, then," she said, exactly as if he had answered. "The Molotov cocktail should have done some damage and evidently it didn't. I can't help but think it's because it didn't get to the source of the field. Do you suppose there's an intermediate space between the doorway and the transmitting mechanism? If there is, we could find that nothing we do outside the main place will be effective."

She looked at Charlie with that same unfathomable expression. She knew those were his thoughts, his assumptions.

She went on, "There has to be a space large enough for people. We know people have disappeared through the doorway and some of them came back out. So there has to be a space big enough for more than one person at a time. We know that. It could be that there's something like an airlock separating the doorway from the control room, or whatever it is. And to damage the control room, the bomb has to get to it."

"The moon suit," John Loesser said, understanding now. "It has its own air supply, insulation?"

Constance nodded.

"I could do it," he whispered.

"So could I," Constance said.

"No! You're out of your ever-loving mind!" Charlie jerked up from his chair and attacked the fire, sent sparks flying up the chimney. He faced it and said angrily, "My job. You get that? Both of you? It's my job. You'd blow yourself up, either one of you."

"You'll just have to see to it that the bomb is idiot-proof," Constance said. "And instruct us. Nothing electrical about it. Or mechanical, probably. What's left?"

Charlie turned toward her, his knuckles white against the poker.

"You can't get within range," she said quietly. "You know that as well as I do. And it's going to take all three of us. Someone has to make sure that no motor is turned on while one of us is inside the thing. What if that happened? Would you get out again if the doorway closed down because electricity came on? We can't risk it. And someone has to help John get to the place. No accidents along the way. And remember, he'll be on skis for the first time; he'll need both hands for his poles. Someone's going to have to carry stuff, help him up when he falls down. Help him into the moon suit when it's time. You know you always needed help, someone to check it out. It's going to take all of us, Charlie."

"I won't let you go anywhere near it!"

"I'm immune," she said. "Exactly the way John is. It attacked me, gave me a fierce headache, a blinding headache for a few seconds, and then went away. I talked to Polly back in California and she said the same thing. We all know that some people within range weren't affected, some were. That part's okay."

"It's not okay!" he yelled at her. "You don't know a damn thing about what's behind that blackness! Neither does he! You think it's going to let someone go in and blow it up, just like that? You think it doesn't have defenses? It could double, triple the field effect, for all we know, as soon as someone gets near that door."

"It didn't, though," John said. "Remember, I was close enough to toss stuff through. Nothing changed. And you can use a flashlight. Mine was pretty small, but it didn't have any effect on it. I can go through, Charlie."

"Goddamn it, John!—"

"Carson," their guest said. "John Loesser died a long time ago. I'm through hiding behind him. Carson Danvers. It's time I finished something that began over six years ago."

"Let's check out the moon suit," Constance said, as if she had suggested they play Scrabble. "Someone's going to wear it eventually."

Charlie went to the basement storage room and returned with a suitcase. He opened it and pulled out the suit. He had not had it on in thirteen years or more, but it was in perfect condition. How they all hated the suits, he was thinking distantly, as he explained it to Carson Danvers. Turkey roasters.

But only if the turkey didn't have enough sense to back up and get out in time. "It's awkward and cumbersome, but it protects against chemical fires, toxic fumes, even radiation up to a point and for a limited time. But you can't move much once it's on. Can't bend over very well. So you need help in getting into the boots, getting the seals right. And the air tank on the back is a bitch to manage without help. These straps can hold whatever you need in the front pouch. The charge will go there. You can't put it on until you're actually in the hotel, of course. You'd never reach it with the suit already on. And you can't see too well with the helmet in place, kind of like blinders on a horse. But you need the helmet, or the air won't work."

He explained the parts, how to regulate the airflow, how to grasp with the oversized gloves on, how to turn your head to get a wide-angle view of whatever was in front of you, and all the time he was doing this, he knew that Carson Danvers would not be the one to go in. That thing wouldn't let just anyone enter, only someone already carrying its signal, already primed. The honeybee with pollen. If a wasp tried to enter the beehive, it would be swarmed over and killed; only the bee with the right credentials would be allowed in. And he had the credentials to go through the door; the thing would recognize its own. The thing in his head wanted to go back home, wanted to take him home, and he wanted to go too. He would be allowed in; not Carson Danvers, not Constance, but he, Charlie, would be allowed in. It would be like going home.

18

Jud Hendricks, Herman Kohl, and Bobby Toluri were hanging out at the Lake Pike Diner, kidding around with La Belle, who was too old for them, but was a looker. A few other kids were there in other booths, and a couple of men at the counter, wearing parkas, dripping ice water from their boots. One was

Jake Dorkins, the Dork, who taught algebra and coached basketball at the high school. The other was Ralph Wasilewski, just
in from plowing Old Ferry Road.

Herman Kohl—who had a basketball scholarship to Penn
State, if he kept out of jail, they liked to say—started to yell
something at La Belle; Bobby Toluri punched him in the arm.

"Shut up and listen. You hear what Wasilewski's saying?"

At the moment he was saying nothing, having finished, and
was now staring off in the misty, greasy, odorous miasma of
the diner.

"Not a hell of a lot," Herman Kohl said.

"Yeah. What he was saying is that those guys in the four-by
are holed up at Mel's camp. What the fuck for?"

"Poaching," Jud Hendricks said. He was the youngest of the
three, still a junior; the other two were seniors. It wasn't too
often that they let him hang out with them.

Bobby gave him a withering look, a warning that he might
be sent packing if he didn't shape up. "They're army, dope. My
old man knows stuff like that. He says they're army, they're
army."

"Okay, they're army. Army can't poach?" Herman Kohl waved
to La Belle and held up his Coke can. "Anyway, there's nothing
up at Mel's except snow. Let them freeze their balls off. So
what?"

Bobby was thinking, his forehead creased, his eyes narrow.
"Look, first old man Tierney goes batty and shoots up the place.
Right? Then Doc Gruening shoots his own head pretty damn
near off. Right? Then the army moves in up at Mel's. Right? I
bet they're testing a weapon or something up there."

Jud groaned and closed his eyes. "You're a nut. You know
that? A real nut. Another conspiracy?"

"Maybe. What about Feldman? Lost in the woods! What a
crock! He invented the woods around here."

"I read about some new weapons," Jud said. "They use su-
perconductors, you know, the stuff that has to be way below
zero for electricity to flow through it. They could be testing
something like that."

"Sure," Herman said. "Why bother going to the North Pole
when you can go to New Jersey?"

"They'd pretend to be hunters. Why not? Did you see the van that went through this morning? Just like in *E.T.* I bet it was crammed with electronics."

They did not really believe any of it. They did not really believe there was a connection among the several instances of craziness that had hit, the deaths that had resulted. It was winter, after all, and Lake Pike in the winter drove people batty. Their basketball game had been called off for that night, and all three were on the team. But Marshfield High was still snowed in. The Marshmallows couldn't make it; they knew they'd get their asses whipped, the Lake Pike boys agreed, but it was an empty victory. They were bored. By now they were tired of the toboggans and sleds and ice skates. They drew closer together and tried to figure out a way to spy on the army. After a few moments, Bobby called, "Hey! Mr. Wasilewski, is Childer's Park Road open yet?"

"What for?" Wasilewski called back.

"Good toboggan runs up there."

"It's open." He returned to his conversation with the Dork and dismissed the restless high school kids.

"What then? Hike back up the mountain?"

"Shit no. We go down the back side of the mountain, across the valley, and then drag the toboggan to Mel's. We don't know anyone's there until we're nearly on top of them. Our plan was to toboggan down from Mel's on the road, only now the road's plowed and we're stuck. So they give us a ride to town. What's wrong with it?"

After another five minutes, they stood up and left the diner. All three of them were over six feet tall, Herman Kohl six feet seven. They were grinning broadly. At the counter Jake Dorkins, the Dork, watched them with unease. Bored kids spelled trouble, but what the hell could they get into with the whole damn county snowed in? Finally, he dismissed them too.

The drive had not been as bad as Constance had feared. There had been one stretch that required chains for about twenty-five miles; all the way traffic had been slow and cautious. She had concentrated on driving, keeping a wary lookout for cars out of control, for patches of ice. Charlie had maintained a brooding silence. Carson had said that when it was over, he probably would go to California, open a restaurant there, see Beatrice. He had sounded wistful and Constance had said something appropriate if not startling; then silence had returned. Suddenly Charlie broke it.

"Take the next right turn," he said.

Constance glanced at him; her hands tightened reflexively on the steering wheel. He was stony-faced, almost rigid, staring ahead. Gone, she thought, nearly crying out, except this was different somehow. She slowed down, searching for a road to the right.

Everything was prepared, she told herself. They had the suit, they had skis; Carson had proven he could move on them. They had the charge. A very simple-looking thing. Too simple? She shook her head slightly. Charlie said it was enough and he knew. Two-phase device, he called it. You pull the pin and that lets two chemicals mix. After about ten minutes they start a heat reaction that will reach eighteen hundred degrees and that sets off the plastique that acts like TNT but isn't TNT. Enough to blow up a bank vault. She made the turn off the state road. The secondary road was plowed, but hardly wide enough for two cars, and certainly not wide enough for a car and a truck, if a truck should appear.

Even if they were getting close, he couldn't feel *it* with the engine running, she wanted to explain to Charlie. He couldn't. It didn't work when the engine was running. She imagined the bank vault blowing up, pieces flying everywhere, showers of green bills. Her mind was skittering because she was so afraid, she told herself, and her mind skittered off again, this time to the image of a submarine exploding in the sea, with a shower of green and gold fish. That was wrong, too. The black door did not lead to anyplace on earth or in earth's seas. They had accepted that without discussion. The transmitter, the parent device, was in space somewhere. The door was a dimensional portal that led to space.

"The next left," Charlie said.

Not with the engine running! She slowed down again. She had studied the map, but now was confused. The last turn was not one she had planned; the coming turn was not on her mental map. On both sides of the road farmland had yielded to forests: black traceries of trees against a sullen gray sky, snow banked over five feet high making the narrow road a tunnel, pressed in on all sides with no retreat. No way to make a turn, to go the other way. Forward only, following the road that wound around hills, made turns too sharp, considering that there could be a truck coming. The hills had become steeper, higher; had become mountains.

On either side of the road there were occasional clearings in the trees, private roads or driveways that vanished in the hills. Few of them had been plowed out. Charlie was staring past her to the left of the road, his whole body stiff with tension. They passed a narrow, tortuous driveway that climbed up the side of a hill, and Charlie sagged.

"We've come too far. Find a place to turn around."

"Charlie, there wasn't any place to turn off back there."

"We'll have to dig it out. Won't take too long."

At the next driveway that had been opened, she turned carefully and retraced their way, past the next plowed drive, searching for the one Charlie knew was there. He caught her arm in a hard grip.

"There it is." He nodded at the opening in the trees. "Our driveway is on the north side of a valley. That last driveway is on the southern side of the same valley. Let us out here with the snow shovels and you take the car back up one of the open driveways and give us half an hour or so, then come back. You can't park on the road while we dig."

She stopped the Volvo and turned off the engine, then looked at Carson Danvers in the backseat. He had become almost as tense as Charlie. His scar was a bright red line along his cheekbone. He held his breath a second or two, then nodded.

"It's okay here," he said finally.

It was fifteen minutes before three. In two hours it would be getting dark. She said, "I'll come back at a quarter after three. Charlie, promise you won't go beyond the road here."

"Sure. We might not even be done yet. Let's get at it."

She knew he was not really seeing her, that he was simply impatient to get on with the job of digging. His eyes had a flat hard look that she had come to recognize over the years; he was looking inward at a landscape no one else would ever see.

The men got the shovels from the trunk and were already

attacking the ridge of snow piled up by the plow when she drove on. She turned again at the next opening, and when she passed them a minute or two later, neither looked up. Four miles farther down the road she came to the village of Lake Pike. There was a diner with steamy windows, a tiny Grand Union grocery store housed in a gray stone building, two churches, a gas station, a variety store. A typical lakeside village with a hotel at the far end, off the main street, presumably with a view of the water. She did not drive past the hotel for fear that Byron and Fred Foley were already in town. She stopped at the diner to have the thermos filled with coffee; they had drunk it all when they stopped to take off the chains earlier. The diner was overheated and loud with raucous teenagers and country rock music. A state trooper examined her as she waited for the thermos. His face was cherry-red, his hair carroty. She nodded politely, paid for her coffee, and hurried back to the car. Now she had drawn attention to herself, she thought angrily, and so what? She had a right to be out driving alone, had a right to want hot coffee, had a right to have three pairs of skis on her car that had no passengers. She drove out of town without glancing back at the diner. Four and a half miles to the driveway they were clearing. There had been virtually no traffic on the road earlier; there was as little now.

At least the stretch where she stopped was relatively straight. If a car did come, there was room for it to go around her. She got out and walked to where Charlie and Carson were finishing a passageway. It was wide enough, but just barely. Both men were red-faced and breathing hard.

"How deep is the snow?" she asked, nodding toward the driveway that was visible only because no trees grew on it.

"Maybe eight or nine inches," Carson said. "I went up a couple hundred feet; doesn't seem to get any deeper, and there aren't any drop-offs. It's okay as far as I went."

"There's coffee," Constance said, and pulled on her knit cap. "I'll have a look at the drive before I start in."

"You're going to drive?" Carson asked dubiously.

"She was born in a snowbank," Charlie said with a flash of his old amusement at his athletic, outdoorsy wife.

"Dad never got a son," she said to Carson. "So he decided his daughters would have to do. I think I was skiing by the time

I was three. Down Iron Mountain when I was six. I've been driving in snow all my life."

Thank God for the southern exposure, she thought a few minutes later, as she followed Carson's prints. And that it was warmer here than back home. No snow had melted in upstate New York since the first had fallen, but it looked as if this had melted off more than once. It was wet, heavy snow, maybe with ice under the top few inches. She stopped and looked around when she came to the end of the tracks. So far so good, she decided. She could make it up to this point. On one side the valley dipped slightly—not bad. On the other the hill started to rise—again, not bad. The curve had been gradual and by now the road was out of sight. Even if they parked here, no one would see them. She made a soft sound of derision. They had already put up markers by clearing the driveway; their tracks would be enough.

When she got back to the car, the men had already put the chains on and stashed the shovels in the trunk; they were ready to go in. She took her place behind the wheel and started the engine again. She backed up first in order to make a wide turn and enter more or less straight. "The trick is," she said to Carson, grinning at him slightly in the rearview mirror, "to go very steadily, no accelerations or slowing down or sudden turns. Just go in slowly and keep going. Set?" He looked terrified. She glanced at Charlie, who was again without expression. "Here we go," she said, easing forward; she turned, aimed at the snow canyon, and then felt the front wheels hit the resistance of snow.

No one spoke then. Ice, she thought distantly; she had been right. There was ice under there. The car swerved a little, not much, and then the chains dug in. She did not slow down. It really was not bad, she thought, feeling the car wheels find purchase, aware that when the front wheels spun on ice, the chains compensated. Not bad. Her father had taught her well.

Then she stopped. She had come to the end of the tracks, Carson's and hers.

"Why'd you stop?" Charlie demanded harshly.

"I need a trailblazer." She took a deep breath. "Listen, Charlie. I drive only if Carson goes ahead and signals that it's okay to keep going. And I don't mean the road. We sit in the car and wait for his signal. With the engine off."

Charlie knew she was right; there was no argument against her reasons. But he knew where *it* was. He could point to it now, go straight to it. That frightened him very much because he also knew he should not be able to sense it in the car with the engine purring away. Before he could make objections that would sound false even to him, Carson opened the back door.

"I'll go on ahead." He walked away, pulling on one of Charlie's knit ski caps.

Constance watched him, thinking he was a good man, a very good man who deserved to go to California and open his gourmet restaurant and keep company with Beatrice until they decided to make it permanent. She hoped they would do that. Carson walked around a drift, tested the snow beside it to make sure she would have room to get through, then went on. She turned to speak to Charlie but he was gone again.

The black space, confined, close, airless, and still. This time he felt himself moving through it, not very far, not very fast, just moving, seeing little but aware of the nearness of the walls, aware of another abyss ahead.

A shudder passed through him and he felt Constance's hand on his arm. He blinked. "It's right over there," he said in a thick voice. "At the end of the valley."

"I can't see anything."

"I know. Let's get the skis off the car while we wait. They can stick out the rear window. God knows it can't get much colder in here than it is now."

They had to get closer, he thought, unfastening the skis from the rack. He had no idea how far away *it* was, only that it was over there. He could cross-country ski, but not well enough to carry the suitcase and manage two poles, and he knew he could not ski at all with the suit on. They had to get close enough for him to make it alone, no steep hills to negotiate, and then . . . And then he would know what to do.

Constance had just opened the trunk to get the suitcase out when she heard another car engine. "Charlie!"

He had stopped moving. "I hear."

Carson was not in sight. Charlie propped one pair of skis

against the car and Constance closed the trunk lid. "I'm going to get us stuck," she said. "Stay clear." She ran past Charlie, got in behind the wheel and turned on the ignition. Charlie jumped back when she revved the engine and plowed into the snow with wheels spinning, digging in, hitting ice, then simply spinning again. A black car pulled up behind her. It looked misshapen with oversized wheels and studded snow tires, a modified Buick that probably could go anywhere it damn chose.

A heavy man in a dark coat got out and came to Charlie. "What the hell are you doing in here? What's she trying to do?"

Constance stopped gunning the motor and got out. "We're stuck," she said brightly.

"You're trespassing. What are you doing in here?"

"We wanted to go skiing," Constance said. She looked accusingly at Charlie. "He said it was a good place. He used to come here all the time, he said. And now look at us, stuck."

"You dug through that snowbank to go skiing?" the man said in disbelief. "Come on. You're getting out of here."

"You the owner of this place?" Charlie asked then.

"Caretaker," the man said. "Out!"

With great patience, speaking the way a kindergarten teacher might talk to a backward child, Constance said, "We are stuck in the snow. My car won't come out. We can't leave. Will you please drive to town and call a tow truck for us. We will sit right here and wait. No skiing or anything."

The man walked to the front of the car, looked at the rear wheels. The Volvo was clearly stuck. He kicked the rear tire and scowled, then went back to his own car and spoke in an inaudible voice to a second man who had not got out. Now he did. He inspected the wheels and both men withdrew and consulted.

They both came back to Constance and Charlie. "We'll take you to our camp," the heavy one said. The other was lean-faced, and almost albino-pale. "We'll send a truck to pull your car out and deliver it to you at the camp. Come on."

"I don't think so," Charlie said. "We'll wait here for the truck."

The lean one reached into his pocket and pulled out a wallet with ID. "Buster, you'll do what we tell you. Police officers. Now move."

"Hold it a second," the other one said. "Who's with you?" He was looking at Carson's tracks.

"I was looking for a good place to park," Charlie murmured. "Out of the traffic, you know. Funny kind of ID you had there," he went on, studying the lean one. "Mind if I have a closer look?"

Now the heavy one withdrew his hand from his pocket. He had a gun in it. "Search them," he ordered.

The lean man was efficient and thorough. When he was finished, the other one said, "Mr. and Mrs. Meiklejohn, get in the car. Now."

Charlie walked to it, talking easily to Constance. "Actually they'll take us to Fred Foley. I was sure this road would lead us to him, but wrong. Can't win them all."

"You're looking for Foley?" the heavy man asked, clearly confused now.

"Yep. And Sid Levy. Wrong turn, though."

"You got that right. Come on, get in."

"Look, what's your name? FBI agent what?"

"Lovins. Mel Lovins. He's Jack Windekin."

"And I'm Charlie Meiklejohn, retired New York City Police force. I've been on this case with Fred and Sid from the beginning. Take my wife to your camp and I'll wait for a tow and join you. Is Fred up there yet?"

Charlie knew the instant he had gone too far. Lovins got mean again and snapped that no one stayed in this place, orders. For a second Charlie eyed him and his partner, thought about trying to run in foot-deep snow, thought about being tackled and dragged back, and he shrugged and got in the car. He was joined by Jack Windekin. Constance sat in front with Mel Lovins.

19

Carson watched the car back out. He had heard nothing, but the actions had spoken eloquently. The FBI, army, police, whoever they were, were already trying to cordon off the area, not very successfully yet, but it would get tighter, he knew, remembering the entrances to the Old Town, the blockade, the patrols on the ridge. For a moment he felt a wild desire to jump up and down and wave his arms, go with them to some safe place, let the cops handle it all. The urge passed swiftly; the car was out of sight. Only then did he leave the clump of snow-shrouded brush he had been crouching behind. He had gone another two hundred yards or so without feeling the charged cobwebs, but even if he had doubted Charlie's certainty that this was the place, the bit of action he had just witnessed solidified his own conviction that this was it. He was sweating under the heavy clothes that Constance had insisted he put on.

Always before he had been able to drive up to the front door, take his gas can inside, do the job, and drive away. This time he didn't even know where the damn thing was yet. Briefly he cursed Constance for deliberately getting stuck, but then he realized that if she had not done that, they would have driven the car out, and with it the skis and the suitcase, and the bomb. Charlie had insisted that it was not a bomb, but rather a two-phase device, but to Carson it was a bomb. He and Constance had watched silently as Charlie explained how to activate it. Simply pull this ring all the way out, he had said, lifting the ring. No way it could accidentally come out. No electrical device needed, nothing mechanical. Sometimes you get fancy with wires and stuff only to have them melt too soon. He reached the Volvo, and, just as the two strange men had done, he examined the wheels and gave up on driving farther without help. Stuck. He looked inside and let out a sigh of relief when he saw the keys in the ignition. He took them out and opened the trunk and stood for a moment looking at the suitcase. It was not very heavy, not a burden to carry, but he knew he could not carry it and use the skis too. Constance had been right about that.

He took out the suitcase, tossed the keys to the front seat, and started to walk again. The road must lead to the hotel, he told himself, and it couldn't be very far, a mile and a half, no more than two. As soon as he was within view of it, he would consider cutting across the valley in a straight line, but until then he was better off on the road. In truth, he did not trust the valley, which widened as he went farther into it. It seemed that the snow was deeper in the clearing than here against the rising hill, and he was afraid there might be a brook somewhere under the snow. He could see himself falling into an icy stream, soaked through and through, resting, drifting into the comfortable sleep of hypothermia. And in the spring some kids would find the suitcase, open it, and pull the string. . . .

The lower reaches of Childer's Park were where families went for picnics in the heat of summer; little kids played in the shallow stream that ran through a meadow. There was a pond that froze solid every winter, fine for ice skating. Up a bit higher was where the eight- to ten-year-old kids took their sleds, boys and girls. Higher than that was the turf of the junior high kids, all boys. No girls would risk the snowball fights, and fistfights, that broke out regularly among them. The highest part was reserved for the high school boys. The sled runs were long and somewhat dangerous, curving around drywalls hidden by snow, winding through stands of trees. Here the toboggan runs began, and they were the most dangerous of all. By the time the boys were old enough to try to join in the fun at the top of the mountain, they were also old enough for beer, for pot, whatever was making the rounds at the time. The cops cruised the road up there, and for the most part the boys tired of the snow games early in the season and were always searching for new ways to get the town cops out of the cruiser into the snow, whereupon the boys would leap on their long sleds or toboggans and flash down the slope. It was a game they played every year; the local police cooperated by yelling and sometimes giving chase, and more often getting back in the car to try to beat

the boys to the bottom of the run in order to bawl them out
and threaten them with charges everyone knew would never
be pressed.

That afternoon there was a serious snowball fight, with the
jocks holding off what seemed at times to be the rest of the
high school population, but in reality was about a dozen other
boys. Herman Kohl was bored with snowball fights, but Jud and
Bobby were really into them, and he had to go along or get
clobbered. In his mind he was planning their slide down the
back of Childer's Park. No one ever went down that way, although it was as good as the front side, because they knew they
would end up over four miles from town, and going down the
front took them nearly to the elementary school. He had been
over every inch of the ground with his father in hunting season,
starting when he was twelve, and he knew exactly where the
drywall was that would be their turning place, knew exactly
how to get past the old Miller Hotel, coast through the valley,
and halfway up the hill to Mel's camp. From there it would be
a five-minute walk to the camp itself. A snowball hit him in the
head and he turned to retaliate, but inside he was furious with
himself for being in a fucking snowball fight. It seemed particularly childish that day when he had other things on his mind.
This was kid stuff; he wanted to take on the whole fucking
army.

Mel's camp was for hunters, and had never been meant for
anything more than primitive shelter and a place to cook meals
and eat them, and to play cards after a long day in the woods.
There was a large common room with a plank table that could
seat sixteen at a time, and four card tables with folding chairs.
Other folding chairs were scattered around the room, some at
the plank table, others apparently at random. The windows
were niggardly in size, bare. Electric lights hung on cords from
the ceiling, which was finished with rough boards. The walls
were made of the same rough lumber. The floor was bare and
echoing. There was a back door, to the kitchen evidently, and
halls leading off from the central room. When Charlie and Constance entered the building, there were three men there. One
was at a portable typewriter typing, two at the plank table. A
coffee urn was on the end of the table.

Mel Lovins went to the table and spoke to one of the men, who got up and walked to Charlie and Constance. He was round-faced, nondescript, as bland-looking as a junior-high civics teacher. "Brooks Sussman," he said, extending his hand. "FBI."

Constance pulled off her ski cap and gloves angrily and slammed them down on one of the card tables. "Mr. Sussman," she said, "your associates have forced us to come with them at gunpoint. They forced us to abandon our car. I protest this kind of treatment and I want it on record. I don't know what in the world is going on here, but I just intended to go skiing and I was kidnapped."

Charlie blinked, then raised his eyebrow at Brooks Sussman, who appeared taken aback. Not my fault, Charlie seemed to be saying.

"Mrs. Meiklejohn, please just try to be patient until we get in touch with Agent Foley. They're trying to reach him now in his car." He looked at Charlie questioningly. "I thought you said you were in on this, have been from the start?"

"I am not a police officer," Constance snapped. "And I never have been, and whatever he's in on is his business. Where's the bathroom?"

Charlie spread his hands helplessly; after a brief hesitation Sussman nodded toward the hall. "Down there." Constance marched off.

"She doesn't like guns," Charlie said. Weak, but he did not have a clue about what she was up to, what the act was for. He caught a look of sympathy that flashed across Sussman's face.

"Well, it's unfortunate that you missed this road and went in over there instead. If you know anything about any of this, you know more than I do right now. Our orders are to keep everyone out of the valley."

Oh, I know something about it, Charlie thought. On the short drive up to the camp he had felt as if he had circled *it* almost completely, that he could draw the coordinates to locate it with precision. What he lacked was the correct reference to calculate distance.

"How far are we from the hotel?" he asked.

Again Sussman hesitated. Then he shrugged and motioned Charlie to come to the table with him. "Just under two miles.

We're plugging the various ways into it right now. Didn't expect anyone to dig through that bank, though."

A map was opened on the table, a topographical map with a red circle that stood out like a target. Sussman put his finger in the circle.

"There," he said. "We're here." He touched another place outside the circle. "You drove in about there." The spot he indicated was also outside the circle, about as far from it as the camp was.

Exactly how he had envisioned it, Charlie thought, gazing at the map. He wondered if Carson had made his way into the red zone yet, and decided probably not; he was too inexpert on the skis. He had a lot of falling down to do on his way to the party.

A door slammed and there was the sound of boots stomping on bare wooden floors. Constance reappeared and cast a withering glance toward the table. She crossed the room, making a lot more noise than was necessary, moved a chair under one of the tables, straightened another one, continued past the table, where Charlie and Sussman and the other two men watched her, and went into the kitchen.

"Maybe she'll find something to do in there," one of the men said almost meekly.

She came back and Charlie realized with near awe that she was casing the joint, looking for other exits, making a head count, right in front of them, openly, blatantly. At the same moment he was swept up in the other images that overrode what was actually before his eyes. Blackness, the too-small space, the other doorway that called, called . . .

"Mr. Meiklejohn? Hey, are you all right? Mr. Meiklejohn! What's wrong with him?"

He felt the hand on his arm and he was back, straining to see, facing away from the table, facing toward the hotel that was still calling him. Constance moved into his line of vision.

"He's very ill," she said coldly. "We think it could be smallpox." She kept moving, this time toward the second hall.

"Shit!" Sussman said under his breath. The look he gave Charlie was solicitous. "Maybe you'd better sit down. You want some coffee?"

"Coffee," Charlie said. "That sounds good. Actually it's a form of epilepsy, very mild. I hardly ever even fall down."

He had to talk to her, find out what she had learned, not make it obvious. How many agents were up here already, where were they? Two men entered the building together, breathing too hard, looking cold. Sussman motioned Charlie to the coffee urn and joined the two at the door, where they spoke in voices too low for Charlie to hear. Sussman cursed and motioned to a man at the table.

"Get your stuff on and go help them. Take Lovins with you. I'm going to the van a minute, see if they've raised Foley yet. Sit down, Meiklejohn. Just relax."

Help them do what? Charlie wondered bleakly, after Sussman left. Search the hotel in the valley? Set up spotlights? Find someone lost in the woods? He hoped it was none of those things. The coffee was bitter with an aftertaste of aluminum. He held the Styrofoam cup with both hands and tried to add up how many agents he had already seen. Seven, at least, and one in the van probably, and a couple more out there on patrol without a clue about what they were looking for or guarding against. Ten or more. Probably all armed. All antsy on a screwball assignment. He scowled at the coffee, not liking his addition at all, not liking the way Constance was behaving, feeling the need to talk to her well up stronger and stronger, because he was afraid she had already made a plan and was tidying up details with all this stamping about, the bitch act that was almost too good.

Sussman returned and looked at Charlie curiously. "Foley wants you to hang around until he gets here, half an hour or so. He's on the road. He says you could tell me what the hell is going on, but you probably won't."

Charlie shrugged. "The hotel is haunted. I'd keep away from it and keep my men away from it if I were you."

"Shit!" Sussman said.

"Actually it's more like Dracula," Charlie said thoughtfully. And that seemed right to him. Dracula's sharp kiss on the neck claimed his victim for all time. He could call his victim home when he desired another kiss. That felt right. He drank the bitter coffee.

Sussman said in a level voice, "Foley also said that I could tell you what's going on here, that you might even have advice for us." It was obvious that this was hard for him, and also that he needed advice right now. "Look, Meiklejohn, we don't know what we're dealing with, that's for sure. One of my men has vanished in the area, not a sign of him all afternoon. Okay. We're marking trees, following that circle on the map, and we'll rope off the area. No one's to go in. You know how big that perimeter's going to be? Anyway, we'll do it. But meanwhile I have a man missing out there. Do you know what's in that hotel?"

"No," Charlie said flatly. "And neither does anyone else."

Windekin, the pale man who had escorted them from the other side of the valley, entered the building, stamping his feet, blowing on his hands. "I drove the Volvo up after we got it pulled loose. Jamieson's in the truck at the end of the drive they dug out."

Sussman nodded, then saw Constance hurrying from the hall. "I want to see my car," she said. "If you've damaged it, you pay, you know. You can't just go around pulling a car like that with a truck. If you hurt the transmission . . . Give me my keys!"

Sussman sighed. "Let her look it over," he said, waving Jack Windekin back out. "You keep the keys," he added. "They're both staying here until Foley says otherwise."

Constance glanced at the men imperiously and swept up her cap and gloves from the table on her way out. "He'll tell you a fairy tale about the hotel," she said, and slammed the door behind her. Charlie sat down at the map table. Again, it was happening again, more and more often, with more power each time. He would *not* turn in that direction, he told himself even as he turned to look, tilted his head in a listening attitude.

Sussman swore and sat down. He hoped the bitch decided to clean the car or something.

Constance forced herself to breathe normally, forced herself not to run to the Volvo. Instead, she approached it with Windekin and examined the front end with great care. The gravel parking area had been cleared by the snowplow; there were four other cars in it, and the black van that had no markings or windows. No one was in sight anywhere outside. She frowned at the side of the car and said accusingly, "You drove it up here with the chains on!"

"Yes, ma'am," Windekin said. He was stony-faced.

She looked inside. Three pairs of skis. Carson had decided not to try to ski in alone. She was not surprised. He was a such a novice with snow; he thought he had a better chance walking in. Two miles, Sussman had said. Could Carson walk two miles through snow that might be up to his knees in some spots, up to his hips in others? She thought not. A Virginia boy, he had called himself. What did he know about snow? She continued around the car to the trunk and demanded the keys again.

"Sorry, ma'am," Windekin said. "I'll open it for you." He opened the trunk lid, and this time she could not prevent her sigh of relief. The suitcase was gone.

"Leave it open," she ordered. "I'm going to put away some of the stuff from the front." She moved the snow shovels to the rear of the trunk, cleared a space. The Volvo had a lot of space. She continued on around the car; now it was between her and the building, between her and the van. She opened the back door and pulled out her skis. Her father had given them to her when she turned eighteen and suddenly measured five feet ten. She put the poles on the snow beside the skis, and her gloves on the floor of the backseat. Ready. Windekin was watching her, looking slightly puzzled but saying nothing, too cold to protest. She took two other poles to the trunk, and he followed.

He never could explain exactly what happened next. He thought she was falling down and he reached out to help her, and then she clamped her hand on his wrist and pulled; as he started forward, her forearm caught him in the midriff. He doubled over and somehow his feet slipped and he ended up in the trunk of the car, winded, unable to call out, to move even, and the lid closed.

She closed it on the strap of one of the poles, just to make sure he had plenty of air when he began gasping in long painful breaths. Now she moved very fast, back to the rear seat to put on the skis, thrust her hands through the pole straps. She looked at the building and the van; nothing was moving, no one in sight, and then she left the parking area through the snow, heading toward the hotel.

They had fooled around too long at the top of Childer's Park, and then Jud had started to whine that if it got dark, his mom wouldn't be willing to drive up for them to get the truck. And Bobby had started to chicken out. What if no one was at Mel's camp and they had to walk four miles to town dragging the fucking toboggan?

' "You want to walk down, start walking. You going down with me, come on," Herman Kohl snapped. He held up the truck keys, made a show of thrusting them in his pocket. He started to pull the toboggan toward the back side of the mountain. "It's no different this way," he said without looking back at the other two. "Better even; faster." By the time he reached the best place to start they were with him, looking glum as they all surveyed the unbroken snow ahead. It wouldn't be faster, Herman knew; the other runs had turned to ice long ago, and this was fresh, deep snow, but it was steeper on this side and that would help.

Herman was the one with woods sense. He knew any patch of woods he had ever walked through, and he had been all over the hills here. He never thought consciously of what lay ahead, but as soon as a new feature came into view, he recognized it, like a clump of birch trees to the left. And the rotten oak that rattled brown leaves as they slid by under it. He knew to steer away from a clump that might have been snow-covered bushes, but was in fact a large erratic boulder, moved from somewhere else by the last glacier, out of place here in New Jersey. And it was great to break through the snow, to be the first ones ever to go down the back of Childer's Park. Tomorrow a dozen guys would want to try it, but he was the first. He saw four pine trees and made an adjustment in their direction. Jud was laughing just behind him, and now and then Bobby let out a whoop, and the three boys leaned this way and that and picked up speed, then slowed down again. They made a good team, worked well together on the toboggan.

They were coming up on the drywall. Herman could not have said what landmark alerted him, how he knew, but he did. The unmortared walls turned up here and there all over the hills, dangerous summer and winter. In the summer you might put your foot down on a snake snoozing away in the shade of a wall; in the winter you could get killed if a runner hit a wall. The snow drifted on one side usually, and barely covered the stones on the other, hiding them, but not cushioning a fall, acting as instant brakes that stopped a sled or a toboggan and sent the rider flying, often to smash into the wall itself. He started to make the sliding turn away from the wall that was not yet visible, when everything changed.

Herman was blinded by a sharp pain in his head that made him duck with his eyes closed. He heard Bobby yell something, and the front end of the toboggan hit the wall. Herman was thrown, and when he landed, he did not move for several minutes. He drew in a sobbing breath and tried to sit up. He was in a drift that had almost buried him. He struggled to get free; the headache was subsiding and he no longer was blind, but he couldn't make out where he was. Then he heard Bobby and Jud fighting up near the wall, and now he saw that he had been thrown over it, had rolled twenty feet or more down the hillside before the drifts stopped him. Jud was screaming shrilly, like a girl. Herman got to his knees in the snow and yelled at them both to cut it out, but it was not that kind of fight. He could see Bobby's back, Jud's arms flailing; the screams grew in intensity. He yelled hoarsely at them; at the same moment Bobby half lifted Jud, turned with him, and smashed his back against the wall. Jud's arms went limp and the screaming stopped abruptly. Herman yelled again, and this time Bobby lifted his head and turned slowly until he saw Herman. He did not move away from Jud, instead he picked up the boy's head between his hands and smashed the back of his head into the wall, then did it again, and again.

Herman threw up in the snow. "Jesus!" he whimpered. "Jesus, Jesus, Jesus." He was slipping down the hill, watching Bobby, who was still facing him, but with a look that was not human. "Jesus! Jesus!"

Bobby let Jud fall and got to his feet, watching Herman. He took a step toward him, moving as if he were blind, his arms swinging loosely at his sides. He tripped on the wall and plunged over it, landed facedown in the snow. Herman struggled to his feet and tried to run. He fell, got up, and pulled himself through the deep snow, fell again, struggled up again. Every time he looked back Bobby was stumbling through the snow after him, sometimes falling, sometimes rising, always coming after him.

"Jesus, Jesus!" Herman kept sobbing. "Oh, Jesus!" He was heading toward the old hotel in the valley, instinctively seeking the nearest shelter, a place to hide, to find a weapon in—a board, anything.

Carson Danvers had to think deliberately about every movement. Lift the left leg, drag it out of the snow, move it forward, put it down. The problem was that he was not able to lift his leg out of the snow; he was dragging it through instead, and it was a leaden weight. He was within range, and had been for a long time; they were all around him, pressing against his head, brushing his face. He staggered and caught himself against a tree and took several deep breaths. That did not help. A burning pain shot through his lower back when he pushed himself away from the tree after a minute. Both thighs seemed on fire. He heard himself laughing at the thought of walking into the hotel on fire; he took another deep breath. Lift the right leg. . . . Then he stopped again in bewilderment. Tracks. He looked at them hard, something large, breaking through the snow like a plow. Then he laughed again.

A Woozle! He was tracking a Woozle! The laughter was more like a sob than anything else. He had to rest a minute or two. The image of Gary swam before his eyes, Gary with his eyes shining in delight at Pooh and Piglet tracking the Woozle. He had to rest. He dragged the suitcase with him to a tree trunk where he could stop for a few minutes, rest. He sat down in the snow with his back against the tree, his knees drawn up to ease the pain. After a moment he put his head down on his knees. Just for a minute or two, he told himself. How long had he been wandering in circles tracking the Woozle? Elinor and he always took turns reading to Gary, each of them loving it possibly even more than the boy. *Winnie the Pooh* was their favorite. If he tried hard, he thought he could even remember the words, the sentences.

"One fine winter's day when Piglet was brushing away the snow . . ."

20

Constance knew Carson was ignorant of the treachery of snow, how it could trick the eyes, dazzle the senses; how it could drain energy and heat so insidiously that a person would not even be aware of fatigue until collapse was certain. Then, after the battle had tilted, one would crave rest, just a few minutes of rest, and those few minutes would ensure muscle stiffness and charley horses, and more rest would be required. She did not try to ski very fast, not on fresh snow that was unknown, through woods that were unknown. A rock, a stump, a log, any of them might suddenly appear, or worse, not appear, leaving no time to avoid the hazard. She was cautious.

She did not know how much of a head start she had. Fifteen minutes? If she was lucky. Ten? Possibly. Unless they had a crack skier among them, they wouldn't come that way. By the road? Again, possibly. They would not let Charlie take off after her, she hoped, prayed. Not Charlie. He couldn't catch her, but he might try, if they allowed it. He knew he had to stay out of range, but she no longer trusted his awareness of his own danger in competition with the strong pull the thing seemed to exert on him. When the trees thinned and she could see a good stretch ahead, she speeded up. She had to find Carson, find the suit and the device that Charlie insisted was not really a bomb. First she had to find Carson; down the hill, across the valley, somewhere on the other side of it he would still be struggling in the snow, trying to reach the hotel. Unless he had collapsed already. She speeded up again.

"I'll tell you a fairy tale," Charlie said to Sussman when the other images vanished. He was shivering.

He started to tell about the thing in Old West, disregarding Sussman's look of skepticism, which soon became one of baleful disbelief that he made no effort to soften.

"So why'd Foley tell me to keep away altogether? Why not take a generator down there and turn it on if that stops it?"

"Because the boys in white lab coats want to study it," Charlie said with great weariness. This was what Carson had run into. No one could believe it who had not personally seen the effects. A fairy tale. An agent he had not seen before stuck his head in the door and called out.

"They found Hershman. They're bringing him in."

Sussman went to the door, Charlie at his side. They waited on the porch for two men supporting another one between them who was covered with snow. He moved like a zombie. Like poor Mrs. Eglin, who screamed and screamed, and then turned into a zombie. This one was not screaming. Charlie felt nausea and hatred well up together. A couple more men appeared, talking in low voices. They all looked cold, not dressed for treks through the snowy woods; they looked frightened. When they reached the building the two small groups had merged and they all entered together. Some went for coffee, with much foot-stamping. No one was talking above near whispers.

"What happened to him?" Sussman demanded as the two holding up Hershman lowered him to a chair. He sat where they positioned him without movement. His face was vacant, his eyes dull. When he sat down, his hands dangled at his sides.

"We found him crawling in the snow," one of the agents said. His voice trembled. He turned and went to the table that had coffee.

"Jesus Christ!" Sussman stared at the casualty, then turned abruptly. "There are cots in there. For God's sake, put him to bed. We'll get a doctor."

"What was that banging?" asked one of the agents, averting his gaze from the two men who were leading the zombie into the hall.

Sussman glared at him. "What banging?"

He tilted his head, shrugged, and returned to the table to add sugar to his cup.

Suddenly Charlie saw again the seconds before Constance had slammed the door on her way out, striding across the room, sweeping up her cap and gloves. How long ago?

"Good God!" He tore across the room, out the door, hearing

Sussman's curse, then hard steps pounding after him. He ran to the Volvo with several men close behind, one with his gun drawn, but now they could all hear the banging, and it came from the trunk of the car. Charlie was first to reach it. He saw the keys in the snow beside the rear tire, and he stepped on them, mashed them down into the snow, scuffed more snow over them as he hit the lid with his fist. There was an answering bang.

"Windekin," he said mildly, and stepped back out of the way. The agent who had already drawn his gun was right by him. He looked too young to be allowed to carry a gun, and too frightened. Charlie glanced inside the car; two pairs of skis. Then he looked at the snow and saw the tracks that vanished into the woods.

Someone found a crowbar and they forced the lid open, helped Windekin out. He had vivid red spots on his pale face. When he saw Charlie, he took a step toward him and nearly fell down. His legs were too cramped for him to walk alone.

"Where's the woman?" Sussman demanded.

Windekin shook his head. "She slugged me and shoved me in there. That's all I know."

"She's gone down the hill on skis," someone called, and they went to the side of the car and looked at the tracks.

"She's gone down there? What for?" Sussman glared at Charlie. At that moment a new car appeared on the driveway. Fred Foley, Byron Weston, and another man had arrived. Looking infinitely relieved, Sussman hurried over to speak to Foley.

Charlie went down on one knee to examine the wheel closest to the roadway; the chain had broken. He clucked softly and went to the wheel near the snow and looked at that one and shook his head sadly. He found and pocketed the keys he had buried in snow earlier, then got up and brushed himself. He sauntered over to Foley and Byron Weston.

". . . with a scar on his face. May be dangerous. I want him brought in, and I want him undamaged. Understand. Not a scratch."

"And the woman?"

Foley shrugged. "Bring me that man."

Charlie waved to Byron, who yelled, "Is Loesser down there? Charlie, he can't burn that hotel! Not this time! Is he around?"

Foley had got out of the car to talk to Sussman; Byron Weston was still inside. The driver started toward the building. Sussman motioned to his men; they all trudged back to the hunting camp.

Charlie waved again to Byron, this time in farewell as the car left him in the parking area. The young agent was still with him, in the rear of the group heading back to shelter and warmth. Charlie snapped his fingers in exasperation, wheeled about, and hurried back to the Volvo. The young agent went with him. At the trunk of the Volvo Charlie leaned over, inspecting the lock. When the agent drew near, Charlie straightened up suddenly and hit him in the jaw. It was too fast for defense, too unexpected; the young man dropped. Charlie took the gun from his hand, got in the Volvo, started, and made a crunching turn in the parking area, throwing gravel. He raced down the plowed driveway, turned on the road at the end of it, and sped on toward the next driveway that he and Carson had dug out. He was afraid they would radio the truck there to drive in all the way and wait with the engine running until further orders. And if Constance had reached Carson already, if they had reached the hotel, had found the black door to hell, had gone through it, they would be trapped inside when the running motor closed down the mechanism.

The truck had backed into the space Charlie and Carson had opened. It cleared the banks but left no room for anyone to enter the driveway. Charlie stopped in front of it and got out, taking his keys with him. The driver opened the window of the truck as Charlie scrambled over the bank to approach the side door.

"Get that thing out of there!" the driver yelled.

"They're trying to reach you by radio," Charlie called back, passing the door on his way to the rear of the truck.

The driver stuck his head out of the window. "What?" Who?"

"Sussman. Call him now." Charlie waited until the head withdrew, then pulled out the agent's gun from his pocket and shot the left rear tire at very close range. There was a scream of outrage from the truck cab, which he ignored as he took aim at the right tire and shot it, then a second time just to be sure. He started to trot through the snow, following the tracks of the Volvo. The truck driver was yelling obscenities at him.

He had to slow down when he reached the spot where Constance had got the Volvo stuck. Now there were only the tracks that Carson had left, a multitude of tracks. One trip out to scout the way, then his return, then his departure a second time. Charlie could see where he had dragged the suitcase through the snow. Now he moved carefully as his fear mounted. Where did *it* start? When would he cross the line? He knew it was there, operative; he could feel it calling him stronger than ever. He knew that if he stepped into range, it would claim him.

When Constance crossed the line on her skis, she nearly panicked with the suddeness of the sharp headache that struck. She swerved momentarily, then caught herself. The headache was blinding this time; it did not double her over in pain. She blinked. Exactly as Carson had described the sensation, charged cobwebs all around her head, brushing her face, pressing against her forehead. She continued to follow Carson's erratic trail through the woods. He had staggered here, had fallen, rested, had sat against the tree there. She found the suitcase; he had taken the suit out, abandoned the suitcase, too heavy to drag farther. And now the light was fading; if she did not find him soon, it would be too late. They would need a search party with lanterns, and that meant they would have to drive in and *it* would close the door.

After that it would be in Byron's hands, and his colleagues'. She thought again of the minuscule Martians trying to reason with the probe that swallowed and analyzed them as fast as they neared it, thought of ants trying to reason with a descending boot, thought of a man blowing up his television because he did not like the program, thought of Charlie going rigid, listening, hearing something she could not even imagine. She stiffened; gunshots! Three shots! Silence returned and she went forward again, and the next second she spotted Carson.

"I'm all right," he said thickly when she touched him. He tried to get to his feet, his motions very slow, as if he were drunk, or too recently roused from a deep sleep. He had the suit wrapped around his arm. The device was strapped to the front of it, accessible when the suit was on.

"Carson, get up. We're very near the meadow. It's not very far now. Just get up and walk, Carson." She took the suit as she talked. The flashlight, she thought, and felt in his pocket for it. "Carson, can you hear me? I'm leaving you. You have to get up and walk to the meadow, keep moving. I'll come back as soon as I can, but I won't be able to find you in the woods if it gets dark. Carson!"

He nodded, and let his head nod down to his chest. She pulled on him until he managed to stand up. "Follow my tracks, Carson. Just to the meadow. You can rest at the edge of the meadow. Can you hear me?"

"Follow," he said, and stumbled after her when she started to ski.

The meadow was very close; he had skirted it for a long time. She went straight through the woods toward it. When she looked back Carson was still moving—unsteadily, staggering, but moving in her direction. Very soon she was out of the woods, and no more then three hundred feet away from the building. There were tracks all around it.

Warily she drew closer, very watchful now, taking her time. She had come almost to the porch, and could make no sense at all out of the prints. People had stamped the snow, apparently heading toward the woods, only to double back. More than one, but she couldn't tell how many; the snow was too trampled. The porch extended across the entire front of the building, deep and free of snow. All prints ended, with only packed snow here and there to indicate that the people had crossed it more than once. Suddenly a figure ran from the building, screaming in terror.

He ran to her, clutching at her arms, although he stood much higher than she. A boy, she realized; he was only a boy.

"Bobby's crazy!" he sobbed, dragging her down. "Help! Help! Oh, Jesus!"

She wrenched free and released her skis, looking past him. "Get out of here," she snapped at him. "There's a man in the woods over there. He needs help. Follow my ski tracks and get him to the road. Get out!"

He kept grabbing her arms, her shoulders, sobbing in fear. She slapped him neatly, took his hand, and turned him in the direction she wanted him to take, all the while guarding the suit and the pull ring from his clutching hands. There was an-

other scream, not his, and he sobbed louder, "Jesus! Jesus!"
She gave him a hard push.

"Get out of here! Help that man!"

He lurched forward, then began to scramble through the
snow. She did not watch him, kept her gaze instead on a
crouching figure that was moving off the porch. "Dear God,"
she breathed. This had to be Bobby. The trampled snow now
told the story. One tried to run away, Bobby came after him,
and he sought refuge in the hotel, someplace where he could
try to hide. Over and over. She moved carefully, sideways, and
Bobby's head turned. She had become the target.

She knew the look of psychopathy. During her graduate
years she had worked in many institutions, some for the criminally insane. They can't be reached, her instructor had said
sadly, not when they are having an episode. No reason could
penetrate. Their brains sent no signals of pain or fear, hunger,
cold—any of the inhibiting checks on behavior that governed
others. And Bobby was criminally insane, murderously insane.

She continued to move with caution, trying to get closer to
the porch without breaking into a run. That could be disas-
trous. He moved with complete disregard for what lay ahead.
If he stumbled and fell, he would simply rise and keep coming.
If she could reach the porch, get inside, she could elude him,
she felt certain. The frightened boy had dodged him; she knew
she could, but first she had to get inside, stay out of reach of
his great hands. She feared him in a way she never feared another person. Her aikido training had always served her well,
but only with rational opponents who could realize that it was
pointless to keep coming against her only to get thrown down
again, perhaps suffer a broken bone the next time. He could
have no such realization.

He was making a harsh noise deep in his throat. Not an
attempt at speech, not anything she had ever heard, a noise so
atavistic it made the hair on her scalp rise. She glanced at the
hotel; the porch continued around the corner, a deep veranda
for wicker chairs, where guests could rest at leisure and sip
lemonade in the heat of the day. There were more stairs on the
side. She edged in that direction. He followed, getting nearer,
the animal sound growing louder. He would lunge, she knew,

and then she would run. Not until then. She wanted to be closer to the sanctuary of the building first, but he was getting nearer. On the porch if he made a grab for her, she could handle it and flee, but here in the snow that was growing deeper with every step, even if she threw him, she would still be nearly helpless against his greater size.

She was within ten feet of the side steps when he screamed and rushed her. She plowed through the snow, then her foot caught on something covered in a drift and she fell down; he grabbed her by the ankle. She kicked out with all her strength and her boot hit him on the shoulder, sent him sprawling backward. She scrambled up the stairs and raced toward the door that had been forced open; she could hear him clambering up the steps. At the door she looked back and moaned. He was dragging the suit.

Charlie walked in dread. Distantly he heard the truck revving, then silence again. They must have driven it out to the road to allow a different vehicle to try to get through. He paused, listening, but could hear nothing. He walked on. Then he reached another drift, this one more like an avalanche that had swept down the hillside, into the valley proper. He tried to see past it and failed. It would stop a car, he decided, and felt a tension within him relax a little. Carson's footprints went around the drift, down the hillside, into the woods. He started after them, and stopped again. There was a tree limb crossing Carson's trail. The snow was trampled all around the area; Carson had found the branch, had dragged it here, and placed it very deliberately across the route he had taken. Charlie's mouth went dry as he considered it.

He heard someone calling him and looked about, settled for a mound of snow to duck behind. Not much protection, but better than out in the open. He sat down and examined the gun he had taken from the agent. A .45, good gun, three bullets gone.

"Charlie? You hear me?"

"I hear you, Fred."

"We're getting a jeep from town, Charlie, and we're taking it in there. And we don't want any trouble. You hear that?"

"Loud and clear. I won't let it pass, Fred." He could see for about fifty feet down the driveway where several men appeared slogging through the snow. "You can't get around the drift here, anyway," Charlie called. He could tell by the way they were looking around that they did not know yet where he was.

"Charlie, for God's sake, what are you trying to do?" Byron called. "Is Constance in there? You know the danger! Charlie, we can't let Loesser burn it out again! God knows when and where it'll turn up next."

Charlie knew all that. He did not respond this time. They were close enough now that they could locate him by his voice, close enough to see the mammoth drift that would block even a jeep. Of course, he thought, they didn't realize how near the line was. Could a jeep drive through the snow and cross it? He was afraid so.

"Charlie, give it up," Fred Foley yelled. "I've got men coming down the hill behind you. For Chrissake, just come on out and give it up!"

Charlie felt his stomach tighten. "Call them off, Fred. Not over there! They shouldn't be over there!"

The cluster of men moved toward him: Fred Foley, Byron Weston, a third man who was unknown. Charlie looked behind him at the hill, hoping Fred had been bluffing. He had not been. At least three men were slipping and sliding in the snow on the hill above the drift.

"Send them back!" he yelled. "Byron, tell him! They're within range if they come down there!"

Byron hesitated, started to reach out to touch Foley's arm, then drew back. One of the men on the hill screamed hoarsely and let go of a tree he had been using to ease himself down. He began to slide, yelling. A second man was doubled over, holding his head. The third one stopped in his tracks, then slowly, very carefully began to back up.

The man who had slid down the hill came into view, walking like a blind man in the direction of the hotel. Blood was shiny red on his face.

"Selene!" Foley yelled. "Selene!" He took a dozen steps that brought him close enough to talk in a normal voice to Charlie. "What's the matter with him?"

"Sometimes they are called in," Charlie said. "At least he's not homicidal. Sometimes they are."

Foley looked about almost wildly. Now he could see Charlie sitting with his back against the hill. Charlie waved the gun, then rested it on his knee. "Who's the new kid on the block?" he asked, motioning toward Byron and the other man.

"Michael Newhouse," the man said, joining Foley. "Physicist. Meiklejohn, we have to have the opportunity to study this phenomenon. You're not an ignorant man. You should understand the importance of this thing." Too cool, too self-assured, almost movie-star good-looking, except for his dark eyes, which glittered and were too small.

"Charlie," Byron said imploringly, "don't make trouble. If Loesser burns it out, we'll just have to go to the next place it turns up. You know that. We can't let this opportunity escape us. You know that, too. We're going to bring in the jeep, and now that we know about where the range starts, it should be fairly easy to get the machine close enough to shut everything down long enough to get the area cleared. If Loesser's in there, we want him, Charlie. He's the only one who can go in and do the tests that Newhouse thinks might answer some questions. Think, Charlie, if it's an alien artifact, what that could mean to the world."

"What is that, Byron?" Charlie asked pleasantly, listening hard for the sound of another engine.

"Charlie! We have the tools to trace it back to its source, to communicate with them, to establish contact. It's the breakthrough every scientist on earth has been waiting for."

"What if it doesn't want to be probed and tested?" Charlie asked. "What if it has a defensive system your tests might trigger? You know what it does to people now. What if that's just a side effect of *its* tests?"

"Meiklejohn, believe me, we know how to take precautions," Newhouse said with a touch of irritation. "That's why we want this whole area cleared, to protect the innocent. We work with very dangerous materials all the time and to date our accident record is unblemished."

Charlie laughed. "What if poor old John Loesser doesn't want to be your errand boy? Volunteers? Would you volunteer to go in there, Newhouse?"

"Loesser will agree," Foley said. "You know what kind of prison term he'll get for all those fires?"

"You have proof?"

"We have your evidence," Foley said viciously. "Remember?"

Charlie shook his head. "I don't believe I ever did make a written report. Seemed little point to it, actually. And I do recall some speculative, rather idle conversation, but not much more than that."

Foley faced away with a disgusted look. "He'll cooperate," he said.

They all heard the jeep and no one moved as the sound came closer. Then Charlie raised the gun. "Fred, if it gets this far, tell him to stop, or I'll shoot the driver and the gas tank. You know I can do it, Fred."

Fred Foley studied him, expressionless. "What are you up to, Charlie? What the hell do you think you're doing?"

"Later. Just flag him down if he gets in this far."

Foley shook his head. "You son of a bitch! You know I won't."

Charlie knew. He had known Fred Foley for a very long time. Sussman might have agreed, not Fred. He sighed tiredly and stood up. They heard the safety being released. What the devil was Constance doing in there? And Carson? Why didn't something happen? There had been time enough, unless neither one had ever reached the damn hotel. Maybe she had taken a fall in the woods and lay unconscious? She could have broken a leg. What if she had been wrong about being immune? Too late. Too late for second-guessing her. She was in there by now, either immune or insane.

He would have stopped her if he could. Now all he could do was make certain no one turned on an engine, not until she was out of that goddamn place. If they trapped her inside that black door to hell, he would kill the lot of them. His hands were moist. He shifted the gun and wiped one, then the other. If she had got through the black door, the abyss, had pulled the ring, and then the jeep went through and the door slammed behind her, she would be there when the device went off. It could not be stopped once the reaction began. The three men watched him holding the gun steadily now. They waited for the jeep, listening to its laboring engine as it came through the snow.

Then he felt *it*. Not now, he wanted to cry out, aware of

Foley and the others, but more aware of the call of the abyss. He could almost understand what it wanted of him, almost hear real words, almost name the sensations that swept him. He felt his head turning in spite of his efforts to resist, and from a great distance he could hear Foley speak.

"Jesus Christ! What's wrong with him?"

He started to move, one foot, the other, the gun forgotten, dangling as he felt himself drawn stronger than ever, a filing being taken to a magnet. He stumbled against the snowdrift, fell, and someone jumped on him, tried to get an arm around his throat. The shock of the snow on his face, the attack, made the summons fade; this reality took precedence. He half-rolled against the snow, enough to dislodge Foley. Charlie sank down against the drift and raised the gun.

"Back up," he grunted. "Just back the hell up."

Brushing snow away, Foley backed up, cursing. Charlie glanced at Byron and Newhouse. Neither had moved. Byron was staring at him with a shocked expression. "He's been affected by it!" he whispered. Then he turned frantically to Newhouse. "He's been affected. We're not in range here. If his wife's in there, and Loesser, they must have a plan to really destroy the source of the radiation this time, not just burn it out. We have to stop them!"

"How's Polly?" Charlie asked, and realized he had turned the gun to point it directly at Byron; it felt right aimed that way.

"I don't know. She's dropped out for the rest of the year. Listen, Charlie, tell us what they're up to. If you were attacked and survived, and Loesser can go in and out at will, and maybe Constance, you must see that it's not as dangerous as we all thought before. We'll lick it."

"Tell that to Polly," Charlie said. "And Mike and poor Mrs. Eglin up at Orick, and the sheriff's men at Old West. Tell that son of a bitch wandering around in the woods, and the one they found crawling in the snow—" He stopped. The jeep was coming.

21

Constance ran across the room she had entered and ducked through an open doorway, where she stopped to listen. She could see the irregular entrance with pale light beyond, and then the boy's figure eclipsed it. His steps were heavy and loud on the bare floor. She did not move as he swung his body this way and that. Looking for her? Listening? His movements were not human; it was impossible to guess his intentions, if he even had intentions now. Again he made the hair-raising animal noise deep in his throat and lurched forward. He was still dragging the suit.

The hotel was very dark away from the lobby area. She could see nothing in the room behind her, and very little of the lobby that the boy was crossing, the insane noise echoing, reechoing until it seemed sourceless. He passed from her line of sight. Now, she thought, she probably could outrun him, get outside, get her skis. . . . The other boy must have tried repeatedly to get away, and each time this one had heard, had seen, had known, and had given chase. She bit her lip, listening for his receding steps. What if he caught the ring pull on a nail? Hearing him made her realize how vulnerable she would be if she moved. Soundlessly she took off her own boots. She nearly dropped them when there was a new noise. She peeked around the doorframe and could see nothing. It sounded as if he were kicking a wall, maybe trying to kick it down, and his guttural voice rose to a near scream, dropped, rose. It was inhuman, full of pain and fury.

She closed her eyes hard and took a deep breath, then another. She knew she could get to the door without his hearing her. The other boy must have pounded like an elephant across the lobby each time he made a run for it. And then? She knew that was no good. She had to find the doorway to the alien mechanism. She had to get the suit with the device out of the boy's hand. She had to stay alive, with a chance of escaping after the device had been delivered.

When she opened her eyes, only a second or two later, they had adjusted to the dimness enough for her to see that she was in a large room with boarded-up windows, completely bare. The strippers had been here. Hardwood flooring had been removed, exposing the rough underfloor. Paneling must have been peeled off the walls, leaving lathwork, with gaping holes in it. Pencil-thin lines of light revealed the outside wall and windows. She looked again into the main lobby where the boy was howling, and this time she could see a figure trying to climb the skeleton of a staircase. The strippers must have taken the stairs away. Hardwood, carved, whatever, they must have had value, and now there was no way for him to get to the second floor. She shuddered. He wanted to go home to it and he couldn't, so he howled his frustration. The realization struck her that she could not reach the doorway to the abyss either.

For an instant she knew there was no point in staying here, that the only sensible thing to do was run to the porch, put on her boots, find her skis, and get away. The boy was trying to climb a long narrow board that had been left standing when the stairs were removed. He got up a few feet only to slide back down, screaming. She could almost see Charlie in the bulky figure, and knew it might become Charlie if they didn't stop the thing here in this place.

Back stairs? Servant's stairs? There had to be service stairs, and they would be plain, not tempting to strippers. Silently she left her refuge and crept around the wall to a spot close to the entrance, where she put her boots, to be picked up on her way out, she told herself. She began to search for back stairs. She had thrust the flashlight in her belt, and now took it out, but did not dare use it until she had crossed another room. The boy's cries were distant now. Another dining room? Another door. Another room, smaller, darker. The slivers of light coming through the boarded-up windows were growing paler. And the cobwebs were everywhere, brushing, pushing, trying to get in. She imagined them seeping through her eyes, entering her ears, her nostrils, her mouth. Shuddering, she stopped, forced herself to breathe deeply, then went on. Another room. Suddenly the boy's voice was close, and she drew back, afraid he had noticed her movements; then she realized that she had made a circuit of half the lower floor, unless she had missed part of it in the darkness. Had one of the rooms been a kitchen? She was almost certain she had not yet been in a kitchen; there would be signs even if everything had been taken out. Cabinets, a pantry, something would be there, and the back stairs would be nearby.

Many doors had been removed; a few still in place would not open, and the darkness grew deeper, windows smaller, with less light penetrating the gloom. Offices? She jerked her foot when a splinter dug in and she realized that she had not heard the boy's voice for several minutes. Had he fallen, hit his head? Made it to the top finally? Resting? She listened, then shook her head and went on to the next room. She did not believe he could move silently; he was not capable of thinking of the consequences of making noise, alerting her. But he might have glimpsed her light, she thought, although she was using it as sparingly as possible, guarding it with her cupped hand. She brushed invisible cobwebs away from her face, listened, crept across one room after another, through narrow halls, and at last she knew she was in the kitchen. There were cabinets— no sink, no appliances or table, but there were cabinets with doors ajar. She hurried across the space, through an opposite doorway, and found the back stairs, intact. The boy was still quiet, or tricks of architecture swallowed his voice. The thought struck her with sickening force that he might be handling the suit, tearing it apart, that he might have enough mind to won- der about the ring.

Her hands were shaking so hard, the spot of light danced on the stairs. "Stop it!" she said under her breath, and gripped the light with both hands until it steadied. She went up the stairs. Here were the bedrooms, an eight-foot-wide corridor, closed doors on both sides. The blackness was complete; her flashlight the only light. Somewhere near the center, Carson had said; that's where it always was. She started with the door to her left, opened it, shone the light around the walls, closed it again. Nothing but cobwebs, both real and invisible, charged cob- webs. The next door. The next. She crossed the hall to look inside the opposite room before moving farther down.

The light revealed the ruined walls, with their exposed plas-

ter and lathwork and peeling wallpaper. Very pale slivers of
light cut across each room, across closed closet doors, or sometimes doorless closets. She opened another door, began her
quick sweep of light over the walls, and stopped. The light was
absorbed by a blackness more intense than any she had ever
seen. Before, the light touched a surface, reflected something
back. But this time, it stopped dead. She caught her breath
sharply. The light swerved; she brought it back and trained it
along the outline of the black abyss. Too large for a closet door.
A door connecting two rooms. She backed out into the hallway.
She had closed each door after looking inside, but she left this
one standing open. She made sure it was the only open door
near the stairs, and then started back down. Now she had to
get the suit away from the mad boy.

Constance made her way back to the lobby. She located the
boy from the noises he was making, but she could not see him
yet. Near the destroyed staircase was all she could tell, in a
shadow that hid him thoroughly. The light coming through the
broken door was almost gone, too pale to reveal the boy. But
did he still have the suit? If he had dropped it, maybe she could
creep in close enough to snatch it away and run.

She took a step into the lobby, the hall to the kitchen behind
her, and then she aimed the light at the spot where the sounds
of his breathing originated. When she turned on the flashlight,
he was not there. She had to sweep the floor back and forth
before she came to him, in a fetal position, sucking in great,
choking gasps of air, the suit held like a blanket against his
chest. As soon as the light was on him, he screamed and
jumped up, clutching the suit. She turned and ran, and he followed, his boots thundering on the wooden floors. She did not
dare enter any of the rooms along this hall; many of them did
not have another exit and he was still coming. Over the thumping of his boots, and the hoarse, inarticulate sounds he made,
she thought she could hear the air tank thumping also, and her
heart pounded even harder. The suit would be useless without
air, if the tank were damaged, which seemed likely.

She reached the kitchen and darted across it, crouched near
the door on the far side, and waited. He came a second or two
later, blundered into a wall, into a cabinet. He was barely visible
in the failing light, no more than a great hulking shape. In

despair she hung her head, trying to catch her breath. If only she could get close enough to hit him with the flashlight. Even as she thought it, she knew there was no point in it. She would need a sledgehammer to stop him. As a weapon the flashlight was useless, but suddenly she thought of how Candy, their cat, could not resist chasing a light, and she shone it against the far wall. His shape moved toward it. One of his hands tried to grab the beam, then smashed into the cabinet the light was on. She moved the light; he followed, futilely trying to snatch it. She turned it off and he bellowed.

Trying to make no sound, she edged along the wall to the nearest cabinet. She placed the flashlight on a shelf, aimed at the opposite wall, and then turned it on. He ran toward it, still dragging the suit, the air tank scraping the floor with every step he took. When he stopped at the spot of light, she started to crawl toward him. He banged his fist into the cabinet again and again, yelling, sobbing. If it didn't move soon, she knew, he would lose interest in it. She crawled faster until she could reach out and touch the suit. She did not try to take it from him, but found the air tank and let her hand slide around it, under the suit to the pouch strapped on the chest. She moved as cautiously as she could, but tried to hurry. Any second he might jerk away, go back to the lobby. Her fingers found the pouch, and she felt around it until she came to the cold metal of the ring. She pulled it.

He felt that and roared, kicked out. His foot caught her in the thigh; she stifled a scream and scrambled away. Her leg had gone numb. If he had groped for her then, he would have found her, but his brain was issuing no orders, reasoning nothing. When he heard her, he tried to smash her. If he saw her, he would follow. As soon as she was silent and invisible, he forgot her. He went back to the light, but only for a second this time. She could see the darkness of his shape moving away, heard his boots, his screams. She couldn't let him go back out there to the lobby, start his useless assault on the old stairs again. She forced herself up and hobbled to the cabinet that held the flashlight, reached it and took it out, waved the light in a circular pattern, then lowered the beam to the floor. He came after it.

She knew he would not let go of the suit. It was a pattern

of behavior that some madness induced. A patient sometimes grasped an object from morning until night, until sleep relaxed the fingers enough for a nurse or doctor to take it away. She led him from the kitchen, playing the light on the floor, on the wall, on the open door. She led him to the stairs and started to back up them. He was coming faster now, spending less time trying to catch the the spot of light, his animal noise louder. He would run over her, she realized, and swung the light around, shone it in his eyes. He screamed and kept coming. She turned and ran up the last dozen steps, ran to the open door, where he caught up with her and hit her on the side of the head with the back of his hand. He knocked her across the room, into the wall. She hung for a moment, then slid to the floor unconscious.

She stirred and moaned with her eyes closed. As soon as she cut off the sound, silence returned. When she opened her eyes a wave of nausea swept her. The light was still on, halfway across the room, shining at the hole where a baseboard had been. Groggily she crawled to it and picked it up. Still on her hands and knees, she hung her head trying to remember what it was she was supposed to do. Memory hit her and she snapped her head up. Pain followed so sharply it brought tears to her eyes. He was gone. She turned the light to the abyss, still there. How long? She had no way of knowing how long she had been unconscious. Steadying herself with one hand on the wall, she forced herself upright and started out, trying to hurry, but very aware that her leg was dragging, that she was mired in one spot, that there was no way she could negotiate a flight of stairs and get out of the hotel.

The jeep stopped twenty feet away from Foley. Two men climbed out; one remained behind the wheel. Foley looked from the jeep to Charlie. His face was set in hard lines, his voice grim. "It'll be dark very soon, Charlie. We're going in while there's still light."

"Someone will be hurt," Charlie said softly.

"Then someone will be hurt," Newhouse said in a clipped voice. "Send them in."

"Is that how it is?" Charlie asked Foley. He examined Newhouse with more interest. Foley waved to the man behind the wheel of the jeep, and Charlie raised the gun. "He'd better get out and look over the situation first, don't you agree? He might not be able to get around this drift."

"I'm tired of stalling," Newhouse said and, turning his back on Charlie, went to the jeep and got in. The driver shifted gears. Foley started to say something, but Charlie tightened his finger on the trigger. And then everything stopped.

It was like being caught in a hurricane, but without wind, or in an electrical storm without lightning. For a second there seemed to be no air, as if a giant vacuum had sucked them all in. Then the charged cobwebs were everywhere, pressing hard against everyone simultaneously, at the same time sucking them empty. Charlie dropped to his knees, both hands over his ears, as if what he experienced was pure sound. Foley fell down twitching. Byron staggered a few feet and fell face-first into the snowdrift. Newhouse clutched his head and screamed.

Carson Danvers and the boy were knocked down by the effect. When Carson began to stir, he thought he heard Gary sobbing. He crawled to him and cradled him in his arms, saying nonsense words over and over, rocking him. The boy sobbed against his chest. Not Gary, just a hurt kid, Carson thought finally, but he did not release him until they were both ready to stand up and start moving together.

When Charlie was able to move, Foley was pulling himself up. "Come on," Charlie cried hoarsely. He staggered to the jeep and dragged out the unconscious driver. On the other side, Foley hauled Newhouse out. Charlie drove around the snowdrift, the jeep tilting perilously, then back up to the driveway and through the snow around the side of the hill toward the hotel. Neither man spoke. Now there was a fierce glow in the sky, sparks were leaping up into the darkening air. Charlie drove too fast, the jeep skidded and slid and threatened to die altogether in too-deep snow, but he kept it going until they were in the meadow, and there the snow overwhelmed it. He stopped and stood on the seat, scanning the area around the hotel. And he saw her, sprawled in the snow. He left Foley and waded through the drifts to her.

She was conscious, but barely. He lifted her and then sat down, holding her in his arms while she shook. "Look at the mess you made," he said in her ear. "Warm?" The heat would drive them back in a minute or two; it was melting the snow around them already.

"Oh, Charlie," she cried, "there was a boy. A poor, mad boy! He took it in!"

"*Sh. Sh.* It's over. It's over."

He held her and watched the fire and waited for someone to come get them. They would call it an earthquake, or a meteorite, or a gas explosion, or some damn thing. They were good at that. They would gather in the hurt, the dead, the destroyed who might live a long time and never know they were destroyed, and before long it would all be forgotten. But what if they had taken it to San Francisco, to Berkeley, or any place with a lot of people, what if they had triggered it there with their tests? He shook his head. He had known it was armed to defend itself if necessary; he had known it.

Foley joined them. "Well," he said heavily. "That's that, I guess. Let's go."

"She can't walk," Charlie said. "No shoes."

Constance wailed, "I lost my boots, and the skis my father gave me when I was eighteen! He was about eighteen." She put her head against his chest and wept. He held her and watched the leaping flames, the flares, the shower of sparks, one of the most beautiful sights on earth.

Sweet, Sweet Poison

1

Al Zukal drove into the driveway of the new house with caution. You never knew out here in the country, he thought; things happen, dead animals, trees down, sinkholes. . . .

"They ain't got here yet," Sylvie muttered. And, in fact, no one else was in sight.

There was the gravel drive close pressed by evergreen trees at the county road and dense undergrowth that neither recognized, with grass that already needed cutting and probably would need it on a weekly basis. The driveway curved a few times, and at those places neither the county road nor the house was visible; it was like being in a wilderness, they both thought uneasily. The yard had not been maintained for many years. Untrimmed roses sprawled with dead lower branches; lilacs grew as high as trees and made a thicket with too many spindly new sprouts. Spent blossoms hung in brown clusters. Sumac had crept in and threatened to claim the entire acreage but was contested by many young trees—maples, pines, a few oaks—all too crowded and weak-looking. There were fourteen acres altogether, reverting back to a natural state where nature would do the thinning.

But no moving van was in sight. Al pulled in behind the house, where he stopped and turned off the motor. There was a two-car garage, unusable until tons of junk were cleaned out. He looked at Sylvie.

She had been a red-haired girl when they married, thirty years ago, and she would die red-haired at the end, no matter how long-delayed it was. He was used to her red hair and liked it. He liked her pear shape, too, and would have admitted readily that they made a good couple, each pear-shaped, with her rounder end down, and his up. It made for better sleeping that way, he liked to think.

"What if they don't make it today?" she demanded, not yet moving to open her door and get out.

"They'll make it. They want to get paid, they get here. Simple arithmetic. Come on, gives us time to make sure where we want the bed."

Actually the only thing they were moving of any consequence from their Bronx apartment was the bed. "That was my mother's bed!" Sylvie had said early on, as if that settled that. And it had. Just about everything else in the van that had not yet arrived was new. The new station wagon had boxes of bedding, two feather beds, also inherited from her mother, God bless her soul, and a mishmash of dishes, no four alike. But Sylvie knew when and how they had acquired each and every one of them, and when the missing pieces had vanished, or had been broken. "I want them all," she had said through tight lips, and there they were in the wagon waiting to be lugged inside. There were also boxes of new clothes; at least she hadn't insisted on keeping every rag they ever owned.

He said, "Well, why don't you get on out and let's get at it?"

Actually he said, "why doncha," and when she responded she said, "Well, aincha the impatient one!" But they didn't hear it like that and presently they were both standing before their new home. It was a two-story building, the lower half finished with river stone, the upper section white clapboard. It had an attic that would sleep many grandchildren, and a basement that would probably hold more junk than they could accumulate in the years remaining to them—they were both in their fifties. The house was large, five bedrooms, a den and breakfast room besides the kitchen, a big dining room, and even bigger living room. The biggest apartment they had ever lived in had had three bedrooms, and one of them was really a dining room or a parlor or something. But with four girls growing up in the house they had needed bed space more than eating space or sitting space. Now they looked at their new home with silent awe.

Looming over the many trees behind the house the mill rose, and that was theirs also. The mill had been built in 1848 and operated until World War I, or thereabouts, and used as a school at one time, and a bootlegger's production site at another, but for the past twenty years it had not been used for anything.

Sylvie cleared her throat and said, "Listen." It came out as a whisper.

"I don't hear nothing."

"That's what I mean."

Before, when they had come out to their house, they had been with the real estate man, and then with their daughter Flora and her husband, Bobby, and their two kids, and there had been noise. But now there was a breeze shaking the trees a little, and off beyond the mill the rustle of water, and a faint sound of the falls, not much, not enough.

"I don't know, Al," Sylvie said softly.

"Jaysus Crackers! Now you don't know! Come on, grab that first box and let's get at it. Wait and see. When Flora and Bobby are here, and the kids yelling, the radio and stereo blasting, it'll be just like home."

They began to carry the boxes inside and stack them on counters in the kitchen, and soon the movers came, and the sight of the four-poster with the pineapple knobs comforted Sylvie. She began to relax. She fussed at Al for getting in the way, and he cursed the movers for bumping the bed against the stair rails, and everything was normal again.

The movers also brought in a new sofa, new chairs and tables, dining table, kitchen table . . . a new stove, a Jenn-Air that had a grill and six burners, and a refrigerator with two doors. Al had stared at it in the store. "Jaysus Crackers! You know what I grew up with? A little box this big, with a chunk of ice delivered every Monday, and by God it had to last until the next Monday."

After the movers had finished, Al nudged Sylvie with his elbow. "Well, watcha think?"

She nodded. "We need more furniture than I thought we would. It's a big house, Al."

"You don't have to fill it, you know."

She was surveying the living room with narrowed eyes and did not answer. The spanking-new and factory-clean furniture looked barren somehow, and that was because there was no clutter, no piles of newspapers and magazines, no sneakers in corners, no beer cans on the tables, no pretzel bags, nothing to make it look like home. It even smelled strange, Al realized, not liking the untouched, unlived-in look and smell. Sylvie would fill it, he knew, and after the kids got here, they would help, and for now, well, there was work to do.

A while later she was stashing things in cabinets in the kitchen when he decided to do the shopping they had agreed on ahead of time. "You coming?"

She shook her head. "Too dirty. I thought they just had this many cabinets in them fancy magazines with houses that no one really ever lives in."

She'd fill the cabinets, too, he thought gloomily and left her there. Spender's Ferry was less than three miles away, one hour and twenty minutes out of New York City, with a commuter train station and everything. Goddamn suburbanites, he thought in surprise. That's what they had suddenly become. Al's father had come over from Czechoslovakia to strike gold and had set himself up in a butcher shop, which Al inherited in due time. Then the Bronx caught on fire. That was how he thought of it. The shop vanished, and Al got a job butchering for a supermarket. At least, he often thought when things got tough, they always had meat on their table. Stolen meat, meat carried home in pockets, in his lunch box, meat sometimes slipped to Sylvie when she came in to shop. When things got really bad Sylvie worked too, cleaning offices in the middle of the night. Somehow they had made out okay. Not great, but okay. Then, almost a year ago, Al Zukal had spent five dollars on the lottery and had won big. Just like his father always said, he thought: work hard all your life and you'll make it. Guaranteed income of two hundred twenty-five thou a year, he thought, as he had very, very often over the intervening months. Goddamn suburbanites!

Jill Ferris was leading the way across a swinging bridge below the mill at that moment. "Dad's always maintained the bridge, just because he likes it," she said over her shoulder to a tall man behind her. Jill was thirty, a bit underweight, with long pale hair, no longer really blond, although she had been very blond as a child. Now it was the color of darkening golden oak; it gleamed with red highlights when she moved into sunlight.

The man following her was Sebastian Pitkin, a few years older than Jill; he had a solemn expression, lank hair darker than hers, and large blue eyes that bulged a little. The bridge swayed and he clutched the handrail involuntarily; she seemed not to notice.

Jill stopped near the end of the bridge and pointed. "Pretty, isn't it?" Below them was Spender's Lake, seven acres in all, with a short strip of beach at the upper-right end. That was on the side of her father's land, several hundred acres, mostly woods, with an orchard that was invisible from here. On the other side of the lake was the university experimental farm. The narrow bridge, twenty feet across, swung a few inches above the dam; the waterfall had a drop of eight feet. The stream that wound away through a gorge was only two feet wide below the dam, although farther on it widened again to become Spender's Creek. The setting was incredibly beautiful, untouched-looking. The trees were massive in the forest, the lake shockingly blue, grasses edged the water in places, and even the picturesque swinging bridge was like an illustration in a book from the turn of the century.

"See, that's state forest land," Jill said, pointing again. "Dad's land borders it on this end and the creek and mill property make up the boundary here. The experimental farm is on the other side of the mill property. No one will ever be able to encroach in any way. Perfect, isn't it?"

Sebastian was nodding thoughtfully, eyeing the mill that towered over them. The waterwheel looked intact, although some of the buckets probably would need replacing. Hard to tell, though; there was too much moss on the lower portion. . . . No water flowed through the diversion trough, but of course it wouldn't, not with the mill shut down. "You say the mill's in good shape?"

"Absolutely. They built it out of cypress, cedar, and oak, and they built it to last forever. The upper floors would be great for dormitories and the entire lower part could be classrooms, mess hall, kitchens, meeting rooms. Wait until you see." She started to walk again; the bridge began to swing again. He caught the handrail and followed cautiously.

There were mammoth double doors that had admitted horse-drawn wagons loaded with grain at one time, but no longer opened. Weeds grew thick at the base of the doors, all around the mill. White Queen Anne's lace, blue forget-me-nots, pink and yellow sweetpeas trailing everywhere. Almost too pretty, too planned. Jill led the way around to a normal-sized door that opened at her touch. The interior was dim; makeshift partitions had been added at one time or another, obviously temporary additions that never had been torn down again.

"See," Jill said, in the center of one of the small rooms, "a private meditation room, or a sleeping cell, or even a meeting place for a group of four or five." The room was about eight by ten, stifling, bake-oven hot. The single window appeared to be painted shut.

They left the room and were in the central, open space where the mechanism for the grinding of the corn and wheat was all there, gears and wheels and chains and pulleys, but the stone grinding wheels had been removed. This section was pleasantly cool. They went up very sturdy stairs and looked around, came down a different staircase, and roamed the back part of the lower floor.

They were emerging from around one of the partitions when Jill gasped at the sight of a figure in the open doorway.

"Who are you? This is private property," Jill said, louder than she intended, startled.

"I could say the same," the woman snapped back at her. "It's private property, all right, my private property, me and my husband's. What are you doing in here?"

Jill could only stare at this awful woman, with her awful, thick Bronx accent and voice that sounded like a demented duck quacking. She was dressed in awful dirty, baggy pants, with a dirty shirt, and she had awful red-dyed frizzy hair poking out from under a grass-green kerchief.

"I'm sorry," Sebastian said. "We certainly didn't mean to invade your privacy. I thought the property was for sale. Mrs. Ferris was showing it to me. Please forgive us." He smiled gently. "This is Mrs. Ferris, and I'm Sebastian."

For a moment, with his light blue eyes fixed, his gaze on her so directly, she felt confusion. A kind man, she thought, understanding, but then the girl made a noise and Sylvie looked at her, the moment broken, gone, leaving a bewildering set of contradictions in its place. Sylvie crossed her arms over her

chest and nodded. "Right. Well, the mill and the house ain't for
sale, not no more. Me and Al bought it all last week and we're
moving in right now."

"Come along," Sebastian said to Jill then. "It's a mistake, after
all. No harm done."

Sylvie watched them narrowly as they left the mill and
stepped onto the bridge. She waited until they had vanished
among the trees on the other side before she went back to the
house, muttering to herself. A politician, or a preacher, she
thought. She shook her head. Preacher. Not just because no
politician would ever own up to a name like Sebastian, but the
way he looked at her. Making up to her, she thought with surprise. The kind who got on Sunday television and looked at
you like that, like he'd be all over you in a flash if he could,
like if he could just lay on a hand, you'd say yes no matter what
he asked. Making up to her, at her age, she muttered angrily.
Sylvie didn't trust religion that relied on sorrowful blue eyes
and the laying on of hands, and the intimate little smiles that
suggested he knew your secrets. Religion should be cooler than
that, she thought, more dignified. And that skinny girl. Putty in
the hands of a man like that. Her lips tightened at the thought
of the girl. *Who are you?* Like she owned the world. Well, she
showed them, Mr. Sebastian-let-me-save-your-soul, and Mrs. I-
own-the-world Ferris.

She was still grumbling under her breath when David Levy
turned up at the kitchen door of the house. He was a stick of
a boy, way over six feet, with a great big pumpkin grin, and
wanting a haircut, like always. Ever since she knew him, he had
needed a haircut. Must get it done sometime, she thought, but
it never showed. Great mop of black hair. Rosa, their youngest
daughter, had told David they were looking for a place in the
country, and David had told them about this, and now here he
was to lend a hand. A good boy. And Rosa didn't know good
when she saw it, off in California on a scholarship, studying to
be some kind of ocean scientist, and some other girl would see
David Levy and not be so blind. . . .

"What can I do?" David asked. "I wanted to come earlier but
we've been pretty busy at the farm. Anyway, here I am." He had
a backpack slung over his shoulder. He put it on the table and

she began directing him exactly the same way she directed Al
and the girls and their husbands and children.

Pretty soon Al came back with the station wagon loaded with
groceries, and they got to work carrying them inside. "I told
my boss about you," David said, putting a box down on the
table. "I hope it's okay if she comes by to meet you."

"Grand Central," Sylvie muttered. "Fine, David, fine. Al, put
that on the table until I have a chance to see what all you've
got. Did you buy some hot dogs like I told you?"

"Sure, sure. And buns, what you didn't tell me. And catsup.
And beer. And I'm for a beer right now. David?"

He shook his head. Al opened two cans and handed one to
Sylvie. David rummaged in his backpack and brought out a thermos. "Lemonade," he said, and drank.

He put the thermos down and went to the door then. "Here
she comes," he said. In just a moment a woman appeared and
he opened the door for her.

"Dr. Wharton, these are my friends, Mr. and Mrs. Zukal."

She was dressed in jeans and a T-shirt and sneakers. She had
the kind of sturdy little body that would let her wear clothes
like that for many more years. Her hair was short and straight,
dark with streaks of gray at the temples. When she smiled, a
dimple appeared in her cheek and her eyes smiled along with
her mouth.

Sylvie nodded. "You want a beer?" she asked. And then,
"You're a doctor?"

"Just a professor. And call me Lois," she said. "I'd love a
beer." She was looking around at the furniture, at the boxes,
and cartons with undisguised interest. "This has been a hell of
a day."

Al Zukal popped another can and handed it over to her and
she drank thirstily. "For us, too," he said. "Moving's a bitch."

"I was really surprised when David said you had bought the
place," Lois said. "Not you, but anyone. This property has been
on the market for years."

"Two looks," Al said. "All it took. Two trips and me and Sylvie, we seen it was exactly what we're after. Believe you me,
we looked at a lot of dumps, real dumps, and a lot of mansions,
too."

Sylvie began to talk about some of the other places they had inspected, and Al was still talking, now about the Realtors who would sell a doghouse and call it a palace. Lois finished her beer and caught the look of affection and amusement on David's face. She grinned again and although both Al and Sylvie were talking, she did, too.

"Anyway, welcome, and thanks for the beer. I have to go and scrub. I'm all over muck. Why don't you join us for a cookout? David, you know the way up the trail, don't you? You can be guide. Seven or thereabouts."

Sylvie and Al exchanged glances; hers said sure, why not, and he nodded.

"Good. No one should have to cook on moving day, and restaurants are just too much trouble if you've been working hard. Don't dress up or anything. It's a real cookout, first of the season, and with the weather cooling off the way it does as soon as the sun goes down, it's not likely to be a late-night affair." She reached out to put down her empty can, and somehow her arm brushed David's thermos and it teetered, then fell with the unmistakable sound of breaking glass.

"Goddamn it," Lois said with a sigh. "David, I'm sorry. As I said, it's been that kind of day. I'll replace it, of course." She bent over to pick it up, but he was there first.

"It's all right," he said hurriedly. "Really. Don't worry about it."

But she would get him a new one, Sylvie thought. Lois left then, and Sylvie turned to the bags and boxes on the table. "Now, let's see what you got and try to figure out where it should go."

Al was looking thoughtfully out the door. "David, she said up the trail, walk to her place. Where? There ain't no place out there that I know about."

David squirmed uncomfortably. "I didn't know she'd invite us all over," he said, not looking happy. "I mean, she's my boss, a professor, Dr. Wharton, and all, but she's also Mrs. Wollander. She lives in the big house at the other side of the lake."

As Lois walked away, she continued to hear Sylvie's raucous voice, and Al's equally raucous voice in some kind of weird harmony. She was still grinning.

"What's so funny?"

She looked up, startled, but not really surprised to see her husband, Warren, approaching with both hands outstretched.

"Hi! Didn't see you there. Sun in my eyes maybe."

He drew her close and kissed her. Warren Wollander was six feet tall and large through the shoulders and chest, strong-looking at sixty-two. "I didn't intend you should see me," he said, softly. "That's just about where I was standing the first time I saw you. Remember? I like watching you when you don't know I'm there."

"Who could forget?" she said, and put her arm about his waist. His arm was across her shoulders as they started up the trail.

He had taken the walk that day even though there was still snow in every shadowed cranny, thick on the north slopes, piled up behind stone walls. And across the lake he had seen a person who, he thought, was spiking the experimental trees. A short, shapeless figure in a down jacket, heavy pants, boots, with a red stocking cap that had a long tail that swung back and forth as she applied a drill to a tree, braced for purchase, and started to drill.

"I thought you were a yeti," she said gravely, and they both laughed. Actually, she had been drilling out core samples to measure for growth. He tightened his arm around her shoulders. "I was smiling at our new neighbors," she said. "Mr. and Mrs. Zukal. I invited them to the cookout. And David, too. It's time you met David, I think."

The pressure of his hand on her shoulder tightened, just for a moment, and perhaps not in response to what she had said, she thought. She did not look up at him, but watched the trail. It was well-groomed, with dense mayapple colonies on both sides.

"Well, well, the place finally got sold? That will surprise Jill, I suspect."

"I guess so," she agreed, and suddenly felt tired, and unhappy about the invitation that she had issued without thought. "Do you mind that I asked them over?"

This time she knew his hand tightened, but it was a reassuring pressure, and reassurance was in his voice when he replied. "Lois, this is your house, not Jill's. Remember? You're the lady of the house. You want company, invite them. Tell me about our new neighbors."

She began to talk and presently he was chuckling, and then laughed louder. "God, it will certainly surprise Jill."

She laughed, too, but she was bothered about his daughter, Jill. What if Jill came on in one of her bitchy moods? She could do that. And this man, this guru, whatever he was, what if he was impossible? She knew that Jill's husband, Stanley, would be all right, and Warren would treat the Zukals exactly the same way he treated everyone. With a politeness that would be excessive if he didn't like them, and with warmth and humor if he did. She sighed and wished she could take back the spontaneous invitation. And even with the thought, she found herself denying it. No, by God, she thought firmly; this *was* her house, she *was* the lady of the house, and Jill had to be reminded now and then. Jill had arrived for a visit three weeks ago and Lois was beginning to think of her as the Woman Who Came to Dinner. Yesterday Jill had announced plans for a cookout, even though the late April weather could be as fickle as any poet ever suggested. She had invited a stranger, Sebastian, and had taken it for granted that it would be fine with everyone else. Well, it was, only the party had suddenly increased by three.

Sometimes she wondered if Warren was fully aware of the cautious maneuvers she and Jill used with each other, and usually she knew the answer was that he was fully aware. She suspected that he knew exactly why she had invited their new neighbors, and she suddenly felt ashamed of herself, and immensely grateful for his support. His position was not enviable either, she knew. He was deeply in love with her, no doubt about that, and he loved his daughter without reservation, even though she could be . . . *difficult* was the kindest word Lois could think of. She gave his waist a little squeeze when they had to separate to walk single file. She appreciated these short periods together more than he could realize; she knew he was the wisest man she had ever met, and if he thought it would all work out, that made her think so too. Most of the time anyway.

2

This was one of the worst evenings of his life, David Levy thought as he and the Zukals approached the big house. They had come up the trail, as Dr. Wharton had suggested, and Mrs. Zukal had been watching for animals or snakes or bugs the entire way. Now they emerged onto a meticulously maintained lawn that stretched out forever. Already, some people on the patio behind the house had turned to watch them. David felt like a pinned butterfly. He swallowed hard and deliberately looked past the group of people to study the house.

The original structure had been tall and narrow, three stories up with a peaked roof, but wings had been added, and now it sprawled and the central part looked almost like a ship's mast to which the lower sections were tethered. The patio was flagstone; a long trellis covered with the first extravagant flush of red and white roses screened what lay beyond.

Although he intended to keep focusing on the house, his gaze was drawn to Lois as she came to meet them. She was dressed in chino pants and a gray silk shirt that made Sylvie's blue polyester pantsuit look tawdry. She got between Sylvie and Al to take their arms and steer them to her husband. Her greeting was warm and cheerful; she made it seem natural for the three newcomers to be part of the group, and to David's surprise no one else seemed to think it strange either. He mumbled something to Mr. Wollander, and then to his daughter, Jill, who looked like a movie star in skintight jeans and a scoop-neck sweater that accentuated her sharp collarbones. He nodded to the other man, whose name was simply Sebastian.

"You've certainly come to a beautiful setting," Sebastian said to Al as they shook hands. "We were just marveling over the lake."

It was about twenty feet lower than the lawn where they

were standing, and in the evening sunlight it gleamed like a sapphire without a ripple to mar it.

"Yeah, it's pretty, all right," Al said, and Sylvie said something at the same time; behind them David suppressed a groan. But Sylvie shut up and the moment passed.

"I have pictures of the mill that go back sixty years or more," Warren said then. "I bet you'd like to see them."

Before they could respond, Jill said to Sylvie, "This afternoon I acted like an idiot. You gave me such a start. We used to play in the mill, you know how children will get into a place like that. We told ghost stories and there you were suddenly, just like out of one of the stories. I'm sorry."

"You started me, too," Sylvie said. "I thought you was squatters or something. No harm done."

"She was absolutely forbidden to go there, just as I was," Warren said, laughing. "We did the same thing when I was a boy. Come on, let's look at those pictures."

As he led them inside, Lois began to relax and she wondered why she had been tense at all. Jill had behaved like a perfect lady, and had taken the news of the addition to her party with such good grace that Lois had felt ashamed. She went to one of the long tables where drinks had been prepared.

"David, Sebastian? What would you like?"

They both took juice and she had gin and tonic. Jill helped herself to white wine. Sebastian was still regarding the lake.

"I had no idea this was back here in the hills," he said after a moment. "I'm surprised that people aren't swarming to it. Isolation and peace are priceless commodities these days."

"Too small and too out of the way," Lois said. "And hiking's better on the other side of the village, up into the mountains. But when hunting season opens, they swarm." She stood at his side and also gazed at the unlikely blue of the water. "You realize that color comes from the fact that the lake is dead?"

Sebastian looked at her with disapproval, she thought, surprised at his expression. "Acid rains did it in," she explained. "Unfit for fish or plant life. It's doing the same to the experimental farm," she added, and heard the bitterness in her voice.

"Perhaps," Sebastian said in his gentle voice, "we are seeing a warning sign that must be acknowledged. A lake here, a farm there. The earth is speaking to us. But who is listening? Perhaps there has been too much experimenting already."

Lois felt a surge of anger that caused a trembling in her fingers. "Not just a lake here and a farm there," she snapped. "Whole forests are dying. In Bavaria, the whole damn Fichtelgebirge forest is at risk. More than fifty percent of the mature trees are dead. And it's happening in Vermont, on the West Coast. Not just a little patch here and there, I'm afraid."

"I understand the peril," he said gravely, "and what I suggest is that if we can restore the harmony of humans and nature, of living with nature instead of pitting ourselves against it over and over, perhaps even this peril can be overcome."

He believed it, she realized, when she turned to study his face, to see if he was mocking. He looked as if he wanted to touch her, to soothe her, calm her; he looked as if he ached because of her pain and anger. Suddenly she remembered a high school teacher, more than twenty years ago, who had looked at her pityingly and said, "Do you really believe we can pollute all the oceans of the world?" Then, as a girl, she had been comforted by such knowledge, such serene wisdom, such absolute faith. This man, Sebastian, with his understanding, his sympathy, his empathy, his firm convictions could be just as soothing, just as comforting. He would dispense faith, trust, harmony with a word, a gentle smile. And meanwhile the trees were dying from causes so complex that few people even attempted to define them, and those who studied them walked in fear. Looking at him, she had the wild impression that he was following her thoughts, that he was telling her she did not have to live in fear, that she could recapture the same kind of tranquillity that softened his face. The tranquillity of ignorance, she said to herself sharply, and lifted her glass and forced herself to look away from him.

She drank, and then remembered that she had not yet asked David about his weekend plans. She turned toward him. "Are you free this weekend? I thought we might start the lime before another rain comes."

Too late she realized that Jill had been talking in a low voice with David; she bit her lip in exasperation. "Sorry. I can't leave my work behind, it seems." But David had left Jill with an embarrassing swiftness and was already at her side.

"I wasn't going anywhere. The lime shipment came this afternoon. And a couple of the hands will be around."

She shook her head, and waved him away. "No. No more work today, no more talk about lime or trees or acid rain." Then, as if to prove her point about no more work talk, she returned to the table with the decanters, and asked over her shoulder, "Sebastian, can you leave your work when the day is over?"

"I'm going to the village to pick up Stanley," Jill said, and walked stiffly off the patio to vanish into the house.

Lois sighed and refilled her glass.

"But how does one say a day ends?" Sebastian asked as if bemused. "One day flows into another, and then another endlessly. And my work . . . That, too, is endless. I am never not working, if that is even the right word."

Lois glanced toward the house, wishing Warren would come back and bring Al and Sylvie with him, let them do the talking. She said to David, "Sebastian is a . . . what, counselor, preacher, teacher? What do you call yourself?"

For a moment, when he had come to her side to talk about lime, David had looked almost at ease, now he looked wretched again. But Sebastian paid no attention to him, he kept his gaze fixed on Lois.

He smiled. "None of the above, I think. A guide at times, when I have found a piece of the path myself. But most of the time I think I am a student, a searcher, and the few stretches of path that have opened to me have revealed that the path is as endless as the day, as my work. . . ." He stopped speaking and regarded her for a moment. "You have a headache?"

After a brief hesitation she said yes. "Tension, I know. Stiff neck, stiff shoulders. Working too hard, racing the clock most of the time. It will pass."

"Let me demonstrate one of the techniques I found along the way," he said. "It will help very fast, or not at all. But first you have to sit down."

It was a challenge, she thought, one she did not have to accept. But his expression was guileless and kindly, and with reluctance she seated herself at the table. At the other side of the table David swirled his ice cubes around and around in his glass.

A few minutes later when Warren returned, laughing with Al and Sylvie, she was still seated at the table. "Warren, let Sebastian show you how to get rid of a headache. It works like magic!"

Sebastian demonstrated on them all. Sylvie was stiff all over as he approached her, confirming her worst suspicions, that he was a laying-on-of-hands minister, and Al was wishing they could go back inside and look at more pictures. What a house, he thought. Made theirs look like kid's stuff. David was wishing he had never been born. He had known this would be the worst evening of his life, but he had not known just how bad it would get. Seeing Dr. Wharton—Lois—with her husband, and then with Sebastian's hands on her neck and shoulders . . . He had thought he was braced, but that was before he had realized just how bad it could get. Women were fussing with another long table and that gave him hope that they would eat soon, and the evening would end.

"See," Sebastian was saying to Sylvie. "You are stiff with apprehension, and that causes the muscles to contract, and that is the source of pain."

"I ain't even got a headache," she said.

"But you are not relaxed, either." His voice was soothing and kind, and when he felt her neck, his fingers were gentle at first; they became probing, and hurting. He pressed at the base of her skull, and then at the top of her shoulders, and it seemed to her that she did loosen up a little. But there wasn't no miracle cure, she added. He went on to Al, who steeled himself as if getting ready for hand-to-hand combat. Sebastian laughed.

Soon after that Jill returned with Stanley. His arm was around her waist, her hand over his on her hip, as if to keep it anchored there, not let it roam. His face was round and smooth, his eyes pale blue. Like a little doll, Sylvie thought. A bright and smiling little doll. She guessed that Jill had told him about the company for supper; he acted like a proper little gentleman with Sebastian, didn't look him up and down or anything, just shook hands, and then turned to her and Al. At first, she expected him to cold-shoulder them; he looked like one of the magazine ads for the type who made a million before thirty and had no use, thank you, for anyone who didn't. But instead, he was like a schoolkid with her and Al.

"Wow! You guys won the big one! Hey, that's great! Do you have a financial advisor yet?"

Warren burst out laughing. "He can turn carrot juice into oil fields, folks. If he gives out advice, listen."

Al surveyed Stanley thoughtfully. "Financial advisor? What's he do?"

"You don't, do you? Oh, God! Let's take a little walk." When Al started to move toward the side of the patio where the trellises were heavy with roses, Stanley took his arm and drew him instead out onto the lawn. "No flowers. Allergic. Mostly to bees, but it's been my experience that if you avoid flowers, you're more likely to avoid the little bastards. Now look, you need someone who makes it a career thinking about money, someone who really likes to see it grow, see. . . ."

It wasn't that he had snubbed Sebastian, Lois thought, but he had shown no enthusiasm either. She listened absently as Jill explained to Sebastian that with Stanley money was a vocation, and a hobby, which made him a happy man since there was so much of it to work and play with. And Sebastian murmured something to the effect that Stanley might be very good for Al and Sylvie. With a start Lois understood that Jill had been apologizing for her husband and that Sebastian had accepted the apology. Lois wondered if Jill had planned this whole cookout simply to bring Sebastian and Stanley together in a friendly manner, and she decided she simply did not care.

David didn't know exactly how it happened, but Warren Wollander asked him a simple question or two, and the next thing he knew he was talking about the need to introduce new foods that would grow in marginal lands, the need to supply complete proteins in crops that could be maintained by peasants everywhere. The need to develop fast-growing trees that would supply fuel and food and fodder and hold the soil, restore the balance of atmospheric gases. . . .

"You can't do it," Jill said flatly when he paused for a breath. "You can't keep up with human fertility through food. You have to educate people, reduce fertility first, and then maybe you will accomplish something."

"But you can't just let them starve if they're already here," Sylvie said.

Al and Stanley returned, apparently having reached an agreement of some sort. Al looked at Sylvie fondly and said, "First thing, we get that check, and first thing, ten percent right off the top, to charity. Her idea."

Stanley groaned.

"And where do you stand in this perennial problem of distributing the world's largesse, Sebastian?" Warren asked. Lois felt herself become very still at the tone of his voice, too polite.

"When enough people find the path, realize the human potential, experience the wholeness that is available to all, then there will be no problem," Sebastian said softly. "It doesn't take everyone, just enough to lead the way. We all find different ways to help bring this about, some through the green revolutions that arise, some through other means."

"Well, the means I intend to apply this minute are at hand at the grill," Warren said. "Steaks in five minutes."

It turned out that neither David nor Sebastian would eat meat; Lois felt, with a twinge of irritation, that she should have known, and she went inside to advise Mrs. Carlysle, the housekeeper, that they would also need a lot of cheese. Her headache had come back.

The steaks were superb. Al asked for the name of the butcher, the grocery, wherever they got them. The supermarket he had worked in never had meat like that. Mrs. Carlysle had found smoked salmon that David accepted, although Sebastian did not. "To hell with it," Lois said distinctly under her breath. Sebastian was not her problem. Let Jill see to his diet. Warren talked to Sylvie about growing up here, how he and his brother, who was killed in Iwo Jima, had played up and down the hills, in the mill. Stanley talked to Al about money matters and to Jill about the hideous mess the painters were making in their New York City condo that was being redecorated. Jill shrugged. "I told you to move into a hotel until they're finished. You keep telling me how awful it is, but you don't do anything about it. You knew it would be a mess." She was quiet for most of the meal, her smile forced and mechanical. Sylvie caught her glancing from David back to Lois, and saw the little glint in her eyes as she reached some kind of conclusion. "You swim every morning, don't you?" Jill asked David, who blushed and nodded. Jill shivered. "I couldn't stand the idea of leaving a warm bed and plunging into that cold water before breakfast even."

It was innocent, Lois told herself. It was. David looked agonized and averted his gaze to his plate. Sebastian and Stanley launched into a tortured philosophical discussion about the ethics of feeding the poor. Sebastian's voice was melodious, his accent softened by a touch of the South. Now that Lois had disengaged herself from trying to entertain him, she listened to the rhythms of his voice instead of the actual words. It was almost as if his first language had been French perhaps, or Spanish, and he had learned English from a southerner who had lived many years in the North. Lois smiled to herself over her own tortured path in trying to identify his origins, and she wondered what Warren had seen in the man to cause his distrust. Aside from the fact that he was some kind of guru, she added.

"But don't you think it would be cruel to give them vitamins and adequate food for a limited time, knowing that tomorrow they will be starving again?" Sebastian asked. His voice had become sorrowful.

"You have to work with it one day at a time," David said, sounding nearly desperate but unable not to join the discussion, his words too fast and sharp. His New York sound, Lois thought.

Sylvie had grown increasingly restless, certain that none of them was talking about real people, just ideas. "What you're saying is just like don't go to the doctor today because maybe you'll get sick again or get hit by a truck tomorrow. Well, maybe if your belly's full and you're healthy tomorrow, you can face whatever's around the corner better." Her voice rose in indignation. "It's crazy to just give up. Might as well not be born in the first place. Or have a bat ready to bash every baby's head the minute it shows up. Is that what you mean?"

"Of course not," Sebastian said. "But I think people should accept what happens. Endless, futile struggling destroys whatever peace is available, and peace of the soul is more important than a full stomach."

"Yeah, but peace is easier with a full stomach than an empty one," Sylvie muttered. "You don't know that, you ain't talked to the right people."

Warren laughed. "She's got you, I'm afraid."

It was the signal that that conversation had drifted too far into unpleasant matters to continue at the dinner table, Lois knew. Apparently Stanley understood the message also.

"Speaking of vitamins and such," Stanley said, "I read that if you take bee pollen in increasing doses, you can build up a tolerance to stings."

Jill toyed with her food and looked terminally bored.

David began to talk about the health food and vitamin catalog that he ordered his vitamins from and Sebastian promised to send him a price list from the company he used, less expensive, he said, than David's supplier. Stanley asked if they carried bee pollen, and Sebastian said coolly that anyone with the right thoughts, the right attitude, reverence for all living creatures never got stung to begin with.

"Right," Al Zukal said with a satisfied grunt. He pushed his plate back, finished. "And them people can whistle snakes up out of baskets and climb ropes that ain't hooked on nothing, and their shit smells sweet. Yeah."

There was a long silence, broken when Warren rose from his chair. "I'll see if coffee's about ready," he said, his voice strained.

Belatedly Lois realized that he was nearly choking to keep from laughing. "I'll help," she said, and followed him inside, where they collapsed holding each other in the hallway to the kitchen, laughing out of control.

That night in bed, Al said, "Well, watcha think?" And Sylvie said, "Doncher get ideas."

"What's that supposed to mean?"

"We're not their kind and they know it and so do we."

"Stanley's all right."

Stanley had insisted on driving them home, to Sylvie's great relief. She had been terrified of the dark trail, and the probable dangers it held.

"Sure he is. They all are. But don't get ideas. Listen. What's that?" They both listened, and she said, "Wolves."

"You crazy or something? There's no wolves anymore. Except on TV. Dogs."

They lay in rigid silence listening to howling that sounded more like wolves than dogs.

"Stanley gave me some good advice already," Al said after a

moment. "And he's coming over Sunday to talk before he goes back to town."

"What advice?"

"He said . . . Well, not all that much, I guess."

"Spit it out," Sylvie said. "You won't go to sleep and neither will I until you do."

"Yeah. Well, he said I should first thing, next check next month, take out insurance, a big policy."

She was silent for a long time, then said, "You already got insurance."

"I mean big. Really big. You know that lottery ticket was mine, and if I kick, that's all she wrote."

Sylvie drew closer to him. Out here in the country it was cold at night, not like back home, she thought. "Well, don't kick," she said finally. "Why should you? You're as healthy as a horse. Listen. What's that?"

After a moment he said, "Frogs or something. Crickets maybe."

After another minute or two, she got up and stood at the window looking out. The blackness seemed to start right at the end of her nose. "I can't see a thing, not a light, nothing. Black as a coal bin out there. I want a dog."

She groped her way to the bathroom, where she switched on the light, and then returned to bed, leaving the door open a few inches. Now the dimly lighted bedroom seemed more natural, like the bedroom in their old apartment, where street-lights had filtered in no matter what she did.

"Dog's a good idea," Al said as they adjusted themselves to fit each other again. Her feet were like ice. "Yeah, real good idea. Tomorrow, you and Flora should do that, go out and get a watchdog."

They both began to think about the visit of their daughter Flora and her husband, Bobby, and their two children, and the noise they would bring with them, and they thought that some-how light would come with them, too. Finally they could drift off to sleep.

The dog was a golden retriever, two years old, female. They named her Sadie. Al regarded her with great distrust. They had never owned a dog before—who wants to clean up dog shit on the streets? Or take it out for a walk in the rain? But out here it seemed the dog took care of herself. And she slept on the porch, so no one had to take her out. But his distrust was focused on the fact that she acted like a kid, just like Flora's two kids, running, romping, having a good time. Not like a watchdog should act, he decided. Mikey held her while Janie went off to hide, and Sadie tore out after her when he let go and found her in two shakes. They tossed a stick and she brought that back. She played Frisbee like a pro. So, Al brooded, good-time Sadie, what good was a dog like that, one that loved everybody? And she did, it seemed, love everybody. She laughed at the kids and smiled at Flora and Bobby, and treated Sylvie like she was a Marine sergeant and Sadie a recruit in love with being a Marine.

On Monday morning when Lois appeared on the swinging bridge Sadie stiffened and growled, although she couldn't see that far, or hear either, Al was sure. He and Sylvie went with the dog to the edge of the property where Lois was just about to step onto their land, and Sadie was shivering, growling. She began to bark and Lois stopped in her tracks. It was the first time Al had heard the dog bark, he realized with approval. Not that she should bark at Lois, but it was a good sign.

Sylvie had to introduce Sadie to Lois, real polite and formal like; the dog sniffed Lois all over, and then wagged her rear end in approval. It was embarrassing to Al the way Sadie stuck her nose in Lois's crotch, but she seemed to have to do that; she had done it to everyone she was introduced to so far.

"She's beautiful!" Lois said when the inspection ended, and she had been accepted. "Has she been in swimming yet? Retrievers usually love the water."

Al hadn't even thought of letting the dog in the lake. But that afternoon he and Sylvie went down and he tossed in a stick, and Sadie tore out after it as if she were half fish. By then he was sold on her, anyway, but it was another good sign. If one of the kids ever fell in, or anything like that happened . . . he thought vaguely, not quite ready to admit aloud that he sort of liked the silly animal for herself. She had set up a hell of a ruckus when the carpenters came to work on the mill, and after they left she went over every inch of the ground they had walked on, everything they had touched. She repeated this the next morning, and the next; they had not introduced her to the carpenters whom she continued to treat as trespassers. But she met Lois at the bridge and smiled, waving her plumy tail, and escorted her to the break in the fence that separated this property from the experimental farmlands. She did not step through with Lois and she refused to go on the swinging bridge unless under direct order by Sylvie.

Now, when Al and Sylvie went to bed, they didn't lie in rigid silence, holding their breath, listening. Sadie was on the job.

On Saturday Flora, Bobby, and the kids came back, and the kids wore themselves and Sadie out again, as they had done before. When the kids had gone on to bed, Al shook his head at the dog, lying in exhaustion on the porch. "That's how it's gonna be," he said. She raised her head and smiled at him. She thumped her tail on the porch once, sighed, and made no further attempt to be polite.

Al was the first one up the next morning. He went to the kitchen to start coffee, and glanced out for Sadie. She would take food from him now, and he liked to feed her, but she wasn't on the porch. He walked out and whistled, expecting her to come bounding in from the fringe of woods, or up from the mill, overjoyed to see one of her people, the way she was every morning. He had disturbed the early birds, silenced them; gradually their twitterings resumed, and there was a slight breeze in the treetops, but no other sound. He walked a few feet from the house and whistled once more, a little louder; when she did not appear, he started to walk toward the mill and the water, vaguely concerned that she might have fallen in, even though he had seen her swimming like a fish before.

A lot of trees had grown up between the house and mill, not as thick as the real woods, but enough so that he could not see the mill until he stepped out from the thicket, and then he came to a full stop.

"Sadie? Sadie!" He ran to the dog, lying on her side in high grasses. "Jaysus!" he whispered hoarsely and knelt on the ground near her, not close enough to touch her. "Oh, Jaysus," he said again, and it sounded like a whimper.

3

The problem was that when she was gone the house changed, Charlie Meiklejohn brooded, sitting at the kitchen table, scowling at the rain that continued without letup. It had rained yesterday, too. Too damn much. It was a comfortable house, if a bit untidy at the moment because he believed in carrying out papers and stuff only when they began to get in the way, and that point hadn't been reached yet. This was Wednesday, and Sunday's paper was still there; soon it would be time. But this little bit of clutter wasn't the real difference, he knew, even though when she was home, clutter seemed to disappear without anyone's doing anything about it. When she was around, he would see something and think vaguely that next time through he would pick it up, but next time through, more often than not, it was gone.

For one thing, he thought then, pursuing the cause of the difference in the house, it felt too big and too empty, and when she was home it never occurred to him that the house might be too big. Three rooms upstairs, one of them her office with her computer now nicely covered, everything in place, awaiting her return. Their bedroom, and their grown daughter's bedroom that was now their official guest room. His office on the first floor was a jumble of miscellaneous stuff. He kept the door closed, he said to keep the cats out. There was the living room, where they spent most of their evenings, a dining room, and a tiny room that they never could figure out what to call. They had put the television in there. Earlier that day he had made a tour of the house, wondering that he never had noticed before that there was too much room. And that was when the mystery had started. When she was home the house was exactly the right size, and with her gone, it was ten times too big.

There were dishes in the sink from last night, and from that morning, and eventually he would rouse himself and cram them all into the dishwasher, but not yet. There was this mystery to solve: What was it that vanished with her gone? How could her presence fill an entire house no matter where she was physically within it? The house was the same. The yard beyond the sliding glass door, with flowers in bloom, the patio awash at the moment, but not changed, everything tangible exactly the same as usual, but everything different anyway.

Even the cats were different. Brutus was not speaking to him at all, disdainful of any attempt at friendliness, accepting food grudgingly, without appreciation, and spending far too much time simply staring at Charlie through slitted eyes that could turn into devil's eyes altogether too easily. That cat was too damn smart for his own good, Charlie brooded. He had come to them in New York, nearly full grown, and street-smart; he had looked them over, looked over their apartment, examined the two other cats and found them acceptable, and moved in. But he had never fully forgiven them for retiring out to the country, not yet, probably never would. And he blamed Charlie; that was obvious in the way he stared at him through devil eyes. Ashcan, the cowardly gray-suited one, kept prowling about, as if Constance might be found under the sofa, or behind the drapes. And Candy, the big-mouth, had gone into her invalid act. She did it very well, dragged herself from room to room, lay without motion for hours at a time, and looked at him with her butterscotch eyes in a way that suggested death was near, and it was his fault.

It wasn't perfume, he knew, returning to the mystery; she seldom wore any. But she had a fragrance that came from her shampoo, her own physical body, whatever. That was part of it. Not enough. Her soft steps throughout the house, the sound of the sliding door opening and closing, her low murmurs to the cats. Another part of it. Not enough yet. A few days ago Mrs. Grayson had come to do her weekly cleaning and she had talked to the cats, and had even elicited a response from them, and that hadn't been enough to fill the void. So it wasn't just another person, another voice that was lacking.

He missed her in bed, of course, the warmth of her body next to his, the rhythm of her breathing, a sigh now and then, and that wasn't enough either. After all, he didn't spend all day every day in bed with her. Not anymore anyway. A grin softened his face, smoothed out deep lines, as he thought of the various times they had tried to do just that. Stop, he told himself. That made it worse.

Charlie had been a New York City fireman, an inspector, a city detective, altogether more than twenty-five years, and he had seen enough, had done enough to put those lines on his face. It was as if when Constance was home, a curtain was drawn somewhere in him that screened out all those lines, those many years, and with her gone, the curtain was removed, his past was written clearly on the landscape of his face. Although he had taken an early retirement, it became evident when he was alone that it had not been too early. He was not generally introspective, and never gazed on his own face except during the act of shaving; he had no way of realizing the change he was fretting about was internal, and he continued to try to find a cause for the palpable difference in the surroundings of the house.

When the phone finally rang he scooped it up before the first peal ended. "Do you believe in auras?" he asked.

"Sometimes. Charlie, are you drunk?"

"Nope. How is she? How's your dad? How are you?"

"She's coming along fine. We get to spring her on Friday. Dad's going crazy. And I'm lonely. How are you?"

"Swinging from the chandelier. The Mitchums are so concerned, they've taken to sending the boys over to keep an eye on me."

She chuckled. Now that the crisis with her mother was over —gallbladder surgery that had gone sour—she could laugh again, but for several days the strain in her voice had made him feel as if he were choking. Another mystery. They chatted; he read her a letter from an associate of hers who wanted permission to reprint one of her papers in psychology; she reported on her father's eccentricities in restaurants—nothing with sauce because you never knew what they were trying to hide—and they both laughed. When he hung up, the house felt emptier than ever.

Candy was regarding him with tragic eyes. "All right," he snarled at her. "She didn't ask to speak to you. So there."

He started to load the dishwasher then and was still at it when Pete Mitchum tapped on the back door. With him was another boy. Young man, Charlie corrected himself, as he crossed the kitchen to admit them. Pete was about twenty and his friend looked a year or so older. Dressed in dripping ponchos with hoods, rubber boots, they looked like Christopher Robin twice.

"Hi, Mr. Meiklejohn. This is David Levy, the guy I told you about."

Charlie motioned toward a chair under the wide overhang out of the rain, and they deposited their wet gear and then came on inside.

David Levy was very tall and angular, with a lot of thick black hair, and blue eyes. "Thanks for seeing me, sir," he said as they shook hands. His grip was surprisingly strong.

Sir, Charlie thought with a feeling of resignation. He asked if they wanted a beer, a Coke, coffee, which he was at that very moment going to make, and motioned them toward the table. They both refused his hospitality, and he abandoned the coffee project and joined them.

"Before I ask you anything," David said awkwardly, "I should find out your consultation fees, I guess."

Pete looked mortified and Charlie said seriously, "Advice is cheap, so cheap that it's held to have no value, and no one takes it anyway. For advice, no fees."

Pete had already told him a long story about how he had met David, through a network of mutual college friends that seemed to stretch out over the country. His friend, he had said, needed some professional advice, would it be okay to bring him over? Since at the time Charlie had been at the Mitchums' dining room table eating chicken and dumplings, it would have been churlish to refuse. Now he regarded the young man patiently and waited.

"What I need to know is how do you go about proving that someone poisoned a dog. I mean, if it's something you really know happened, then what?"

"Your dog?"

"No sir. You see, I work at the university experimental farm over at Spender's Ferry, about forty-five minutes from here, I guess. And my friend Rosa's parents won the lottery last year and they were looking for a place in the country and I told them about the old mill over there. . . ." He took a deep breath.

"Take it easy," Charlie said. "There's no rush. Rosa's folks won the lottery. She's your girlfriend?"

David blushed. "That's what my dad asked. It's not like that, sir. I mean, she's female and she's my friend. I think men and women are friends more than they used to be maybe. Anyway, her parents won the lottery. And they decided to move out of the city. They've always lived in the Bronx, I guess. And because I'm doing graduate work at the farm, I knew about the mill. They were looking for a big place. Anyway, they liked it and bought it, and Mrs. Zukal bought this dog, a beautiful golden retriever, because she was afraid out in the country. And someone poisoned the dog. We all know it was poisoned. But now what?"

"Did they send you? Mrs. Zukal and her husband? Why didn't they come themselves?"

David shook his head. "No one sent me. They don't even know I came here. I guess I feel sort of responsible because I found the place and suggested they look at it, and all."

Charlie grunted and stood up. "I'm going to make that coffee. You guys sure you don't want something? Cold drinks are in the fridge. Help yourselves."

Pete helped himself. "He just drinks juice or herb teas," he said, opening a can of Coke.

"Sorry," Charlie said. When *she* was home there was always freshly squeezed juice, but he never thought of it. He busied himself with coffee and then returned to the table. "Okay," he said. "There is a problem with proof. Dogs get into things. You said a mill. Maybe rat poison, something like that. Maybe a neighbor put out something that he ate and died from. Did a vet look at him?"

David shook his head. "Her," he said. "Her name was Sadie. They found her the next morning, I guess. She was good and dead. No point in the vet. Mr. Zukal buried her."

"Then you don't really know what she died from."

David shook his head even harder, a stubborn look settling in on his face. "One day she was playing, chasing a ball, in great shape, the next morning she's dead. We know. And the mill hasn't been used in half a century maybe. There aren't any rats there. Sadie was trained in a special school to be a watchdog. She wouldn't go chasing around the neighborhood. She had to be poisoned on her own property by someone. I just don't know what to do about it. How to go about finding out anything."

"Okay," Charlie said briskly. "You haven't ruled out accident, you know. She could have caught a diseased animal, or a poisoned animal. A squirrel or a rabbit, even a rat. They're everywhere even if you don't see them. And no doubt dogs are susceptible to a host of things you also don't know anything about. So the first thing you'd have to do is find out what killed her. That means exhumation. You would take her remains to a veterinary pathologist and have tests run. Then you have something to start with. Right now all you have is suspicion. Is there any one person you suspect?"

David had turned very pale at the word *exhumation.* Charlie pretended not to notice.

"I can't think of anyone, or a reason," David said faintly.

"Right. So, after you learn the actual cause of death, if it was poison, you would call the county animal control office and ask if other poisonings have been reported. If there have been, they might take over at that point. If not, you're still on your own. But the first step, in any event, is to find out the cause of death."

"If I find out that she was really poisoned, will the sheriff investigate? Or the animal control office? Will anyone?"

Charlie felt a stab of pity for this earnest young man burdened with his load of guilt and responsibility. "Maybe," he said slowly. "But, David, I won't kid you, unless there have been other cases, and unless livestock gets involved, probably not much. Someone might ask the Zukals a few questions. But it's almost impossible to prove something like this unless you actually catch the person in the act, and even then, chances are good they'll get off with a slap on the wrist. And the animal pathologist will charge, you know. It will be expensive, and you'll run up against indifference. Just the way it goes."

"That's really shitty!" Pete protested.

"Yep."

David stood up then and held out his hand. "Thanks, Mr. Meiklejohn. I appreciate your talking to me about this."

Charlie wanted to pat him on the head, but he knew that would not be welcome, and besides, he would have had to get on a chair. Instead, he shook hands with David, and then stood

in the doorway watching the boys walk across the backyard in
the rain. So young they probably would splash in every puddle
they came to, getting a sampling of how truly shitty the world
could be. They would climb the fence, walk through the pasture
that separated the Mitchum house from his house, and that
would be that, he thought, almost wishing he had told Pete no,
not to bring his young friend around. The advice he had given
had left a bad taste in his mouth.

Saturday morning Lois was surveying the greenhouse that held
her cloned trees. Some of them were outgrowing the bench
already and would have to be moved onto a lower one, and
that was going to be a mess, she knew. It would take several
hours to do them all, and meanwhile she had the metabolism
studies to work on, and the measurements. . . . She glanced at
her watch again. At ten-thirty she walked outside and started
for David's apartment, but then she saw Tom Hopewell emerging from his corn rows, and she slowed down.

He waved at her and she waved back, glanced toward the
apartments, and waved again.

"Are you busy right now?" she called.

"Sure. But I can stop. Why?"

Sometimes she felt a bit of confusion with Tom, but she had
no idea of what caused it. He was a year or two younger than
she was, and he dressed like a ragged child, and like a child he
could grin so disarmingly that people often forgot that he was
a truly fine botanist with a Ph.D. There was something unfathomable about him, about the way he looked at her, the way he
could stop what he was doing just like that. He looked and
acted like a child playing at being a scientist, his hair too long,
knees out of his jeans, dirty hands.

"It's probably nothing," she said as he drew near. "David's
so late, and I need him. I was going to go wake him up, but it
might embarrass him if I walk in. Would you mind?"

"Oh, it might embarrass him indeed," he said gravely, but his
eyes were dancing with amusement, and she didn't know what
he found funny.

They walked on to the apartments together, and she knocked
on the door. There was no response from inside. Tom entered

and continued on through to the bedroom; Lois stood in the doorway uncomfortably, keeping her gaze averted.

"Oh my God!" Tom said in a voice that was low but carried to where she was standing. "Lois, there's been an accident or something."

She ran into the apartment, into the bedroom, where he was standing ashen-faced, staring at the bed, at the figure that had covers drawn up to his chin. She reached past Tom and touched David's cheek, then jerked her hand back. She heard a moaning sound and did not realize she was making it until she found herself standing at the sink, hanging onto it as if to keep from falling, and behind her she could hear Tom on the telephone.

The day before, Friday, Charlie had gone to the city to give a deposition in an arson case he had worked on, and he got talked into a poker game that lasted too long, but made him feel filthy rich afterward. And because on Monday Constance was due, he stayed in town to meet her at Kennedy, and then they celebrated by staying the rest of the week and seeing two Broadway shows. By the time they returned home, the weather had changed dramatically, into summertime, and the house was filled with her presence and once more was exactly the right size.

He had forgotten David Levy and his problem and never would have thought of him again, except in a passing moment, if Constance had not come looking for him in the basement a few days later.

"Charlie, there's a man to see you. A Mr. Levy. He's pretty upset."

"David?" Charlie put down the spinning reel he was trying to fix. It kept snarling the line, and for the life of him, he thought moodily, he couldn't see why. He wiped his hands and followed Constance back upstairs. It was a pleasure to watch her move. She was long and lithe and moved like a dancer. When they emerged from the dimness of the stairs into the sunlight in the kitchen, he got another jolt of pleasure in seeing her hair gleam when she moved through the brilliant light. Only God knew how much of that color was the original color, how much was because the original color had started to turn into spun platinum. His own black crinkly hair was unmistakably turning gray, but she was keeping her secrets.

She preceded him into the living room, where a tall, gangly man stood. "This is Mr. Levy," Constance said.

Charlie felt bewilderment. Not David. He started to extend his hand, but the other man stepped backward, swaying. He looked very ill, cadaverous almost, with sunken eyes and a pallor that suggested confinement, hospital, sickbed. Deathbed.

"My boy came to you for help," Levy said heavily. "He did what you told him and they killed him. I just wanted to look at you. See you. What kind of a man are you to turn him away like that? Send a boy off to get killed."

4

Charlie watched in icy shock while Constance took Mr. Levy by the arm and maneuvered him to the kitchen table with a cup of coffee before him. She said little as she managed him, and what she said made no difference; Levy allowed himself to be led and now he picked up the cup and sipped from it.

"Tell us what happened," Constance said gently when he put the cup down again.

In his mind's eye Charlie was seeing the lanky boy unfold himself from that same chair; he remembered his own impulse to pat him on the head, remembered watching the two boys trudge out into the rain toward the Mitchum house.

"They called me," Levy said. "They said there's been an accident. They said they had to do an autopsy. They released him to me and I took him home and buried him. Today they said the investigation is over, accidental death. They said he used drugs and overdosed."

He looked into Charlie's face across the table from him and shook his head. "My boy didn't do drugs," he said with finality.

"No, he didn't," Charlie said. "Mr. Levy, do you know why he came to see me? Did he tell you?"

Constance would have taken it slower, he knew; she would have gentled Levy some more, got him to relax some more, but Constance hadn't met that string bean of a boy. Maybe she didn't realize that Levy was a dying man. Constance didn't have the icy rage that filled Charlie at that moment.

"He told me in a letter," Levy said after a hesitation. He pushed his cup back.

"Hold it a minute, Mr. Levy," Charlie said, his voice suddenly harsh. "Just hold it a minute. He came here for advice and I gave it to him. Did he tell you if he followed up on it, what he learned?"

Levy faced Constance, directed his words at her. "He couldn't get anyone to help him, the sheriff, the animal agency, no one. Your husband. I told the sheriff about the dog, what Davy was doing, and he said Mr. Meiklejohn was high-priced and wouldn't get involved with a dead dog, that no one in his right mind would get involved with it. He said Davy took the drugs himself and that's that. He didn't even read the letters. Pretended to, that's all. He already had his mind fixed on what he thought he knew."

Constance was totally bewildered by all this information. Charlie had not told her about David Levy or a dead dog. And this poor man, she thought, had not fully accepted the death of his son, no matter if there had been a funeral; he still had hope behind the desperation in his eyes. And he was so very ill. The skin was drawn tight over the bones of his face; his eyes were bloodshot, sunken, the rims red. There was a tremor in his hands.

"Mr. Levy," she said, "did your son find out who killed the dog? Did he tell you?"

He sighed deeply and shook his head. "I think he knew, but he didn't say who it was in the letter. I'd better be going. It's a long drive."

His pain was so wrenching that Constance wanted to hold him and soothe him, and she knew that would be absolutely wrong. Not now. "Mr. Levy," she said, and Charlie heard her professional voice, the crisp manner and tone of a trained psychologist, "you made an accusation about Charlie that we have to air. When did your son die?"

"Saturday, the twentieth, in the morning. Today they said the investigation was over. I came to get the stuff they were holding and to show them his letters. No use."

Charlie's eyes were narrowed in thought. He shook his head. "He couldn't have followed my advice already. Listen, let me tell you what we talked about the day he was here. That was on Wednesday, late afternoon. He said the Zukals' dog had been poisoned and I said he would need to exhume it and have tissue examination tests to find the cause of death. There's no way on earth he could have done that and got the results in two or three days, by Saturday."

"Just like the sheriff," Levy said with weary bitterness. "You're all alike." He started to get up.

"Just sit still, will you?" Charlie snapped at him. "Maybe there's a connection and maybe not. I sure as hell don't know at this point and apparently neither do you. But, Mr. Levy, neither do I believe your son took drugs of any kind. Now let's talk about it."

"Why?" Levy asked. "I can't afford to pay you anything."

"For crying out loud! Do you have a buck? Just haul it out and put it on the table."

Levy looked from him to Constance, and then withdrew a shabby wallet and fished out a dollar bill.

"You're paid in full. Now, just answer a few questions, will you? Honey, is there more coffee?"

Two hours later they walked to his car with him, a twelve-year-old Ford. Home for him was a veterans' hospital in New Jersey, a long drive.

At the car he hesitated briefly, then held out his hand to Charlie. "Let me know what you find out," he said, and got in and started the engine; he looked almost surprised when it turned over. "All he wanted to do was help feed the world," he said softly, looking straight ahead, his cavernous face twisted. He shook himself and engaged the gears and left without speaking to either of them again.

"We'd better find out something pretty damn fast or he won't be around to hear it," Charlie said as the old car backed out to the road. "Let's go read those letters."

In the kitchen once more, Constance gazed at the dollar bill that had been pushed aside to make room for the letters that Levy had produced. He was dying, he had said candidly; he and his son had pretended that death could be put off until David was through with school. And now he could go ahead and die, Constance thought, but she knew that he would try to hold on until he knew the truth.

She began to arrange the letters chronologically. David had been a faithful correspondent, had written at least once a week; there were a lot of letters to go through. Levy had also left a box of personal effects that the sheriff had released to him— snapshots, a few magazines, a calendar, catalogs, a grocery list, bills, a checkbook, and several bank statements. It was a pitiful assortment.

"Look at this," Charlie said a few minutes later in a grumpy voice. "Three pages about the party at Wollander's place, a blow-by-blow account of a cookout! And half a page with one line about the goddamn dog, the last letter he wrote."

Constance nodded.

Charlie read it in disgust: *Remember Sadie, the dog that got killed, I think I'm onto something about that. More next time.*

He tossed the letter down on top of the others and stood up. "Want to go for a ride in the country?"

"Where to?" she asked. "Spender's Ferry?"

He grinned at her. "Why ask anything ever? Just say the answers. Works just the same."

"Charlie." She began to gather up the letters. Watching her hands, she said, "If a boy came through that door right now and asked what to do about a possible dog murder, you'd tell him just about what you told David Levy, and you know it."

"Yeah," he said. "I know that. Somehow it doesn't seem to help much. And, like the sheriff said, maybe there's no connection."

"The sheriff must be Greg Dolman," Constance said a few minutes later in the Volvo, drawing up a memory of the sheriff. Middle-aged, paunchy, amiable, good politician, and he did not want trouble. That was how he put it, he didn't want trouble, kept a clean county. At one time, it was said, he also had run a speed trap that had netted someone a lot of money that never seemed to show up on the books. The next election his vote had been bigger than ever; his constituents understood the value of free enterprise and approved. But someone had put a stop to that, without publicity, without scandal; it just stopped.

Having sorted him out in her mind, Constance began to regard the passing scenery with great pleasure. God must have been having a very fine day when he invented June, she thought. Today the sun was warm, without the cruel heat that could come later in the season; the leaves were at their brightest, most tender stage, flowers abounded, and even the traffic seemed manageable, civilized and polite.

They drove through Spender's Ferry slowly. Like most New York villages, it had been discovered by tourists, and it played up its picturesque appearance. A grocery store with a boardwalk in front, and a mammoth parking lot behind it; three antique shops, one with a sign that said: CUSTOM-MADE ANTIQUES. A gift shop. A church with a white steeple and a golden bell. Redbrick elementary school, a restaurant that probably was very good, housed in a beautifully maintained Victorian three-story house—it had a sign that said only HAZELTINE'S.

"Hokey," Charlie said.

"But nice."

"You betcha. Pays to look nice."

She sighed as the fleeting romanticism disappeared. Beyond the village, working farms stretched out on the right, fields and fields of satiny corn six inches high, and on the left the experimental university farm began. It looked very little different from all the other farms they had passed. Then Charlie turned into the driveway of the Zukals' house.

"Now, this is nice," Charlie murmured when he drew up to the house and stopped. He opened his door and got out as Constance got out on her side, and they both stood very still.

A woman's raucous voice was screeching; a man's equally raucous voice was yelling at the same time. Just then Sylvie and Al appeared from the trees behind the house. She had a green kerchief tied on her head; wisps of red hair had escaped and clung to her sweaty brow. She was dressed in baggy pants and a man's shirt. He was in jeans that rode too low on his ample

belly, and sneakers with shoelaces flying. He had a fringe of
pale hair and a bright red scalp.

"You want they should nail you to the floor? Why doncher
just leave them to their work?"

"You hear anyone saying I'm in the way? You hear that? I
don't hear nothing like—"

They broke it off when they saw Charlie and Constance, and
now the sound of hammering could be heard, and a loud radio.

"You another lousy inspector? Go inspect already! Watcha
waiting for? Go inspect until your eyes fall out!"

"Mr. Zukal? Mrs. Zukal?"

"Yeah, who you think, Queen of Sheba or something? It's
over there!" Sylvie began to stamp toward the house, muttering
over her shoulder to Al. "And stay out of their way! They don't
need help!"

My God, Charlie realized suddenly, with amazement, he had
missed this! He had known people like this all his life and he
had missed them. Constance had come to his side; he took her
hand and walked forward.

"Hold it, Mrs. Zukal. I want to talk to you about your dog."

Well, he thought, satisfied, as they both froze, he had their
attention. The stillness was short-lived, and one of them was
demanding to know what for, and the other who did he think
he was, and either or both, what did he know about their dog,
and other things that got lost in the tumult. He held his hand
up, shaking his head.

"Let's sit down and talk," he said firmly. "I'm Charlie Meiklejohn, and this is my wife, Constance, and we are not inspectors
of any sort. We are private investigators. Can we talk?"

Sylvie looked them both up and down, and then nodded
toward the house. "But don't you go to the living room," she
snapped at Al. "All that sawdust!"

They went inside the house and stopped at the kitchen. "This
is fine," Charlie said; he pulled out a chair for Constance, another for himself, and sat down at the kitchen table.

The Zukals sat down after hesitating briefly, and Al demanded, "Now, you. Who sent you and what you want here?
And what do you know about our dog?"

"Not enough by half," Charlie said, and went on to describe
David's visit again. "Today his father hired us to look into Da-

vid's death," he finished. "His father doesn't think he ever took drugs in his life."

"See!" Sylvie cried. "See! I told you! That David, he wouldn't even drink beer!"

But Al was scowling fiercely at Charlie. "You sure as hell didn't do David no good."

"I know that," Charlie said quietly. "That's why I'm here now. Will you answer a few questions?"

Sylvie yanked the kerchief from her head and ran her fingers through her red hair until it looked like the hair of the bride of Frankenstein. "You axe, then we see," she said.

"Yeah, just axe. No promises," Al said.

"Right. First. Did David actually dig up the dog?"

"Nope. Didn't even know he was thinking about it. Never said a word."

Sylvie contradicted him instantly. "He nearly cried when I told him. He would go stand by the grave and just look. You knew what he was thinking, all right. It hurt him. He was such a good boy. Rosa should have seen it, that he was such a good boy."

Charlie asked where the dog had come from, and was rewarded with an avalanche of information. He let them both talk without interruption.

"Brenda Ryan's kennels over by Albany. Me and Flora, she's our girl, me and Flora and the kids took the wagon and went over. I thought it might need lots of room in the car, you know, chains and stuff like that, but she was like a puppy, after Brenda introduced us, I mean. Introduced us like she was a person. Sadie, this is Sylvie, and this is Flora, and this is Mike and this is Janie. Just like that, and the dog smelled us, and then began to wag her whole rear end."

"And when they got her home, we had to take her all around the place and let her pee now and then, and smell the trees," Al chimed in. "She had to do that, you know, to find out where she lived. And if we wanted her to be nice to people, we had to do like Brenda done and go, Sadie, this is David, or Sadie, this is Lois. Don't do no good to put it any other way. I mean, you can't just go meet the gang or nothing."

"Brenda Ryan weighs three hundred and forty pounds," Sylvie said suddenly, in awe.

"Jaysus Crackers! What difference does that make? You told me that a hundred times already. Who cares?"

Sylvie turned to Constance. "I just axed her right out. That's the way. People don't care if you just go ahead and axe instead of beating the bush like. She said lady dogs are even better than boy dogs to guard things. They take their responsibility seriouser or something. I thought it would be one of those great big ugly black dogs like on television all the time, you know, all big teeth and hair like painted on. But Sadie was real pretty, and she liked to play—"

"Sylvie, who cares if she was pretty! Let the man axe his questions, will you?"

Constance glanced at Charlie, who looked absolutely at ease and relaxed, as well he might, she thought. This was going to take the rest of the day.

Slowly he drew the story out of them. Sylvie had brought the dog home and for the next few days they had felt secure, well guarded, and then the dog died. They had it one week.

"But dogs don't just die any more than people do," Charlie murmured at that point. "They die of something."

Al and Sylvie exchanged uneasy glances.

"Who did you introduce the dog to during those days?"

"David, of course. He was in and out all the time, just like he was at home like. And Lois. Mrs. Wollander. She cuts through the property walking to work and home."

"So on Sunday morning you found the dog dead?"

"Yeah. Stiff already. Puked a lot first, then kicked."

"Were you here Saturday night?"

"Sure. And Bobby and Flora and the kids. They come on weekends, but as soon as school's out, they're moving in with us. Anyways, they was here. Kids played with Sadie right up to bedtime. Crazy about her. Real smart, she was. They'd hide things and she'd go find them. Real smart."

"Where did Sadie sleep?"

"On the porch most nights. But she'd be up prowling around all hours. Investigating noises, I guess."

"And did she eat outside, too?"

"Yeah. On the porch . . ." Al's voice faded out and Sylvie said, "But we found her dish way over by the mill. Remember, Al?"

"Yeah, just thinking about that. But the kids was hiding it on her. They must have left it there." The certainty that had been in his voice was gone, however.

Charlie was feeling more and more unhappy as they talked, and when Al asked if he wanted a beer he nodded gratefully. Al brought one for Constance, too, and, bless her, Charlie thought with appreciation, she pretended she wanted it.

"We'll have to exhume the dog's remains," Charlie said a few minutes later. "Can you tell me anything about David? He didn't tell you he was coming to see me, I know. I asked. But something made him decide to poke around himself. Any idea what it was?"

Al began to pick at the beer can as if the painted-on label might be peeled off, and Sylvie began to pat her hair down, suddenly aware that it was unkempt.

Charlie waited. If there was anything people like the Zukals could not stand, he knew very well, it was silence.

"It was the insurance," Sylvie muttered. "Set him right off."

"I'll be damned if it was. It was them letters. You had to go show him, didn't you?"

From then on Charlie listened. The Zukals had met David when he and their daughter had attended a special science-oriented high school in the Bronx. The kids had become good friends and David had spent a lot of time at their apartment. His father was ill even then, in and out of the hospital, and David was lonely. They had treated him like a son, and maybe that was the problem with him and Rosa, Sylvie added thoughtfully. Anyway, they didn't try to hide things from him. When they were broke he knew it, and when they struck gold, he knew that, and when the letters came, it had seemed natural for Sylvie to show him. Gently Charlie drew her back to the letters.

"Yeah," Sylvie said heavily. "They don't want our kind here, you know. Don't much blame them, but here we are. And here we stay, like it or not. Anyways, Monday, after Sadie died a letter came, nasty like. *Go back where you belong.* That's all. Looked like a kid must have wrote it. And the next Monday another one came. *What does it take? A bullet? Would that penetrate your thick skulls?* David seen that one and I told him about the first one."

"And two days later he came to see me," Charlie said. "Did

you keep the letters?" They both shook their heads. "Have there been any more?" They shook their heads again. "Okay. What about insurance?"

"Nothing to it," Al said. "Sylvie got spooked, is all. See, Stanley, Wollander's son-in-law, he tells me I should get more insurance just as soon as the next check comes, seventh of July. He's talking a big policy, something no-load, or front-load, or something like that. I can borrow on it even, and Sylvie tells David, and he goes maybe it's not so safe out here for us. But, hell, wouldn't do nobody around here no good if I kicked."

"Someone might think Sylvie wouldn't hang around out here if you were gone," Charlie mused.

"Well, someone's got another think coming," Sylvie screeched.

And now Al told in great detail how his two sons-in-law were geniuses. "See, we get the big check and first thing Sylvie tops it right off, ten percent by Jaysus, to a school for girls."

"Well, there's boys' camps everywhere, homes for troubling boys, special schools, and girls get the short stick every time. Sure I did, and next time another ten percent."

"Yeah, yeah. We been all over that. Okay by me. See, we got these four girls—"

"And whose fault is that, Mister? You got the special doohickey that makes a boy baby, not me. Rosa told me all about that," she explained to Constance. "She's a scientist. Or will be someday. Real smart, Rosa."

"Jaysus! Will you let me finish! Anyways, we was going to spread the dough around, you know, let the girls and their husbands have some, and they all got together and talked it over, and they go, not the way to do it. If we really want to help, we'd help Bobby and Harmon start a business, this year and next, and then help Les and Nola get a bait shop they been wanting, and like that. Seeds, they call it. So Bobby and Harmon—Bobby can make things out of wood, really good stuff, chairs and tables, stuff like that, and Harmon can do business, sell stuff. They make a good pair. They're going to have the mill for a shop. Handmade furniture. Won't make a fortune right off, but it'll grow. Bobby comes out and looks it over and he goes, you know, Pop, that mill can make electricity, all we'll ever need, and more, and the electric company has to buy all the leftovers. We'll break even right off the bat, and that means profits faster than anyone thought at first." Al looked puzzled, then shrugged. "You can have leftover electricity? I don't know about that. But . . ."

Now Sylvie chimed in and her voice overrode his. "That's what we mean, you get it? We bought this place, and they can send inspectors and zoners and whatnot, but we're here. And we're here for good."

Charlie asked a few more questions and got more answer than he wanted each time. They had not seen David after his visit to Charlie's house. What with the kids all over the place Saturday and Lois working David's butt off over at the farm, Al said, it hadn't struck them as unusual not to see him. And she's working her butt off, too, remember, Sylvie put in, and they went on from there.

They hadn't even known anything was wrong until Lois had come to tell them. When David didn't show up on time, even though it was Saturday, she had gone to his place looking for him, and she had found him dead. She was real shook up by it, Al said soberly. It hurt her real bad.

"So she came to tell you?"

"Yeah. She thought it wasn't right for us to find out in the village, or something like that."

"Did you believe he overdosed himself?"

Al and Sylvie looked at each other, and she said in a low voice, so low it was hard to catch her words. "You know, we're from the Bronx. We wanted out, want to get our kids and our grandkids out of there. Sure, we know it's not everyone shooting up, snorting, messing themselves up, but who's to say who is and who ain't anymore? I didn't believe it about David but I don't know. We seen too much. Been fooled too many times. You know what I mean?"

Charlie nodded. He knew.

He asked Al to show him where they had found the food dish, and where the dog was buried, and for permission to dig it up for tests. And when Al asked him with incredulity if he was going to dig it up himself, Charlie shuddered. He said he would send someone. They all went out to walk over the grounds, down to the bridge, around the mill, to the mound that was Sadie's grave, to the spot where Al had found her dead.

Al and Sylvie talked over the noise of the carpenters in the mill with their radio turned on at maximum volume. Lois was going to help choose which trees had to come out. Al was going to put in a little beach at this end of the lake. Here was the place in the fence that Lois used every day to go to work. They planned to put in a real gate and fence off the bridge, because of the kids. . . .

Charlie paused at the break in the fence and looked back at the mill, several hundred yards away; the loud music was dimmed by distance but still too clearly audible. A path led from this point, skirted the lake side of the mill and continued to the swinging bridge. No comparable path led to the house through the tangle that many years of neglect had produced. Beyond the break in the fence the path was even more sharply defined, three stone steps down, then a hard-packed trail.

He glanced at Constance and nodded toward the path. "Let's see a bit more of it."

"It's like a sidewalk," Al said behind them as they started down.

And it was, almost. It led them through a few feet of brambles and low sumac and suddenly they were in a grove. The ground still sloped, but more gently here, hardly noticeable as they walked slowly. On the left the trees were all about twenty-five feet tall, straight up to a canopy, but on the right the trees had been allowed to keep their lower branches and they made a thicket that would be all but impenetrable. They had been planted precisely, meticulously, and looked totally artificial in almost military ranks. Every tree was tagged.

Constance looked at the experimental trees with a sense of unease. No grasses, no vines, nothing grew under them, but more, the trees themselves looked alien, foreign to her. Not like oaks or maples or conifers, these had smooth, pale tan trunks, leaves too shiny and thick, and many small round nuts no bigger yet than peas, and they also looked alien. Orchards were always arranged carefully, she reminded herself; she had planted their apple trees according to the book, so many feet from one to another, but every one was different from the next, gnarly, unique, with the differences more apparent year by year. And these were all the same.

They came to a different section, smaller trees, obviously

younger, identical. . . . Abruptly Charlie stopped, shaking his head. The path continued but it wound here and there and the end was not in sight. Neither was the lake. Stippled sunlight, rows and rows of identical trees, and finally silence; they had gone far enough to lose the rock music.

"How far to the farm?" he asked Al over his shoulder.

"Three, four hundred more feet of trees and the buildings start. It's all like this, all the way. Up at the fence you coulda turned toward the lake, and that's different, right down to the water, but let me tell you, I sure don't like this way."

"Yeah. See your point," Charlie said, and turned back. "Is this the way David came, through the trees?"

Al nodded. "Closest this way. Lois uses the path every day. Lots of people seem to, why it's all packed down."

They returned to the mill property and the noise of hammering and music. They walked to the bridge and surveyed it and the dam.

"That dog, Sadie? She wouldn't set foot on the bridge," Al said. "Can't blame her none. Bridges ain't supposed to move when you do, way I see it."

Silently Charlie agreed. Finally, he and Constance got in their car to leave and he felt that he had missed whatever it was he had been looking for.

"You think the dog was poisoned, don't you? Deliberately," Constance said as he backed and turned around, headed out to the road. "But, Charlie, a dog trained the way that one apparently was wouldn't take food from a stranger, would it? And how could anyone have gone in that far? The dish was at least three hundred yards from the edge of the property."

He grunted. "On my list," he said. "Both items. Tomorrow we ask Brenda Ryan a thing or two. And not how much she weighs."

After a moment, Constance murmured, "Lois Wharton Wollander is the only one outside the family who was introduced to the dog, apparently. And David, of course. And David worked for her."

"It'll be a busy day tomorrow," Charlie said, slowing down at Spender's Ferry. "Brenda Ryan, Lois W. W., Sheriff Greg Dolman. A busy day. Let's check out Hazeltine's." He drew up before the Victorian mansion that housed the restaurant and turned off the engine. "You know who Wollander is?"

"Vaguely familiar name. Tell me."

"What Al would call a crowner. A kingmaker. A man who knows which closets hold skeletons, and how to unlock the doors to get at them, and where every body is buried."

"Oh, dear," Constance said. "Al said all those inspectors, zoning people."

"Yep. Someone must have sicced them onto him."

5

That night after dinner in the Wollander house, Warren Wollander said, "Jill, would you mind if we all go to the study for a little talk?"

Lois felt her muscles tighten at his tone of voice. Carefully she placed her napkin on the table and just as carefully she did not look across the table at Jill.

"Let's talk here," Jill said. "What now? I feel like I'm twelve years old again."

"You're not a child," Warren said evenly, "and that's part of the problem. People are talking in the village about your . . . involvement with Sebastian and his group."

"What I do is my own business," Jill said coldly. "I don't give a damn what they're saying in the village. And you never used to."

"Now I do. Mrs. Carlysle tells me you've ordered a special diet for yourself and tonight you barely touched your dinner. Is that at Sebastian's suggestion?"

Jill flung down her napkin and started to jump up, then decided not to, looking intently at her father. She took a deep breath. "Yes. He understands nutrition thoroughly. I am to eat meat sparingly, drink a lot of milk and juice, no alcohol in any form, make sure I have plenty of fresh vegetables and fruits, many of them raw. I am to watch my weight and not gain more than sixteen pounds, and get plenty of exercise."

"My God," Lois said softly. "Jill! That's wonderful!"

Warren looked confused for a moment, then a wide smile spread over his face and he blinked rapidly. He jumped to his feet and took Jill's hands, drew her from her chair, and wrapped his arms around her, held her hard against him. After a moment he pulled back and examined her face; his eyes were bright. "Are you sure? I thought you couldn't . . . Your mother said—"

"She was wrong," Jill said. "That's what the meditation has been all about, why I've practiced and practiced. And it worked. I had to learn to relax, to center myself, become receptive. It worked! That's what Sebastian was trying to explain out here: If you can master yourself, you can do anything."

"Let them talk," her father said then, and laughed and hugged her fiercely again. "Let the bastards talk all they want. When? How are you? Have you seen a doctor yet? Will you stay here until it's time, afterward if you want?" He looked at her closely again. "Stanley doesn't know yet, does he?"

Jill turned helplessly to Lois and shrugged. "I wasn't going to tell anyone for a couple more weeks. It's too soon. But *I* know. Next weekend, when Stanley comes up, I'll tell him, now that it's out anyway. But let me be the one. Promise. Not a word yet."

Lois nodded, smiling. And Warren said, "We should have a toast in champagne. A tiny preliminary celebration."

Jill shook her head. "No alcohol, remember? Don't tempt me. You two go ahead. I want to walk a little bit and then read, and then sleep. I should get as much sleep as I can, too."

She kissed Warren's cheek, nodded to Lois, and started to leave the dining room. At the door she paused, her hand on the knob, her head bowed. She looked like a too-thin adolescent in her long pale skirt and tank top. Her arms were nearly fleshless, her hands sharply boned. She turned to look at them and said softly, "Dad, I'm really sorry. The things I said when Mother died. I'm sorry. I was a little bit crazy. And, Lois, I'm sorry. You've been wonderful to me, and I've been a bitch. I know. I know. I'm sorry. Can we all start over, now, tonight?"

Warren started to move toward her; she waved him back

again and smiled slightly. "No emotional upsets, either. Let's just pretend this is day one and go on from here. Okay?" She gazed at him steadily, then at Lois, and nodded. "Thanks." Then she opened the door and left.

Lois tried to convince herself that the glint in Jill's eyes had been happiness, not triumph.

"Well, let's take a walk, too," Warren said then to Lois. He was beaming, his eyes glistening.

They walked slowly down to the lake, and then along the tiny beach to where there was an immense log. All around them the night sounds were like music not quite in harmony, stopping and starting, speeding and slowing. Cicadas, crickets, tree frogs, the whir of wings—a night hawk or an owl. Overhead, the sky was clear, midnight dark with myriad pinpricks of stars. The air was warm, but cooling fast. It rarely stayed warm throughout the night, not until late July, or even August.

They sat on the log, his arm around her, her cheek on his shoulder. "I'm so happy for her," Lois said. "And for you."

He squeezed her slightly. "She surprised the hell out of me. The last thing I expected her to say. She made me forget altogether the other matter I wanted to bring up with both of you."

Lois started to pull away a bit, but he held her firmly.

"I've been in the spotlight for more years than you've lived," he said after a moment. "I've made enemies. And some damn good friends. But there are enemies. And some of them are nothing but slime."

Lois shivered, whether at the falling temperature or the harshness of his voice she could not have said. The chill entered her and stayed.

"I want you to promise me something," he went on.

"You know I will."

"Maybe you will and maybe you won't. We'll see. Promise me that if you get any poison-pen letters, you'll bring them to me. Will you promise that?"

She jerked away from him with a suddenness he could not counter. She leaped up and backed away from him. "You've had letters like that? About me? Someone's found out, hasn't he? I told you it would happen!"

He stood up and caught her hands and held them tightly. "Not about that. That's what I'm afraid of, that someone will send such a letter to you. I've had filth like this before in the past. Slime can't face a man directly, they act like this, under-handed, mean, nasty, hurting. Today I got a letter about Jill and Sebastian. Last week one about you. Both lies. Meant to de-stroy, to kill something fine and wonderful."

"About me? What about me?" Her mouth had gone dry, and she was shivering uncontrollably.

"It doesn't matter what it said. Believe me, I know how this kind strikes out. They don't want to hurt you, just me. And they know the way to do it is through the two people on earth that I love. They always know how. If he doesn't see a reaction from these first two, I'm afraid he might send you a letter. If he does, will you just hand it to me?" He pulled her to him and held her, and she stared, unresponsive, dry-eyed at the lake. Starlight reflected from its surface in an unquiet shimmer that appeared and vanished with the motion of a breeze. Dead lake, she thought, and felt as dead as she knew the waters were.

"It must be Coughlin," she said finally. "He must have found out what you're doing."

"*Shh*. No jumping to conclusions. It could be a number of people for a number of reasons. Let's leave it at that for now."

She might not have heard. "If it's Coughlin, he won't stop. He'll dig and dig until our grandparents' private lives are on the line."

Warren sighed. "Darling, this has no payoff. You can specu-late all night, all week, for nothing. You'll just lose sleep. Either this slime will keep it up or he won't. Either he'll make de-mands or he won't. Either he'll send you a letter or he won't. I just wanted to prepare you, in case. Now we leave it alone." He released her and stretched. "Speaking about grandparents, how about Jill? My God, I'll be a grandfather! And you a grand-mother!"

They began to stroll and he talked about his strategy for keeping his daughter here, at home, during the pregnancy. "Can't pressure her," he admitted, thinking out loud. "Through Stanley. He'll see that it's for her own good, fresh air, rest, no stress of the city, no muggers. That's the ticket. A little chat with Stanley. No pressure."

She said the appropriate things at the appropriate times, but her thoughts were on Bill Coughlin, who had told Warren to keep out of his way because he had every intention of becoming governor first, and then president when the time was ripe. Over my dead body, Warren had murmured, and Coughlin had nodded. If it takes that, he had said. Two weeks later Warren had started writing his memoirs. But no one could have learned what he was doing, she told herself firmly. No one knew yet except her, and his secretary, and, no doubt, Jill. His secretary, Carla Mercer, had been with Warren for over twenty years; she knew more of his secrets than he could remember, he sometimes said. When Warren began to chuckle, she realized she had heard nothing for a long time, and she realized that her thoughts and worries were spinning in all directions and had become too chaotic to track.

Later that night, unable to sleep for thinking about his grandchild, grandson, he corrected firmly, Warren stood at his darkened window gazing at the land his grandfather had bought so many years ago. A moon sliver shed enough light to see the oak tree that he had built a treehouse in, and had fallen out of. But even without the moon, he knew every inch, where every shrub lay, every rise and fall of his land. And now another generation to maintain it, preserve it, love it.

He always had known that Jill would come home, he thought then. She had spent her first eight years right here, and after those good years, at least half her time had been spent here, absorbing the countryside even if she had not realized it then. She knew this piece of land as well as he did, it had reached out to claim her exactly the way it had claimed him, and her son would know and love it, too.

Suddenly he stiffened. A figure was hurrying up the driveway toward the county road, a woman dressed in a long black coat with a hood, a raincoat from the downstairs closet, he knew. She was out of sight almost instantly, behind the clump of birch trees.

He felt leaden as he turned from the window. His room was too dark to see anything, but he crossed to the door, out into the hallway, where dim lights were always on. Moving like a stone man, he walked through the hall to the wide stairs. Halfway down he realized that he had no slippers on, but he kept going, to the first floor, to the den, which was dark. Without turning on a light he went to the bar and poured a drink from a decanter there; he knew it contained scotch. He added no water. He took the glass across the room and sat in his favorite chair, his father's favorite chair before him, and he drank deeply.

At first he had thought to await her return, confront her, accuse her? Even that, he admitted to himself. Accuse her. Drive her away? Possibly, he admitted, and got up for another drink. The first half hour passed, then a second half hour. He was certain he had not dozed, certain he would hear the door open, would hear steps eventually, but the deep silence persisted. Another half hour. Then he cursed himself under his breath. She could have entered through the back door, or the side door. He wasn't even sure which door she had left by. He went to the front hall and looked inside the closet. The black coat was there, as usual. Heavily he returned to his room, where he stood for a long time regarding the border of light outlining the connecting door to Lois's bedroom. He did not touch it.

Behind the door Lois lay with her face pressed into her pillow. Trapped, she kept thinking. This was what it meant to be trapped. She couldn't stay, and neither could she leave. She was not weeping, although her eyes felt afire with unshed tears. And the word, *trapped*, repeated like a drumbeat in her temples. She had told Warren in the beginning that it wouldn't work, and he had assumed she meant the difference in their ages. *No, no, no!* she cried and had told him about her first husband. They had been in Hazeltine's, a corner table, she remembered distinctly. The vase had two irises in it, a velvety deep blue one, and one that was only faintly touched with blue.

"He got in trouble at school," she had said that night, speaking of her first marriage. "He was my advisor, and then we married, and my name was on the paper along with his. We both were in trouble. He . . . he fudged some results and it was discovered. He was ruined, and I dropped out and went to California to start the degree process all over, using my maiden name, Wharton. When I applied here, in New York, I had to tell the committee, of course, but no one else knows. Not my colleagues at the farm, no one. The name on the paper was L. Malik, his name; L. Malik is dead and buried, and she has to stay dead and buried. She could ruin both of us if anyone ever makes the connection."

Warren had looked blank. "History," he said. "What does it have to do with us now?"

"You don't understand how serious something like that can be. If anyone brought it out, smeared me with it, I would have to go away. But you could be hurt, too."

He reached across the table and put his finger on her lips. "One question," he said softly. "Did you do anything wrong?"

His finger pressed against her lips. She shook her head.

"I thought not. Will you marry me?"

Lois turned over in the bed and stared at the ceiling. She should have known, she thought wearily. She had known. Secrets always surface again. Nothing stays buried. But now that Jill was pregnant, Warren would have his grandchild, his heir. . . . She bit her lip. Six months ago she had brought home a new prescription for birth-control pills, had filled her little silver box, and then had stood holding it tightly for a long time, and finally had put it away without taking a pill. She had prayed, if only she could give him the heir he so desperately wanted. She had not told him, afraid that if nothing happened, he would be too disappointed, and now she was relieved that she hadn't mentioned it, hadn't talked about it. And she realized that she had better start them again.

She did not move yet, but continued to stare straight up at the ceiling. And the pulse in her temple beat *trapped, trapped* over and over. When she finally rose to take a birth-control pill, she could not find the container, the little silver one-a-day dispenser that she had bought the day after Warren's proposal and her acceptance. She was so tired she could not remember where she had put it, when she had last seen it even. It was three in the morning and she was too tired to think anything. She dragged herself back to bed.

Then, in that state of not yet sleep, but not awake either, she realized that Warren must have taken the pills. In her mind's eye his face shaped itself, smiling at her, coming closer and closer, and she smiled back and held out both hands to him, and they laughed together and made love.

"What they needed was a good watchdog, and a good dog for kids, and good around water. Sadie all the way," Brenda Ryan told Charlie and Constance the next morning. She was probably more than three hundred forty pounds and she was enraged. Her face was red-splotched, her jowls shook as she talked. She wore a tentlike garment with great pink blossoms of some improbable flower, and the garment shivered and rustled and shook also, as if her rage had communicated itself to her clothing. Only her hair, a mass of tight golden curls, did not move. They were in her office outside Albany.

Very mildly Charlie said, "You're sure the dog wouldn't have taken food from a stranger?"

Brenda snorted and everything about her shook harder. "Look, I train those dogs myself. You don't want a dog that'll take poisoned meat from a burglar, now do you? I see to it they don't. We see those caper movies just like the burglars do, and we take care of that. Mr. and Mrs. Zukal, they could feed her, that's it. And I'm not too sure about him. Her, I know. I trained her, too. Mrs. Zukal, I mean. If she doesn't handle the dish, handle the food, Sadie doesn't eat. It's like that. I tell her, Mrs. Zukal, I mean, it's good to have a backup or two. I mean, she gets sick or something, dog doesn't eat from strangers, dog dies. I never saw it happen, but it could, that's how they're trained."

"You never even met Mr. Zukal, did you?"

"No. I told her how to teach Sadie to take from him, too. They both handle it for a few days, and then he can do it alone. Not until two, three days. One of them kids could have dropped a steak under her nose and she'd leave it there. That's how they're trained. Poisoned? God, I don't see how."

She talked on about the dog, wanted to show them the kennels, demonstrate how she trained them, but Charlie and Constance declined, and left in morose silence.

He slouched in the passenger seat and she drove. "Maybe Sadie wasn't poisoned," she said.

"Maybe. Maybe Sylvie did it herself."

"Hah!"

"Right."

Miles later she said, "Maybe Al did it."

This time he said, "Hah!"

It was midmorning when she pulled to a stop in front of the administration building of the experimental farm. If there hadn't been a sign on the door, they might have mistaken it for a farmhouse. There was a wide porch and a nice lawn out front with well-trimmed hedges and specimen shrubs but nothing to suggest that it was a university facility.

Charlie had the feeling that if he rang the bell, a plump little housewife in a starched apron would appear and the fragrance of apple pie would fill the air. He ignored the bell and tried the doorknob instead. The door opened onto a long hall. On one side there was a narrow table with metal in and out baskets, some of them nearly overflowing with mail, others empty. Above each basket was a hand-lettered nameplate. He looked them over and spotted one that said Dr. Wharton; the basket below it was empty. There were several closed doors on both sides of the hall and a staircase. No carpeting, no other furniture, no other person.

Somewhere a typewriter was going and there was the sound of an air conditioner that apparently was in serious trouble. A door closed somewhere out of sight. Charlie shrugged at Constance and they moved on down the hall looking for a person, anyone. A door opened and a young woman in jeans and a faded Pink Floyd T-shirt stepped out carrying papers. She regarded them uncertainly.

"Are you looking for someone?" she asked.

Charlie turned to Constance. "See? I told you we weren't the last man and woman on earth." To the bewildered young woman he said, "Dr. Wharton."

"Oh." Her relief was evident, she even smiled. "Out back. You can go through here."

She indicated the hallway, possibly to a second door to the outside.

"And after we are in the open air again, then where?" Charlie asked gravely. They all looked at the stairs as a man began to descend, speaking to someone still out of sight on the second floor.

"Just tell them if they can't be in and out again within two weeks, we'll have to get someone else." He saw Charlie and Constance then. "Hi. Can I help you?"

"We're looking for Dr. Wharton."

"I'm going that way. Come along. I'm Tom Hopewell."

Charlie regarded him with interest. One of the hand-lettered nameplates had been Dr. Hopewell, but this man looked more like a ragpicker than a doctor of anything. His worn shirt was a faded, red-tinged mud color, and both elbows were out. His jeans were shabby, one knee out, never hemmed, and now ragged at the bottoms. He had what looked like a two-day-old stubble. Thirty-five at the most, slender with narrow shoulders, and very dirty hands.

"Lois is back in the tree section," Tom Hopewell said, setting a brisk pace through the hall, out to the back of the building. The appearance of a family farm stopped abruptly here. Rows of tomato plants came to the door almost, and they seemed to be all tagged. Beyond them were rows of immature corn that looked bedraggled and stunted. Some of the plants had plastic tents over them. Some had plastic bags over portions of them only. Small boxes spotted the ground here and there. Tom Hopewell ignored it all and maintained his fast pace. Suddenly he stopped and pointed. "There she is. I've got to go." Although his words indicated a need to hurry, his body seemed of two minds about it. The lower part started to turn, the feet started to move in the other direction but his head did not move immediately as he gazed another moment at the woman he had pointed out. Then, abruptly, he turned all the way and trotted off.

The woman had just emerged from a greenhouse near the start of the tree plantings; she stood in the doorway talking over her shoulder to someone still inside. She nodded and walked toward a Quonset hut. Another farmhand, Charlie thought, another worker dressed in jeans, T-shirt, and sneakers. Doctors were not what they used to be, he added to himself, as he and Constance went forward to meet Lois Wharton Wollander.

They caught up with her outside the Quonset hut. "Dr. Wharton," Charlie said, "can we have a few minutes?" At first she had appeared to be as young as the woman in the building—thirty maybe, with very attractive gray streaks in her dark hair that were dramatic enough to have been added at a salon—but close-up it was obvious that she was a bit older than that. She wore no makeup and was very good-looking in a careless sort of way, as if she hadn't thought about other ways to fix her hair, or how beautiful her wide eyes actually were.

She glanced from him to Constance and back. "Why?"

He introduced himself and Constance. "We've been hired to investigate the death of your student, David Levy."

One moment her expression had suggested preoccupation, a bit of impatience, and not a lot of interest in them, but now she simply looked startled and puzzled. "But why? I thought . . . The sheriff said he overdosed."

"Yes. But his father isn't convinced, and, frankly, Dr. Wharton, neither am I. Can we talk?"

She hesitated, then nodded. "I have an office in the admin building. I guess we could go there."

"Where did David live?" Constance asked suddenly. "One of the units over there?" Off behind the greenhouse, only partially visible, was a long, low building that looked like a motel of the fifties.

Lois looked at her more sharply and nodded again.

"I stayed in a place just like that years ago, a summer at Indiana State," Constance said. "I bet they used the same plans. Can we talk in there?"

Reluctantly Lois said the units were open and they started to walk. "Is the whole operation here organic?" Constance asked, and this time Charlie looked at her sharply. "The bees," she said. "All those little boxes. Hired bees. You can't bring in bees if you're using sprays. Well, some sprays, I guess, but not most."

"It's all organic," Lois said. "That's why we're understaffed and overworked and underfunded. We have a continuing grant for the next four years. We're six years into this project."

The apartments they were approaching were very ugly, institutional ugly, with aluminum windows and doors, no porches or even stoops. There were eight doors.

"No one's staying in them now," Lois said, leading the way to the end door. "They're all due for painting, refurbishing. Thorough cleaning. The usual summer maintenance. This one was David's."

She opened the door and they walked into a cramped, L-shaped living room with a kitchenette; one door to the right opened to a bath, and another straight ahead to the bedroom. There was only one narrow bed, but the room had been designed for two; two chests of drawers, two chairs, two desks were crowded into the space. Constance nodded. Exactly like the one she had shared with another student many years ago. By the end of summer they had been ready to throttle each other.

"Of course, nothing of David's is still here," Lois said, standing near the door as Charlie and Constance looked over the apartment. The spartan rooms were stripped to such essentials they looked uninhabitable. The apartment felt loveless and gray.

They returned to the living room, where they all sat down on plastic-covered chairs with very little padding. Charlie regarded Lois steadily and asked, "Do you believe David took drugs? That he took an overdose?"

Miserably she looked down at her hands. "I don't know. I didn't. Then the sheriff said he must have done it. I just don't know."

"Okay. Tell us something about him. Good student?"

She nodded. "Good, but not brilliant. He was idealistic. His plan was to get his degree and then go to some third-world country and teach. He could have done that."

"Why don't you just talk about him. How he got along with the others here. Who his friends were. Anything that comes to mind."

The picture she painted of David Levy in halting words, with pauses and hesitations, was that of a shy young man with few friends among the other graduate students. He was not asocial but he didn't do the same kinds of things they did, and he was an outsider. He didn't dance, or like rock music, or drink anything alcoholic, or do drugs. He was a strict vegetarian, a health food advocate. He got along with everyone, as far as she had been able to tell, but he wasn't intimate with anyone. When the school year ended only two other graduate students remained and they lived in an apartment in the village. They both had been away that weekend.

"So he was over here by himself?"

"Yes."

"How did he appear to you the last few days before he died?" Charlie asked.

Lois shrugged helplessly. "I didn't notice anything out of the ordinary. We were working very hard, seven days a week usually, and he was as busy as I was. It isn't as if we had much time for socializing."

"Okay. What about the day he died. You found him?"

She took a breath and nodded. "We have two hundred cloned trees that need daily tending. Saturday, Sunday, it doesn't matter. It was David's job to see to them early every morning, and that Saturday he didn't show up. Over the weekends it was just for a few hours, but it had to be done, and I had other work to do myself, and after a while, about ten or ten-thirty, I was becoming angry that he wasn't there, I'm afraid. I assumed it was the usual kind of thing; you know, the clock didn't go off, or too late a night, something of that sort. Anyway, I started to come over here." She paused. Her face was pinched-looking, strained. Now she looked nearer forty than the thirty she had seemed at first glance. "I saw one of the scientists here, Tom Hopewell. I asked him to come with me. It occurred to me that if David was in bed, it would be embarrassing for him if I showed up."

Charlie nodded encouragingly at her.

"We both came to the door. I knocked, and called David, and tried the knob. It turned, and I opened the door, but Tom actually entered. I stood in the doorway and he went on into the bedroom and found David."

"Did you go into the bedroom at all?"

"Yes. I couldn't believe . . . I thought . . . I don't know what I thought. I just ran across the room and to the bed. I . . . He was dead."

"Okay." Charlie studied her for a moment; she was pale and strained, too tight, but in control. Too controlled? "Dr. Wharton," he said then, "was anything out of the ordinary that you could tell?"

"I don't know what would be ordinary," she said, shaking her head. "I never had been in here before. It was very neat. David was fastidious, nothing out of order, nothing out of place. I didn't see a glass or a bottle or anything like that. The sheriff asked."

"What happened next? You saw him. Was he covered by the blanket or anything?"

"Yes. I touched his cheek. Then . . ." She paused again. "I'm really not sure. I was standing at the sink, holding onto it while Tom was on the phone to the police. I kept thinking, he intended to make an omelette. I remember thinking that he wouldn't have his omelette. I was crying," she added in a low voice, her eyes downcast.

"What made you think of omelette?" Charlie asked. "What did you see at the sink?"

She shook her head helplessly. "I don't know. I was crying, and holding on, and hearing Tom on the phone saying he was dead. I must have been in shock for a minute or two."

Charlie caught a signal from Constance, nothing she said, nothing she did, no motion she made, nothing that would have been discernible to anyone else on earth, he knew, but there it was, almost like a hand on his back, fingers digging slightly into his spine. He held the next question. Constance stood up and went to Lois, took her arm.

"Let's go to the sink, the way you were then," she said.

For a moment Lois resisted the pressure, but then she got to her feet and walked slowly across the room to stand stiffly at the sink. It was dull metal with little dents here and there. Water had discolored a trail to the drain. A few inches of the same dull metal made up drain boards on both sides. A three-burner stove was to the right, a tiny refrigerator to the left.

"I think," Constance said, "you should move closer, hold it the way you did that morning."

With obvious reluctance Lois moved closer and grasped the edges of the sink and bowed her head.

"Now, close your eyes and see what you saw that morning," Constance said, as if this were the most natural thing in the world.

Lois obeyed, and after a second or two she said, "There was a yellow rubber dish drainer on that side, with a small pot in it. Two eggs were on the other side, and a piece of cheese. And a glass. His vitamins were on that side, too. Several containers of vitamins." She lifted her head and looked startled. "I smelled orange juice," she said. "I forgot that before, and the eggs. I forgot them. There was an omelette pan on the burner." Her startlement increased. "Dear God, there was a towel, wet." She spun around and looked at the room. "A chair was right here," she said indicating the place in the tiny kitchenette. "There was a towel draped over it. He must have been swimming. He swam every morning before breakfast. We had to walk around the chair to get to the bedroom."

They waited, but there was nothing else. She had not seen bathing trunks, but she had not gone into the bathroom. After Tom Hopewell called the sheriff's office they had gone outside to wait.

When they were finished in the apartment, Charlie stood just outside the door looking around. The units had been placed close to the boundary of the grounds. Behind the structure the experimental trees started. From the door nothing of the greenhouses or the Quonset hut was visible. Trees were in the way, and the trees continued down to the lake. He studied the layout unhappily. David's apartment could be entered without anyone on the farm seeing a thing. For these few seconds that he looked over the grounds, Lois stood silently also.

"It just won't work, will it?" Lois said in a very quiet voice that seemed almost resigned. "He wouldn't have gone swimming, had his juice, and then take anything like quaaludes. He wouldn't have taken phenobarbital before his chores were done."

"No," Charlie agreed. "It won't work."

6

Tom Hopewell got to his feet and brushed dirt off his knees when Charlie and Constance approached him at the edge of one of the corn patches. A few feet beyond him there was a twelve-foot-high fence made of posts with netting. Beans were starting to spiral up the lines. Hopewell was just as ragged-looking as Charlie remembered.

"Dr. Hopewell," Charlie said, "would you mind answering a couple of questions?" He introduced himself and Constance, who was eyeing the bean trellis thoughtfully.

"About David Levy?"

Charlie raised his eyebrows.

"Well, what else?" Tom Hopewell said with a shrug. "First Lois, now me. I thought that whole matter was handled a bit fast."

"How will you pick them?" Constance asked then, still studying the trellis.

Hopewell glanced at it, then back to her, and grinned. "We hire very tall workers." When she grinned back, he said, "Actually we want the biomass more than the beans. For compost. And we need the windbreak. Those are scarlet runner beans, not even a true bean. They'll cover the netting, with any luck, and pollen from the corn down past the peas won't blow this far and mess up this stand." He shrugged and added, "We're working with very limited space here, I'm afraid."

Charlie waited patiently as Constance asked another question or two about the farm, but when it appeared that Tom Hopewell intended to take her away on a tour, Charlie cleared his throat quite loudly. Constance smiled at him.

"Another time," Hopewell said to her. Then to Charlie he said, "And you want to know about that morning, I guess."

"Yep. But first, how well did you know David?"

"Hardly at all. I was down in Peru all summer, their summer that is, and came back in April with seeds. Corn seeds. I was on a collecting trip. We're looking for better strains, more resistant, hardier, faster to yield, more yield. And perennial strains, of course." He was like a little boy who wanted to show off a new kite. When Charlie cleared his throat again, he looked apologetic. "Yes, David. Anyway, I met him in April, and we worked together a little, not as much as you might think, though. Lois had him pretty well tied up. Properly so, I might add." He grinned suddenly. His grin was infectious and made him look too young to be off in Peru collecting seeds, too young to be a doctor of anything. "We're always trying to snare each other's grad students, of course. Free labor, and God knows we can all use more help than we have. Early on I tried to lure David, to get him to put in a few extra hours. No dice. That was probably the only time I ever really talked to him, more than passing the time of day, I mean. Anyway. I hardly knew him."

"Who's actually in charge here? Who was around that weekend? Besides you, I mean."

"In charge," Hopewell said. "That's Dr. Clarence Bosch, the head of the farm here, our boss. His daughter got married that weekend. He took off on Friday and got back Monday. There were the hired helpers, locals for the most part, but not that early on Saturday. A couple of them were due at ten, for half a day. They were mine. The other two grad students were off for the weekend. All the rest had already left for the year. School's out, off they scoot, credits in their grimy little fists."

"Okay. So that morning, what happened?"

His expression became sober. "That morning. I got here after eight or eight-thirty, I guess. I don't wear a watch, you see, and I didn't check the time anywhere. After I'd been busy for a bit, Lois called me, and I met her near the apartments. She was sore and didn't want to go in herself." He glanced from Charlie to Constance and said ruefully, "Levy had a crush on her, although I don't think she knew that. But I did, and I didn't blame her for not wanting to go in and catch him in his underwear or anything like that. Anyway, she knocked and tried the door, but I went in first. She followed me inside, but just inside the doorway. I found him in bed. Then she came on into the bedroom. We went back to the other room, where I called the sheriff's office. Then we waited outside for them to get there."

Charlie nodded. "Let's back up a step. When you went into the bedroom, she was standing at the door. Was she still there when you called her?"

Hopewell's face tightened. "The sheriff asked me if she could have removed anything, and I told him no. The way the apartment is set up, it's a straight line from the door through the kitchen space and into the bedroom. I saw him, and looked back at her instantly. She hadn't moved. I said some dumb thing, like there's been an accident. Something in my voice made her run into the apartment, straight through to join me by the bed. She reached down and touched his face, that's all. Then I took her arm and moved her to the sink. Frankly, I was afraid she might upchuck or even pass out. She went dead white, and she was crying. I kept an eye on her while I made the call. She just stood there hanging on to the edge of the sink. Then I took her outside. I was watching her every second."

He had not seen a container for the pills, had not seen anything out of the ordinary, accepting that he had no way of knowing what was ordinary. "I never had been in his apartment," he said. "Like I said, I hardly knew him."

"So you have no way of knowing if he did drugs," Charlie said.

"Exactly. But I'd guess not. He just wasn't the type. Now, *my* grad student, Preston Heywood, that's different. But he left in mid-May. And he was in Peru with me, so he knew Levy even less than I did, I guess."

"Maybe he could have sold something to Levy," Charlie suggested hopefully. "You don't have to be bosom pals to deal."

"Not unless it was coke. I said he was in Peru with me."

He had started to fidget restlessly, and glanced at two workmen who were standing several hundred feet away under a tree, apparently waiting for him.

"One more thing," Charlie said, dissatisfied. "Do you know the Zukals?"

Hopewell looked surprised. "Sure. To be neighbors with them is to know them. So?"

"You ever go up to their place?"

"What the devil does that have to do—? As a matter of fact, when they bought that mill, they closed down one of the favorite lovers' lanes hereabout. But I haven't been up there for a spell, not since last summer, at least."

"They came down here?"

"No. I saw them by the lake. Look, I really do have work to do." His impatience was turning into real irritation. He waved to the waiting men and started to edge away.

Charlie might not have noticed his growing restlessness. "Did they have the dog with them?"

Hopewell looked at him angrily. "No. I've got to go now."

They watched him take a couple of steps. Then Charlie called after him. "What did you do when you found out that your student had smuggled coke into the country?"

Hopewell was caught in midstride. He wheeled about, pale-faced. "I didn't say he did."

"What did you do?" Charlie repeated softly.

"I fired him. Are you through now?"

"Oh yes. See you around, Dr. Hopewell."

They watched him stride away quickly. He looked stiff.

"Well," Constance said. "If you wanted to get his goat, you succeeded."

"I did, didn't I?" He took her arm. "Let's go see the sheriff."

Sheriff Greg Dolman was grayer than Constance remembered, and a bit stouter, but his smile was just as wide, just as false as it ever had been. His eyes did not know the rest of his face was smiling.

"Charlie! You're looking great. And, Constance, prettier than ever. Come on in and sit down. How are you? How's the little plantation? What can I do you for?"

He ushered them into his private office in the county courthouse and stood beaming at them until they were seated in the two wooden chairs. Then he went around his desk and took his own seat.

"It's about David Levy, Greg," Charlie said. "His father came to see us."

"Poor guy," Dolman said, shaking his head in sorrow. "Walking dead man. Only son. You know how that goes."

"Uh-huh. Fill us in, will you? About the boy."

"Nothing there, Charlie. Like I told the old man. Just nothing there. Kid takes an overdose. What're you going to do? Can't supervise them all their lives."

"I'd like to see the reports," Charlie said, just as amiable as the sheriff, his eyes just as hard.

"Charlie, the case is closed. Did the old man hire you? What with? He doesn't have two dimes to rub together."

"The reports, Greg. Medical examiner's report, you know. He hired me. Got to earn my keep. You know how it goes."

Dolman regarded him flatly for a moment, then smiled his expansive smile again. "Sure, Charlie. But I can wrap it all up in a couple of sentences. The kid took methaqualone and phenobarbital together. A real bad combination. Real bad. Took them with orange juice, on an empty stomach, the worst way. Took all he had. We did an analysis on everything in that dump, vitamins, aspirins, juice. Not a trace of anything. He took them all, probably flushed the paper they were in. Then he went back to bed. Just not a good morning for him, I guess." He smiled again. "Frankly, Charlie, between you, me, and the woodwork, I don't give a shit if the dopeheads go out that way."

"That sounds exactly like what we've been hearing," Constance said. "Poor Mr. Levy. It won't take more than a couple of minutes, I think, to make copies of the various reports. Then we can write our report for his father. Poor man."

Dolman looked at her suspiciously before his smile returned, but she was as innocent as dawn. "Yeah," he said finally. "Why not? There's just nothing there."

Fifteen minutes later they were back in their Volvo, Charlie driving. "Pretty slick," he said. "I take it you wanted out of there."

"Damn right," she said. "He's worse than ever."

Charlie chuckled and rested his hand on her thigh. "Let's go home and do some reading."

Years before, when they bought the house in the country, long before they could spend much time in it, Charlie had said in a burst of exuberance, "When we retire, it's fifty-fifty, kiddo. We take turns with chores, okay?"

"Like what chores? I say we hire some things done, like snow-plowing."

"Maybe. I meant in the kitchen. You cook, I cook, tit for tat."

"Wonderful," she said, laughing. "And, Charlie, I won't forget, you know."

And she hadn't. If either of them was really crushed for time, that was different, but generally it was tit for tat. But with a new case on their hands, Charlie was thinking at the kitchen table, maybe they could discuss it again.

Constance broke into his thoughts. "Charlie, I'm glad we worked things out in advance, cooking, things like that. It could be awkward on a day-by-day basis, couldn't it?"

He examined her carefully; her clear, pale blue eyes were guileless, her expression serene. He sighed. "Fish on the grill," he said. "Later."

"Wonderful, darling," she murmured. "Look, here's the list of the stuff they examined in David's apartment. He was a real health-food addict." She continued to read as the orange cat, Candy, sidled up to her nonchalantly and sneaked onto her lap,

as if hoping she would not be noticed and sent off to Siberia.
Constance adjusted to the cat and stroked her absently. Candy
began to purr. Constance was reading over the shopping list
they had found, more of the same: tofu, yogurt, black beans,
lemons, herb tea. . . .

He sat opposite her at the table and started on the medical
examiner's report. For a long time neither spoke. Candy got
bored and flowed out of Constance's lap like a sluggish mass
of syrup. Brutus stalked in and glared at them, stalked out again
twitching his tail. Constance was skimming the early letters
from David Levy to his father. When she got to April she began
to make a few notes. Charlie was making notes too.

They would both read it all, and then discuss everything. But
Constance was having a harder and harder time with the boy's
letters to his dying father.

Finally she put one facedown and stared out the screen door
to the backyard. The early bulbs were all finished and now irises
were making a show, and baby's breath had come into bloom,
making the irises appear to rise from white clouds. Yellow, orange, bronze marigolds, calendulas in lemony colors, some almost white. A cardinal flitted past, then two chickadees. All too
pretty to introduce such ugliness into, she was thinking. Peaceful, bucolic even, the air alive with buzzes and hummings, the
twitter of birds, a song now and then—

"Tough going?" Charlie asked. He reached across the table
and covered her hand with his.

"He didn't kill himself," she said quietly. "He didn't do drugs
in any form. He was murdered."

"I know. And we'll find out who and why. I'm going to start
the grill."

She set the table on the patio, and now the three cats
prowled between her and Charlie, who was cursing softly. The
grill never seemed to work exactly right without starter fluid,
and he was opposed to using a chemical in his food, not even
one that had long since burned off. He danced around the cats
and cursed fluently and finally had a bed of coals, not ready
yet, but coming along. When he backed away from the grill with
a satisfied nod, she put a glass into his hand. He tasted and
nodded more vigorously. Gin and tonic.

The fish was delicious, the salad superb, the wine chilled just right, potatoes crisp and brown and tender. They sat with coffee as the first stars began to appear in the postcard-blue sky.

"Okay," Charlie said then. "Okay." He leaned back in his chair. " 'Star light, star bright, first star . . .' You do that when you were a kid? Make a wish on the first star?"

"Absolutely. ' . . . I see tonight. Wish I may, wish I might, have the wish I wish tonight.' " She closed her eyes a moment and when she opened them it was to see him regarding her with a soft expression.

"Bet I know what you wished," he said.

After a second she nodded. "I think you do."

"Enough of the mushy stuff," he said. Then very briskly he went on. "The way I read it, David Levy got up at six that morning and went down to the lake for his swim. He went back to the apartment and had orange juice and his vitamins. He got the eggs and cheese out but he wanted a shower before breakfast. He showered, shaved, shampooed, and dried off and put on his shorts, but by then he was feeling sleepy, or dopey, or something and he crawled back into bed and fell asleep and died. Death between eight and nine at the very latest."

Constance poured more coffee. The tiger cat Brutus was stalking the grill, planning his attack. Charlie had given them fish already, but with cats *enough* was a meaningless word. "I can see why Greg had a problem," she said after a minute.

"Yep. They opened the vitamins, all what they said they were—A, B complex, E, C, mineral supplements, there's a long list. Not many of any one of them, but all okay. Containers okay, no trace of anything other than the legitimate contents, all as they should be. The juice was okay. All the food okay. Nothing in the aspirins but aspirin. One missing from a container of twenty-five, expiration date last summer. The kid just didn't take things. Period. And unless Lois Wharton Wollander or Tom Hopewell removed something, there was no container for any other drugs. But they had to come from somewhere. And if he did unwrap them and flush the paper, that means he did it himself. And there's no way we can prove or disprove a thing."

"He could have had company," Constance said after a moment. "Someone else could have made the juice and fixed a glass for him with the dope in it, and then washed it out again."

"I really hate that a lot," Charlie said, frowning. "It's the damn time element. That junk had to be in his system by six-thirty. He comes in from swimming and someone says, Here's your juice, and he drinks it and goes to shower and comes back out in his shorts. That someone must have been a good friend, and he didn't have good friends at the farm. Okay, he could have had a robe on, and could have taken it off again to go to bed. He wasn't expecting company for breakfast—two eggs only. I just hate that a bunch."

"Were any of the vitamin containers empty?" she asked after another minute or so.

"Nope. Our friendly sheriff is an asshole, granted, but he's thorough. He thought of that, too. A few of this, a few of that, and so on, but something in each of them, and no container in the trash. He was running low, but the new supply must not have arrived yet. He ordered them from a mail-order company." He sighed. "Your turn."

"Not much we don't already know, I guess. It's pathetic, how he wrote to his father pretending nothing was wrong, that his father wasn't a dying man. He must have told his dad everything there is to know about the work he was doing. There's a lot about Lois Wharton. He really did have a crush on her. He mentioned Tom Hopewell's arrival and Hopewell's fight with the other student, and he told his father when the bees were delivered. He told him about cloning the trees, and a fight they all had over space and priorities. Apparently they are really strained for space. He referred to a time when they all thought Lois might approach her husband to buy the mill and the grounds there for her work with the trees. The other scientists begrudge her the space that trees take. He didn't refer to it again. I guess it was just a wish on their part. I haven't got much further. The Zukals are due, that's when I stopped reading."

"That damn cat," Charlie muttered, and then yelled wildly. Brutus was on his hind legs, straining to see the top of the grill. He dropped to all four feet and streaked away. Ashcan slunk off into the bed of irises, and Candy crouched near the door, her eyes enormous, her hair standing up like a razorback hog's, her ears flattened. Charlie went to the grill and closed the lid; when he turned toward the door, Candy bellied away from him. "Let's get back to that stuff," Charlie said cheerfully. Anytime he had all three cats buffaloed at once, he thought, he had earned his Brownie points for the day.

"You'll give them all traumas," Constance said.

"Good. I'll take the coffee, you bring the cups."

It was nine-thirty when Lois got home that night, so tired that she felt numb. Until she had a replacement for David it would be like this, she had told Warren. The metabolism tests had to be done within a limited time period or they would be meaningless. Even a week made such a difference. . . .

"He said you knew," Mrs. Carlysle said helplessly when Lois asked where Warren was. "One of those committee meetings."

Mrs. Carlysle was a kindly woman in her sixties, white-haired and a bit overweight. She had been with Warren for twenty-eight years. Now she said, "I'll make you something to eat. You must be starving."

A few minutes ago Lois would have agreed that she was starving, but now she felt only her fatigue. "Just a sandwich," she said. "I can do it." She started to walk through the hall toward the kitchen, Mrs. Carlysle close behind her.

"We have ham, and there's some tuna fish, of course. Cheese. You just tell me what you want and I'll make it. You look so tired."

Lois stopped at the wide staircase and felt her shoulders droop. "Tuna fish would be fine," she said. "And milk. I'll go up and soak in the tub for a few minutes. Thanks."

When she called to tell him she would be late, he had not mentioned a meeting, she felt certain. She would remember that. But she had forgotten that tonight was Jill's night to go to Sebastian's meeting. Every Wednesday night they did chants or something. She tried to relax in the warm water, tried to remember what Warren had said, but nothing came. Nothing. He hadn't said anything. All this week she had been taking her car to work because she no longer had time for the leisurely stroll over to the farm, and then back again. And this morning she had left before Warren was up. Had he been too abrupt on the phone? Or had she? It had been a short conversation. "I'm sorry, but I'll be late. Go ahead without me and I'll have something when I get home." Had she said more than that? She shook her head irritably. What difference did it make? He had a meeting, and he had forgotten to mention it.

But something was wrong, she thought. Something was slipping away and she didn't even know what it was, or how it was happening. The poison-pen letter he had received had something to do with it. He had refused to tell her exactly what it said. Lies, all lies, was all he would say about it. And then he forgot to mention a meeting. Or she forgot that he was going out. Wearily she climbed out of the tub and toweled herself dry, put on her gown and robe, and went to the bedroom, where Mrs. Carlysle had left a tray. A sandwich, salad, milk, coffee. Even a bowl of strawberries. Lois found that she could eat little of it. All she wanted was to lie down and stretch as far as she could and close her eyes.

She would hear him when he came upstairs, she thought. She always heard him in the next room, moving around, opening a drawer, opening his closet, his bathroom door. Water running. He would come in to tell her good night, kiss her good night. She turned onto her stomach.

Three years ago when she tried to explain why they should not marry, she had said, "I have this work to do. I don't mean that it's something I just would like to do if it's convenient. I have to do it. I can't explain it any other way."

"And you don't have to explain it any way at all. That's one of the things I love about you, your determination, your unswerving march to your own goal. I promise I'll never get in your way. I won't ever try to get between you and your work. I love you very much, Lois. More than I know how to tell you."

"People will say I married you for your money. Your own daughter will think that."

"Now you listen to my secrets," Warren had said soberly. "Two years ago I had a heart attack. Not serious, just a warning, the doctors told me. Jill doesn't know. She was in Paris with her mother. I went on a cruise to think and rest, and I decided that all my life was a lie. I lied to myself and to the world, pretending I was doing public service. Public disservice is more like it. You've read how a person changes when death comes too close? Believe it. I changed. When I came back, I began to sever ties, to disengage myself. It's been slower than I'd like, but I'm still working on it. I don't know what I'll do with the rest of my life, but not what I've been doing. People who look up to me look up to an illusion, nothing more. You think I care what they say about you, about us? Jill's mother married me for money and it killed her. Addicted to everything that money can buy, she died of money. She was respected because she was from a good family, and she sold herself like a common whore. You would do me great honor if you will marry me. I know I'm rushing you, but I'm afraid of time. Maybe I see salvation through you. Don't say anything else now. Maybe we've both said too much for one evening. I'll take you home."

Lois rolled to her side and breathed deeply, remembering. Salvation. But now with a grandchild on the way, with reconciliation between him and Jill, everything had changed. It was like looking into a kaleidoscope that had been still for so long that she had forgotten how swiftly the pattern could change.

This was ridiculous, she told herself as she slipped into sleep. He would come in to kiss her good night. She would remember that he had mentioned a meeting. She would get a replacement for David and not have to work such long hours. And they would walk hand in hand in the garden again.

This way! This way! he called, and she ran toward the sound of his voice, up there, past a gate, running without effort. Then she stopped in terror. All around were ghost trees, pale and stopped of leaves, rising from drifting sand. The sand made a whispering sound as wind stirred it; nothing else moved. The trees had been denuded of smaller limbs, and those that remained were stilettolike, gleaming in a light without a source. She backed away, but was mired in sand; when she dragged one foot loose, the sand whispered. *This way!* His call again. All the trees were gray, silver, unmoving, the trunks too thin to hide anyone, but she could not see him, could only try to follow the sound of his voice. Her legs ached with the effort and when she would have fallen, she found herself unable to touch one of the ghost trees for support, staggered instead to her knees, and had to work desperately to stand up once more.

Now the sand started a slide, and she was caught in it, dragged along downward, twisting and turning to avoid the sharpened tree branches, breathless with fear. Below was the sapphire lake, unreal, painted-looking, but then churning with motion. *Alive*, she cried out in her dream, laughing and crying at once, eager to finish the slow-motion slide. As she watched the boiling water, a figure emerged, upright. David! His hair swirled about his face, then was plastered to his cheeks, across his open, staring eyes. He rose as far as his shoulders, and began to sink again as she gazed with horror.

This way! No! She tried to scream, and the sound was no more than a moan as her slide toward the lake continued. The water was subsiding, becoming still again, unreal again.

Standing in the open doorway between the bedrooms, Warren watched her toss and twist. The sounds she made were unintelligible; her thrashing and her moans reached a crescendo and for a moment he thought she would surely wake up, but instead she sighed deeply and then became still. In the dim light he could see a sheen of sweat on her forehead, her cheeks. Silently he backed into his own room and closed the door.

When she woke up it was six in the morning.

7

O kay," Charlie said on Friday afternoon. "We're stymied until we get the report on the dog. Right?"

Constance nodded. They had learned so much in the past few days, she thought, mildly surprised again by how much of everyone's lives had been recorded, filed away, remembered by unlikely people. Clarence Bosch, in charge of the experimental farm, world-famous for his introductions of various vegetables, bigger and better tomatoes, better peppers, earlier melons . . . Jill Wollander, a wild girl in years gone by, now respectable, married to a millionaire . . . Lois Wharton, brilliant in silviculture circles, introducing a new tree that would grow twenty feet in a season in the north . . . Warren Wollander, power behind the visible power. The reason no one could construct any of them, Constance knew, was that there were great gaps in all of their lives. Jill had flitted back and forth between mother and father for many years. What had she done in those years in Europe with her mother, who apparently had been in and out of sanatoriums for the last ten years of her life, addicted to alcohol, drugs, who knew what all? Even Clarence Bosch. He had sued Warren Wollander for a million dollars fifteen years ago, charging malicious slander. It had been dropped, but the mystery persisted. What had that been about? Lois Wharton. She had appeared with a Ph.D. in hand and had been hired on at the farm out of nowhere. Six years of her life a blank. Nothing on record for those years. And Sebastian. Con man? Preacher? Enlightened? Just suddenly there in the picture, looking into buying the mill for a school, or possibly a temple. Or something. They had found nothing yet about Sebastian.

There was no point in calling Wilbur Palmer, the pathologist who had dug up the dog Sadie. He would simply snap at them and hang up until he was ready. There was little they could do until they had his report. There might be little they could do even after they had the report.

Charlie's thoughts were equally gloomy. This was the kind of case he had hated back when he was a New York City detective. Pointless deaths. No direction to strike out in. No direction for questions except the obvious one: Did you kill that boy? He had dumped out the contents of the box Mr. Levy had left with them, and morosely moved stuff around. Such a pitiful little pile of stuff. A few bills, a checkbook, postcards . . . He had lived on practically nothing, had no extravagant habits, damn little to show for having lived at all. He put it all back inside the box.

"When David came to talk to you," Constance said then, "he didn't know who killed the dog. So, if there's a connection, something must have happened in the next day or two to make him suspect he knew. Or maybe he did know by then. But, Charlie, no one would commit murder to keep something like that hidden."

"A nut might."

She rolled her eyes. He had more faith in crazy people behaving in crazy ways than she did, he knew, but nuts did nutty things all the time; they earned the title. And killing David Levy seemed to be in the category of nuttiness.

"So, let's make a case," he said, tapping his fingers on the table. "Someone wanted to buy the mill property, but the Zukals got there first." She made a noise; not an interruption, she never did that, but still. . . . He paused, waiting.

"Maybe it wasn't that someone wanted to buy it, just that someone didn't want the Zukals there," she said. "For a lot of reasons. Starting a furniture factory, trucks maybe, traffic, noise. All those grandchildren at play, Sylvie and Al themselves yelling. Or maybe for a reason we can't even guess—a treasure buried on the grounds." She spread her hands. "There's so much we can't even guess about."

Charlie nodded. "I know, but let's assume a scenario, that someone wants them out, for whatever the reason. So someone decides to drive them away. First the dog. Give them a scare. Then David catches on, and he has to go." He looked at her and shrugged. "Won't play in Baltimore, will it?"

"I wouldn't buy it."

"Me neither. Let's go to to Sebastian's service tomorrow."

Sebastian had private, invitation-only meetings every day for one thing and another, they had learned, but on Saturday he had open services.

"We'll have to sit on the floor," Constance said. Charlie made a face.

Lois watched Jill and Warren climb the bank from the lake that Friday evening. For days she had been unwilling to go near the brilliant water; even glancing at it filled her with dread. Jill and her father were talking and laughing. All this time, Lois was thinking, how she had wished they would be close again, father and daughter, friends, loving, confiding in each other. The kind of relationship she had yearned for with her own father, who had died too soon for it ever to happen. Warren's first wife, Shelley, and then Jill, had hurt him so much; Lois had ached for him, and now he had his daughter back. She knew she should be rejoicing, but her stomach felt leaden and her head throbbed with a persistent pain. She sipped her wine and forced a smile when they drew near.

"Al Zukal has come up with a fantastic scheme!" Jill said. "He's going to put in a beach at his end of the lake. Limestone. He's planning to ship it in from Tennessee or Kentucky. It'll look like snow!"

Lois looked past Jill and Warren. From up here she could see only the upper end of the lake, but now Al and Clarence came into sight. They were strolling back in the direction of the mill, their heads lowered. Limestone? She felt a rising excitement as she considered it. Every rain, every snow would dissolve some of it. How much would it take? Maybe if they did their beach over . . . She looked at Warren; he averted his gaze.

"I've got to change and meet Stanley's train," Jill said as she hurried to the house. "I made a reservation for us at Hazeltine's, but we won't be out very late."

As soon as she was gone, Lois said, "Warren, what's wrong? What's happened?"

He shook his head. "I'm just a little tired. I'll lie down before dinner."

Her hands were shaking. Carefully she put down her wineglass and took a step in his direction. "Something's happened, hasn't it? Warren, what is it?" Her voice rose and she stopped abruptly as he walked past her.

"We have to talk about it," she said, controlling her voice so much that it sounded strange to her own ears. "Whatever it is, we have to talk about it or this weekend will be hell for all of us."

He paused and turned finally to regard her. "I'll be here when you want to tell me what you're hiding." He entered the house then.

She sank into one of the lawn chairs and stared blindly at nothing. For a long time she could not track any single thought from start to finish; they merged and blended, and disconnected things joined one another haphazardly. Last night Warren had pressed Jill for an explanation of exactly what it was that Sebastian taught, exactly what she meant by enlightenment, by the rapture of nothingness.

"Nothingness," Jill had said hesitantly, "has to be by choice. But if you choose, you are actively involved, and that can't be real nothingness. But it can't be simple mind-wipe fatigue, because that's negative, and it has to be positive." She had thrown up both hands. "I can't explain. You have to ask Sebastian."

"It sounds exactly like my problems with algebra back in the good old high school days," Warren had said, smiling. "I followed the teacher's explanations, watched the steps on the blackboard, and each time I thought I had it finally. It was so clear, so simple, logical. Then I would tackle the homework and it was all gone again."

Jill had set her mouth stubbornly. "It's not like that."

Lois had left them to return to her Quonset hut and the metabolism studies she was trying to finish. Now, thinking about that conversation, about nothingness, she felt that she had come back from nothingness herself, and it had not been enlightening or rapturous. The shadows had lengthened perceptibly and the only thoughts she could recall had to do with nothingness. Tired, she rose and walked into the house. She told Mrs. Carlysle she would not be home for dinner, collected her purse from her room, and left.

Much later she was still staining one slide after another, studying it under the microscope, making the cell count, and recording it. Her eyes burned and her headache was like the surf—pounding, receding, pounding.

"I taught you well, didn't I?"

She dropped the slide she was holding and spun her chair around. "What are you doing here? Get out!"

"Just wanted to see for myself." Earl Malik was slender, wiry, with black hair untouched by gray. His eyes were very dark, and bloodshot at the moment. His eyebrows nearly met and were bushy, much too heavy for his thin face; they gave him a made-up look, like a performer inept with the tools of his trade. He leaned against the doorframe, looking about the lab with contempt. "They're going cheapo, all right," he said.

There was her workbench with the microscope, the tray of slides, notebooks, a computer with figures in columns on the monitor. Behind her station were two more workbenches, sinks, shelves of flasks, burners. . . . Many high schools were better equipped.

Lois stood up and pushed her chair aside. "Get out of here, Earl. Now. I don't have any more money. I don't have anything at all for you. Warren suspects you're around, and if he finds out for sure, he'll make a lot of trouble for you. Just get out and leave me alone."

"But, Lois, I'm your collaborator, remember? I taught you everything you know, and that's my work you're messing around with. Let's be reasonable. I don't want your money. I want us to work together like we used to."

"You've been drinking," she said with disgust. "How did you get out here?"

"Took a little walk, not that far, couple of miles. I waited for you last night, and the night before, and tonight I said to myself, Old friend, she's not coming, so you'd better get your ass over there and see why not. So here I am."

"Earl, listen to me. I don't have any money left. I don't have access to his money, and even if I did, I wouldn't give any to you."

He shoved himself clear of the doorframe and stood swaying. "We'll work together, Lois. Like before. So you won't mess up again. I'll check things out this time."

She went to the computer and saved what was on the screen, turned it off, and began to stow away her materials on the workbench.

"Too early to stop now," he said. "Couple more hours, finish up here. My work, Lois. Remember that, it's my work."

"It isn't!" she cried, suddenly furious with him, with herself for not knowing how to get him out again, furious with the whole bloody mess, she thought. "You botched it once, remember? You botched it. I started over from scratch, and this is my own work and it's damn good work. Now get out of here!" She was screaming at him, trembling all over. She drew in a deep breath. "If he does find out, I'll tell him you're blackmailing me, Earl. I will! He'll put you in jail!"

He smiled and took a step toward her and she rushed at him and shoved him backward, back through the open door to the outside. He staggered, caught himself, then fell into the hydrangea bush, cursing hoarsely. She grabbed her purse, flipped the light switch off, and pulled the door closed and locked it. He was scrabbling in the bushes, still cursing, when she ran to her car and got in and locked the door. Gravel flew as the wheels dug in and spun before the car jerked away and she raced up the drive to the road.

"What the hell are you doing?" Al Zukal demanded Saturday morning. Sylvie was bustling around the kitchen as if preparing a holiday dinner, and it was just eight-thirty.

"Apple kuchen," she said with a withering look. Any idiot could tell that much if he just took the trouble to look.

"Yeah, yeah, I seen that. What for?"

"Stanley might like a bite of something. You ever seen anyone turn down hot apple kuchen?"

"He ain't coming for no breakfast. This is a business meeting, like I told you."

"He don't eat none, the kids'll polish it all off later. Won't go to waste."

"Yeah, yeah." Flora was due with the children by noon. This weekend Bobby was tied up at his job. With only two more weeks there, he was trying to clean up things, not leave his boss in a lurch. Good guy, Bobby. Considerate like. Al looked at the table and groaned.

He had spread brochures and folders all over the kitchen table, but he knew he was out of his depth here. Stanley had sent the stuff ahead of time to give him a chance to look over the various proposals, and Stanley would be here before nine to review them with Al, but so far none of the stuff had made any sense at all. Insurance come-ons, certificates of deposit, trust deeds, treasury notes, equity loans. He understood none of it. Sylvie put two pans in the oven and a strong whiff of cinnamon drifted across the kitchen. He'd end up doing whatever Stanley thought best, Al had already decided. It was like a game with Stanley, Monopoly or something. See how much money you could make with money, watching it every second, keeping track, knowing when to move, when to sit still. And it was a headache bigger than the house for Al.

When he heard a car in the drive, he went to the door to watch Jill come to a stop near the turnaround at the garage. The new station wagon was still parked outside the garage, but maybe this week he'd get to work hauling the junk out, hauling it away. Stanley got out of the car and crossed in front of it to stop at Jill's side. He leaned in and kissed her and then stood watching until she made the turn, headed out, and disappeared at the first curve in the driveway. When he turned so that Al could see his face, he was grinning like a kid with his own strawberry jam pot.

He started to walk toward the house, then veered in the direction of the station wagon and went to it instead. Mystified, Al watched him pull open the back and then scream hoarsely and throw both hands up over his face, backing up, screaming.

"Jaysus!" Al ran out of the house, crossed the yard, and came to a stop. Stanley had fallen down and was rolling over and over, and clustered all over him were bees, hundreds of bees. Stanley convulsed suddenly, his back arched; he shrieked and went limp.

8

Ellis Street was lined with venerable maples that met overhead and made a tunnel with diffused lighting. Parked along the street that morning were two Cadillacs, one Continental, one Saab, several Volvos, and half a dozen other cars far less remarkable. Charlie found a parking space and pulled in. When he got out he noticed that their three-year-old Volvo needed a good washing. He took Constance's arm and they strolled back to number 1242, a neat, well-kept two-story frame house with a postage stamp–sized lawn closely sheared. On the porch they were greeted by a pretty, slender woman in white pants, a white silk shirt, and a blue sash at her waist.

"Welcome," she said softly and opened the door for them. They entered to find a closed door on one side of a foyer, and open double doors on the other. Many shoes were lined up in the foyer. They added theirs and went into the meeting room where a dozen other people had already assembled.

An assortment of cushions was at the end wall. They selected one each and looked around for a place to settle. The others in the room were in many attitudes, some lotus position, but not many. One woman was kneeling. Most of them were cross-legged or had their legs sprawled out. Charlie felt a touch of relief at that. He knew damn well that he could not sit cross-legged for more than a few minutes, and as for lotus, forget it. He indicated a place that would allow him to see the double doors, as well as a single door in the back of the room, and they sat on their cushions and waited.

At the far end of the room was the only furniture—a tier of long tables covered with white cloths held many arrangements of flowers. Like a funeral, Charlie thought gloomily. On the floor in front of this was a red cushion on a white rug. A pagan funeral, he added. The windows were covered with white drapes that admitted light. On each side wall were two pairs of gold sconces with tapered lamps in them. The floor was covered with straw mats. Very simple, very soft sitar music drifted in from somewhere; there was no other sound except for the occasional rustling movement of one of the other attendees.

Already present, and seated, were eight women, four men. Most of them were simply dressed, in white or pastels. Most of them were waiting with their eyes closed, breathing evenly, some so deeply that it appeared they were in a trance state. Charlie recognized Jill from many newspaper photos when she entered. She was in white, a jumpsuit of some sort with a scarlet sash. She sat down cross-legged, bowed her head, cradled one hand in the other, and did not move again.

Sebastian's entrance was so underplayed that it would have been easy to miss it. He glided into the room and took up a lotus position on the red pillow; the sitar music ended abruptly. Most of those gathered bowed, some touched the floor with their foreheads, and then they resumed their silent, unmoving positions.

"The student came to the master and said, 'In my village is a very powerful man, a very rich landowner who tells me I must finish my studies quickly in order to return home and enlighten my fellow villagers and thus lead them to a happier life more quickly.' " Sebastian's voice was pleasant, low-pitched, and conversational. He seemed to be making no effort whatever, but his voice carried throughout the room. He looked totally relaxed, his expression both serene and eager as he gazed at his

listeners, first here, then there, including everyone in a very
personal way that was engaging. He was dressed entirely in
white, even his sash.

When his gaze lingered on Charlie, the effect was strangely
unsettling. He had the gift, Charlie thought then, the same gift
that carried politicians into high office, that made evangelists
draw thousands to their television sets, to stadiums where they
preached. Myopic, Charlie told himself, that accounted for the
peculiar staring quality of the man's eyes, but he knew it was
more than that. Sebastian liked him personally; he liked everyone in that room personally. They all felt it and responded.
That was the gift he possessed, the ability to project such
warmth, such acceptance, liking, even loving the other, the
stranger. Uh-huh, Charlie thought, and watched as Sebastian
turned his myopic blue eyes here, then there.

" 'What should I tell this powerful landowner?' the student
asked. The master laughed delightedly and raised his staff and
whacked the student across the head. 'Just this,' he cried. 'No
more, no less.' "

Sebastian smiled widely, as if he shared the master's delight.
"What a beautiful story," he said. "What a beautiful man was
this master, how fortunate this student. But let us examine this
student. A student is one who is receptive, who comes empty,
yearning to be filled, who comes with no thought of what he
has left behind, but only of what is before him. The student
must sever his ties to the past, because the past shackles him
to his ignorance, to his preconceptions, his false thoughts. . . ."

Charlie's legs were going to sleep. He glanced at Constance,
who had taken her aikido position of sitting back on her heels,
her hands loosely joined before her. She looked as comfortable
as Sebastian; she looked as if she could stay that way for hours.
He had tried that position once, only to find that after ten
minutes he could not straighten his legs at all. He had hobbled
for an hour, he remembered bitterly. He knew she was thinking, *I told you we'd have to sit on the floor*. He refused to look
at her again, but began to ease one leg inward, thinking if he
could just bend that knee a little, then work the other leg in a
little. He caught a glance from one of the women, and stopped
moving temporarily.

". . . can have but one master. A student can have no
thoughts for those he left in his village, whether family, friends,
lovers, whoever. . . ."

He had not even got to the rich man yet, Charlie thought,
and began to ease his leg again. Across the room a woman went
from lotus to simple cross-legged. When he realized that no
one gave her a glance, he drew in his right leg. Several people
looked at him, their concentration broken.

"How long had this student been harboring this burdensome
problem that he evidently brought with him to the ashram? Lost
time, every second of it gone, never to be recaptured, and he
would have to start . . ."

Jill had not yet moved. How could she do that? Her head
was turned so that he could see only the tip of her ear, a bit
of her chin. Too thin, much too thin. Anorectic, like most young
women, he decided, especially most rich young women. Why
did the ones who could afford to eat anything so often choose
to eat practically nothing?

". . . did not say young man, or old man, a wise man or a
fool, a good man or an evil man. No, he defined him in the
simplest terms available, and the most untrustworthy: a powerful rich man and a landowner. . . ."

Charlie looked at Sebastian with awe. He was still going on
about the student. But it seemed he intended to slop over to
the landowner any day now, any month now. . . . And he, Charlie, was going to die right here, gangrene would set in, both
legs would fall off.

Suddenly Warren Wollander stood in the doorway looking at
the group. Charlie recognized him, too. There was a flutter of
stirred air, as if his presence affected the charge, and molecules
were rushing back and forth in a dither searching for equilib-
rium again. Warren spotted Jill and went to her quietly, whispered into her ear, took her arm, drew her to her feet, and
took her away.

Sebastian's voice faltered less than a second, then he resumed his analysis, although most heads had turned to watch
the exit of father and daughter.

Charlie jumped to his feet as soon as Warren led Jill out of
the room, but one of his legs really had fallen asleep, and he

would have plunged headlong into his nearest neighbor if Constance had not caught and steadied him. Leaning on her heavily, he hopped from the room, dragging his useless leg.

They reached the porch in time to see Warren depositing his daughter in the passenger seat of a Buick that he then entered and sped away in.

"I'll be damned," Charlie grunted. "Now what?"

"I don't know. Wait here and I'll get the car. Flex that leg to get the blood running again. Be right back."

"I can make it," he protested.

She was already moving. "You hold on to that rail and exercise. I'd rather get it alone than carry you down the street."

She hurried away and he bent his knee, straightened the leg, bent it again. He was now getting pins-and-needles, and they were all red-hot.

She drove to the curb moments later and he walked to the car, determined not to limp or hobble. "Fine," she said, grinning. "Where to?"

"Let's just drive past the Wollander house, and Al's place. See if anything's stirring."

Actually they didn't get farther than Al Zukal's house, and it was clear that whatever had happened had taken place there. The sheriff's men were on the road, waving traffic on, and a medic unit was pulling out when Constance drew near.

"Make a U-turn, back to the farm," Charlie said, craning to see something besides the traffic cops. The medic unit had left without its siren blaring, meaning no one inside it would benefit by being rushed to a hospital.

He slouched down in the seat. First the poor dumb mutt, then the boy next door, and now what? Al? Sylvie? He remembered Al's words: "You sure didn't do him no good." Christ, he thought then, there was another possibility they had left unexamined: What if Al or Sylvie was really the target of the murderer? But who out here could want either of them dead? He scrunched down in the seat scowling.

Constance made a turn and headed back. She pulled into the driveway of the farm, and there was another police car with an officer leaning against the door.

This officer's instructions had been simple: keep those people at the farm until the sheriff got through up at the mill.

Nothing about keeping anyone out, or stopping anyone from talking to anyone else. He didn't interfere when Constance parked and she and Charlie got out of the Volvo and entered the building.

"What's going on?" Charlie asked Tom Hopewell, who had opened a door to peer out when he heard them enter.

"Come on in," Hopewell said, and swung the door open farther to admit them. "Clarence, Mr. and Mrs. Meiklejohn. Private investigators. Dr. Bosch," he finished, and closed the door again.

They were in a small office cluttered with too much furniture and too many file cabinets. There were also three computers and monitors, all working with blinking lights and ever-changing columns of figures. Clarence Bosch was standing at the window when they entered, a slender, pale man in his sixties, with thin gray hair that did not quite cover his scalp, and oversized glasses with dark frames. He seemed confused by their presence.

"What are you investigating?"

"David Levy's murder," Charlie said.

Clarence Bosch sank into a chair behind the desk, staring at him. "Good God!"

"What's going on up at the mill?" Charlie demanded. "Why are the cops here?"

Bosch shook his head helplessly and Tom Hopewell said, "I was hoping you could tell us. All I know is that Lois went tearing out about forty-five minutes ago, and soon after that the cop outside arrived and said we should hang around and wait for the sheriff." He spread his hands and shrugged, then sat down at one of the computers and gnawed on his finger, watching the numbers scrolling past.

"Come on," Charlie said to Constance.

"But we're supposed to wait," Bosch said.

"Wait then. See you later."

They went through the hall, out the back, past the rows of tagged and tented vegetables and on to the Quonset hut. Charlie stopped and looked at the gravel scattered on the path, on the single step that led inside.

"He said she left in a hurry," Constance said.

"Twice. Come on."

They continued to the path among the tagged trees, and a few minutes later they emerged onto the mill property. They had almost reached the house before one of the deputies spotted them and escorted them to Sheriff Greg Dolman, which was where Charlie wanted to be at the moment.

"How the hell did you get in here?" Greg snapped.

"Just out walking in the woods and came to call. What's up?"

They were near the driveway where the station wagon was parked at the side of the garage. Half a dozen deputies were standing well back from the station wagon. Squinting, Charlie could just make out the box inside the wagon. And bees seemed to be everywhere, zooming back and forth purposefully.

"We're waiting for the guy who owns the hives," Dolman said. "He knows how to get that hive out of there. We're not about to touch it."

Charlie nodded. "Who opened the back?" he asked grimly.

Dolman gave him a quick look and nodded. "You read it right," he said with a sigh. "Stanley Ferris. Dead. And old man Wollander's after someone's scalp for this."

It took several seconds for the name to register. Ferris, Jill's husband, Wollander's son-in-law. He exhaled softly. "Boy oh boy, Greg. You've got a hot one this time."

"Yeah. Punk kids did it, trying to tie a can to Zukal's tail, get him out of here. Pothead friends of that Levy, I bet. Got high, thought, What a gag it'd be. And now Ferris is dead. I'll get them, Charlie. You better believe."

"How are the Zukals?"

"Real shook up. Pretty bad. She told me about those letters. Guess they're getting a message all right. Goddamn punk potheads!"

"I'll go see how they are," Constance said in a low voice.

Charlie squeezed her arm slightly and she left them standing near each other regarding the hurrying bees. She went to the kitchen door and peered through the screen to see Al and Sylvie at the table, both voices going.

"Damn it, it's getting in my eyes."

"I can't help it. You're hot as a firecracker. Ice melts soon as it touches you. Hold still."

"Let me have that."

Constance entered. Al had been stung too. His face was puffed on one side, and both hands were blotchy with red welts. Another one was on his neck.

"Did someone take the stingers out?" she asked over their voices.

"Miz . . . Miz . . ."

"Just Constance. Did the medics treat him?"

"Yeah. They used tweezers and got the stings, and they said to keep ice on them, but he won't sit still."

"I'm sitting still, but it's running down my neck and in my eyes. Damn it, Sylvie, watch it."

She had turned to speak to Constance and was jabbing a cloth with ice cubes wrapped in it against his ear.

"What my mother used to do," Constance said, "was use baking soda. You have any?"

Sylvie nodded toward the cabinet, and presently Constance had a paste made and began to dab it on the stings. "How about some vodka?" she asked.

"You want a drink?" Sylvie asked in wonder.

"No. Just another trick from the old country."

Sylvie went out and returned with a bottle of vodka. Constance put ice cubes in two glasses and added an inch of vodka to them and swirled them around a few seconds, then took them both to the table and handed one to Sylvie, one to Al. "Aspirins?" Al lifted his glass and downed the vodka in a gulp, and after a second Sylvie drank hers.

"Aspirin in the bathroom, down that hallway." She kept smearing the baking soda paste on Al.

Constance found the bathroom, and aspirins in the cabinet, along with cotton balls, and brought both back to the kitchen. "Another thing she did," she said, mashing a dozen of the tablets in another glass. "The paste dries out and falls off. Makes a real mess, I'm afraid. But when it did, she would swab off the sting with this solution, clean it, and then put more paste on." She poured vodka on top of the aspirin granules and stirred it. "Helped us. How are you doing?" she asked Al kindly.

"I'll live," he muttered. Some of the paste on one of his hands was already flaking off. Constance dipped a cotton ball in the vodka-and-aspirin solution and cleaned the sting, and then reapplied the soda paste. Al's wrists were very hairy.

One of the deputies appeared at the door, wanting keys for the station wagon. The bee man had moved the hive, he reported, but he wanted to move the wagon away from the area because the bees kept going back inside it.

A few minutes after that Charlie appeared at the door. "I'm going down to the farm with Dolman. Won't be long. How are you, Al?"

"Not bad. Not bad. Constance knows a trick or two them medicine men could use."

"I bet she does," Charlie said, grinning, and trotted off.

Sylvie cleared all the brochures and pamphlets from the table and brought the apple kuchen over along with the coffee.

"See," Al said as she moved back and forth arranging things, "Stanley, he was a genius with money, and he was coming to be my advisor. What he said, my advisor. Early, before the kids get here making a whoop and holler all over the place."

"They're coming pretty soon," Sylvie muttered. "I don't know, Al. This just about does it for me. You know what I mean?"

"Yeah, yeah. I know. So he's coming over, like I said, and Jill drives up and turns around, and he gets out and smooches her real big through the window and off she goes. And I'm thinking now he's coming on in, but he turns to the station wagon and pulls the back open and the bees are all over him. Just like that. He's yelling and throwing his hands over his face trying to get them off, and he falls down, and by then I'm going out there, and I'm trying to get them off him and pull him away. I tried artificial resitation. I took a class once, but it don't do no good. He's a goner even before I reach him. Bees on his face, even his eye, all over his arms."

"And I'm right behind Al and I seen him fall down and I run back in and call that emergency number wrote down on the phone book and the bitch goes, You gotta stay on the line, and I go, No way, I gotta call Wollander, and he shows up about the same time them near doctors get here in their truck and when he sees that Stanley is a goner, he goes tearing out for Jill."

Sylvie dabbed more paste on Al's cheek, and they all ate kuchen and drank coffee and Sylvie and Al talked about staying here, or going back to the city, or getting a hotel room for a few days, and about installing a real professional security system on Monday, and maybe trying another dog. And finally Charlie came back with Greg Dolman.

The sheriff's tone was solicitous. "You doing better now?" His eyes were as hard as ever. Al nodded, and he said, "Look, if you get any more letters, give me a call, will you? And if you decide to go somewhere else for the next few days, let me know where I can find you. Wouldn't blame you for leaving for a while. But we'll get them kids. We'll get them."

He started to leave, then paused. "My guys have been holding the reporters off, but when the word gets out that it was Stanley Ferris, they'll be thicker than fleas out here. I'll leave someone to hold them off while I go talk to Wollander. Another hour, hour and a half." He nodded to them and went out the door.

Wordlessly Sylvie got up and poured coffee for Charlie. She examined the paste on Al's stings and cleaned off a couple of them. "What'll we do, Al?" she asked then, subdued. "That sheriff ain't going to do us no good."

"Yeah. I don't know. Maybe we'd better just take off."

"Al," Charlie said gravely, "your station wagon still has some bees hanging out in it. The beekeeper plans to come back after dark, after they're all back in the hive, and take the hive back down to the farm. Meanwhile some of the bees seem confused and keep homing in on the wagon."

Al shuddered and Sylvie made a moaning sound so deep in her throat it sounded inhuman.

"Our car is down at the farm," Constance said. "After your daughter comes and you send her back home, you can go down through the trees and take our car. You can go to our house and wait for us. Do you mind cats?"

Charlie blinked at her, then nodded slightly.

"Cats?" Sylvie asked uncertainly. "Your house? Where's that?"

"We'll give you a map," Constance said. "Three cats. They'll hate having you show up in our car, and they may even just take off and sulk. Don't worry about them. You can relax and try to decide what you want to do without any reporters bugging you. We'll wait until the beekeeper comes back and clears them all out and then join you."

Al and Sylvie looked at each other, then looked more closely at Constance and Charlie, and in the end they nodded and began to talk about what they would take with them. "Not too much to lug through them woods," Al said, and she said, "Three, four days of clothes. Is the suitcase in the attic or the basement?" When they began to talk together, Charlie leaned back in his chair and grinned faintly at Constance.

"Well?" Constance asked later, when she and Charlie were alone in the house. The daughter and grandchildren had come and gone, the Zukals had left. The reporters had not landed yet.

"No one knows when the hive was taken. It could be one that was put under the trees in April when the trees were blooming. They're checking now. You can move a hive at night, no problem. Probably it was done overnight. The sun heated up the wagon and the bees got mad when they couldn't get out and tend to business. And that's about all. No fingerprints on the hive, or the wagon."

"It's so ugly," she said after a moment. "What if one of those children had opened the station wagon first?"

"Everyone's thought of that," he said quietly.

She told him the story Al had told her. He didn't know why Stanley Ferris had opened the station wagon. There wasn't any reason for him to go near it that Al knew. He and Sylvie had used it yesterday and there wasn't anything in it, nothing that should have been of any interest to Stanley.

"They know it was meant for them," she said matter-of-factly. "They're taking it a lot better than I would be doing."

Charlie nodded. He knew he would be out with a gun looking for someone to shoot along about now.

The reporters came to the porch and Charlie got rid of them. He didn't know where the Zukals had gone, he was house-sitting for them, he didn't know anything about anything. That was the station wagon, and it still had bees in it; if they wanted to go get pictures, fine. They left. Constance straightened up the table and put the baking soda away again, put dishes in the dishwasher, and stood looking at a can of dog food left in one of the cabinets. Sylvie's green kerchief was on the counter, and the stack of brochures that Stanley had sent them. She sighed and turned to the door as someone knocked. More reporters, she thought.

But it was Lois Wharton Wollander. She was very pale and had been weeping; her eyes were inflamed and puffy.

"Oh," she said uncertainly when Charlie opened the door for her. "I came to see how Al is."

"He'll survive," Charlie said. "Come in. How's Mrs. Ferris?"

Lois shook her head. "It hit her pretty hard. She . . . she miscarried. The doctor has her sedated now."

"Hospital?"

"No. She was only a few weeks pregnant, he said that physically it shouldn't be too serious. She just needed calming down for now." Lois sank down into one of the kitchen chairs. "Have Sylvie and Al left for good?"

"Probably not. They're tough, and once they get over the shock, they'll be ready to fight back." Charlie studied her thoughtfully, then asked, "Were you interested in buying this property?"

Startled, she shook her head. "What for?"

"Your work, maybe. For the school, maybe. I don't know."

"That's a crazy idea. It never occurred to me."

"What's the cause of the hard feelings between Clarence Bosch and your husband?"

She flushed. "I don't know that there are hard feelings."

"Mrs. Wollander," Charlie said, drawing out a chair and sitting down, "murder has been done here twice now. A lot of questions are going to be asked, and if they aren't answered, a lot of digging will be done anyway. There aren't many secrets that will stay under wraps from here on out. If there's something between Bosch and your husband, it'll come out."

"Ask them," she said sharply then. "Why are you asking me things like that? Ask them."

"I will. And I'm asking you because you're here. There's been a death in the family, your stepdaughter's had a miscarriage, your husband must be devastated by such tragedies, and you're inquiring about a neighbor you just met recently. I'm surprised you're not over at your own house holding someone's hand, or making tea, or answering the phone. You know, rallying around."

She rose stiffly. "I was on my way to lock up the lab. I won't be in it for days, of course. I just stopped in to see if Al was all right. I'll be going now." She went to door and paused. "The sheriff is calling Stanley's death accidental. Some boys were playing a prank on Al Zukal and it got out of hand."

Charlie nodded. "I know what the sheriff is saying, but I'm still investigating murder, Mrs. Wollander."

She walked out, and he watched her return through the yard toward the break in the fence. She had just reached the area where trees and unruly undergrowth would hide her when Tom Hopewell and Clarence Bosch emerged from the tangle. The three scientists stood together talking for a few minutes. Lois turned and headed toward the mill and the swinging bridge. Hopewell watched her go out of sight, then he and Bosch continued to the house.

"Reporters," Tom Hopewell said with disgust when they entered. "They're getting a human-interest story from some of the workers. We decided to duck out until they're done."

"Did Al and Sylvie get out before they arrived?" Constance asked, ushering them both into the living room. The furniture was very good in here—two sofas, comfortable chairs, and pleasant lamps; all subdued colors, ivories and tans with green and blue accents. One of Sylvie's scarfs was on the sofa, a beer can was on an end table, a child's toy vacuum cleaner stood in the corner. A window seat at a bow window was completely covered with children's coloring books and crayons.

Tom Hopewell nodded. He seemed about to say something, but held it back. All the friendliness that he had shown them earlier was gone now. He looked angry and upset.

"Al said you would be up here until dark, and I thought this would be a good time. I wanted a word with you," Bosch said. "You made a serious statement earlier. You said David Levy was murdered. Why, Mr. Meiklejohn? On what basis?"

Charlie shook his head. "Let's just say it's what I believe. Why were you feuding with Wollander?"

Bosch groaned. "This is what I was afraid of," he said. He was perspiring and took off his coat. He had on a short-sleeved shirt, open at the throat. His arms were tanned up to the edge of the shirt sleeves, and when he moved, the white above the sleeve appeared and vanished. "Questions. The past dug out and aired all over again. That's old history. It has nothing to do with the present."

"If anyone knows, I'm bound to find out," Charlie said reasonably. "Why not let me have the real story?"

When Bosch hesitated, Constance said, "I can see the tabloid headlines now: ATTACK OF THE KILLER BEES. OLD FEUDS SETTLED AT LAST." She looked at him kindly. "You know that's how it will be treated."

"I know. It's just a silly thing, sordid and unpleasant, but not relevant. And I know you're right, it will come out again. Back in the seventies, you remember all the turmoil on campuses, everywhere. It was here, too. Wild kids, rebellious, experimenting with LSD, magic mushrooms, whatever came down the road. They got out of hand here, too. I threatened them with expulsion—there were eleven graduate students, supposedly young adults, too old to require supervision. Anyway, there were parties, and people from around here were upset because some of the local kids got involved. I had my students in and warned them that at the next party I'd call the sheriff and round them all up. And I did. One of the locals who got hauled in was Jill Wollander. A kid, fifteen, sixteen. And Warren threatened to have my head. He said things he shouldn't have said and in self-defense I got an attorney and slapped him with a suit. To shut him up, stop his threats. It worked, and he hasn't spoken to me since."

"What kind of threats?"

"What you might expect. He would close down the farm here, or have me removed, things like that. Called me incompetent, said I provided the atmosphere, and maybe even the drugs, let things get out of hand. It was ugly."

He looked grim, his mouth set in a tight line. His soft, slender appearance had been deceptive; now with his coat off, his arms revealed wiry muscles when he moved, and his expression was obstinate. He would take on Wollander again if he had to, Charlie thought. A tough old bird who would fight city hall and all the king's men, whoever got in his way.

"And now your bees kill his son-in-law. Oh yes, it will be aired again, I'm afraid." Charlie regarded him with commiseration. "Tell me something about the bees. Could anyone have gone in there and just picked up a hive and walked out again?"

"Walked out, maybe. But our night watchman says no one drove in or out after Lois left at ten-thirty. The sheriff practically accused him of lying about it, falling asleep on the job, or something, but I believe him. He's a good man, and he's been with us ever since I've been there, twenty-one years. There's no reason for him to lie."

"How heavy are the hives?"

Bosch glanced at Hopewell and shrugged. "Seven, eight pounds. They're lightweight, meant to be carried out to fields or berry patches. And if it was the one left under the trees, it didn't have to be carried far."

"If you don't think it was neighborhood kids, who do you suspect?" Charlie asked softly then.

"I didn't say that," Bosch protested. "I'm just saying they didn't drive in with a truck and collect a hive. And if the hive was up in the trees, they wouldn't have had to drive in. Maybe they spotted it earlier and knew it was just a few feet from the fence. That fence is down here and there, has been for years. Harry wouldn't have seen them necessarily if they had gone in that way, through the trees, but he would have seen a truck. There wasn't one. That's all I'm saying."

"What happened to Jill after the cops collected her?"

Bosch shook his head. "I don't know. I think Warren packed her off to live with her mother. Maybe they put her in a convent. Where she belonged in those days. With a high fence topped with barbed wire. The next time I saw her, four, five years later, things were different here. That crazy phase had ended."

"Does she speak to you?" Charlie asked.

"Sure. She's been over a time or two to bring Lois mail that the rural-delivery woman leaves over at the house. Jill is as friendly as a pup. But Warren will never forgive or forget."

Tom Hopewell was getting restless, tapping his fingers on the arm of his chair, crossing and recrossing his legs. Charlie glanced at him. "Anything you can add?"

"Nope. I agree with Clarence about the truck. Actually, what I suggested we do is inspect the fence line and see just where the breaks are, and if there are traces someone might have left. And we decided that we shouldn't do it ourselves, alone, I mean. We thought maybe you would come along." He stood up and began to move about the room.

"You really don't want the sheriff to pursue the truck idea, do you?" Charlie murmured. "Afraid of a blot on the reputation of your watchman? What is it?"

Bosch looked more obstinate, more irritated than before. "That's partly it, of course. We don't want a blot, not now. I'm due to retire the month after our grant runs out, three years, six months, nine days. And I don't want to get into another fight with Warren. He could start a lot of trouble, talking about dangerous, uncontrolled bees, that sort of thing. He couldn't shut us down, but it would be a nuisance that I frankly just don't have time for. But more than that. You said that David Levy was murdered. Presumably you have your reasons. Lois said the dog was poisoned. I assume she has her reasons for believing that. And now, the bees. Someone obviously has launched a campaign of terror directed at the Zukals with the possible intention of driving them away. And it's just a matter of time until the rumors start flying that one of us at the farm may be behind it." His voice had gone very dry, his words precise and clipped. "It is no secret that I tried to get our board to buy this property on two different occasions. The second time it seemed a possibility, but then funds vanished and there simply wasn't enough money to make it feasible. But that's the sort of thing people will be saying if this doesn't get cleared up quickly. And if the sheriff is off searching for an illusory truck, it won't be cleared up quickly or any other way. I told him about the fence being down and he sent an incompetent to have a look, but that was the extent of his interest. I thought you might be more interested, if you are seriously looking for a killer."

Charlie nodded. "I think we should go look at that fence. How *I* heard it was that when Lois Wharton married Wollander, it was assumed that she would add the mill property to the farm."

Bosch shook his head vehemently. "Rubbish. Warren would be just as likely to cut off his arm and present it as a gift. Let's go inspect the fence."

Tom Hopewell had been standing at the bow window gazing out; abruptly he swung around. "Wait a minute," he said. "You know where rumors like that lead. If it wasn't bad kids playing bad jokes, it must have been an outsider, someone who tried to move in on the old families by marrying one of the big shots. They sure don't need you to suggest any such thing, Meiklejohn. They'll think of it all by themselves. Come on." He strode from the room, out of the house, and led them to the break in the fence. "I found it on one of my rambles years ago," he said. "There's another section down nearer the road, and of course the one at the lake end. Everyone knows about all of them."

"We talked about fixing it at a board meeting," Bosch said dryly. "But it's mill property, not ours, and there's just no money for anything extra."

On the mill side of the fence there were fine old maple trees with a thicket of straggly new shoots that competed for light and room. Closer to the fence there were sumacs and a few blackberry brambles. The break wouldn't be noticeable to anyone not aware of it. Then the ground was too rocky to support even that underbrush, and here the fence had been bent over. The break could have been used recently, or not; it was impossible to say.

"Deer do it getting down to the lake," Bosch said, surveying it. "Snow piles up, they walk over it. Comes a thaw, it's low enough they still walk over it, or maybe jump over it. Two, three seasons and it's all the way down."

They stepped over the fence and kept to the rocky ground for fifteen or twenty feet where more sparse undergrowth struggled, and then they were among the experimental trees.

"Where was the hive?" Charlie asked.

"I don't know. Lois's chart will show where it was placed. But you can see that I was right, no one had to drive in. No one had to carry the hive more than a couple hundred feet."

Charlie nodded slowly, and said even more slowly, "I see. And you're right, it would have been easy for anyone who knew the hive was up in the trees here, and who knew there was a broken section of fence, and who knew his way around in the dark, and who didn't mind leaving a car or truck parked somewhere and walking in nearly half a mile. Doesn't sound a hell of a lot like your typical teenagers. How I hear it is that they won't walk to the mailbox if they can help it. And probably not your typical transient from Toledo."

Bosch returned his skeptical gaze steadily. "Warren probably knew all those things. He's a good walker, and he knows every inch of all this area, dark or light."

9

What do you think?" Charlie asked a few minutes later. He and Constance were walking at the edge of the lake on the farm grounds. Across the lake the woods had ended at a grassy slope; the upper part of the Wollander house was visible, as if rising from an emerald carpet.

"I think that if our culprits are neighbor kids, the sheriff is in a much better position to find them than we are."

"Granted. What about Bosch?"

She knew that Charlie had a lot more faith in instant analysis than she did, and that he believed implicitly that she had the ability to peer through all layers of masking to see to the core. She had disputed this too many times to try yet again. Instead, she said slowly, "He's driven to complete his work, of course. I plant half a dozen vegetable varieties that he developed and introduced. Tomatoes, peas, some peppers. He's done very important work in horticulture. I can imagine the fights he's had just to get where he is, spending the last ten years of his professional life doing exactly what he wants. The bureaucracy probably put up roadblocks all the way, but he won. I wonder what really lies behind his hatred for Warren Wollander."

"You don't believe the story about the bust, about Jill being caught in the net?"

"Oh, certainly. But I suspect he knew ahead of time that she would be. Maybe that's why he called the police," she added thoughtfully. "It really isn't how the system works. You have to see the university as a clan; those who wear the tartan keep the problems at home, keep the family secrets hidden away, they don't call in the police and get their own into that kind of trouble. They just handle it in-house, the way Tom Hopewell handled his student. Nothing on the record, no police, no bust, matter ended. And Clarence Bosch has been a clansman his entire life, as a student, then a teacher; it's the only world he's ever lived in. He wouldn't have done that unless there was something else behind it. And it seems to me that Warren must have overreacted to the incident if Jill just happened to be one of several. But if she was a target, then fifteen years of hostility isn't so excessive, is it?"

Charlie nodded, and gripped her hand tighter. That hadn't occurred to him, and he believed every word of it. See? he wanted to tell her. See what you can do without any effort at all. He said nothing like that because they had had that debate too many times, and it was one he couldn't prove or win. But he knew. He nodded toward the general view before them.

"Pretty, isn't it?"

On this side the ground sloped gently to the lake, with knee-high grasses, waist-high in spots, and wildflowers in bloom. Butterflies and bees were everywhere, but here they seemed benign, a piece with the setting. On the other side the grass was clipped, and the slope was steeper and higher. They had drawn even with the small beach, a length of golden sand twenty feet wide, fifty or sixty feet long. It looked as artificial as it was, but it, too, was pretty, uncluttered and clean. How much value did Warren Wollander place on this serenity, this privacy, this quiet? Charlie tried to imagine the lake filled with loud-mouthed youngsters, and Sylvie and Al's voices raised in warnings, and radios blaring, bonfires blazing, hot dogs burning. Paradise lost? Maybe, he decided. Maybe.

Yet the thought was swiftly followed by another; he preferred the chaotic imaginary scenes he had conjured. Knowing the lake was beautiful and dead, that the water flowing into it brought only more death tainted the beauty; unbidden, unseen, unidentified evil had insinuated itself into the pristine valley and now owned the dead waters. Silver wind ripples played on the surface, a mockery. He forced his gaze from the lake.

"What I'd like to do is walk to the end, see how hard it might be to cross the stream up yonder. Game?"

She nodded. "I suspect what you'd really like to do is walk

across the water and beard the lion in the den," she murmured, her expression calm, her eyes busy taking in the landscape.

He grunted, and they walked on toward the end of the lake.

It would be hard, he had to admit a few minutes later. The lake narrowed until it became a swift stream that ran ten to twelve feet down a rocky gorge. Not wadable, he decided, unless you didn't mind rock climbing, and getting soaked, and then what was the point? You might just as well swim across the lake itself.

"You know," he said, "there might not be a connection, and that's why we can't see it. Like the little man on the stair."

"Three murders—if you count Sadie, and I do—and no connection? How likely do you suppose that is?"

"Not very, but possible," he said grumpily. "And I'll be damned if I can link them. A dog that's trained not to take food from anyone but the owner, poisoned. A boy who doesn't do drugs, overdosed. The wrong schmuck opens the car door, dead of bee venom."

"You agreed to look into the death of David Levy," she reminded him. "Just that."

"Yeah, yeah. But the other two tag along like kids from the first marriage. What does David's death have to do with forcing the Zukals out of here? Why on earth would anyone here want to kill the Zukals? What kind of nut would kill someone just because he saw him toss bad hamburger to a dog?"

"Maybe someone whose reputation is extremely important to him," she said after a moment.

"And we don't have anyone around here like that," he grumbled. "Just a few world-famous scientists, a presidential advisor, and a guru."

She laughed softly. "You're just hungry. Al and Sylvie will eat our food, we eat theirs. Let's go see what kind of food they provide."

When they reached the break in the fence that Lois always used, they saw a woman waiting for them. She was middle-aged, with gray hair, wearing a simple skirt and blouse, and sandals; the sort of woman, Charlie thought, whom you saw in supermarkets and discount stores clutching coupons and comparing prices, and whom you forgot instantly.

"Mrs. Meiklejohn? Mr. Meiklejohn? I'm Carla Mercer, Mr.

Wollander's secretary. He would like to talk to you this afternoon, if it's convenient."

She did not offer to shake hands, and got no closer than ten
feet. Charlie imagined that she could type up a storm. He nodded. "Fine. We were hoping to get to talk with him, too. When?"

"He suggested three."

"We'll be there. Up through the woods okay? The station
wagon has been invaded by bees and we're on foot."

"It's the best way," she said seriously. "I'll tell him."

They watched her cross the swinging bridge, staying well in
the middle, not looking down at the water at all. Holding her
breath, Charlie thought; when she reached the other side, he
heard Constance exhale softly. He chuckled and took her elbow. "Food. And I don't care what it is as long as it's soon."

Lois sat in a small room they called the flower room, a solarium,
sun-drenched in the winter, filled with greenery and blooming
plants that got carried out to the patio at the start of summer
each year. The room was white, with tall windows, and window
seats; although it looked stark now without the greenery, in
winter it was a cheerful haven from the often-bitter cold, and
it was her favorite room. She held a book in her lap but she
had not read any of it since entering the room; it was a shield,
to be used only if someone came in. She did not expect anyone
to come in.

Now and then she heard herself say under her breath, "Poor
Jill." But it was mechanical, as if someone else were saying it.
Dissociated, she thought, remembering an article she had read.
One of the stages of schizophrenia was dissociation, in which
the person saw herself as if she were an actress in a play. And
that was exactly right. She kept seeing herself at different stages
of her life, herself as a child, as Earl's bride, as a student, facing
her committee. Warren's bride. It was strange that the figure
she saw was so identifiable and yet so distant.

Her mother screaming at her father: "Don't you see that she
doesn't want you pawing her like that?" Her father drunk, trying
to draw her close, his arm around her shoulders, swaying and
leaning on her more and more heavily. "You love the old man,
don't you, sweetheart? You know I don't blame you, don't

you?" Until then she hadn't even considered that he might blame her for anything; until then she had loved him, although she tried to avoid him when he was drinking because at those times she was afraid of him. The fear was too general to have a real basis, she knew, but it was there, strong, pounding, making her shrink away from him then. At that moment she had realized that she was to blame for his failure; if she had not been born, then maybe he would have become the scientist he yearned to be, not the junior high school teacher he actually was. Her fault, she accepted, and she shrank away from him because he might have to punish her for destroying his life, and finally the fear of his drunkenness had a cause.

Ten years later, her father long since dead, her mother insurance-rich, she had been confronted by the ghost of the past. Earl, drunk, weaving back and forth, lurching against a doorframe, clutching the table for support, cursing the committee that was persecuting him. And she shrank away from him because she was afraid of him. She could say nothing, because anything she did say would provoke a tirade aimed at her; he would lash out, once he even swiped at her and fell heavily onto the couch when he lost balance. And the next day he would forget, or pretend to forget, all of it.

Now the ghost was walking again, had entered her life again, and it brought the same fear as before, the same helplessness. She could see the twelve-year-old child pleading with God to make it not happen, to make it stop. "I'm sorry," the child whispered into her pillow. "I'm sorry." She could see herself at twenty-two: "I'm sorry. I should have checked everything closer. I should have double-checked. I shouldn't have been so trusting, so confident. So stupid." That time she whispered into the dark in their bedroom while Earl crashed around in the living room beyond the locked door.

Last night, when he crashed into the bushes outside the Quonset hut, her fear and helplessness had been exactly the same as the child's many years earlier. Nothing had changed.

She stared out the window at an oak tree unmoving in the sunlight and wished for a storm, a hurricane, a volcano to erupt, a tornado to wipe everything away, a flood, anything. Exactly the way a child wishes for a catastrophe, she thought wryly, and turned to see Warren standing in the doorway. How long he had been there she didn't know, but she had the feeling that he had been watching her.

"I have to tell you something," she said then, surprised at the steadiness in her voice. "Earl Malik is hanging around. I tried to pay him to go away again, but I don't think he will."

Warren shook his head, as if trying to recall who Earl Malik was, or why she was bringing this up now. She felt a wrench at the sight of him; for the first time she realized that at sixty-two he was starting to look old.

Before he could say anything she went on, "I wasn't going to tell you. You were right, of course; I did have a secret. I didn't want to worry you with my old problems, but with so much other trouble now, there can't be anything like this getting between us. I'll handle him someway, Warren. I don't want you to get involved with him."

"Maybe he's behind all this trouble," Warren said. "That would explain it."

She shook her head. "Not Earl. He wouldn't do anything like that. He just wants money, and recognition, and . . . I don't know what all he wants, but he wouldn't deliberately harm anyone. He isn't dangerous that way."

"You're still protecting him," Warren said harshly, sending a shock through her. "Why, Lois? What's that man to you now?"

She put down the book she was holding and very carefully walked across the room, trying to quiet her shaking hands, trying to control her breathing. She felt as if there wasn't enough air to go around, that he could breathe, or she could, but not both of them. He moved aside as she drew near the door.

"I was trying to protect you," she said finally. "And maybe myself. I don't care if Earl Malik is alive or dead." She walked past him stiffly, out into the broad hallway, and stood still, no longer knowing where she could go in this house, where she could feel safe, not like an intruder, an unwelcome guest who had lingered beyond decency.

Half an hour later she was pacing in her room, back and forth, to the window to gaze at the wide expanse of lawn that looked painted, back to the door where the wood grain revealed a multitude of faces, some in profile, some full view, one grinning, one leering, back to the window again. She watched

Carla Mercer scurry up from the woods and cross the lawn, and envied her. A break from her work, then back to mind-numbing details. She yearned for her own work, her tiny laboratory and the endless slides to examine and catalog. She was at the window when Warren tapped on the connecting door between their rooms.

"It's open," she said, not turning around.

"Lois, I'm sorry."

She looked at him then. He did not move into the room. She waited.

"Too many shocks, too fast," he said hesitantly. "And I'm a fool."

Slowly she crossed to him and then reached out her hands. He took them and drew her to his chest and held her. After a moment he said, "My first reaction was to call the sheriff and tell him to look for Malik. An easy out, I thought. But I didn't. Then I called Diedrick and asked him what he knows about Meiklejohn, and he called back to say we can trust him. He's discreet and he's thorough. I sent for him. We don't have to tell anyone else. Let him find some answers. If Malik isn't involved, that's that. And if he is . . . We'll go on from there. But, at least, there won't be publicity."

It didn't occur to her to wonder when he had found time to call Diedrick, his attorney, when Diedrick had found time to learn anything about the private detectives, when he could have sent for them. She felt only a great relief as she stood sheltered in his arms, secure again, safe. Not until they were in the study with Charlie and Constance did she realize that this must be why Warren had been searching for her in the solarium, to tell her that he was bringing in private investigators. And by then she had already told them about Earl Malik.

They were in Warren's study, with its good old cherry furniture, green-leather upholstered chairs and sofa, floor-to-ceiling shelves with neatly arranged books. Very nice, all of it. Charlie had glanced around with obvious approval, then said bluntly, "Why us, Mr. Wollander?" Wollander's retainer check was on the desk; Charlie had not touched it yet.

Warren Wollander was equally blunt. "I don't want anyone to make any connection between those unfortunate occurrences and this house. My . . . resources . . . would surely establish an interest on my part. I want someone to be very discreet. Since you are already on the scene asking questions, you seem the obvious choice."

"What is the link you want to keep under wraps?" Charlie asked. His voice was bland, his eyes as hard as obsidian chips.

Warren studied him for a moment, glanced at Lois, then said, "My wife's former husband has been hanging around—a stranger in these parts. And we all know a stranger is the likeliest suspect if there's trouble. I want that to stay unpublicized. Unless, of course, he is actually involved. But we doubt that he is."

Charlie looked at Lois, who now had two patches of high color on her pale cheeks, as if rouge had been applied hastily; it gave her a look of vulnerability. She held her head up and sat with her back straight; only her hands, clutching one another, betrayed her nervousness.

Briefly she told them about Earl Malik. When she was finished, Charlie shook his head at her. "You know we want more than just stripped facts. Is he the one who knocked over bushes outside the Quonset hut last night?"

The color left her cheeks and her hands clutched spasmodically. She nodded. "He came there and I ran out. I drove around awhile to calm down and then came home. But he wouldn't have moved the bees. He couldn't have known anything about them or the station wagon, or anything else up there. Besides," she finished in a very low voice, as if she had cause to feel shame, "he was very drunk. He wouldn't have been able to carry out anything. I . . . he used to go to sleep and not wake up for ten or twelve hours when he was that drunk."

She didn't know, she said, what time she had left him; after ten was as close as she could come. She didn't know what time she had arrived home; she had driven around to calm down, and had stopped at a diner somewhere for a sandwich first. This morning she had not seen him and the lock had not been disturbed on the Quonset hut. When she finished, she leaned back, visibly relieved.

"What does he expect of you?" Charlie asked. "Did he mention buying the Zukal property, having you buy it?"

"Of course not," she snapped. "That's a ridiculous idea."

"I agree," Charlie said, nodding. "But so is blackmail when you come down to it. You've paid that man over twenty thousand dollars, you say, just to get him away from here, and yet he hasn't gone. How much more does he want? How much more are you willing to pay? Is it going to be a monthly annuity for him? For how long? You say he showed up in April. Before anyone knew the Zukals were interested in the mill. Why not consider that he might have wanted it for his work, his and yours? You see, the problem is that you don't usually pay blackmail to someone simply because you don't like him. In that case, you sic the dog on him, or call the cops, or tell your husband, who takes steps. When did you tell your husband, Mrs. Wollander?"

At that moment everything fell apart again, and the pieces shattered into dust, and the dust was in her mouth. She realized that Warren had sent for Charlie before she had confessed that Earl was in the area. With a startled look she turned to Warren, who was gazing out the window as if none of this concerned him, and she knew that the security she had felt in his arms, the safety she had found there was an illusion, that this large, important, self-assured man whom she had thought so wise was a stranger.

She swallowed painfully, and said in a steady voice, keeping her gaze fixed on Charlie Meiklejohn, "I didn't tell him until today. I knew he would do something, just not what. And I knew that Earl would go to the press and betray me. If Clarence learns that I have been involved with Earl in the past, he will let me go. He made Tom fire his student a month or two ago. He won't keep me either if I become a liability. It's his project; he pushed it through the administration, through the committees, he wrote the grants and got the money. It's all his, and he has the power to hire or fire. He saw to that. No tinge of scandal is to be allowed, or the entire operation might be suspect, and it's important work. I don't blame him. I might do the same in his place. It is very important work."

When Charlie spoke again his voice was gentle. "The trouble with paying blackmail is that sooner or later you run out of money. Have you considered what you would do then?"

Tiredly she shook her head. "I told him I don't have any

money, not the kind of money he's talking about. I have my salary. I gave most of it to him already. I told him that Warren and I signed a prenuptial agreement that I had insisted upon. I can't touch Warren's money. Earl chose not to believe me. And then, I don't know what I will do. My salary, as long as that satisfies him. I don't know. I haven't thought ahead that far."

It was interesting, Charlie was thinking, how at the beginning of this conversation she had glanced again and again at her husband, as if for reassurance, support, something. And now she was apparently oblivious of him. As she might as well be; he was as remote-looking as the Sphinx.

"Why did you confess this now if you don't think there's a connection with the trouble at the Zukals' property?" he asked then.

She felt her muscles go stiff in her effort not to look at Warren. "There were some letters," she said, "sent to Warren. One about me. I don't know what was in it, but obviously someone must have seen me with Earl, or something. And if someone knows, no doubt, there will be talk now. The sheriff may learn about it. I thought if there are questions, we should both be prepared."

Charlie turned to Warren Wollander. "May I see the letters?"

"I burned them." He continued his fascinated study of the great outdoors.

"Uh-huh." Charlie got up from his comfortable chair and crossed the room to the desk, where he lifted the check made out to him. "Mr. Wollander, presumably you want an investigator who won't ask embarrassing questions, and to whom you can lie. I'm not that man, sir. Sorry."

"What the devil are you talking about?" Wollander swung around.

"I mean, what's the point of hiring me and lying to me? There are letters. There were other letters that the Zukals received. There are links and cross-links all through this crazy case, and you burned the letters you got. Fat chance, Mr. Wollander. I rather think you handed copies of them over to your lawyer, or those other resources you mentioned earlier, and at this very minute someone is trying to find the author. Or has someone already found the author? You think you can hand out a smidgeon of information here, another smidgeon there, another to the sheriff, and when we all bring in our crumbs you can piece them together and make a cake?" He looked at the check regretfully and then tore it in half and let the pieces fall to the desk. "I'm already hired, you know. So I'll just keep on asking questions here and there and do the best I can."

Well, he thought, he hadn't whacked him over the head, but he might as well have. He certainly had Wollander's attention. Suddenly that attention was diverted and Wollander was on his feet, deep concern etching his handsome face.

"Jill! What are you doing up? You should be resting."

She entered the study to stand by the door. "I called Sebastian," she said. "He said he came and they stopped him at the gate. I want to see him. Call them and tell them to let him in."

"Jill, baby, you need to rest. I told Duane I'd call him when you woke up. He's standing by."

She shook her head. She was very pale, with the waxy unnatural look of a gardenia; the long dressing gown she was wearing was pastel green, so little tinged with color that as she moved it went from a suggestion of green to silver. The green reflected from her skin eerily. Her hair was mussed, as if she had been tossing and turning quite a while. "No more of your cronies. No more of the good old boys. No Duane or Richard or Herman. I wouldn't let Richard touch me with his fat pink fingers and I don't want Duane talking about his fat pink God. No more. His God took my mother and my baby and my husband. No more. I want to talk to Sebastian. Call them."

"Honey, you're hysterical. Just lie down and rest—" He moved to her side and she flinched away from him, shaking her head. Her eyes were wide and too bright, the pupils pinpricks.

"I wouldn't let him touch me but I took his pills and I dreamed. I was showering Mother with money, tons of money. Crisp, green, like lettuce leaves, so pretty in the sunlight. Up to her knees, her hips, and she was spinning around with her hands out, laughing, trying to catch some of it. Then I woke up. I know what it means. I have money now. More money than I ever dreamed of. I can go anywhere, stay anywhere. You can't stop me. I would give it to her if she were alive. God, to see her happy like that! I could do it. And I can see Sebastian. Here or at his place in town. You can't stop me, Father! Call them at the gate!"

"For God's sake, Jill. This is shock, hysteria. You don't need company." His voice had become peremptory, harsh. "I'm going to hire a nurse. You need nursing care, bed rest."

Now Constance got up and went to Jill. "She isn't hysterical," she said briskly. "But she's doped to the eyes. I think you should call and tell them to admit Sebastian. She certainly can't go out this way."

Jill looked at her gratefully, and when Constance took her hand, she did not resist. Neither did she allow herself to be drawn from the room. She watched Warren Wollander, who finally went back to his desk and lifted the phone; he spoke to his security people. When he replaced the receiver, Jill turned and walked out with Constance.

"I'll stay with her until Sebastian arrives," Constance said over her shoulder.

For a time no one in the study moved. Lois looked frozen in her chair, and Warren stared at the open door blankly. Charlie had not left the desk. When he stirred, Warren glanced at him and then seemed to remember where they were, what they had been saying and doing.

"Sit down," he said. His voice was flat, tired. "The letters are in my safe-deposit box. I'll get them on Monday. No, Tuesday. Funeral's on Monday. In Bridgeport."

Charlie nodded and sat down. "And the report on Sebastian."

Lois looked surprised, but Warren merely nodded, almost absently. "That, too. I couldn't leave it around here because Jill would have found it and been angry." Again he seemed to make an effort to collect himself, and more briskly he opened the desk drawer and withdrew his checkbook.

Charlie got the address where Earl Malik was staying. He asked a few more questions, but nothing of consequence, and when Warren pushed a new check across the desk, he took it without comment. "I'd like to walk around the house and grounds a little," he said. "And when Constance comes back, we'll leave. I'll see you on Tuesday, around two."

Warren Wollander nodded, and now Lois was watching him with concern. Charlie was anxious to get out of the room, out of the house, where it felt as if an impossibly heavy weight had descended. And Warren looked like a man shell-shocked, he thought, as he began his stroll. He corrected himself. Warren Wollander looked like a man who had only this minute realized how passionately his beloved daughter hated him.

Jill's room was spacious and all over the same pastel green that she was wearing, and gold and white. A white, fluffy rug was mashed down in a regular pattern, from window to bed to bathroom, as if she had paced miles around and around. The bed was a heap of sheets and a satin spread, a pillow on the floor. Jill stood in the center of the room and seemed to shrink, to become a child in front of Constance's eyes.

"He always does that," Jill said. "Says do this, do that, stop doing this, stop doing that . . ." She felt her hair, glanced down at her gown. "Excuse me." She went into the bathroom and closed the door.

On a white-and-gold table flanked by two white-and-gold chairs there were magazines, fashions and decorating, one of them French, and a number of pamphlets and booklets, all spiritual material. One of them had a smiling Buddha on the cover. A large music system lined one wall; another had a portrait of a beautiful woman. Constance studied it. Jill's mother, she decided, dressed almost exactly the way Jill was dressed now, in a flowing gown of silvered green, a large emerald on one finger, her eyes almost as green as the gem.

Jill returned and stood at her side. "Isn't she beautiful? How could he treat her the way he did? She loved light and gaiety, dancing, music, everything alive, and he wouldn't leave this mausoleum. Never. He treated her like a hired prostitute, made her sign an agreement never to leave him, never to even ask for a divorce, never to demand anything more than their contract allowed." Tears were streaming down her cheeks as she gazed at the portrait of her mother; she seemed unaware of them. She continued to talk rapidly about her mother, life here, life in France and Switzerland, as if all these words had been stored in a container too tight for them and, now that it had been opened, the words were not to be denied.

Constance moved away from Jill and went to the bathroom, where she wet a washcloth and wrung it out. She glanced swiftly over the counter at twin gold basins, hastily opened both cabinets and looked inside, then returned to Jill, who had not moved and was still talking in that out-of-control staccato. Constance didn't miss a word, and when she gently wiped the girl's cheeks with the cool cloth, Jill seemed as oblivious of her as of the tears.

Jill was talking about the parties, about the house they had had outside Paris. "And she was so ill, so much of the time, but she never let anyone know. She was so brave. When she was too sick to stay home, I came back here and she went to a rest home in the country. And then she got better and called me and I flew back. I hardly even needed an airplane. She could have had any man in Europe, but he wouldn't release her, and she had nothing. Nothing. And so sick so much of the time. And she had to take care of me. I tried to make her leave him anyway, and she was afraid. What would become of us? Of me? Always it came back to that—what would become of me?"

Suddenly she stopped talking and snatched the washcloth from Constance. "Oh, God, look at me!"

She dashed into the bathroom and turned on the water.

"Let me brush your hair," Constance said, following her. The brush was gold and very heavy. She began to pull it through Jill's hair. "Are you bleeding very heavily? Perhaps you really should see a doctor."

Jill drew in a shuddering breath and held the washcloth to her eyes. "It isn't that bad," she said dully. "Lois talked to her gynecologist. He told us what to watch for, made an appointment for me, in a few weeks, I forget when. I'm all right."

Constance finished with her hair; it was silky, with a slight wave. "Well, come sit down for now, and keep the cloth on your eyes."

A minute or two later, when there was a tap on the door, Jill was composed. Constance opened the door to see the housekeeper and Sebastian. He ignored her and went straight in, and before the door closed, she saw him kneeling at Jill's chair, taking both her hands in his.

10

As soon as they left the lawn and walked behind enough trees
to hide them from the Wollander house, Charlie stopped and
caught Constance up in his arms. He nuzzled her hair, and
kissed her, and then kissed her a second time.

"Well," she said. "Well."

"Touching base with reality," he said, grinning, and took her
arm, steered her toward the path back to the mill. "What happened?"

Dreamily she said, "I think that could catch on. Sharing reality. Your reality or mine, baby? What do you think?"

He pinched her bottom.

"Oh well," she said. "Beautifully furnished room, lots of
white and gold and pale green. If she sat still in that dressing
gown, she would melt right into it and be invisible. No books.
A few magazines, some religious material, booklets. One on
meditation, one titled *Unwinding the Universe*. Stanley was a
hypochondriac, lots of prescription medications, more over-
the-counter do-it-yourself nostrums. Stomach, bowels, muscle
tone, hair loss, you name it, he was probably treating himself
for it. Plus heavy-duty sleeping pills, chloral hydrate, a prescription. And high blood pressure medicine. And allergy medications, ointments, pills, Caladryl lotion and tablets, and a sting
kit still sealed."

"Good Lord," Charlie said when she paused. "You were gone
ten minutes."

"I know," she said regretfully. "If she hadn't talked so much,
I probably would have had time to snoop around a little. Let's
see, what else did I intend to mention? Oh yes. A portrait of
her mother. Remember that scene in *Tales of Hoffmann* where
Beverly Sills plays the girl who sings a duet with her dead
mother? I always forget the names of the various women, but
you know the one I mean. The father either is or has been

dealing with the devil, and it's time to pay up. Anyway, it reminded me of that. Jill looks very much like her mother, and of course the mother is highly idealized in the portrait, great tragic eyes, honey silk hair, boneless hand draped beautifully over her pale arm. Dressed in a pale green satiny thing with lots of highlights. I guess it's too late for me to have a portrait done, isn't it?"

Charlie dug in his heels on the path and brought her to a stop for a second time. "The biggest mistake I ever made was in packing you off to learn self-defense. Otherwise I would threaten to toss you over the hill into the lake. What did she *say?*"

"I was just getting to that," Constance explained. "It was all about her mother. That's why I prefaced it with the portrait, you see, just so you would have a basis for underst—" She broke it off to say warningly, "Now, Charlie. It seems that her father kept her mother on a very short leash for a very long time. He had her sign a prenuptial agreement, and if she insisted on it, Jill didn't mention that. The agreement stated that if she left him, divorced him, she would take only what she had brought to the marriage, an inheritance of ten or fifteen thousand. He would pay for the education of any children and their maintenance, but not a penny alimony. If he broke it off and got a divorce, an arbitrator would settle the financial terms. He had an obsession, Jill said, about no divorce, the need to keep a good public image of an intact family, just in case he decided to run for office himself instead of pulling wires from behind the screen. So they all lived here when she was a young child, and then the first Mrs. Wollander split for France and never came back. In and out of hospitals, boyfriends, drugs, alcohol, the whole Fellini bit. When she was too disabled, she sent Jill home, but she never stayed more than a few months at a time, and then back into the party with Mother. She died a little over four years ago, and Jill married Stanley a few months later."

"Wow. And Wollander has a clean image, electable by a landslide."

"I'd say so. It's quite an in thing to admit to dependency treatments, attempts at cures. And he stood by her through thick and thin." Her voice had become detached and too thoughtful, too professional, as if she had Warren Wollander on a slide and was interested the way a doctor might be interested in a bacterium. "I wonder if the current Mrs. Wollander really believes the idea of a prenuptial agreement was altogether her own." She paused, then added, "Something came up today that shook her. Remember? It had to do with when she told him that her ex was in the neighborhood. She changed completely after that."

He remembered clearly. Now they had reached the place in the path where they had to walk single file, and he stood aside for her to go first. He liked to watch her move, liked the way the low sun was filtered through the trees to touch her hair again and again, the way her hair changed from brilliant to pale. The path was a pleasant walk, never steep, and, except for this one stretch, comfortably wide. Here the trees had funneled the trail to a scant two feet, and even that was nice, the fact that they had let the trees have their way. She looked very nice here among the trees in the soft dappled sunlight. When they emerged from this section, the lake was visible again. Constance turned to reach for his hand, and paused at the look in his eyes.

"Another reality check?" she murmured.

"You're a wicked woman. And it's not too late to have a portrait. By God, it's not!"

This time she kissed him.

The beekeeper came and Charlie watched closely, but there was little to see. The man looked inside the station wagon and nodded in satisfaction. It was not altogether dark, but the bees had had it for the day, apparently. He simply picked up the box by handles on each side and put it on his truck, and that was the end of that. "Italian strain," he said. "They're real peaceful if you treat them right." He got in the truck and drove away.

When they got home, after winding through several unfamiliar roads to make certain they were going home alone, they found Al and Sylvie in the television room playing gin. The television was turned on too loud, and they were arguing, and Al was holding Brutus in his lap. Brutus barely acknowledged Charlie and Constance.

"I'll be damned," Charlie muttered. "Perverse beast." Brutus hated strangers, had always hated strangers, and wasn't too crazy about people he knew.

"This one's a pussycat," Al said, stroking the cat. "Aincha, tiger? The others ain't showed up."

"He thinks he's back prowling city streets," Charlie said, and Sylvie said at the same time, "Betcha you're starving, aincha? Me and Al, we snacked some but we ain't ate. Thought it'd be polite like if we waited. We got Polish sausages and potato salad and a couple other things. We seen this little store on the way over here and stopped and we got plenty lost when we come out again, got real turned around, but then we got on the right track again."

Al's stings were all but gone now, no welts, not even an itch, he said proudly. "Some tricks," he said to Constance. "What we thought," he said then, "was that while Sylvie's finishing up supper, I'd show you the stuff we wrote down today. Everything we can think of that happened with David after Sadie kicked. Ain't much, but who knows?"

"That's right," Sylvie said. "Who knows?"

They all went to the kitchen to keep her company and Charlie looked over the notes they had made while Constance set the kitchen table.

Sylvie talked disparagingly about her cooking, and Al talked about the security system he had in mind, the kind where if someone moves without you doing nothing, the lights come on and an alarm, and she said that they would just shoot out the lights, and he said that would be a signal too, they could fix it like that.

Charlie found it hard to read what they had written down. Sylvie capitalized every noun, and Al capitalized nothing at all. Neither seemed to have much use for periods.

Sylvie was a superb cook and dinner was too good to talk through; it was late by then and they were all very hungry. Sausages and potato salad with a sweet-and-sour creamy dressing like none that Charlie had ever had before, with bits of green onions and olives chopped up in it. She had made a green bean casserole with mushrooms, and a tossed salad that had shredded raw beets and carrots and even pine nuts. He sighed his contentment when he finally pushed his plate back half an inch, his signal that another bite would do him in.

Constance made coffee and Charlie brought in brandy; they all cleared the table and sat down again, and this time Charlie actually read some of the items they had written down.

"Them with checks," Al said, "that means we both seen him together."

Charlie went to the beginning of Al's paper. David had come to the mill to see how things were going on Monday; Al began to talk about the work being done in the mill, and with great concentration Charlie managed to blank out his voice and read on. Thursday of that week David had dropped in briefly to visit with Al while Sylvie was shopping. Now she talked about Betsy, the lady with the new antiques, whose son made them and made them look old by torturing the wood. They don't torture it, Al said, they just torment it a little, make holes in it with a drill. They worry it, that's what they do. Charlie looked up helplessly and found Constance following their talk with very bright eyes and not a trace of a grin. Betsy might even show some of the furniture Bobby made, Sylvie continued, pointedly ignoring Al, but not pretend it was antique, and Bobby sure wouldn't think of torturing good wood.

Charlie gritted his teeth. On Friday David had brought their mail in; that was confirmed by both of them. He stayed for a glass of milk and a couple of cookies. Sylvie talked about how thin he always had been. That night they agreed they had him for supper.

Sunday he brought her head scarf, found it on the beach or somewhere. Filthy. Past washing. She had got used to wearing them when she cleaned offices in the city. No one had any idea of how filthy some doctors and lawyers could be. Maybe out here in the country she would get out of the habit, but her head felt naked. . . .

Monday, Sylvie told David about the poison-pen letters, and he had got real upset, she said soberly. Al nodded. Thursday, the day after he had talked to Charlie, although they didn't know nothing about that, but it was just like him, anyways, he had asked Al exactly where the dog died, where they had found her. Sylvie said he stood at the grave and looked real troubled, and he walked around the mill, troubled real bad. Al nodded again.

"We figured that maybe he was trying to come up with his own answers," Al said. "And maybe he did."

"Next day," Sylvie said, "we both seen him tossing sticks in the water. He looked just like the little Robin boy with his teddy bear. You know how they stood on the bridge and threw sticks in the water? Only he wasn't playing no games. He looked worried and bothered, and then he walked down the side of the lake and we didn't see him no more."

"Sticks?" Charlie said faintly, and put down the papers in defeat. He would read them tomorrow.

"Little sticks. Twigs, like." Al measured about three or four inches with his hands, then adjusted them a bit. "Little sticks. Charlie," he said, leaning forward, "something that we both seen. Everything bad that happened was always on a Saturday. You see that? Sadie dies. Then David dies, and now Stanley dies. Always on Saturday."

Charlie nodded. "I noticed."

Al looked disappointed, then brightened again. He and Sylvie exchanged a meaningful glance and she nodded. Al said, "Something else, Charlie. Me and Sylvie, we think you want to be more careful. I mean, if there's a high school kid out there with ants in his pants, that's one thing, but if there's a nut out there, you want to be careful. You're too trusting, Charlie."

"How's that?"

"Well, like you let us come here and we coulda robbed you blind. You don't know if I'm a nut or a thief or what have you. See what I mean?"

"It goes both ways, Al. We could have robbed your house."

"She wouldn'ta." Al nodded toward Constance, who nodded back emphatically.

"Well, she's the one who invited you to come here, if you'll recall." And *she,* he thought, a bit disgruntled, didn't pipe up to say he wouldn'ta, either.

"You wouldn'ta axed us?"

"Not on my own, probably."

Al nodded in satisfaction. "That's okay then."

"I told you," Sylvie said.

"Something you might be able to tell us," Charlie said then. "How did David get over here to see me that day? Do you know?"

"Sure," Al said, and Sylvie said at the same time, "In Lois's car. He borrowed it."

"Then probably everyone at the farm knew he was going somewhere, even if not where. And maybe at Lois's house, too. She could have mentioned it, I guess."

"Gonna buy us a gun or two," Al said suddenly, making an abrupt right turn in the conversation without warning.

Charlie groaned. "Do you know anything about guns? Ever do any shooting?"

"Nope, but all them punk kids in California know, and just about everybody on television. Even the president's wife had a gun, you know? Can't be that much to learn, even if she did say it was just a little tiny one."

"You'll kill yourself, or Sylvie," Charlie muttered unhappily.

"You think we should go back there without no protection at all?"

"Why don't you take a little trip? Just a few days, a week. Go to Atlantic City and play the slots or something for a few days."

Sylvie screeched something and Al said something, and altogether it added up to no. They weren't going to be driven out of their house after all these years. Sylvie began to talk about her grandparents who had come from Poland, and Al talked about his father setting up a butcher shop, only to be burned out, and now they were trying the same with him and Sylvie. . . .

"Okay, okay," Charlie said, shouting over both of them. "Let me go over the security system when it's in place, will you? Before you go back, I mean."

"Sure," Al said agreeably.

"My grandmother had a stove like that," Sylvie said, pointing to the wood-burning stove that wouldn't be used again until fall. "And one of the places we seen, they had a stove like that. Remember, Al? The place with the horses?"

"Yeah. Horses. Never get them stables smelling like roses in a million years. You know horses, Charlie?" he asked with a thoughtful look. "Big. Real big."

Helplessly Charlie nodded. "Yes, Al. I know."

"We gotta go now," Sylvie said, standing up. "We called a hotel we seen on our way here, and if you'll just point us in the right direction, maybe we can find it again." She sounded as if she doubted it. "It sure is dark in the country, you ever notice?" she asked Constance. "Real dark. You'd think they could put in a streetlight or two, for appearances or something."

They both talked and Charlie went out with them and pointed directions and then rejoined Constance inside. "Well," he said, "watcha think?"

"I think they're swell," she said judiciously. "And I think we had better catch that nut who's keeping them from enjoying their new fortune."

While Constance finished straightening up in the kitchen, Charlie went through the house turning off lights. He was carrying one of Sylvie's headscarfs when he came back; she had left it in the television room. All three cats were prowling around the kitchen now to see if any interesting tidbits had fallen, and Candy was complaining bitterly, her hoarse voice very like Sylvie's. Charlie watched the cats approach to investigate the scarf, which he had draped over a chair-back to be returned the next day. He was thinking of Sylvie cleaning offices, Al butchering for a supermarket, four girls growing up in a small apartment, all four of them getting educated, and he agreed with Constance. They should be allowed to enjoy their place in the sunshine, their place in the country. Candy kept getting closer to the scarf, then backing off suspiciously, and she kept complaining. He felt certain her raucous words were very obscene.

Constance flicked off the light at the sink; he put his arm around her waist, and they went upstairs, leaving the cats to decide if the green scarf was friend or foe.

11

Sunday was a bust, Charlie decided in midafternoon. They had read all of David's letters, and the papers Al and Sylvie had left with them. They had gone over David's other belongings and there was nothing new. He had been pitifully poor, saving for three months to buy a new pair of running shoes, doing without a new watch when his old one quit, making do. Just making do with what he could afford, and writing letters week after week to his father. His checking account had bottomed out each month while he waited for his scholarship money, but he never was overdrawn. He had done without instead of bouncing checks. It all made Charlie grouchy and on edge.

Constance brought in peas and asparagus from the garden and he prowled around the house and yard, making the cats uneasy. They kept starting at noises he couldn't hear, and staring at objects he couldn't see, and casting swift, frightened glances over their shoulders at nothing at all. After dinner Charlie announced that he wanted to see a movie.

"What movie?"

"Any movie. Preferably a western, with lots of shooting and frantic riding around on the prairies and deserts."

"Oh, that kind of movie." She found the weekly local newspaper and scanned the two ads for coming attractions. It really didn't matter which movie he saw when he was in this state, but if she had to sit through something with him, and if there was a decent choice, she preferred to make it herself. When Charlie said any movie, he meant it. He might see it, or maybe not, or maybe some of it. It was as if at times he had to have something taking place before his eyes in order to let his brain get on with its own business of making sense when no sense was apparent. Later, he might walk endlessly. Other times he might play solitaire, but now it was a movie that he needed.

She drove to the theater in Woodbury, ten miles away, and

they entered to find a Woody Allen movie already started, full of New York scenes done in sepia. Charlie settled down contentedly with a bag of popcorn, and she watched the movie. When it was over, she had to nudge him with her elbow.

They went out and walked the half block to the Volvo and she got behind the wheel again. Halfway home, he grunted, and said, "Where are the damn vitamins?"

"Didn't the police lab destroy them when they were looking for drugs?"

"I mean the new package," he said softly.

She thought, recalling David's belongings, and then said, "Oh! Of course."

In just a few minutes they were back inside their house, with David's personal effects once again spread on the table. Charlie found the police report and the list of vitamins they had destroyed: A, E, B-complex, C. . . . Constance found the other list of what the sheriff's men had taken, and later had returned to David's father. No new package of vitamins. She picked up the catalog that David had ordered from and began to look for a price list, an order form. It had been torn out. But there had been a check made out to the company, she remembered, and now looked for that in the register.

"He ordered a three-month supply on May twelfth," she said a few minutes later. "And before that, back in February. Orders spaced just over three months, one hundred of this and that. It's an in-state company, wouldn't take more than a few days for the order to be processed and delivered."

Charlie made a noise that wasn't really a response. He was comparing the catalog to the list from the sheriff's office of destroyed vitamins. "Four of this and five of that," he murmured. "You'd think with one-a-day type vitamins, the numbers would be the same. And he was almost out of them. As close as he was with money, if the new supply hadn't been delivered before he died, they should have been in the next week while the police were collecting his mail."

"Four of some, five of others? But, Charlie, if the drugs had been in vitamins, there'd be some trace, wouldn't there? I mean, Greg Dolman uses a good lab technician, surely. And who could count on David's taking the drugged ones? That's just too chancy."

He nodded. Then abruptly he read down the list again. "Ill be damned," he muttered. "The fives are all capsules, the fours tablets."

Constance waited, trying to reason it out, drawing a blank.

"Try this," Charlie said at last. "You see that there are a lot of small containers, each one with five vitamins, and you take away the ones with capsules. You replace them with identical containers of capsules that have been tampered with. It doesn't matter which ones he takes of the capsules, they're all poison, but they'd look normal, and still have the right smell. Then, after he's taken the doped capsules, you return the containers with the harmless vitamins, and there are still five in each of them, but only four in each container that held tablets. Tablets are too hard to duplicate, but capsules are a snap to empty and refill. No trace of drugs would be found, obviously, since none of these ever had drugs in them."

Slowly Constance nodded. "Someone could have taken the new package, his new supply, and tampered with them, thrown away everything afterward." She began to study the catalog list again. "Some of those capsules would have been awfully big—a thousand milligrams of C, with rose hips, for instance, in a time-release form. That means hundreds, even thousands of little individual bits, like beads, to dissolve over eight hours or so. That begins to get pretty large for a single dose. Some of these are in the megavitamin category, really big, but would there have been enough of the capsules? Enough space for a lethal dose?"

"I don't know. We'll have to get some and see."

"Oh!" she said then. "Look, he ordered cod-liver oil. A lot of drugs could have been dissolved in it, and the taste and smell would hide just about anything."

Charlie looked over the list of things the sheriff had tested; no cod liver oil was there.

"Maybe he was just going to start it," Constance said.

"We'll sit on it for now," Charlie said. "I want to get the damn pathology report on the dog. But I think we've got this link. And it sounds a lot more plausible than a six-in-the-morning visitor."

"Just one more thing," Constance said then. "This other price list. Did you notice it? I thought at first it was more of the same, but look." She held up a list and pointed to the top margin, where words had been scrawled: *The list I promised. S.*

Charlie looked from it to her and shook his head. "So?"

"It's a different company altogether," she said. "And he could have saved nine dollars by ordering from this one. And who do you suppose *S* is? And why didn't David order from this company instead of the higher-priced one? They seem to be offering nearly identical items."

"S," Charlie said then. "Sebastian? Remember David's letter about the party at Wollander's? They talked about bees and about vitamins."

"I know."

"Well, well," Charlie said then. "Interesting, isn't it? No matter where we toss our net, the same fish keep swimming into it. I told you I wanted to see a western movie."

She suppressed a groan and he started to put everything back into the box.

Early Monday they found the address Lois had provided for Earl Malik; it turned out to be a trailer court, Hunt Acres. The manager's name was Petey Wilson, and he looked like a wrestler, with great bulging muscles and a neck that was the same diameter as his head. His head was shaved and it was deeply tanned, as was the rest of him. He was wearing an undershirt, cutoff jeans, and sandals. Even his toes appeared muscular. His eyes were bright blue and clear.

"Earl? Sure. Third trailer from the end, left. But he's not here."

"Say when he'd be back?" Charlie asked.

"Man, he hasn't said anything for days. Haven't seen him in nearly a week. His tough luck. He's paid up in advance; I should worry. If he isn't back by the end of the week, I'll clean out his junk and rent the unit to someone else. I could care less."

Charlie nodded and surveyed the trailer park. Ten trailers were visible and probably there were others beyond them in a grove of trees. A gravel drive wound around them all. At the moment the whole complex seemed almost empty, but in hunting season, he suspected, it filled to overflowing. A blond woman in pink short shorts was sweeping her two steps endlessly, watching them. She was heavily made up, as if for a performance.

"You live out here, too?" Charlie asked Petey Wilson.

"Yep." Petey pointed toward the road and the first trailer in the place.

"So anyone coming or going would have to pass right by your place."

Petey looked somewhat disgusted and shrugged. "If they come in this way, they do. There's a back entrance in from Huntaker Lane. Lots of them use that one. Closer to Spender's Ferry that way."

Charlie was eyeing the third trailer from the end, not yet moving toward it, but evidently intending to do so. Constance said, "Haven't I seen you on television? Wrestling? Or was it football?"

Petey peered at her suspiciously, then nodded. "It's been a long time."

"But you've kept in such good shape! You look as if you're ready to go back to it right now, this minute, if you wanted to."

He flexed his biceps. "Could. Pays to keep in shape. You watch wrestling?"

"Pretty often in the past. It's not the same now, for some reason. I knew the minute I saw you that you were familiar. Did you ever get hurt much? It always looks so cruel."

"Naw. We learn to take it, that's all. Nobody watches it much anymore. All fake now. Not like it used to be."

She nodded sympathetically, then turned to Charlie. "Why don't you take that stuff to Earl's unit? I'll wait for you here." Then she looked at Petey again. "Mr. Wilson, is it really true that those matches are all decided in advance?"

Petey glanced from her to Charlie and back, then he shrugged slightly. "Now maybe, but not in my day." Charlie left them talking.

The door was locked, but even a kid on his first solo burglary could have opened it. Charlie slipped his plastic card in and opened the door. The trailer was hot, and smelled foul—too many spilled drinks, too many fried onions and hamburgers, too many cigarettes, never enough air. It was dirty and messy, with clothes scattered about and magazines and newspapers everywhere, and a thick coating of greasy dirt on the window frames and the back of the stove. There were many books, science books, biographies, books about trees, plants. . . . The refrigerator smelled even worse than the apartment, but there were steaks and apples, milk, butter, eggs. A broken egg had dried on the bottom of the refrigerator. On the only table was a notebook opened to a page of numbers and cryptic notes. It looked like the same sort of thing that had been scrolling on the computer monitor back at the farm. A stack of computer printouts with more of the same was by the side of the notebook. Earl Malik was keeping up, apparently.

There were two unopened bottles of bourbon, one of gin, three bottles of beer, some collins mix, and a trash can filled with empties. Charlie was hurrying, trying to get a picture of the man, and the picture was too uneven. A pig, but a smart pig was the best he could do. A tiny chest of drawers held a few shirts and socks; two drawers were empty, and a pair of slacks and a jacket were in a small closet. All the pockets were empty. He ran his hand under the mattress on the sagging bed, and he looked under the cushions on the sad-looking sofa. Nothing. He picked up a crumpled map near the table and opened it. Then he folded it and tucked it inside his pocket and stood surveying the place for another second before he left. A real search by experts might turn up something, he thought morosely, but he doubted it.

Constance was still in an intent conversation with Petey when he rejoined them. The woman in the short shorts had stopped pretending to sweep; she was simply watching them now. Constance looked at Charlie brightly. "You wouldn't believe some of the tricks they use now to fool the audience!"

"I'd believe," he said. They all looked toward the road as a siren blared nearer and nearer, then passed. Medical rescue unit, Charlie thought distantly. The road was hidden by trees.

"Well—" Petey started; he stopped again as another siren wailed, approaching.

"Let's go see," Charlie said, taking Constance by the arm. "When Earl comes, tell him we'll be back. Just say Charlie. Okay?"

Petey nodded, following the sound of the sirens. A third one was approaching.

Charlie drove back up the gravel driveway to the county road, and waited there for a sheriff's deputy to pass with the siren screaming. His face was without expression as he watched it go by. He listened briefly, then pulled out after it.

"The farm!" Constance exclaimed a few minutes later.

They were waved off the driveway to the front parking lot, but no one stopped them when they entered the admin building and hurried through and out the back door. Charlie was nearly trotting as he led the way past the rows of plants to a group of people near the Quonset hut. They were farmworkers and a few others that Charlie had not seen before. Tom Hopewell was with them, his hands jammed into his pockets, his shoulders hunched. Everyone was watching the activity at the apartment units, although deputies were keeping them all well back.

Tom Hopewell started, then nodded to Charlie and Constance when they reached him; a deep frown lined his face, aging him many years. "My God," he said. "My God!"

Charlie looked past him. Several of the apartment doors were wide open, one unit had windows broken out. Greg Dolman was near it, but no one, as far as Charlie could tell, had entered.

"What the hell?" he muttered, and then he got a whiff of gas. He gave Constance's arm a slight squeeze. "Wait here," he said, and strode toward Greg Dolman.

A deputy moved toward him, to intercept him probably; he ignored the man. "Greg, what the hell is going on?" he called.

Dolman scowled at him and motioned the deputy away. "Gas," he said unnecessarily. "Place was full of it when the painters opened the door. Thank God, no one tossed a cigarette or match in."

Charlie nodded. "Someone's in there?"

Dolman's expression turned suspicious, and Charlie said irritably, "For Christ's sake! What are the medics waiting for if there isn't someone in there?"

"Just to haul him away," Dolman muttered. "He's been in there a long time apparently. Too long. Bosch took one of my guys up to the main building to try to find a fan. But that sucker in there, won't matter to him."

Charlie's hands bunched up into fists, and he stared at the apartment, every muscle taut now. Another one, he kept thinking. Another body.

The fan was produced; someone had to go find an extension cord, and finally it was working to air out the apartment. Bosch was the color of wet newspaper, and said not a word. He stood near Charlie watching the apartment as if he expected to see fireworks. He looked as tightly wound as Charlie was.

When Dolman approached the apartment, Charlie followed. No one seemed to notice. He entered, sniffing first just to make sure, and then stood well out of the way, keeping his arms tightly crossed, observing. A dead man with dark hair, dressed in jeans and short-sleeved shirt, running shoes. On his side in the kitchen area. Bedroom door closed, bathroom door closed. The technicians—death technicians, he thought bleakly—did the usual things; some took pictures, then more pictures, while others dusted for prints here and there. Dolman prowled around purposefully, and finally they turned the man over and there was blood-soaked hair matted on that side. Charlie left.

Bosch had joined Constance and Tom Hopewell. "Who is it?" Bosch asked. A little color had returned to his face, but he still looked bad. A tic jerked one eye again and again.

Charlie shrugged. "They didn't find any ID. It may take a while to identify him. I never saw him before." He looked at Tom Hopewell, included him in his question, "What happened?"

Bosch said quickly, "I was in the admin building when I heard people yelling, running for a telephone."

Tom Hopewell was looking everywhere, and likely seeing nothing. His gaze flitted here, there, somewhere else too fast for anything to be registering. Charlie touched his arm and he jumped. Very quickly he said, "I was in the field. One of the painters opened the door, and, thank God, he had enough sense to yell for me to turn off the gas. I looked in through the window, and saw that someone was in there. That's why we broke the windows. I covered my face with my shirt and went in, but there wasn't any point to it. So we waited for the sheriff to get here."

"Did you touch anything?"

"No! Just the body, and only enough to make sure he was

dead." He looked like a man who had only this minute finally come to believe in the irreversible fact of death. And he looked like a man lying in his teeth. Charlie wondered if he had become this pale, this ancient when he found David's body, if he had looked this guilty then. Would finding a third body finish him off entirely?

Greg Dolman came to the small group. "Why don't you folks go back to the main building. I'll want a statement when we're through here, and a list of everyone who's been around the last few days. You could get it together while we're finishing up."

Charlie lingered as Bosch and Hopewell started toward the building. After a glance at him, Constance followed the two scientists. Tom Hopewell was moving so fast she would have had to run to keep up.

"Any ID?" Charlie asked Dolman then.

"Nothing. Transient. I think this wraps it all up, Charlie."

"Is that how you're going to play it, Greg?"

"That's how it is," Greg Dolman said flatly. "A bum moved the bees. Who knows why? Then he went out in an accident. Finis."

"Was there a bottle in there? I didn't see any."

"No. Why?"

"Wondered, that's all."

"Well, stop wondering. I don't give a shit about a bottle. I say it's complete as it is."

Charlie shook his head. "It won't work, and you damn well know it won't."

"Butt out, Charlie. Just butt the hell out." He turned away abruptly and strode back to his men still working in the apartment.

When they reached the admin building, Clarence Bosch sent Tom Hopewell to talk to the rest of the staff, and get the list of employees. "If those two people show up for interviews, tell Wanda to keep them in the front office. I'll get to them as soon as I can." He busied himself with making coffee. "Something about coffee," he said absently. "I think it's just something to do, keep the hands busy, that's why we always think of it."

Constance agreed; she studied the room they were in. Apparently this had been the original kitchen of the house that had been turned into the administration building. There was a sink, some cabinets painted brown with the paint flaking off, and a refrigerator, but there were also file cabinets, a computer and workstation, and an array of test tubes and flasks on two of the counters, also a coffeemaker. A box of latex gloves was on the table, and a metric scale.

"Ever since the Zukals came," he said, stopping in the middle of measuring the grounds into the basket. "It's as if they brought a bad wind with them. Nothing but trouble."

"That piece of ground is so small, just fourteen acres. It's hard to believe anyone could want it so desperately as to cause all this trouble."

"No one wanted it for more than ten years," he said, and finished measuring the coffee, plugged in the machine. "Frankly, I was glad to see someone buy it, maybe put an end to the lovers' lane reputation it had. Ever since I can remember, since I was a boy, it's been that, a place to rendezvous."

"You grew up here?"

"I, my wife, Warren, his first wife . . . all kids together." His gaze was distant, as if he were looking into the past. "We used the mill, too, in those days," he said with a faint smile that was so fleeting it might not have appeared at all. "Things were different, though. No drugs, a little beer, maybe; now and then a little booze. Then we all grew up and went our own ways. Warren to Harvard, I to Penn State. Warren got Shelley, and after a few years I got Barbara. And we were all grown up."

"I understand that Jill's mother was very beautiful."

"Oh yes. Every one of us wooed the beautiful Shelley, and Warren won. Or lost. Who's to say anymore?"

He turned his back on her and began fishing around in cabinets, pulling out a cup here, another there. Constance knew she was pushing it, but she kept up the questions as if she simply wanted to pass the time with him, distract him from the gruesome business at the apartment units.

"Was she really as wild as rumor has it?"

He laughed harshly. "Rumor can't even touch the reality," he said, and counted the cups he had assembled, went back to rummage for more.

"And was Jill like that?"

He stiffened and stood motionless for a second or two, then turned to regard her carefully. "I've been rather naive, I'm afraid," he said. "You're working, aren't you? I forgot."

"I'm working," she admitted. "Dr. Bosch, the present doesn't exist independently of the past. The gun that was loaded thirty years ago sometimes is fired in the present, but the question remains: Why was it loaded at all?" She had heard Charlie enter the building, but he was not coming into this room yet. She sensed that he was on the other side of the closed door, listening, letting her carry it for the time being.

"Our past has nothing to do with the troubles going on now," Bosch said almost primly. "Believe me, it doesn't."

"Probably you're right, but there are such big blanks. You called the police and turned in Jill Wollander when she was an adolescent. There are many ways to interpret that action. Revenge. Hatred for the Wollanders. Hatred for Warren in particular, striking at him where he was most vulnerable." Clarence Bosch's face looked frozen, his eyes unfocused. Very gently Constance said, "And another way to interpret it is to wonder if maybe you were trying to save Jill. You knew what her mother had been like, and you could have seen a chance to prevent the daughter's following that path."

He closed his eyes for a moment and shook himself slightly. He looked down at the cups on the table and moved one, then another aimlessly, keeping his gaze on them. "I . . . loved Shelley very much. Most men did. And she taunted me when she became engaged to Warren. She said he would do anything she demanded, and that he had money and position, things I didn't have. I was going to be a teacher, a poor teacher. She laughed at me. And suddenly I hated her. Just like that. Later, I pitied her, I think. And then Jill was slipping across the lake at night, meeting the students in the mill, in the apartments. I don't know. She was so young, so ignorant. I told my wife, and she tried to talk to Warren, but he . . . he wouldn't hear a word against Jill. I called the police, knowing he would have to pay attention, be aware. I knew the price I would pay, that we all would pay, but she was so like Shelley in those days. Barbara, my wife, agreed with me, that we should at least try to help her, even if it meant scandal and hostility and an end to our relationship with Warren." He looked up finally and shrugged. "As you see, it has nothing to do with what's been happening around here."

Constance nodded. "I think your wife must be a very fine person."

He blinked in surprise. "Of course. The coffee smells done, don't you think?"

He was pouring coffee when Charlie entered the kitchen. Constance watched Charlie make a swift survey of the room, and she knew that later, if necessary, he would be able to list proportions, contents, windows, everything about it. Training, he said; she called it magic.

Bosch looked at Charlie with an expression that was almost pleading. Charlie shook his head. "The sheriff will be along in a couple of minutes. We'll take off before he gets in. Just a question or two first, if you don't mind."

Bosch ran his hand through his thin hair. "Go ahead."

"Right. When will Dr. Wharton return to work?"

"Tomorrow."

"And you're interviewing her applicants for her? Will you hire them, or one of them?"

"No, of course not. I told Lois I would simply determine if they are qualified. It would have been best to contact them both and put off the interview until tomorrow, but with the weekend, and they were already on the way. . . ."

"I understand. Dr. Bosch, when this project is finished, you'll retire, won't you? And Tom Hopewell? What will he do?"

"You'll have to ask him. I imagine he'll cast about for another position where organic methods will be approved. It's far enough in the future that we haven't really discussed it."

"And Dr. Wharton, she would have to start a job hunt, too?"

This time Clarence Bosch shifted uncomfortably. He sipped the coffee he had been holding and paying no attention to. "I really don't know. Her situation is different, of course. A commitment to trees is a commitment to time itself. A lifetime is really too short."

"You haven't discussed it with her?"

His discomfort increased and a flush of color tinged his pale cheeks. "We talked about it," he said. "She said at the time that she didn't know what she would do."

"Did she discuss the possibility of continuing her work without the sponsorship of the university?"

"She didn't, but I did. Not on the mill property, not on fourteen acres. But damn it!" he said with his first show of real passion, "Warren owns over four hundred acres, much of it in pasture, there's a big apple orchard, open land. Good land. I suggested that she could work at home, and she was adamant about not doing that. That was the end of the discussion."

"Do you know that the organic project will end at the ten-year mark?"

"Absolutely. They'd like to phase us out now, if they could. The high-tech bioengineering people can't wait to get in here. That's already in the planning stage."

Charlie cocked his head, listening, then said quickly, "Just one more thing, Dr. Bosch. Who would know if a liquor bottle was found anywhere on the grounds over the past couple of days?"

"I'd know," Bosch said, looking bewildered. "The groundskeeper reports to me. If anything unusual had turned up after the bees were taken, I'd know. Believe me, everyone's on full alert, a bit late maybe, but they are now."

"Thanks," Charlie said. "You've really helped, Dr. Bosch. We'll be on our way." He took Constance's arm and hurried her through the hallway out the front of the building as Greg Dolman entered the back.

"Are we on the lam?" Constance asked, seated in the Volvo, with Charlie behind the wheel.

"Not yet," he said, engaging gears. He waved to the deputy, who waved back, and drove out the gravel driveway to the county road.

"Was it Earl Malik's body?" she asked after a moment.

"Probably."

"And did you mention that to Greg?"

"It didn't come up."

She nodded slowly. "Eventually he'll find out that you suspected it was Earl Malik and that you deliberately withheld the information. How long do you suppose it will be before we *are* on the lam?"

Charlie chuckled and patted her thigh, and then let his hand rest there.

12

Today no cars were parked along Ellis Street. The postage stamp–sized lawn was just as immaculate as it had been on Saturday, but when Charlie knocked on the door, the young woman who answered was wearing jeans and a T-shirt.

"We would like to see Sebastian," Charlie said.

"I'm sorry, do you have an appointment?" She looked sorry to the point of tragedy. She was a pretty young woman with very long dark hair held off her face by a blue ribbon, no makeup, no jewelry. Her eyes were a lovely clear brown. She looked as if her sorrow might lead to tears momentarily.

"Just tell Sebastian that I am a private investigator employed by Mr. Wollander, and I would like to talk to him."

Her eyes widened and her mouth made a little O; she withdrew and closed the door. Charlie glanced at Constance and winked.

"Ten seconds," she said gravely.

It was no longer than that before the door opened again, and this time Sebastian appeared. He motioned for them to enter.

"You were at the lecture Saturday," he said.

"Indeed we were," Charlie said agreeably. He introduced himself and Constance. "This won't take long. I know you must be a very busy man, what with services and lectures and private counseling and house-hunting, and all."

Sebastian smiled and shrugged. "My office," he said, and opened a door in the foyer. The office was small and had no desk. It was painted white, with a soft gold carpet, and soft gold draperies. There was a rack of books and pamphlets on one wall; Constance recognized titles that she had seen in Jill's room. There were many cushions piled along the opposite wall, and between the two walls were several upholstered chairs. Still smiling, Sebastian motioned them to chairs.

"I noticed that you found the seating arrangement not altogether satisfactory the last time," he said.

"Very observant," Charlie said as he and Constance sat down in chairs. Sebastian stood near the window. "Are you still looking for a place to buy?"

"I have not looked at all for a place to buy, much less still." His eyes bulged slightly, and his lank hair fell continually into his face. He used both hands to push it back again and again. The slight smile did not waver.

"Ah. I understood that Mrs. Ferris was showing you the mill property a few weeks ago."

"Many people show me many things, Mr. Meiklejohn."

"I bet they do," Charlie murmured. "Mr. Pitkin, there have been several deaths in and around the mill, as you well know. We can play games, or you can level with me and I'll go away."

"Please, just Sebastian. And believe me, I want very much to help in your investigation. I'm afraid I have a small problem, however. I don't quite understand exactly what it is you are investigating."

"The murder of David Levy. And the death of Stanley Ferris."

He sobered at the words, and now looked sorrowful. "Murder? David? Surely not. I met him only one time, I'm afraid, so I have no knowledge of his usage of drugs, but I assume that when the authorities decide a death by self-administered drugs is accidental, they have sufficient grounds to make that assessment."

"Murder, Mr. Pitkin. You gave him a list of vitamins. When was that?"

"Vitamins? Oh, yes. I remember. We talked about vitamins at that cookout. Weeks ago, the same day Jill escorted me through the mill. He was paying far too much. That company is without a conscience, I'm afraid. I did tell him he could buy less expensively through the company I recommend to my own people, and a day or two later I gave the list to Jill to pass along to him. She said she would give it to her stepmother, who would actually give it to David. I heard nothing more of the matter."

He looked so self-satisfied, so *superior*, Charlie thought, that he wanted to give him a swift kick. "And you said that evening that a person with the right attitude wouldn't get stung by bees, didn't you?"

Sebastian shrugged, and his hair fell into his face; he pushed it back. "It's possible I said that, of course, because it is true. But I confess that I don't recall saying it."

"Is it also true that if you have the right attitude, you won't get bitten by a dog?"

"Of course. You see, Mr. Meiklejohn, you are the bee, and you are the dog, and the tiger, and the snake." The cadence of the words, the rhythm suggested thinly disguised mockery. "Naturally there are many quite self-destructive people who haven't grasped that yet, and they are at risk, but with understanding and acceptance, there is no longer any danger with anything of nature."

Constance had been watching him intently, but now she left her chair, as if bored, or perhaps simply restless. She moved about the room and came to a stop at the books and pamphlets. At first Sebastian watched her movements with annoyance as she strolled farther and farther from Charlie, forcing Sebastian to turn his head from side to side to include both of them in his sweeping gazes. When she began to examine the various books, he seemed to give up and concentrated on Charlie, only now and then glancing at her as she browsed in the reading material as if unconcerned with the questions and answers.

"Uh-huh," Charlie said, ignoring Constance. "If you aren't looking for property to buy, what were you doing at the mill with Jill Ferris?"

"Looking." He held up his hand and shook his head. "Don't be angry, Mr. Meiklejohn. Your questions are difficult because they carry so many presuppositions, so many assumptions. Why is it, I wonder, that you ask only questions that you already believe you have answers for? Anyway, at one of our discussion meetings here, the matter of a school came up. I did not bring it up myself, but it was the subject of discussion once it did arise. It was suggested by one of our people that if we had a school, a large enough building to accommodate sleeping space and lecture rooms, that then some people could use it for a retreat, immerse themselves more fully in study and meditation without the interference of pressures of the outside world. A cloistered retreat seemed idyllic to many of us, I admit. But I have no money and I did not pursue the idea. Since then, several people here have offered to show various properties that they had reason to believe might be suitable. Jill made such an offer and I accepted. Not with any intention of buying, however, because I can buy nothing."

Charlie regarded him for a moment, and then said, "And if one of your people takes you on a tour and you find the ideal place, and if that person then says, 'Hey, don't sweat it, I'll buy it for you,' then you're in like Flynn. Neat."

"There are many paths to enlightenment, Mr. Meiklejohn. That may well be one that one of our people will follow."

"How long has Jill Ferris been coming here?"

Now Sebastian shook his head, in sorrow as deep as his receptionist's had been. "You know I won't talk about any of my people, Mr. Meiklejohn. I came here in March this year, and I met Jill Ferris soon after that. She never offered to buy a building for me, or to help me financially to purchase one, and that's all I intend to say on the subject."

"I see. Was she driving all the way out from the city, just to attend your meetings? When did she become a regular?"

Sebastian shook his head again, harder, sending his hair flying out both sides. "You will have to ask her."

"Oh, I will. Do any of your . . . what do you call them? Parishioners? Disciples? Students? Do any of them ever stay here in this house?"

Sebastian folded his hands before him. "Exactly what are you implying now, Mr. Meiklejohn?"

"Just curious. You got here in March. Jill turned up for her prolonged visit in April, I understand, and yet she's become quite an adept in meditation. Makes me wonder how she had time to advance so fast."

"Some people are ready to progress rapidly. Others never are able to see beyond their own noses. I really must go now, Mr. Meiklejohn. Is there anything else?"

"One thing," Charlie said, rising lazily. "Why did you agree to see us at all? You had no intention of telling us anything, did you? And did you notice that I asked not a single question about where you're from, how you got into the soul business, your qualifications to counsel troubled people. Nary a question. No doubt, that sort of thing will be neatly wrapped up in Wollander's report on you. If I see that I need more, I'll come back."

Sebastian did not move, but his stance changed subtly, his hands became tighter in their grasp, one of the other. "What report are you talking about?"

"Did you really think you could set up camp in his backyard and not be investigated? Now that is really naive. Especially where his daughter is concerned. I haven't asked you about your movements over the past couple of weeks, last Friday night particularly, or if you've been over to the farm, communing with the bees, your alter egos. We'll see how much of your time is already accounted for."

"I have nothing to hide, and nothing to fear from any investigation," Sebastian said with tight lips. He strode across the room and yanked the door open, then stood aside for them.

"Thanks for your time," Charlie said good-humoredly as they went through the foyer to the front door. "Be seeing you around, Mr. Pitkin."

Sebastian's lips tightened even more, and his eyes looked strange, more bulging than before, as if suppressed rage was pushing on them from behind. A high flush was on his cheeks now. He said nothing.

Charlie opened the door and let Constance go out first, then pulled the door closed hard. He did not let go, however, and did not allow it to latch. Silently, with an amused expression, he counted to seven and then pushed the door open an inch or two in time to hear Sebastian's voice:

"Goddamn son of a bitch! If they come back, tell them I'm in Poughkeepsie! That bastard Wollander!"

Silently Charlie pulled the door closed again, this time releasing the knob. Grinning, he took Constance by the hand and they went down the front steps.

"Made you mad, did he?" Constance said softly.

"Damn right. But I made him madder. What was that with the books?"

They reached the car and got inside. He turned the key and then waited for her answer.

"All his own work. I was just curious. Jill's reading matter seemed a bit odd—high-fashion magazines and spiritual material. I guess he hands out the pamphlets and articles, or sells them, to his people."

"His people," Charlie snorted. He started the car, began to drive. "I'm in the wrong racket. Nobody ever bought me a school or a church, or even a house."

"You could grow a beard and wear a serape, or a ruana, or even a simple blanket—go barefoot, of course—and talk about taking the right road, scorning the wrong road, not being distracted by enticing signs, like luncheonettes, or anything that . . . Where are we going?"

"You know damn well we're going to have lunch and mull things over."

She smiled slightly.

"What I want," Charlie said in the Spender's Ferry Coffee Shop ten minutes later, "is a roast beef sandwich with lots of gravy." Constance cleared her throat, and he added, "But what I'll have is the tuna salad with tomatoes and dressing on the side." He looked at her balefully. "Okay?"

"Very good," she said, and ordered the same. "And coffee right away."

"We need a spy," he said, and fell silent until the waitress poured coffee for both of them. As soon as she was gone, he continued, "I want to know the minute that crew gets home over at the Wollander house."

"Charlie," she said, a little shocked, "they're at a funeral!"

"I know. Jill can hightail it to her room if she wants. But you can count on it that Greg Dolman won't waste any time in telling them the whole thing's settled. They've got their bum, in the best possible condition as far as Greg's concerned. He sure as hell isn't going to deny anything. So, case closed with even better speed than he managed when he closed the case of David Levy. The county's clean and all's well with the world. I want to get there first, that's all."

She nodded thoughtfully. Not the Zukals, she decided. They were probably still at the hotel. Not anyone at the farm, too many unknowns concerning all of them. Not anyone. "I could hang out at the mill. I wonder if you can see enough from there?"

"No way. Not you."

She looked searchingly at him then. No trace of amusement was visible on his face.

"Honey, there's a real killer loose in that neck of the woods. Someone as opportunistic as hell and pretty damn smart. And desperate by now, I expect."

"Can Greg make a case for Earl Malik? Will it stick?"

"Not if I can help it. They'll find a high alcohol level in the blood, no doubt, and Greg will think that cinches it, but he can't have it both ways. If Malik was drunk enough to fall down and bash in his head, he was too drunk to be lurching around the woods carrying a beehive. They didn't find a bottle, remember. He didn't sober up and then start drinking again. And there weren't any prints on the stove. Whatever was on the doorknob was messed up by Hopewell when he opened the door. No prints. So Malik goes in the apartment and turns on the gas, and wipes off his prints, and then obligingly falls down and knocks himself out. Won't work."

"Then he must have seen whoever got the bees, and that's the motive for killing him."

Charlie nodded. Their salads arrived and neither said any more for the next several minutes. "What they'll do," Charlie said then, "is mill about for a while after the funeral, more than likely. Say they start for home again around three. Be back by seven. I guess our best bet is simply to be on hand and wait for them."

"We'd better go through the mill property," she said. "The security people probably won't let us in the front gate."

"Right. So we go home and brood about that damn dog, and light a fire under Wilbur Palmer if he hasn't got his report ready yet."

"You brood. I intend to freeze peas and speak encouragingly to the tomatoes." She had left most of her tomato on the plate. It was picture-pretty and tasted like plastic.

When Charlie called the animal pathologist that afternoon the report was ready. "One of the organophosphates," Wilbur said. "More than a dozen trade names for the stuff—insect sprays, dusts, that sort of thing."

"A smart dog would eat something like that?"

"Charlie, the word *smart* is relative, right? So the dog's smarter than a possum, what's that mean? You mix this stuff with some canned dog food, and watch."

"But if it was insect spray, she could have got into it accidentally."

"If there's a store of it around. There was a lot in the body. Still is. I doubt that even a pretty dumb dog would lap up that much unless it was mixed with something. Oh, maybe some fruit got sprayed heavily, but dogs sure don't eat many apples or pears, now do they?"

Charlie thanked him and hung up and then stood at the patio door watching Constance move about in the garden. She picked a pea pod and ate it and continued with the chore of picking enough for the freezer. Hers was an organic garden, no poisons. You could go out there and eat whatever struck your fancy, he thought, and shuddered at the idea of the meal that had been fed to that poor dumb dog. "But how?" he muttered to himself. How had anyone managed to get her to eat it?

Someone out there was an opportunistic and smart killer, he thought again. Too smart. Taking advantage of every opening to get whatever the hell he was after. Or she, he corrected himself. First the dog Sadie, feeding her poison when she was trained never to take food from anyone but her owners. Then David Levy with drugs when it was known that he did not do drugs. Then the attack on the Zukals with the bees. If Al were allergic, he would be as dead as Stanley. One of the grandchildren, both of them could have been killed. And now the man he was certain was Earl Malik. Each one killed, using materials at hand, leaving no trail, hitting and vanishing in good terrorist form. Kill and run. If Greg announced the end of the mystery, the closing of the case, then whoever was responsible could strike again, and again, until . . . until what? he thought bleakly. Who next?

The phone rang in the kitchen as he stood watching Constance. He took the call before the answering machine got its act together. It was Al Zukal. The sheriff had called, he said, and they could go back home. The crazy killer was dead.

13

Lois felt like an interloper, an intrusive guest who was always in the way, no matter what she did. Coming home from Stanley's funeral, Warren had held Jill as if she were a small child, her face against his chest, his arm protectively around her shoulders. One of the security men, Robert something, had driven the Buick, and Lois had been superfluous. The Ferris family had virtually ignored her, and again she was superfluous. That family's grief was so consuming, so overwhelming that even Warren and Jill had felt excluded somewhat; no one had suggested they linger after the funeral services, after the obligatory wake that had been cut short when Mrs. Ferris left the room on the arm of her husband. "We'll go home now," Warren had said, and they got in the Buick and Robert drove them home. No one had uttered a word during the drive.

Worst of all, Lois thought, gazing at the landscape without recognition, she had gone blank. She tried to think of work and nothing came. Two people to be interviewed, she reminded herself, and forgot them again. Where had she stopped the metabolism studies Friday night? No answer came. Had she put everything away on Saturday? No answer. Would Clarence think to check the moisture level of the cloned trees in their pots in the greenhouse? Would Tom? When the Buick stopped at the front of the Wollander house, she seemed to come up from a trance state that left no memory.

Mrs. Carlysle admitted them to the house and Jill started up the stairs silently. She was deathly pale, and looked as if she had lost five pounds in the last day or two. Should she be made to see a doctor, be examined? When Lois had asked hesitantly if she was bleeding heavily, if she needed anything, Jill had simply shrugged. "I'm all right." Lois saw again how she had looked Saturday in the brilliant white jumpsuit, with the blood-red sash, and blood running down the legs. Jill had looked mortally wounded. At the stricken look on Warren's face, she knew he was seeing that same image again. She wanted to take his hand, but their new awkwardness permitted no such intimacy now.

"Mr. Wollander," Mrs. Carlysle said in a soft voice that was almost fearful, "there is a message from Mr. Meiklejohn."

"For God's sake! Not now!"

"I'm sorry, sir. He said to tell you it's extremely urgent, that it can't wait. He left a number to call." She held out a slip of paper, but Warren pushed past her and went into the study. Lois took the message, and Mrs. Carlysle looked relieved and grateful. "Thank you," she whispered, with a frightened glance toward the study. "He said it's vital and even told me what to write down, or I wouldn't have brought it up now."

Lois watched her hurry away down the broad hall toward the kitchen, and then opened the folded paper. *I have to talk to you both immediately. It's about Dr. Wharton's former colleague.* There was a telephone number.

She watched the paper start to shake, and realized that she was trembling all over. She closed her eyes and took several deep breaths, and then went into the study.

She offered the note to Warren, who was standing at the window looking out toward the front of the property. He ignored the slip of paper.

"I'm going to call him," she said.

"Leave it alone until tomorrow. My God, that man knows we've just come from the funeral!"

"I know he does. That's what makes it frightening." She went to the desk and dialed the number, watching Warren's back all the while. He was suffering, she knew, losing his son-in-law, his grandchild, maybe his daughter . . . being brought face-to-face with his own mortality again. Charlie's voice sounded in her ear.

"I got your message," she said. "Can't it wait until tomorrow?"

"No. Tell your security people to let us through. We're at the mill property. We'll be there in five minutes."

"But what's hap——"

"Five minutes." He hung up.

"They're coming from the mill."

Warren's shoulders seemed to hunch as if he were bracing against a cold wind.

"I'll go meet them," she said. She started to leave, but stopped again and said pleadingly, "Warren..." He didn't move. She left the room after a moment to wait on the patio.

They never had needed security before, she was thinking distantly. She had felt as secure as a child in her parents' home, protected, safe from the world and everything it might threaten her with. And now there were men on duty to keep out reporters, sightseers, curiosity seekers. Killers? Maybe even that. And the more security they hired, the less secure she felt. She felt as if the threat existed at her elbow, not out there at all. She started to walk across the expanse of manicured lawn, feeling more exposed with every step.

She waved away one of the guards when Charlie and Constance emerged from the woods. They were an odd couple, she thought, still with the distance that seemed to be her self-protective armor. He was so dark and bearlike, she so tall and slender and fair. Lois liked the way they looked at each other. One plus one made a bigger one, she thought then, and thought of them that way, bigger than one, but still one. She felt a rush of envy, and she had an impulse to warn them that the cleaver could fall, even on them. They wouldn't believe her, any more than she would have believed such a warning just a few weeks ago.

"What's happened?" she asked as soon as they were in range.

"Let's save it for you and your husband," Charlie said. The crinkles at the sides of his face were gone, and deeper lines etched his features now.

Her fear returned, redoubled; she nodded and led them inside the house. They went straight through to the study, where Warren was now seated in his favorite chair, with a drink in hand, an invisible wall all around him. It started at his eyes; they were cold and hard. He nodded curtly at Charlie, and ignored Constance altogether.

"This shouldn't take very long," Charlie said. "Today another body was found in the apartments at the farm. The sheriff will be around either this evening or in the morning. I wanted to get here first."

Lois went paper-white and sank down into a chair, her eyes wide and staring. "My God," she whispered. "Who?"

"Unidentified at the moment."

"Earl?" she whispered. "Was it Earl?"

"I never met him or saw a picture of him. Hard to say for sure. But I think so."

Warren's eyes had narrowed and he looked different; he looked dangerous. This must be his political face, Charlie thought. Briefly and succinctly he told them what he knew about the body in the apartment, watching them both closely. Neither moved until he finished.

Charlie caught a motion from the corner of his eye and glanced at Constance, who was moving toward the study door. She opened it. Jill stood there.

"Come on in," Charlie said. "You heard enough to know what's happening, I take it." No name had been mentioned, he knew; Lois's whisper *Earl* could not have carried to Jill. What she had heard would be broadcast news, and it made no difference. The interesting part was that she had learned it this way, by eavesdropping.

She had changed her clothes and was wearing jeans, a black shirt, and sandals. She looked childish and ill. She went to the sideboard and poured gin, added tonic and ice cubes, and sat down without a word. She looked too young to be drinking anything but a Coke or juice.

Lois stirred finally and said, "I'm sorry. Do you want a drink? Sit down please." She looked at Charlie and Constance in turn, but without real invitation behind the words.

"You were right to tell us first," Warren Wollander said then. "A man without ID. Died the same night that the bees were taken. He probably did it himself, then. They may never find out who he was." He looked steadily at Charlie as he spoke in a very deliberate voice.

"They'll find out," Charlie said just as deliberately.

"Meiklejohn, I hired you to do a job for me. I find now that I made a mistake. Keep the retainer, but you're no longer in my employ. I think that's all we need say. Our business is concluded as of this moment." He lifted his glass and drank, and set it down on the table by the side of his chair.

"Dr. Wharton," Constance said then, "we have to talk, you know."

"My wife is under no obligation to talk to either of you," Warren said coldly.

"Mrs. Wollander may be protected by your name and your position and your wealth, but Dr. Wharton is at grave risk," Constance said.

Lois was watching her, pale down to her lips now. She glanced at Warren, who returned her look, stony-faced. Suddenly Jill jumped up, knocking over her glass that she had put on the arm of her chair. Everyone ignored it.

"Look at you!" she cried, facing Lois. "Mrs. Wollander will obey! I always envied you, did you know that? I did! Your degrees, your brains, your work, your freedom. Your freedom! You could tell the world to fuck off if you wanted to. But you're just like the rest of us! One look from him and you're just like the rest of us. I thought someone finally would say no. That's all, just *no!*" Tears were streaming down her face by now. She wiped at them with the back of her hand. "Shit! I'm going down to the lake." She ran from the room and a moment later a door slammed, the sound muffled by distance.

"What do you want to know?" Lois asked. Her voice was harsh, grating.

Of them all, Charlie thought at that moment, only Constance appeared unruffled by the scene Jill had made. And Constance had a thoughtful expression—her professional expression, was how he thought of it. And since it was her show now, he waited for her to go where she was heading.

Constance nodded to Lois, but turned to Warren and asked, "Why didn't you ever run for office?"

He started at her question. Jill's outburst had affected him deeply, it was apparent; he looked very tired, and very old. After a second he said, "I don't even know her. She's like a stranger over and over." He took a breath. "I'll get you both a drink. Lois?"

He busied himself at the sideboard, handed out gin and tonics, and then said to Constance, "I thought I could be of more service in the background." He stood at the sideboard watching her.

Constance sipped her drink, then put it down again. "Thank

you," she said. It wasn't clear if she was thanking him for the gin and tonic or for responding. "And in the background there would be no public scrutiny, no inquisitive press hounding your every movement."

He shrugged. "That too, but I have nothing to hide, nothing to fear."

"Maybe not personally. But what about the first Mrs. Wollander? What would have come up about her?"

His jaw muscles tightened noticeably, but he controlled his voice so much that it was flat, expressionless. "It was never an issue."

"I want to tell you something about your daughter, Mr. Wollander, but first you must tell me something. Why didn't you divorce your first wife? What was her hold?"

Charlie tensed, then made himself relax again. Wollander looked murderous, but he was not moving, not threatening. And if he did, Charlie thought, Constance would flatten him like a pancake. He waited.

When Wollander remained silent, Constance said gently, "She was a lovely young woman, much sought-after. She could have had her pick, and she accepted you. She made demands that you were happy to concede to. And the demands were binding long after the time when you would have divorced her if there hadn't been a hold. Isn't that right, Mr. Wollander?"

He was regarding her with disbelief. "Who told you any of that?" He rubbed his eyes suddenly and left the sideboard where he had been standing, took his chair again, and looked at nothing in particular. "You have it pretty much as it was. I agreed to sign over the property here to her, in the event that I ever divorced her. I agreed that no illegitimate child could inherit the estate. We were drinking champagne, celebrating her acceptance, laughing, joking. I thought we were joking, playing a game. I agreed in advance to a divorce settlement that seemed as remote as Mars. Divorce was the last thing on my mind then. I was deeply in love with her, crazy in love, I think the expression was in those days. I doubt that she could have suggested anything I would have balked at."

"I thought it must have been something of that sort," Constance said, still gentle and thoughtful. "You see, Mr. Wollander, your daughter believes that your prenuptial agreement bound your first wife financially in such a way that if she sued for divorce, she would be penniless. Did Jill have any money of her own?"

He shook his head, looking baffled now. "Just an allowance. But that's a preposterous idea." His expression changed, became harder. "Shelley did it deliberately, to turn her against me. She had an instinct for that, finding the sore spot, knowing how to turn people against people. She told Jill a half-truth; if she sued for divorce, she would have been comfortably fixed, but without power over me. She wanted me to start the proceedings and I wouldn't. That explains so much. I knew she lied to me about Jill, I just never considered that she also lied to her about me. I didn't think of that." He turned to Lois. "That's what she meant, that she was envious of you. It didn't make sense. But if she thinks I held her mother in bondage—"

"And now me," Lois said. She looked at Constance in dismay. "We had a talk with her and Stanley, before we announced our engagement. We told her about our agreement, and I tried to make it clear that I wasn't interested in the money or the property, that I didn't want to get between father and daughter in any way. I thought it was important for her to hear that from me. And she must have assumed that we were repeating what she thought she knew about her mother and her father." Her voice trailed off and she shook her head. "We'll have to talk to her again."

"It won't be easy to overcome a lifetime of believing something else," Constance said. "You may need help."

And now she was finished, Charlie realized, and could not have said how he knew that.

"I have copies of everything," Warren said. "She'll have to believe."

Constance shrugged and did not reply. She glanced at Charlie.

He turned to Lois. "How drunk was Malik Friday night? Staggering, falling down, incoherent?"

Lois started, and then closed her eyes hard for a moment, as if she had to clear out the present revelations in order to think back to Friday night. "Coherent," she said then, faintly, "but weaving back and forth. Unstable."

"How did you push him? Stand up, show me. I'm Malik and you're coming out."

She hesitated, and he said impatiently, "Stand up and show me."

With reluctance she stood up, still uncertain. Charlie motioned. "Here's the door. I'm blocking it, is that right?"

She nodded, and now picked up her purse and put it over her shoulder. She glanced around, at Constance, at Warren, and took a step forward toward Charlie. When he did not move, she reached out with both hands and shoved him in the chest. He took a step backward and sat in a chair. "He fell like this, straight back? Into the bush?"

She moistened her lips, nodded.

"Then what?"

"I ran to my car, it was only a few steps away, and got in and drove off."

"Did he get up?"

"I don't know. I didn't look at him again."

"How did you pay him off? Cash?"

She nodded.

"Where?"

"I met him on the road, at the entrance of the trailer court. He got in my car and I drove about half a mile to a turnoff. I parked there a few minutes and he took the money. Then I drove back."

"Where did he live?"

"I don't know. He said in the city, that's all."

"Was he using his own name?"

"I don't know. Probably."

"Did you ever enter the trailer court?"

"No."

"Did you give a vitamin list to David Levy?"

She looked bewildered and shook her head.

"Did you give work printouts, computer printouts to Malik?"

"Yes. He insisted on knowing what we were doing."

"Did you find David Levy's thermos at the farm?"

"I don't know what this is all about! What difference does it make? No. He kept it in his backpack."

"Could Malik have moved a hive of bees in his condition?"

"No. I don't know. He was staggering. Maybe if he slept

awhile and sobered up. But he didn't know anything about the bees or the mill property, or the Zukals. He didn't even know where I lived. He thought this house was miles away, that the only way to get here was by car. He came by train and stayed a couple of days and then left again. Then he came back. But he knew nothing about this area. No."

"Was he ever fingerprinted? In the service? Arrested?"

She shook her head. "I don't know. Not that I'm aware of."

"Did he have a family, close ties who would start a search if he stayed missing?"

"No, not that I know." She looked exhausted. She bit her lower lip when it began to tremble visibly.

Charlie looked at Warren Wollander, and without moderating his tone, he said, "Did you have Malik investigated?"

"I think I've had just about enough of this," Warren said coldly.

"It hasn't even started," Charlie said in a voice even colder and harder. "You had him investigated and that fact will come out. This is going to blow up in your faces and you know it. When did you have it started?"

"Last week," Warren said finally. "But my men don't talk about private work."

"Last week?" Lois asked in a faint voice. "You told me you didn't believe the letter."

"I didn't believe it," he said harshly. "My God, I thought you were faithful! It never occurred to me to believe it until I saw you leave that night. The night Jill told us she was pregnant. I couldn't sleep for thinking of it and I saw you, someone, going up the driveway. I came down to wait, to speak to you, someone, I don't know what I intended, but no one came back in. When I went upstairs again, your lights were still on. What was I supposed to think? The next day I called Myers and had him look into it."

"And a few days later Malik is dead," Charlie said softly. "Mr. Wollander, you know this isn't going to stay a secret."

Lois was staring at her husband with incomprehension. "I didn't go out that night, or any other night, not to meet him, or anyone else."

He looked at her with a penetrating gaze and finally rubbed his eyes. "It wouldn't have been Jill," he said slowly. "Why would she sneak out in a black raincoat like that? She was with that man Sebastian for hours every day, no need to meet him like that. Who else? Mrs. Carlysle?"

"Show me," Charlie said then. "You were where?"

Warren went to the window and pointed. "She vanished behind the copse of birch trees. I didn't see her again. I thought I'd hear her when she came back in but I didn't."

Charlie dismissed it. "Okay. Is it possible Sebastian believed that Jill had enough money of her own to buy the mill? Did she have money of her own?"

"No, of course not. Stanley was more than generous, but it was his money. Now it's hers, of course. What Sebastian believed, who knows?"

Lois seemed to have shrunk into herself; she sat huddled in a tight mass, her arms hard about her body. She looked from Constance to Charlie, and she asked quietly, "You think they will find out that dead man is Earl, don't you? No matter what we do or say, they'll learn that?"

"Routine police work usually uncovers an identity," Charlie said. "It may take a little time. Maybe fairly soon. What will you do if they bring around a picture and ask if you know this man?"

Before she could speak, Warren said, "I'm sending my daughter and my wife away for a rest. My daughter has had two terrible shocks and needs complete rest, and she needs a companion."

"No," Lois said, still not looking at him, keeping her gaze on Charlie. "I have my work to do. That won't help. Running away never helps." She moistened her lips. "Tell us what to expect."

"Right. I expect the sheriff already knows I'm in here with you, and that's enough to make him come calling this evening. He'll be polite and insist that the case is neatly tied up, the killer is dead of gas inhalation, accidental death, and that's that. But the routine will take place anyway. They like names to attach to corpses, after all. And he'll find out. That will bring him back here with more questions. And he'll find out that you've withdrawn large sums of money from your bank account. He'll find out that Mr. Wollander has had a private investigation of Malik. He already knows about the campaign to get rid of the Zukals. Probably there will come a time when he'll say to himself, What if this Malik character and Dr. Wharton decided they wanted the property themselves in order to continue the work they started together so many years ago? And he'll come back with even more questions. Somewhere along the line, they'll connect material found on Malik's clothing with the bushes outside the Quonset hut, and someone will remember the stones that were thrown up by tires, and someone will remember two sets of skid marks, two fast departures. Someone will suggest a scuffle between Malik and his former wife on the night the bees were moved. Now Greg Dolman doesn't like trouble, but the way this is shaping up, the Wollanders are really out of it. This is between a flatland foreigner who is now dead, and a lady scientist who doesn't really belong here anyway. That will reassure him and he'll keep coming back with more and more questions."

Abruptly Warren snapped, "Stop this! This is nothing but speculation! It won't get that far!"

Lois regarded him very steadily, as if he were a stranger. "Why not?" she asked quietly. "You know me better than anyone else here, and you were ready to believe the worst. You still believe the worst." She turned to Constance. "I was naive. But now I understand what you meant. High-priced lawyers may be able to save Mrs. Wollander, but Dr. Wharton is doomed, isn't she? Dr. Wharton cannot survive another scandal, especially of this magnitude. Suspicion, innuendo, accusations, even if it never gets as far as an arrest."

There was a soft knock on the door and Warren strode over to open it. "What is it? We're busy in here."

Mrs. Carlysle nodded. "Yes, sir, but it's the sheriff. He says he has to see you."

"Our cue," Charlie said when Warren looked over his shoulder into the room again. "We'll leave by the back door."

"I'll show you," Lois said, rising. "I doubt that he'll want to see me at this stage." She led them out without another glance at Warren.

They went through the wide hallway, into a narrower one. Good, old-money comfort, Charlie was thinking, glancing around with approval, not new-money chic; there wasn't a trace of an interior decorator more recent than the turn of the century. Good woods, cherry and walnut, chestnut paneling, stained-glass windows here and there. Very nice.

They came to a side door and Lois paused after opening it.
This was the side of the building; a short brick path led to the
wide lawn; beyond the lawn was the trail through the woods.
The sun had set; violet, shadowless twilight yielded to darkness
under the trees.

"Thank you for . . . for preparing us," Lois said formally then.
"Mr. Meiklejohn, you think that all this is connected, don't you?
David's death, the bees, Earl."

"Oh yes. Starting with Sadie."

"Sadie?" Momentarily she lost the tight control. She closed
her eyes and drew in a long breath, and then said, "Thank you.
I'd better go back in now."

Charlie and Constance walked across the lawn in silence. At
the edge of the woods he stopped to look at the driveway that
curved around the birch trees and vanished. The woods were
close on the other side of it. It was a wonder Wollander had
been able to see anyone moving there, he decided, and took
Constance by the hand and entered the woods. It was getting
dark fast and under the trees it was almost too dark already.
Still, the trail was easy to follow.

"Charlie," she said in a low voice, "that scenario you outlined, I think Greg Dolman would buy it in a second if things
get that far."

"Oh, so do I."

"And it will come out that she was friendly with Sadie. She's
the only one beside the Zukals who was."

"Yep. I know."

"And she certainly had access to David's apartment."

Charlie took out a penlight and they walked single file, and
then they were out of the woods at the end of the swinging
bridge. They had taken only a step or two on it when bright
lights came on at the corners of the mill. Charlie grunted. Al's
new security system was up and running.

"If our killer decides to strike again," he muttered unhappily,
"those lights won't mean diddly."

14

They turned down the offer of dinner from Sylvie and inspected Al's security system for a second time. Smart lights that came on when anyone got within twenty-five feet, dead bolts, sensors on doors and windows. All very good stuff, Charlie admitted, and knew that none of it would matter in this particular case with this particular opportunistic killer. He did not tell Al and Sylvie this. Instead, he merely cautioned them to be alert and not to put too much faith in the sheriff's pronouncement that the case was over and done with. Then he and Constance drove to El Gordo's, where they ordered Mexican pizza with green chilies and authentic white cheese that was very like Feta, and a seafood platter for two, Vera Cruz-style.

"With a pitcher of margaritas," Charlie said firmly. "Soon."

"A whole pitcher?" Her protest was mild, without conviction. He pretended not to hear.

"Okay," he said as soon as the waiter, Rene, appeared with the pitcher that was so cold it looked frosted. "All right!" He poured for them both. "You were saying?"

"Not a thing." She sipped, then took a real drink. "Charlie, what about the thermos? Why bring that up with Lois Wollander?"

"Funny that it's missing, that's all. Not listed among his things. Just wondered."

She drank again and settled back against the leather seat. The furnishings in El Gordo's were authentic—massive black tables and chairs with dark leather. The service pieces were heavy pewter that retained heat no matter how long the diners lingered. A nice place, she thought contentedly, and the margarita was not the only reason, although it helped.

"So," she said after a moment, "he used the thermos for tea or lemonade. Not the sort of thing you would leave in it overnight, especially if the next day you planned to work only a few hours, with a late starting time. I think he was out of lemons, at least none were mentioned in the inventory, and he had them on his grocery order. You especially wouldn't leave tea overnight," she added with a grimace. "The dishes were all washed and put away. The thermos should have been put away too, or at least on the counter ready for use. Then what?"

The way she did this, voiced the thread that was running through his mind, sometimes bothered him, sometimes amused him, most of the time startled him no matter how used to it he pretended to be. Once or twice, many years ago, he had asked her to explain how she did that, and she had looked puzzled and said simply, "I don't have an idea in the world what you're blithering on about." The one time the question had taken the form of a demand, she had turned her pale blue eyes on him in a way that reduced him to a thieving boy caught dead to rights in the act. His demands had been very infrequent over the years.

Tonight he followed her reasoning with a grin and nodded when she finished. "Then what, indeed," he said. "I wish I knew. And who took a late-night walk in a black raincoat on a warm night without rain? Why? As Warren Wollander said, Jill spent hours every day with Sebastian, no need to meet him like that. And as Lois said, Earl Malik never went to the house. I guess he didn't. I found a map with the farm marked on it, but not the house. Remember, he was on foot. That's a long walk by road, seven or eight miles from the trailer court. Just over two miles to the farm from there. That road curves and recurves before it passes by the Wollander place."

The pizza arrived and they became silent as they ate the spicy food that was piquant just to the point of pain, and drank the tangy margaritas. A couple they knew, the Martinsons, passed by their table and stopped briefly to chat. Rene brought the seafood platter and lifted the pitcher in invitation. Charlie shook his head regretfully. Rene shrugged with artistry and went away.

"Tomorrow," Charlie said, "I want to mosey over to the county board of zoning commissioners and bat the breeze a little. And I think I'd like a chat with the real-estate company that handled that piece of property. Routine stuff. No point in dragging you through it." Routine that he disliked, he thought, but did not add that. She already knew. This was the sort of thing he used to have underlings take care of. Sometimes he missed that privilege, of giving orders that would be followed without question, more or less the way he expected them to be.

"You know, your aunt Maud's birthday is coming up fairly soon," she said thoughtfully. "And there's an anniversary present for my parents to shop for. Maybe I'll browse the antique stores in Spender's Ferry."

"Aunt Maud is an Aries," he said coldly. "And your parents aren't entitled to celebrate more than once a year, just like the rest of us. We sent them something back in March."

"But shopping takes so much time," she said. "Never too early to begin."

"Christ," he muttered. "Tell me something. Do you think any of those people are crazy?" She rolled her eyes and sighed. "All right, not crazy, just demented, psychotic."

"I see. But not crazy. Clarence Bosch is determined to try to keep the project up and running for the duration of his grant. How far would he go to do that? Pretty far. Lois Wharton Wollander is determined to continue her work; she is driven by her need to accomplish good work. How far would she go to get rid of anything in her way? Pretty far. Warren is determined to protect his daughter, his property, and his wife. Same question, same answer. Pretty far. The Zukals are determined to keep that land. And so on. Crazy people? Of course not, but obsessional people, yes."

"You left out a couple," he said after a moment.

"I know. Sebastian. Charlatan, simpleton, or believer? A bit of all, I suspect. Did Jill make him a promise to buy that land and the mill? How far would he go to get it? I think the answer depends on the strength of his faith in what he's doing, and I can't judge. I haven't seen enough of him to have an opinion. Do you think he's a complete charlatan?"

He hesitated, then shook his head. Not really, he had to admit. He wanted to believe in Sebastian as one hundred percent charlatan, but not yet. He had that particular gift, and in Charlie's experience people with it usually came to believe in what they preached, to some extent, anyway. "Jill?"

Constance looked remote. "She's been twisted out of shape by too much hatred. Shelley must have been extremely clever, also twisted out of shape. I think Jill is going through a terrible time. Coming of age shouldn't be this hard, but she's waited a long time to start the process. I wouldn't like to be Warren."

"What about when he tells her the truth about the prenuptial agreement? What will that do to her?"

Constance shrugged. "Probably not what he wants. She may take it as an attempt to whitewash him, and to turn her against her mother, whom she obviously loved. She could become even more furious with him for not telling her years ago, for allowing her to live the lie of her mother's invention. She could simply start running and never stop until she's back in Paris or wherever she lived with her mother. It takes a certain amount of readiness to begin the reconciliation process and I don't think Jill is ready just yet."

Charlie thought about this for a time, and then asked softly, "And what about Tom Hopewell?" It pleased him that she looked surprised.

"You've noticed?"

"Come on," he said. "Think I'm that blind?"

"I don't think he's even aware of it himself."

"Let me have a go at him," Charlie said. "He sees Lois as a brilliant, very attractive woman, exactly as I see her. Well, maybe not *exactly* as I see her, but anyway, as a colleague that he respects and admires, and he thinks that she's wasted on an old man like Wollander."

"I doubt that he's thought through any of that."

"Yet."

"But what could he hope to accomplish by driving the Zukals away?"

"I don't know. Maybe he thinks that Lois could have bought the property and they could have worked on it together."

Constance shook her head. "He's into corn, not trees."

"Right. But two other men who looked at Lois with lust in their hearts are dead, remember. Speaking of lust, let's hit the trail. I have this little proposition I've been meaning to bring up practically all day."

———

"The game plan," he said the next morning, slowing down in Spender's Ferry, "is that we meet at Al's place. You wait there if you're done first, or I wait. You're sure you want to hike out?"

"It's only two miles or so," she said. "Of course."

"And, honey, watch your step. I think that crazy or not, there's someone hanging around who is sure deadly."

"I do, too," she said.

He stopped at a corner and she opened her door, then leaned across the seat and kissed him. "I wouldn't be Lois Wharton Wollander for anything," she murmured, withdrawing. "See you later."

What the devil was that all about, he wondered as he pulled away, and watched her in the rearview mirror. She waved, smiling softly. And he thought he knew. He began to hum under his breath. And the people she grilled today wouldn't even suspect a fire had been lighted under them.

In the first antique shop Constance compared a milk-glass bowl to a Depression-glass vase, and priced a set of iron sconces. She asked a few questions and listened, and asked a few more questions. In the next shop she examined a wicker chair and end table, and listened. And so it went for over an hour. She dropped in at the bank to cash a check and met the sister of Carla Mercer, who was Warren Wollander's secretary. She remarked on the resemblance and listened some more, and moved on. Midway down the street she saw the blond woman who had been at the trailer court; today the woman had on yellow slacks and a yellow tank top. The dark roots of her hair made her look like a sunflower.

Constance nodded to her as they neared one another; the other woman paused, then stopped.

"You were out at the court, weren't you?"

"Oh, that's where we met!" Constance said in apparent relief.

"You're new around here, aren't you?"

"I'm just waiting for my husband. He has some business to take care of and I'm burning up. I was thinking of a nice cool drink. Iced coffee, maybe. Is there a place around here for something like that?"

"Sure. Coffee shop up in the next block."

"Want to keep me company? Have a coffee with me. Charlie

said fifteen minutes but he's been hours already. And my feet hurt."

"Husbands!" the blond woman said eloquently. "Up this way."

Her name was Ellen Thurmond and her husband was canvassing the county for a national survey company. *He* had said it would be fun for her to come along for the ride, but then he parked her in the trailer court and took off every morning. *Husbands!*

It was cool and dim in the coffee shop. They sat in a booth and Constance sighed. "This feels good. That looked like a pretty nice trailer court, I thought. And that Petey! He's something else, isn't he?"

"But what? That's the question. It's a good thing your husband got there yesterday. Would have been too late by now, I guess. That Earl, he's something else, too. Flits back and forth to New York like a commuter flight or something."

"I never got to know him, but Charlie seems to think he's pretty weird."

"Weird! That's putting it mildly. A nut is more like it. Your husband a process server?"

Constance looked around, then said conspiratorially. "Something like that, why?"

"Thought so. It figures. See, Earl comes to the court and he's there alone, without a car, and I'm there all day alone without a car, and I think, Well, he's someone to talk to, at least. Can't talk to Petey. All he wants to talk about is Petey. So I go over to Earl's place and look in, and the place is a mess. I mean a real mess. And there's all these computer printouts everywhere. And he acts like it's national security time suddenly." She fell silent as the waitress brought their coffee. Then she leaned forward and said in a harsh whisper, "I think he's one of those hackers who breaks into the big computer systems and does them dirt or something." She sat back, satisfied with herself, and began to sip her coffee.

"Oh dear," Constance said. "I wonder if Charlie suspects anything like that. Go on."

"Well, the way he goes back and forth into New York City, I mean, why doesn't he just stay there if it's that important? Anyway, this morning a guy comes and says he's Earl's buddy and he's supposed to pick up his stuff for him. He has a letter from Earl and some extra rent money for the inconvenience. He says he wants to keep renting the place for another couple of months, and even pay extra just to hold it, in case Earl decides to come back and finish his work. And he even signs the register for Earl." She glanced swiftly about the coffee shop, exactly as Constance had done, as if checking for eavesdroppers, and then added, "But he spelled the name wrong. Earl Marker. That's how he signed it."

"But that's awful! I don't even know his last name. What is it?"

"I don't remember. But not Marker. Maxwell, something like that. But it's Marker now."

"It really sounds as if there's something funny going on," Constance said with a frown.

"Yeah. Let me tell you. You know how when you want to make a phone call, you put in your money and get the other person, and you talk. Right? Not Earl. He puts in his money and says a word or two, and hangs up. Then in a couple of minutes the phone rings, and he's right there, and this time he talks. We don't even have phones in those dumps. Petey's afraid we're going to run out without paying up, I guess. It's a pay phone out by his apartment. In clear view from my place. I saw him with my own eyes, twice. Like in the movies or something." She finished her coffee. "Anyways, I think he got wind that the process server was closing in or something like that. And he's skipped."

"I guess you're right," Constance said. "But that's how it goes." She listened to Ellen go on for a little while longer, but when it became apparent that nothing of interest would be added, she looked at her watch and then asked, "Would you like more coffee?"

"No, thanks. I've got to get over to the store before it gets much hotter. It's a long walk home. And *he'll* come in wanting supper on the table like always. I tell him it's a long walk, but he's out in the air-conditioned car all day, what does he care about that?"

A few minutes later they stood on the sidewalk and Constance waited to see in which direction Ellen was headed, and then walked the opposite way. She dropped in at the drugstore, and looked over the racks of magazines and books, then chatted with the pharmacist while she mulled over the numbers on the sunscreen lotions and finally chose a number twenty. He approved. Skin as fair as hers needed protecting, he said. Finally she decided she was ready to start the long walk to Al and Sylvie's house. She felt her morning had been well used.

She wished she had paused to make some notes, but that would have been too conspicuous; now, since she hadn't done that, she began to review the facts. Just the facts, ma'am, she told herself, rubbing sunscreen on her nose as she walked, sometimes in the sunlight, then in a shady area. The trailer court was only half a mile from town, not at all the long walk that Ellen had complained about. She passed it. The houses were far apart now, farmhouses mostly. The road was narrow and curvy, bordered by fields of corn, a truck garden, a small apple orchard, and some abandoned cherry trees that were gnarly and beautiful, and alive with birds eating their fill and making a raucous, joyous cacophony.

The experimental farm started, fields of corn that were planted in blocks, not like the uninterrupted fields of commercial farmers. Although from the car the farm looked like the others, on foot it was easy enough to tell the difference; there were many labels here, rope dividers, and interplanted with the corn were other crops—a block of amaranth with furry, red flowers already; squash vines sprawled; blocks of what looked vaguely like bush beans. . . .

When she reached the entrance to the farm, she turned in. She walked around the admin building, nodded to workers here and there, and kept walking toward the Quonset hut where Lois worked. When she drew near the second greenhouse, a plump young woman in shorts came out carrying a clipboard. She looked as if she had fallen asleep in the sun. Her nose was bright red; her cheeks, her forearms, and thighs all glowed.

"You looking for Dr. Wharton?" she asked.

"Yes."

"In there," she said, pointing to the greenhouse she had just left. She hurried on to the next one and went inside.

"Thanks," Constance said after her, and stood in the open

doorway peering in. Toward the far end she could see Lois Wharton and another young woman. Lois was watching this woman do something with an instrument that from here looked like a complicated hybrid of thermometer and syringe.

"Hi," Constance called.

Lois looked up, spoke to the other woman, and came toward Constance. She looked haggard, in jeans and a tank top and sneakers, her face moist, her hair stuck to her forehead here and there. There was a smudge of dirt on one cheek.

"It all comes back to me," Constance said with a smile when Lois got near. "The reason I chose psychology instead of one of the hard sciences. Actually there are several reasons, I'm sure. I never could remember to keep both eyes open when I used a microscope, for instance. I always felt that if they wanted you to use both eyes, there should be two eyepieces."

"Mostly there are these days," Lois said. She was smiling slightly now. "When your husband introduced you, he said Leidl, but I didn't make any connection with the name, I'm afraid. One of the grad students is awed, though. He's studied some of your work, he says. I'm not very good with people, associating names, remembering things that are important to others." There was hardly a hint of apology in her tone even now when it was clear that she intended to be apologizing.

"That's a strange relationship, isn't it?" Constance said. "Student and teacher, I mean. I've had students act as if they really believe I was born with a Ph.D. They sometimes seem to want to deny that we put in the hours, did the classwork, were disciples of teachers who were as difficult taskmasters as the ones they face in us. TAs, waiting for the acceptance notification, summer workshops, never quite enough money, the orals, they seem to think we skipped all that. Especially the women students," she added. Neither of them mentioned Jill.

Lois was nodding emphatically. If she noticed that Constance had started them strolling toward the trees that screened this part of the farm from the opposite side of the lake, she gave no indication. "What I was always so terrible with was the politics in academia," Lois said, her gaze on the ground before her. "Somehow I kept forgetting that everything ended up being political, no matter where or how it got started. I still do. I guess, coming out of psychology, you were better at that part."

Constance laughed with a touch of bitterness. "What I seemed to be good at in those days was butting my head against walls. Idealistic and all that."

Lois glanced at her with understanding. "Me, too."

They had reached the trees, where the shade and the breeze coming off the lake were both welcome. Constance lifted her face and breathed in deeply. "I was pretty hot," she said. Before Lois could respond, she went on, "I was thinking of you last night, the patience it must take to work with trees. I had a friend once who was going through a difficult time with a physical problem that was quite undecided. She planted half a dozen trees on their property during the period when she was stewing over the outcome of tests. I thought it was an act of supreme faith. The trees are very lovely now."

"And your friend?"

"She succumbed after five or six years but she nourished the trees to the end. She said they were her legacy. A butternut for the squirrels; a red twig dogwood for beauty in winter and for the birds; a noble fir for protection of wild things when the weather was brutal; a sugar maple . . . Each one was chosen for a particular purpose. It was, I think, a great act of love, to leave this legacy."

For a time they were both silent as they gazed at the lake that was such an unnatural, sapphire blue. The wind played on the surface in random patterns. It riffled a section that smoothed out again, then another, and another.

Suddenly Lois sat on the ground and hugged her knees tightly. Constance sat down near her. They both kept watching the unending patterns rise and fade on the surface of the blue water.

When Lois spoke again, Constance was taken aback by the harshness of her voice. "It isn't patience," she said, "it's desperation. So few people understand the situation we're in, how fast it could become critical. Tom Hopewell, Clarence, a few others. Earl knew at one time. You build a generating plant back in the Midwest, Gary, Indiana, or Chicago, somewhere, and the vapors rise and years later come down as poison, rains so acidic that lakes die, trees die, plants twist and writhe in their own brand of agony. Fish, frogs, aquatic plants, algae, all gone. And the lake looks like a reflection of heaven. Isn't that ironic, that it should be so beautiful and so deadly?"

"But can't it be countered?"

Lois continued to stare at the lake stirring in the soft breeze. In her in mind's eye she saw the ghost trees, saw the figure rising from the waters, David's blind eyes wide open. . . . She shuddered. "A seedling puts down a deep taproot," she said, almost as if lecturing. "A zone of undifferentiated cells forms where the rootlet and soil merge, and then the acid releases the aluminum in the soil and that means the tree is doomed. The tree no longer absorbs the potassium it needs, the calcium, magnesium, manganese, whatever nutrients it relied on before; aluminum replaces them or seals the cells that would take them in. Desperately the tree puts out surface roots and they take up the nitrates that also rain down from the heavens. In this form, in this amount, more poison. Or else drought comes along and the shallow roots wither. Our need for electricity, heat, light, our need for crops, fertilizers, they doom the forests. Can we undo it? No one knows. No one."

The breeze that had felt so welcome only moments ago now was chilling; the lake that had been so incredibly beautiful now seemed a mockery. Constance hugged her arms about her. "Why are you telling me this now?"

"You said patience. But that's not it," Lois said, following her own line of thought, paying little attention to Constance. "Patience is benign, maybe even saintly. Sebastian has patience. People with too much patience are dangerous. They're the ones the world listens to, wants to hear, wants to follow. Not us, the doomsayers. Do you have any idea what kind of hours we're putting in here at the farm? Clarence, Tom, me? We're not driven by patience!"

"Yet you were willing to drop your work and come chat with me," Constance said. "Why?"

Lois pressed her forehead hard against her knees. Her voice became muffled and thick. "You, your husband, you have to leave all this alone. It's over with. The sheriff's satisfied, everyone else is. I have to get back to my work. We all do, yet as long as you're still asking questions, saying it's still open, no one can."

"Why do you drive to the farm now? I thought you enjoyed the walk?"

Lois looked up then and said sharply, "It's late when I stop work, too late to walk home. I'm too tired."

"Or afraid to walk through the woods in the dark suddenly?"

"That's absurd."

"I think it's very sensible not to be alone in the dark around here," Constance murmured.

Lois took a deep breath, started to say something, and turned to look at the poisoned lake instead. Very quietly she said, "There's nothing in this for your husband. Warren paid him; he won't stop payment or anything. Just leave, let us all get on with the work we have to do."

"Your husband thinks he can delete Earl Malik from living memory?" Constance asked.

"Last night," Lois said, speaking to the wind, the water, the air, "Warren and I talked a long time. There's something he has to do, something very important to him that he must do. He had a heart attack a few years ago, before we were married. Coming that close made him reexamine his life, everything he's ever done, and he realized that the most important thing is . . . what he has to do now. Anyway, we have to get all this . . . this trouble behind us so we can both get on with these other things. We simply have to." Her words rushed out suddenly, and she was almost whispering. "He knows how to manage things, make things work out. He always has known how to do that. For him there's no mystery to politics, how to make people do what he wants them to do. It will be weeks before Jill can touch Stanley's money, but he will lend her some so that she can go back to Paris, where she wants to live. She has friends there. That poor girl never was here long enough to make any real friends, always back and forth, back and forth. He told me last night that she never quite finished high school. She went to a private school in France, and another one in Switzerland, another one in England, but altogether she never actually graduated, never went on to college. That explains her outburst about me, her jealousy of my work. She never had a chance."

"And Charlie's warning last night, that an identification will be made eventually? What about that?"

"You don't understand!" Lois said, her voice rising. "Warren can manage all that. He can manage Charlie, too, if he has to. I believe him. He's always been able to manage things. Except for Shelley. How shrewd she must have been to get that agreement signed early. She understood him thoroughly. She used to taunt him about inheriting the land here, about selling it piecemeal, plowing up the lawn to put in tract houses or something. She was a devil! She taunted him about Jill, how the line had run out, how there'd be no heirs to keep the property in the family. She made him believe Jill could never bear a child, that the land would go to strangers and be destroyed. I knew how important it was to him, to leave the property to his own blood. I even stopped taking birth-control pills last year, thinking that maybe I would be the one to provide the heir." She laughed bitterly. "I was so convinced of the rightness of providing him with a child that I actually lost the pills, misplaced them beyond finding again. Is that a Freudian slip or something?" She put her forehead on her arms again. Her words became nearly inaudible. "I know the order of things now. I guess I always did but I let myself pretend to be stupid. His daughter, his grandchild, his land, and then me. That's the order of things. And it's all right. Jill is young enough. She'll marry again and present him with grandchildren. I have my work. He has his memoirs to complete. And we have to get on with it. We have to!" When she raised her face, it was tear-streaked. She ignored the tears that were still flowing. "We'll do it Warren's way. He'll take care of everything. Father knows best and all of that."

Constance regarded her for several seconds, then turned to look at the lake again. "When did *your* father die?" she asked. "You loved him very much, didn't you?"

Lois scrambled to her feet. "What do you mean?"

"Oh, you married your mentor years ago, and you let him take you into dangerous if not illegal waters. Although he finally betrayed you, when he turned up again, you paid him handsomely, out of pity, out of remorse, out of fear. Only you know why. And now you are willing to let another father figure plan your future for you, take you into dangerous waters, perhaps betray you. And this time, through enough love, enough pa-

tience, enough forgiveness perhaps you can atone. Children
feel such guilt, such betrayal when parents die prematurely that
occasionally they spend a lifetime trying to rewrite that particular past. It never works, you know. Actually, it's one of the
most egotistical fantasies of childhood, that you as a child could
bring about the death of your parent through wishing. The
more sinned against you feel, the more forgiveness you must
offer."

Constance had been gazing at the blue lake, but now glanced
at Lois, who stood rigidly before her as if paralyzed. "You and
I both know that Clarence Bosch is well aware of your past. As
director of this project he would have been informed. That's
how the system works, and we know it. He values your work
and your honesty or you wouldn't be here, and you know that,
too. He'll keep you until the grant runs out, unless you are
arrested. He has nothing to lose by it—not at his age, with
retirement coming. And he has much to gain through your
work." She shrugged slightly, stood up, and began to brush
traces of leaf mold from her slacks. "No, you're not going along
with this just for yourself and your work. But why? To protect
your husband? I wonder why you think he needs your protection. A deep-seated psychological need of your own, or a concern of greater immediacy?"

Lois turned ashen and swayed. She held on to a tree for a
moment, then pushed herself off and ran staggeringly. She
bumped into another tree a second later, steadied herself, and
continued to run toward the Quonset hut. Constance watched.

When Lois was out of sight, Constance started up the path
that led to the Zukal house. She was startled when Charlie
stepped out from behind a tree and held out his hands to her.
Wordlessly he drew her close and held her, stroking her back.

When she pulled away after several minutes, she studied his
face. "You were watching?"

"For a while. I got here first and decided to walk around the
farm a bit. I didn't want to interrupt you. Are you okay?"

"Fine," she said wryly. "Doctor's fine, patient is a mess." They
started to walk together, his arm around her shoulders, and
she told him what Lois had said, that Warren would arrange
things. "Manage things, is how she put it," Constance said. "In-

cluding you. He could be a very difficult enemy, Charlie. He has a lot of power around here."

Charlie tightened his grasp of her shoulders and did not reply.

15

When they were within sight of the mill, Charlie stopped and said, "Anything interesting in town?" He was watching men stack lumber torn down from the interior of the mill; the little rooms were all gone now to make way for the large work space Bobby would need. Next week, he thought distantly, Bobby and Flora and their two children were due to move out from the city.

"It's a fascinating little village," Constance said. "I think if a grasshopper sneezed in that town, word would be out to everyone within ten minutes. And anything to do with the Wollanders or the farm is prime news, of course. And the people who work out here for the most part either live in town or have relatives who do. Every sneeze is reported."

"So tell me," he said in a growly sort of way.

"I am," she said in her equable sort of way. "First, Clarence Bosch didn't drive to his daughter's wedding the weekend that David died, after all. His wife drove over to Long Island on Monday of that week and he flew out of Albany at noon on Saturday. They drove home together, arrived Sunday night late."

Charlie grunted. "What on earth made you go after that tidbit?"

"Curiosity. Usually the wedding is in the hometown of the bride. I just wondered why not this time. It's because the groom is in the navy and had a very short shore leave, and his parents live on Long Island and could swing the affair, and he had to report for duty again on Sunday at noon. They all decided that on the whole it could be managed better without extra traveling for the bride and groom. And Clarence Bosch didn't have to leave home until after ten-thirty on Saturday to make his flight."

"Check. Next."

She told him about Ellen from the trailer court, and about someone's cleaning out Earl Malik's possessions. This time he cursed softly.

"That's Warren Wollander's doing. He's managing things, the bastard. Go on."

"Warren's secretary's sister is a teller in the bank where Lois banks." She said this rather flatly, not liking the implications. "Everyone in town could have known that she was withdrawing large sums of money. On the other hand, Jill had charge accounts everywhere and Stanley wrote the checks. He was very generous, they say. She lost a rather expensive gold bracelet a few weeks ago and he just bought her a new one. And you never know where you're going to see her flashing past in that little *foreign* car of hers."

He chuckled as her voice took on the tones of disapproval she had registered when listening to the townspeople. She was a good mimic.

"And the mill was a regular den for years and years, but recently it's been quiet, for the last ten years anyway. It's because those kids don't have to sneak around to do things now the way they used to. They just live together openly and don't care who knows it." Again she was mimicking one of the people she had talked to that morning. It didn't matter which one, Charlie knew; if he ever talked to that person, he would recognize that voice instantly.

Constance gave him a complete summary of her talk with Lois and they were both silent after this for several moments.

"You know," he said at last, "the case I made for her being It could even work. She certainly had reason to kill Malik."

"And David?"

"He could have tumbled to the fact that her ex was hanging out, that she was seeing him."

"And Sadie? And the campaign against the Zukals? I believe Clarence Bosch, that this little parcel of ground would be meaningless for the work she does."

"Yeah," he said. "I know. But maybe Malik knew more than

she told us about the setup here, the bees and all. Maybe he actually did it the way Greg thinks he did, and then she had to kill him, to keep him from striking again."

"Good heavens!" she cried. "What for? Malik, I mean?"

"David because he caught on to his being here. Sadie because he hated dogs. The bees because he wanted to worry Warren to death so Lois would inherit the plantation and he could step in and run it."

Gravely Constance nodded. "And then Lois told him about her prenuptial agreement, that she won't inherit, after all, and he hit himself in the head, turned on the gas, lay down and died out of remorse. I'd buy that."

Charlie scowled. "What else did you hear?"

She told him a few more things she had heard in town, mostly confirming what they both had already known. Wollander had this county in his pocket; it was hinted that he owned the sheriff, that he was the one who had made Greg Dolman stop operating a speed trap years ago, but that he had allowed it to go on until Greg had made a killing first.

"Your turn," Constance said finally.

"Not as much as you turned up," he said. "An anonymous phone call to the zoning commission started the whole investigation from that department. Everything's in apple-pie order. No one knows if it was a male or female who called. Period. And no one even looked at this place for the past four years until the Zukals showed up. There was a little interest earlier, but nothing serious."

"That reminds me," Constance said. "Apparently Sebastian has at least half a dozen rather wealthy patrons showing him real estate all over the county."

Charlie grimaced. "And one of them will buy a place for him, want to bet?"

"No way. You know very well that I never bet."

He laughed outright and took her hand. "Let's pay our respects to the Zukals and be on our way."

"You're not going to Wollander's house?"

"Nope. If what Lois said is right, there's no point. Let him stew about it. Next time we talk, let him come to me."

Sylvie had one of her green kerchiefs tied on her red hair. She had on baggy pants and an orange-and-blue plaid shirt with the shirttails out. She was standing with her fists on her hips, glaring at Al on the porch, when Charlie and Constance reached the house.

"Charlie, tell him what they do when you shoot a deer out of season. Just tell Mr. Thick Skull, will you?"

"Dear God," Constance breathed. "Did you buy a gun, Al?"

"What's this, a third degree, all of a sudden? I ain't got a right to have a gun?"

"Did the deer keep you up all night?" Constance asked him.

Al gave her a suspicious look. "Yeah. Lights go on, lights go off, on, off, all night. And you look out and it's like they're getting ready for Christmas or something, getting ready for the long ride." He looked at Sylvie with a scowl. "I told you, I ain't going to shoot *at* them, just shoot and make a noise, scare the bejaysus out of them so they'll go have a meeting somewheres else. What's the crime? A man can't shoot a gun?"

"All night," Sylvie said. "You wouldn't believe it. All night. The lights go on and you look out and it's this monster with horns like this." She spread her arms wide. "Just looking back at you. Red eyes. Like the devil in the movies, you know what I mean? Real red eyes. And just standing looking back. Like they own the world or something." She frowned in puzzlement. "I thought deers was supposed to be scared of people."

While Constance talked to Sylvie about deer and the hypnotizing effects of light, Charlie went with Al to inspect the gun, which turned out to be a twelve-gauge shotgun. He gave Al the name and address of an expert who would teach him to load it and how to shoot it, and extracted a promise that Al would not even try until he had instruction.

"Well," Constance said in the car, driving home again. "If he does try to shoot that thing, it will buck and he'll think he's broken his shoulder. A shotgun!" She glanced over at Charlie, who was scowling at nothing in particular. "Don't you have any ideas? This is giving me the willies."

His scowl deepened and he didn't even bother to answer.

In his dream Charlie was hiding bitter pills in bleu cheese and feeding them to Brutus, who gulped them down as fast as Charlie could prepare them. He woke up enough to hear rain and reluctantly got up to take care of the windows. He closed the bedroom door without a sound and dodged all three cats as he made his way through the house, checking windows. The cats always became manic if anyone got up at night or if anything unusual took place before breakfast. Ashcan wove in and out between his feet, and Brutus sniffed his ankles, his knees, and swatted Candy, and made a nuisance of himself. Then Candy and Ashcan raced after each other, and Brutus ambushed them both at the door to the dining room, and all of them wanted to go outside. If he was up, they forgot about their own swinging door that he had installed to end the doorman's job he had inherited somewhere along the line. Doorman to a bunch of dumb cats, was how he had put it then, and he repeated the phrase now as he stood with the door open, and they sniffed the air suspiciously, and then cursed him for making it rain.

He poured himself a bit of bourbon, added water, and went to the refrigerator for a piece of cheese, and Brutus was back inside at his feet magically, watching for a dropped crumb. He could move faster than thought if cheese fell, and he could hear the refrigerator door from anywhere in the yard, especially in the middle of the night. He could hear the can opener from the next county, Charlie thought sourly, dancing around the cat. Cues, Constance had said. He had learned all those cues and they were indelible in his brain, new synapses had been formed, and probably never would be erased again. At least, not without extensive countertraining.

Charlie sat at the table and found that he was no longer thinking of the insatiable cat, but of Sadie, who also had learned cues. The trainer had transferred the cue to Sylvie, he was thinking. A word, maybe, or something in the introduction that let the dog know it was all right to take food from her new mistress. And in turn Sylvie could transfer a cue to Al. He remembered what she had said, they both had to handle the dish and food for a few days, and then Al could do it alone. Scent, Charlie decided. That cue was scent. Sylvie's scent had to be on the dish while the dog was learning to accept Al, too.

He nodded to himself. The rain stopped and the sky was lightening, not in a proper dawn because there was still too much overcast; he realized he did not really want the bourbon. He got up to make coffee instead. A moment later he caught a flash of movement as Brutus jumped on his chair and snapped up the pieces of cheese Charlie had left on the table. The cat streaked away as Charlie watched in resignation.

A little after seven Constance stood in the doorway as Charlie moved about the kitchen muttering. Muttering in their house could mean either that the person speaking needed reminding that what was being said was unintelligible, and at those times it was okay to interrupt, to join in, to ask questions. The other muttering was different: it was not to be interrupted. Muttering at seven in the morning, alone in the kitchen, was definitely the other kind. He was making pancakes, his voice a soft rumble; the aroma of coffee was rich and irresistible. She entered the kitchen without a sound, and he looked at her with an almost blank expression and said, "But why?"

"I give. Why? What why?"

"I think I know how someone got rid of Sadie, but Jesus, why? What was the point?" He glanced at the clock on the stove. At seven-thirty he would call Brenda Ryan, and it was taking hours for the time to creep to that number. Several hours had passed since the last time he looked at the clock, two minutes ago.

Constance blinked, and he grinned at her. "I'll bring coffee, you sit." He poured a cup for her and brought it to the table, where she was yawning. "I'll pretend you're awake. Ready?"

"In a second." She drank some of the coffee first, then nodded.

At nine-thirty they drove up to the Ryan Kennels. The sun had broken through the clouds and the morning was brilliant and pleasantly cool, fresh-smelling, sparkling with water droplets everywhere. The trembling drops looked as pure, sweet and life-giving as they were meant to be.

Brenda Ryan was waiting for them. This morning she was wearing a bright-pink-and-white print dress, and pink earrings that looked like bracelets. Three hundred eighty pounds, Charlie thought, shaking her hand, no matter what she had told Sylvie. She had a very firm grip. A large black Labrador retriever was at her side. Brenda's fingers brushed the dog's head, and it began to wag its tail languidly, as if out of duty rather than interest.

"This is Duchess," Brenda said. "And if you can get her to eat, I better go into another line of work."

"You held back part of her food this morning, so she'll have an appetite?" Charlie asked, suddenly not quite as certain as he had been only moments ago. He was carrying a shopping bag.

"Sure did, but it wouldn't make any difference. I mean, most dogs will eat whenever food's available, hungry or not, unless they're really overfed. And I don't overfeed my dogs."

For a moment she looked as if she dared him to comment on that, but he pretended no automatic comment had come to mind, and he and Constance moved into the office, which instantly became very crowded.

Brenda watched as he began to rummage in the bag. First he pulled out a plastic-wrapped package of latex gloves. He pulled on the thin rubber gloves without a word and felt inside the bag again. This time he took out a package that held a scarf. He handed it to her unopened.

"Would you mind taking out the scarf and tying it on your head a couple of minutes?"

She hesitated, watching him through narrowed eyes, then shrugged, sending her patterned dress into a flurry of motion. Her hair was bouffant, curled, sprayed, dyed, with smells Duchess would recognize instantly, Charlie thought, hoped. He watched her put the scarf over her hair and tie it loosely. Next he took out a can of dog food, and finally a can opener.

He held up the can for her inspection. "Gourmet dog food," he said, unnecessarily; she was already nodding at it. "Just tell me this," he said, opening the can. "Is there anything in particular that you do or say when you feed her?"

"Nope. She's trained to stand back and wait, and then eat. Don't have to do anything more than put it down for her."

"Good. I was afraid there might be something else." The top came off, stuck to the magnetized opener. He put it on the desk. "If it's going to work, that's probably time enough for the scarf," he said. "Let's finish. I'll take it now."

His uncertainty was increasing by the second. Duchess had not shown so much as a flicker of interest at the sound of the can opener, or the malodorous contents of the can. Brutus would be climbing his head by now, Charlie thought gloomily. Brenda handed him the scarf and he spread it out on the desk and began to spoon dog food onto it. He put a few spoonfuls down and cast a doubtful look at the beast who sat there looking as inscrutable as a damn Buddha. Sighing, he wrapped the food enough to move it, and lowered it to the floor, and stepped away from it.

"Now, I guess we just wait," he said. "You didn't give her a signal to sit still or anything, did you?"

Brenda was looking very interested now. She shook her head. "She's waiting to see if I'm going to give her a signal. See her look at me?"

Charlie didn't see the dog move a muscle.

"If this works," Brenda said soberly, "I'll have to change my methods, take it into account." She became silent now as Duchess began to shift.

The dog stood up, still apparently waiting for a sign, and when none was forthcoming, she ambled over to the food on the scarf and sniffed it with interest, then sniffed all around it, and back to the scarf again. Then she gulped it down in two bites. She licked her chops and sat down again.

"Goddamn it!" Brenda muttered. "I never thought of that. Of course, you'd have to have an in, get something that belonged to the owner, but even so, it's gotta be trained out. Goddamn it!"

Charlie looked at Constance, who was smiling, more at his relief than at his victory. "So now we know how," she said. "But why?"

She drove back. He talked.

"We made such a fundamental mistake," he said. "The dish was found at the mill and we assumed that food had been put in it over there. Let's rethink the whole thing. Someone doctored the dog food and put it at the edge of the property. Sadie wouldn't have barked unless someone actually stepped over the line, and that wasn't necessary, after all. Just reach in and lay down the scarf with the food on it, then stand back and wait. You saw how that mutt wolfed down the food. Two bites and done. Then the poisoner reached in and grabbed the scarf back and was finished. David found the scarf and returned it to Sylvie. I'd guess he didn't realize until later what it meant. There could have been traces of the food on it as well as grease, or he could have seen someone with it earlier. He saw something, that's for sure. So he was next."

He became silent, brooding about it. Finally Constance said, "Charlie, it doesn't make much sense, does it?"

"Why not?"

"Well, killing David because of the dog poisoning, and then killing Earl Malik because of the bees. It just doesn't make sense. Neither of those things, killing a dog or moving bees to the station wagon, was a capital offense; a reprimand, a fine, that's all either warranted. Murder to prevent discovery is just too much. In each case the response to being found out was too great. It keeps getting muddled in my head. I mean, it seems to be what happened, but it's so senseless."

She was a good driver; when she needed to pay close attention she focused on the road and other traffic, then her thoughts were tightly contained. After the road was clear again, the other thoughts took precedence. It was an automatic process that she didn't question. Now traffic thickened a little and she passed a Grand Union truck, and a Honda, and a few minutes later she glanced at Charlie and started to speak. He was slouched in the passenger seat, his chin tucked in, a scowl on his face.

She held the words and looked straight ahead again. Beside her, Charlie stirred, and the words were in his head just as if they had been uttered. He grunted again, considering. They had made a second, more serious fundamental mistake.

Warren Wollander was going over the several days' stack of accumulated mail with his secretary, Carla Mercer. Pleas for money; would he put in an appearance at a dinner for Representative Lorenzo; two committee meetings were coming up, an agenda was needed . . . a policy meeting in Washington . . . Tiredly he rubbed his eyes when the phone rang. He motioned for her to take it, and he leaned back in his chair with his eyes closed.

"I'll ask," she said. "It's Richard at the gate. He says Sebastian is out there and is asking permission to come in."

With a jerk Warren sat upright. "Let him come in. And you can get started on that stuff. We'll continue this afternoon with the rest of it."

She spoke softly into the phone and hung up. She gathered up papers, checked around the desk, and left for her own office down the wide corridor, toward the rear of the house. Warren went to the window to watch for Sebastian.

Sebastian's car, a powder-blue Cadillac, came into sight at the exact spot where someone had vanished the night Jill had announced her pregnancy. He rubbed his eyes again, harder this time, as if to erase the memory that was filled with pain, and he walked through the study, through the hallway to the main house entrance, and admitted Sebastian before he had a chance to ring the bell.

"I would like to see Mrs. Ferris," Sebastian said.

"Come in. This way." Warren pushed the door shut and started back to the study. When Sebastian hesitated, he motioned with his hand. "Come along."

At the study, he waited until Sebastian was inside, and then closed that door and stood at it. "Sit down, if you'd like. This won't take long, but you may as well be comfortable."

"Mr. Wollander, I have no wish to take up your time. I really would like to see Jill." He remained standing in the middle of the room.

"I know. I'll call her in a minute." He studied Sebastian for another moment, then started walking slowly toward his desk. When he spoke again, his voice was machinelike, completely expressionless, as if he were reading from cue cards. "Sebastian Pitkin. Boy evangelist. Petty thief. Trick knee that keeps you out of the army but permits you to sit in lotus. Married twice, divorced twice. One son, sixteen years old now. Expensive tastes and the ability to indulge them without any taxable income. Out of the country for seven years, never accounted for."

Not a flicker of expression crossed Sebastian's face. He listened almost gravely, as if checking off the items against a list in his mind. When Warren stopped, Sebastian said, "I would like to see Jill, if you please."

"Of course." Warren had come to a stop at his desk. He moved around it and reached for the phone and paused once more with his hand on it. "I have very little influence outside this state, but for various reasons a good deal inside it. Did you know that many IRS investigations arise from information gathered first at the state level?" He picked up the phone and touched a button. The wait was brief. "Jill, Sebastian is here, in my study. Will you come down, please?"

Sebastian's expression continued imperturbable. Warren sat down and leaned back in his chair and neither said anything more until Jill entered.

"I came to see how you are," Sebastian said, studying her face intently. "I was concerned about you."

"Well, as you see, I'm fine. In mourning, but okay."

"Are you doing your meditations? Are they helping?"

She shrugged. "Not really. That served its purpose, and I appreciate all you did for me, but I think I'm through with that now."

"Jill, you are the best student I've ever had. You have enormous promise. Don't let it slip away because of this tragedy. Let this experience strengthen you; find its meaning and grow from it."

"See it as an opportunity?" she said bitterly. "Look, Sebastian, for a time I believed I could follow your path, but no longer. I'm sorry."

"I have the name of a camp, up in the hills about an hour's drive, they tell me. It's a private camp that has come on the market. Go there with me, Jill. A ride up into the hills, a walk under the trees. We won't even have to talk if you prefer silence during this healing period. Silence brings its own power to heal the soul if you let it. And, yes, see it as an opportunity to learn, to grow, to contemplate the absolute in a way that has never been available to you before, because you were not prepared before to face it."

She was moving restlessly about the room. She looked irritable and impatient when she took a breath and said, "Leave me alone, Sebastian. I wish everyone would just leave me the hell alone."

"I know he had me investigated, and that he told you things that he learned, but, Jill, I already talked about those things in our group meetings. Think back. You know I already talked about those things. Each one, every mistake filled with pain and regret became an opportunity to grow. And we grow or we cease to exist. We all have things in our pasts that are better left behind. We talked about that, too, Jill. Remember?"

She whirled around to face him. "What are you saying?"

"Only the truth."

"Well, listen to me, Sebastian! I don't have anything in my past that can hurt me now. Nothing! And I have no intention of helping you finance a school, or a church, or a camp, or even a barbecue! Now leave me alone!" She ran from the room and slammed the door after her.

"You'd better go," Warren said in a flat voice.

Sebastian looked at him, then looked past him out the window. "There is an image in my mind," he said softly, "of a puppet master whose fingers drip venom that runs down the wires that control the puppets, and the puppets absorb the poison, more and more until they are sickened and die of it."

He turned and walked from the room. Warren swiveled in his chair to watch out the window until the blue Cadillac curved around the birch trees and disappeared. He felt chilled and there was a tightness in his chest that he hadn't felt since his heart attack five years ago. His hands were clenching the arms of his chair so hard that when he forced them away, they hurt.

Gradually the noises of the house and yard returned. The sound of a riding mower swelled and receded; he could hear the rustle of Mrs. Carlysle in the hall, and a door closing somewhere in the back of the house. Outside, birdsong that had been silenced by Sebastian's departure now resumed. Slowly he arose and walked out through the side hall, out into the yard, where the overnight rain had refreshed everything. Two gardeners were at work in the flower beds where majestic delphiniums made a deep blue backdrop for golden irises, and masses of pink sweet williams and carnations were intermingled with clouds of baby's breath. The lawn glistened with raindrops in the shade where it had not yet evaporated. So much beauty, he thought. So much beauty. He found himself standing under the oak tree that he thought of as his tree and he touched the bark almost tenderly. He wanted to wrap his arms around it as far as they would reach, press his cheek into the trunk, and weep.

16

When Constance came within sight of their house, she slowed down. A pale-blue Cadillac was in the drive and leaning against it was Sebastian.

"Well, well," Charlie murmured. "Well, well."

She pulled into the driveway and stopped a short distance from the Caddy; Sebastian straightened up. He looked grim and very angry. "Hi," she called pleasantly, getting out of the Volvo; she headed for the front door with her key in her hand.

"I want to talk to you," Sebastian said to Charlie.

"How'd you even find me?" Charlie asked, following Constance.

"Jill said you lived around here somewhere. I asked at a gas station down the road. I said I want to talk to you. Do you mind?"

"Well, of course not. Come on in." He looked at Sebastian with disbelief. "You don't mean out here, do you?"

"It will take just a second."

"In the house," Charlie said firmly and entered without glancing back again.

Constance had gone on through to the sliding door to the patio, which she opened, and then continued to the kitchen, moving around cats without paying any attention at all to them. Candy was complaining in a loud voice and Brutus was looking his slitty-eyed meanest. As soon as they saw a stranger, Candy streaked away, back through the cat door to make her escape, and Ashcan pretended he was a rug.

"Well, sit down," Charlie said to Sebastian, motioning toward a chair at the dinette table. "Honey, you going to make coffee, or you want me to?"

"I'm doing it. Or would you rather have tea, Sebastian?"

"Neither one," he said. He did not sit down, but glared at

Charlie, who did. "I have a message for you to deliver to your boss, Wollander. Just tell him that if he, or anyone else, harasses me in any way, I have enough information to make life uncomfortable for him, and I'll not keep it to myself."

"You mean about that woman? What's-her-name?" Constance asked from the kitchen end of the long room.

"That's what I mean. I'm sure he would prefer not to have everyone in the county looking at him with raised eyebrows the next time he presides at a committee meeting. Especially the one on ethics in government that he's so fond of."

"Gave you the bum's rush, did he?" Charlie asked with interest. "But Jill's still on your side, isn't she? I mean, she's of age and all."

Abruptly Sebastian pulled out a chair and sat down. He looked uncomfortable, and for a moment Charlie wondered if he should offer him a cushion for the floor instead.

"Jill's completely dominated by him," Sebastian said. "I didn't believe she would fall into that kind of trap again but he's controlling her; she's like a doll that he moves around here and there."

The fragrance of brewing coffee began to float around the room. Constance brought cups and saucers to the table, then cream and sugar. She talked as she moved about, almost as if absently, "Of course we can tell him that, but I don't see what difference it would make, do you, Charlie?" Her back was turned when she paused, not really long enough for him to answer. She picked up the carafe and came back to the table with it. "I mean if everyone already knows . . ."

"Well, everyone doesn't know that he had a motive for killing David Levy," Sebastian said harshly. "I can rake that over a few times and see how he likes it."

"Oh, really," Constance murmured, and now she sat down and poured coffee for them all. "Do you take sugar? Cream?"

He looked down at the cup before him in surprise, then back to her. She was smiling easily.

"Why don't you tell us about it?" she said. She looked at Charlie with raised eyebrows and he nodded almost imperceptibly. "You see, Sebastian, we aren't working for Mr. Wollander anymore. He fired us, I'm afraid. But we are working for Mr. Levy; we are investigating the death of David Levy."

Sebastian set his mouth in a tight line. He pushed back his coffee cup and seemed ready to leave.

"The sheriff is convinced that David's death was accidental overdose," Charlie said evenly. "I'm convinced that it was murder. But the sheriff may have the last word. Again, I just don't see why Wollander would give a damn about what you think."

"The sheriff will say what the puppet master tells him to say. Wollander would go to any length necessary to prevent a word of scandal from touching his wife, and David had more than just a word. He had a whole history to talk about. That's motive enough." Now he stood up.

"Sit down," Charlie said sharply. "Are you really so naive that you think you can get away with blackmail, especially with someone as powerful as Wollander?" Sebastian didn't move. Charlie waved toward the chair, the coffee on the table. "You'd better sit down," he said tiredly, "and hear me out. You see, the natural response to your little blackmail threat is to say that you had even more motive. You wanted the property for yourself—"

"I didn't. I told you, Jill didn't have a cent. I wasn't expecting to get that property at any time."

"I know quite well what you told me. Now I tell you things. I said sit down, damn it! I'm getting a crick in my neck."

Sebastian's eyes were bulging more than ever, but he sat down, his face flushed, his hands clenched.

"Use your own method and relax," Charlie muttered. "My God, you'd think I had a gun to your head. Relax, damn it. See, this is how Wollander could play it. David sees you and Jill together, maybe he even hears her telling you there's nothing she won't give you if you can help her get pregnant. And that means the mill property. Then the Zukals arrive and they have to be driven out again. First the dog, then David." He paused, then looked at Sebastian with a hopeful expression. "By the way, you haven't come across a stray thermos, have you? David was missing one."

"No, I haven't. And you're stringing a line of BS and you know it."

"Oh well," Charlie said blandly, and continued. "Anyway, the Zukals dig in, get their backs up, and another dirty little trick is called for, this time the bees in the station wagon. And this time a transient sees what's happening, and he has to get it, too. But now Jill has inherited a mint, and, no doubt, the Zukals will clear out, and the mill will be up for grabs again, but suddenly Jill's giving you the cold shoulder, telling you to get lost, and you want to retaliate by spreading dirt on the old man. That's how he'll play it, Sebastian. Believe me, I've seen the type many times, and that scenario will hold up. Yes indeed, it would work just fine. If anyone has to leave a tidbit here, another there to clinch it, I'd guess tidbits will be strewn around." He sighed and drank his coffee. "And as you said, the sheriff will buy whatever he has to sell."

Sebastian's head began to shake from side to side, as if he had nothing to do with it, was not even aware of it. His lank hair swayed back and forth. His gaze remained fixed on Charlie, who had to turn away because it was too damn eerie, he decided.

"It wasn't like that," Sebastian said finally. "It wasn't. She never even mentioned pregnancy until after Stanley was dead. I had no idea. She never promised me anything for anything. I was in the role of guide to meditation, nothing more than that. And she was a good student. That day at the mill was the only time we were ever alone together for more than a counseling session a few times at the house, where there were always others about. I have witnesses. He can't stick me with anything like that. I have too many witnesses."

"She seems to have found plenty of time to blab to you about the family, about David. Not in front of all those witnesses, I'd bet."

"No. Of course not. We had private counseling sessions. She was very disturbed in the beginning, very. She seemed to derive comfort, serenity even, from our sessions—for a time, at least. She never had anyone to talk to before, not even her mother, certainly not her father or stepmother. She needed to talk to someone and I filled that role for her. She talked a lot about her father, how much she hated him, and the reasons. Good reasons, I can see now, but the emotion of hatred was harming her, truly harming her." He looked very earnest, very sincere. "That emotion, hatred that fierce, does far more damage to the hater than to the one who is hated. I was teaching her that lesson."

Constance got up and took away his coffee, which had become cold. She refilled the cup and brought it back and this time he lifted it and sipped.

"So Wollander found out that David knew something about Lois and might tell it out of turn," Charlie said. "Is that it then? Just that? Will you keep adding more details as needed?"

"What more?" Sebastian took a deep breath. "From what Jill has said about her father, that was more than enough, Mr. Meiklejohn."

"Just Charlie," he said, then added with a grin, "Doesn't have quite the same ring as when you say, 'Just Sebastian,' but it's the best I can do. And, no, that isn't enough, not even for a man like Wollander. What's the rest of it?"

"Never mind," Sebastian said. "I'll tell him myself."

"I doubt it. You had a chance and blew it. Don't be an ass now. You wanted us to do your dirty work for you. Pass the word that you're talking to people, no matter about what, just talking. He would then go to Jill and ask what you could possibly know that gives you any clout, and she would stew and steam over it, and maybe even come up with an item or two, and then the high and mighty Mr. Wollander would treat you with respect. Or at least leave you alone. But, you see, Sebastian, you're playing in a new league here, a new game, new players, and you don't know the rules they play by. You don't even know the name of the game. It's *Put the Bugger in His Place.*" He stood up lazily and stretched. "I'm afraid, Sebastian, old buddy, that you've been used, and now you're being sent packing. Just the way it goes." He smiled kindly at him. "And you know very well that I won't help you in a blackmail or extortion scheme, now, don't you?"

Sebastian glared at him and pushed himself up from the table. "Try this one, then," he said harshly. "Who was the man Lois Wollander was keeping on the side in the trailer court? Does the whole world know about that little affair?" He stalked from the room, with Charlie close behind. Constance began to clear the table.

"I wonder just how much about that he actually knows," she said when Charlie returned, grinning.

"Remember that question we asked about Sebastian back in the beginning?" he said. "I've got my answer. How about you?"

She tilted her head, considering, and then said, "I think we probably agree. Poor man," she murmured. "He's trying so hard to keep his toe in the door. You really shook his tree for him, and you offered no comfort at all to soften it."

"Hah! That's my mission for today, shake trees, see which nuts come tumbling out. And as for him, he tried to put the bite on the wrong woman, that's his problem. And Daddy came to the rescue. I'll give Pete Mitchum a call now."

Three times Charlie had had to tell Pete, nothing yet, still working on it. The boy's disappointment had been hard to take each time. Mr. Levy's disappointment had been much harder on the two occasions that Charlie had returned calls from him. Soon, he thought, soon.

"Nothing definite yet," Charlie said to Pete when he appeared a few minutes later. "I could use some help, though."

Pete nodded with enthusiasm. "Whatever I can do, Mr. Meiklejohn." Although he had been disappointed, his faith was undiminished.

Constance brought a plate of cookies and a can of soda. Now and then she made Scandinavian delicacies that her grandmother had spoiled her and her sisters with, and she always gave most of them to the Mitchum boys. Too much butter, too much cholesterol for Charlie, who could stand to lose a few pounds, she thought, but she didn't nag about it. Instead, she made the special cookies that he loved and let him have a few, and gave the rest away. And the reason, she knew, was the way the boy was looking at Charlie at that moment. Charlie pretended not to notice that the Mitchum boys had a serious case of hero worship, and he harrumphed if she hinted at it, but there it was. Fortunately he had never said anything like give me a hand, will you, or one of them might well have run for a saw.

"What I want is four or five guys about your size," Charlie was saying, opening the map he had found in Malik's trailer. Pete Mitchum stood five inches taller than Charlie, and his brothers were just as tall and broad. He nodded with a serious expression now that they had got down to business.

"Here's Spender's Ferry, out the county road here to the farm," Charlie said, pointing. "And the mill property. Now, as soon as you cross this bridge, all the land on the left is state forest." He traced the curvy road, and then stopped. "And this is the Wollander driveway, in about ten feet from the fence here. State forest on the other side of the fence." He pulled out a felt-tip pen and drew a wavy line on the map, the boundary, and then drew in the Wollander driveway. "Along about here, I think, is a clump of birch trees that will be your guide. The driveway turns just past the trees and goes on to the house. I want you guys to start at the county road, on the state forest side, and search the woods from the fence on in for about three hundred feet, from the county road on past the birch trees another thirty feet. It's a lot of ground to cover."

"Naw, it's not that much," Pete said. "What are we hunting for, Mr. Meiklejohn?"

Charlie glanced at Constance. "I'm looking for a thermos," he said. "And you might not find anything at all, but I want a good show of a bunch of guys searching. Carry big bags, wear gloves, pick up anything and everything that doesn't belong in the woods, even beer cans. Now, someone will probably come over to see what you're up to, and just tell them you're working for me, and you're searching for a thermos. You might even find a thermos, but I don't want you to fix your mind on that. Chances are you won't find it. If you do find one, don't open it, just chuck it in the bag and keep on searching until you cover the area. Got it?"

"Yes sir!" He looked like a horse at the starting gate.

Charlie thought for a second. "It could be that the sheriff or a deputy will come along and order you to leave. Don't argue. Just tell them you're working for me, and that you're on state land and have a right to be there. Tell them where I am, at the Zukal place, if they want to talk about it. If they insist that you leave, do it. Bring your loot over to the Zukal place. I'll be there."

"What if they try to take the bags away from us?"

"Well, don't let them," Charlie said mildly. "One of the things you'll have to have is a whistle. Use it if they want to steal your loot. I'll come running. But I doubt it will come to that."

Pete looked ecstatic. "They won't get it away from us, Mr. Meiklejohn. Don't worry about that."

"Okay, I won't. Now, about time. It will take you a while to gather your forces, round up the bags, the whistle, gloves. Do you think you can have it all together by four?"

"Yes sir!"

"Good. When you finish, come over to the Zukals' and leave the bags, and you're done."

Charlie watched Pete cross the yard at a run. When he reached the fence this time he didn't bother to climb it; he put one hand on top and vaulted over as easily as a deer.

"One more little chore, and then lunch, and then off to the wilderness to shake a few more trees." He grinned at Constance, who looked up from cutting dense wheat bread. She already had roast beef out, and lettuce, and other good things, he saw with approval.

He dialed the Wollander house. Carla Mercer, Wollander's secretary, answered on the second ring.

"Charlie Meiklejohn," he said. "I'd like to speak with Mrs. Carlysle, please."

There was a pause on the other end, and then she said, Just a moment; he nodded in satisfaction when he heard a click on the line. He put his hand over the mouthpiece and silently formed the words: "They're taping it."

He waited almost two minutes before Mrs. Carlysle's tentative voice said hello.

"Mrs. Carlysle, this is Meiklejohn," he said in a brisk voice. "I need some information that I think you can help me with. Would it be convenient if I drop over at about one, or one-thirty?"

"Oh, no, I couldn't. I mean, I'm working. What is it?"

"Not over the phone, please. It won't take more than a minute or two, I assure you. And it has nothing to do with you personally." She made a throat-clearing kind of sound which he ignored. "I don't want to bother the family anymore and I believe you can tell me what I need to know. About one, then. I'll come around to the kitchen." He hung up, and looked over at Constance. "Is it lunch yet?"

At one-twenty-five he and Constance walked from the woods onto the Wollander lawn. Since he had planned to make them wait until almost one-thirty, he was satisfied with his timing. He was humming under his breath.

"I think we have a reception committee," Constance said softly.

"Pretend you don't notice."

Warren Wollander and Lois were on the patio watching them all the way. Warren moved stiffly to the edge of the flagstones as they drew near.

"I want to talk to you," he said.

It sounded to Charlie much more like an order than an invitation. "I have some business with your housekeeper, and then I'll be on my way," he said pleasantly.

"I don't think you have any business with anyone in this house. And I don't want to broadcast what I have to say. Will you come up here, please."

Still not a real invitation, Charlie thought with regret. He shrugged, and he and Constance changed course and headed for the patio. "All I really want to know is who hauls your trash away, and to where," he said, still on the lawn a few feet away. "I thought the housekeeper was the logical one to tell me."

Lois was staring at him in bewilderment. "Why?" She looked as if she had not slept enough for a month, and the effects were ravaging. There were hollows under her eyes and she was very pale.

Warren gave her a sharp look and she sat down abruptly in a chaise. Charlie could imagine the scene that must have taken place a short time ago: Warren in his good, gruff, masculine voice saying, "I'll handle this. You just keep still."

"I'm still on the trail of that missing thermos," Charlie said with a shrug. "The way I figure it, David had to take the pills somehow, and it could be that he dissolved them in lemonade and did it that way. But then, where is the thermos? See? If it turns up in a landfill somewhere with traces of quaalude and barbiturates, then we'll know, won't we?"

"You're still harping on that?" Warren said in disbelief. "My God, everyone else is satisfied that it was an accidental overdose. What I want to tell you, Meiklejohn, is that I am convinced, as is the sheriff, that the culprit was that transient in the apartment. We're both satisfied that nothing more is to be done except get on with life now. I don't want you nosing around here anymore. You are no longer in my employ, and if you enter this property again, you will be treated as a common trespasser. Is that clear?"

"Mrs. Wollander," Charlie said, looking past Wollander, "was that thermos you bought a regular, glass-lined one, or stainless steel?"

"Just a regular one, glass lining, I guess." Her voice rose. "Are you going to search the landfill? For a thermos?"

"If it comes to that. First the woods. I thought of the lake, but an empty thermos would float, you see, so I gave that up. I thought that if David took it with him when he swam that morning, he could have left it at the edge of the water, but someone would have spotted it, either there or floating around." He was pointedly ignoring Warren Wollander, who was livid with fury now. Charlie gazed across the lake. "I'm hiring a few of the workers to put in some overtime, after-hours, to search the farm. Eventually I may have to tackle the landfill."

"There could be a dozen such thermos bottles in the landfill!" Warren Wollander said harshly. "You're wasting your time, and right now you're wasting mine. Get out, Meiklejohn."

"I know there could be others," Charlie said. "And we'll haul every damn one in for laboratory examination. You realize how hard it is to hide something if people make a determined effort to find it? Very hard, Mr. Wollander. Very hard."

Lois had risen, and was gazing at the lake also. Hesitantly she said, "It could be in there. At the bottom. If he didn't put the cap back on, it would fill with water and sink." She looked at her husband. "I think we should call in someone to make a search of the lake. If they find it in there, that will pretty much settle it. Then we'll know."

"I already have someone lined up," Charlie said. "But that's good reasoning. I don't think you leave the cap off myself, because you might lose it, but it's possible. If nothing turns up at the farm, or in the woods, bright and early tomorrow morning you'll see people in the lake. Even if it's in the water, filled with water, there probably will still be traces of the drugs. It doesn't take much to show up in a good lab with good technicians. I have them lined up, too."

"I won't tolerate this," Warren said. "I won't have people here in the lake."

"But the Zukals will," Charlie said easily. "I looked it up in the county records. They have as much right to the lake and what goes on with it as you do. And my people will enter through their property, not yours. Are you going to give me the name of your trash collector, or do I have to do that the hard way, too?"

"Get out of here!" Warren turned and stamped back inside the house. After a moment, Lois followed him.

"She looks dreadful," Constance said in a low voice as they retraced their steps across the lawn.

Charlie shrugged. His face was set in hard lines, his eyes were flinty, like chips of coal. "Let's go see Bosch," he said.

Constance felt chilled. This was how he had become just before they both retired: hard, merciless, finally showing as little sympathy for the victim as for the criminal. The fact that he had become like this was what had made her declare an ultimatum: He had to quit the force, or she would leave him. It came back over him from time to time, that unswerving, unpitying coldness that once had threatened their marriage, threatened everything in her life that she cared about. When he turned into this kind of iceman, the chill extended out from him to enwrap her.

In fact, Charlie was not thinking of Lois at that moment, nor of Constance, either. That order, "Get out of here!" reverberated in his head. All his years on the force, as a fireman, an arson investigator, a city detective, he had been subordinate to men with power just like that, power to decide when to prosecute, when to plea bargain, when to persist, when to call off everything. The power to order, "Get out of here!" and never have to look back to see that they were obeyed. You stay with it long enough, something rubbed off on you, he had come to understand finally. Something that couldn't be washed away. Not as simple as hatred, or contempt, not necessarily corruption. But something rubbed off that lingered, that made you see them all as pieces moving in an insane game—the politicians, prosecutors, judges, cops, those who lashed out and those who were lashed, victimizers, victims, all players in the same hellish game. Each and every one of them willing to do whatever it took to survive the game. Even him, Charlie knew, and the knowledge filled him with icy fury, because he wanted, needed, a world built on sanity and reason and law, and they, the ones who made the game rules, had destroyed it, and had forced him to participate in the destruction. By the time you were smart enough to realize that something had rubbed off, you were a bona fide member of the wrecking crew, and the stain, the something, had penetrated right down to the bone marrow.

With those few words, *Get out of here!* Wollander had established his place in the game, Charlie's place, Lois's, everyone's. Those few words had caused to surface a deeper bitterness than Charlie had experienced for a long time.

He felt Constance take his hand, and then squeeze it hard, and he looked at her with surprise.

"Nothing," she said. "Onward. Let's go shake Clarence Bosch's tree."

Charlie grinned at her, but it was superficial. It did not touch his eyes. His eyes looked like dull chips of stone.

"Look, Dr. Bosch," Charlie said a few minutes later, "I don't give a shit if you like it or not. I want to hire your people. If I can't, then I'll bring in outsiders. I'll get a court order if I have to, but I want the search made today."

They were standing outside the admin building. Bosch was grayer than ever, more troubled than ever. "Do you have any idea of what all this nonsense is doing to us? Do you? We're weeks behind schedule. Weeks! I told you my caretaker here found nothing. Nothing!"

From the corner of his eye Charlie could see Tom Hopewell approaching, not in a big rush, but covering the ground. "Did you get a look at that man in the apartment?"

Bosch shook his head. "No. I looked in the window, but he was just a man on the floor."

"How long have you known about Lois Wharton, who she is?"

Bosch looked startled. He glanced at Tom, who was only a dozen yards away, and motioned him not to come closer. In a low voice he said, "I won't have you dragging any of that into this mess, Meiklejohn! That's uncalled-for. It has nothing to do with anything here and now. Lois Wharton is a brilliant scientist, doing brilliant work, and that's all I intend to say on that matter."

"Why didn't you mention that you left town for your daughter's wedding late the morning that David died?"

"Oh, my God, what are you driving at? I didn't conceal it. It simply never came up."

"I bet." Charlie waved to Tom Hopewell to join them. Brusquely he said, "I'm hiring some of your workers here to search this end of the farm when they knock off for the day. Any objections?"

"What the hell for?" Tom Hopewell demanded.

Why didn't he buy some new jeans? Charlie thought irritably. He was tired of these worn-out clothes, worn like a badge of merit, a symbol of his dedication to work, his unawareness of the amenities.

"If David took pills dissolved in lemonade, he might have left his thermos at the edge of the lake, or he might have dropped it on his way back to his apartment. I want a thorough search made of the grass at the lakefront on this side, and through the undergrowth from the lake to the apartment units. Understood?"

Tom Hopewell blinked, and Clarence Bosch raised his eyes beseechingly toward the sky. Bosch said, "You know how much area you're talking about? The whole side of the lake?"

"Absolutely. Do you know precisely where he went in, where he came out? Do you know precisely where he might have sat down to take a drink? Or the exact path he followed back to his place? The whole damn side!" Grimly he added, "If we don't find it today, I'm sending in divers tomorrow to search the whole damn lake bottom!"

"Jesus God," Bosch whispered in despair. "Let's get them started and get it over with. For God's sake!" He looked at Tom Hopewell. "Tell Henry, let them do it now, for God's sake." He reentered the admin building.

Tom Hopewell looked at Charlie, then at Constance bitterly. "This is a damn fucking mess. Come on, meet Henry Tremont."

When they returned to the Zukals' house, Al and Sylvie were both yelling at a strange man, who was dressed in olive-drab shirt and trousers. A red slash insignia was on his shirt pocket. "I don't care! I don't want no deers looking me in the eyes all night. You can't fix them lights so no deers set them off, what good are they?" Sylvie was screaming. Al was saying, an octave lower, but more menacingly, "I think youse guys loused it up so we'd buy more of your fancy systems. Systems! Systems to get dough!"

"You're from Frederick's Security?" Charlie asked the man, who was very red in the face.

"What's the matter with these people? They nuts or something?"

"Al, I've been thinking about your problem," Charlie said soothingly. "Let me talk to the man, okay? I'm Meiklejohn," he said. "You?"

"Bergman. Carl."

Charlie took his arm and steered him toward the mill.

Al hesitated, started to follow, hesitated again. "Leave them alone!" Sylvie said. "Let Charlie take care of it, like he said. You deaf or something?"

"Sylvie, could I have a drink of water?" Constance asked then.

"Water? Hell, we can do better than that for you," Al said in evident relief that he had an excuse for not following Charlie. "A beer? Vodka? Even coffee. I say a beer would go all right. Come on in."

A few minutes later, when Charlie joined them in the kitchen, Constance was pouring freshly brewed coffee over a tall glass of ice cubes. "And that's all there is to it," she was saying. "Once when I ordered iced coffee the waiter brought me a steaming cup of coffee with a single ice cube melting away in it."

They all looked at Charlie. "Al, Sylvie, I guarantee that no deer will keep you awake tonight," he said. "And, Al, if you have another beer, that sure would go down just right."

17

A few minutes after four Greg Dolman arrived. Charlie watched him leave his sheriff's car and walk toward the Zukal house, stiff with anger. The trouble with Greg, Charlie thought, was that he looked like a bookkeeper, not a lawman. Or even a preacher, he decided; Greg would look at home at the pulpit. Not a fire-and-brimstone type, but the soft-spoken, even mournful type who suffered over the sins of his congregation, and frequently told them so.

Charlie leaned against the porch railing, his arms crossed, a slight smile on his face as he imagined Greg sadly exhorting the sinners to sin no more. "Afternoon," he said.

"What the hell are you up to?"

"Just leaning against a porch rail, taking life easy."

"You're messing with the wrong people, Meiklejohn. I told you—"

"Is that the sheriff?" Sylvie yelled from inside the house. She, Al, and Constance trailed out to the porch. "I want to know what's the good of having a sheriff who don't do no sheriffing," Sylvie said. And Al said, "We think, Mr. Sheriff, you don't look too hard when it don't suit you. Charlie here, me, and Sylvie, we don't think that tramp carried no bees nowhere."

"I don't give a damn what Charlie thinks," Greg snapped.

Charlie lifted an eyebrow and glanced at Constance. "I think we should take a little walk, Greg. Constance, you want to come along?"

She nodded.

"This won't take too long," Charlie said to Al and Sylvie. "Greg? Let's wander down this way a bit."

They walked toward the mill. The sound of workmen had diminished, and the numbers were down now, but there were still several of them coming and going. Today, a Con Ed truck was parked near the mill between a van and a pickup.

"What the devil are they doing now?" Greg muttered.

"Looking it over to see if the waterwheel is in good shape, looking over the dam, the sluice gate, things like that," Charlie said. "This is going to be a working establishment very soon now, it seems."

When they were past the mill, on the edge of the property overlooking the lake—which appeared bluer than ever—Charlie stopped. Briefly he wondered if the acid content of the recent rain had already affected the lake. How blue could it get? He glanced at the sheriff and said, "Greg, there's a murderer running around doing murderous things, and I intend to get him. I take it the boys have shown up by now in the woods, and that Wollander sent you over to give me a warning. Right?"

"Charlie, do you have a shred of proof? Do you have anything better than the scenario I have? If you do, unload it, and then let's talk."

Charlie shook his head. "The problem as I see it," he said in a meditative way, "is that I'm not real sure who you're working for. I mean, is it the Zukals? Then why didn't you find out who killed their dog, and who's been making life hell for them? Is it the public at large? Then why didn't you go after David Levy's killer? Is it Wollander? If it is, then anything I say will end up on his table, and that would put a crimp in my plans."

A vein throbbed in Greg Dolman's temple, and his face became redder. "If you have information, it's your duty to tell me," he grated. "And if you don't cooperate, I'll go after your license. And you know I can take it if you're playing games with me."

"And you haven't answered my question," Charlie murmured. "You see, what I thought I might do is contact Captain See at the state police detective bureau. I've known him for more than twenty years; we used to work together back in the city now and then. Good man, See."

"You're trying to blackmail me!" Greg Dolman cried in disbelief.

"Gentle persuasion," Charlie protested. "I've had a lot of role models around here these past few days. Wollander's washed-up, Greg. Did you know that?"

The sheriff snorted and jammed his hands down into his pockets.

"Oh, he probably would deny it himself, but that's the way it is. He's bowing out voluntarily, he thinks, but actually I think his days are numbered by forces even bigger than he is. Writing his memoirs, I hear."

A new intentness stilled Greg. He glanced from Charlie to Constance.

She said, "You remember when Eisenhower retired, Greg? He gave this impassioned warning about the industrial-military complex. Rather like biting the hand, don't you think? And Admiral Rickover? He did about the same kind of thing when he retired, a dire warning about the dangers of nuclear submarines, nuclear weapons of all sorts. This seems so common, doesn't it? The insider who gets out so often has an overwhelming desire to tell all. Educators do it, preachers do it, politicians. Even actors." She gazed thoughtfully at the quiet lake. "Funny, isn't it? When they start to tell about whatever it is they are leaving, they don't seem to stop. They go all the way."

"I don't believe you. He wouldn't bow out, no matter what. The game he's playing is the only game he knows."

"But he's tired of it," Charlie said quietly. "Too many upstarts. The New Age politicians probably turn him off. Managerial types with their clipboards, spin-control specialists, four-second sound bites. It's not his game any longer, and he knows it. And he knows a lot of other things, too. He's been around a long time."

Very softly Constance said, "Think about the little remarks you must have heard in the past few years, the never-confirmed rumors you must have heard. Probably you didn't want to have to think too much about them, but I suspect they're floating around. Aren't they?"

He looked at her sourly. "There are always rumors." He turned to Charlie. "For Christ's sake, what are you after? Give me something."

"A killer. I told Wollander the same thing. I simply want him to leave me alone to do my work. If I ask his wife a question, I don't want his answer. Or the housekeeper, or the daughter. And I want to know that if I tell you anything, it stays with you. I don't want him second-guessing my every movement. And I sure as hell don't want you getting his permission every step along the way."

Greg Dolman looked meaner than ever, his eyes little more than slits. "Not enough, Charlie. He says you're after a thermos, guys searching the woods over there, people searching the farm on this side. Hell, it's all over town that you're after a thermos. Why the thermos? Tell me something I don't know about the thermos."

"It's the key to the mystery," Charlie said, and if Greg Dolman heard the undercurrent of mockery in his voice, he gave no sign of it. "If we find it in the right place, it'll mean David Levy probably took the drugs himself. If it turns up in the wrong place, it'll prove murder. See what I mean? The key."

Greg Dolman's indecision was painful to watch. He glared at Charlie with an expression of near-hatred. Abruptly he faced away. "Beat it, both of you. I have to think."

"But not too long, Greg. It's going to be you or Danny See. I want an official lawman around if the thermos turns up. Wouldn't like to be accused of rigging the sails the wrong way. Know what I mean? We'll be up at the house." Charlie took Constance's hand, and they left Sheriff Greg Dolman standing near the swinging bridge staring out at nothing in particular.

"Charlie," Constance said as they walked back, "did you ever really work with Danny See?"

"We need definitions," he began.

"I thought not."

"Dolman doesn't know one way or the other and the very thought of bringing in the state police makes him ache in a place he can't reach with ointment. But Danny did come to town a couple of times, you know. He took some workshops in investigating arson. It just happens that I conducted a couple of them. So there."

She nodded. "I wonder if Greg fully realizes that he's between the rock and the hard place."

"He does now. Bet he'll be back in half an hour, and then he'll hang around like an attached shadow. Bet?"

"You know I won't. Besides, why do you suggest a bet only when you know you'll win?"

"Because I hate to lose," he said with complete honesty.

Constance looked through picture albums with Sylvie and made all the right comments about the pretty daughters and beautiful grandchildren. Her comments were true, it was a handsome family. And Al and Charlie played the "Did you know X?" game. It had turned out that Charlie was on a special investigative force during the period that the Bronx was burning most fiercely, the time that the butcher shop Al's father had started was burned out.

"Did you know Mort Wurstman? Over on Trinity?" Al asked.

"Yep, and the son Dooley."

"A bad one, Charlie. Real bad. Got sent up."

"I know. I was part of the crew that sent him."

"Really? Good job, but it shoulda been done years before. Did you know Sal Maldane?"

"The hock shop? Sure. He's okay."

"Yeah, for a hock-shop guy. He got burned out, too."

"Prettiest case of arson you could ever hope to see."

"Yeah? Thought you said he was okay."

"Doesn't mean he can't light a fire, now, does it? He *is* okay."

Then the sheriff came back, still glowering, but his mind made up. "You hanging out here these days?" he asked Charlie meanly.

"Until the boys get through and bring the stuff over. And the people at the farm check in. Want some dinner after that?"

"Yeah. And talk. Especially talk."

Tom Hopewell arrived first with Henry Tremont, who looked a bit like a tree himself, brown and tough. No sign of a thermos on the farm grounds, he said truculently, and he'd swear to that.

Charlie thanked him nicely, and asked Tom, "Will people be around at the farm for a while?"

"Are you kidding?" Hopewell said fiercely. "Most of the night is more like it. I tell you, we are running a little bit behind, like three weeks behind by my figuring."

Henry Tremont seemed to plant his feet even more firmly, and cleared his throat. "Dr. Bosch," he said deliberately, "he don't like the idea of people coming and going all night, taking bees, getting in the apartments, and such. We're putting on a

couple of extras at night for the next week or so." He said this
as if it implied a warning to Charlie, who nodded gravely.

Then several cars pulled into the driveway; Tom Hopewell
and Henry Tremont stalked away, and Pete Mitchum and his
friends spilled out of the cars and expanded like foam monsters
released from too-small boxes. Pete shook his head in regret,
no thermos, and Charlie said that was all right. He said hi to
Pete's two brothers and was introduced to the three boys he
did not know. He introduced them all around, and it was obvious that they didn't want to leave, but he thanked them
nicely, too, and sent them away. They had deposited four plastic garbage bags on the lawn before the front porch.

"We had witnesses to it all," Pete said before he left. "Sheriff
deputies stayed right with us the whole time."

Charlie grinned. "I thought they might."

Pete grinned even broader. "I thought that's what you
thought," he said in triumph. He swung around and returned
jauntily to his old Ford that he kept looking spiffy.

Charlie regarded the bags, and shrugged. "Might as well have
a look," he said. "I bummed a tarp from the carpenters." He
spread the clear plastic tarp on the ground. Al helped position
it and weight it down with rocks, and then Charlie emptied the
first bag. About what he had expected: mostly beer cans, a few
soda-pop cans, a few bottles. A beret. A leather glove that had
started to mildew. Sodden newspapers. He used a stick to push
stuff to one side as he went through it all. Nothing of interest.
Greg Dolman held the garbage bag open and Charlie and Al
lifted the tarp and dumped the stuff back in and tied it. The
next bag had a syringe with a rusty needle, partly dirt-filled, and
a broken Swiss Army knife in addition to miscellany much like
that in the first bag. There were many spent shells; hunters
made use of that land in season. The third bag was more of the
same. Two condoms, and a string of dime-store beads, and a
little silver-colored pillbox were among the junk. Charlie
pushed the pillbox to one side with the stick, and Constance
picked it up carefully by the edges, using a tissue. The fourth
bag had nothing to interest Charlie.

"What's that?" Greg motioned toward the silver box that Constance had put on the porch rail.

Charlie was through and all the trash was again packaged

up. He looked at the pillbox without touching it. "You have any gear in your car?" he asked. "Might as well check for prints. Probably aren't any, but let's give it a go."

Greg went to his car and returned with a fingerprint kit. There were only smudges, worthless. Charlie picked up the box then and turned it over thoughtfully. "Real silver," he said. "It's just beginning to tarnish."

"That's too small to hold dope," Greg said.

"I know." The box was only an inch and a half on the side, and about a quarter-inch deep. Charlie opened it, empty, and then slipped it into his pocket. "It's a pretty little thing." He stretched. "Let's leave these people in peace for now," he said. "Al, Sylvie, thanks for the use of your place. See you later."

Greg Dolman followed Charlie and Constance to the Volvo. "Now where are you going? Is that it for today?"

"Dinner," Charlie said firmly. "Remember? We take you to dinner? I suggest you follow in the police car, or do you want to ride with us?"

"I'll follow," he said. "Where?"

"I spotted a roadhouse about ten miles out of Spender's Ferry. Don't know a thing about it, but that's where we're headed."

"Now," Greg Dolman said in the roadhouse. They were seated in a booth with drinks before them.

"Now," Charlie agreed, studying Greg thoughtfully. He knew Constance didn't trust the sheriff any more than he did, but she had said sensibly, "What choice does he have but to go along with it?" Charlie wished he knew.

"First," he said finally, "I'll want you to stick closer than a tick the rest of the night. Deal?"

Greg flushed a deep red, but nodded.

"I don't want any alarms going off, or any of those private security people nosing around. You, as a representative of the law, can handle them if they do turn up. Okay?" Again the sullen nod. "Okay. I've been all over the place today baiting a trap, and I'm pretty sure that it will be sprung tonight. Late tonight. I'll want you, or someone, to be there."

"Tell me what you're up to, Charlie. No games; no puzzles, just what you're up to." Greg took a swallow of his bourbon, straight up, and added, "You know I cut loose today, damn you. Wollander suggested I talk to you and let him know what you were doing. Well, I haven't gone back since. So, I guess you could say I'm committed." He sounded very depressed.

"Right. All day I've been broadcasting my belief that David Levy was drugged by the contents of his thermos. And the thermos is missing. That you already know. Everyone in the damn county must know it by now. I made it plain that if the thermos doesn't turn up in the lake, or on the edge of it, or on his route back to his apartment, it will prove beyond a doubt that he was murdered, and the investigation will go forward. But if it does turn up, I'll have to accept that he probably did it to himself. I think everyone concerned with this mess wants it over with, wants me to accept that David killed himself accidentally."

Greg scowled. "Goddamn it, Charlie, what if the damn thermos is in the lake? Then what?"

"It isn't. Not yet anyway. I think someone will make an attempt tonight to put it there."

"Oh shit," Greg said in a low voice, disgusted and discouraged. "You're fishing. You don't have anything, do you? You've been around, Charlie. You know there's people you don't play mind games with."

He was not even questioning his own acceptance of the game rules, Charlie knew, and Charlie understood without a doubt the process Greg Dolman was going through; looking inward, searching for his own way out of this predicament, probably examining the words he would recite to Wollander. Brusquely Charlie said, "When I walked away from NYPD, I walked away from those people who like to tell you what to do and when. I'm calling the plays tonight, Greg, and, by God, you're in! Shut your face and stop the bellyaching!"

He couldn't stop Greg if the sheriff decided to take a walk, Charlie knew, not short of pulling a gun anyway; and he didn't have a gun along. The moment hung there while Greg made up his mind. Finally he lifted his drink and finished it.

"He didn't take the thermos to the lake for a morning swim," Charlie said, exactly as if neither of them knew what had gone on during that brief interlude. "He had a routine. Up early, a swimming workout, back to the apartment for breakfast, and then to work. You don't take a thermos for a workout when

you're a minute away from home. No, the killer took it. Maybe to plant it on someone else, maybe to lace lemonade with dope to make it look like that's how he took the stuff, maybe for some other reason altogether. But the accidental death was accepted so easily there wasn't any real need to do anything with it. It's been stashed away somewhere all this time. If it was tossed,
then our killer probably has a new one in hand. I'm betting on it."

"You're planning to stake out a whole damn lake in the middle of the night?" Greg shook his head.

"Part of it, Greg. Just part of it." Charlie pulled out a notebook and began to sketch rapidly. "Here's the lake." It looked like a teardrop. "Over here, the farm, with extra guards patrolling, and lights on. Not a good way to approach. Next, the Zukal place. Security lights everywhere. Even worse. On around the state forest land, and to the Wollander property. Again, guards everywhere. On past, and there's the orchard. Dirt roads back among the trees. Short walk to the lake from there. So, just this end, near the Wollander beach. It's the best place, after all. Toss the thermos as far as possible. It lodges among the rocks on the bottom and looks like it rolled in when David swam that morning." He took a gadget out of his pocket and placed it on the table. It looked very much like an infrared television control. He pushed it across the table to Greg. "I had the Frederick's Security Company put in a light, a portable unit. This controls it. It'll light up most of the lake. We'll catch our killer in the act of getting rid of the thermos, and then the real work can begin, the nitty-gritty detail work that cinches things. First you have to have a direction, then you can run with it. You know that's how it goes. I know it, too."

"You've got someone in mind?" Greg asked, a new intentness making his face taut, his eyes narrowed.

"Oh yes. And a lot of little things to corroborate it, but we need something big now."

Their dinners were brought then and they were silent until the waiter had left again. They all had ordered steak because they didn't trust anything else on the menu. The steaks turned out to be very good.

"Start at the beginning," Greg said. "Give."

"You won't like it," Charlie said; he stopped chewing to speak. "You see, it starts with the dog, Sadie." Greg made a low groaning sound and Charlie said, "Sorry about that, but that's the way it goes." He looked thoughtful then and said in a wondering sort of way, "I just remembered Captain Bertlesman. For God's sake, good old Cap Bertlesman. He used to come in to deliver lectures when I was a green-as-grass rookie, back when the dinosaurs roamed. He used to say, 'Get the who and the how, and let the shrinks take care of the why.' " Charlie looked apologetically at Constance, who had made a noise that was not quite a snort. "Didn't say he was a nice man," Charlie murmured. "Anyway, that's what I have for you, Greg. But only the how for the time being. If there aren't any slip-ups, you'll get the who in a couple of hours. Why will take care of itself."

For a moment Greg Dolman simply looked puzzled, but then a dull flush spread across his face. "You son of a bitch!"

Charlie nodded. If there were any slip-ups, he knew he needed that card in the hole; he might have to persuade Greg to tag along another time. Greg looked as if he wanted to reach across the table and choke him, and that was all right, as long as he didn't move in that direction. Charlie waited.

"Go on," Greg finally muttered.

Charlie described how he and Constance had demonstrated how to get a trained dog to take food from a stranger. "So, no problem," he said. "The killer dosed dog food with insect spray and killed Sadie. But then David came across the head scarf. Maybe the killer saw him with it, or they even talked about it. Anyway, David had to be next."

Greg was attacking his steak ferociously, as if this might be his last meal. Indigestion in the making, Charlie thought sadly.

"So, everyone knew about David and his vitamins, and his morning swim." When Greg made a growly sound, Charlie explained about the cookout and the meticulous report David had written to his father. "So, as I said, everyone knew. Everyone involved in this mess, in any event. No one was questioning the death of the dog, and now if David's death could be made to look accidental, so much the better. And the vitamins showed up. Heaven sent," he added drily.

Greg shook his head. "How you going to prove that, Charlie? No way."

"Wrong, Greg. Two facts. One, the company David ordered his vitamins from shipped them on the fourteenth, from Rochester. They would have been delivered by the sixteenth, but they aren't listed among his effects. Two, examine the autopsy report, the contents of the stomach. You see, a few of those vitamins were time-release doses, the vitamin C, for example. No vitamin C is listed, and it would have been there in granular form for many hours, only gradually dissolving, being absorbed. Our killer entered the apartment, swiped the new shipment of vitamins, doped some of the capsules, and substituted them for the ones on the counter. Then, when David was dying, or even after he was dead, the killer returned and took away the doped containers, replaced the untouched ones, and it was done. There was one too many of each one that was in capsule form, but who would notice? Who did notice?"

"And the thermos?"

Charlie shrugged. "An ace in the hole, probably, but one that wasn't needed, not until right now, anyway." He looked with regret at his plate; his steak was nearly gone and he had no real recollection of eating it.

"So," he said. "Two down. No hubbub. No real investigation. On to the next item, moving the bees. And the tramp. You know, Greg, if you had found a bottle, that would have been much harder; much, much harder. But either the guy was so drunk that he turned on the gas and forgot about it and then fell down and bashed his head in, or he was sober enough to walk through the woods carrying a hive of bees. But not both. Let's say he was sleeping off a drunk under a tree and he hears someone messing around with the hive, and he follows out of curiosity, or even calls out. Our killer has to act fast now. A witness is the last thing on earth needed at this moment. Probably he said something like, 'Let's duck inside one of the apartments and talk. The watchman will spot us out here.' Something like that. And he picks up a rock. Inside the apartment, a quick bash on the head, turn on the gas, close up the place, and get back to the work at hand. There must have been a wallet, and he lifts that, just to muddy the waters. You could see the outline in the hip pocket," he added. A distant, thoughtful look crossed his face. "It might even turn up," he said. "And the rock, of course, gets tossed into the lake, one among five million others."

"And not an iota of proof," Greg Dolman muttered. "Not a single print anywhere."

"But that's proof," Charlie said. "Why would the tramp wipe his prints from the gas stove? Now that wouldn't have made any sense at all."

The waiter cleared the table and they sat in silence until he returned with coffee, and then left again.

"I don't like it," Greg said. "We need more people. Three's not enough. Too much territory to cover."

"Too many people and you start tripping over each other."

"How you plan to go in? Your car's a dead giveaway and so's mine."

"We'll park in the Zukals' driveway, about a third of the way to the house, where it curves, out of sight of the road and the house."

"And those damn lights they installed blast you. You said yourself, that's out."

"Um. The lights won't come on after ten tonight. I fixed that with the security guy today. He's the only one who knows," he added. "Not even the Zukals are in on it."

Greg thought some more, and they ordered more coffee.

"Have you considered that the damn thermos might have been ditched someplace not accessible now?" Greg asked finally.

Charlie looked at him in surprise. Constance had asked the same question. "Sure. But I think *a* thermos will end up in the lake tonight, if it gets that far. One's pretty much like another, and who would pipe up and say it's not the same one? And I'd put up money that it will have measurable amounts of methaqualone and a barbiturate," he added grimly.

Greg was not happy about any of it, Charlie knew, and he also knew there wasn't a thing he could do about that. It was chancy; the killer might not have the thermos, or any thermos. He might be throwing a party that no one would show up for. Maybe the damn thermos was already in the lake. Maybe David had lost it himself days before his death. He understood that Greg was going along with it for now, this one night, and if it didn't work out, he'd be back in Wollander's pocket tomorrow. Case closed, again.

What if he was wrong? He didn't believe it, but it was a possibility he began to consider. What if they had read all the signs wrong? What if. . . ? He felt Constance's hand on his thigh under the table and looked at her. She knew, he realized, and she was saying, It's okay. He felt some of the tension seep from him, and he covered her hand with his.

Constance now said to Greg, "We both have dark raincoats in the car. Do you have something to put on? That shirt will be like a beacon."

It was going on nine-thirty. Right or wrong, Charlie thought, it was time.

18

Charlie had positioned both Greg and Constance, and he no longer could see either of them. Greg had complained. "Hey, it's been a long time since I pulled an all-nighter."

"So go to sleep. You'll wake up when the lights come on."

"If."

"When. But, Greg, if you start snoring, I'll come over and kick you in the butt."

Constance was invisible, merging with a clump of bushes until not even a nighthawk would have been alerted to her presence. Charlie admired, and even envied, her ability to go into a meditative state—alpha state, she called it—effortlessly. She would be wide awake and alert and totally relaxed for as long as it took. That had been part of her aikido training and she had mastered the skill, but he had not been willing to learn it himself and he could not say why. She had explained it, rather too airily, he thought. "You aren't willing to give up any control, even to yourself." Maybe that was it, maybe not, and now, he was wishing he did not have a cramp in one leg, wishing that time would pass faster, wishing this was over.

Greg was against the bluff at the edge of the beach, his back against the rise, no doubt. And no doubt he was asleep. Now and then Charlie had heard his rustlings, but not for some time. Charlie was farther down where the bluff was not so high and he could see over the edge if he tried. Some large round rocks were on the top here, and he hoped his head appeared to be just another such rock when he stood up to look.

At first, he was thinking now, you didn't hear anything. Or only those noises that were expected, insects, cicadas, crickets, distant traffic sounds, a whippoorwill and a faraway echo of an answer. Then other sounds became noticeable—a bird flapping its wings, a bat's high screech, a small animal moving in the grass. No fish jumping, he thought with regret; no frogs yelling *here I am*. Two does and a buck had come down to drink and had stood outlined against the sky briefly, but they were not fooled by human immobility; they had left fast, the sounds of their feet loud, and with a snorting sound almost horselike.

No new stars had appeared in a long time. At first, he had been able to pick out a section of sky and study it, count the stars in it, close his eyes for a count of ten, and when he looked again the number of stars in the sector had doubled, tripled, quadrupled. But the slow swing of the heavens was impossible to see without a reference point; he tried to align certain stars with a tree branch, only to lose them when he closed his eyes again. Too many of them now.

He cupped his hand over his watch face; it was twelve-forty. He had not expected any action until after twelve, after one even, but time was being contrary; it had slowed to an unbelievable crawl. He stood up to scan the area again, and now that his eyes had adapted so well to the night, he could make out individual trees, individual bushes. He hoped Constance was stretching from time to time, and he knew that Greg had done that earlier, but not for too long a time. He inched away from his position and eased himself to where Greg was propped up, sound asleep.

He shook him lightly, and put his fingers over Greg's lips. "Get up and move back and forth a couple of minutes," he said softly. "I'll keep an eye out."

Greg made a mumbling noise and pulled himself upright jerkily. He had become stiff already. He bent and stretched a few times and then walked down the beach and back, then again.

"Okay," he whispered. "Thanks."

"Yeah. It's nearly one. Thought you'd want to know."

Charlie carefully made his way back to his position and studied the landscape again. Nothing. He wanted to go check on Constance but he couldn't do that. He would be silhouetted if anyone happened to be watching. But, he told himself, he had put her where he did because he knew he could trust her not to fall asleep and not to stiffen up, and he had put Greg where he did because he knew Greg would do both.

The doubts that had troubled him earlier kept swimming back into his mind. What if nothing happened? What if he was overestimating the lure of the bait he had spread around altogether too thick all day? He personally would suspect a trap, he told himself, and then told himself to shut up. If it didn't work, well, he'd think of something else. But the other part of his mind, the part that resisted the idea of achieving a meditative state, and that now was arguing with him over the futility of this night watch, that part would not shut up. Instead, it was saying, if it doesn't work, there probably won't be another day for you, asshole. He would lose Greg's cooperation, and did he really think he had enough evidence to stir up any interest with the state cops? Dummy.

He shifted his weight. Now he was keeping a close watch over the top of the rise, but even this, that other voice was saying derisively, how long could he keep this up? He was damned uncomfortable. His was the worst possible position he could have claimed; nowhere to rest his weight, no way to lean against a tree for relief, just stand upright and watch, or sink back down on this side and be blind. He was cursing himself silently when a figure appeared.

His hand closed over the infrared control in his pocket and drew it out. The person had vanished again, blended into the shadows of trees and shrubs. He didn't move, barely breathed, and presently he heard a sound that was new, then another. Footsteps on grass, hardly audible but there, coming closer, apparently hurrying.

Charlie caught an eclipse of a cluster of stars as the figure started down the slope to the lake, and now he counted silently, *one, two, three, four.* He pressed the button on the infrared control, and was blinded momentarily by the brilliance even though he had been expecting it.

He already had started to run the dozen steps to the woman in the black raincoat when she lifted her face and screamed. Constance had materialized at her side, one hand on the thermos held in the air ready to be thrown, the other on the woman's wrist.

"Hello, Jill," Charlie said and took her other arm. Greg was right behind him.

Charlie had to admit that Greg behaved admirably during those first few seconds. He blinked a lot, but that could have been from the blinding lights. He looked at Charlie with large questions in his eyes, and when Charlie nodded firmly, he managed a nod also.

Two security men were racing toward the beach, one with a gun drawn, both with flashlights that were no longer needed. The portable spotlight array had turned the entire end of the beach into noontime glare.

"Mrs. Ferris," Greg said soberly, "I'll have to ask you a few questions. Let's go inside." He swallowed hard, and then recited her rights in a swift monotone.

Charlie gave Constance a quick look; she nodded, very somber, tired. She carried the thermos; it was filled, the top on loosely, ready to slide off any second. Charlie kept a grasp on Jill's arm; the sheriff waved the private security men out of the way, and they all walked toward the Wollander house, where lights were coming on upstairs and down.

By the time they reached the patio Warren was hurrying toward them, tying his robe belt. "What the devil is going on?"

"I couldn't sleep," Jill said shrilly. "I was taking a walk by the lake and found the thermos in the water and then they all jumped me."

"Take your hands off her!"

"Inside," Charlie said. "Come on, inside."

Wollander grabbed at the thermos, and Constance easily fended off his hand and kept moving with Charlie and Jill. Warren looked past them and yelled at his security men, "Get these people out of here! Right now!"

"Mr. Wollander," Charlie said patiently, "it's over. Now, let's just go inside and talk. The sheriff will have to use your phone to call his deputies, and while we're waiting, we can talk things over."

"You heard what my daughter said. She found that damn thermos."

"Filled with tap water. I heard. Greg, do you want to just go straight in with her? Constance can bring a car around if that's the only way to handle this."

At the door to the house Lois said, "Come in." She held the door open as they all passed her, and then pulled it closed again. She was in a long gray robe and slippers, her hair disheveled.

Warren glared at Greg. "Do you know what you're doing?"

"Yes, sir. I'm afraid so."

Lois led the way to the study and when they were inside closed that door also. "What happened?" she asked then.

Charlie released Jill's arm. "You'd better sit down," he said, not too unkindly. She sank down into one of the leather chairs and drew up her feet into it. She looked childish, like a sick little girl. He felt in his pocket for the silver pillbox and handed it to Lois. "Do you recognize this?"

She turned it over and over, then looked at him sharply. "Where did you find it? That's mine. Or just like mine."

"I think it's yours."

Warren walked stiffly to his desk and sat down. He picked up the phone and began to punch numbers. "I'm calling my attorney."

Charlie shrugged and spoke to Jill. "When they arrest you," he said, "the first thing they do is search you thoroughly, and there will be a medical examination. By a gynecologist." He heard the phone clatter back to the receiver but did not turn to look at Warren. "I'm not a doctor," he went on, "but I have it on good authority that there are certain physical symptoms that are present in the event of pregnancy; even if a pregnancy has recently terminated in any way, the signs are still there. Will they find the right symptoms, Jill? The right hormones, the right physiological changes?"

She was staring at him speechlessly, the color gone from her face, her lips.

"When they send the thermos to the lab, will they find tap

water? And maybe methaqualone and phenobarbital? You know
the sheriff will have to search your rooms here. You must have
had access to those drugs recently if you put them in the thermos. Are they still up in your room? Will they find them?"

"There's medicine," she said, keeping her gaze on him as if
hypnotized. "My medicine. Stanley's. Maybe what you're talking
about—"

"Jill, for God's sake! Just shut up! You don't have to answer
his questions. Just shut up until an attorney is here to advise
you." Warren's hand was on the phone but he did not lift it
again.

She turned her wide, staring gaze to him, and began to shake
her head. "Just shut up. Be still. Be good. Do what Daddy tells
you. If I'm not good, you'll send me to Mother, and if she gets
tired of me, she'll send me back to you. Back and forth. Back
and forth. I saw the letter she wrote to you. She showed it to
me, laughing and laughing. We both laughed. See another doctor. Get more opinions, and more, and more. Remember? It
can't be true. I don't believe it. See this man, he's good. Remember? She dragged me to one doctor after another in their
prissy white coats, with their prissy fat fingers, and they kept
telling her the same thing, didn't they? All of them. Over and
over. Then a new letter from you would come: Try this one,
that one, this treatment, that treatment. And she wrote to you
again and again, and still, try this, try that."

When she became quiet, Charlie said in a low voice, "You're
barren, aren't you?"

"Yes," she whispered.

"And he's known that for many years, hasn't he?"

She nodded. "Yes."

"Did you take your stepmother's birth-control pills and use
them?"

She nodded again.

"To make it appear that you had had a miscarriage?"

"Yes! Why are you asking me all this? You already know the
answers! Yes! Yes! Yes! To everything."

"And the only victim you ever really had in mind was your
husband, Stanley."

"Yes. Of course. Yes!"

Behind him Charlie heard Warren Wollander make a choking, sobbing sound. He did not look at him. He was gazing instead at Lois, who was pasty, and looked as if she might faint. The fury in his low intense voice was startling when he said to Lois, "He's known from the start about the fake miscarriage, about the fake pregnancy, about the killings. He was going to throw you to the wolves if necessary to save her skin."

Behind him he could hear Warren Wollander using the phone. His voice was toneless. "Get over here," Warren said. "We have desperate trouble. Come now."

Greg called his deputies then, and asked Warren if he would need a search warrant. Warren said yes, but Jill said no. Greg spoke into the phone again, ordered a search warrant drawn up, and began to say what it should include when Charlie interrupted him again. "Tell the judge you're also looking for a solid gold bracelet carved with flowers." Greg looked mystified, but included the bracelet.

"We'll have to wait," he said uncomfortably when he was done.

"I'll make coffee," Lois said. She left without a glance at Warren.

Charlie looked at Constance, almost expecting her to go after Lois, but she moved her head fractionally and did not get up from her chair.

In a very low voice Warren said, "Greg, you don't have to do this. We go back a long ways."

Greg Dolman looked more uncomfortable but Charlie noticed that Constance tightened her grasp on the thermos. Son of a bitch, he thought, she still didn't trust Greg Dolman worth a damn.

"Jill," Charlie said softly, "one question. Why did you take the thermos?"

"You mean there's something you don't already know?" she asked bitterly. "When I went to the apartment to switch the vitamins, I found that I had left the cod-liver oil here, and I couldn't replace it. I panicked. I was afraid someone might connect it to the dope, and I thought that I could mix the drugs in the thermos if anyone questioned anything."

The deputies finally arrived and they all watched as the thermos was decanted into a sterile jar that was sealed and labeled, and then the thermos was put into a bag and sealed and labeled. The attorney Warren had called turned up, looking mean and sleepy. Charlie and Constance began to edge toward the door. Greg followed them.

"I'll want more," he said tiredly. "Tomorrow, sometime. What's that about a bracelet?"

"Tomorrow," Charlie said, just as tired as Greg. "I told Sylvie and Al we'd drop in around one. And before that, our phone will be off the hook and the doors sealed tight."

Greg didn't argue. He nodded, called one of the deputies to drive them over to collect their car, and turned back to the routine that awaited him inside.

Charlie looked past him for just a moment; the lawyer was in a chair drawn up close to Jill's. His face was inches from hers and she was still huddled with her feet under her, still looked like a sick little girl. He took Constance's arm and they left.

When they were once again in their own car, heading for their own house, Charlie said with a groan, "I am wiped out from here to Thursday and I ache from top to bottom."

"When we get home, soak first and then I'll give you a Swedish massage."

He squeezed her thigh. "You're good."

"And after I do you, you can give me one," she added. He squeezed her thigh again and she covered his hand with hers.

19

Charlie woke up grinning, and was still grinning broadly when he entered the kitchen to find Constance making waffles. Fresh strawberries were marinating on the counter. She eyed him suspiciously.

"So you ate the canary, after all?"

He laughed out loud. "Dreaming. I was dreaming that I was married to Sylvie and I kept trying to dump her in the lake so

I could run away with you. See, even in my dreams, I'm chasing you like a fourteen-year-old with two bucks running after the only whore in town."

She raised her eyebrows and looked like a schoolteacher with a recalcitrant eight-year-old. "You're just after my body. I always suspected that."

"Damn right," he said, nuzzling her neck. "And I would dump Sylvie in the lake, or run Sophia off a cliff, or ditch Elizabeth in a second to get at you."

She reached behind her and gave him an indecent tweak that was just short of vicious. He howled and danced away, tripped over Brutus and Candy, and ended up at the table, laughing and cursing.

"Are you ready for breakfast, by any chance?" she asked demurely.

"If they only knew," he said as soon as he could speak. "Oh, if only they knew, all those people who are ready to canonize you. Saint Constance. Hah!"

She brought him a steaming waffle covered with strawberries, and a pitcher of cream on the side. "You realize that this is your ration of high-caloric food for the day," she said severely. "Steamed fish for dinner. Fruit and carrot sticks for lunch."

He caught her wrist and kissed the palm of her hand. She leaned over and kissed the top of his head.

Al Zukal met them in his driveway. He had a look of total disbelief on his face. "Charlie! Lois said Jill's the one! That skinny girl? What for?"

"Is Lois here?"

"Yeah. Sylvie said you said she should call Lois and get her over here. She's been crying real bad, Charlie."

They turned to see the sheriff's car coming in the driveway.

"I didn't know we was going to have a party," Al muttered.

"Sorry," Charlie said. "I thought this would be the best way to wrap things up. You and Sylvie will want to hear where you stand now. And Lois needs to know a few things. Okay?"

"And if it ain't? Yeah, yeah. Come on in."

They sat at the kitchen table, where Sylvie had coffee ready, and two kuchens, one apple, one cinnamon. Constance shook her head firmly at Charlie. Greg Dolman, he noticed, aggrieved, had a very large piece of both coffee cakes.

Lois was in jeans and a T-shirt and sneakers. Her working clothes. Her eyes were red-rimmed and swollen. She did not speak when they came in, but ducked her head and moved her cup around and around in the saucer.

"This won't take very long," Charlie said briskly. "Constance and I came to the same conclusion at the same moment, I think. We had been misdirected royally, and as soon as we admitted that, the rest began falling into place. Actually, Constance is the one who said it must be Jill."

"Everything pointed to her," Constance said, "but we were all so busy looking the other way we couldn't see her as a suspect."

Lois looked at her in bewilderment. "Nothing seemed to point to her. I thought she was pregnant and I lived in the same house with her."

"I know. But when I went to her room there wasn't a single book about pregnancy, no books on babies, no books on how to achieve pregnancy. None of the things you'd expect an anxious mother-to-be to have around. The drugstore in town has a nice selection, so it wasn't that they aren't available locally. She simply wasn't interested. And I kept wondering why she was here. It's obvious that she is not fond of her father, and she has no friends here, so why was she here?"

"They were redecorating their condo in the city," Lois said. "The place was completely torn up."

Constance shook her head. "She could have gone on a trip, or to an apartment, or to a hotel, or to visit friends, a number of things. But she came here, and stayed. Anyway, once we decided we had made a fundamental mistake, we backtracked, and it kept coming around to Jill when we asked: What if Stanley had been the intended victim from the start? After that it was obvious." She lifted her coffee then and Charlie knew the rest would be up to him.

"We backtracked all the way back to the day you and Sylvie came here," Charlie said, nodding to Al. "And that made us realize that Jill already had a plan in mind by then. I'll just take it step-by-step. She has no money of her own and is jealous of Lois because she is independent. She saw her mother as a kept

woman all her life, and resented it, and she saw herself repeating the pattern with her husband. Out here he could be
with her only on the weekends and it gave her time to think
and make her plans. It's really very hard to arrange an accidental death in the city, without drawing suspicion, you know. But
out here? She learned about the bees, no doubt, when they
arrived." Lois looked up, startled, and nodded slightly. Charlie
went on. "Stanley was allergic to bees. It could be made to look
accidental if he got multiple stings, and no suspicion would be
attached to her, especially if she was a grieving widow who also
had lost her child. But how to get him to where the bees would
attack? That must have presented itself as a massive problem,
until she found Sebastian. I think she brought Sebastian out
only to verify that she had gone into the mill, into some of the
little rooms with him. She had no hope of buying any property,
or anything else. Stanley gave her gifts, and paid her charge
accounts, but you can't buy a piece of property like this on
your Visa card. So, why take Sebastian into the mill, unless she
had a different purpose altogether? She claimed to have lost a
heavy gold bracelet, remember?" He glanced at Greg, who nodded.

"We found it in her room."

"I thought you might. Anyway, she said it was lost, and Stanley filed an insurance claim, and got her a new one. But if she
could get the bees into one of those little rooms, and close the
door on them, and then tell Stanley that she remembered that
she had worn it the day she showed the mill to Sebastian, she
could get him to open the door to go look for it. The rooms
would have heated up just fine by midmorning; the bees would
have been swarming around in a rage, just as they were later.
It would have worked. The mill used to have a reputation as a
hangout; kids could have moved the bees as a prank, and poor
Stanley. She would have turned her big eyes on you and said
she had no idea why he went in there, just as she did later
about the station wagon."

He turned to Sylvie, "But you showed up. And then a dog
arrived. And carpenters began taking the mill apart. Everything
she had planned was going to hell all at once."

"She killed Sadie?" Sylvie cried. "But how? Sadie didn't even
like her. And why?"

Charlie detailed how Sadie could have been poisoned. Then he asked, "Sylvie, when David found one of your scarves and returned it, was there anything funny about it?"

"Filthy. It was filthy and I threw it away. I didn't even want to wash it."

"Mud? Grass stains? Filthy how?"

"All that and greasy." Her eyes widened.

"Greasy," Charlie said. "David found it and later on he must have made the connection. How he connected it to Jill I don't know, but he did, and she had to get rid of him, too." He shrugged. "As for why she killed Sadie, that's pretty obvious now. She still needed to be able to cross the bridge to collect the bees, and she needed a place to put the bees so she could send Stanley to them. Not on the Wollander property, too suspicious. If not the mill, then this house, or the station wagon, but not if a watchdog was barking its head off at her. It must have come to her, there was the perfect smokescreen; she could arrange things so that it looked like an attempt to get the newcomers out of the neighborhood; kids could take the blame."

His face tightened. "But David saw something and found the scarf. Maybe he saw her toss it. Maybe he even asked her about it, accused her of killing the dog."

"I don't understand what the fuss was over the thermos," Lois said. "What were you doing?"

"Well, it was missing. So the killer must have taken it. I was sure she had tampered with the vitamins, but why take the thermos? And I thought, if she had taken it, she would see this as a chance to sew things up good and tight. Let someone find it in the lake and be done with it.

"So now everything is in place for Stanley's death. She has announced her pregnancy, everyone is jubilant, even though Warren Wollander actually knew she was barren. He kidded himself at first about believing her, I imagine. She had taken the birth-control pills in order to plan exactly when she would start bleeding, and, to a certain extent, how much."

Al looked uncomfortable and shifted in his chair, and Sylvie's mouth pursed; Charlie was talking about things men didn't talk about, their attitudes clearly said.

He went on. "That night Warren saw her walk on the driveway to the place where it comes very close to the state forest.

Why the midnight walk? Why the raincoat? Not to meet Sebastian. The raincoat was to hide under. A shadow moving out among shadows. Lights were still on, people still awake and she didn't want to be seen. And the reason could have been to throw something away. Not in the house trash because she already had said she had lost a bracelet and people might be sifting through trash more carefully. She had enough pills for her purposes, the rest could be flushed down the john, but there was the silver pillbox, and she had to get rid of it. She could have returned it to your bathroom, but if you knew it was missing before, that would raise questions, and she didn't want any questions about birth control or pregnancy to come up."

"You were looking for that?" Lois exclaimed.

"Not really. For something. I didn't know what she had tossed, or even if she had tossed anything, and it could have been the thermos, although I didn't think so. But that's what they found.

"So everything was ready, at last. Stanley came up for the weekend. He had a medicine cabinet full of medications, including some heavy-duty sleeping pills. If he didn't take one himself, she could see that he got it. And in the night she went over to move the bees to the station wagon. Then a witness showed up, a transient. He was drunk, but he saw what she was doing, and must have started to make a ruckus. She got him to enter the apartment and hit him on the head, turned on the gas, and left to complete her real mission of murdering her husband."

Al made a grunting sound and Sylvie shifted in her chair, but no one spoke. Lois didn't move at all.

"Saturday morning Stanley has an appointment with Al, here, and she has her regular class, service, whatever it is, with Sebastian. What's more natural than that she would drive? Stanley doesn't like wandering in the woods; allergies, you know. She pulls up in the driveway to turn around, where she can see in the wagon, make sure the bees are still there. She says, 'Oh, I think I lost my bracelet in the station wagon. Seeing it has just reminded me. Be a darling and get it for me, will you? It's in the back. Do it before you start talking to Al, or you'll forget.'"

Lois made a deep throaty sound and closed her eyes.

"Right. So now it's done. I suspect that she stopped in the driveway, out of sight, long enough to hear the yelling, and then went on to Sebastian's meeting. Daddy shows up and rushes her home, she gags herself in the bathroom, takes out the tampon, and becomes an ashen-faced widow who has just lost a baby. But she won't let a doctor near her. There's only one more thing she has to do and that's get Sebastian over and tell him she was pregnant. She said he knew, that he was already advising her, and she has to make sure that he actually knows, just in case someone mentions it. She makes a big scene about seeing her spiritual advisor, and finally she can relax, wait for her inheritance to work through the legalities, and take off for France."

There was a long silence, broken finally by Lois. "And last night, it was all planned? All just a trap for her?" she whispered.

"Sure. There was no proof yet. I was pretty sure that if a scene started with her father present, taking over, giving orders, she would confess." *Get out of here!* She had killed three men to escape those orders. Charlie had not simply been pretty sure; he had known beyond doubt that when she saw that trap closing yet again, she would escape in the only way remaining. He said no more now, but watched Lois, and wondered if she saw escape as a possibility.

Lois sat unmoving for several seconds, then she shook her head hard. "He must have known, but he was so desperate to believe," she said, nearly inaudibly. "And he was as happy as a child. She lied about her pregnancy exactly the same way that her mother lied, to hurt him, to make him know he had to choose." She closed her eyes very tightly for a moment. "No man should be forced into that lifeboat with his wife and child," she whispered. Abruptly she turned to Greg Dolman. "Sheriff, I'd like a word with you alone."

Constance stood up. "We should be on our way, too. Dr. Wharton, is Jill under a doctor's care now?"

"Yes. They took her to jail and did the usual, I suppose, but then the lawyer got a psychiatrist in to talk to her. He will attend her. Why?"

"I just thought that if that is the case, we may never hear any more details, when she did this or that, or how, or who that man was in the apartment." Her gaze was very steady as she regarded Lois. "Between a doctor and a lawyer, she may never have a chance to make another statement. This is what she feared and dreaded most, isn't it? Never to be free, to be independent. She really is to be pitied, and so is her father. And you, of course. But you have your work. You may be the most fortunate of the three."

Lois moistened her lips and slowly she nodded.

"We can step outside, if that's all right with you," Greg Dolman said then, rising, pushing back his chair.

"It's nothing," Lois said, her voice low, but decisive. "I should be getting back." She held out her hand to Charlie and then to Constance. "Thank you both." She walked away, back toward the mill, toward the swinging bridge.

Greg Dolman shrugged. "We'll be tying up loose ends for the next few months, more than likely. We found the bracelet and the drugs, and the water in the thermos is tap water with something in it. They're analyzing it now. We'll have the doctor's report on Mrs. Ferris in a few days. I'll be in touch." He also held out his hand. Lois's hand had been like ice, his was sweaty.

"And I have to pick up that portable light unit and return it," Charlie said. "And youse guys don't have to worry none about being drove outta here, get it?"

"It don't work, Charlie," Al said. "The words are okay, maybe, but the tune's wrong, know what I mean?" And Sylvie said, "Watcha acting like that for, Mr. Wiseguy? Aincha got no manners? He don't mean nothing by it, Charlie."

In a few minutes Charlie and Constance were walking hand in hand toward the farm lakefront where the portable spotlights had been set up.

"One more little thing to see to," Charlie said, and gave her hand a squeeze.

She tried to think of what they had omitted; nothing came to mind. When they emerged from the tree sections, Charlie turned toward the row crops and began to peer up the paths. He waved when Tom Hopewell showed up between two rows.

"I'd like a word," Charlie called.

Tom came to them, his hands covered with moist dirt. "I heard," he said. "Everyone's heard. It's really over?"

"Yep. I suspect Lois Wharton will be back at work in a few

days and gradually things will return to normal. There are a few missing pieces, but nothing we can't live with."

"Well," Tom said doubtfully, and eyed the corn row he had just left.

Charlie helped him look down the row. "You know, if I had gone into that apartment first, I would have been overcome with curiosity about the identity of the dead man. Especially since I rather like Lois Wharton and wouldn't want to see her injured in any way. But then, if I snitched a man's wallet, I might not know what to do with it, might even be tempted to keep it around, and I would resist that temptation the way Adam should have resisted the apple." Tom Hopewell's face turned crimson. Charlie patted him on the arm. "Since I didn't find any such thing, I'm not going to worry about it. Just wanted to say so long. And pick up those lights. See you around."

After they retrieved the lights and were in their car again, Constance said, "I can't believe you told him to get rid of that wallet."

"You've got a nerve! After you told Lois to clam up? And right in front of the sheriff, too."

"Well, that's different."

Charlie began to chuckle and after a moment he was laughing out loud. His laughter died when he turned south to start the drive to New Jersey. In the back of the Volvo was the box containing David Levy's few possessions. They had to be delivered in person; this report had to be made in person. Constance rested her hand on his thigh as he drove.

Just before Christmas that year Lois paid them a visit. At first she was awkward. "I really just wanted to tell you," she said, "Warren is very ill, did you know? Last week he had his lawyer in and destroyed our agreement and changed his will. He set up a trust fund to care for Jill as long as she lives. But she may never be able to leave the institution. Anyway, he also transferred the property, the whole parcel of ground over to me, to use as an experimental farm."

Constance took her arm and led her to the kitchen and saw her seated, then began to make coffee. Lois looked almost dazed.

"There will be enough money to run it. I intend to hire Clarence when he retires, as a consultant. And Tom, if he ever stops chasing corn in Peru." She looked up at Constance and said in a tone of wonder, "I told Warren the story about your friend who planted trees as an act of faith. Last summer when I was planning to leave him, I told him that, and he asked me to stay and help him through this crisis. He needed someone." She shook her head. "No. He needed me. I am grateful that he's lived long enough to know I forgive him. We are at peace. I wanted to tell you." Before Constance could say anything, she went on, "We're already working very hard to get things ready. Al Zukal put in his limestone beach and it looks exactly like snow. Maybe it isn't too late."

She didn't stay long. At the door, ready to leave, she hugged Constance hard, and kissed her cheek. "Thank you," she whispered and was gone.

They watched her back out of the drive and then looked at each other. "He'll stop chasing corn in Peru when Warren kicks," Charlie said. He glanced at the sky; it had started to snow. He closed the door.

And won't she be surprised at what he'll have to say!

Charlie didn't know if she had said the words, or if he had, or if either of them had uttered a sound. He cast a suspicious glance at Constance and then sighed. She was smiling that certain smile she sometimes had, and it didn't matter.

Torch Song

Charlie had finished cutting up the apple trees he had felled back in February. Delimbing, debranching, disjointing, disarming—he grinned—at least sawing them into manageable lengths; he surveyed with satisfaction the mess he had made. "Get 'em before the sap rises," his neighbor Hal Mitchum had advised, "and you can burn the wood come fall." They were old, tired trees that yielded too little to stay and caught every disease known to the apple kingdom, and worse, they threatened the well-being of the half dozen new ones he and Constance had planted. He had gotten them before the sap rose, and then rain and snow had alternated week after week and Constance had said, "Charlie, you can't just leave them all spring, all summer. They'll be covered with brambles and weeds the day after spring comes. And you can't drag them out after the daffodils are up," she had added in a way that warned she meant it. She had planted the daffodils and probably knew where each one was, when it was due.

"Why don't you just hire someone to come in, do the job, clean up, and be done with it?" he said, mimicking her very well. He should have answered, Because you don't hire someone every time there's a little job to do, not when you're supposed to be retired. But she would have nailed him on that one; there had been a couple of pretty lucrative jobs he had done in the past six months.

He started down the slope toward the barn to get the tractor fired up, find a chain, start hauling the butchered trees to less sacred ground. Slipping and sliding on a layer of snow over a layer of ice that rested uneasily on a layer of oozy mud, he made his way without a glance toward the house until he had nearly reached the barn. Then he stopped when he saw a man emerge from the barn and another one watching his progress from the back patio.

He shifted the chain saw and continued to walk. City men, dressed in topcoats, the nearer one in shiny black shoes that definitely were not meant for snow and ice and mud.

"Hey, Charlie," the man at the barn said. "Carl Pulaski, remember me? We met twelve, fifteen years ago."

Charlie had never seen him before. "You just dropped by for a little visit?"

"Sort of. In the neighborhood, remembered you, knew you were around here somewhere. I'm with ATF, you remember?"

Charlie passed him to enter the barn. He glanced around swiftly but couldn't tell if anything had been moved, touched, or added. Pulaski followed him in.

"Gee, Charlie, Mr. Meiklejohn, I'm sorry you don't recall our meeting. That would have made this easier." He held out ID.

"Yep, Carl Pulaski, says so right there," Charlie murmured after a glance at it. He headed for the rear of the barn, where coils of rope and lengths of chain hung on pegs. "Thought you guys were all south for the winter—Waco, someplace like that."

"I'm in the area on official business," Pulaski said stiffly. "My associate and I want to talk to you."

"Well, I'm pretty busy right now. Like to get that wood hauled before it snows, rains, or sleets, or all three. Why don't you tell me what you want, and I'll remind you that I'm not official anything these days, and we'll both be able to get on with our work."

"Why are you on your high horse, Meiklejohn? You know you can make this as hard or as easy as you decide."

"See, Carl, when I was a wee lad, my mother taught me that if you want to pay a visit, you ring the doorbell and wait for someone to answer it. If no one shows up, you go away. You don't go snooping around outbuildings."

"We're investigating the Fircrest fire, Charlie. We need to talk to you."

Now Charlie studied him with interest. Pulaski looked frozen. His face was lean and very red at the moment. About fifty, give or take five, bareheaded and gray, pale blue eyes; he looked very earnest, sincere, like an accountant about to tell you how badly you screwed up your tax forms last year.

"What about the fire?" Charlie asked. "I know what was in the papers. You can probably still get them at the library."

"Let's go inside the house and talk," Pulaski said with an edge in his voice. "My feet hurt from the cold, and my hands are numb."

Charlie shrugged and nodded. He led the way, secure in his heavy boots now that the ground was level. Pulaski had trouble with his footing. At the patio, the second man waited. "My associate, Cy Gorman," Pulaski said, starting for the sliding door. Gorman kept his hands in his pockets.

"This way," Charlie told them, and led them to the back porch entrance, where he began to pull off his boots. He looked pointedly at Pulaski's feet, and the agent took off his shoes. Gorman's shoes were clean; he had had enough sense to stay on the walk, which had been cleared about a hundred times that year. Inside the back hall, Charlie hung his jacket on a peg; they kept their coats on.

He took them to the living room, where he poked a smoldering log into life, added another one, and drew aside as both agents crowded closer.

Gorman was softer-looking than Pulaski, and younger. His face was pudgy, pink from the cold, and he took in the room and Charlie with darting glances that didn't seem to linger long enough for anything to register. He was blond, with thick dark eyebrows that looked pasted on.

"Anytime," Charlie said, settling into his morris chair. He motioned toward chairs, the sofa. Ashcan, the cowardly gray cat, had gone rigor mortis–stiff when they entered the room, had blended invisibly into the covering of an overstuffed chair. Now, when Pulaski approached, Ashcan moaned and fled. Pulaski pretended not to notice, but his lean face tightened and became sharper, as if he suspected Charlie had set him up for a fright. He took off his topcoat and tossed it on the couch, sat down, and stretched out his legs toward the fire. Gorman, still standing on the hearth, shrugged out of his coat and held it. They used the same tailor, Charlie decided, and the tailor had stock in charcoal worsted. Even the ties were the same inoffensive blue-gray.

Deliberately, Pulaski said, "We're conducting an official investigation of the arson fire at the Fircrest Nursing Home during the night of March tenth. Where were you that night?"

Charlie shook his head. "Wrong approach. See, first you tell me why you're here asking questions, why ATF is involved and not the locals, and then we'll see if I can give you answers."

The other one was mute, Charlie thought then. Actually, he thought dumb, then changed it, because no one in his right mind would suggest the ATF could do anything dumb at the moment, not with tanks and heavy artillery out in force in Waco. Gorman was watching him closely, not moving, not speaking. Charlie decided to ignore him. Instead, he watched Pulaski wrestle with an interior dialogue.

At last, Pulaski said, "I'm going to give it to you straight, Charlie. We looked you up; we know your record, your background, your years as an arson investigator, then homicide, everything that's public knowledge, and more. There are mixed feelings in the agency about you, your reasons for quitting on fires, where they say you were very good. Problem is, we got a tip three days ago, a woman from the nursing home who called to report that she saw a man toss something in a car trunk that night, minutes before the fire broke out. A white car. She got three of the numbers, and the computer came up with a match for your license. That's why we're here. Where were you that night?"

"My license and how many others have those numbers?" Charlie murmured. "She called you in Washington? Not Werner Kolb over at Fircrest?"

Pulaski glanced at Gorman before he answered. "Yeah, she called us."

"That's some savvy lady," Charlie said. "Course, you guys have made it big in the news department; that might explain her knowing about you. Got her on ice?"

Pulaski set his mouth in a firm line. "I'm asking the questions, Charlie. What about Wednesday night?"

"Here."

"With your wife, I suppose."

"I think I had a dancing girl in that night. You're sure the caller was a woman?"

This time when Pulaski glanced at Gorman, Charlie was watching to catch the signal, too. A slight shake of his head, easy to miss, easy to spot now that he was looking for it.

"Loosen up, Charlie," Pulaski said. "This is a preliminary,

that's all. Someone calls in a tip, we check it out. You know that."

Charlie shook his head. "Uh-huh. Like the FBI checking out a tip on a local shooting. Give me a break, Pulaski. You got a whispery voice on the phone with a phony tip, you did a background check, and three days later here you are. You don't have the caller; you don't even know if it was a man or woman. What are the other dates you're interested in?" He was satisfied when Gorman's eyes widened, then narrowed.

"We haven't mentioned any other dates," Pulaski said altogether too fast.

Charlie stood up. "You'd better move a bit away from the fire," he said to Gorman. "Your britches will scorch there."

Gorman took a step away from the hearth. "They said you were quick," he said, breaking his long silence. His voice was thin and high. "You figured we're looking into serial arson fires?"

"I figured," Charlie admitted.

Gorman nodded, then, keeping his gaze on Charlie, he said, "Give him the dates."

Pulaski rattled off five dates, the first one a year ago in February. "Can you prove where you were on any of those nights?" he demanded when he'd finished.

"If all those fires started between three and four in the morning, probably not. Can you?"

"No one said when they started," Gorman said quickly.

Charlie was glad then that Pulaski was doing most of the talking; Gorman's voice was already an irritant. He shrugged and glanced at his watch, checked it against the mantel clock, and nodded. "Gentlemen, it's been interesting. Now I'm afraid I'm going to have to ask you to get the hell out of here. Chores to do, you know how it goes."

Pulaski got to his feet, crossed the room to pick up his coat, and put it on. "It isn't just arson fire; it's also murder. Four people have died, others injured, some of them seriously, including two firemen, millions in damages. . . ."

"Will you consent to a polygraph test?" Gorman asked.

Charlie gave him a look of disgust. "No." He said to Pulaski, "You picked him too green. Toss him back out in Wyoming to ripen on brush fires a year or two." This time, Gorman's face flushed, and there was a gleam for a moment in Pulaski's eyes. "Come on, out the way you came in, or you leave your shoes here." He walked before them to the kitchen, out to the porch, and watched Pulaski put his shoes on, tie them. They left without another word; he watched until they rounded the side of the house, and then he went to the living room, where he continued to watch until they appeared in the driveway, got in a black Chevy, and drove off. Pulaski drove.

By then, Ashcan had come out from hiding, and Candy was in the living room sniffing around, first the hearth, then the chair where Pulaski had sat, the couch. Charlie watched the orange cat as she stood on her hind legs to smell the couch cushion.

Slowly, deliberately, Charlie opened his fists and flexed his fingers. Those sons of bitches, he thought, believed their cock-and-bull story.

Constance sometimes pretended that the community of Fircrest had built the recreation center just for her. It was not a big establishment as such things went, but it had a good pool, and a good gymnasium, where she conducted self-defense classes for women three times a week and twice a week worked out with several women who were almost as good as she was in aikido. Very satisfactory, she thought that morning outside the low, sprawling building. She felt extraordinarily good, as she usually did after a workout, and there were crocuses pushing up through a crust of snow at the edge of the sidewalk. The air was cold and the sky threatening, but the crocuses knew their business, knew when it was time to melt their way through whatever lay above them.

She pulled her scarf closer to her wet head and hurried to the car. She was starved, and Charlie would be hungry after wrestling with those trees all morning. She hoped he had spent the morning getting them out of her orchard. If he hadn't, she thought, grinning at the idea, she would nag until he did. He could be so stubborn. Oxtail soup, she thought then. She had some in the freezer. She was humming by the time she completed the ten-minute trip home. Snow lingered in the fields across from the house, under the evergreens in front, in sheltered nooks and crannies, but the air smelled of crocuses and spring.

All three cats met her at the door. Candy complained hoarsely, Brutus stalked about looking furious, and Ashcan looked as if he feared she might kick him. "Don't do that," she scolded. She had never kicked a cat in her life and by now he should know he was safe. She hung up her jacket and took her scarf to the kitchen to dry, walking through cats as if they weren't there; she stopped inside the kitchen door. Newspapers were scattered across the table and Charlie was scowling at them.

"You're looking for a garage sale," she said. Then she saw a headline: NURSING HOME FIRE. And he was as furious as Brutus, she realized. His eyes had that strange, flat agate look, and his jaw was tight, his back rigid. "What happened?"

"Sit down," he said, "and I'll tell you."

She forgot her hunger and sat at the table with him and did not interrupt as he told her about his visitors. Then she said, "Cy Gorman. Wait a minute." She went up to her office on the second floor. Charlie began to refold the newspapers. He was finished and had them back in the recycle bin by the time she returned.

"A forensic psychiatrist," she said, moving past him to get the soup from the freezer.

"Might have known," Charlie muttered. "A goddamn shrink. He looked like one, acted like one. No offense," he added darkly.

"None taken, since I'm not a goddamn shrink," Constance said. She was a psychologist, retired more or less, just as he was retired more or less. They were the busiest retired people she had ever heard of. She put a bowl of frozen soup in the microwave. She had made the soup on the woodstove, which even then had the house a touch too warm, but for thawing and reheating, it was microwave every time. She returned to the table and sat down again. "What are you going to do?"

"Nothing. They think they've got a case, let them prove it."

"Have you talked to Werner Kolb yet?

He shook his head. "They've already got to Werner, told him to dummy up," he said.

"Probably, and if he stalls you, you'll know it for a fact and

I'll get Marion to set up something." Charlie gave her a look and she shrugged. Marion had been in her class last year. "Did you see the expression on Werner's face when she put that football player down at the exhibition? He'll talk to you."

"To you maybe," Charlie said, and he knew he was simply being contrary, but he seemed powerless to stop himself. Talk to her, talk to him, same thing. He remembered the exhibition Constance and their daughter, Jessica, had put on; he would never forget that.

The microwave dinged, and Constance got up to stir the soup; she returned it to the oven, then brought out placemats and bowls, a loaf of bread and butter. Charlie started a pot of coffee. Of course, he wasn't going to do nothing, he thought savagely, but damned if he knew where to start. Arson fires that went back more than a year. *They* had the manpower, the equipment, the necessary information. Same method each time? A letter of warning, or a gloat after the fact? A calling card left at the scene? It wasn't merely that they had all started around the same time of night, either; arsonists often started their fires between midnight and dawn. But something tied them all together, and they knew what it was. And if they had looked up his record, talked to people, they knew he wouldn't take this without fighting back.

"I think they are stymied and see this as an excuse to get you to work on their case for them," Constance said.

He wished to hell she wouldn't do that, apparently follow his line of thought, and even complete it. "Is it soup yet?" he asked coldly.

It was, and they sat down to eat and didn't talk now. Constance finished first. "Good soup," she murmured. Then she said, "If you have the dates, we can find out where the fires were from the computer database."

Charlie pulled his notebook out and opened it to the last entry, the dates Pulaski had rushed through. Constance studied them and then stiffened.

"Charlie, where is that letter you got last winter? You know, the threatening letter?"

He put down his spoon and left the table. He knew exactly where it was, in the file labeled "Threats." Not the same date, he thought, hoped, when he pulled out the folder and extracted the last item he had filed there. The letter was post-marked in New York City on February 11 of last year; the first date he had jotted down was February 10. He returned to the kitchen and put the envelope on the table between them. They both knew the contents: words cut out of a newspaper, pasted on a sheet of lined paper. There had been no fingerprints on the letter, and only smudges on the envelope. The letter said: "You will feel my pain."

Constance did not touch the letter, she looked at the post-mark and then at Charlie. "I'm scared," she said softly.

He got up and went to stand behind her chair, put his arms around her. "Take it easy, honey," he said, and kissed the top of her head. Her hair was still moist and fragrant. "We don't know that it's connected. Some nut out there wanted to get my goat, that's all. How many letters like that do you suppose I have in that file? Dozens, starting way back."

She did not relax. "If someone's been planning this for over a year," she said, "time's on his side. We don't have a clue about what else he might come up with."

"Then we'd better get moving," Charlie said, and kissed her head again. "Enough of this lollygagging about. I'll go start on the computer."

She cleared the table, put the dishes in the dishwasher, and finally opened the envelope and read the message again. "You will feel my pain." It was connected. She knew it was. That had been step one. The tip to the ATF office step two. Four people had been killed in the fires, many others injured. Suddenly, the house felt cold.

"Good heavens," Constance said when Charlie appeared later holding a printout with dozens of entries.

"Right," he said. "A fireman's job is never done." He had a map under his arm that he now spread on the table, and they began to locate the sites. At first, Charlie penciled them in with small x's, but after a moment Constance left to get a jar of dried beans; then they continued, placing a bean on the name of each town and city in the northeastern part of the country that had reported fires on the dates Pulaski had provided. Buffalo, a two-bean city; Poughkeepsie; New York City, too many to fit on the map; Middletown; Pittsfield . . . After several minutes, Charlie straightened and grunted. Slowly, he began to remove the beans. He left four.

"September fourth, 'ninety-two," he said in a low voice. There were nine entries. After locating them all, he put a bean on Utica. "December seventeenth." Seven entries. He put a bean on Norwich, New York, and drew back to regard the map.

Six beans, six fires, and the most distant one—Danbury, Connecticut—was less than a hundred miles away. The beans might have marked a deformed wheel, with Fircrest in the center.

"I don't blame Pulaski and his crew," he said. "I'd have come here, too."

Constance made a note of the towns and then gathered up the beans silently. They would have to verify them, she knew, but no doubt the list was right: If you're making a noose, you make it tight enough not to slip off.

That afternoon, they drove over to the Fircrest Nursing Home. It was a three-story gray-stone building, built in 1889, a school originally, a prison for a short time, a government building during World War II, vacant for many years after that, and refurbished as a nursing home seventeen years earlier. The stench of recent fire was in the air. He hated that smell more than anything else he could think of.

Dense shrubbery would have screened a car from view here on both the first and second floor, he decided, driving slowly past the front of the building. From the third floor, only the top part would have been visible, no license plate, no trunk opening. On the side of the building he had already passed was a paved parking area, and beyond that were high evergreen trees. He drove around the other corner. Both sides of the building had columnar evergreens five feet from the stone, a screen for the inhabitants, allowing them to open windows, get some air, and still have privacy, but also blocking their view of the street. He continued to creep along the street to a drive that went in behind the building, no doubt a continuation of the other one that went to the parking lot. Here a tall streetlamp would have cast enough light, he thought, but again the shrubs and the angle indicated that no one from inside could have seen a license plate.

"You're not going in, are you?" Constance asked in her most neutral voice.

"Nope," he said. "Just wanted to see. When I get a lawyer, we'll come back and take pictures, prove a point."

She gave him a sharp look. "Have you figured out why anyone would try to burn down a stone building?"

He whistled softly and entered the driveway. He stopped the car at the center of the rear of the building and they both gazed at it. The back part had been expanded at some point, and the expansion had been made of wood, which was charred, and in some places burned completely away as high as the roof. The burn pattern formed steep, jagged peaks, like the stock market at its craziest. From here, they could see that the interior had been gutted.

Before Charlie shifted gears to start driving again, he saw in his rearview mirror an ancient blue Ford pull into the driveway. He turned off his motor and waited. The car pulled in close and Werner Kolb got out, came to his window. In his bulky jacket, he looked like a moving barrel.

"Charlie, Constance, how you folks doing? Thought I saw your car heading this way."

"It got away from you, didn't it?" Charlie said, nodding toward the building. "How the devil did it get up there so fast? Somebody take a blowtorch to it?"

"Pret near, I guess. We figure it was gas in a sprayer, a paint sprayer, or the kind you use for trees, something like that."

"Someone's living dangerously," Charlie muttered, thinking of gasoline under pressure. "The others like this?"

"Same pattern, far's they can tell. I'm not supposed to be talking to you."

"Figured that."

"Well, I told them they were barking up the wrong tree, but that's not what they wanted to hear. Told them how you come over to the station couple times a year, talk to the boys, give them pointers, all that, and they said that could be part of the pattern, keeping your hand in, irresistible urges or something. Told them if anyone's crazy around here, it ain't you."

"Where were the others?" Charlie asked.

Werner told him; it was the same list Constance had already

written. "Gotta go," Werner said. "Marion's always complaining it takes me longer to go out and buy a jug of milk than it takes the cows to make it. See you around, Charlie." He started to move away, stopped, and drew an envelope from his pocket. "Oh, 'most forgot. You might want to look this over." He handed it to Charlie, waved to Constance, and turned to leave.

"Hey, Werner," Charlie said as he ambled away, "I owe you. Next time you have a benefit, I'll come twice."

Werner chuckled and kept walking.

A sprayer. Charlie thought of Pulaski in his barn, examining his sprayer, sniffing it, maybe photographing it. Constance put her hand on his thigh as he started to drive and after a moment he covered her hand with his. He wondered if she knew how bad this could get. When she squeezed his leg, he knew she did.

When they got home, Candy met them, demanding explanations in a raucous voice, her tail upright and quivering in indignation. Ashcan begged to be forgiven. Charlie eyed him moodily; that cat never had been able to shake his Catholic upbringing. In the kitchen, they found Brutus asleep on top of the warming oven of the wood cookstove. They ignored him; what it would take to break him of that habit would be having his tail catch on fire.

"The classic question now is, Do you have any enemies?" Constance said. She went to the freezer to contemplate packages and packages.

Charlie snorted. "Does a vulture have bad breath?"

She closed the door empty-handed. "I think three to six months would be long enough to consider, don't you?"

He waited. He had taken the papers from the envelope Werner had handed him.

"I mean before the first fire, of course," she went on, gazing past him absently. "But I simply can't think of anything you did in that period that would bring a response like this." She tapped her lips with her finger. "Maybe six months is too short."

"Go for the last thirty years," he said, and started to scan the six fire reports with the details that never made it to the daily papers. Now he simply looked them over; later he would read them thoroughly. February 10, 1992, Danbury, Connecticut: a

movie theater. March 28, 1992, Middletown, New York: a strip
mall, one shopkeeper killed. July 9, 1992, Pittsfield, Massachusetts: two warehouses destroyed, one watchman killed, one
transient. September 4, 1992, Utica, New York: a paint factory
burned down, a vice president killed. December 17, 1992, Norwich, New York: a high school damaged. March 10, 1993, Fircrest, New York: a nursing home. He tossed the reports on the
table. "I'm going out to finish that damn wood," he said.

She nodded. He could always think better if his body was in
motion, or at the very least his hands. Now he would fool
around with his trees and think. She read the reports and then
began to pace the kitchen, the living room, and finally upstairs.

When Charlie came in, it was getting dark, and although the
temperature had been dropping steadily, he was sweating. He
sniffed: lamb, green beans, tomatoes, lots of garlic and onions.
"Aye, and it's a good woman you are, Constance," he said.

"God knows I try," she said demurely. He swacked her bottom as she walked by him.

"What's all that?" he said, pointing to many papers on the
table—faxes, from the looks of them.

"Shower, change, relax. I'm about to have a glass of wine,
and when you come back all dewy fresh and fragrant, you can
have some, too." This time when he reached out to give her
another pat, she caught his wrist, and he knew she could have
put him down in the middle of the floor if she had wanted.
Instead, she drew his arm around her waist and kissed him.
She stepped back and shook her head; her nose wrinkled. "Just
as I thought. You are in great need of a shower."

Laughing, he went upstairs to shower.

"Now," she said later, showing him the faxes while he sipped
his wine. "I kept thinking of all the work you did last year, all
white-collar crimes. Those men will never go to trial. They'll
deal with their companies, pay fifty cents on the dollar, and
retire."

He nodded. He had come to the same conclusion.

"And I tried to think of all the people you've made angry
around here over the years. A very long list," she added gravely,
"but not enough for anyone to retaliate this way. You have a
knack at winning poker and you might make some of your bud-
dies sore, but this sore? I don't think so."

He nodded, keeping his expression as serious as hers, enjoying this.

"So I called Loretta Halliday," she went on, startling him. "I got a list of people who were released from New York State or federal prisons for the three months before the first fire. Another long list, I'm afraid."

Charlie stared at her, awed. He had planned to get that list, but it had not occurred to him to call and just ask for it. Loretta Halliday had been on the state corrections board for as long as he could remember, and she was a dragon. "What in God's name do you have on Loretta?" he asked. "I might want to use it someday."

"Now, Charlie. I simply told her you received a threatening letter and refused to take it seriously, but that I did. Since she thinks men are such idiots, that seemed a logical approach. She was very cooperative."

He laughed and drained his glass. Besides, he might have added, Loretta knew the information was available to anyone who wanted to dig a little.

"The trouble is," she said, "I don't know many of these people from a long time ago, from when you were still with the police. It's going to be up to you to sort it all out."

By the time Constance had dinner on the table, Charlie had culled thirteen names from the list. In each case, he had been the investigating officer, the arresting officer, or had testified in court, often all three. He was gazing at his short list moodily when Constance called him to dinner.

"Ah, memories," he said, putting his list on a table by his chair. Then he demanded, "Why is it when you cook, I have a lapful of cats in here, and when I cook, I have the kitchen full of the damn beasts?"

"I feed them before I start," she said, "as I have told you more times than I can count."

He made them wait, he thought, tossing Brutus off his lap, so they could have table scraps, which was the natural order of things.

He did not mention his short list during dinner, and only when they had coffee and a leftover apple kuchen did he say almost casually, "I think I know who it is."

She put her fork down. "You're kidding!"

He went to get his list, and then said, "These struck me as possibles." He pointed to the first name. "John Scovotto used a knife and got caught. Bad temper, very bad. Acted on the spur of the moment, a flash of rage with an irresistible impulse to kill. I don't think so." He pointed to the next name. "Lincoln Trowbridge liked a baseball bat, drug stuff. Nope. Gary Thomson, armed robbery, several times, I believe. He forgave me on the spot. The way he saw it, he was doing his thing and I was doing mine. Reasonable sort of fellow. Barbara Jelinsky killed her pimp in a fight. Not her style—arson, planning." He went on down the list, remembering all of them. . . . He paused at one and said thoughtfully, "I considered him a bit longer. Wade Lee. He killed his wife, her mother, and a neighbor who happened to be in the wrong place, wrong time. Then he set the house on fire. After insurance, and really stupid. Too stupid." He shook his head and pointed again. "Don Flexner. He was plenty sore, but he couldn't plan far enough ahead to get a bus transfer." Finally, he pointed to a name he had skipped over.

"Peter Eisenbeis," he said. "A great-looking kid, tall, blond, blue eyes, football type. A real planner, too." He could tell from the alarmed expression on Constance's face that she remembered him.

The look of fear vanished; her face became expressionless, and she asked in a low voice, "When did they release him?"

"December tenth, 'ninety-one."

They were both thinking about the anonymous threat: "You will feel my pain."

God, Charlie thought suddenly, all this was making him feel old. Thirteen years ago, yet he remembered as if it had happened last week. Pete Eisenbeis had scoped out a warehouse on the East River, not far from where his girlfriend lived. One Friday afternoon, he had gone there to apply for a job and, application in hand, had roamed the building with no one paying much attention. At four, an armored truck arrived and at the same time a fire broke out in half a dozen places at once. The kid had walked up to the truck just as the guard on the passenger side opened his door and stepped out. The kid had shot and wounded him, had taken his place, and the truck had sped off. With all the confusion of alarms, fire equipment arriving with sirens blaring, workers rushing around, the truck was lost.

Charlie had found Pete's prints on the application, on a door facing, a metal girder, and he had gone through the neighborhood with his description and had come up with a name, Peter, and his girlfriend's name, Marla Sykes. No one approached her; they waited. Two days later, Peter Eisenbeis returned. Charlie should not have been involved in the chase, but he and the stakeout were trying to decide if they should wait outside the tenement or go in after him, when Marla and Pete reappeared; he was carrying a baby. He spooked, shoved the girl and baby inside the car, and raced off. Charlie's car was the one that hung on his bumper through the Upper East Side. By then, other cars were converging, and the kid crashed his car. He was barely injured, a few scrapes; the girl was hurt slightly more. The baby was thrown thirty or forty feet and suffered massive brain damage. Pete was sent up. The baby lived, but he would have been better off if he hadn't, from all accounts.

"You will feel my pain."

"They didn't find the money," Charlie said, remembering. Pete had taken them to the spot where he'd hidden the truck, out on Long Island. They had found the driver's body chained to a water pipe in a bathroom of an empty house; he had suffered a heart attack. Pete swore he had left everything in the truck. His plan was to get Marla, take the cash, and get out of the country. At least $280,000 in cash vanished, and millions in checks, paper of various kinds.

Constance was thinking of the two youngsters. Marla had been seventeen, Pete nineteen. Her mother had told her to get out with the baby; Pete said he did it for her, for their son, so they could have a life. The public defender took a plea bargain for him: twenty-five years. But now he was out. She rubbed goose bumps on her arms.

"Hey," Charlie said softly, taking her cold hand. "At least we have a place to begin, more than we had a couple of hours ago." He was grateful she didn't tell him to take this business to Pulaski. He could imagine the pitying look on that lean face, because he was certain he had worn such a look many times when a suspect cried, "I've been framed!"

When Constance went downstairs the next morning, Charlie was making blueberry waffles, whistling. Water droplets still clung to his crinkly black hair; it was hard to tell the droplets from the few gray hairs. She liked his hair, she was thinking, pouring coffee, when the phone rang.

They listened to a woman's voice explaining why she wouldn't make it to the aikido class that morning. When she finished, Constance said, "I'll give Sandy a call and have her take over for me." Sandy was good enough to lead the group, she had decided during the night as she lay staring into darkness. Charlie had been up and down several times and she had been awake every time he left the bed without a sound.

"I don't think so," he said, at the counter, taking a waffle from the iron. "Look, perfect, is it not?"

She agreed. He gave it to her on a plate and poured in more batter. "I'm going to be on the phone all morning. Pete's probation officer, where he reports, what he's up to, what he did in the jug, where Marla is now . . . stuff like that. You might as well be doing the usual thing. Let them worry that we're not taking any of this bullshit seriously. Okay?"

She nodded, her mouth full.

He was on the phone in his little downstairs office when she left for the recreation center, and he was on it when she returned two hours later. She waved to him from the doorway and he nodded, listening. He looked tired, she thought with dismay. Now and then, she caught him in a certain light, in a certain pose and realized that he was growing older before her eyes. Most of the time, such thoughts never came to mind; he was young in every way she could think of. But in fact, he was getting gray, and at the moment he looked tired. He hung up and regarded her with those strange, flat eyes that he sometimes showed her, and she knew it wasn't just that he was tired; he also was frightened.

She held her breath for a moment, then grinned and said, "I think a workout was just what I needed. How'd you make out?"

He shook his head. "I shouldn't have let you go out alone. I'm acting like a fool, honey."

"Why? What happened?"

"Nothing. I began to think: If our guy is really Pete Eisenbeis, what hurt him most? Going to prison or losing his lover and his child? I don't want us separated until we see this through. Okay?"

She could feel his fear radiating out to her, enveloping her. She nodded wordlessly and went to him at his desk, held his head tightly against her; he wrapped his arms around her and drew her even closer.

"He's dropped out of sight, broken probation," Charlie said, the words muffled against her breast. "He's out there some-where, maybe watching us, watching you."

Dear God, she thought. Oh dear God!

The phone on the desk rang. He drew back and picked up the receiver. "Yeah," he said, then listened and made a note or two. "Right. I'll call if there's anything else. Thanks, Brian." Brian Posner was an investigator he sometimes used in New York City.

"Let's go sit down and I'll tell you what I have," Charlie said. "Hungry?"

She shook her head. Hand in hand, they went to the living room, where he sat in his morris chair and she in the wing chair, close enough that they could touch each other.

"Okay," he said. "He got out and two days later turned up at Marla's place. She has a house down around Tuxedo Park, been there all these years with the boy. She said she sent him away, and no one's laid eyes on him since. He's skipped, prob-ably with two hundred eighty grand. She hasn't heard from him. That's for openers. She married Steve Boseman a year after Pete went up, and a year later Boseman was killed. They figure he was in the drug game or numbers; it had the marks of a gangland killing—hands tied behind his back, shot in the back of the head. He was dumped in a creek and drowned a few miles from where they lived. She's been alone since then. But she visited Pete once a month all the time he was in the pen."

"Why? If she married someone else . . ."

"Don't know. We'll ask."

Constance nodded. Crazy, she was thinking.

"What I thought we might do," Charlie said, "is take a little spin over to Utica and then down to Norwich. If you're really not hungry yet."

"We can get some lunch along the way," she said. "I'll change first." She was wearing sweatpants and a sweatshirt, running shoes. He thought she looked good the way she was.

She drove. It was less than an hour's drive to Utica. He directed her to Grant Street, where the paint factory had burned down. And it would have burned to the ground, Charlie knew; it had been made of wood. Explosions, toxic fumes, roiling, poisonous smoke . . . The site had been cleared and fenced. This was an industrial area with ugly gray buildings and trucks, ugly gray slush, a railroad siding. . . . A road led around back of the property; the fence was new. Anyone could have parked within a hundred feet, walked in, sprayed the place, tossed the match, and out.

He directed her past a hospital, past Utica College, onto State 12. Another good road, she thought, driving. All the places had been on good roads, accessible. Rain started to fall. Don't freeze, she ordered. Just don't start freezing.

In Norwich, an hour later, they drove around the high school building. The gymnasium, an annex, had been destroyed; the school building had been saved.

Constance stopped for a bunch of teenagers who couldn't decide if they wanted to cross the street or not. They didn't seem to notice that they were getting wet.

Charlie scowled at the kids. He'd be leaning on the horn, he thought, and they'd flip him off and make him even madder. He'd end up yelling; one of them would pull a gun. . . . They moved out of the way and Constance edged past them; they didn't seem to notice the car. She turned to circle the school again, and Charlie touched her arm.

"Let's go find something to eat," he said. This was a bust. The school would have been a cinch at three in the morning. A quiet neighborhood, everyone sleeping. Something was nagging at him, and he couldn't get at it. Something was screwy, he thought, then realized he was thinking like an arson investigator. What was behind the fires? Not killing anyone, not a spectacular show. He couldn't have hung around to watch, he thought, or said—he wasn't sure which, because Constance made a sound that sounded like agreement. A stranger in a small place like this would have been noticed. Even in Utica, around the warehouses, no stranger would have gone unnoticed. And Fircrest? Forget it.

Constance interrupted his train of reasoning. "What you should do," she said grimly, "is find us the quickest way home, without going over mountains on narrow roads."

He looked at her questioningly.

"The rain's starting to freeze," she said.

By the time they reached their driveway, three hours later, the car was riding on ice like a hockey puck. Charlie let out his breath as she pulled into the garage. "Ya done good, babe," he said.

She gave him a mean look. "I'm just about ready to faint from hunger. You cook."

That night, Charlie dreamed of the fire, his fire. He was in the endless corridor, where every doorknob burned his hand as the fire roared behind him, forcing him on until he couldn't breathe and his knees were buckling. He woke up, to find Constance's arms around him. He drew in a long breath, another, and said, "Thrashing about a bit?"

"A bit," she said.

He was soaking wet, the way he always was after that dream. "Shower," he mumbled, pulling away from her. A moment later, as he stood under the hot water turned on full force, her shadow fell on the glass door; she opened the door and stepped in beside him.

"Wanton hussy." He reached for her.

"Damn right," she said.

Charlie hated it that he never could sleep later than seven, but there it was. They had remade the bed last night, and the last thing he remembered was seeing Constance turn the clock away. She intended to sleep late. He grinned; on the whole, he felt better than the few hours of sleep warranted. He was whistling as he made coffee and fed the cats. Constance was right; they stayed out from underfoot as he scrambled eggs. He took his plate to the table and only then glanced out the glass doors to the patio, and he stopped whistling. Iced in. Ice coated everything. He turned on the radio for weather news.

When Constance came down at nine, at first he thought her

radiant smile was for him, but then he saw that she was gazing past him at the world turned into fairyland.

"Oh," she said, and went to the door.

"And good morning to you, too," he said huffily.

A thin coating of ice glistened on every blade of grass, every twig, every tree branch; already it was starting to drip diamonds. The weather forecast said it would be gone by noon. If he could go out there with a giant heat machine, he thought, he'd do it, and it would be gone now. He continued to watch her at the door, and when she turned away finally, whatever it was on his face changed her smile into an expression tender and private. Charlie didn't think anyone on earth but him had ever seen that look.

"I'll make you some scrambled eggs," he said. "I'll even bring your coffee."

She nodded and sat down, then eyed the table curiously. He had brought out the road map, a calendar, his notebook, and the faxes of ex-cons' names, and she couldn't tell what else.

He brought coffee and went back to the counter near the sink. "Onions, cheese?" he asked.

"Everything. I'm starved."

He laughed and began breaking eggs, enough for both of them; he was starved again, too. When they were both eating, he said, "I looked for a pattern for the dates—zilch. Two on a Saturday, one on Tuesday, and like that. No pattern. And they're spread out over the months, too. Not the first week, or the last, just sort of random. No pattern there, or in the intervals between fires." Always look for patterns, he had advised rookies in training. But you don't always find them, he now added.

"So, what's the plan?" she asked, motioning toward the papers he had pushed to one side.

"First, I want to see the other sites, just to check them out. I don't know what I'm looking for, to be honest. Then, a visit to Marla."

"You think he might be hanging around her?"

"Maybe," he said soberly. "I hope to God he is."

He would take his gun, she knew, and no doubt Peter Einsenbeis would be armed. Slowly she said, "Charlie, listen a minute. You know a lot of people, and most of them will be like

Werner, on your side. An APB on Pete might catch him in a day or two. You don't have to do this by yourself."

"The people who really count won't be like Werner," he said. He had already considered this; he gave her an abbreviated version of where his considerations had led him. "First, he skipped out on his parole officer, so they already have a bulletin out. Second, he might lead them to nearly three hundred thousand in cash and millions in paper, so they're looking. Third, even if they get him, I'm not off the hook, because he's bound to have as good an alibi as mine, or better. Fourth," he finished, "they already think they know who torched those buildings; they aren't looking for anyone else." What they were doing, he knew, was sending flocks of agents out to every location, asking questions about a white car, a stocky man with dark hair turning gray, flashing his picture. . . .

"So where do we start today?" Constance asked when he became silent.

"Toss a coin. We can go over to Pittsfield and on down to Danbury, and Tuxedo Park, or we can go down to Middletown first and then Marla. Can't do all three sites in one day and still get to Marla, I'm afraid. I thought we'd pack a suitcase, pile up in a motel tonight, then hang around Tuxedo Park tomorrow and ask a few questions."

"It will be mountain driving all day if we go to Middletown," Constance said, and he said, "Right." They decided on Pittsfield and points south. An hour later when they started, the ice was gone, and most of the lingering snow with it.

Charlie drove today, mostly on the interstates, and too fast. "Pittsfield," he said as they neared the town in Massachusetts. "Two adjacent warehouses, one furniture, the other a wholesaler for craft supplies. Two dead, a watchman and a transient, who apparently sneaked in and went to sleep." Soon they had entered a district of warehouses and car lots. Again the building sites they were looking for were closed off with a new fence, and again access would have been simple without the fence. Just warehouses with loading docks, drives, parking areas, a road behind everything, fields behind that, and nothing in the way of anyone with a sprayer filled with gas. He could have been heading out U.S. 7 before an alarm went off. What he couldn't have done was hang around and watch the show.

Charlie was tempted to skip the next one, but since he was driving on U.S. 7, and Danbury was on the way, he headed for the theater site. It would be the same, he thought, disgruntled, pondering the question of how Pete had been able to find such ideal places in such a short time. Had he drawn a circle on a map and worked only within the circumference? It looked like it. What he would give, he thought then, to find such a map with Pete's prints all over it, with each town circled in red. . . .

"You don't suppose he knew any of those people who died, do you?" Constance asked. She was looking at the descriptions of the victims: a shopkeeper in Middletown, fifty-eight, lived there all his life; a chemist who had lived in Utica for twenty years, vice president of the paint company. The transient had been twenty-four, bumming around after serving in the navy for four years; the watchman, sixty-four. . . . She gave it up. Charlie didn't bother to respond. He didn't suppose.

The theater in Danbury was constructed of brick and wood; it had been repaired, the first of the buildings to be burned, the first one fixed again. It would have been the biggest challenge, too, Charlie thought as he drove through an alley behind the building. On the other side of the alley was a medical complex with a large parking lot, and a Methodist church on the corner, but the alley was narrow, and this was practically in the center of town. He must have driven exactly where Charlie was edging along. This was the only place where he had run any risk at all. But at three in the morning, who would be up looking? He suspected Pulaski would be concentrating on Danbury, maybe going from house to house, betting on the theory that someone was always up and looking. The fire had not done as much damage here as in the other buildings they had inspected. Pete had been learning on the job. By the time he hit the warehouses in Pittsfield, he had been a real pro who did not take risks.

An hour and fifteen minutes later, they checked into a motel in Tuxedo Park and got directions for Cedar Falls, which turned out to be a hamlet a few miles to the west. Charlie nodded as he drove through Cedar Falls: a supermarket with prices posted in the windows, and a smaller, more discreet grocery without signs in the windows, an antique shop, a few small houses set back off the highway. A Porsche and a Cadillac were in a gas station being serviced. A fine Victorian house partly hidden by trees had a sign swinging in the breeze: CHELSEY HOUSE.

"Restaurant," Constance said. "Look at the size of that parking lot!"

The road narrowed when they left the tiny town: a slender black snake frozen in motion. The woods were dense here; the only indications that there were also houses were the many driveways that vanished among trees and shrubs. Most of the entrances had gates or chains. Some of them had signs with names. He spotted the name Boseman with a sigh of relief. That driveway had neither gate nor chain, but it wound among trees just like the rest, to a large, handsome split-level house with a lot of windows and a turnaround at the front entrance.

"Well," he said, "little Marla struck it rich."

She could have used a yardman, Constance thought as they went to the front door. The grounds were unkempt, overgrown with shrubs and flower beds that had been neglected for years and were a mass of decaying flower stalks, weeds, and leaves. Seedling maples had been allowed to grow, crowding one another, all spindly.

The door was opened by a young woman who looked surprised to see them. "Oh, I was expecting someone else. What do you want?"

"Can we talk?" Charlie asked pleasantly. "We're looking for Peter Eisenbeis."

She started to close the door; he held it open. "I don't know where he is," she said sharply. "I told them that already."

She was slender and pretty, dressed in jeans and sneakers and an oversized white sweater. Her hair was black and long, caught up in a ponytail tied with a red ribbon. She looked almost exactly the way he remembered her from thirteen years ago.

"Mrs. Boseman—Marla—Pete's in very serious trouble. I have to find him before it gets even worse." His voice was gentle; he made no motion to push the door open.

She looked from him to Constance, back. A slight frown appeared on her forehead as she studied him. "Who are you?" she asked, nearly whispering.

"Meiklejohn. I arrested Pete thirteen years ago."

"Why did you come here? What's he done? I told you, I don't know where he is!" She stepped back from the door.

They followed her into the house. "Let's just talk," Charlie said. "Maybe you know something and just haven't thought of it."

She shook her head but made a vague motion toward an arch on one side of the foyer they had entered. Inside the house, the same lack of attention showed that was evident on the grounds; there was dust on a sideboard near the door, and an empty vase, also dusty. A pale blue rug that was deep and soft was also dirty, with a trail of footprints embedded in it. The room she led them to was spacious, with twin sofas, many chairs with damask covers, everything dirty, dusty, uncared for, all the expensive furnishings untended. She waved toward the sofas, and she perched on the edge of a chair. Almost immediately, she stood up again.

"I have to do something," she said. "I'll be right back." She hurried from the room, and after a moment Charlie and Constance followed. He kept his hand in his pocket, where he had put his .38.

They trailed after her up a short flight of stairs and saw her enter a room. Moving without a sound, they went to the open door, and now they could hear her voice; it had softened and sounded musical.

"Honey, I won't be long, and Roy will be here any minute. He's running a little late today, he said. Do you want me to put on a movie? . . . *Beauty and the Beast* again? . . . How about *The Canterville Ghost*? I'll just raise the chair a little. Here we go. . . ."

She continued to speak in a soothing, comforting tone. Looking through the doorway, Charlie could see the boy, her son, an elongated figure on a reclining wheelchair—so thin, he hardly raised the sheet. For a second, he looked bald, but then Charlie could see pale, fuzzy hair. His head appeared oversized for the thin neck; his arms on the sheet were skeletal, and he did not make a sound. The elaborate wheelchair was near French windows leading to a balcony, and a mammoth television was against the wall opposite his bed. A round maple table and a single chair were close to the bed. Silently, Charlie drew back when he felt Constance's fingers on his arm. They returned to the living room and sat without speaking until Marla reappeared in the arched doorway. The sound track of a movie was barely audible.

Before Marla could enter the room, the doorbell rang, and she ran to open it. "Roy, thank God! He's had a terrible day, and he's so tired."

A large man walked past the arch, his head cocked as he listened to Marla. "I think if you just let him soak for a long time and then give him a massage, maybe he'll relax enough to eat something." Her voice faded as they passed out of sight.

A minute later, she was back, and this time she sat down. "I'll tell you what I told the others," she said. "And that's all I can tell you."

She was as rigid as a department-store mannequin. Her white-knuckled fingers clutching the chair arms looked frozen.

"Pete came here a day or two after he got out," she said in a low, fast monotone. "I told him to leave and he did. I haven't seen him since and I haven't heard from him."

Charlie held up his hand. "Not quite so fast, Mrs. Boseman."

"Don't call me that," she said sharply.

"All right," Charlie said. "But you see, we really do need to find Pete. Mind if we look around a little, just to make the record complete."

She jumped up. "You think he's here? I'm hiding him? I told you, we had a fight and I threw him out. Be my guest, help yourself, look. I'm going to make Nathan something to eat." She left the room swiftly, without a backward glance.

When Charlie stood and glanced at Constance, she shook her head and walked out after Marla. He started to explore the large house.

Constance followed Marla to the kitchen and stood back out of the way as she began to prepare food for her son. The kitchen was spotless. It was ultramodern, with a cooking island, stainless steel everywhere, white tiles, white appliances, all gleaming. An adjoining room that overlooked the back of the property held a television, comfortable chairs with russet-and-green covers, a dining table and chairs. That room looked used, as if this was where she spent her time. Half a dozen fashion magazines were on a sofa, jewelry and garden catalogs.

Marla was cutting up cooked carrots; she put them in a com-

mercial blender and whirred them briefly, added milk and
whirred them again, and scraped them into a small plastic bowl;
she tasted the puree, added salt and a half teaspoon of sugar,
stirred, and tasted it again. She put a lid on it and began to cut
up potatoes to repeat the process. The food had the consis-
tency of cream. A piece of well-done steak was next; she
blended it with stock until it was like a thin soup. When the
dinner was prepared, she put the bowls into a microwave.

She washed the blender and made a milk shake with frozen
strawberries, a banana, half an apple, milk, and a scoop of ice
cream. She poured it into a plastic glass and snapped on the
kind of top used for toddlers just learning to drink from a glass.
She put it in the refrigerator.

Finally, she looked at Constance. "What are you, an investigator for the health department or something?"

Constance shook her head. "It must take him longer to eat
the food than for you to prepare it. Will he eat much of it?"

Marla seemed to sag, then straightened again and walked to
the table across the room. "He eats enough," she said, gazing
out the wide windows.

A long ramp went to the back of the yard; there was a concrete walk that curved around bushes and trees. Thick, high
shrubbery screened the entire back; no other house was visible.
The back section looked well tended, with several raised flower
beds. "You work out there?" Constance asked.

Marla nodded. "He likes to be outside, watch me plant
things, weed, pick flowers."

"Why do you stay here, so isolated? It must be lonely for
you."

"Boseman did that to me," Marla said after a moment. "I can't
sell the house, or his car, or anything. I can use it for as long
as I want to, but I can't sell out. I'm stuck here. He did that."

"What about Boseman?" Constance asked. "How on earth did
such a man enter your life, yours and Nathan's?"

Marla went to the window and pressed her forehead against
the glass. "Funny," she said. "No one ever asked that. They
asked everything else, but not that." She glanced at Constance,
who had moved to stand beside her at the window. "He got
the gun for Pete, and the car; he knew all about it. Later, when
Nathan was in the hospital, he came around, to collect what

Pete owed him, he said. I told him to go talk to Pete. He wanted to make out with me. You know? And I said no. He asked what it would take and I said a ring, the piece of paper, the whole works. He laughed. But then he said, 'Why not?' I thought he meant it, but he had me sign papers, and after he was gone, I found out what I'd signed. We can stay here, I can drive the Buick, but nothing's mine, except the Datsun. His mother gets it all the day I leave." Tiredly, she added, "I'll stay; it's a good home for Nathan, better than anything I could afford."

Constance wished Marla would sit at the table so she could sit across from her and study her face as she spoke. The profile told her nothing. Her sweater was a very fine cashmere and the earrings were dangling garnets. Not cheap, but not insurable jewelry, either. She didn't look destitute, Constance decided, and got no further than that with her examination.

"At first," Marla was saying in a low voice, "he thought I knew where the money was, where Pete had stashed it, and he thought he'd get me and the money sooner or later, but when he saw that I really didn't know, he began to change. He taught me how to drive and bought the little Datsun for me. He wanted to take a trip, a late honeymoon."

"Ah," Constance said thoughtfully. "So he didn't object when you continued to go visit Pete."

Marla gave her a sharp look. "He wanted me to go. He thought Pete would tell me someday."

"How did Pete take it when you got married?"

"Look, we thought he was going to be up there for twenty-five years. He knew I couldn't keep Nathan without help. He was all for it. 'Take him for all you can,' that's what he said."

"And you kept visiting him all these years," Constance said. "Why did you, Marla?"

She shrugged. "You think I haven't asked myself that more than once? Habit, maybe? The only guy I felt safe around, maybe? I met a girl who makes jewelry. She showed me some pieces she was taking to show her husband. He's in for life. Anyway, it was neat stuff, earrings, necklaces, things like that. She gave me these," she said, fingering an earring. "I told her she could sell jewelry like that and she said no way. She had three kids, a full-time job, and lived up by Saranac Lake. She never even saw New York City. So I bet her I could sell it. I took a few pieces down to SoHo and sold them, and she gave me twenty-five percent. It was like fate gave me a break. If I hadn't been going to see Pete, I never would have met her, and others like her. I'm a jewelry rep—can you believe it?"

Constance nodded, but before she spoke, Marla faced her and said angrily, "You want to know what a bind is? Let me tell you. It's when you have a sick kid and no money and have to get a job, but if you leave him to work, the state will take him away and put him in an institution so he'll get the kind of care he needs. That kind of care would kill him. That's a bind."

"The state pays for his medical care, doesn't it?" Constance said, not so much a question as a statement of fact.

"They have to. They did it to him; they take care of him. Someone like Roy an hour or two a day, and respite care. You know what respite care is? I get a day and a half off each week. At first, I wouldn't leave even that much. They were just looking for an excuse to take him away from me, claim I was neglecting him, something like that." Her cheeks flared as she spoke rapidly. "I fainted a couple of times and the doctor said it was stress, that I needed to get away now and then and that no one could hold it against me. It was my right. If I got sick, they'd take him in a hurry, and if I didn't have some time off, I'd get sick. Sheila showed up with her jewelry about then and I was in business. I take my respite days all at once, five, six days in a row, make my rounds, take the jewelry down to New York, and next month do it again. Nathan hates it, but I figure he can put up with someone like Roy for a few days if it means I get to keep him with me the rest of the time. And it does."

"That's a terrible burden to shoulder alone," Constance said. "Why didn't Pete tell you where the money was, help out that way?"

Marla went to the hallway and cocked her head, listening. No sound came from upstairs. "He knew they'd be watching for me to come up with money," she said scornfully. "That would really have been stupid." She stayed by the hall door now, still listening.

"I suppose so," Constance said. "It just seems so unfair. Did he think you'd get back together when he got out?"

"Yeah," Marla said after a moment. "He thought so, and I guess I did, too. He said he had a few things he had to take care of first, and we had to be cool, not lead anyone to the money, just wait for the right time and then take off for Spain. We talked like that, and it was like having a dream over and over. You know? You hate to wake up because it's such a good dream. I used to take Nathan's pictures to show him, and I told him how Nathan was getting along. Pete knew all about him. But when he walked in and took one look, he said we'd have to put him in a hospital or an institution. We had a fight. I kicked him out and he stayed out. I guess he got the money and went to Spain or somewhere like that."

Constance shook her head. "We think he's still hanging around. How did he get here from Attica? He got out on the tenth and came here on the twelfth. Where was he those two days?"

"He didn't say," Marla said coldly. "He called me from the bus station in Tuxedo Park, and as soon as Roy got here, I went over and picked him up. The next day when Roy got here, I took him back." She added bitterly, "He slept on the sofa that night."

She stepped into the hall to listen again, and this time when she came back, she checked the wall clock in the kitchen. "Look, why don't you and your husband just leave. I told you he came here and then he went away. That's all I know. I haven't seen him or heard from him, and I don't expect to. I've got to go up and see to Nathan and feed him some dinner. Just go away."

Almost as if on cue, Charlie entered the kitchen then. "Ready?" he asked Constance.

She nodded. "We'll come back tomorrow," she said to Marla. "Just a few more details we need to clear up. It shouldn't take long. Is this Roy's usual time? Between three and five?"

"Get out of here!" Marla cried. "Just get the hell out of here!" She hurried across the kitchen and punched in numbers on the microwave, turned it on.

Charlie took Constance by the arm and they walked through the house to the front door and left. Neither spoke until they got inside the car and were heading back out the narrow black road. Then Charlie asked, "What was that all about?"

"She's lying," Constance said. "I'm not sure yet how much,

or when she turned the lies on and turned them off. She alternated, I think. But she most certainly is lying."

"You sure?"

"Yes indeed. She claims to be living in poverty and yet she's wearing a five-hundred-dollar sweater and earrings that cost about that much. And she called you my husband, but no one mentioned anything like that to her at any time. Did we?"

He squeezed her thigh lightly.

"Okay," he said when they were in their motel room. "Change of game plan. We can't see Marla until after three, and there's no need to ask too many questions around these parts, so let's breeze over to Middletown in the morning and come back here in the afternoon."

She eyed him narrowly. "You turned on Roy's talk switch?"

"Sure did, but you first. Give. Or do you want something to drink first?"

The motel room was a minisuite, a king-size bed on one side and a little sitting room on the other, with a sofa, two chairs, and a low table, where Charlie's feet now rested.

"Drink," she said, getting up to cross the room to their suitcase and a shopping bag. She took a bottle of wine from the bag and held it up for him to see. "No expense account, no room service. Right? I came prepared."

Then, as they sipped wine from water glasses, she told him in detail what Marla had said. "My problem," she said when she finished, "is that I know she was lying, but not about what or when. For instance, I think she noticed that I had appraised her earrings, and she came up with a story that sounded plausible at the moment but really isn't. A woman scraping by with three kids doesn't give away jewelry that would bring in hundreds of dollars. And that sweater, not what you wear in the kitchen pureeing food. Splatters . . ." There were other things not quite right, she was certain, but she needed time to sort them out. "Your turn."

"Roy lives on the road between Cedar Falls and Tuxedo Park," Charlie said. "He knows everyone in the county. He thinks she's a saint and she's blind to the truth about the boy. She gives him parties, puts up a Christmas tree, the whole thing. He has the brain waves of a vegetable, according to Roy, who is a hospital orderly, by the way. Up until two years ago, they didn't have the ramp, and she carried him downstairs to take him outside, gave him his baths, and had in a handler when she had to go out, and for the five or six days she takes off. That's what he says he is—a handler; the kid's past therapy. A couple of years ago, the boy began to grow, until she couldn't lift him. Roy stops in there every morning, gets the boy out of bed and into the wheelchair, and goes back later to give him a bath and get him back in bed." He poured himself more wine and stood at the table, swirling it in his glass. "It's been hell for her," he said quietly. "She's done it all alone."

Constance knew he was remembering the day of the wreck, when the infant Nathan had been thrown out of the car. She made a motion as if to reach for him, but, oblivious, he returned to his chair.

"So," he said, "Roy was there the day Pete arrived. She went out and brought Pete back. The next day, while he was giving the boy his bath, she said she had to go out again, that Pete was leaving. They were fighting, he said, yelling at each other. Everyone in Cedar Falls probably saw her drive by with Pete; they all knew the ex-con was there, and they were afraid he might stay. They saw her drive back without him. Roy says if she sneezed, the whole town held its breath for fear they'd catch whatever she had. She scandalized them the first time she showed up at the supermarket with food stamps. She was a loner from day one and is still a loner. Roy thinks she has a boyfriend out there on the road, hopes she does. He said she comes home with presents now and then, but she doesn't confide in him, hardly even talks to him except about Nathan. She's real close with money, does things herself or lets them go for the most part, and she nurses the cars along. He says she takes the gangster car, Boseman's Buick—they call him Grossman around these parts—out on the highway to keep it running well, because that's her emergency car for when Nathan has to go to the hospital for a checkup or something. He's had about a dozen operations over the years, and he has seizures. Other times, she drives a little red Datsun that's twelve years old, Boseman's wedding present. Everyone in Cedar Falls hates that Datsun. They don't think a person like her should be allowed to live in a big, expensive house and let it go to ruin, and drive a heap like that around to shame them all."

His voice had gone very flat. "So there it is. Pete came and Pete went away. I think we're back to where we started from, honey."

They were both silent then until Constance asked, "How much does this room cost?"

"Ninety per. It's off-season. Why?"

"I don't know. It's just that if she's so broke, how can she afford to stay in motels every month, eat meals out for five or six days? How much money could she be making with that jewelry? It seems she must be spending it all just to survive on the road."

"If it's her therapy, maybe she figures it's worthwhile even if she loses money," he commented.

She felt a twinge of annoyance with him. Someone had paid for that ramp, she thought, and the expensive wheelchair with a motor. The state didn't provide that kind of chair. And the pricey sweater and earrings . . . and insurance for two cars, utilities for a house that size . . . Even as she thought this, she felt disgust for herself rising. So what if Marla had a rich friend? Or what if she was into something illegal herself? Her devotion to her son was real; her care in preparing his food, her steadfast refusal to surrender him to anyone, to risk losing him, that made up for a lot. She had no doubt that Nathan would have died long ago without her constant attention.

A few minutes later when Charlie said maybe they should think about food pretty soon, she agreed readily. No more brooding about Marla and Pete, she told herself. Think food thoughts, she added, remembering the Victorian house they had seen. Not being on an expense account did not mean they had to eat at McDonald's, she also told herself, and she suggested aloud that they should call Chelsey House for a reservation.

The restaurant was as good as they had expected; Constance had sweetbreads. Charlie said he wished she wouldn't do that and she said at least she never made the dish at home, and he said she should wait until he was out of the country to eat it at all.

It was close to nine-thirty when they left Chelsey House.

Charlie drove to the supermarket, stopped, and gazed around Cedar Falls. There was a dim light in the market, another, dimmer light in the grocery store across the street from it, and a light at the service station. The antique store was dark. No one was in sight.

"What I'm thinking," he said, starting to drive again, not toward Tuxedo Park, but back up the road toward Marla's house, "is that it was too public, the way she got rid of Pete. A fight for Roy to hear, driving through town, where everyone would be watching, dumping him and coming back, knowing she'd be watched all the way. She could have stopped, let him get out and hop in the backseat, scrunch down out of sight."

"Where are you going?"

"Just looking. This sure is a dark road, isn't it?"

Dark, narrow, with occasional lights showing from houses that were not visible, the road wound uphill more steeply all the time. He slowed down and grunted in satisfaction. "I thought so," he murmured, and made a turn to the right onto another narrow black road. After winding about for a bit, this road led downhill. A few miles later, there was a well-lighted intersection at State Highway 17. The information sign said that I-84 was four miles to the left, Tuxedo Park three miles to the right. Charlie turned right, and within minutes they were back at their motel in Tuxedo Park.

"Escape hatch," he said. "Thought there might be one. So our boy Pete could have gotten in that big black Buick and been gone without anyone ever suspecting he'd been around."

There had been nothing in Marla's house to indicate that he had ever been there, but Pete was smart—he would have erased his tracks thoroughly. Charlie thought of upper New York State, Pennsylvania, New Jersey, Vermont, Massachusetts, Connecticut. . . . He could be anywhere out there, secure, waiting to make his next move. Marla would be in touch with him, he felt certain. She would tell him they were sniffing around; they had done exactly what he had wanted them to do. Pete was toying with them, and there wasn't a thing he could do about it, except follow where the trail led, knowing that Pete had planned it this way, that the trail might be mined, booby-trapped a dozen different ways that no one could anticipate and avoid. Time was on Pete's side and he had enough money to carry out whatever plans he had made during his thirteen years in hell.

The drive to Middletown the next morning was quick and easy. The sun came out and all traces of winter were gone; that was deceptive at this time of year, Charlie had learned, but for now, today, the early spring made him cheerful. He found the strip mall without any trouble, and they drove behind it to look, as they had done with all the other buildings. This strip had a dozen shops—shoe store, florist, Chinese restaurant. . . . Charlie's good humor faded as he studied the rear of the long, narrow structure: cement-block construction, metal window frames, barred windows. There were a few pallets leaning against the wall, two Dumpsters, a few stacks of cardboard boxes strapped together . . . and nothing that would burn more than ten minutes. Yet a shop had been destroyed, the owner killed. Mervin's Novelties, he remembered, and made a sharp turn at the end of the alley to drive by the front of the mall. No Mervin's Novelties. That business had not rebuilt. Although the mall was open for business, there were few cars, few pedestrians. He pulled into a parking space and studied the layout of the strip mall.

"I see how the fire got inside," Constance said, reading the report about this fire. "The back window to Mervin's shop was open; gasoline was sprayed in. He was in the rear section of the store."

Charlie nodded, unhappy with it. You can't burn down a cement-block building, he thought grumpily. You don't leave a window open at three in the morning, even if it is barred. You don't sleep through alarms and get burned up when the outside door is a few steps away.

"Let's buy a flower and ask a question or two," he said, nodding toward the florist shop. "For Auntie Geraldine." The shop was in the space where he had expected to see Mervin's Novelties.

"Hi," Charlie said to the woman in the florist shop. She was quite round, with iron gray hair and a pleasant smile. "Maybe we can find something in here, honey," he said to Constance, and then turned to the woman. "We're on our way to Monticello, her aunt's birthday, and thought we should pick up

something, since we left her present on our kitchen table. I left
it there," he said woefully. "Guy I know said there's a novelty
shop around here somewhere, but we can't find it."

"I'll just look around," Constance said, peering at a birthday
card. She replaced it and picked up another one.

"Well, people always like flowers," the woman said. "A nice
arrangement? Or a garden bouquet?"

"I don't know," Charlie said. "Is there another mall like this
down the road? Maybe the shop's in a different one."

"You said a novelty shop. Like trick lapel buttons that squirt
you? Whoopee cushions? For her *aunt?*"

"Is that what he meant?" Charlie said, aghast. He took a step
backward.

"Well, if it is, the shop's gone. Used to be that space where
your wife is looking for a card. I expanded when Mervin got
burned out last year."

"Gone," Charlie echoed. "Burned out?" He looked around.
"You, too?"

"No, hardly any damage in here, but his shop was destroyed.
He died in the fire, poor man."

"Gee," Charlie said, and leaned in closer again. "Really? Right
there?"

She nodded, then said in a low voice, "He must have been
dead drunk. They say he opened his back window and fell
asleep on the floor, never woke up. He was a lech," she added,
and pursed her lips. "Some of the stuff he had, well, porno-
graphic comes to mind, but maybe others didn't see it that way.
Well, I'm not saying he's paid for his sins—that's not up to me
to judge—but he's gone, and that's for sure."

"I can't imagine what my good buddy was thinking of, telling
me to go to a place like that with my wife! Junk like that! What
kind of stuff did he handle?"

"Oh, inflatable animals, lions, even a dinosaur, inflatable
beds, anything you could blow up, he had. Dolls. Dolls with
. . . you know, parts? Real junk. He had an inflated woman in
his window for about a year, looked like a maid, you know, the
high heels, little tiny skirt and apron, cap, everything. People
would stop and pretty soon they'd be laughing, but some of
his stuff wasn't funny, I don't think. I told him all that gas was
dangerous, but he wouldn't listen to anyone, not him. You

know gas explodes and spreads the fire something awful when it gets too hot."

"Gas," Charlie repeated. "He kept gas in there?"

"You know, for blowing up the balloons, the animals and people, all that. Real dangerous to keep gas around."

"It's surprising that he could manage a business, what with chasing and boozing. . . ."

"Oh, he chased, all right, but he wasn't a real drinker. That's why it was surprising that time. But why else would he have stayed after the fire started? Unless he was out cold," she said triumphantly. "Never went home that night. Got himself a bottle and started in and didn't quit until he passed out. Just that one time, and that one time's the one time the place catches on fire. Makes you think, doesn't it?"

"What do you mean he never went home? You mean he slept in his shop?"

"Just that one time . . ." she started again, and again made his head spin.

He tsk-tsked. "Makes you think," he said. "Sure does." He looked at the rear of the shop, where Constance was reading another card. "Honey, just pick one, will you? Auntie Geraldine can't see it, anyway."

"It has to be right," Constance said primly; she replaced the card and picked up another one.

"We all think he had a girl in there. He had these books and magazines he kept locked up, and sometimes he'd pull his shade down and put the 'Closed' sign up, and we knew he was in there with someone, probably showing her dirty pictures or something. He closed early that night, but he didn't leave."

Charlie stared at her in disbelief. "That one time . . ." he said. She nodded vigorously. "What did the police say about *that?*" he asked in a hushed tone.

Now she drew back and looked at Constance. "I don't guess anyone mentioned it. You know, his wife, Shirley, I mean, what was the point in hurting *her?* She had enough to put up with when he was living and chasing, no cause to bring her more grief." She was watching Constance.

"Honey," Charlie called sternly, "if you're not through in two seconds, I'm leaving without you."

Constance marched to the counter and put down a very large

card with a red velvet rose. "And that box of chocolates," she said, pointing.

"That's fifteen dollars!" Charlie exclaimed.

"If you hadn't left the birdcage on the table, we wouldn't have had to stop to buy anything. Pay the lady."

A block away from the shop, she opened the box of candy and handed him a piece, took one for herself. They began to laugh.

"Birdcage!" he said.

"This is the one time that . . . I can't do it." She laughed harder.

"That one time was the one time that . . ." He sputtered to a stop and ate the chocolate.

After a moment, he said, "I think it's a break. Someone might have seen something that night."

Traffic was not bad, but still he had to pay attention. It was Sunday, and drivers who had not touched a wheel all week were out flexing muscles that were stiff and uncooperative. A Dodge passed him doing eighty and then slowed to fifty a car length ahead of him. Two other cars were dawdling in the passing lane. A U-Haul passed them on the right. Telephone, Charlie was thinking. He needed help. He spotted a gas station and diner and left the highway.

At a pay phone outside the diner, he dialed Brian Posner's number in Manhattan. A machine answered, as he had known it would, and he said, "Meiklejohn. I'll call back at one. Answer the damn phone then." It was ten minutes before twelve, giving him plenty of time to decide exactly what to tell Brian.

His smile was beatific when he turned then to Constance. "Know what occurred to me out there on the dieway?" He took her arm and steered her toward the restaurant. "Ten percent of roughly six million smackeroos. Reward money for recovering the loot from that job Pete pulled thirteen years ago. You want a Danish with coffee? Let's live it up, kiddo."

In a booth, sipping coffee that was very bad and nibbling on a Danish that was good, he made notes for Brian. "Keep her in sight," he muttered. "From three until five every day, get any phone number she might call. . . ."

"And through the night," Constance said. "She could leave any night in the Buick. Who would know? Nathan won't tell."

"You think she'd leave him alone like that?"

"She does what she has to do for the greater good," Constance said.

He made another note. This would get spendy, he knew, but eventually Marla would lead them to Pete. He wrote again in his own peculiar shorthand: "Find out who was in the novelty shop with Mervin, when she left, what shape he was in, when he opened the window, or if she did." No doubt she was afraid of publicity, afraid to come out with it, but she could be found, questioned. Not by him. He was determined not to give Pulaski a clue about where he was heading with this. His guys would be all over the place showing Charlie's pictures, describing his car; they'd know he was snooping around, too. He might have gone too far already with the woman in the florist shop, but that was done; he doubted that she suspected she had been questioned. But he couldn't go back. Ten percent of 6 million, he thought. Worth the risk of keeping the ATF in the dark.

"I don't guess we could get a list of all the artists she deals with, the shops where she sells the jewelry," Constance said thoughtfully. "She mentioned one woman, Sheila, who gave her the idea, and who has a man in Attica for life. What if Pete is staying with someone like her, upstate somewhere?"

Charlie shook his head. They couldn't even throw such a wide net, much less follow through—contact all her clients, investigate them all. There were federal and state agencies who could, but he wasn't part of them. Marla had to lead them to Pete. And she would, he added. She would. It was nearly one. He left Constance to go make his phone call. As he walked, it occurred to him that if he had an hour alone in Marla's house, and if she kept records, addresses, he would find them. He tried to dismiss the idea and dialed Brian's number.

When Charlie pulled up to Marla's front door, Roy's station wagon was already there, still ticking as the motor cooled. They had watched it drive by from a driveway down the road, had waited two minutes, and followed. Marla opened the door almost instantly. She was wearing a heavy sweatshirt, and she stepped out onto the front stoop, pulled the door closed after her.

"You can't come in," she said. She sounded hoarse and

looked as if she had not slept. "You got Nathan too upset yesterday. We were up all night. You can't come in and do it again." She drew in a quick breath. "I called a friend this morning, and he said to tell you about him, about us. I don't have Pete here, and I don't know where he is. He won't come back. I told him I have a friend and he won't come back! I see someone every month. Up by Lake Champlain. He has a cabin up there where we stay." She was hugging her arms about herself as if she was freezing.

"His name, Marla," Charlie said.

"Scott Breckinridge. He teaches at Bennington and he has an art gallery. People come there to bring jewelry for me to take to New York, and then we go to his cabin. I go out to meet with other people during the day, and back there at night."

"Where's the cabin? When did this start?"

"Benson's Landing, in Vermont. I met him years ago. You think that's so awful, that I have a man, a boyfriend?" She flushed angrily. "Well, that's how it is. Now just go away and leave me alone!"

"I think it's perfectly normal," Constance said. "The only strange thing is why you don't get together on a more permanent basis. A few days a month isn't much."

"I can't!" Marla cried. "I can't take Nathan out of the state! You think Vermont would pay for his operations? For a therapist for him? Hah! And Scott can't just leave his job. He has tenure! He can't just walk away from it."

"Does Breckinridge use the cabin when you're not there?" Charlie asked.

She shook her head. "Maybe in the summer."

"Did you tell Pete about him?"

She shrugged and muttered, "Yeah. I knew he'd understand how it's been with me, and he did. He said I needed a little attention, a little fun, but then he blew, after he got out."

She opened the door behind her and tilted her head, listening. "Look, I told you all I'm going to say. Now leave me alone. I won't talk to you anymore. If you come back, I'll call the police or something." She laughed bitterly. "That's a joke, isn't it? Me call the police on you!" She opened the door farther and stepped inside, closed it softly behind her.

Back at the car, Constance asked if he wanted her to drive

and he said yes. Marla was hoarse because she had been up all night reading to the boy, he was thinking. Roy had said she did that, read to him for hours at a time when she claimed he was upset. Roy said there was no way to tell if he was upset or not, or even if he could hear what she was reading, but she thought it helped him through bad times. He said each meal took two hours, and she chattered away all the time she was spooning baby food into his mouth and wiping off most of it when it dribbled down his chin. She chattered, he had said, even while she was changing his diapers.

Charlie slumped in his seat and gazed ahead and saw nothing of the scenery they passed, nothing of the traffic that Constance navigated through. They didn't talk now. She always knew when not to talk.

At home, they ignored the cats and listened to the answering machine messages; Charlie instantly forgot what the messages were. If any had been important, he would have noticed, he thought, and sat down to call Breckinridge. When he hung up, he said, "Tomorrow. He'll meet us at the cabin at three. He gave me directions." He looked at her. "I feel prickly."

"Me, too." It had been too easy, she thought then. Why had Marla told them anything? She could have slammed the door.

"She got orders from Pete," Charlie said softly.

"We turn left at the sign for Benson's Landing," he said the next afternoon, watching for the sign. He suddenly thought of the distances out west, drive two days and not leave Texas, ten hours to get across Oregon, a lifetime to travel from Southern to Northern California. All the distances in the Northeast were child's play comparatively. The drive from home up here to Benson's Landing had been only two and a half hours. He saw the sign, two miles to Benson's Landing, turned left, and checked the odometer. One mile and turn left again, then watch for Breckinridge's sign.

There was more snow up here than they had seen all day, and now they could see the lake, with pale patches of ice against dark water. His next turn was onto a gravel driveway that wound through pine trees to a gray cabin. The lake was a short walk through the woods. The air smelled good.

"We're so early," Constance said. It was two-thirty.

"I figured he'd probably get here before three," Charlie said. "Give us time to look things over before he shows up."

They had both worn boots, not knowing what to expect in this area, but the drive was clear of snow, as was a walkway bordered with pale, round rocks that led to the cabin door. The structure was of unpainted cedar that had weathered to a nice silver gray. Patches of thick pine-needle carpeting showed through the snow, melting its way to the light. Constance went to a window and peered in; the shade was drawn halfway down. Kitchen, with a gas stove, scant cabinets . . . She wrinkled her nose. And a dead mouse. Two dead mice. She drew back just as Charlie yanked her arm, jerked her away from the house and into the snow, where she staggered to get her balance. He kept his hand tightly on her arm and pulled her farther away.

At that moment, another car crunched on the gravel drive, and they turned, to see a Land Rover come to a stop and a short heavyset man get out.

"Breckinridge," he said. "You're early." He was carrying keys and walked quickly toward the house.

"Don't go near it!" Charlie called. "Stay back."

"What?" Breckinridge paused. "What's that?"

"Gas," Charlie said. "Stay back." He stopped and picked up a large rock and heaved it at a window. Almost instantly, the smell of gas was in the air. "Where's the main?" he demanded.

Breckinridge looked stunned. "You broke the window!"

"Where's the goddamn gas main?"

He pointed to the side of the cabin and Charlie strode off in that direction. Constance and Breckinridge followed. "I need a wrench," Charlie snapped.

Constance ran back to their car and opened the trunk. There were always some tools there. She found a wrench and hurried back with it. Charlie turned off the gas. He glanced around the back of the cabin, but the snow was too deep for any rocks to show. Silently, he went back to the front and lifted another rock.

"For God's sake, you don't have to do that," Breckinridge cried. "Just open the door." He started to go to the cabin door and Charlie caught his arm.

"Don't even think of touching that door," he said darkly, and pointed. A narrow strip of metal was visible at the bottom of the door. Breckinridge backed away; he looked confused.

Charlie broke another window, took a rock around back, and broke a window there. The smell of gas was sickening all around the cabin. They went to stand by the cars.

"What are we going to do?" Breckinridge asked helplessly.

"Wait a while and then open the back door. Is there a key for it?" He took the key from Breckinridge's fingers.

"*He* did this! My God, he tried to kill me!"

Charlie grunted, thinking of the unbroken snow at the back of the house, some of it drifted up over the doorsill. If that door had been opened, booby-trapped, the snow would have been disturbed, he decided, and went around to unlock the door. First he examined the frame, the single step, the door itself, and finally he inserted the key and turned it. A light wind was blowing, would be blowing through the house, he knew, and a lot of gas had already been released, replaced with fresh air. Enough ventilation? He decided it was, and he pushed the door open and quickly stepped back as a cloud of poisonous air rushed out.

He waited ten minutes before he entered the cabin through the back door. It stank of gas, and would for quite some time, but it was no longer a primed bomb. He stopped to examine the front door: solid wood, like the back door, with weather stripping, a good tight threshold, and a narrow strip of metal nailed to the door on the inside, bent to fit under it. Inside the door, a metal plate was like a deadly welcome mat. It would have done nicely, he decided, and opened the door carefully, using a handkerchief, watching for a spark. If one came, he missed it, but he felt certain that it had sparked, and if the door had opened an hour ago, the house would have gone up in a gas explosion.

Constance had followed him in through the back door and now took his hand without a word. Breckinridge approached cautiously. He was pasty-faced.

"Keep your hands in your pockets," Charlie told him. He squeezed Constance's hand and released it. "You'll have to go to the nearest phone, in Benson's Landing, I guess, and call Bruce Wymouth over in Albany. I don't know anyone in the FBI in Vermont. Tell him what we found here, why we came—checking out a tip that Pete might have holed up in the cabin—and tell him that we haven't called in the locals yet."

After she left, Charlie pushed open the doors to the bathroom and bedroom, both empty. Bedding was in a jumble on the bed; Breckinridge looked away in embarrassment. "Let's go sit in your car and wait," Charlie said. "Smell's giving me a headache."

Breckinridge led the way, his head bowed, hands deep in his pockets. At the car, he said, "I won't say anything until the FBI gets here."

Charlie shrugged. "Suit yourself." They got in the Land Rover, where Charlie slumped down in the passenger seat and gazed at the cabin broodingly.

After a short silence, Breckinridge said, "She's so pretty." Charlie made a noise, and Breckinridge went on. "She's only thirty. All the trouble she's had and only thirty now. I'm forty-two," he added. "She's the first girlfriend I ever had . . . real girlfriend." Then, haltingly, fragmenting it, jumping around in time, he told it all.

She had been coming to Bennington for a couple of years before he met her. One of his students had made a necklace and earrings and wanted to put a price tag of a thousand dollars on the set; Marla had said six hundred, and they came to his gallery for an opinion. He did appraisals, he said. He had said two hundred. Two months later, Marla had dropped in to tell him she had gotten six hundred, and they had gone out for coffee. He mentioned the cabin a month or so later, and they had met here, and she had stayed all night. . . . He trailed off.

She hung around his gallery for a few hours and the artists brought their pieces to her, he said a few seconds later. He always came out first, fixed things up, bought wine, things for dinner, made a fire, then she came. He was sure no one suspected that he was letting her use the cabin, that he met her there.

"She's so paranoid," he said unhappily. "She's afraid someone will accuse her of being an improper mother or something and take Nathan away from her. I tried to talk her out of the notion, but that's what she believes. So I had her for a few evenings a month, and those were the happiest times of my life."

"You've broken up?" Charlie asked when the silence continued this time.

He nodded. "Not altogether, but . . . I asked her to marry me. I told her I'd pay for a hospital, that she didn't have to worry about that. I said she could move up here, we'd get a house. . . . She walked out and I didn't see her for three months. Then I went down there, to her place. She was furious that I showed up, but she let me in, and I saw Nathan. She didn't have a minute for me all afternoon, through the night, and the next morning she made me leave. She read to him nearly all night," he mumbled. "All night. I could hear her voice outside his door. I begged her to start coming back the way she used to, and finally she said she'd spend a night in the cabin, and that's what it's been like for a year now. But I'd be happy to have her one night a year, if that's all I can have."

Charlie probed a little, and Breckinridge obliged with answers. Then Charlie asked, "What did she say when she called this time?"

"I knew about Pete," he said. "She said you thought she knew where he was, that you were making Nathan miserable, making her miserable, and she had to tell you about us, make you believe her. I told her to tell you." For a moment he looked defiant. "I don't care who knows. I never tried to keep it a secret. I would have danced in the streets if she had let me talk about it. I want to marry her," he said miserably. "I haven't seen her since January! We had that blizzard in February; she couldn't get here. I call and leave messages; she doesn't even have time to talk to me."

They both turned to look when a car pulled into the driveway. Constance was back. She got out of the Volvo, carrying a cardboard tray with three Styrofoam containers.

"Coffee," she said. "We may have a little wait."

She sat in the backseat and they drank the coffee. In twenty minutes, a car pulled in, then a second one. They went out to meet the feds.

Six men emerged from the two cars; five of them were nameless, and they went straight to the cabin and entered, carrying little satchels, cases of various sorts. They looked like a flock of doctors making a house call on a head of state. The sixth man introduced himself. "Robert Chelsky," he said. He looked as if he belonged out on a whaler, as if he had spent most of his years at sea, where the salt spray and wind had chiseled his face down to the bare essentials and colored him red. He took their statements, made notes, and then snapped his notebook shut.

"We'll know more what to ask after we've gone over the cabin," he said with a heavy New England accent. He studied Charlie. "Eisenbeis has been out for over a year. Took you a while to get interested in tracking him down."

"I've been out of touch," Charlie said. "Just found out recently."

"Um. All right. Mr. Breckinridge, I reckon you'll want to stay and cover up those windows. Maybe we can turn on some heat in the cabin and talk a little. Mr., Mrs. Meiklejohn, if you want to leave, there's no reason not to. Long drive back down to your place. Appreciate it if you keep this quiet for now."

"Trust me; we will keep it very quiet," Charlie said gravely. He shook Breckinridge's hand, pitying the wretched man even more than he had before. He suspected that Chelsky would find out when he lost his first baby tooth before this night was over.

In the car, Constance asked, "Do you think he knows about the ATF investigation?"

"Probably not."

"Will the FBI tell Pulaski about this?"

He laughed. "Does the dog tell the cat?" He patted her leg. "Want to make a note of some dates before I forget them?" They both knew he would forget nothing of what Breckinridge had said, but she got out her notebook and he filled her in.

She studied the dates thoughtfully. "He proposed in September of 1991. December twelfth, Pete showed up at her house. On December twentieth, Breckinridge showed up. She agreed to resume their relationship on her terms and has had access to his cabin ever since. You don't think Pete's been there all that time, do you? With Breckinridge there one night a month, too?"

"Maybe he hid under the bed," Charlie said. Now, he thought, the big guns would go after Marla's contacts, her clients; there would be a list. He began to ponder the problem of how he could get his hands on it.

"I bet he hasn't been there at all," Constance said after a long pause. "Until last night, anyway. It's too far from Marla's place, and there's no telephone in the cabin. He certainly wouldn't have gone into town to use a phone, too public."

And they are in touch, Charlie finished silently for her. He said, "You know, it really doesn't take both of us. We could take turns staying home, tending the fire." This time, she patted his leg.

That night, holding a book that she was not reading, Constance worried. Had the trap at the cabin been step three? First the threatening note, then the tip to the ATF, next an explosion and fire, possibly another death. If Breckinridge had gotten there first, he would have been killed; Charlie would have been found on the scene of another fire with another body. Step three? But there had been no guarantee that Breckinridge would open that door. It might have been her, or Charlie, who . . . She shivered. "It hadn't mattered," she said under her breath. "He didn't care who got killed."

Charlie put down a magazine he had not been reading and said, "Listen."

She didn't hear anything.

"Wind," he said in disgust, and stood up.

Now she heard it. It was March, and a certain amount of wind could be expected, she thought but did not say. He hated high winds; he got twitchy. The cats hated the wind and they got twitchy. So now for a day or two, they would all twitch at her, she thought in resignation.

"What are we going to do next?" she asked.

"Not a damned thing we can do but wait," he said, still listening to the rising wind. "Wait for Brian to check in, or for Pulaski to show up with a warrant, or for Chelsky to come around and ask polite questions for twelve hours, or for Pete to make his next move."

Twitchy, she thought. Waiting was going to be very hard.

All day Tuesday, he stayed busy doing something or other to the car in the garage; she didn't ask what. And she stayed busy doing something with apples in the kitchen; he didn't ask what. Late in the afternoon, he sniffed at the woodstove, where she was stirring a very large pot of something. "Umm," he said, and put his arms around her, nibbled at her neck. She turned and nibbled at his earlobe. The first time she had done that, thirty years earlier, he had growled, "What the hell are you doing?" and she had said, "Stimulating an erogenous zone." A second later, he had said, "I'll be damned!"

Now, thirty years later, he was still surprised. She pushed the kettle to the back of the stove, closed a damper most of the way, and arm in arm they wandered upstairs. Outside, the wind shrieked and the rain pelted down.

Wednesday, the cats were all snapping at one another. When Candy came in drenched, he reached for her, a humanitarian gesture—he just wanted to dry her off; she snarled and hissed. Brutus watched him through evil, slitted yellow eyes. Ashcan slinked around, hiding behind a chair, behind the couch, underfoot, whimpering. Constance snapped that the apple butter was tasteless, and she fussed around adding spices; he had to take the spark plugs out and put them back in before the car would start. The gutter had filled up with spruce needles that had blown like snow, and he had to get the ladder out and clear the channel; he came in as wet as a human could get without having being dumped in the ocean.

"That doesn't happen if you live in a decent apartment building," he said coldly, removing layers of wet clothes.

"You're dripping on the floor," she said, just as coldly.

They both stopped when the telephone rang and Brian's voice came on. Charlie raced to pick up the phone. Constance finished making the coffee she had started and got out the bottle of Irish.

They sat at the kitchen table when he hung up. He sipped his coffee, raised his eyebrows, saluted her with the cup, then drank again. "Ah," he said. "Okay, first Marla," he said then. "Chelsky and company paid a call yesterday. Stayed two hours. As soon as they left and Roy showed up, she got in the Buick and went tearing out to the interstate, down the highway to an exit with a gas station and phone, ran to the phone, then turned and got back in the car and raced home. No call. She hasn't shown her nose since." He took another drink of the Irish coffee, savoring it. "The real scoop is on Sal Mervin," he said then. "The guy with the novelty shop." She nodded. "They found an empty bottle, scotch, and the story is that he drank until he passed out; then he got up to open a window later and passed out again. Trouble is, his widow says he couldn't drink more than one mixed drink or maybe two during a whole evening or he fell asleep and was out for twelve hours at least. He was on allergy medication, and that along with alcohol put him out fast. Anyway, a passing cruiser checked the mall at midnight and the window was closed, lights out."

She said doubtfully, "He could have come awake enough to open a window? But what was the woman doing all that time in a dark shop? Sleeping?"

He gave her a look. "Come on. Try this. For some reason, Pete had to get rid of him. He goes to the shop, gives him a couple of drinks—" He ignored her skeptical look. "Anyway, Mervin passes out and Pete unlocks the back window so he can open it from outside later, and he leaves."

"Every time you said 'Pete,' you could have said any other name that occurred to you," she pointed out. "What you mean was, someone did this, someone did that."

He scowled, but she was right—it was too iffy. No stranger could have counted on Mervin staying asleep with only a drink or two in him. Would Mervin have been chummy enough with an ex-con to tell him he couldn't drink? He stood up and took his cup to refill, just coffee this time. Why hadn't Pete just hit him in the head and been done with it? It wouldn't have tied in with the serial fires, he told himself. The arson murder was meant to be laid at Charlie's door along with the others. If the trap had been sprung at Breckinridge's cabin, that would be on his head, too.

Thursday was not quite so twitchy; the wind had died down again. The cats all went outside and spent most of the day in the sun; Charlie fooled with his fly rod in the basement, and Constance pretended to answer mail, pay a few bills, but she accomplished little. The thought nagged at her: They were missing something. In the basement, Charlie thought in annoyance that there was something right over there, just out of sight; if he could turn his head fast enough, he would have it.

Chelsky called and then dropped by on Friday morning. "Just need to fill in a few details," he said, shrugging out of a heavy plaid jacket. He had taken off his boots and left them outside the front door, he pulled on felt slippers. "March," he said, "hard month. Too hot, too cold, blizzards, wind. You sure can't count on anything in March."

Without comment, Charlie led him to the living room, where Chelsky took a chair close to the fire. "Nice," he said. "Smells good in here. Apples, cinnamon, cloves. Like the apple butter we make back home."

"Would you like some coffee?" Constance asked. "It won't take a minute." Charlie gave her a look. She was falling for the nice "just home folk" line. Chelsky said coffee would hit the spot.

"What can I do for you?" Charlie asked brusquely.

"Reckon you could do a lot, but what you'll do is pretty much what you've already decided on." Candy appeared and sniffed his feet, then jumped onto his lap. He stroked her. "Way I see it," he said, gazing at the comfortable fire hissing in the fireplace, "you either started a lot of fires and you're aiming to pin them on Pete Eisenbeis or else he started them and is doing a pretty good job pinning them on you." He glanced at Charlie; his eyes were a sparkly blue. "Mrs. Boseman says you're crazy," he added.

"You get around," Charlie commented.

"Yep." He gave it two syllables. "Why don't you just fill me in on Pete, Mrs. Boseman, all of it, from day one."

Charlie shrugged and told most of the story.

Then Chelsky started asking questions. Constance brought coffee and he added sugar and cream to his and went on asking questions. Why Eisenbeis, not one of the other cons who got out about the same time? How long did the drive to the cabin take? Had he known Boseman? How long had they been at the cabin before Breckinridge arrived? Had anyone touched anything inside the cabin? He was thorough.

In the middle of a question, which already had been asked and answered, Charlie held up his hand. "You didn't find Pete's prints, did you?"

"Nope. Not a one." He started to say something else, but Charlie shook his head, thinking.

"How tight is that cabin?" he asked after a moment.

"Good and tight. Cold up there, windy. It's tight."

Charlie visualized it: solid doors, all that weather stripping, storm windows, bedroom and bathroom doors closed. Now he remembered the gas stove with one burner on less than a quarter turn.

"The fireplace damper was shut down, I suppose," he murmured.

Chelsky nodded and remained silent.

"It could have been set up anytime—a week ago, a month ago, anytime since the end of January," Charlie said at last. "Not aimed at me, but at Breckinridge."

"Looks like it," Chelsky agreed. "Would have passed as an accident more than likely. It would have burned to the ground, isolated like that, old wood." His eyes were twinkling again as he asked, "Haven't been chasing around Vermont the past six weeks, have you?"

"Nope." But Charlie was thinking. There was something, something elusive that he should have noticed.

Abruptly, Constance stood up. "If you don't need me any longer, I should put on some dinner." She hardly waited for the agent's polite response as she hurried to the kitchen, where she stood rubbing her arms, chilled through. Step three was yet to be taken. The cabin wasn't it; that was simply opportunistic, unplanned as far as Charlie was concerned; he just happened to be on the spot. Step three had him at the center.

Chelsky stayed another half hour. As soon as he left, Charlie came to the kitchen muttering, "No one, absolutely no one believes Pete's anywhere in the state, maybe not even in the country."

"Charlie," Constance said from across the kitchen. Her voice was low and charged, intense. "There has to be one more fire, doesn't there?"

He stopped near the table. "Go on."

"Breckinridge would have opened that door whether you turned up or not."

He nodded.

"He was meant to die. But his death wouldn't have had anything to do with the serial fires. It was separate." Step three was in the wings, she thought, planned, ready. She said, "It has to be something bigger, something so incriminating, you won't be able to get out of it. They'll arrest you. You can't prove a negative, that you didn't set the fires, and there's no one else, not really."

She was thinking out loud, Charlie knew. Softly he said, "And then what?"

"Remember the note: 'You will feel my pain.' Prison won't be enough. I'll be killed, or disabled." Suddenly, she went white. "Jessica!" she whispered.

"Just sit still," Charlie said. He had taken Constance to the living room and stirred up the fire, added a log. He felt as clammy as she did.

"She's coming home next month," Constance said in a strained voice. "And he's so patient." She started to get up. "We have to call her, tell her not to come."

"We'll call her, but not at midnight, their time. What I'm going to do is make us an Irish coffee; later I'll do one of my famous omelettes." When he started for the kitchen, she got up to follow him; she stood within reach as he brewed coffee and then rooted around in the cabinet for the Irish. "You want whipped cream?" he asked. His voice had returned to normal; until that moment, he hadn't realized how forced it had been minutes ago. She shook her head.

He stopped fiddling with the Irish and cups and took her into his arms. "Ah, honey," he whispered.

"That's the worst thing, isn't it?" she whispered back. "Having your child threatened."

He nodded and then kissed her neck and returned to the coffee. "Let's sit down and talk it through," he said. "We're missing something. It's nagged at me for days."

That wasn't right, she wanted to say; they never talked it through until they had more to go on. First he had to think and think, and then they talked. She bit her lip, and they went to the living room with their Irish coffee.

"Let's start with Pete," he said after a moment. "He's up for thirteen years, plenty of time to plan anything. Maybe she took him clippings, anything she came across concerning us." He was thinking of the article that had appeared about Jessica when she was selected as a Rhodes Scholar. She was in Oxford, due home in April. The article had spelled it out. He shook himself. "So he gets out and two days later he turns up at Marla's house."

"Why two days? Why not go there directly?"

"He had to collect the money and stuff."

She shook her head. "Marla had the money. I told you. She must have been careful about how and when she spent any, but she had to have it. The television alone cost over a thousand dollars, and the custom bed, the wheelchair. . . . Did you look at it? It's custom-made. It will make a bed; that's why she could have Nathan in it from morning until evening. And that sweater."

"Breckinridge? He has money."

"Some of that stuff predates him. Just think of her other expenses, insurance for two cars, utilities. Heating that house must run over two hundred a month. She had to have the money, Charlie. She only works four or five days a month, remember? Then one day in New York. She simply isn't handling the kind of jewelry that would bring in that much money with so little effort."

She had told him, and he had dismissed it, he realized. He had seen the disarray, the dirt, the lack of yard care, no help with housework, no help with Nathan except what the state provided. . . . So, he thought soberly, Pete lost his girlfriend, his son, and the money.

Constance started to say something, then stopped, seeing the look on his face. She sipped her Irish coffee. He had forgotten his, on the table by the side of his chair.

"She observed all the holidays for Nathan," he said finally. "Put up a Christmas tree in his room, decorated for Halloween, gave him a birthday party every year. Complete with balloons. Roy said they floated around his room for days, until she got tired of them and took them out."

Constance gazed at him. Balloons, she repeated to herself. Helium balloons? If they floated . . . "Oh," she said then. "Mervin's shop. He kept tanks of gas for balloons."

"Maybe," he said slowly. "Maybe." The nagging feeling of having overlooked something was gone, he realized suddenly. "I wonder if Mervin had a butler to go with the maid he kept in his window," he said softly.

"Charlie," she said with a touch of exasperation, "where is this going? What are you getting at?"

Gazing at the fire, speaking in a low voice, he said, "Pete called and she made him wait until Roy was there. People got a good look at him; they knew who he was. Roy got a good look at him. What if Pete stayed alive just long enough for her to tape a real fight, and that's what Roy heard the next day? Suppose she had the inflatable butler all ready for the next act, Pete's jacket on it, a cap, and away she went, past the gawkers in Cedar Falls, up the road, nearly to Tuxedo Park, to make the time right, and then she stabbed Jeeves and deflated him and drove back alone. But Mervin knew what she had bought."

"If she was a regular customer, she probably rented helium tanks now and then, left a deposit, gave her name and address," Constance said after a moment. "He probably talked to her a lot. She could have known about his allergy medicine."

They were both silent for a time, considering. "Poor Pete," Constance said then. "She punished him every time she went to Attica, didn't she? Pictures of Nathan, stories about him, her marriage to Boseman, her car . . ."

The real bind, Charlie thought then, was sitting on a quarter million dollars and spending it a nickel at a time because otherwise they might haul her in for questioning, put Nathan in a hospital or a home of some kind.

"She's obsessive about Nathan," Constance said in a low voice. "She'll do whatever she has to to keep him with her, and punish those who hurt him."

"Crazy," Charlie said under his breath. He got up to make an omelette, thinking that they had not even a shred of evidence. Chelsky had not taken seriously his suspicion that Pete was carrying out a vendetta. How much less likely was it that he would believe the saintly Marla could entertain evil thoughts?

What if he, Charlie, had become obsessive? he thought suddenly, and stopped grating cheese. What if the arsonist was someone else, someone not connected to Pete and Marla? A nut out there with a real or imagined injury, getting revenge. Slowly, he returned to the job of making dinner, more shaken than he would have admitted. He had nothing but a gut feeling about Marla and Pete, he admitted to himself; she could be exactly what she appeared to be—a devoted mother nursing a hopeless invalid child.

They ate the omelette, delicious as it was, without comment. Constance pushed her plate back fractionally, got up for coffee, and then said, "What do you suppose she talks to him about for hours and hours every day?" When Charlie looked blank, she said, "You told me Roy said she talks to him all the time, while she's feeding him, giving him a drink, cleaning him up, and each meal takes about two hours. Up to eight hours a day, more? What can she find to talk about?"

Charlie thought about the things *they* talked about, trivialities for the most part: spruce needles in the gutter, emerging crocuses, what the cats had been up to, neighbors, their daughter and her future plans. . . . Trivial, but necessary. The real punishment of solitary confinement was having no one to talk to. People needed to talk.

"Let's think about this," he said.

She brought coffee for both of them; they pushed their plates aside and thought about it.

The next afternoon at five-thirty, Charlie made the turn onto Marla's driveway and slowed to a stop long enough for Constance to get out and vanish into the shrubs. He continued to the house. "If it doesn't work," he had said, "I'll leave and accidentally tap on the horn, and you hightail it back to the road. In any event, in exactly ten minutes, you be back there. Right?"

She had nodded. And now she was out of sight. He parked and went to lean on the doorbell. Constance ran lightly to the rear of the property, zigzagging in the overgrown brush. There was a board fence separating the front and backyard. She didn't even try to find a gate, test for a lock, but simply pulled herself up and over the fence, then trotted to the first door in the rear. Locked. The next door was locked, and the kitchen door. Without hesitating, she ran to the end of the balcony outside Nathan's room and jumped up a few inches so that her fingers caught the edge, and again she pulled herself up and over the rail and crouched down.

"Look," Charlie was saying to Marla at the front door, "I know you sent lover boy to booby-trap the cabin. Okay? I mean, that's a given. Let's get on to something else."

"I told you to get out or I'll scream for the cops."

"Scream, doll. Scream. But first think about ten percent of six million dollars. Want a calculator?"

Constance felt too exposed on the balcony, even though she was keeping low, hiding behind the rail as much as possible. Too open. If anyone happened to glance this way . . . The sliding door had a drape closed over it, but light came through; she would be silhouetted. She covered the last few feet and stood against the house at the side of the window. The screen door slid without a sound when she nudged it. The glass door was locked. Charlie had said there was a security bar, but probably it wouldn't be in place this early; if it was, he had said she should leave. They would find another way. She pulled a strip of metal from her pocket and worked it into the tight space between the door and facing. She had practiced at home. Charlie had shown her exactly how to do it. . . . She had to start over when the metal strip jammed. This time, she felt the lock click, and she let her breath out.

"Marla, stop playing dumb," Charlie was saying harshly. "We're talking big time here. I want a piece of it, and I intend to get it. I'll split with you. I'm generous. But first we agree that Pete's just a little detail that we can dispense with. Right?"

"You're crazy! I told them you're crazy. I don't know what you're talking about!"

The glass door moved; the bar was not down yet. With the door open an inch, Constance stood there listening. Roy's voice sounded very distant; there was the sound of rushing water. Swiftly, she opened the door and slipped inside, hesitated only a moment behind the drape, and then darted across the room to the table where Marla sometimes worked jigsaw puzzles or sat and read. She knew exactly where everything was; Charlie had made her a map. She had the backing off the tiny listening device before she reached the table. She pushed the device into place at the top of a leg, where it joined the tabletop. Roy's voice sounded louder.

"Okay, buckaroo, that's it."

She ran back to the sliding door and out just as he entered the room, carrying Nathan. Very gently, she pulled the door closed, then the screen door, and in a crouch she retraced her steps across the balcony to the edge. There was the ramp; Charlie had said maybe she should use it, but they had known it would be too exposed; she ignored it again. She swung her legs over the edge of the balcony and dropped to the ground.

"Honey, we do it my way or I'll send you up exactly like I sent Pete up. The kid will be a number in a hospital. I want Pete, doll, and I want him bad. You know where he is. We deal. Sooner or later, we deal. I'll be in touch."

"I'm calling the FBI. I'll tell them you threatened me, threatened to burn down the house if I don't give you the money. We'll see who goes up." She slammed the door.

When Charlie stopped at the end of the drive and Constance opened the passenger door and slid inside, he was breathing harder than she was. He put his arm around her and drew her to him for a moment. "Okay?"

"Fine. Done." She pulled back and stripped off rubber gloves. Her hands were hot. "You know, Charlie, if you would work out with me a couple of times a week, you'd be in much better shape."

He wanted to slug her as much as he wanted to kiss her. He shifted gears and started the drive home. Done, he thought. The tape recorder and receiver were in a waterproof box in a shallow depression at the edge of the driveway, hidden by a log. Every day, Brian would retrieve the tape and put in a new one. Brian didn't want to know more than that; Charlie didn't plan to tell him more. Illegal as hell, he knew, and done.

On Sunday, Brian's colleague delivered the first tape, made on Saturday. After twenty minutes of listening to it in Charlie's office, Constance left the room, looking stricken. Charlie listened for another twenty minutes before he had to turn it off. Prattle of the sort a loving mother mouthed to a two-year-old. "What a good boy you are. . . . One more bite. . . . It's chicken breast, your favorite. . . . Oh, the sun was so good for you today! You're getting a suntan. . . . Just a sip, that's right. Strawberry milk shake, isn't it yummy? . . ." Her voice was low and musical, lilting. There was not a trace of impatience in it.

He joined Constance in the living room. "It's going to be tough. She's telling him what they'll do next week, next month."

"We don't have to listen together," Constance said. "We can

take turns, half an hour at a time, something like that." She stood up. "I'll go."

Charlie went out to make himself a drink.

"We'll put in a new flower bed," Marla's voice was saying happily when Constance turned the tape player on again. "Remember all those catalogs we got last winter? We'll use them and pick the prettiest flowers we can find. One more bite now, a little one. That's good. . . . I'll tell Roy to take you out every day if the weather's good. He'll do that, and you won't even miss me. . . . I think there's just a little more of the milk shake, hardly even a mouthful. . . . You have such an appetite! . . ." Constance closed her eyes; she felt stiff and rigid as the voice went on and on, rising and falling. Then it was Charlie's turn, and she went to the kitchen, where she found a martini waiting for her. She drank it gratefully. She should start some dinner, but she did not move.

"Honey, come here," Charlie said from the doorway a few minutes later.

She followed him to the office. He had turned off the tape player and now turned it back on. Marla's sweet voice filled the room.

"I'll just cut off those roses right at the ground and that's where we'll plant our seeds. The roses will go in the trash. No funeral for flowers, you just haul them away if they die. You remember what a funeral is, don't you? That's for people, not plants. Oh, look, no more chicken! . . ." Charlie turned it off again.

"Nathan knows what a funeral is," he said. He sounded remote.

"She could have buried a bird, or a cat or something," Constance said faintly.

Charlie looked at his watch. "Let's go buy another tape recorder. I want to tape segments like that so we won't have to listen to the whole thing ever again." He took the tape from the player and put it in a wall safe. "Let's eat while we're out. I sure as hell don't want to cook."

"Neither do I," she said.

At dinner, she said, "It's like free association, what she says. One thing reminds her of another and off she goes. Eventually, if she keeps on, she'll tell everything, but we'll never be able to use any of it for any purpose."

For their purposes, it would do just fine, he thought, but she was right. Legally, it was useless. He said, "I think I goaded her enough yesterday to make her change her timetable. She'll want me off her back sooner rather than later."

That night, listening, he knew he was right.

"I know you hate it when I have to leave," Marla said. "And my regular days are coming up next week, but I'm afraid I'll just have to. It won't be for long, I promise, and not tonight. Tonight let's watch *Beauty and the Beast*. I think that must be my very most favorite movie." The tape went dead momentarily.

It was voice-activated but did not record electronic sounds, Charlie's supplier had told him. "How does it know?" he had asked, and the man had said mysteriously, "Magic."

He listened to Marla giving Nathan a drink of water. It took fifteen minutes and she prattled, then finally said good night. She would be in later to see if he wanted anything.

The tape went through the morning and into the afternoon, when Brian had lifted it and replaced it with a new one. It took Marla an hour and a half to feed Nathan breakfast and she said nothing worth retaping; then Nathan took a nap, and when she was back, she told him they would go out to the balcony. Charlie cursed when her voice faded out.

Later, feeding Nathan lunch, she said, "You have to eat a little more if you want to grow big and strong like your father. He was over six feet tall, and you're going to be that tall. I can tell."

Brian brought the new tape the next day and Constance called Charlie to listen to a segment she had retaped. "Time to go to work," Marla said, laughing. "What do you think? Six hundred? I think I got six hundred for that one. Isn't it ugly? So six hundred. And four hundred for the pin. When that FBI guy asks my clients what kind of business I do, won't they give him an earful! I'm the world's greatest saleswoman! See this? It's tigereye. Isn't that a nice name for a stone? You can see the light in it, just like an eye. I think eight hundred, don't you? . . . Maybe that's too much. That would be three thousand eighty dollars. My cut . . . seven hundred seventy . . . I guess that's okay."

"She began talking about buying him a cowboy hat then," Constance said. "What in the world was she doing?"

They listened to it again. "I think she's settling for twenty-five cents on the dollar," Charlie said finally. "She sells something for a hundred, says she got five hundred, and pockets twenty-five percent of that. No questions asked about her income; she has records, and happy artist clients, and probably fake receipts for shop owners in New York. My God, she could go through the whole schmear that way." He glowered at the tape.

"The FBI will interview her contacts and they'll all come on like boosters," he said aggrievedly. Then he said, "But that means she has the money within reach, in the house!"

"The figures she was using don't add up," Constance pointed out. Then she said, "Oh, it doesn't really matter when or even if she sells anything, does it? Not if she's making up prices, paying off her clients with stolen money, collecting commissions on sales she might or might not make."

"Twenty-five cents on the dollar," Charlie growled. "God, she is crazy!"

And very smart, Constance added silently.

Marla talked about her mother, on the streets of New York, she said, just where she belonged. She talked about her father, whom she had never seen, about Breckinridge, a fat little toad. She talked about the weather, about Nathan's hair coming back in so thick, just like his father's used to be. Drivel, Charlie thought in disgust, listening to her read the descriptions of flowers from a catalog. Throughout the day, he had retaped no more than a few minutes and had listened to hours of drivel. Constance took his place and he left to do something about dinner; it was his day to cook.

It was six o'clock Monday evening, and they were listening to the tape that had been made of Marla starting Sunday at three through Monday afternoon, when Brian had put in a new one. It made Charlie nervous to be a day behind all the time, hearing today what she had said the night before, no clue about what she was doing at the moment.

"Charlie!" Constance called. He hurried back to the office, where she was rewinding the second tape recorder. "She was reading from the catalog and he fell asleep, I guess. She just came back on." Constance pressed the play button.

Marla said gaily, "Oh, I thought you might be awake by now. I can't come too close. I stink like gas. I'll just take a shower and be right back."

There was a pause. Constance held up her hand. Then Marla was back. "Now I'm decent again. Did you have a good little nap? Roy will be here pretty soon and I'll make you turkey. And asparagus. You love asparagus! Tomorrow when I go out, I'll get some new library books, something we've never read . . . and groceries. We're almost out of ice cream. . . . And I have to put gas in the Buick, and check the oil and the tires. It would be terrible if I had road trouble, wouldn't it? There are car-jackers out there, just waiting for a woman to have trouble in the middle of the night. Did you know that? I wonder which would be worse, a carjacker or a cop. Anyway, it won't happen, because I'll have the Buick checked out. . . . I know what I want to read next. . . ."

Constance turned off the machine. "She talked about stories and then Roy came in. Charlie, she serviced the Buick today, and yesterday she smelled of gas."

He rewound the tape and played it again. Hours more on the tape, he thought then, and it was after six now. With few exceptions, they had to listen to it all in real time. They couldn't finish with this one before midnight. Too late? Right now she would be in with Nathan, feeding him, talking, talking. Call Chelsky, tell him everything? He shook his head. He didn't know where Chelsky was, how long it would take him to arrive, or if he could persuade him to come out now, tonight. And for what? He didn't even know if there was a reason to call for help. He went to the door. "I'll rustle us up a sandwich or something. You keep listening. Okay?"

She reached for the on switch. Roy was there; she fast-forwarded the machine until she caught Marla's voice again and listened until Charlie came to the door and motioned for her to turn it off.

"Anything?"

She shook her head.

"Come on out, take a break," he said. He waited and they went back to the kitchen. "What I'm going to do is go down there and grab the new tape the minute she turns off Nathan's light. Eight, eight-thirty, about then. I'll listen to it in the car. Be back around ten. And that's just about all we can do right now." When she started to object, he said, "And I want you to get on the pipe to Chelsky. Run him down if you can and tell him what we think is going on. If he doesn't call back in an hour, go after Bruce Wymouth up in Albany, and if he's not available, as a last resort try to get Pulaski." He put a sandwich in a plastic bag as he talked, and kept a second one on a paper plate. "You know the old saying, Eat and run. 'Fraid I'm going to run and eat. Made a couple for you, too." He glanced around as if checking whether he had forgotten anything, and then he said casually, "Of course, no one's going to believe you."

"Probably not," she said. "But someone might be curious enough to come around. Especially if they realize you're out somewhere."

"Especially," he agreed.

She gave him one of her looks that sometimes made him think he was as transparent as a crystal skull filled with spinning gears in rainbow colors.

"Charlie, when you don't show up again by eleven or twelve, do I tell Chelsky or whoever it is that you're keeping the vigil at Marla's house?"

He was pulling on a heavy jacket and stopped moving for just a moment, then grinned and said, "Honey, Brian has a cellular phone. If I decided to do anything like that, I'd call you. Honest." He was ready to leave. On the way out, he said, "Try not to give them the tapes if possible."

"Resist torture to what point?"

"It won't get too serious before I get back. You can hold out."

She walked to the garage with him, watched him back out and leave, and then locked the door and returned to the kitchen. It felt empty and cold. She called the numbers Chelsky had left with them and left a message on a machine with the first call, and left the same message with a man who wanted to know why she wanted Mr. Chelsky. Then she took a sandwich to the office and turned on the tape player again.

She couldn't eat and listen to Marla, she realized after only a minute or two. She put the sandwich down and listened to the sweet voice cajoling, laughing, lilting as Marla fed bite after bite to her son. Then Constance stiffened and turned on the other tape recorder.

"That toad called again. I don't know why he doesn't catch on. But he's dumb, even if he is a teacher. If he knew how much we hate hospitals, he'd never say that word again. I know what's good for you. Just look how you're growing. . . . Hospital! I know how much you hated it there, how mean they were to you. I won't see him ever again, I promise. I won't go near him again. . . . I put just a little cinnamon on it, exactly the way you like it. . . ." She began to talk about getting a motor home, a little one, and the vacations they would take.

At ten minutes before eight, Chelsky called. He asked for Charlie.

"He isn't here," Constance said. She drew in a deep breath and then said swiftly, "We have vital information you should have immediately. We think there will be another fire, probably tonight. We prefer to talk to you about it, but if you can't make it, then I'll call Bruce Wymouth in Albany."

He was skeptical and he kept asking where Charlie was, when he would return, where they thought a fire might happen. She cut in sharply. "Mr. Chelsky, those fires never started before three in the morning. There's time for someone to get over here and talk about this and maybe avert a disaster. If you can't or won't come, say so, and I'll call Bruce Wymouth."

"Now, Mrs. Meiklejohn, don't get in an uproar. I didn't say that, now did I? Happens I'm in Albany myself. I could take a run down that way. You expecting Mr. Meiklejohn back soon?"

"Around ten or eleven, or he'll call," she told him, and he said he'd be there at ten, or a little after.

She ate her sandwich; the bread had already gone too dry. Then she ate an apple and drank a cup of coffee and finally started to listen again. How could Marla keep it up? That pleasant, cheerful prattle, on and on and on. Laughing over nothing, pretending he understood, responded. Constance began to pace the office, and she thought suddenly that she simply couldn't stand this any longer. She clenched her fists and after a moment sat down again.

When she took a break later, she made a pot of strong coffee. This would be a long night, she thought despondently. She had copied only two sections of tape since Charlie left; both of them had to do with hospitals, how everyone wanted Nathan in a hospital, how much they hated them. Slowly, she returned to the office and rewound the machine a little and listened again.

". . . and there won't be any more talk about that. But they'll think of something different. They just don't give up, do they, honey?" Constance rewound it farther back. "I'll make them stop talking about putting you in a hospital. I'll wave my magic wand and there won't be any more talk about that. . . ."

Marla went on talking about magic, about fairies who lived under flowers. . . . That's what she would start checking out of the library, she went on very happily. Everyone loved fairy tales.

When Chelsky arrived at ten minutes past ten, three other men entered with him. He introduced them: Carl Pulaski, and his assistant, Larry Dell, and his own colleague Stan Lehman.

"Where's your husband?" Pulaski demanded before he had his coat off.

"I'm not sure," she said. She pointed toward the hall closet and let them hang their own coats.

"When did he leave?"

She ignored him and said to Chelsky, "I have to start at the beginning for this to make any sense."

He nodded, but Pulaski demanded harshly, "Mrs. Meiklejohn, I want some answers, and I want them now!"

"Seems she wants to talk to us, if you'll just let her," Chelsky said in a mild way.

She nodded. "I have a map on the kitchen table. It will be helpful."

Pulaski's face was a tight furious mask, but he followed when she led the way to the kitchen and he remained silent until she told them what she and Charlie had surmised about Marla. Then he snorted.

"She's been investigated more than once and there's nothing. Where's Meiklejohn? What's he up to now? I'm warning you, if there's a fire tonight and you don't cooperate, you'll be an accessory."

"He's watching Marla's house."

"Do you mind if we look around?" he said gratingly, and started for the back door.

"Do you have a search warrant?" she asked coldly.

"No. Not yet."

"Then you can't look around."

He reached for the wall phone, and she said, even more coldly, "And don't use the phone. Charlie will call any minute now."

He jerked his head at his assistant and they went out the front door. Constance watched them, and when she turned back to Chelsky, she caught a glint in his eye that looked suspiciously like a sparkle of silent laughter. He leaned over the map without comment.

The phone rang and she snatched it up. "Hi, honey," he said cheerfully. "You have company?"

"Mr. Chelsky is here, and Mr. Pulaski," she added when he reentered the kitchen.

"Everything under control?"

"So far."

"Okay, put on the speakerphone. Let's chat."

If she had had to reveal the tapes, she would have said so; they both understood that. When she turned on the speakerphone, his voice sounded as if he were in a deep mine. He told them he was at Marla's keeping watch and he suspected that she would venture out to set a fire that night.

"Could use some backup," he said blandly.

"You know we can't do that," Chelsky said. "Not with no more than we have."

"Come on in, Meiklejohn, and let's talk," Pulaski said harshly.

"I think he's getting a search warrant," Constance said then. Pulaski glared at her.

"Uh-huh. You got a bug in place yet, Pulaski?" He didn't wait for an answer. "I'd guess not yet. I'll call back in half an hour or so, give you time to put things in place. Talk to you later."

"Charlie! Wait a minute," Constance cried. "If she tries to leave, can't you block the driveway? If she has the gas—"

He chuckled. "Honey, I'm afraid Brer Pulaski might claim I was out salting the mine or something. And she'd claim she was out to get a breath of air. Hang in there, kiddo." He hung up.

Chelsky asked questions about Marla; she answered. They all drank coffee, and after a prolonged silence, Chelsky glanced at

Pulaski. "You boys have a car down anywhere near Tuxedo Park?" Pulaski shrugged. "Neither do we, I guess. Not familiar with your roads around here. How long you suppose it'd take to get a car or two in the area?"

Pulaski motioned for Chelsky to go to the living room with him. They left together and murmured inaudibly. When they came back, Chelsky said to Constance, "Problem is, if your husband's telling the truth, won't do much good to have an APB out on the Volvo, now will it? I mean, he wouldn't try to follow anyone in a white car like that. You happen to know what kind of car the other fellow's driving?"

She didn't know.

He motioned to his companion, Stan Lehman. "Why don't you bring in another phone in case we decide to make some inquiries?"

Lehman went out as silently as he had remained since arriving. He was a tall young man who never seemed to take his gaze off Chelsky. They went to the living room together and spoke in low voices when he returned.

Charlie called again at twenty minutes to twelve. "Speakerphone," he said. Constance felt a tremor pass over her at the sound of his voice. "Listen up, guys," Charlie said over the speakerphone, sounding as distant as the man in the moon. "Find out where the kid has hospital treatments, where she takes him for checkups. I think that might be the target." He hung up.

"Hospital!" Pulaski whispered. "My God, is he going to burn a hospital?"

Chelsky snapped at Lehman, "Find out."

"Not just checkups," Constance said then. "Where he had surgery within the past few months." She was shivering.

Chelsky eyed her narrowly and then nodded to Lehman. "Get on it."

"His hair is just now growing out again," Constance said. "He has seizures, and sometimes they operate to remove a blood clot or something."

They waited. In various combinations, the four men went to the living room and spoke in low voices, returned.

Finally, Charlie called again. "She's leaving," he said. "We're

keeping with her. Be back on as soon as she hits the interstate."
He disconnected.

"Mrs. Meiklejohn," Chelsky said, "if you can sort of point me
in the right direction, I could probably work your coffeemaker
just fine."

She stirred. But she had made a pot. . . . It was empty. She started a
fresh pot, grateful to Chelsky for giving her something to do.

Charlie slouched in his seat while Brian drove. He stayed far
enough behind the Buick not to alarm her, and now and then
he drove with his lights off. He was good. He stayed with her.
Charlie called home again. "Heading north on I-Eighty-seven,"
he said. Pulaski wanted to know what they were driving. He
hung up. But he was worried: It was early for her to be heading
out. How far did she intend to go? He kept his eyes on her
taillights. Somewhere with a hospital where Nathan had been
operated on. He kept hearing her soft, musical voice: "Such
beautiful hair, and they shaved it all off. My poor baby. But it's
coming in thicker than ever. Just like your father's. They won't
do that to you ever again. I promise you. After tonight, they'll
never hurt you again."

She held at seventy miles an hour. Traffic began to ebb and
flow, growing heavy at each entrance to the interstate, thinning
again. Suddenly, Charlie straightened and pressed the redial on
the phone. Brian said, "There she goes." She had turned onto
State 23.

Charlie reported in. "Anything about the hospital yet?" he
asked. Chelsky said there wasn't, and asked where he thought
she was going. "Don't know," he said. He gave them the number of the cellular phone and then said, "Constance, you okay?"

"Yes," she said in a low voice. "You?"

"Sure. Oh, oh. She's going to turn again, or pull over or
something. Hang on." She was signaling a turn, and now his
stomach began to hurt. "She's on State One forty-three," he said
in a flat voice.

He heard Constance make a soft noise. "Take it easy, honey,"
he said softly. "We'll know more when she gets to I-Eighty-eight.
You still have a lot of company?"

"All of them, four guys," she said, and she sounded perfectly
normal.

He grinned. "I'll be back in a couple of minutes," he said.

Marla was going to his house, taking the route he used, the quickest way from her place to his. He bit his lip. There was little traffic on 143; Brian had to keep farther back than he liked. Could use a little backup, guys, Charlie thought darkly. He called Constance again in a few minutes. They were about ten minutes from the interstate. Constance answered his first ring.

"Honey, if there are cars out front, maybe it would be a good idea to get them in the garage, or around back, out of sight."

"Thought of that," Chelsky said. "We're moving them now. We'll turn off lights, make it look like it usually does this time of night."

Marla turned left at I-88 and then made the next turn onto the county road that led to his house. Brian hung back as far as he dared; he was muttering under his breath, and driving without lights half the time. When they passed the house, it looked like a house should look at one-thirty in the morning: an outside light on the front stoop, a dim light from an upstairs window, empty driveway. Marla drove past slowly, then speeded up a little.

"Don't turn on anything yet," Charlie snapped into the phone a minute later. "She's turning around, making another pass."

Chelsky said very calmly then, "Meiklejohn, don't touch the brakes. If she's suspicious, the brake lights will give it away."

"We'll pick her up here," Pulaski said, "just as soon as she goes by." He and the two aides hurried to the garage.

This time, she slowed to a crawl as she drove by the house, then came to a full stop for a second at the boundary where a ditch separated the property from Hal Mitchum's.

Charlie was speaking into the phone throughout, worried. She had pulled too far away before they had been able to make a turn and resume the chase. Her lights were distant and fading fast. He saw a car pull out of his driveway and go after her, but he was cursing softly.

"See what she did out there," Chelsky said to Stan Lehman, who had come back in and now went scurrying out. He returned with a sprayer.

"It was in the ditch," he said.

Then Charlie was back on. "We lost her," he said in a harsh voice. "We're on this side of a train with Pulaski; she's on the other."

"Where?" Chelsky asked, looking again at the map on the table.

"About seven miles from the house, four miles from the interstate. Pulaski will head north with me; his guy will go south with Brian as soon as we hit the interstate again." He sounded very grim. "Pulaski's holding a gun on me," he added. There was a choking sound close by, and Charlie said, "Well, then take your damn hand out of your damn pocket."

"Easy, easy," Chelsky said. "We'll have people on the interstate as soon as possible."

Charlie hung up.

Chelsky was on the kitchen telephone, speaking in a low voice; Stan Lehman was on the cellular phone, arguing with someone. Constance sat at the table, feeling helpless. Lehman made some notes then and disconnected. "Got it," he said.

Over the past five years, Nathan had been treated in two hospitals in New York City and had had surgery in one in Albany last November.

"Let's go," Chelsky said, and they ran to the garage. Constance was at his elbow when he reached the car. He hesitated briefly, then yanked the back door open, and she got in. Lehman drove; Chelsky stayed on the phone.

In the other car, Pulaski listened to Chelsky and relayed the message to Charlie. "Children's Hospital, Albany. If this is a wild-goose chase, Meiklejohn, I'll have your ass."

"Just shut the fuck up. Address."

Pulaski told him and he snapped, "Get on the phone, someone to lead us in, tell us the best route to take."

Pulaski began speaking again.

Charlie watched taillights, drew close enough to see if it was a black Buick, passed whatever it was in front of them, and then did it again. Traffic was light, but as they got closer to Albany, it picked up. Pulaski made a choking sound again when Charlie swerved and passed a semi. "No sirens," Charlie snapped. "No fanfare, no fire trucks. Understand? She'll spook and take off for parts unknown to dump the gas. God only knows what she'll burn then."

"Right," Pulaski said, and repeated the message into the phone.

A few miles out of Albany, they picked up an escort—two unmarked dark cars, a Chevy and a Dodge, one to lead, the other to follow. Pulaski kept the phone line open now and the three cars left the interstate and headed for the hospital.

Two blocks from the hospital, the lead car turned down an alley, and the following car passed them and continued out of sight. "We stop here and you drive," Charlie said. "You're a doctor on a call. Park near an entrance, get out, and go into the hospital. I'll duck down out of sight in case she's already around watching the place." She was cautious, he thought, paying no attention to Pulaski's objections as he stopped at the curb. "Another doctor arriving for an emergency—she probably will accept that, but she knows me. Now."

They changed places and Pulaski drove into the parking lot near a side entrance where several other cars were parked. There was a Buick there, but it wasn't hers. Pulaski got out, stretched, and walked to the entrance, into the hospital.

The hospital was close to the street in the front; the ambulance entrance was on one side, well lighted. Here in the back, the parking lot was lighted with a few lamps, and had great shadowy areas, with cars scattered here and there, clumped near entrances, some all the way to the far edge near the sidewalk. The other side of the building was flush with the sidewalk. It would be back here, he thought grimly—if she came at all.

He had been too busy driving and searching for her to worry until now that they might be in the wrong place altogether. Maybe they had made a false assumption and she was heading for another warehouse, a school, the governor's mansion. He eased the car door open and slipped out, keeping low. She would drive by, make sure it was safe, maybe drive by more than once, and then . . . She wouldn't enter the lot, he thought; she would park out on the street, walk in, ready to run back to the car and take off as soon as she tossed a match.

How many agents were already there, in parked cars, in the

building, across the street? He couldn't see anyone, but he knew they were there. They'd better be there, he thought grimly. A car drove in; a man and woman got out and hurried inside the hospital. He heard another car leaving. A nurse came out, smoked a cigarette, and reentered. Another car pulled in, parked. No one emerged this time. He didn't move.

He eyed the building; what she'd do was park over on the street, walk around the block maybe, approach from this side, spray it and light it, and have only a dozen feet to the car to cover. They hadn't come down that side street; he didn't know if the Buick was there or not.

The building was old and shabby, brick and wood, lots of wood on windows and doors, and a lot of dead ivy clinging to the bricks. It would carry fire to the roof, he knew. A couple of wooden benches were near the entrance, no shrubbery, no place anyone could hide, just a walkway around the building, and the parking lot. His ears had become attuned to the night sounds now—traffic out front, an occasional car on the side street, a light wind rustling in the dead ivy. Then he heard a different sound, soft footsteps, and he carefully looked around the back of the car, into the parking lot. At first, he thought he was seeing a boy with a backpack, but it was Marla, dressed all in black—jacket, jeans, shoes, a black visor cap pulled low. She was walking openly through a drive lane, making no attempt to stay hidden behind cars, and she looked like a boy going to work late. Then figures appeared from parked cars, and others from the building, and he heard Chelsky's voice.

"Stop there, Mrs. Boseman."

She was holding the wand of a sprayer, Charlie realized; the backpack was a sprayer tank. Don't anyone shoot, he prayed. Marla hesitated, raised the wand, and then continued toward the building.

Charlie went cold all over when he heard Constance's voice. "Marla, you have to stop now. If you don't, someone will shoot, and you'll die. Who will care for Nathan if you die?"

Marla swung around, aiming the wand toward the car where Constance stood. Charlie began to move quietly then. Her back was to him.

"You!" she said in a low, harsh voice. "Now he'll know what it's like to see someone you love crippled, hurt."

"Marla, if you spray me, someone will shoot. The sprayer will explode if it gets hit. You'll die. No one will watch out for Nathan, see if he's making progress. Who else will even notice if he's getting better? They'll let you see him, visit with him, make sure he's getting things he needs."

Charlie was nearly close enough. Don't spray her, he prayed. Don't do it. Don't.

"Who else will read to him, Marla? Who will tell him about the flowers? No one else believes he can understand. They won't read to him, talk to him, but you will be able to. They'll let you see him."

"You're lying!"

"If you're dead, he'll die, Marla. You're keeping him alive. You know that."

Charlie knew others were moving, too, although he didn't take his gaze off Marla, off her hand holding the wand pointed at Constance. She had something clutched in her other hand.

"He'll miss you, wonder if you've forgotten him, if you're ever coming back. No one will even tell him that much, because they don't think he can understand. He'll suffer, Marla. He will."

Charlie jumped then. He threw one arm around her neck and grabbed her hand on the spray wand. As she tightened her finger on the trigger, he forced the wand down; gasoline sprayed on the pavement at their feet. She raised her other hand, and he swept it back in a brutal, swift motion. Something fell with a clatter. Abruptly, she relaxed; her whole body seemed to lose tone, and her hands hung limply at her sides.

"I have to go home now," she said. "He's waiting for me."

Charlie held her while someone came and removed the back-pack sprayer gingerly. She didn't resist then or when two agents took her by the arms and led her away. He took a step toward Constance, who was running to him. They held each other hard, not speaking.

Then Chelsky tapped Charlie on the arm and cleared his throat. "This yours?" he asked. He opened his hand to show them a disk, the size of a silver dollar. He opened it, a locket, with Constance's picture in one half and Jessica's in the other. They were both wearing *gis,* their martial-arts clothes. Marla must have been at one of their exhibitions, he thought with a chill. The last one had been over a year ago.

"It's what she dropped," Chelsky said when Charlie shook his head. "That probably would have done it, that and the sprayer at your place." He started to walk away, then said, "You folks go on home. You need a ride?"

Charlie shook his head. "Brian can take us."

"Someone has to go take care of Nathan," Constance said, facing Chelsky.

"We'll see to him. He'll have to be put in a hospital tomorrow."

When Constance turned back to Charlie and took his hand, he saw tears gleaming on her cheeks. Brian took them home and no one said a word all the way.

The next morning Charlie left Constance in bed and he and Brian drove down to Cedar Falls to collect the Volvo. He went on to Marla's house after Brian headed back to New York. He retrieved the tape recorder hidden by the driveway and parked behind several other cars; Chelsky met him at the door. It appeared that an army was going through everything inch by inch.

"They took the boy to Children's Hospital this morning," Chelsky said. "We found the money, certificates, checks, all that's left. And a map," he said heavily. "Every arson neatly circled. Few other things, but that's the big one."

Charlie shook his head. "I'd go dig up the roses out there," he said, motioning toward the back garden. That was the big one, he thought.

It was late afternoon before Charlie returned. Constance met him at the door, examined him closely, and said, "You look terrible."

"I have a right," he said. He told her about the money, then said, "Pete's body was under the rose bed, along with an inflatable butler. The kid's in the hospital."

They went to the kitchen, where he poured himself a shot of bourbon and drank it down. "About the money," he said then. "Had a talk with Chelsky. I think if we recover expenses, that'll be okay. Don't you?"

She nodded. "And the rest?"

"Oh, I don't know. Children's Hospital, something like that."
She kissed him.

He needed a nap, he said, and she said she would help him
take a nap, and they went upstairs, just to nap, they both understood, but it was nice to fall asleep holding her, being held
by her.

Two weeks later, Chelsky called and asked if it was okay to drop
in, since he was in the neighborhood. He took his boots off
outside the door and pulled on his felt slippers; then he settled
into a chair before the fire. "April showers," he said. "Not too
bad, though."

Constance brought in coffee.

"The boy had a seizure couple days ago," Chelsky said, gazing at the fire. "He didn't pull out of it this time. They couldn't
save him."

No one spoke for several moments. Finally, Constance asked,
"And Marla?"

"They told her last night. She hanged herself in her cell."

The silence stretched on and on. Chelsky stirred his coffee
and put the cup down again.

"You came all the way down from Vermont to tell us," Charlie said.

"I reckon," he said slowly. "It'll be on the news later on. Just
thought you should know first." He stood up and said more
briskly, "Guess I'll pass on the coffee. Things to do." They
walked to the door with him. "Sometimes it's hard," he said.
"Sometimes it surely is hard. You both take care now." He
shook hands with Charlie and then kissed Constance on the
cheek. "You take real good care now."

They went back to the living room. On the table by the cup
of untasted coffee was the little bug Constance had put on the
table in Nathan's room. Charlie picked it up and regarded it
and for a moment he heard that soft, sweet, musical voice.
From the look on Constance's face, he thought she was hearing
it, too. There was nothing they could say. *Sometimes it's hard*,
he thought, and she nodded.

Christi's Tears

1

April Fool's Day," Charlie said, ripping March from the kitchen calendar with some enthusiasm. Rain, snow, wind, summery days alternating with ice storms too fast to fathom—March was a good month to be done with. "April Fool's Day," he repeated with a grin. "Wonder why that seems so appropriate."

Constance made a snorting sound, a wordless comment he had no problem interpreting. For people who had been married as long as they had, words could be superfluous. He chuckled. On Thursday a priest he knew from the city had called to introduce someone else by phone. Someone Else had at first demanded, then pleaded for an immediate meeting in Manhattan. Saturday, Charlie had said, and at his home in upstate New York. That was the whole point in being retired; you did things your way or skipped them.

"All right," Someone Else had said. "That will give you time to check us out. I'll bring two others."

After hanging up, Charlie had gone straight to his computer and checked them out, and had returned bemused. John Webber, alias Someone Else, was a high muckety-muck in the Catholic Church, right hand of God maybe. Carlos Villanueve Ortiz was a high muckety-muck in the Mexican embassy. And Willy Bols was an ex-con. April Fool's Day.

When the group arrived at ten, a fourth person was present: a young woman on stilts was Charlie's first impression as he watched her approach from the driveway. But she simply had very high heels, very long legs, a very short skirt, and a lot of improbable red hair out every which way. Charlie could see a new Toyota parked behind a Continental in the driveway.

Bols was easy to pick out: slightly built, furtive, keeping his distance from the other two men. The Mexican was easy too: not very tall, almost rigidly erect, with a mass of black hair, nattily dressed in a gray three-piece suit, spit-polished shoes.

Typecasting, Charlie thought derisively. Webber, in a sports coat and slacks, could have been the corner grocer, a druggist, a high-school teacher. He was tall and wide, with wind-tossed blond hair a touch too long, which was interesting since no wind was evident. He had played center for Notre Dame.

Charlie went to the door to admit them. Constance followed to help with coats, and the introductions were made in the foyer. The woman was Noreen Raditch; she had a Brooklyn accent. Then, in the living room, Charlie watched them sort themselves out: Willy Bols and Noreen Raditch on the love seat, as close together as two people could get without surgery; Ortiz and Webber on opposite sides of the room, as far from each other as the room allowed. He took his morris chair, and Constance her usual wing chair, and he said, "So, tell me. What do you want?"

"We wish to engage you to pursue a matter of great delicacy."

Ortiz. Born and raised in the States, a Princeton education, he had not even a trace of accent.

"Your name was suggested; your reputation for discretion was looked into, and your past achievements . . ." Webber. Roughneck kid, rough Chicago neighborhood, the Church. His accent would never desert him.

"We need you to find something. . . ." Bols had not quite squeaked through high school. *Neeja, finsumpn.* . . . The Bronx all the way.

"Mr. Webber," Charlie said, "since you called, why don't you lay it out for me?" Webber was a priest who had advanced by way of the Office of Antiquities Acquisitions, but Charlie was damned if he'd say *Father* to a man ten years younger than he was.

"Yes," Webber said. "We should follow the original plan," he added, frowning at Ortiz.

"Your plan. Always your plan."

Charlie began to tap his fingers on the arm of his chair. "Mr. Webber, if you will," he said firmly.

"Our plan was to let Mr. Bols tell his story first, and then fill in our roles. It began with him."

Charlie turned his gaze to Willy Bols, who was looking more and more uncomfortable. Noreen's white-knuckled grip on his arm would leave bruises, he thought, waiting.

"Yeah," Bols said. "Yeah. See, I was working in the infirmary up at Attica, and there was this real old guy dying in there. One day he wanted me to look in a box for some pictures, and I found a Bible. And I says, Hey, Ed, you never told me you could read Spanish, and he says he can't. They sent it to him when his Pa died. He never even opened it, didn't even know it was a Spanish Bible. He was in for life," Willy added somberly. "Anyway, I'm looking for the pictures and moving stuff around, and this envelope falls out of the Bible, and I say, Hey, Ed, your Pa must have wrote you a letter, and you never even opened that neither. And he gets all excited. He's little, like a dried-up monkey, and he's crying and blubbering for me to read it to him. So I open the envelope and there's two letters, one of them in English and one in Spanish."

Willy shifted repeatedly on the love seat, his gaze darting about the room. He kept fingering the buttons on his shirt. "Okay, the letters. See, they were both old, real old, and they'd been through a lot. Most of the writing was gone, the papers stuck together like they'd got wet and sort of glued together when they dried again. It wasn't no letter from his Pa," he said. "It was real fancy, full of stuff like, Your holiness, blessed mother of God, stuff like that. And poor old Ed, he's crying, and he begins to talk about this thing that happened when he was a little kid. He forgot about it until I read him that letter, and he doesn't remember it too good, a little bit at a time, for the next couple of weeks."

The year was 1904. Abe Worsham had lost his wife and two children to a pestilence ravaging the South. He took Ed, his surviving son, and an old draft horse and cart and headed north to look for work. Somewhere along the way he was hired by a group that included two men in black dresses and three Indians with a lot more gear than they could carry. They loaded up stuff on his wagon and continued. One Indian died the first night, and they buried him. The other two were nearly dead, but they held on for another day, got too sick to move, then died. They buried them and most of the gear; now the priests were also ill and had to ride. The American priest died next, and there was only the Spanish-speaking priest left, a raving maniac. The American had written a letter and paid Abe to mail it for him in the first town they came to. Now the Spanish-speaking priest wrote another letter, added it to the first one, and sealed the envelope. When he died, Abe buried him, and he and his son went on their way. He never mailed the letters.

Willy had kept the Spanish letter, hoping to find someone he could trust to read it for him, but after Ed Worsham died finally, he forgot about it.

"So I get out back in 'ninety, and me and Noreen get together again, and that letter sits in my junk until two years ago when she finds it and gets all hot and bothered, thinking some woman's been writing to me and I never even mention it."

"What I thought was that it should be read," Noreen said bitingly.

"Yeah, right, and you blab it all over the place, and next thing I know these dudes are climbing my back," he said aggrievedly, motioning toward Ortiz and Webber.

"I asked a *priest* how to find out something about two other *priests,* for crying out loud! A priest! If you can't trust a priest, then who? And I asked a Spanish high-school teacher to read it for me. A teacher! I knew the dude from way back, and he goes straight to him!" She nodded toward Ortiz. "A spy, that's what he is, a spic spy!"

Ortiz and Webber both had followed Willy's narration with fierce concentration, as if they never had heard the story before, or as if they hoped he would add a new tidbit this time. Charlie let it go for the moment. "How did you both find your way to him?" he asked.

Ortiz spoke first. "She gave the letter to an acquaintance of mine, pure happenstance. The teacher knows I am interested in antiquities, and he sent me a copy, since the letter was obviously quite old," he said smoothly.

Charlie nodded and turned to Webber. "And the priest she talked to happened to be your acquaintance?"

"Not at all. But he searched a database for whatever information he could find concerning those two priests, and that alerted my office. Accordingly, I went to talk to him, and here we are."

Charlie nodded again. "It's an interesting little bit of Americana, but why are you here?"

Webber smiled slightly. "You know the parable about the blind men and the elephant? One thought it was a wall, one a rope, and so on. We're those blind men, and we've come to you because you're sighted. We each know things, but not enough, and obviously no one is willing to divulge everything to either of the others for fear that one will rush to the graves. I'm afraid Willy knows a great deal more than he has revealed, enough to send him off on his own private expedition to search. Fruitlessly, I might add. We've had many discussions, and finally hit upon the notion that an outsider, someone trustworthy and intelligent, with proper investigative training, might be able to configure the elephant for us."

"Knock off the bull about elephants!" Noreen cried. "Look, it's simple. Everybody tells you everything they know, like in private, and you figure out where the treasure's at. Okay?"

"But why me?" Charlie asked again, ignoring Noreen. "I never heard of any of you."

"We all submitted names, many names," Ortiz said with a little sigh. "On investigation, none of those suggested seemed appropriate. Then Willy mentioned your name. We investigated. No one has any objection to hiring you."

For several seconds Charlie had been aware that Constance had been trying to get his attention. When he glanced at her, she was watching Willy Bols intently. He didn't even sigh.

"Why are you so nervous, Mr. Bols?" Constance asked then. Charlie leaned back, waiting.

"Me? Well, hey, if they know everything in my head, they don't need me no more. Right?"

"Well, that seems cause enough," she said slowly. "Charlie, let's ask Mr. Bols to step into the other room for a moment." She stood up and started to walk from the living room.

Ortiz leaped to his feet; Charlie waved him down again. "You gentlemen can amuse each other." Willy Bols had drawn back into the love seat as far as he could; he looked miserable. "Well, come on," Charlie said.

Noreen and Willy exchanged glances, then she began to rise. "Me, too," she said. "Come on, Willy."

Charlie ushered them toward the den. At the door Constance mouthed to him: *Wired*.

In the den was the television, a red leather-covered couch, three comfortable chairs, an old banged-up desk where they kept household accounts, and bookshelves. Each window had potted plants on its sill, hanging from the ceiling nearby, or on the floor before it.

Charlie stood at the door and said to Willy, "Strip."

Willy and Noreen were in the center of the room. "What?" Willy cried. "What?"

"Strip, or beat it."

"They know," Noreen said nervously.

"Shut up!" Willy yanked off his sports coat and began to tear at the buttons on his shirt. No one spoke as he opened his shirt to expose a cassette recorder taped to his stomach. Gingerly he began to pull at the tape. With a scowl Noreen reached over and yanked it off. He moaned with his eyes closed.

Charlie took the cassette recorder and pulled the wire loose, then put the small gadget on the floor and stamped on it. He picked up the crushed pieces and handed them back to Willy. "The microphone?"

Without a word Willy ripped a button off his shirt and handed it to Charlie.

"Who put it there?" Charlie asked then.

Willy shook his head. "I can't tell you that," he whined. "He'd kill me."

Constance put her hand on Charlie's arm. "Are we going to take this on?"

"Nope. Out of our line."

She studied him intently for a moment, then shook her head. "We are. Let's go hear the rest of the story."

When they returned to the living room, Ortiz jumped to his feet; then, belatedly, Webber stood up. Constance motioned them down and Charlie said, "Just give it to me as straight as you can, guys. What's buried in that grave?"

"You need a little background—" Webber began.

Ortiz said quickly, "Many artifacts, many of them property of the Mexican government, the Mexican people."

"They are the property of the Roman Catholic Church," Webber said coldly. "Mr. Meiklejohn, please ask Carlos not to interrupt, so that we can discuss this matter in a civilized way."

"Robbers, scavengers, worshippers of death . . ." Ortiz muttered. "Let him talk, then I'll tell the true story."

"You first," Charlie said to Webber, his patience near the limit. "The short version."

"Around the turn of the century there was great turmoil in this hemisphere, as you know. Mexico was in revolution; there was the Spanish-American War—" He looked to the ceiling beseechingly when Charlie scowled at him. "All right, I have written material for you to read. In Mexico, the Church was increasingly nervous about the security of many precious items. Religious items. The decision was made at the highest levels that many of the items were to be packed up and shipped to Rome for safekeeping."

Ortiz made a deep, snarly sound. Webber continued without pause.

"Some items were shipped through the Gulf of Mexico to Cuba and on from there, but that became unfeasible, and this particular dispatch was shipped to New Orleans to be transferred to a steamboat that would take it up the Mississippi River to St. Louis, and from there by train, and so on. However, the material did not arrive at St. Louis, and now, after ninety years, we have a clue about what happened to it. Clearly, it belongs to the Church."

"Pah!" Ortiz exclaimed. "The items, many of them, are pre-Columbian, priceless art of the Aztecs, the Mayas. They were confiscated, stolen, spoils of conquest. My government demands that that which is ours be restored to our people; this is our culture, our heritage, not booty of war. To him, to his Church, they are merely trifles; to us they represent the soul of our people."

"Right," Charlie said. "Gotcha. Okay, you said you each know something the others don't know. What next? You tell us what those little extras are, and let us puzzle it out? Is that the plan?"

"Exactly," Webber said.

Ortiz nodded.

"But then what?" Constance asked. "What if we actually can puzzle it out? You draw swords and fight over who gets what? Pistols at dawn?"

In the silence that ensued, Willy Bols studied his shoes; Noreen worked on her cuticles. Webber frowned thoughtfully at the ceiling, and Ortiz leaned back with his eyes closed. Charlie winked at Constance, and neither of them made a sound.

At last Ortiz murmured, "We have made arrangements with Willy. He has been compensated for his cooperation, and is due a second payment when he confides in you. John and I have agreed to share the expenses of your investigation, and to pay you a reasonable finder's fee. As for the rest, we will make accommodations between ourselves." He did not open his eyes; he sounded almost dreamy.

"Not good enough," Charlie said. "We'll need to know what those accommodations are, know when to put on the bullet-proof vests, when to start ducking, all that kind of messy stuff."

"For now, let's just get at it," Webber said. "If it appears that you're actually on the track, then we'll huddle and come up with a workable plan. We decided fifty thousand would be a reasonable finder's fee, by the way."

Charlie shook his head. "Fifty now, another fifty if we find anything. All expenses paid weekly."

Ortiz sat up straight with his eyes open.

In a pained voice Webber said, "We'll have to talk this over."

"And this, too," Charlie said easily. "Since you both have de-voted flunkies and I don't, if I say I need this or that, you get it. No questions asked. If some of our expenses aren't ex-plained, no questions about that, either, since I don't tell any-one anything until we know exactly what you plan."

"No progress reports?" Webber demanded. "Come on, Mei-klejohn, you know better than that."

"No specific progress reports," Charlie said.

There was another silence, this time a very glum silence, un-til Webber said, "What else?"

"We'll want a contract, and the first payment; then we talk to you one at a time until we have all your little secrets. We'll go on from there."

After a moment Webber sighed. "We should break up this meeting at this point. Carlos, will you be my guest for lunch? We can talk, and return here at two. Is that agreeable?"

"My pleasure," Ortiz said. "We must discuss all this," he said almost apologetically to Charlie.

"Fine," Charlie said. "We'll be here."

As soon as they were all gone, he turned to Constance and laughed. "My God, we're going on a treasure hunt!"

2

Over lunch Constance asked, "You don't really believe we'll be able to find anything, do you?"

"Nope. That's why the fifty grand up front. We'll put in the time, do the work, and end up richer than we are now, with corpses, or what's left of them, undisturbed in their graves, and the priceless treasure still safe in the arms of Mother Earth. How about you?"

"Same," she said. "They've had the leads for two years. They must have tried everything—metal detectors, low-flying planes, infrared devices. . . . Willy thought he knew where to look. . . ."

"And Willy has an angel," Charlie added as she trailed off and finished her salad. "We go after him first. Okay?"

She nodded. Obviously Willy was first. Her eyes narrowed in thought as they both ate. Finally she said, "Charlie, after this is over, let's use some of the money for a cruise."

He groaned. He did not like big boats, speedboats, rowboats, any kind of boat. People were not supposed to go out on the ocean. If something went wrong, then what? You couldn't run away from it. He had seen the movies, the paintings, had read the stories. He knew about the *Titanic;* that's what came of going out on the ocean in a boat. Everyone knew steel did not float, at least not for very long. Just looking at a Turner seascape made him seasick.

"We'll talk about it later," Constance said, her voice low-key, easy, but with a look in her eyes that made him uncomfortable.

Later, after putting two checks in the wall safe along with a signed contract, Charlie and Constance left Webber and Ortiz in the living room glowering at each other and escorted Willy and Noreen back to the den.

"Okay," Charlie said when they were all seated. "You know

the rules. No stonewalling, no evasions, no beating around the bush. Who else did you tell your story to?"

Willy shifted uncomfortably. "This rich guy, DeWilde's his name. See, those two dudes come running around asking questions, and I seen this was big, then they go away and don't tell me nothing. I try calling and get the cold shoulder. Then I seen a story about this DeWilde guy, he paid a couple of million for some old picture, and I think maybe he'd be interested. But he wasn't," he added.

"Who else?"

Willy glanced at Noreen and then out the window. "That's it," he mumbled.

Charlie shook his head. "Forget the rules already? No lying, that's one. Who wired you?"

Willy began to crack his knuckles. "I can't tell you. I mean, it's my ass here. He'd have me put out like a candle. If that messes up the deal, that's the way it's gotta be."

"What we really want to know," Constance said easily, "is the rest of your story. I suppose your other friend doesn't know any more than you do, but does he know more than we do? Let's treat your sketch as an outline and start filling in details."

Willy nodded gratefully. Charlie leaned back in his chair and let her start digging.

What had first attracted Abe Worsham's attention was the sight of a large trunk floating down the river, sinking lower and lower until it was gone. He and the boy had set out on foot to see what was happening—if there was anything more than the trunk—and they spotted the priests and three Indians tying up a very big bundle, as big as a man. They had wrapped up whatever had been in the trunk and some of the empty crates that were strewn about. They dragged the big bundle and a couple of small boxes back a ways; then they made a fire with the empty crates just when it was getting dark.

The next day Abe watched again. They had dragged the stuff less than a quarter of a mile away from the river, and they were all exhausted. He approached them and was hired.

"It's like I said before after that," Willy said then. "They began dying. When they buried the two Indians, they dug one of the graves real deep, and they hauled the big bundle to it and buried it first, the Indian on top of it. He, Ed, was just a little kid, remember, and he was scared to death of those guys. Especially the priests. He said they put a curse on the grave so no one would bother it. He said they couldn't move the big bundle and they had to use the horse to drag it to the grave. He remembered that.

"When the first priest died, they buried a closed box and put him in on top of it," Willy continued. "The other priest was crying; that's what Ed remembered best. Then a day, two days, he didn't know when it was, the last one bit it, and Abe buried him alone. Him and Ed kept going. There was one last box of junk and they dumped it."

"Where were they heading?" Constance asked.

"Paducah," Willy said, after a brief pause. "Ed said him and his Pa sold the horse and wagon, got on a boat at Paducah, and went up the river."

Charlie's knowledge of the geography of that part of the country was too slight to register. Later, he decided, he would get out a map and have a look. For now, he was content to listen.

"What was in the letter you read to Ed Worsham?" Constance asked.

"Hey! That was ten, eleven years ago! I can't remember that stuff."

"Of course you can," she said reassuringly. "I'll help you." She smiled at him. "First, you make yourself as comfortable as you can; put your head back and close your eyes so that nothing in the room here will distract you. What you do is start at the beginning of the day you saw the letter. You woke up . . ."

This was going to take a while, Charlie knew. Willy was fidgety and suspicious, certain there was nothing to remember. On the other hand, Charlie had seen Constance at work; her patience was greater than Willy's resistance.

After a few minutes, Charlie stood up. "Doorbell," he said. "Carry on. I'll get it." Actually he was grateful for an excuse to leave. Constance had Willy at Ed's bedside now; he was still fighting her. Charlie left them.

In the living room Carlos Ortiz and John Webber were both at the front window, peering out. Ortiz was livid, Webber flushed and angry. Charlie walked past them to the foyer and the door.

"Mr. Meiklejohn? Montgomery DeWilde. How do you do."

"Come in, Mr. DeWilde. Join the party."

DeWilde was wearing comfortable-looking chinos, a windbreaker, and running shoes; he had parked a dazzling red MG in the driveway. He was a tall, slender man of fifty or so, with dark, wavy hair and dark blue eyes. He looked amused.

"A party," he murmured, entering the living room. "So it is. John, Carlos." He nodded to them.

Ortiz looked at Charlie and demanded, "Who told him?"

"Not me," Charlie said.

"It was Willy," Webber said in a choked-sounding voice. "That little bastard."

DeWilde said, "Now, John. Such language is not befitting a man of the cloth."

"What's your angle in this affair?" Charlie asked.

"I represent the United States government," DeWilde said.

"And I don't," Charlie said. "So what's your angle?"

"You see, Mr. Meiklejohn, the government has an interest in any treasure found within its boundaries—monetary, ethical, and moral interest. We can't let greedy treasure hunters benefit from simply stumbling across lost objects, sunken ships, what have you, now can we?"

"We know how he operates. First, he skims the cream," Ortiz said angrily. "Then they demand we pay for what is ours. Yours is a money-mad government, I'm afraid. John, we should talk. Is there a private place, Mr. Meiklejohn?"

"The patio. Not too cool, I don't think. This way, gentlemen." He took them to the patio and returned to study DeWilde, who was seated comfortably in Charlie's morris chair.

"You want a cut," Charlie said. "Is that it?"

"I am working for the government, exactly as I stated. I do now and again, you see."

"And you just happened to learn they all came out here," Charlie commented.

"Something like that," DeWilde said with a smile. "We expect you to cooperate with us, Mr. Meiklejohn. Neither of them is to remove what they find before it's been inspected and appraised."

"Funny thing," Charlie said, still standing. "I have the feeling I'm a private citizen, minding my own business, doing my job to the best of my ability, getting by. You having them all tailed around the clock?"

"If they make a move to recover anything, I'll know. Neither one of them has any legitimate claim to the stuff, you must understand. It belongs to humanity. Isn't that the phrase?"

The doorbell rang again and Charlie went to see who else wanted to party. He grinned when he saw who was standing there this time. "Well, well," he said. "Rob Rob! And Peaches. Come in, gentlemen. Come right in."

Rob Rob was Robert Roberts, and Peaches was his attorney, Oliver Pochoda. Rob Rob was getting on, Charlie thought; he must be over seventy, and he had given up the funny hairpiece he used to wear. When he took off his very nice fedora, his bald head gleamed like a wax apple. Pochoda was not much younger; his hair was white and thick. Rob Rob was too fat, but he always had been too fat, and Oliver Pochoda was too thin. They were both elegantly dressed in thousand-dollar suits, topcoats that looked like vicuña, and Rob Rob had on a chartreuse-and-blue necktie that made Charlie blink.

"You're looking good, Charlie," Rob Rob said. No one offered to shake hands.

"And you look like hell," Charlie said cheerfully. "This way. You want to take off your coats, or stand around menacingly with your hands in your pockets?"

"We'll keep them," Rob Rob said. "Getting cold already, that kind of day."

DeWilde stood up when they entered; he looked confused. Charlie introduced them briefly and said, "Excuse me, gentlemen. You can discuss the weather for a few minutes, I'm sure."

He ducked out to the patio, where Ortiz and Webber were talking heatedly in low voices. "I'm afraid Willy's been spilling the beans to quite a few people," Charlie said. "Two more just showed up. One's a big-time crook from New York City, and the other's his attorney." He spread his hands. "Not my doing, but there it is. It could be time to call off the treasure hunt. I'm afraid so many people out there with picks and shovels might do great damage to one another."

"No," Ortiz said. "You can still look into the matter, and report to us your findings. We will be responsible after that."

"Let's see what Rob Rob has on his mind," Charlie said. "You might decide to put this off for a hundred years or so."

When they returned to the living room, Charlie introduced everyone to everyone else. They all stood like wooden soldiers waiting for the bugle to sound, Charlie thought as he eased himself down into his morris chair.

"I want to talk to my client," Pochoda said.

"Your client? Who?"

"Mr. William Bols. I represent him in this affair, and I demand to see him immediately. If you don't produce him, I'll be forced—"

"Peaches, shut up," Charlie said. "That's a cute angle, Rob Rob."

"No angle, Charlie. Willy's a friend; I look out for friends. We figure a percentage, not a flat fee. Willy owes me; he collects, I collect, he pays Mr. Pochoda, you get what you're after, and we all come out smiling. Right?"

"No!" Webber said. "Willy already has an agreement with us."

"Forced on him," Pochoda said. "Verbal agreement, worth the paper it's printed on. I have here a real contract. It is customary to offer a percentage of the appraised value to the finder, which is what we're demanding. Where is Mr. Bols?"

Charlie shrugged. "Funny, Willy didn't mention anything like that before."

"Willy is not a very good businessman, I'm afraid," Rob Rob said. "That's why I'm looking out for his interests. We really do want to speak with him, Charlie. I suggest you go get him."

"You know this man? Is he your accomplice or something?" Ortiz asked.

"Oh, I've known Rob Rob for twenty-five years," Charlie said. He was hoping Constance had made some headway; he was not certain how long he could stall Rob Rob, and no doubt Willy would go mute upon seeing him. "When Mrs. Roberts named her new son Robert, they nicknamed him, of course, and he took the diminutive as an imperative, and has been following it ever since. Nearly sent him away once," he added, speaking to Ortiz. "It didn't take, though. Peaches here pulled some strings, and lo and behold, Rob Rob was back in business."

Rob Rob glanced at Pochoda. "Why don't you go see if you spot Willy in the john or something."

"You know I won't let him do that," Charlie said softly, holding Rob Rob's gaze with his own.

"Let's just talk a couple of minutes," Pochoda said nervously. "We don't want trouble, Meiklejohn. Willy owes Mr. Roberts. It's that simple. No way can he collect unless Willy gets a new contract. Let these gentlemen sign it. Let Willy sign it, and we're out of here. I will be at the appraisal, of course. When Willy collects, he pays his debts. That's not too hard to understand. No skin off your nose."

"Maybe you two should go back to the patio and discuss this new development," Charlie said to Webber. Webber and Ortiz left the room, rigid with indignation.

"Sorry about the wire," Charlie murmured.

"No big deal. Would have shaken my confidence if you hadn't found it. I got you in on this, you know."

DeWilde had been silent, watchful, no longer amused. Now he said, "Mr. Roberts, I should introduce myself more fully. I represent the United States government in this matter. Mr. Pochoda can research the position the government has taken in the past concerning the handling of lost items, sunken ships, buried treasure, whatever. The Supreme Court has ruled favorably and without equivocation that that position is legal and enforceable."

Rob Rob looked him up and down and deliberately turned away. "Yeah, Mr. Pochoda will do that." He took a step back and craned to see out through the dinette to the patio, apparently trying to see Webber and Ortiz. "Get Bols for me, Charlie. Then we'll beat it, let them talk some more. Guys like that, you know the problem with guys like them? Can't make up their minds. Talk, talk, talk, that's what they gotta do. We'll collect Willy and beat it and you tell them the score. Then we'll all have another little meeting. Day, two days. They'll need that, couple of days."

"Maybe they'll just pack their bags and go home," Charlie said.

"Nah, not them. They want what's out there buried somewheres. What they'll do is try to find a way to cut me out, cut

Willy out. Just tell them how the world works, Charlie." He
stopped looking out toward the patio. His gaze was death-cold.
"Just tell them, Charlie. I'll give you a call. You can set up the
next meeting. You going to bring out Willy, or is he?" He nodded toward Pochoda.

Charlie knew it was time. He got up and went to the hall.
"He and Noreen are having a little talk," he said. "Be a minute."

"Talk!" Rob Rob said in disgust. "That's the problem with the
world these days. Everyone's gotta talk, talk, talk."

Charlie went down the hall to the den and entered. Willy
looked asleep; Noreen looked bored. Constance nodded at
him.

"Time's up," Charlie said. "Willy, Rob Rob's out there. I don't
think it's a good idea for you to tell him what you've been doing
in here with my wife. He looks like a jealous man."

Willy leaped to his feet, his face a greenish-gray color.

"Take it easy," Charlie said. "He thinks you've been in here
having a confab with Noreen. Not a bad way to leave it."

Willy moistened his lips and looked at Noreen, who had
gone pale, too. "Yeah. Me and Noreen had stuff to talk over."

Charlie said to Constance, "I'll sing out when the coast is
clear. Come on, Willy. I don't think Rob Rob likes to be kept
waiting."

Willy and Noreen scurried out ahead of him. Rob Rob looked
Willy over and turned toward the foyer. "Follow us," he said.
Then, after one last look of disgust at the men on the patio, he
said, "Tell them the way the world works, Charlie."

He walked out, with Pochoda close enough to be his
shadow; Willy and Noreen rushed after them, pulling on their
jackets as they went.

"Now, Mr. DeWilde," Charlie said, "I think it's time for you
to get in your little red car and tootle off."

DeWilde nodded. "That man can't buck the federal government," he said angrily.

"And just what the hell do you think he's been doing these
past forty years or so?"

DeWilde went to the door. "I'll be in touch."

"I'm sure you will be," Charlie agreed. He locked the door
after DeWilde went out, then he crossed to the window to
watch the various cars leave his driveway.

He collected Constance, Ortiz, and Webber, and they all returned to the living room. He told Constance briefly what had happened, turned to Webber, and shrugged. "It's been interesting, a real fun day, but the deal's off. Sorry."

Constance felt certain Charlie had looked away from her too quickly to have noticed the surge of fear Rob Rob's appearance had sent through her. Why had that man involved Charlie in this—what was he after? The treasure hunt no longer seemed funny. She became guarded, watchful.

"Why?" Webber asked Charlie. "You're not afraid of that gorilla, are you?"

"Sure I am. But that's beside the point. Look, on one hand you've got the United States government on your case; on the other, you've got a big-time gangster wanting in. One or the other will grab the booty, assuming we even get a scent of it. Which, frankly, I doubt. So what's the point?"

"He said he wants to collect a debt from Willy. Would he stop at that?"

Charlie shrugged again. "Maybe, especially since the Feds will be involved. I guess he has Willy on the payroll for the time being—financed his little private expedition, bought him a new car. But he smells real money. That debt could be a million dollars, Webber. Two million. Who knows what he'll say it is? Or if he'll stop there?"

Webber looked thoughtful. Charlie asked softly, "Why don't you guys let me in on it? How much are we talking about here? How high would an appraisal go?"

Ortiz shook his head. "It's inestimable, Mr. Meiklejohn. Earlier I said priceless; I spoke the literal truth. Is a van Gogh worth twenty million dollars? Is a Picasso worth ten million? How does one put a price on art that is priceless?"

Abruptly Webber stood up. "Meiklejohn, I want you to go ahead. We'll give you what we have, you get started. It's going to take time, we all know that. Meanwhile, I'll consult with some of my people. No doubt Carlos will do the same. Maybe a benevolent God will decide it's time for Mr. Roberts to encounter a truck. Deal?"

Watching him, Constance knew Charlie was not calling it off, not now, not with Rob Rob in the picture. Her chill deepened.

Charlie gazed at Webber for a minute before he said, "The first thing you should do is examine carefully those people you plan to consult. Rob Rob has tentacles that reach into very odd places. He already knows whatever Willy knows, and then some. He knows about you two, maybe even what's in those graves. How much does DeWilde know already? I don't think you've considered the resources either of those two gentlemen can snap into action."

"I have my own resources," Webber said in a low voice. "So does Carlos. If, at a later date, we decide your advice is valid, we can always withdraw. The Church can be patient. But now, when we have many of the puzzle pieces, it wouldn't be a bad idea to see how they fit."

"I agree," Ortiz said. "You can make a start. As you intimated, perhaps there aren't quite enough of the pieces yet, in which case, you still benefit. You have our checks. I have no intention of stopping payment. I put myself at your disposal."

"And so do I," Webber said heartily. He sat down again and sprawled his legs out comfortably. "Who goes first?"

3

Obviously the shipment could not be transported overland, it was decided. Mexican banditos, highwaymen, the U.S. Army, innkeepers—all posed a threat. Too many nights in transit, too many loadings and unloadings of what was obviously a very heavy burden. No, it had to be by ship, then by steamboat, then by train. . . . The *Delta Lady* from New Orleans to St. Louis was the answer. Once on board, the chests and boxes would not be moved again until they arrived where men of the faith would see to the unloading and safe transport to Our Lady of Peace and Tranquility Parish Church in St. Louis.

Two priests and six Indian servants boarded at New Orleans. On July 2, 1904, the *Delta Lady* stopped at New Madrid, and was there for four days. Two of the Indians had died; their bodies were removed to the care of the local priest. One Indian fled. The three remaining Indians were locked in the cabin the entire group had shared from the start of the trip. On July 6, the *Delta Lady* departed from New Madrid; its next scheduled stop was at Cairo, Illinois. It was never heard from again.

"Okay," John Webber said. "That's all pretty much in the public record. What isn't mentioned is the pervasive fear the other passengers had of the Catholic priests and their servants, the cholera epidemic raging through the South, the bigotry . . ." His voice rose and with a visible effort he stopped, drew in a breath, then continued. "The priest at New Madrid wrote a letter, too. He said the group on the *Delta Lady* was terrified of overt anti-Catholic sentiment aboard the vessel. There were rumors the Catholics were spreading the disease on purpose, that the vessel itself was doomed, that the captain and his crew wanted to put them off at New Madrid, and so on. Now it appears that the boat did land somewhere and put them off. Previously, it was assumed that the *Delta Lady* sank and everyone aboard perished."

"Your people made searches, I suppose," Charlie said.

"Of course. A dozen or more over the years. They even sent divers down in diving bells at one point. Never a trace."

"Okay. The cargo. What do you know about that?"

Webber moistened his lips. "There were four wooden crates, about fifteen by fifteen, twelve inches deep maybe. One large trunk, three feet by two, by two. Oak with brass fittings and a domed top." He stopped, then said, almost as if he had overlooked this item, "Oh, yes, a small box of some sort. Twelve inches by twelve, about eight inches deep, with a domed lid."

"Oak?"

"I believe it was carved teak. Brass fittings."

He had a list of the crew members and passengers, he said; they all had been investigated thoroughly. None who remained on the boat ever showed up again after July 6, 1904. The Indian who had fled probably died soon after running away.

"Quite a few of the passengers disembarked at New Madrid; many of them died. The survivors were located and questioned. They confirmed the hostility, the fear. They reported talk among some passengers that they should seize the trunks."

He filled in a few more details, and promised to send documents by messenger to provide the history of the different searches, along with anything else Charlie wanted.

When Ortiz entered the den, he was carrying a folder. He bowed stiffly to John Webber, who was on his way to the living room, bowed again toward Constance and Charlie, then watched Webber for a moment before pulling the door closed.

"My government was negotiating in good faith with his church," Ortiz started.

"No more history for the moment," Charlie said.

"I just want to tell you this," Ortiz said.

Charlie hated it when anyone just wanted to tell him what he didn't want to know. He said, "That's all history, Mr. Ortiz. I take it you have sufficient cause to believe you have a stake in finding that stuff. Let's let it go at that."

"We thought they were negotiating in good faith, as well," Ortiz said. "They stole away in the dead of night, and by the time we knew, the ship was gone, they were gone. We sent horsemen—"

Charlie stood up and started for the door. "No more history," he said.

Ortiz jumped to his feet. "Please," he said. "Forgive me. It's simply that their claim is so unjust."

Charlie went back to his chair, and both men sat down again. "You searched, too?"

"Yes, several times, and we observed their searches as well. And we made a land search after Willy Bols turned up. *Nada.*"

"Okay," Charlie said. "I want the Spanish letter."

"Of course. Not the original, however. It is in very bad shape. But photographs, photocopies, and our translation. Meanwhile, I have here my memory of what I read in that letter. It's exactly word for word what you will find there, but much of it was indecipherable. Our best people cannot make out more than I have reproduced here."

He opened the file folder and withdrew a sheet of paper. "See, this is how it looked, to the best of my poor ability to render a facsimile. Willy did not handle it with care, obviously; pieces flaked off, he pulled it apart. . . ." He sighed, and they all peered at his drawing.

He had sketched a rectangle in heavy black lines, and within it the outline of the letter—an irregularly shaped fragment only, the top almost completely gone, the bottom part gone, part of the middle gone.

"I have studied this letter for many hours," he said slowly, taking another sheet of paper from the folder; this one had writing on it. "These are the phrases and words we have to work with." He placed the letter on the coffee table by the couch.

Charlie and Constance studied the letter on the low table. ". . . take Christ's tears to his grave. *Por dios.* . . . May I be worthy of such suffering . . . followed the finger, beckoning . . . in His footsteps . . . torrents unceasing, how the beast struggles . . . no rain will wash away Christ's tears, never a softer pillow . . . cursed rain, cursed mud . . . *Madre,* have mercy . . . Patrick's tears, Christ's tears flow together where the angels dance. . . ."

Charlie looked at Ortiz with incredulity and frustration. "That's it? You expect that to get us anywhere?"

Ortiz spread his hands. "The original is in such poor condition. We used enhancing techniques to make this much legible. Patrick was Patrick O'Bannon, and there was enough of the signature to reconstruct the other name, Domingo Sanches. But there are clues, Mr. Meiklejohn. Among our people, the setting sun on a rock can be seen as a finger beckoning, the sun on a dead tree spur, a planet sinking below the horizon, Venus perhaps. . . . If we know where to start looking, we may see the signs."

"And you might see angels dancing," Charlie said morosely. He put the sheets of paper in the folder and closed it. "Ortiz, what's in those graves?"

"We've told you. Many items, some of them religious items, some pure art. What more can I say?" He smiled; his teeth were perfect.

"How heavy would those things be?"

"Very heavy," he said gravely. "The big chest, very heavy indeed. Even the smallest cask would be heavy." He smiled again.

Charlie, aware that his own teeth were not perfect, aware of a gold cap that showed when he opened his mouth, did not smile. "Let's go talk to your pal and wrap this up for now."

In the living room he said, "Rob Rob will give me a call in a day or two. What do I tell him?"

"We want to see the contract, have our own attorneys look at it. I've been thinking," Webber said. "If he has a legal contract, with witnesses and the weight of the law behind it, he stands to make a bit of money legitimately. Why try anything illegal?"

Charlie shrugged. "So what do I tell him?"

"We can have our attorneys get in touch with Mr. Pochoda. Let the legal beagles snap at each other for a few months. Is that agreeable, Carlos?"

Ortiz nodded.

"I want to see any contract you come up with," Charlie said unhappily. They both nodded.

4

I say we tell them to find someone else," Constance said after all the guests had departed.

"My first idea exactly," he admitted. "But, honey, we have fifty grand I'd sure hate to hand back. And since there's no way we can find anything, what's the harm in digging a little?"

"Digging where?"

"Beats me," he said with a grin. "You get any more from Willy?"

"Not much. And it's so scrappy, it's worthless. I jotted down phrases as he remembered them, and they may or may not be in any particular order. He said a lot of it didn't make any sense at all, and I believe him."

She produced the sheet of paper she had written on, and they read the phrases together. ". . . after . . . overland through the canyons and valleys . . . God sent the Negro to us and showed the way . . . buried Pedro and Juan . . . good and faithful servants . . . Pepito first . . . May God have mercy . . . Juan rests on the great parcel . . . God's will . . . Domingo or I will share Christ's tears . . . guard . . . for eternity . . . Pray for a priest in Paducah. . . ."

He looked up, feeling very dim and blank. "Me too," she said. "Ed mentioned that he and his father had been staying close to the river, living off fish, corn, and blackberries. That's it."

"I'll stash this in the safe with the other stuff," Charlie said, then paused. Constance was gazing off abstractedly. Not the cruise again, he hoped. "Something?"

"Something," she said, bringing her focus back to him. "You. We agree that we're not likely to come up with anything. Are you looking for a chance to get Rob Rob?"

"Honey," he said in protest, a touch too quickly, "do you see any way on earth I could do that?"

She shook her head. "But I can hear your wheels spinning. Leave him alone, Charlie. He's part of the past, done with."

He started for the door, carrying the sheet of paper. "Honey, I promise you, if such a thought occurs to me in any serious way, you'll be the first to know."

She could hear his wheels spinning, he thought, going to his office safe. Hah! His wheels were mired in mud. If there was any way on God's green ball of grass that he could get at Rob Rob, he'd do it, but the wheels refused to turn.

Constance was remembering the case he had worked on with his partner, meticulously, secretly, for over six months, making certain that Rob Rob wouldn't find a way out. An airtight case, Charlie had said, so airtight a match wouldn't light in it, and he had done it. The perfect case, a certain conviction of guilty-as-charged for a double murder. Within two hours of the arrest, Pochoda had gotten him out. Rob Rob had an alibi. A United States congressman, a millionaire businessman, and a famous psychiatrist had all sworn Rob Rob had spent the evening of the murders playing poker with them.

First, Charlie had gotten drunk; then, sober again, he had cleaned and oiled his revolver and started out. She had blocked the door. That was the first time she had threatened to leave him. She no longer knew if she would have done it, but neither had he known at the time. They had argued—fought—most of that night; he had raged, detailed more horror than she had known existed, all laid at Rob Rob's feet, and she very nearly had come to agree with him that if the law couldn't handle a man like that, a person had to. But he would have been killed, too, she had understood. One way or another, he would have

died. She had no doubt that if he believed he could get Rob
Rob now, after all these years, he would do it.

On Monday materials began arriving: detailed maps of the Mississippi from Natchez to Cairo; pamphlets about the locks and
dams on the river, studies concerning the levees and natural
and manmade barriers to keep the river where it belonged; a
lengthy report on the many dramatic floods that had made a
mockery of those attempts; a drawing of the *Delta Lady;* topographical maps of the flood plains of Missouri, Arkansas, Tennessee, Kentucky, Illinois; authorized history books on the
Catholic Church and its mission in the New World; a history of
the monastery where the two priests had lived and worked;
other history books on the same subjects, written by nonbe-
lievers; beautifully illustrated books of Mayan and Aztec art,
much of it in church vaults and museums; detailed reports on
the disappearance of the *Delta Lady* and the subsequent
searches that had been made by everyone from the United
States government to insurance companies to the Church and
the Mexicans; an epidemiological study of the various waves of
this and that that had swept the nation from 1882 to the present . . . Charlie and Constance settled in to read.

The crocuses gave way to daffodils; the apple trees bloomed,
turned green. She conducted her regular aikido classes. He
tilled the garden and she planted seeds. Asparagus shoots appeared. One of the cats left a dead rat on the back stoop, and
repeated the act daily for the rest of the week.

Rob Rob called and said the lawyers were *talking, talking.*
Charlie told him to send Willy back, and the next day Willy
appeared with Noreen. It had rained or stormed every day,
Willy said; Ed had told him he sank up to his knees in mud.
They all had to walk because the horse couldn't pull the loaded
wagon in the mud. Ed never said how long they took to get to
Paducah.

Constance worked at getting more details about the letter
Willy had seen, but that, too, was useless. All that holy stuff
made his eyes glaze over, he said resentfully. She suspected that
his reading skills had not been sufficient to get more than he
had.

Ortiz and Webber both called; Charlie told them to leave him alone until he got in touch. DeWilde paid a visit; Charlie was rude to him and sent him away again.

The Mississippi, the Missouri, the Red River, and the Arkansas River were all flooded that spring. Charlie and Constance watched a special on television about the efforts being made to keep the water back, to shore up the levees, to erect new ones. The river danced over the land, Charlie thought, cutting itself a new channel here, there, wherever it wanted, and later they redrew the maps. A bow was cut through to create a crescent-shaped lake, and the river had a new path to the Gulf. A trickle strayed around a hill over a bit of low land; more followed, and there was a new island in the river, another new channel. It flowed south to Cairo, met the waters of the Ohio River, and presently, bigger than ever, turned north again, up to New Madrid. A river shouldn't go north *and* south, east *and* west.

Suddenly Charlie grunted and sat up straighter on the couch in the den. Constance looked at him.

"All those maps we've been studying," he said. "Pointless. We need maps from Nineteen-four. How many times have there been major floods since then? Nineteen-thirteen, 'twenty-seven, 'thirty-seven, 'ninety-three, now . . ."

"Webber can find them," she said after a moment.

"They probably already thought of it," he said, "but they didn't know Willy's part of the story yet. Ortiz is looking westward from the Mississippi, in Missouri. Webber is, too. Let's not clue them in to turn one hundred eighty degrees and start looking there. Topo maps of both sides of the river from Cairo to . . . what? A hundred miles south?"

She was nodding. "The roads have changed, no doubt. We need more than just geological maps; we need farms, roads, towns, everything for miles inland from the river, too."

He grinned. "The distance from the Mississippi to Paducah, plus or minus twenty. Okay?"

"Plus," she said.

"Right." He glanced at his watch. Nine-thirty. Not too late to call Webber. He went to the phone.

"He said there aren't such maps," Charlie said when he hung up. "You heard what I said." What he had told Webber was that Webber should put some cartographers to work and create them. "They'll have to start digging in local county seat records for property holdings, farms, that kind of stuff. They'll start at Cairo and work south. It will take some time."

She nodded. "We have time."

"Poor Webber," he murmured. Then, "What in hell do you suppose is worth this kind of trouble and expense?"

They had not discussed the contents of the various trunks and crates, since it had seemed pointless to speculate. It was a treasure hunt was Charlie's thought, and hers too; a treasure trove of gold was buried out there. Now, however, in answer to his rhetorical question, Constance said, "Christ's tears." She was as surprised as he was by the answer.

He blinked. "Meaning?"

"Well, both letters mentioned Christ's tears. I can't believe those two names alone, Patrick and Domingo, were enough to send a signal on a database. But the names *and* the words *Christ's tears*? Maybe."

"Let's look at those letters again," Charlie said.

He read aloud the phrases from the English letter: "Juan rests on the great parcel . . . Domingo or I will share Christ's tears . . . guard . . . for eternity . . ." He picked up the Spanish translation and read: ". . . take Christ's tears to his grave . . . no rain will wash away Christ's tears, never a softer pillow . . . Patrick's tears, Christ's tears flow together where the angles dance. . . ."

He looked up from the letters to her. "I think you've got it. What it is, God knows, but that's it. Christ's tears. A thing, an artifact of some sort, not just a figure of speech."

"I think so," she said. "Now all we have to do is find out where the angels dance." She was regarding the letters. "You know, this phrase, 'Pray for a priest in Paducah,' why pray for him? I wonder if it doesn't mean pray that there will *be* a priest in Paducah. I wonder if they didn't intend for Abe Worsham to deliver their letters to a priest, not for him to mail them. He could have led a priest back to the graves. If he hadn't been able to find a priest there, that would explain a lot." Ruefully she added, "I wish Willy had asked a few more questions of Ed Worsham."

"Honey, you're doing just fine," Charlie said. "Let's think about where the angels dance. Spanish moss in the wind?"

"Or the play of sunlight on leaves. Birds. Butterflies. Shadows." She shook her head. "Maybe he was delirious and saw angels dancing."

"Was the other one delirious, too? Or did he really see canyons and valleys?"

"How could he?" she asked. She stood up and went to the big Webster's dictionary on a stand in the den. He followed. "Angels," she muttered. "Angel bed, angel cake, fish, eyes." She reread that one, "Angel eyes; bluets," and made a note. "Angel light, pie, red, angel's hair . . . angel's trumpet. Datura." She made another note, and read on down the list.

"What's a bluet?" Charlie asked.

She pulled a book from the garden shelf and found *bluet*. "Knapweed, *Centaurea montana,* perennial, mountains of Central Europe . . . Maybe," she said doubtfully. "It's something like a bachelor's button, I think, pretty common, but is that too far south for it to thrive? Don't know. Angel's trumpet is the datura plant," she added. "That, at least, is from Mexico and farther south. I don't know if it would thrive in such a humid climate; it likes deserts and wastelands." She replaced the book with a sigh. "I just can't imagine describing either of them as angels dancing." She frowned, then said, "Too much thinking. Let's go to bed."

He chuckled. "My kind of woman, direct, straightforward, no shilly-shallying. You're on."

She gave him one of her looks.

Ten days later Webber delivered a package in person. "New maps," he said. "And a report of our last search. I believe we inadvertently left that out of the original report." He lied with such ease, he could have been a television salesman. Today he was dressed in a shirt open at the neck and lightweight slacks. June had brought in a heat wave; the air was thick and sultry, thunderstorm weather.

"Get your contract settled with Rob Rob yet?" Charlie asked, leading him to the back patio, where it was not really cool but cool-looking, with deep shade from vines covering the lattice top. All three cats appeared to be dead, their remains sprawled on the patio; Brutus got up deliberately, hoisted his tail, and stalked off. Ashcan fled in terror. Candy did not move.

"I brought that, too," Webber said with a grimace. "Are you making any progress at all?"

"Following our noses," Charlie said. "Running down ideas. Let's have a look at your map."

The cartographers had started with the western bank of the Mississippi and had prepared a topographical map of how it had been a hundred years ago. "To the best of their ability," Webber said. "That was a difficult order, Meiklejohn. As they fill in more, we'll send it along. The other side is even sketchier, I'm afraid."

He spread the map on the table and pointed to a spot marked with a small red circle. "That's an old fueling station. You know, the steamships had to stop to pick up wood along the way. Accounts for a lot of the deforestation, I'm afraid. Anyway, last summer Carlos and a crew docked a boat there and mucked around for about a week, then left. We went in afterward and poked around. Since we now know the boat put the group ashore between New Madrid and Cairo, that seemed as likely a place as any. It's the only place they could have docked," he added.

The site was on the Missouri bank of the river. Charlie studied it, then said, "Does seem likely, doesn't it?" Why not there? he wondered. Why not the fueling station dock? Across the river from the fueling station was Kentucky. There was no dock on the Kentucky side.

"There must be a clue in that Spanish letter Carlos has," Webber said. "Something sent him over there to look. If the three of us put our heads together, maybe we can uncover it."

Charlie grinned. "How about some lemonade? Hot day like this, we find lemonade hits the spot."

Webber looked petulant as he groped in his briefcase to find the copy of the contract with Rob Rob. He handed it to Charlie, who paid scant attention to it. It would mean exactly what Rob Rob decided it meant. Webber hung around until Charlie politely invited him to go away.

As soon as he was gone, Constance and Charlie spread out two maps on the dining room table—one current, the other, provided by Webber, an approximation of how the area had been nearly a hundred years earlier.

Now and again one or the other murmured something: "This

road wasn't there." "Just a track from one farm to another." "Swampy, must have flooded routinely back then." "Must have been a dirt road to let them put a rowboat in the water or something."

Charlie gave up first; it was his day to cook dinner, and his back ached from too much leaning over. Constance pointed to a road on the current map. "I bet Willy thought that road was the one they took. But it wasn't even there then. They seem to have relocated it miles to the north, around that marsh."

She was studying the maps as he left to see about dinner. Later they ate shrimp sautéed with green garlic, rice and peas, and a lush salad of many mixed greens. They were still eating when the first fireflies appeared and the mosquitoes swarmed. All three cats were lying in wait for their share of shrimp. Constance was thinking about the sick priests, Abe and the child Ed, the Indians, being eaten alive in swampy land in July. Lightning flashed so far away that no sound of thunder carried to the patio. Lightning could be seen as angels dancing, she mused, if one was extremely fanciful. She shook her head and they started to carry dishes to the kitchen.

Charlie stopped just inside the sliding door, both hands filled. "How did they manage that?" he muttered.

"What?" She stepped around him and put her dishes down on the counter.

He moved then, put the bowls he was carrying on the kitchen table, and continued on to the dining room, where he switched on the lights and peered at the 1904 map again.

"They stayed close to the river, lived off fish, corn, and berries. Remember? But there's no road that follows the river."

She looked. Of course, there wouldn't have been, she thought; it would have been washed out over and over. Fields, up and down the shoreline as far as the map showed. She drew back with her eyes narrowed. "Charlie, you never paid a lot of attention to our fields back home, did you?" She had grown up on a dairy farm in Minnesota. "Dad always left a pretty wide strip along each field; we used them as roads for the tractor, for the wagons to bring out the wheat. You have to leave them to have access."

He began to trace the outlines of fields, farms with boundaries marked in some places, not in others. "That's it," he said.

"If they stayed at the edges of the fields, they could have kept close to the river. How big is a farm wagon?"

She shook her head. "Cart. Willy first said a horse and cart. Later everyone called it a wagon, because that's what we're used to. But it must have been a cart, small enough to use the margins of the fields for a road. That's why they were up to their knees in mud. They might never have been on a real road."

Charlie felt a tingling in his spine as he looked at the map. "How high would corn have been in July?"

"I don't know. Field corn in the South—eight feet tall maybe. Why?"

"Valleys," he said in a low voice. "Canyons. As soon as they turned east they were closed in on both sides by corn over their heads."

They were startled by a thunderclap near enough to shake the house. "Stuff on the table," Charlie muttered, and hurried outside to finish clearing away the leftovers.

Brutus leaped off the table, bearing the last of the shrimp. Candy was nearby, cleaning her face fastidiously; Ashcan was sniffing at the patio floor in apparent bewilderment. With a sigh Charlie stacked plates on the platter and carried them inside. Lightning was playing on the horizon in a continuous dance. Thunder sounded again, closer, and they rushed to finish.

She got the candles out and put them on the dinette table, and he found the kerosene lamp, just in case. Then they stood at the door, his arm around her shoulders, her arm around his waist, and they watched the storm approach. He was remembering another storm, a long time ago, when their daughter was still an infant. *What if lightning hit, and people found us like this?* she had asked, and he had said, *They'd be jealous. Not a bad way to go.* He tightened his arm and drew her nearer.

"It's the ozone," she murmured.

"What is?"

"What makes you so horny when it storms."

The lights flickered and went out, and they went to bed, exactly as he had known they would.

The next day they went to a copy shop and made copies and transparencies of the 1904 maps. Then, back in the dining room, they started to work.

"What we know," Constance said, studying the map with the transparency taped over it precisely, "is that they were able to drag the big bundle a quarter of a mile away from the river. Not on a road, or why not stay on it? Abe must have met them on one of the margins of the fields. Not too far from open ground, where they could bury them."

"You don't think they just buried the guys in the cornfields? Why not?"

"Because you don't," she said without looking up.

He grinned. *Because.* As good a reason as any. "They must have been taken ashore in a small boat. Did steamships use lifeboats?"

"I don't know. But you're right. So we need some sort of beach with a trail leading away from it."

"Someplace visible to Abe," he added.

By late afternoon they had located four possible landing sites and traced them with erasable markers on the transparency. They eliminated one of them quickly. Too far from a good place for a grave, she had muttered.

"If that was an unusually wet summer, I just don't see how we can narrow it down more than this," Constance said when it was nearly time for her to start dinner.

"And if it was a normal summer, you see light at the end of the tunnel?" he asked glumly. All he saw was an impossible task—try out one after another of those trails and look for angels dancing.

"Well, yes," she said. "Ed sank to his knees in mud. Remember? That suggests up here near this marshy area if the summer was normal."

"They had rain and thunderstorms every day," he reminded her.

"Well, we do too, almost. And you won't sink like that anywhere."

True, he thought. Their yard had been scrubbed clean by the storm of the previous evening, but there wasn't any mud anywhere. "I can find out," he said then. "There must be a meteorology group talking about weather even as we sit here. I'll go ask."

He went to his office to go online, and she went to the kitchen to cook. His answer was posted at nine that night: that summer had been on the dry side. She smiled sweetly at him.

"Okay, eenie meenie miney time," he said, back at the map. "North or south of the swamp?"

The swamp was eight to ten miles from east to west, a mile or two from north to south. Swamp, then some higher rocky ground, another road several miles north, and more fields.

"We need a timetable," she said after a moment. "Abe and his son met the priests in midmorning, probably. They already had dragged the bundle a quarter of a mile, remember? I don't imagine they made more than five or six miles that day. Then one died, and they had to find a burial site, dig a grave . . . That would have been day two."

Slowly they filled in the timetable as they speculated on how long the events they knew about might have taken. Then they placed the marked transparency over the current map and surveyed it. One of the trails they had marked was a mile or two north of State Highway 62, and even merged with it at two spots. Another was on U.S. Highway 60.

Constance became aware that Charlie was regarding her; when she looked up at him, his eyes were shining, and a grin was playing at his mouth.

"Honey," he said, "what if we could pinpoint it enough to go start digging?"

But it was a game, she started to say, a treasure hunt game. An image of Rob Rob, followed by many men with guns, followed by U.S. marshals came to mind. She looked down at the map, back to him, and she said, "What if?"

"Let's knock off this part and go talk," he said.

The next morning, she found him whistling softly as he scrambled eggs, timed precisely for her arrival downstairs. He always woke up first, and he most often woke up hungry and happy. It was a mystery to her how he could be so cheerful so early, but she liked his breakfasts. His crinkly black hair sparkled with water diamonds.

He served the eggs; the toast popped up and she went to

fetch it and the coffee. Neither talked as they ate, but over his second cup of coffee Charlie said, "They expected someone to find the graves. They marked them somehow."

"The priest in Paducah? He could have hired Abe to take him there."

"I don't think so," Charlie said. "I have to ask Webber, but I doubt they would have trusted a stranger with such a treasure. I bet they wanted him to make certain the letter was sent to a proper authority, either in Mexico or Rome, or maybe somewhere else, which could mean no one would get back to the graves for many months. But the graves had to be findable."

"We need to know more about those two priests," she said thoughtfully.

"Right. We know enough to know what we don't know. That's a real step forward."

"Willy said Ed Worsham told him they put a curse on the grave with the big bundle. I want to ask him a few more questions."

"At some point we're going to have to go have a look," Charlie said almost absently, thinking of two trails, each about forty miles long, with possible graves almost anywhere along either of them. "And without a gaggle of geese at our heels."

"I know," she said. "Any ideas?"

"Lots, but most of them are pretty bad. Let's think about it. How about a little trip down to New York—hole up in a hotel a couple of days and have a go at them all again?"

After a moment she nodded, not at all thrilled by the idea.

5

Three days later they checked into the Grand Hyatt at noon, and an hour after that Carlos Ortiz arrived. He looked at their small room with disapproval. "We don't expect you to stint on expenses," he murmured.

Charlie had to move aside for him to enter. "We practice

frugality," Charlie said. "Years of practice; we're getting pretty good at it."

"You have something for us, something definite?"

"In a word, yes. Did you bring the material we asked for?"

"Of course. Mr. Meiklejohn, do you know where the graves are?" He had turned pale; his voice quavered.

"I believe Mr. Ortiz is feeling ill," Constance said. "Would you like a drink of water?"

Charlie put his hand on Ortiz's arm; Ortiz was shaking. Wordlessly Constance went to the door and opened it; Charlie put his finger on his lips and pulled Ortiz back to the door. When he started to speak, Charlie shook his head and touched his lips again. They left the room and walked out, past the elevators to the stairs.

"What are you doing?" Ortiz demanded on the stairs.

"Safe room," Charlie said easily. "That one's bugged, twice. Probably DeWilde and Rob Rob's doing."

They walked down to the twelfth floor, on to another door, which Charlie opened with his computer key to reveal a suite. A low table had an assortment of bottles, ice in a bucket, glasses. Brian had done it up just fine, Charlie thought with approval. Using a phone in Fircrest, he had called Brian Posner, an investigator he sometimes used, and told him exactly what to do, and here they were. He grinned. There were tubs of plants with a mirror behind them, intensifying a jungle effect. A low couch, four easy chairs, stereo and television . . . No frugality in evidence here.

"A drink? Juice? Coffee? Seems we have it all," he commented, glancing over the table. "I'm going to leave you here with Constance, and in about fifteen minutes bring your pal Webber in. Then we'll talk. Constance has a few questions to ask while I'm gone. Okay?"

Ortiz sank down onto the couch. "Bugged! My God!"

Back in the other room, Charlie clinked a glass, shuffled papers, and once he said, "Just read, then we talk." He waited for Webber by the open door, took his arm, and led him down the stairs to the suite. Constance and Ortiz were sitting side by side on the couch with cups of coffee.

"We bought ourselves a little time, a little privacy," Charlie said, taking one of the comfortable chairs across the table from Constance and Ortiz. "They're on to the trick by now, maybe already looking for us. So we don't want to waste time. I have a list of questions, and I want straight answers. I don't give a damn who tells me what, just so I get answers."

Webber was still standing, frowning at Ortiz. "What have you been telling them?"

"Sit down," Charlie snapped. "First, do you have a portable metal detector that can find the loot if it's five or six feet down? How many guys would you need to dig it out and haul it to a truck or something in the shortest possible time? Do you have people you can trust not to talk, to dig without questions? Who would those priests have written to? Have you paid Willy what you owe him? What do you plan to do about Rob Rob? About DeWilde? If you could put your hands on the stuff, then what? Have you decided how to split it up without bloodshed?" He grinned amiably. "That's enough for starters. Webber, why don't you sit down." He motioned toward a chair across from him.

Webber nearly fell down. While his jaw wasn't really hanging, it gave that appearance. "You know!" he whispered. Huskily he said, "They would have written to the bishop in Mexico; he knew what they were transporting, and he would have sent people to them."

"What did they tell people they were transporting?" Charlie asked.

"The Mexican was a horticulturist; he was in charge of delivering a lot of plant material to St. Louis. O'Bannon had a trunk of books," Webber said. "That was their story."

"If I can get my part of the material to our embassy," Ortiz said thoughtfully, "we'd let the lawyers haggle for the rest of their lives."

Webber nodded. "Same for me. Once the items are secure, what can DeWilde or that crook do? We paid Willy the first half, then that crook showed up and there didn't seem any point in paying him more until the matter was settled."

"Pay him his money," Charlie said. "You'd unilaterally cancel the contract you signed?"

"It was signed under duress," Webber said grimly.

"We could each provide four men," Ortiz said. "For the digging, transporting, security. Four each would be sufficient. We have the metal detectors," he added.

"So do we," Webber said.

"You've come to an agreement on how to divide the stuff?" Neither spoke for a minute. Then Webber said, "He doesn't know everything in that bundle. We have the inventory, not them. There are pieces I would not dispute," he said slowly.

"There are pieces I must have," Ortiz said.

"Christ's Tears," Charlie murmured.

They both started in surprise.

"Their name for it," Ortiz said furiously. "It is a sculpture that predates the conquest by centuries!"

"The Church will never give it up," Webber said with smug conviction. "That piece isn't to be included in the division."

Charlie picked up a bottle of Jack Daniel's and poured some into a glass. He added ice cubes and swished them around. "Okay. I've got my fifty grand. Someday, five years from now, ten, I'll go dig it up myself and sell it to the highest bidder." He tasted his drink with appreciation.

Webber and Ortiz raged, and Charlie looked off into space and sipped his drink until it was gone. He wanted another one, but decided against it.

"They said you were an honorable man," Webber said bitterly.

"Maybe the only one present," Charlie murmured. "I'll tell you the rest of it and let you go huddle some more. We'll want a houseboat, something that will sleep all of us and your eight diggers. A trustworthy crew to take care of it, cook, all that. That's for openers. It could be docked at Cairo, as good a place as any. Don't go near it yourselves or put your diggers aboard until and unless I give the word. It would be nice if it didn't get bugged. I'm sure you have associates who can arrange it. Constance and I are taking a little vacation; we'll be out of touch for a few days. When we get back, I'll give you a call. If you've reached an agreement about the sculpture, we'll go on from there. Otherwise, that's it." He stood up. "Oh, one more thing. You should assume you're being watched, listened to."

He let them fume a few more minutes, then escorted them to the door. "I'll call next week," he said. He closed the door, locked it, hooked the chain, and then said to Constance, "Let's see how much we got."

He moved aside one of the tubs of plants and shifted the mirror to reveal a camcorder on a stand. He turned it off, removed the cassette, and put it in the VCR, and they watched themselves and Ortiz enter the room. The picture was very clear. Charlie left and returned with Webber, and that, too, was good and sharp. Then Charlie walked to the door with both men, all duly recorded. There was no sound.

At two-thirty they went to meet Willy in Shannon's Bar, a dim, loud place with tiny tables and too many patrons. Willy was sitting with Rob Rob, who was too fat to get very near the table. No one was crowding him in the crowded bar.

There were no greetings as they drew near the table, pulled out chairs, and sat down. The waiter came and Charlie pointed to Willy's beer. Constance shook her head. Rob Rob was drinking mineral water.

"Just a few things we want to get straight," Charlie said. "How crazy was Ed Worsham when you talked with him?"

"Crazy. I don't know. He'd start to talk and forget what he was saying and drift off, you know, just nuts, old."

"Think hard, Willy. Did he mention Cairo?"

Willy shook his head. Rob Rob picked up his glass of water, and Willy frowned, thinking. "Nah, no Cairo."

"How long did it take to reach Paducah once they were rid of the baggage?"

"Hey, Meiklejohn, he was a little kid. He didn't know, a couple of days is what he said."

"That figures," Charlie said thoughtfully. "After he reached the road, crossed the bridge, it was a good road the rest of the way, thirty miles, couple of days."

"He said they were heading for Paducah," Rob Rob said. He was watching Charlie like a snake eyeing a bird. "You're thinking of that fueling station. Forget it. There were people there."

"Would you go near a bunch like that if you thought they were carrying cholera?" Charlie asked softly. "Abe and his kid escaped whatever it was, immune maybe. Abe wanted to go to Paducah, on up to Cincinnati, but the priests? Forget it. Why would they head east? They were on their way to St. Louis." He looked at Willy sadly. "You threw us a foul ball, I'm afraid. We've been busting our butts in the wrong place."

"There's nothing like that in any of the records," Rob Rob said. His eyes were narrower than before, meaner.

"So sue me. There's nothing on the record, period. Willy, what about the curse? What did Ed say about that?"

Rob Rob made a disgusted sound, then inclined his head toward Willy. "So, tell him."

"I already told you what he said," Willy whined. He glanced at Rob Rob and said quickly, "Okay, okay. Ed was scared of those guys. The Spanish one, he did the mumbo jumbo at the grave, and threw stones on it, then made them put more dirt on the stones."

Charlie shook his head. "Stones? He picked up stones and tossed them on the grave? What made Ed think it was a curse?"

"He had the stones in a bag," Willy said hurriedly. "I forgot that part. A black bag or something. He cursed them and tossed them on the grave. He did it again when they buried the other priest, and used them all up, and that time he was crying."

Suddenly Constance stood up. "I want to do a little shopping."

"Catch up with you later," he said, and watched her walk out. She walked as if she owned the joint, he thought with pleasure. He liked watching her walk, the loose gait she had, the way she held her head.

"Shop and talk, talk and shop, that's all they know," Rob Rob said, dismissing Constance. "You want anything else with Willy?"

"Yep. A few things." He didn't, but neither did he want them to know he had gotten what he was after. He asked a few more questions. Finally Charlie shrugged. "We wasted two months on that crazy story. Now I have to start over."

"Go tell Roy to bring the car around," Rob Rob said, not looking at Willy, who instantly got up and hurried out. Rob Rob studied Charlie for a moment, then said, "We go back a long way, you and me. You've got something. That's okay, that's what you were tagged for. But, Charlie, don't try to get cute. Nothing funny, nothing cute. We figure the appraisal will come in around twenty million, and we're in for twenty percent. You can do the numbers. You don't want to get between me and my cut."

"Why don't you retire?" Charlie asked pleasantly. "Aren't you afraid all this stress and excitement might be bad for the ticker?" Rob Rob had had a triple-bypass two years earlier.

"See to it that there isn't any stress and excitement," he snapped. "I'll take care of my health, and you watch out for yours." He heaved himself up from his chair and waddled out.

He was not doing a very good job of taking care, Charlie thought, fishing a twenty from his pocket. It was fifteen minutes after three. At three-thirty he had a date. He left the bar and strolled along Lexington leisurely for a block or so, then turned onto a one-way street, walking against the traffic. At three-thirty a Ford Taurus slowed to a halt at Charlie's side, to an instant outburst of horns. Charlie opened the door and got in.

"Hi, Brian, good timing. Probably two cars will be tagging along as soon as they get a fix on your license plate."

Brian had ginger-colored hair, a florid complexion, and very blue eyes. He was forty-three, and good enough that if Charlie ever decided he needed another partner, Brian would be it. Brian was grinning. "Someone's license plate," he said. Charlie leaned back and let him do his thing.

Constance was right, he thought, New York was no place for a sane person to operate an automobile. Traffic was worse than he remembered; every time he came to town it was worse than he remembered. Too damn many people. Too damn many cars. He was starting to think his followers would catch up just by sauntering along when traffic moved forward through an intersection.

"Okay," Brian said. "I'm going to pull into the next lane. Sandy Milosevic will pull up even on your side—green Honda, right behind us now. First stop, I'll let her edge ahead, and you're out of here."

"Right," Charlie said. "Good old Sandy Miles, still playing cops and robbers."

"You got it," Brian said, and eased into the next lane over. Horns blasted the air.

"I'll call when we get back," Charlie said, watching the green Honda draw even with the Ford. Sandy didn't glance his way.

They stopped again; he opened his door, stepped out, opened the back door of the Honda, and slid in. She moved forward and made a last-minute decision to turn at the next intersection as a surge of cars pressed forward—the drivers all thinking, no doubt, that the green light meant they had right-of-way.

"Hiya, Charlie. Jesus, I thought you retired." She was a bottle-blonde with a cute little snub nose and freckles; she was sixty or more, and looked forty. It was the nose and freckles, he had decided years ago when she was forty and looked twenty.

"Sandy, you look terrific," he said.

"Yeah, I know. I've been working out, jogging, eating tofu, you know, all the good stuff. Ma lived to be one hundred and three; my old man ninety-two. I figure I've got some good years left." She talked all the way to La Guardia. When they got there she said he was clean, no tail, and he believed her without question.

"I owe you, Sandy," he said.

"Yeah. Give us a call when you can. See ya."

He checked in at the Delta counter; they were flying as Mr. and Mrs. Brian Posner. He made his way to the departure gate—Delta flight to Louisville, then a regional carrier to Paducah. Fifteen minutes later when Constance walked in, a small knot he hadn't known was there loosened in his midsection.

He kissed her. "Problem?" he asked.

"No. A woman stayed with me for a while: two bookstores, three department stores, but somehow I lost her in Blooming-dale's." She was carrying a bulging Bloomingdale's shopping bag. "I bought us some deli sandwiches," she said. "We can get wine and bad coffee on the plane." He kissed her again. A minute later their flight was announced, and they boarded. It was six-forty-five.

Airborne, they turned down the offer of food and unwrapped their sandwiches. "What were you doing in a bookstore?" he asked. The plan had been for her to buy him a couple of shirts, some outdoor gear and shoes for her, toothbrushes, stuff like that.

"I thought I should consult *Hortus*," she said, and took a bite of sandwich.

He glowered at her, then started to eat. She would tell him in her own time, her own way, and the sandwich was great, a real New York deli creation that no one else could get right. Roast beef, sharp cheese, sharp mustard, pickle . . .

Eventually she told him. "Ortiz described the garden the Mexican priest—not a priest, but a monk—created out of the desert. The man was a world traveler; he collected plants, seeds, cuttings, tubers, bulbs from everywhere and made them grow. That was to be his mission in St. Louis, to create a garden. And Willy said he put stones on the graves, in the graves actually. Stones. Bulbs. They might have survived. So I decided *Hortus* might be better than the dictionary. And it was," she added demurely. "Much better."

He wanted to strangle her. "You plan to tell me, or just tease?"

"I'm telling you," she said in mock indignation. "*Hortus,* as you well know, is the bible of the plant world, the encyclopedia of plants. It has a very long list of common names as well as the official names of just about everything that grows. I found angels dancing, Charlie." When she looked at him, her eyes were dancing, too. "Put this stuff on your tray so I can get rid of mine and I'll show you. I bought a flower book."

They shifted things and she brought the book out of the shopping bag and opened it at a bookmark. She read, " '*Dierama pendulum,* sometimes called angel's fishing rod . . .' " She skipped down and read again, " 'The stems are narrow and wiry, invisible from a distance, and with the slightest breeze the flowers appear to be dancing in the air. . . .' They came from South Africa, and they grow from bulbs," she added. "Stones."

He was looking at her in awe, she realized. "Elementary," she murmured, and retrieved her wine from his tray. He laughed.

The rest was so simple, he was amazed that no one had done this many years ago. In Paducah they visited the county extension office, where they said they were photographers on the trail of anomalous plants, wildflowers out of place, and they were given maps that would have led them to colonies of mayapples, lady's slipper orchids, peltiphylum, and arisaena, and that directed them to two naturalized swatches of dieramas.

"With any luck, they might still be blooming," the young woman at the county office told them. "It's cutting it close, though. And it's illegal to pick them, you understand."

They assured her they would do no picking. Then they drove twenty-seven miles out of Paducah, parked at the side of the road, and started to hike. On one side corn was over their heads already; on the other tall cattails and sedges marked the start of the marsh. They skirted the marshy ground at first, then the trail led through the marsh, out again, and after two more miles, they came to a stop and stared. The angel's fishing rods covered the ground, three hundred feet deep and fifty feet or more wide. The marsh limited them in one direction, rocky ground in the other. The bright red flowers nodded and dipped and danced in the air.

"I'll be damned," Charlie said in a low voice. Constance reached for him and they stood holding hands, watching the angels dance.

Back at the car Charlie studied the map. "Let's leave the other one for tomorrow," he said. That trail was four and a half miles, too much walking for one day. "There's a state park somewhere . . . Ah, here. Let's explore. You want to drive?"

The next day they found they could drive on a one-lane dirt road part of the way to the other patch of angel's fishing rods. The road ended at a trail that made up the edge of the corn-fields. This was the trail they had marked on their 1904 map as a possible route the small group of men would have followed. Another trail led straight ahead through straggly corn. The ground was getting spongier; they had reached the marsh again. After another mile on foot they stopped to gaze at several acres of red flowers dancing in the breeze. Although the trail skirted the mass of flowers, they did not follow it any farther. The grave would be close to this end, they both knew. The dieramas were on their left, marsh on the right.

"Okay," Charlie said, pleased. "Okay. Now we need to hole up somewhere and plot out the next couple of weeks." He was grinning broadly.

Five days later, on a Saturday afternoon, he and Constance met again with Webber and Ortiz, this time on a bench in Central

Park. "Let's take a walk," Charlie said. A jazz band was playing. They edged in closer until the music was loud all around them.

"Have you decided about the sculpture?" he asked bluntly.

"We have," Webber said. "Together we will deliver it to a neutral party and let the decision come from him. Not someone from Mexico or Central or South America."

"And not connected with the Church," Ortiz added.

"Right. Okay. Now listen, and listen good; they might be getting a fix on us already. Webber, next Sunday night at nine you will go to an art-show opening. Go by taxi. Walk straight through to a sign that says 'Employees only' and enter. Two guys will be in there. One of them should say, 'Don't cry.' If no one says that, take off, enjoy the art, and go home. If he does, then you do exactly what he tells you. Without quibbling, without questions. Got it?"

"I'll have to check my calendar," Webber said, then nodded hastily. "Of course. I'll do it, exactly what you've said."

"Right." Charlie gave him the name of the gallery and its address. "Mr. Ortiz, on Sunday night you will arrange a dinner party at a certain restaurant. Get there by eight. At exactly nine, excuse yourself, apologize for having to leave, and make your way to the men's room in the basement. There will be two guys there, with the same message: 'Don't cry.' Follow directions exactly. No password, just leave, finish your dinner, go home."

Ortiz's eyes were shining. He grinned at Webber and nodded. "But of course."

"Okay. Can either of you arrange to have a private plane at Newark Airport that night?"

Webber said quickly, "It will be there. We're to be spirited away, aren't we? Where to?"

Charlie ignored his question. "When you get the pilot lined up, give him this number to call and tell him to ask for Butch. And tell him he's to do exactly what Butch says. Again, no questions, no quibbling. Just do exactly what he's told. Got it?" He handed Webber a slip of paper with a number where Brian would pick up the phone. "He's to call at seven on Sunday night. After seven-thirty no one will answer and the whole thing's off. And he's to talk to no one."

Both Webber and Ortiz looked like kids about to place a

whoopie cushion on the principal's chair. Charlie sighed. "Let's walk. There's more." A trumpet solo had silenced the crowd listening to the New Orleans jazz band.

They walked and stopped when the band got loud, and Charlie told them what else he wanted. Then they walked some more. Finally, Charlie said, "This is going to get pricey, but I plan to do exactly what you hired me to do: find the treasure and get it into your hands, without government interference, without appraisals, without Rob Rob. Are we going to haggle over expenses?"

"Four million dollars' worth?" Webber muttered.

"Nowhere near, but pricey."

Without hesitation Webber and Ortiz agreed not to question the price.

"Are you going to remember everything I've said? You want to go over it again?" They walked some more, and finally separated. On South Park Avenue Charlie made a thumbs-up gesture, certain that DeWilde's men had caught it, Rob Rob's crew had caught it, and Brian had caught it.

On Sunday night Charlie and Constance went to a party, a big, noisy affair, the sort of party where people drifted in and drifted out, where drinks and hors d'oeuvres were plentiful, where some coke was available. She was wearing a simple long black dress, very little makeup (as usual), and nice pearls. He was in a dark suit with a red tie. They knew a few of the people there and mingled, nibbled, sipped drinks. At ten minutes before ten Constance drifted down a hallway toward the bathroom. Another small room was opposite it. She entered the small room, and after only a second or two Charlie entered also. Another couple was already present. Swiftly, without speaking, Charlie and Constance began to strip off their clothes. The woman put on the black dress, which fitted her perfectly; she put on the pearls. Her hair was short, blond, sleek, her makeup exactly like Constance's. The effect was uncanny, Charlie thought, pulling a black turtleneck over his head. He put on jeans, and they were done. The other couple had become Constance and Charlie in five minutes.

At ten o'clock the other couple left the party by the back door and were picked up by a green Honda. This time four cars played tag with the Honda, and this time, although Sandy took a roundabout way, she made certain she lost none of them. She was silent all the way to La Guardia.

At ten-thirty, Constance, wearing a wig of permed blond hair and in a red spangly dress that left her back bare to the waist, leaned against a tall pale man who was running his fingers up and down her spine. He put his lips to her ear and whispered, "How did they look?"

She giggled and mock-pushed him away. "Perfect."

He began to draw her toward the door; she wobbled just a bit as they left the party. On the sidewalk, with her still leaning against him, he looked up and down the street, and at that moment a taxi turned the corner, came their way, and stopped. Two men and a woman, all laughing, got out. The woman said, "Hey, Drew, you leaving already? Hey, it's your party!"

"Duty calls," he said. "I'll be back." He put Constance in the taxi and got in beside her. The woman laughed, and the trio entered the building.

The taxi pulled away from the curb and Constance sat up straight. "They were absolutely perfect," she said.

"You put on a pretty good act yourself," Drew said. "You ever want a job, you know the rest."

He was Drew Anaxis—a patently made-up name that he had picked once when quite stoned—but he had grown to like it. He was a very good director. He had said sincerely to Charlie, "Gorilla theater! Shit, real gorilla theater! I love it!"

Ten minutes later Charlie left by way of the roof and a fire escape. This was the only dangerous part of the plan, he thought, walking on Tenth. After two blocks he got into a low black MG idling at the curb, with Brian at the wheel.

The rest stop on Interstate 287 was always busy, but that night it was busier than usual. A very large RV pulled in early that evening and parked. Two unmarked vans pulled in close to it and parked. Soon a little MG drove in. A farm truck carrying bales of straw was next. Then came a battered old Buick, closely followed by a taxi.

Webber emerged from the Buick and Ortiz from the farm

truck, both dressed in workmen's clothing; they entered the RV. Drew kissed Constance on the cheek and left again in the taxi to return to his party, flushed and triumphant. Charlie and Brian hitched the MG to the RV. The two men who had arrived in it went to the two vans, were admitted, and the vans drove away. The whole thing was done without conversation, without consultation.

Then, inside the RV, Charlie grinned at Constance. "You're a knockout in that outfit," he said. He looked at Ortiz, whose eyes were shining with excitement, and Webber, who was flushed. "You did a good job," he said. "This will be our home for the next few days. You'll find other clothes in the little closet back there. We're completely self-contained—shower, cooking facilities, toilet, everything. We can sleep six, but as you see, we are five, so it won't be too uncomfortable. Now I advise you to rest if you can. We have a long drive ahead of us."

"Where are we going?" Webber asked, almost timidly.

"Tell you when we get there," Charlie said. "I'll start driving, then Brian, then Constance. We'll stop for gas, and that's all. When we stop, Brian will take care of things; no one else will get out. And when we stop, keep the curtains drawn. Okay? Questions?"

They had plenty of questions, he knew, but at the moment, they were too intimidated, or too awed, or too *something* to ask them. He went to the driver's seat and studied the console a moment, turned the key, and started. He was humming softly.

Charlie drove into the state park outside Paducah the next night at ten. Constance was in the passenger seat beside him. She patted his leg when he turned off the key. End of act one, they were thinking.

The next morning they explored the park. They were in the section reserved for trailers, campers, and RVs, and the spaces on their right and left were vacant. Charlie had reserved them, too, for the vans. A small group of young people had a spot closer to the river, and they were already splashing and laughing by nine in the morning; another RV was several spaces away in the other direction. Charlie and Brian unhitched the MG.

At ten the vans drove in. Webber went to one to consult with his crew, and Ortiz went to the other one; Brian huddled with his two associates briefly. Some of the diggers had on T-shirts printed with the words *Bill's Bowlers* and a set of pins. Their story was that they were on their way to a bowling tournament, and in no rush to get there.

"Okay," Charlie said, after Webber, Ortiz, and Brian returned to the RV. "We take the two men with dowsing rods. I'll drive the MG, and Brian will drive the van and follow me." Both Webber and Ortiz were nearly quivering with excitement as they hurried to a van and got in. "Inventory check out?" Charlie asked Brian; he nodded. If it hadn't, Charlie would have sent someone back to Paducah to complete the shopping list.

"So, let's do it," Charlie said; he and Constance got in the MG and he pulled out of the park with the van following. "How do they strike you?" he asked Constance.

She had watched Brian teach them both how to play pinochle. "Ortiz didn't care one way or the other; his heart wasn't in it. But Webber's an aggressive player, aggressive to the point of carelessness. He wants to win. I think it's all that football in his past."

He grinned. Soon they were at the turnoff; he signalled and made the turn onto the narrow dirt road. It was a tight fit for the van; he had thought it wouldn't be able to drive in as far as the MG, and he had been right. Well, he thought, that's why Brian was driving it. He'd stay with the van; the others would have to walk an extra mile, and that was appropriate, he decided. Would they go the extra mile for the loot? When he stopped and got out to tell them the bad news, he kept a straight face. It was a sultry hot day already.

"We can drive," Webber said. "Who's going to notice if a few cornstalks get knocked down?"

"You know the ground rules," Charlie said. "When we leave this place, it's going to look as if no one's been here since the Flood. Come on, out with you."

Driving again, he could see them in the rearview mirror, two men with equipment in cases, Webber and Ortiz trudging on the narrow track.

"Don't laugh," Constance said.

"I'm not laughing."

"Oh, yes you are."

They came to the trail where even the MG couldn't go, waited for the others to catch up, and then walked the rest of the distance. The day grew hotter, a sullen kind of heat without a breeze, and so humid that sweat simply piled up on itself. Even Constance was sweaty and flushed, and she never looked anything but cool. No one was speaking when they reached the beginning of the field of red dieramas, which were in motion even though the air seemed completely still.

Webber gazed ahead miserably; he was not in good shape, apparently, or was unduly sensitive to the heat. But Ortiz exhaled and said something under his breath in Spanish, then in English: "Dancing angels."

"Right," Charlie said. "Okay, the drill is that we four stay on the trail, and the two with the gizmos start looking. Start close to the trail and work in, guys, and try not to trample any more than you have to."

They began to unpack their gear, which looked very complicated and heavy with shoulder harnesses and double handles. Charlie had had a metal detector as a kid; it had weighed less than a pound. He had found some change, an old rusty watch, two spoons, and then he had sold the thing to another kid for two dollars, and had come out ahead. For a minute or two he watched the two pros, and did not envy them for a second; then he joined Constance in the shade of ten-foot-tall cattails.

The dieramas were like daffodils, Constance had said; after they bloomed, the leaves would gradually turn brown and wither until the following year. A lot of grass was growing in the field; it would hide their traces, he hoped. Grass was tough; it would spring back after the first rain.

Webber came near and said truculently, "I thought you said you found the graves. This could take a week."

Charlie didn't bother to respond.

"Why here? What led you here?" Webber demanded.

Ortiz said, "The Spanish letter. See, it took all of us to name the elephant."

Webber looked at him in disgust and turned to watch the two men with the metal detectors. They were moving with painful slowness, every step deliberate, measured, keeping their eyes on dials or something.

It took over an hour before one of them raised his hand. Charlie got to his feet to watch as the men consulted, then began to sweep their detectors back and forth in a small area. Webber started to move toward them; Charlie caught his arm.

"They know what to do," he said. "Leave them alone."

After another few minutes both men looked at the watching group and nodded. Working together, one using the detector, they marked the area with thin stakes that vanished in the grass and leaves but would show up clearly under infrared light. Then they rejoined the group on the trail.

"Three and a half feet down," one of them said, repacking his equipment. "It'll be a cinch."

They started the hike back to the van.

At the MG they separated. "You guys go on back to the park and cool down," Charlie said. "We'll be along in an hour or so. No point in rousing suspicion by going out together, returning together."

"I'll have a swim," Ortiz said. "A long, cool swim."

In the little car, Charlie turned on the air conditioner and drew in a long breath. "We'll give them time to get out and take off," he said, his head back, eyes closed, relishing the cool air. "You brought the binoculars, didn't you?"

She had, a set for each of them.

They drove to the end of the state road and parked, then walked to a wooded area overlooking the Mississippi River. They both began scanning the river. Downstream and on the other side was the houseboat, a crew member on deck, no one else in sight. Farther down was a fishing boat, apparently anchored; Charlie grinned. The boat had an antenna—not the usual sort of thing for a boat of that type. It was rocking in the wake of a tug pushing a string of cargo vessels riding low in the water. In the other direction he spotted another houseboat, smaller than the one at the dock, but much fancier. On the deck he made out Rob Rob and two other men, all stripped down to their shorts, sitting under a canopy, drinking. Rob Rob's shorts had big, bright Georgia O'Keeffe poppies. Another fishing boat was closer to the Kentucky side; it too had a peculiar antenna. Charlie laughed.

Bill's bowlers had a cookout that evening; they sang and played guitars for an hour or so, then they went inside the two vans and were quiet. The other RV, occupied by a retired couple in their seventies, became dark by ten. The group near the river stayed up a little longer, but by eleven the park was completely dark and quiet.

The plan was to take both vans, leaving Constance and Brian in the RV, and be in and back out before dawn. There was an opaque tent to raise; they would need light to work by and couldn't risk being seen. They would also need a nursery cart with a sheet of canvas to haul stuff in and out; tarps for the dirt; pallets on runners for the tarps, to avoid mashing the surrounding plants too much; and two big bags of pumice rock to put back in the grave to keep it level when refilled. Pumice, Charlie had insisted, because it would fill the space, and it weighed very little. Let future archaeologists puzzle it out. First they would section off the area, dig out the plants, and put them aside; then they would dig the graves, retrieve the items, refill the graves, and replace the plants, all while trying not to leave any blatant traces of activity.

They started at eleven-thirty. Try to get some sleep, Charlie had said to Constance; he had napped several hours earlier. She stretched out on one of the narrow beds, closed her eyes, and after a time actually dozed. Across the RV Brian was snoring softly. It was one o'clock. She dozed again. Two. Three. At four-thirty she heard the first van arrive.

"Brian," she said softly. He came awake fast. Then, very quietly, men opened the van doors and heaved two large, dirty bundles into the RV; they smelled like earth, like graves. Webber and Ortiz were right behind them, exultant. Charlie, following, looked exhausted.

"Bed," he ordered, when Webber started to move toward a bundle. "We'll get to it later. Brian will be up and awake to keep an eye on things."

He grinned at Constance, then fell into one of the little beds, and to all appearances was asleep instantly. After a moment Webber and Ortiz also groped their way to their beds. This time when Constance closed her eyes she fell into a deep sleep.

The material encasing the treasure had long ago rotted away; they had found the pieces and bones all mixed together, and the pieces were encrusted with dirt. But even so, Constance thought, watching the division, even so, it was obvious that this was a priceless treasure trove. Webber was holding a solid-gold cross, eighteen inches high, inlaid with precious stones. He put it on his canvas wrap. Ortiz was holding a small gold raft with three human figures on it, intricately worked, one holding a spear. He put it on his side without dispute. A silver chalice with a gold band inlaid with emeralds—Webber's. A grotesque gold figure of something inhuman—Ortiz's. A few pieces were disputed and laid aside for the time being. But for the most part there was little disagreement until they started on the pieces they had set aside.

They were arguing about a footed silver bowl when Charlie said, "I suggest you settle this in the next ten minutes, or we won't get to the other site and locate the grave before dark. And I intend to be out of here tomorrow."

Webber said, "You can have it, then."

Ortiz put the bowl on his side. They finished soon after that and carefully wrapped their items in canvas. Two men from the diggers came to stay with the bundles, and Brian stayed with them. He was offering to teach them to play pinochle when the group left the RV. They gathered the men with their metal detectors, took one of the vans, and drove to the other site, where they left the driver behind and walked in.

It was as hot as it had been the day before, and the hike was longer, but it didn't take as long to find the grave this time.

That night at dinner, Charlie said, "It isn't going to take all eight guys to dig this one. That thing's only three feet down. I guess Abe was tired of digging graves. We'll take one van, two diggers from each side, one driver. He can't park on that road at that time of night, so he'll have to come back to the park entrance and wait. He can check after two hours, then every hour until we show up at the trail. Let the others get some sleep."

They left at eleven-thirty, as before. Again they stationed two diggers in the RV, and Brian stayed with them—the diggers watching the RV, watching the bundles, and watching each other, and Brian watching them. Constance knew sleep was impossible. She turned her back on them all and dozed in snatches.

At three-thirty they were back. The cask was intact; the hinges had corroded and fused, sealing it. It was filthy, with dirt that seemed to have melded with the teak.

"We'll leave it until daylight," Charlie said tiredly. Neither Ortiz nor Webber seemed satisfied with that, so Charlie nodded to Brian, who slipped out of the RV and returned with his two men, the two who had driven in with the diggers in the vans. "These gentlemen are detectives," Charlie said. "They are armed. Brian and I both need sleep, and I suggest sleep as a good idea for you guys, too. They'll guard your box." He stretched out on his bed. After a moment, Webber lay down, then Ortiz did. It was a long time before Constance fell asleep, surrounded as she was by a pack of men with guns.

At nine the diggers carried the two big bundles to the vans. One of them produced a crowbar and then Webber, Ortiz, and Constance watched Charlie force the box open. Webber made a choking sound, and Ortiz was whispering to himself.

A golden head lay on a decayed fragment of cloth. The head was clean and perfect. The eyes were dark green, jade perhaps, with pupils of black onyx, and on both cheeks flawless cabochon emeralds were inlaid. The emeralds diminished in size as they descended.

"*Christ's Tears,*" Webber said hoarsely.

"No!" Ortiz cried. "You saw the images of our gods—grotesqueries, monstrosities, because the gods are grotesque and monstrous. No, this is no god. This is a man, a human being. You saw the photograph of the crystal skull, carved from a single quartz crystal; this is the companion piece. Not a god! A weeping man. Perhaps he weeps because of the cruelty of the gods." Tears were on his cheeks. Reverently he touched the gleaming head.

"Don't touch it!" Webber screamed. He lunged at Ortiz, and almost casually Constance reached out, caught his wrist, and put him down on the floor.

"You had no intention of handing it over to a neutral party, did you?" Charlie asked, just as casually. Webber, on the floor, looked stunned and furious.

"Take it, Mr. Ortiz. Get in your van and go. Remember, Rob Rob has a contract with you two. I wouldn't rush into print about this. Six months, a year. That's plenty of time, and you don't ever have to say a word about how you came upon it. I'll need a couple of days to tidy up around the edges, so stay out of sight two, three days. Okay?"

Webber scrambled to his feet, looked at Constance, and edged away from her toward the door. "He can't! We have an agreement. You can't give it to him!"

"I just did," Charlie said. He nodded to Ortiz. "I suggest you beat it, like right now. Can you carry it alone?"

Ortiz looked stricken. He opened his mouth; no sound emerged. He lifted the head in the box and backed toward the door. Webber tried to grab him, but this time Charlie was in the way, and Charlie was holding his old police revolver. Ortiz fled. Seconds later they heard a van drive away fast. It was followed swiftly by a pounding on the RV door.

"Brian and his guys are out there keeping the peace," Charlie said. "I suggest you let your guys know things are okay before war breaks out. You know how it is with peacekeepers—they seem to end up in the thick of things no matter what they intend."

Webber rushed to the door and yanked it open. His diggers were amassed outside the RV; Brian's men were at the van, leaning against it lazily.

"Tell them to relax," Charlie said. "Then close the door."

"I'll be out in a couple of minutes," Webber said in a thick voice that was hardly recognizable.

"What you're going to do," Charlie said then, "is write a letter to a priest, a bishop, anyone like that in the vicinity, and tell him to keep your newly arrived van under guard until you get there, and to feed and bed down the men who brought it. Relax, Webber. As far as I could tell, you got the best of the deal overall. You ended up with most of the loot."

Webber shook his head. "You think I'd cooperate in any way with you after this?"

"You have a choice," Charlie said thoughtfully. "See, I said I intend to take off, and I mean it. Today. Brian's guys can take that van to the nearest dump and leave it, for all I care. Or they can take the stuff to a pawnshop. The van, this rolling house, the little car—we're all leaving. You and your guys, you can all stay here. Or you can write the letter, tell your men where to take the van, and eventually go there yourself to explain things. Your choice."

Webber's eyes narrowed. "I'll bring charges against you, Meiklejohn. I'll see you in prison for this."

Charlie laughed. "You going to tell DeWilde about the treasure? Tell Rob Rob? He thinks he has a contract with you, remember? He could get sore."

Webber glared at him with hatred. Abruptly he sat down.

"Louisville? You know anyone in Louisville? Or St. Louis? It shouldn't be too far away," Charlie said.

After a long pause Webber muttered, "Louisville."

Half an hour later the second van drove away, with Brian's two men as passengers as far as Louisville. "They'll make sure it gets there okay," Brian said to Webber, who was too furious to respond. As soon as the van was gone, Charlie said it was time for some lunch.

"When are we leaving?" Webber demanded. "You can't hold me; that's kidnapping."

"I'm not holding you," Charlie said, rummaging in the small refrigerator. "You can take off whenever you want. Long hike to Paducah, though."

At three o'clock he said it was time to go. "We'll drive the MG, and you can follow with Brian," he said cheerfully. He drove west, toward the Mississippi again, and stopped at the same place as before, near the woods. Brian pulled in after him, and he and Webber got out and came to the MG.

"Now what?" Webber snapped.

"Show time," Charlie said. "There are extra binoculars in the RV, if you want to watch."

Armed with binoculars, they walked in among the trees to find good theater seats. The river was brown; river traffic was up, with two strings of cargo vessels in sight, both heading south. The fancy little houseboat was in place; today Rob Rob was not in sight. The two funny fishing boats were also in place, to all appearances unmanned. No one was in sight on the big houseboat at dock. Charlie scanned the low, eroded bluff behind the dock: ocher-colored mud with no vegetation, gaps here and there, a trickle of water flowing in one of them. He knew exactly where to watch for the actors; he had mapped that side precisely, had told them where to go, where to dig, when to return.

Then the mime show started. The other Charlie and Constance appeared in one of the gaps. She was wearing a wide-brimmed straw hat with a pink streamer, he had a sombrero. Charlie grinned. Maybe he'd buy a sombrero; he liked the way it looked on him.

Behind the first two, Drew slouched along. He had darkened his skin, and had dreadlocks now. He was muddy from head to foot; each step seemed an effort, the mud was so thick on his boots. Now men dragging a makeshift sled came into view. On the sled were bulky bundles of something wrapped in mud. They struggled with it. At the houseboat, four men grasped handles, lifted a stretcher from the sled, and staggered aboard. A second group was arriving close behind them, toiling with another sled and another stretcher; this group was followed by the other Ortiz and the other Webber. Everyone was coated with mud.

Drew went to the rear of the houseboat, where he began hosing off his legs and boots. The others followed him. Someone yelled something; Drew opened two gates on the fencing round the rear deck and began hosing mud off the flooring into the river. The men with the stretchers made their way to the same area and turned the bundles off the stretchers, onto the floor. After that it was a bit hard to follow the action.

The houseboat was tilting slightly with all that weight suddenly on the rear deck: thirteen people, a ton of junk. The deck was awash with muddy water; the bundles were slimy with wet clay. One of the men rose slowly from tipping the bundle off the sled, and was pushed down by someone else. He came back up swinging. Someone else pushed someone else; someone slipped in the mud and went down. Both bundles began to slide, but no one noticed. Drew was still holding the hose; he began to throw water all around wildly, apparently trying to get to the faucet to turn it off. Other people fell; there was more shoving and pushing and punching. The bundles slid inexorably toward the open gates. Too late the other Webber made a lunge for one, and might have inadvertently given it a nudge instead of stopping its momentum. It slipped over the side, and the second one followed. Everyone froze in a tableau of horror.

The fancy little houseboat had begun to move toward the big one. Then engines were cut; it drifted, stopped. Rob Rob was at the rail, again wearing only the shorts with blazing red poppies. His face was turned away, but his body language was eloquent. He raised both fists, pounded the rail, turned, and staggered. Two men tried to catch him; he was too heavy. He hit the deck, and one man ran inside; the other was trying to get something into Rob Rob's mouth. The houseboat turned and picked up speed, running back to Cairo.

"My, my," Charlie murmured, and turned his attention to the two fishing boats. One was speeding toward the dock, faster than fishing boats usually moved; the other one was holding its position. He could see DeWilde on the forward deck, speaking into a telephone.

When Charlie looked at the houseboat again, the other Webber, Ortiz, and the captain were at the rail, the gates were closed, and various diggers were sitting about dejectedly. The captain was shaking his head. The other Charlie and Constance vanished into a cabin, Webber and Ortiz went somewhere out of sight, the captain said something to a crew member, and the crew began preparations to untie the boat at its mooring. Within minutes the houseboat was pulling away from the dock; it made a long, slow turn and started north.

Charlie put his arm around Constance's shoulders, grinning. Webber and Brian moved from behind the trees where they had been watching. Brian looked like a merry jack-o'-lantern, his face split by a mammoth grin.

"My God," Webber said. "My God, those people! Who are those people? It was like seeing a doppelgänger!"

Charlie gave Constance a final squeeze and they started back toward the car and the RV. "Mr. Webber," he said, "there are some things about this whole operation you'll never know. But now you know what happened on that houseboat. I suggest that you and Ortiz get together over a beer and you let him in on it, just in case anyone ever asks a question."

They stopped at the MG. "DeWilde will have a crew check out where the digging happened over there," Charlie said. "They'll find that you folks exhumed everything, bones, treasure, every scrap. He'll have divers in the river in a day or two, no doubt. If Rob Rob is still capable of doing anything, he'll have his own divers out there. You might want to pretend an interest for a time. Or not. Suit yourself. Just stay out of sight for a couple of days, give all those folks time to fade out of sight. DeWilde and Rob Rob will be busy, so they won't be on your case."

Webber looked disbelieving. "They think the items are in the river," he said, as if he had to sort this out in his head. Then, "What was in those bundles? What will their divers find?"

Charlie laughed and opened the passenger door of the MG. "Rocks, dirt, mud. A scrap of burlap. Who knows what's in that river?" He handed the keys to Constance. "You want to drive? It's a fun little car." Then he said to Webber, "Brian will take you to Louisville. I'll send a bill in a few days."

Webber turned to leave, then he swung around again and held out his hand. "Meiklejohn, thanks. I think I've been witness to a miracle. Thanks."

Constance got behind the wheel and adjusted the seat, the mirror. Brian left with Webber in the RV, and Constance pulled out onto the road.

"Another fifty grand coming," Charlie commented happily. He started to hum.

But Constance knew it hadn't been for the money. She had watched Rob Rob collapse. She knew why Charlie had done it, and she did not say a word.

An Imperfect Gift

1

When Al Gruber called Charlie Meiklejohn for an appointment, Charlie's first thought was that someone at the Gruberhaus restaurant had sticky fingers; his second thought was that he would turn Al over to a Manhattan investigator and that would be that. He had no intention of making the two-hour-plus drive to the city. He had suggested as much, but Al had insisted that he needed someone he could trust—Charlie. No one else would do. And now he was here, on Charlie's back patio in upper New York State, sipping coffee and pretending to relax in the September sunshine.

There had been a light frost during the past week, and Charlie had started to put away the outdoor furniture, but Constance had said no, not yet. They were due a nice Indian summer; considering what a cold wet year they had endured, that was no more than simple justice. And she had been right, of course. The weather was very fine. Asters were blooming, roses were budding again for a riot of fall blossoms, and the dahlias were showing off in a profusion of gaudy colors. Very fine, indeed.

But Al Gruber was having trouble coming to the point of the visit. They had discussed his sister, Bernice, and his brother, Daniel; his father, who was in his seventies; the restaurant business, which was quite good. Charlie had known the Grubers all his life, had played with the three kids, and the one who had died of polio. He had eaten more meals than he could count in the Gruber kitchen, and later in the restaurant, which was a family business with an enviable reputation.

"Charlie," Constance had said thoughtfully when he told her that Al was dropping in, "today is your day to cook, remember. Do you want to cook for a chef like Al?" Because the answer was no, he was getting impatient now as Al continued to reminisce about the good old days.

Al Gruber was fifty-two, florid-faced, with a receding hairline. His hair had been quite dark, now it was streaked with white; it was hard to tell if he would go totally white-haired or totally bald first. It appeared to be a dead heat. He was a little overweight, but Charlie couldn't remember a time when he hadn't been a little overweight, and otherwise, he looked good, if troubled.

Finally Al set down his cup and drew in a long breath. "It's funny, Charlie. All the way up here I went over this mess again and again, trying to find the best way to get it all out. Know what I mean? It's complicated."

"Start at the beginning, go to the end, and stop," Charlie murmured.

"That's the only way I can tell you so it makes any sense," Al said. He leaned back in his chair and gazed at the barn at the back of the property. "Just bear with me a little bit. Okay?" He didn't wait for a response.

"You know my father escaped from Nazi Germany back in the thirties when he was just a kid. If you know that much, and about everyone does, you know as much as I've ever known until recently, but these last couple of years, it seems his mind is doing tricks, like he can't remember last week, or even yesterday sometimes, but his early years in Germany are clear as springwater."

He took a sip of coffee, then continued. "Father, his little sister Hulga, and my grandparents Kurt and Anya Gruber, lived in Hanover. Kurt and Anya were part of a group that smuggled people out of Germany in those years; Anya had relatives in Holland, and they were a link to the outside world. From Hanover, over the countryside, across the Wester Ems, and into Holland, that was one of the routes they used. Grandfather's sister had emigrated to America years before and she had begged him to get out, to bring his family to the States, but it was a hard call. He and Grandmother had friends, the restaurant, relatives. . . . It was a hard decision, one he put off too long. He would instruct others on what to pack, how to pack stuff, important papers in waterproof pouches taped to their legs, and to wear loose, dark pants. For the women to sew the family jewels, if they had any, into petticoats and wear them, and dark clothes on top. Convert everything they could to gold or silver. Like that. But more important, he had access to food and could provide a little cheese, sausage, things he could scrounge from the restaurant."

His voice was almost without inflection as he told the story; his gaze remained on the barn.

Kurt and Anya had younger friends, the Waldmans. Marlene Waldman worked in the restaurant and Kelmut had worked there in the summers when he wasn't in school. He became an assistant economics professor, penniless, of course; they had two children, younger than the Gruber children, and Kelmut was terrified that he would be conscripted. He decided to flee with his family, and Kurt and Anya knew it was time for them to escape if they were ever going to. The underground resistance was being infiltrated with traitors; travel permits were hard to get; gasoline and food rationing made travel a nightmare. And everyone knew a broader war was coming. They made their preparations. Kurt began to stash food under Kelmut's house, a few miles out in the country. Anya sewed the family jewelry into the petticoats; Kurt melted down the family silverware and cast small ingots that could be sewn into hidden pockets in his coat; they had a target date, the first week of August, a time when the restaurant closed for holiday and their absence would not arouse suspicion.

But late one night in June the phone rang, and when Kurt answered, the caller said, "I'm sorry. It's a wrong number." Now Al paused and lifted his coffee cup. It was empty and Constance refilled it. Neither she nor Charlie had stirred as Al told his story. She felt immobilized, transfixed, seeing in her mind the frightened family, feeling their dread.

"All right," Al said. "So they had been betrayed; that was the signal to run immediately, to grab whatever they could and run. Grandfather taped the papers to his own leg; Grandmother put on her petticoat with the jewels. Then Grandfather taped a picture to my father's leg. A strange thing to take with them, but it had been in the family for a long time, a painting of the first Gruberhaus." He looked at Constance and shrugged slightly. "Four generations of Grubers, all in the restaurant business, including us now. Anyway, they beat it in their car. They were fairly prosperous, but even so, they had enough gas to drive just a few miles before they had to abandon the car and continue on foot. They were heading for Kelmut Waldman's house, their supply of food, and to warn Kelmut that they had to go now, not in August. But when they got within sight of the tiny farmhouse, it was in flames, and they were afraid the Waldmans had already been arrested. Grandmother cried because they had not brought any food with them, and now they couldn't go near their supplies.

"They walked across the country, and when they could find crops growing, they stole food. It was raining, they were wet, cold, starving, traveling at night, hiding by day, and toward the end, Grandmother collapsed. Grandfather and my father, who was fourteen, carried her after that."

Al stopped speaking, and no one else broke the silence until he started again. "They made it to the rendezvous point, and to their relief the Waldmans were already there, and they had food. Another couple had made it; two others had not shown up and never did. No one could cross the border on foot; it was too dangerous, too heavily patrolled. What they did was hide in a sand and mud cave until the tidal bore on the Wester Ems coincided with the dark of the moon, and then a boat would arrive from the Holland side. Such brave Dutch men, they knew about tidal bores, about inlets and rivers. When the surge flowed back to the sea, they rode the outgoing tide back to the Dutch side. No oars, just a rudder; they didn't dare risk the sound of oars slapping the water. They trusted the tide to carry them."

His voice thickened and he cleared his throat, drank coffee, then went on. "They waited for the tide; the boat came and they got in, but their betrayal had been complete. Suddenly, as they crouched in the bottom of the boat, under canvas, there were searchlights, machine guns . . . screams. The boat began to swing around, uncontrolled, and it started to sink."

He paused once more, and then finished this part swiftly. "I brought a tape we recorded of my father's account. For now let me say only that he managed to drag himself ashore on the Holland side. And there he passed out, and was found the next day by the Dutch; he was naked, a deep gash in his head, delirious. But he was saved, and for years he believed he was the only survivor. He was cared for by his relatives in Goningen, and six months later he joined his aunt in New York."

The sun had dipped behind the barn and shadows were lengthening, darkening. One by one the three cats had appeared, languorous from sunbathing, eyeing the table greedily.

"Let's go inside," Constance said. "I think a drink's in order, a little cheese or something." No one objected.

In the house, as if on automatic pilot, Al Gruber sat at the dinette table, more at home in the kitchen than he would be in the living room, Charlie suspected.

Then, as Constance rustled up some snack food, and Charlie got out an assortment of bottles, Al said, "I don't want to take much more of your time. I'll try to wrap this up. Just bourbon, water on the side, Charlie."

Charlie fixed the drinks and took them to the table.

Al resumed his story as soon as they were all seated. "When my father's aunt died she left him a little money, not much, but some. She had made him go to school, but all he could think of was starting a new Gruberhaus. Six tables in those days. He worked hard and every spare dime went into the business. You know, Charlie. You saw how it was when we were kids. We all worked. But things were okay. Then, back in nineteen seventy-two, he saw an article in the newspaper: Henrik Wall's death was reported; his survivors, a son Eric, a daughter Greta, some grandchildren. Father was overjoyed; they were his old friends, the Waldmans. His father had been Erik's godfather; Kelmut and Marlene had worked in their restaurant, and they and little Gerde had survived, after all. We tried to reason with him, different names, people of wealth, position, not his old friends, but he knew what he knew. Erik, he said, looked exactly like his father. You know how he is, Charlie. Gets an idea in his head, bingo, no room for alterations. He knew. So, he said, they changed their names; many refugees did, with cause in most cases. Nothing would do but for him to write a letter to his old childhood friend Erik Waldman, who was now called Eric Wall."

Al sighed deeply and shook his head. "In time, a long time, he got a stiff little note back, thanking him for his condolences and saying that he was mistaken in their identity. So sorry. Period." He drank his bourbon down straight, followed it with a sip of water.

Charlie and Constance exchanged looks; hers meant, What

is it all leading up to? His meant, I can't tell him to close the curtain and leave now. Neither said a word aloud.

Al glanced at his watch, confirmed the time with the wall clock, and said briskly, "All right. Now, skip forward. What do they say, fast-forward? That's it. Fast-forward to last spring. Bernice and our father—he lives with her and her family—were watching a television show about mansions, palaces, castles, that sort of thing, in America. Suddenly Father jumped up yelling, 'That's it! There's the country inn!' Bernice was scared. Father is seventy-six and, as I said, his mind plays tricks with his memory. She was afraid he was having a stroke or something. He was crying and yelling that it was the country inn, this magnificent estate on the Hudson was a country inn. To calm him down, she promised to order the video and let him watch it again. Meanwhile, he began rummaging through boxes, through trunks, and one day he found what he had been looking for. An old faded photograph, a daguerreotype that his aunt had left him, a picture of his grandfather and grandmother and a bunch of others in front of a small thatched-roof building. A country inn. The first Gruberhaus in the village of Hanover. Not much of the building is shown; it was a picture of the people, but you can see part of the inn."

Charlie did not sigh; he knew he didn't sigh, but Al gave him an apologetic smile and opened both hands palm up. "I'm sorry, but this is part of it. The video arrived and we all watched it, fast-forwarding past the Hearst castle, past the du Pont and Rockefeller estates, past Monticello, until Father said, Stop, watch. And we did. We were looking at the interior of an estate perched over the Hudson River. The show was mostly about the architecture, the gardens and statuary, with a woman leading the camera here and there. She goes into this room and the camera takes a look all around, but she's walking straight across toward a fireplace. There's a lot of art on the wall, not in focus or anything. She begins to turn around to point to something, the camera zooms in on her, and Father yelled again, 'Stop the film!' Then we inched back and forth until he said to stop again, and there on the wall was a painting that looked very much like his old photograph of the first Gruberhaus."

This time Charlie did speak. But gently. "Al, there must be hundreds, thousands of paintings and photographs of old thatched-roof buildings, and to my eye they *all* look very much alike. What's the point?"

"That's the problem, Charlie. Now we grow near the purpose of this *professional* call. We want you to go to that house on the Hudson River and get a very good, very sharp picture of that painting."

Charlie nearly choked on bourbon he had just started to swallow.

"Because, if it's the same, it belongs to my father. That's the painting that his father taped to his leg for their flight from Germany. It now hangs in the home of Erik Waldman, who calls himself Eric Wall."

Al held up his hand in a commanding way. "Let me tell you one more family story. The first Gruberhaus was opened by my great-grandfather, Hermann Gruber, in 1860, or thereabouts. Years later, twenty years or more, a group of travelers arrived, intending to stay only for a night, but one of them arrived feverish and ill. He remained for many days and Hermann and his wife cared for him. When he became stronger, he painted a picture of their inn and called it *A Country Inn*. Hermann was very pleased and wanted no other payment for the interval the guest had lingered in the inn, and that was just as well since the traveler had very little money. Then he happened to see the painter start to paint over the picture, and he grabbed his arm and pulled him away, demanding to know what he was doing, why. There was by then a white swatch on the lower right corner. The painter explained that he had ruined the picture, that he had intended a perfect gift and instead it was imperfect, not fit to give to his benefactors. Hermann stood between him and the painting and demanded that he leave it alone, just sign it, and he and his wife would forever treasure it. The painter refused to sign it, but finally he wrote on the back of the canvas instead. What he wrote was, 'You comforted me in my distress, you fed me when I hungered, you restored me, and, in return, to my shame, I present you with an imperfect gift.' "

Al shrugged. "Flowery, maybe, but it was heartfelt. Then he left and never came that way again. My father grew up studying that painting that hung in his family's living room. He knew the story, how treasured it was, almost like a holy icon. And he carried it, a link to his own past, from Hanover to his encounter with the Wester Ems. It is his."

They had done all the proper things, Al said then. A professional photographer had isolated and enhanced the picture, enlarged it, but what he had not been able to do was see through the head of the woman who had conducted the tour of the mansion. And her head obscured the lower right-hand corner of the painting. They needed a photograph of the entire thing, and then they could decide what steps to take to recover it.

"Erik denied my father once, in 1972, and there's no reason to believe that he would change his mind and admit to the past. If we inquire, he could easily substitute something for that picture, something similar, and say get lost. And once my father is gone, there won't be anyone to make the claim, to give the true history of the painting."

Charlie was watching condensation run crazily down the side of his glass. He traced one of the tracks with his fingertip, and, watching it, he asked softly, "What's the punch line, Al? Not just a painting, is it?"

"No," Al said, just as softly. "The artist refused to sign the painting, but he signed his sentimental inscription on the back of it. He wrote: 'To my friend, Herr Gruber, Vincent van Gogh.' "

2

That night they studied the two pictures under a strong light in the dining room. Using tracing paper, Constance had outlined the Gruber clan who had posed for the daguerreotype, all caught in stony expressions, poses held so long they had started to look pained, or even like painted dolls designed to frighten small children. Al had pointed to various family members, naming them when he could, but he didn't know them all. His father had been a child, as wooden as any of the adults, his eyes bulging somewhat, as if he had been biting his cheek to keep from moving, keep from smiling. With the tracing for a guide, she had cut out an opaque silhouette and carefully taped it in place to screen out the people, to let her and Charlie concentrate on the building better. She had done the same thing to the photograph made from the video of the painting in the Wall mansion. The woman in that picture was in profile, her arm raised, pointing to ornate marble molding, on her way to a mammoth fireplace of green marble streaked with gold. The painting was partly obscured by her face.

Part of a timbered building was in the family portrait, heavy black timbers from the look of them, and part of a thatched roof, flowers, the edge of a shuttered window, little more than that.

"Flowers look the same," Charlie murmured.

"Hollyhocks, sunflowers. He was mad about sunflowers in his later years."

"Everything's so brown, no golden flowers, red roses, just shades of brown."

"The window looks the same, and the thatch."

"They all looked like that." He stood up and rubbed his back. "Could be, I guess."

"Or not," she said.

Charlie had asked Al a lot of questions, and then had said soberly, "You know as well as I do that something like this could drag out through the courts for decades. Proving provenance is caviar and champagne for attorneys."

"That's why we came to you, Charlie, to see that it doesn't drag out forever. Our father couldn't bear it. When he began to recover from his ordeal, he had nightmares; then he started a new life in America and gradually the nightmares went away. Ever since he saw that picture on television, he's had the nightmares again. He's in a hurricane, something like that, with the wind driving rain in his face so hard he's blinded, and choking. And he can hear Hulga, his little sister, crying out for Mama, for Papa, then for him, for Franz. But he can't get to her. The wind, water, something keeps pushing him back, and she cries out for him to help. Then he wakes up in a cold sweat. He's an old man, he can't stand much of that."

As he prepared to leave then, he said, "Don't commit yourself now. Think about it, how to resolve it. You have the video, the pictures, a tape of my father's voice telling his own story; whatever help we can provide, we will. Think about it, Charlie. Give me a call."

Now, leaving the pictures side by side on the table, they went to the living room, Charlie to his Morris chair, where their orange cat, Candy, claimed his lap, and Constance to the wing chair. She watched Brutus terrorize Ashcan into retreating when he tried to take her lap; Brutus claimed it, and Ashcan decided he needed a bath and proceeded to clean himself. "Wimp," she said under her breath.

"We need to hire a cat lap, or else get rid of one of them," Charlie said.

She nodded. "We could hire a helicopter, land on the lawn, say we just dropped by for a visit."

Charlie didn't even blink at the change of subject. "I was thinking along the lines of skydiving in."

"Or take a canoe out on the Hudson, scale the cliff to the property, and enter."

"Apply for jobs, butler and maid, maybe."

"We have to remember tranquilizer darts for the dogs."

"What dogs?"

"Big ones, trace their ancestry all the way back to the original Hound of the Baskervilles." Charlie grinned.

Neither of them suggested that they listen to Franz Gruber's tape-recorded voice recounting his ordeal. Not that night. What they needed was a good look at the original painting, and a sharp, complete photograph of it, front and back, she thought glumly, and without arousing anyone's suspicion that that was what they were after. The two pictures on the dining room table were tantalizingly alike, but that wasn't good enough. What was in the lower right-hand corner of the original; what, if anything, was written on the back?

When Al spoke about his father's nightmares, she had seen Charlie's eyes become almost lusterless for a moment, and she had felt a jolt. He had been a fireman, she had been working toward her doctorate in psychology when they were newlyweds; he had moved up to arson investigations, and she had earned her degree and started teaching and doing clinical research at Columbia. Later, his nightmares had started. He was always in a long hallway with a fire roaring at his back, racing toward him. Every door he passed had a red-hot knob, and he kept trying to go forward, get away, escape. At the moment he realized a blank wall faced him and the inferno was at his heels he woke up in a sweat that drenched him, his pajamas, the bedding. His body was trying to put out the fire.

"You can't live with nightmares like that," she had lectured him, straight out of the textbooks. His was a classical nightmare, she had said; he had to change whatever in his life was bringing it on. Eventually he had moved from arson to the police department, where they had put him in Homicide. Al Gruber, without any study of psychology at all, knew exactly the same thing: Whatever was bringing on his father's nightmares had to change to free him.

She had no doubt that Charlie would do whatever he could. As a private investigator now, with both of them retired more or less, pensioned, with a few investments that had been wise, a daughter who was self-sufficient through grants and scholarships and who seemed inclined to continue to gather degrees for the rest of her life, Charlie worked only when he wanted to. No trailing of wayward husbands or wives; no looking into pilfering at the office; no tracking down runaway kids. . . . Many of the jobs he did, jobs they did together, had been quite lucrative, she had to admit, but he no longer did anything for just the money. First he had to be interested. And he would not be able to turn down his old childhood friend.

"First thing we have to do," she said, stroking Brutus absently, "is find out what we can about the Wall family."

Charlie nodded.

On Thursday, three days after Al's visit, when Constance arrived home from the community center where she conducted an aikido class four days a week, Charlie was at the telephone in his downstairs office. She waved, and continued through the house.

Later, hoping she had done something about lunch, he found her in the kitchen sorting tomatoes that looked green as hell to him. She had a large basket of them, as if she had picked every damn one bigger than a marble.

He watched silently as she inspected a fruit and either put it to one side on the counter, or tossed it into a plastic pail. It was a bright sunny day again, just as she had predicted, and he was mystified.

"Why?" he asked finally.

"It's time," she said.

He knew the routine: Any blemish at all would consign the tomato to the pail and then to the compost; she would wrap the good ones individually in newspaper and gently pack them all into shallow boxes, and later that fall when others were paying a buck ninety-nine a pop, she would bring forth one perfectly ripe tomato after another. But why now? If he asked again, he suspected her answer would be even more irritating. Because. He went to the refrigerator and started to rummage for the makings of a sandwich.

"Another wash?" she asked, turning a tomato around and around appraisingly.

He grunted. He made them both sandwiches; she abandoned her task, washed her hands, and they ate. "I called Phil; I want to know who's in charge of security at the Wall place. He argued." That really meant very little; Phil Stern, their old friend in the insurance racket, head of a consortium of insurance companies, always argued first. "He'll call back. I have to call Al, and I don't have a damn thing to tell him."

He doubted that there was anything left on the public record that they had not uncovered, and that simply wasn't good enough. They had spent hours on their two computers, using every search engine available; they had read newspaper archives and reference books, magazine articles, financial profiles. . . . And what they had found out was that Henrik Wall had fled Rotterdam with his wife and children during the bombing that had reduced that city to rubble. The rest of his family had been wiped out; the family jewelry business destroyed, all records turned to ashes. Henrik, the youngest of the Wall offspring, had not been a diamond merchant, had gone into economics instead, but he had salvaged what he could of the business stock, had carried out of Holland as much as he and his family could manage. From Rotterdam he had escaped to Switzerland, and on to America, where he had quickly established himself as a knowledgeable financier and economist who was fluent in six languages, a great admirer of Roosevelt, and an avid supporter of the war effort. He had done well during the war years, and better in the years that followed.

Charlie suspected that the FBI had a file on him as thick as a telephone book, but publicly there was not a word to be found that diminished his patriotism, his honesty, his integrity in business dealings, or his propensity for making money. And his son Eric was a chip off the old block.

The problem was that the Wall story was as credible as the Gruber story.

The mansion on the Hudson had been built by another quick-money man who had made a killing on the stock market in the twenties, and then was killed by the collapse of the same market. The mansion had gone on the block for taxes; no takers. It had remained an empty mausoleum until Wall had bought it in the fifties, for approximately one-tenth of its assessed value at that time. It was worth millions now.

Concerning his wife, whose name was given as Marta Wall, not a word had been printed until her death was reported in 1966, "following a long illness." The only mention they had found of the daughter, Greta, was that she had survived her mother's death and in 1972 the death of her father. Period. Finis.

The four grandchildren who had been mentioned in the article about Henrik Wall's death were all Eric's children. By now, more than twenty years later, Eric probably had grandchildren. There was no mention of Greta's ever having been married.

Charlie sat brooding over a cup of coffee, and Constance returned to her green tomatoes. He liked watching the little play of muscles in her arms as she moved; she had good muscles, better than his, he sometimes thought. But the way she worked out, she should have good muscles. And, of course, he followed the thought, their builds were so different; he was stocky and she was long and fluid. And golden, he thought then.

She glanced up at him, smiled, and he realized he had been smiling.

"You have to finish them all now?" he asked.

"You just want to put off that phone call."

"Wrong. That's not what I want."

She laid down the tomato she was holding and washed her hands again.

Later, propped up on his elbow, watching her get dressed, he said, "I think I'll call Al tomorrow or maybe on Saturday. Let's take a little ride first, take a few pictures of the picturesque villages along the Hudson. Talk to a few people about this and that."

When Phil Stern called back that evening, he said snappishly, "Pal. That's P dot A dot L dot." Charlie groaned. P.A.L. Security was very good. Like the security around Fort Knox.

He was not at all surprised the next morning to see that there had been another frost overnight, harder than the last one, but still not a deep freeze. It would have gotten the tomatoes, Constance murmured at the breakfast table. Of course, he had thought.

He drove the first leg of the trip, to the village of Longview, and they got out to talk to various people about this and that. At a counter in a gift shop they talked to a woman with pink hair who said she was the chamber of commerce. "You're a little too early for the fall foliage," she said pleasantly. "But you're lucky, too, because then you can't even find a table in a restaurant, and forget motels unless you have reservations a couple of weeks in advance."

"What we're really interested in," Charlie said, "is that castle we saw on television. You know, last spring sometime? I said, as soon as we get the tomatoes in, let's take a run down and have a look at it. To think it's so close and we never even knew about it."

The chamber of commerce shook her pink head. "I'm afraid you won't get a look at it now, either. I don't know a soul who has had a look at it, except on television."

"They don't let the public in? You know, tours, something like that?" Charlie asked plaintively.

"Never. We were all surprised when they let those television people in. And you can't even see it from the road. We have the video, if you're interested in that. And I have a map with other historic buildings. . . ."

In a diner a teenage boy looked at Charlie in disbelief when he said he'd bet the kids in the area had found a way to sneak in.

"You kidding? Man, they got security. Be worth your leg to try to get inside that place."

An old man weeding a planter with yellow marigolds and red petunias said, "They used to drive through now and then, years ago, you know, but since the new highway was put in, they don't even do that." He went back to his weeding. Frost hadn't hit here yet. At home the petunias had become black overnight.

A clerk in a sports shop told them that the Walls never used local people for anything. They hired their servants out of a New York City agency, and *they* were snooty and didn't talk.

Their waitress in a café said, "There used to be a real cute guy come in now and then, a chauffeur or something, he said he was. He'd chat a little, flirt a little. You know? But he'd clam up if you mentioned the folks at the big house. He didn't stay long," she said regretfully.

They were running out of places where they could wander in, browse, ask a few questions, buy a trinket or a cup of coffee. "Library?" Charlie said dourly on the sidewalk, surveying the small town that had been prettified for the tourists with planters of blooming flowers, striped awnings, new paint. Everyone said they should come back when the trees turned; it got real pretty then. And it would, he knew; the maples would turn the ambient light pink, and cars would be bumper-to-bumper on the streets.

"You do the library; I'll take the bookstore," Constance said, as dejected as he was.

The bookstore was tiny and cluttered, with more used books than new ones. Two young women were chatting near a section of mysteries, and an ancient woman was in a rocking chair working a word-find puzzle.

"Help you?" she asked, keeping her pencil on the puzzle. Her pale face was like a maze of crisscrossing lines.

"Just browsing," Constance said, going to the section of local books and gardening books mixed together.

"Help yourself," the old woman said. Her lips moved as she searched for a word.

The two young women moved to the farthest corner of the store and continued to talk, their voices lower now. Constance glanced at them, and abruptly they walked past her, out to the sidewalk, where they stood talking.

"Oh, dear," Constance said. "Did I run them off?"

"They weren't going to buy anything," the woman said; she sniffed. "Never do. You looking for anything in particular?"

"Well, I saw that television show, the one that had the Wall mansion, and I thought there might be a book about it, the history of the building, the gardens. It was so beautiful."

"Used to have two books about it," the woman said. "After that show they both got bought."

"Maybe a dealer could find one of them for me."

"Doubt it. Self-published books like that, they don't get circulated all that much. The library has one you could look at. Shows pictures, great big cobwebs everywhere, boarded-up windows. But you can still see how pretty it must have been before Fielding died. Before the Walls came in."

"Oh, that must have been back in the thirties or forties. Even that would be a find."

"It was a long time ago. I had that book forty years, two copies. Gone now. Probably won't ever be another one. The folks up there like their privacy."

"Oh? Do you know them, the Walls?"

"Of course not! They don't mingle. There used to be a teacher, a speech therapist, something like that, who'd chat. Talked about books mostly. She loved to read and I did too. Still do, but my eyes get tired."

"Speech therapist? At the Walls' place. Whatever for?"

"For the girl. She couldn't talk, you know, not after what she went through, the bombing and all. For years she couldn't talk, and then, when she got her speech back, they had a therapist stay up at the house with her. Had to teach her the way you would teach a baby, and her a grown woman. She used to buy a book for her now and then, children's books."

"You had books in Dutch?"

"No, no. English. She spoke English just like you and me. But she stuttered. A bad stutter. I guess that's what they were trying to cure her of. Don't think it worked, though. You have to get them when they're younger. She was too old by then to correct her problem. Poor thing."

They were still chatting when a young woman ran into the

bookstore and knelt at the old woman's rocking chair. "You were dead right, Grandma. Twin boys. March twentieth. How did you know?"

Constance slipped out of the bookstore and saw Charlie in the passenger seat of their Volvo across the street, apparently studying a road map. She slid in behind the wheel.

"Jackpot?" he asked, folding the map.

"Something. I don't know what it is yet. Home?"

"Scenic route," he said, and directed her to the county road that ran past the Wall estate.

But there was nothing to see, they had to admit minutes later, when on Charlie's side sparse woods gave way to a stretch of mown grass, ten feet wide, backed up by a high chain-link fence. The grass continued on the other side of the fence for about six to eight feet, and the woods started again.

"That's it," Charlie said with resignation. "First fence wired; it's posted, High Voltage Warning. And then, inside the next border, an invisible fence."

"Invisible fence," she repeated.

"Right. Infrared sensors, a signal that sets off an alarm inside the house, the sheriff's office, who knows where else, and also gives a dog a pretty good jolt if it crosses it. Keeps your pooch in your yard. I bet those dogs are trained to charge through at a signal that the first fence has been breached."

"You see dogs?"

"Nope, and you won't, unless you cut through the outer perimeter. P.A.L.'s specialty, electric fences, trained dogs, radio signals. Expensive to install, then practically maintenance-free and cheap to run. . . ."

The high fence followed a narrow driveway that curved behind trees within twenty feet of the road; it reappeared on the other side of the drive. They followed it for another half mile to a T-intersection and Charlie said they might as well take the turn, hit the highway, and head for home.

A few minutes later, on the highway, heading north, Constance recounted what the old woman in the bookstore had told her.

"You scored more than I did. All I got was a floor plan and stuff about the original mansion. Lots of cobwebs. It's renovated, updated, modern plumbing and air-conditioning installed, new wiring. God knows how accurate any of it is." They both became silent.

She was trying to remember an article, a monograph, something she had read years earlier, eons earlier, studies of children who had suffered trauma during the blitz of London in World War II. Eudora . . . Dorothea . . .

"Honey, pull over," Charlie said quietly. His hand squeezed her thigh.

"What? What's wrong?"

"Just pull off the road."

She slowed, turned on the signal, and pulled over to the shoulder. "What happened?"

"Nothing. Not yet. You were doing about ninety. Let's change places."

"Dorothea Hardesty-Wyndham," she said.

"Right. Out with you. I'll drive." He drove the rest of the way home, and he did not ask her a question, or interrupt in any way whatever was happening in her brain any more than she would have interrupted him when an idea was shaping itself, taking form, finding substance.

That night Charlie got out steaks from the freezer, and made baked potatoes and a salad, in no mood to do more than the basics. Constance had gone straight up to her office, without a word, not even a hint of where her mind was wandering, what paths she was following, what goal she had glimpsed. Four hours later she still had not surfaced.

Then, after eating with an absentminded oblivion for his efforts, she said, "Charlie, what would it take? What would it take to prove Al's story?"

"The painting, for openers," he said.

"Not really. Eric Wall could explain it away. A maternal relative named Gruber had it in her family, or something else as convincing as Al's story. It's not enough. It could take years to settle, and Mr. Gruber may not have many years."

"A confession from one of the Waldmans, and we know Eric Wall, or Erik Waldman, isn't about to furnish it."

She nodded. "Gerde," she said softly.

Who might be a loony bird, he thought grumpily. "What's on your mind?"

"Some studies of children who were traumatized by the blitz of London. I had a dim memory, but I needed to pin down some facts. When you talk to Al you might say we're working on it," she suggested then.

"I want to talk to his father. I have some questions for him. For one thing, would he be willing to pay for an expert in old Dutch masters to examine and authenticate that painting?"

"One who is fluent in German," she added. "Written and spoken German. Or would it be in Flemish?" She thought a moment. "I know who would know an expert like that. Malvin Twining at Columbia. You remember Malvin, don't you?"

He didn't have a clue about Malvin, but it didn't matter. She knew everyone at Columbia University, he sometimes thought.

Then, decisively, she said, "Let's put together a list of questions and tell Al we'd like to see him and his father on Monday. I'll e-mail Malvin." She stood up and, without a glance at the remains of dinner on the table, she left.

He decided to call Al Gruber from the kitchen phone in order to keep the cats away from the scraps of meat, which, given a chance, they would snatch and take behind the couch, or to the middle of the bed, or somewhere else he preferred not to have it.

One of the things he needed to know was how rich the Grubers had been. Al had said Waldman was penniless, and the Grubers were prosperous, but that could mean anything from food every day at regular intervals to a family fortune worth a bundle. He needed to know. Henrik Wall's story was that he had fled to Switzerland with a fortune. Where had it come from if that story was a fairy tale and the Gruber silverware and jewels had not amounted to much?

Another thing was information about the other couple who had made the escape attempt across the Wester Ems. Al's father had survived, possibly the whole Waldman family had made it. If there was a remote chance that the other couple had come through, there might be a possibility of tracking them down. He had little faith that it could be done after so many years, but he wanted to know.

And what, if anything, was wrong with Greta Wall? If she was a nutcase, they couldn't rely on anything she had to say.

When Constance reappeared, she snapped, "Brutus! Get off the table!" The cat leaped down with a scrap of meat and fled toward the living room.

Charlie, still on the phone, raised his eyebrows and lifted one hand in apology. He had turned his back. Constance started to clear the dinner dishes, and soon Charlie wrapped up his conversation with Al.

"He says it wouldn't do us any good to ask his father questions. When he begins to talk about the distant past, he automatically lapses into German. So we'll meet Al and Bernice on Monday and hand over a list of questions that she'll ask, and she'll tape-record every word he says and translate it." She nodded, cutting up the leftover meat. She put it on the patio and whistled; all three cats bounded outside, and she closed the door and sat down at the table.

"During the war," she said, "so many children were traumatized by the bombing, the rockets, strafing, all the horrors of modern warfare."

Charlie sat down opposite her and listened.

"There were a lot of refugee children as well as British children sent out into the countryside, where they would be safer," she went on. "Some of them reverted to infantilism, to bed-wetting, autism, dyslexias of many sorts. Stuttering, babbling, ramblings, aphasia, verbal noise. Silence." She paused. "This was the part I thought I recalled, how they treated their speech disorders. Many, maybe even most children, got over their problems with the proper therapy, but some didn't respond. Then, in later studies, it was discovered that the children who responded most favorably were those who were treated by people like them, people with the same accents, the same language usage. Cockney children didn't respond well to the public-school-educated therapists; the upper-class children didn't respond to the Manchester accent, and so on. Not just the words, the language itself, but the inflections, the nuances, the references were important."

Baffled, Charlie listened, watched her, and waited. Her gaze was distant, abstracted, seeing a route that she could point out to him, but one that he never would find alone.

"I wondered," she said, "why Greta Wall didn't respond to therapy. They had money; they were in Switzerland, where there were marvelous doctors; they could afford the best to be had here in the States. Why didn't she respond? It wasn't physical damage, or she wouldn't have broken through her wall of silence in the fifties as she did."

She became silent, her gaze on the distant point only she could see. He covered her hand with his, and she came back to the present, back to him. Very softly he said, "They were using the wrong language."

"I think so. They were pretending to be Dutch. The two languages are so similar, adults, older children could easily go from one to the other, but she was too young. She had to hear the German of her infancy, her formative years."

"When she did start talking, they made her learn English," he said. "And she stuttered."

The next week was very busy. They met with Al and Bernice. She had inherited the gene that brought on premature white hair, but on her it was dramatically striking. Her nearly black hair was streaked with silver. She had been a very pretty girl, and she was a lovely woman, tall and beautifully proportioned, with light blue eyes and a dimple that appeared and vanished as if by magic.

Their father didn't know they were pursuing the investigation of the Walls, Al said, and Bernice added, "It would break his heart to be rejected a second time, to have Erik deny him again. And if it is a mistake, then nothing is to be gained by putting him through it."

She looked over the list of questions Charlie and Constance had prepared, and nodded several times. "This I know. The other couple, they were elderly, and very wealthy. They had come to the Gruberhaus a time or two in a big expensive car, and she wore many jewels: rings, brooches, necklaces. Father doesn't know their names. Our family's jewelry consisted of wedding rings, a watch, a cameo, a brooch with a beryl, things like that. Trinkets by comparison."

Then she looked at Constance with a puzzled expression. "You want to know about snacks, what the children ate after school? Why?"

"Filling in the frame," Constance said. "And don't worry about translating anything. We have a translator lined up."

When they were finishing up, Al asked, almost timidly, "Charlie, of course, we'll pay whatever expenses there are, the translator, the expert, all of it, but how do you intend to get anyone in to examine the picture?"

"By invitation," Charlie said. "It's the only way to get inside that pile of marble."

After that they went to meet the expert Malvin Twining had provided, an attorney who spoke fluent Dutch, German, and French, of course. *Of course*, Charlie had echoed silently. When he heard the name of the expert on old Dutch masters, his impulse had been to reject him out of hand. Smith Duncan Symington. No man with three last names was to be trusted, he thought dourly. He was inclined to dismiss him out of hand a second time when they met. Not only did Smith Duncan Symington have too many last names, he was an insufferable little snob. He received them in his home office in a hotel apartment overlooking Central Park. They had to pass through security, be announced, then be escorted to his floor and watched until he opened the door in person, and he stood five feet two at the most, and weighed at least one hundred ten pounds. His hair was shoulder length, silvery, and he was dressed in a pinstripe gray silk three-piece suit. He looked to be sixty. What he lacked in bulk he made up for in attitude.

He all but ignored Charlie and made a big deal of kissing Constance's hand. "Of course, my dear, if Malvin said I must see you, then I must. And, of course, there is no newly discovered van Gogh. There are a thousand, many thousands of faux van Goghs; a few swipes of a bright color on canvas, and lo, another van Gogh surfaces. But come in, come in. Tell me your little story."

The room he led them to was very large, with tables and chairs in primary colors that seemed to have been randomly scattered about, all from the bears' house of Goldilocks fame. Some too big, some too small, some just right. Two chairs here, three there, a sofa without a table within reach . . . Comic book furniture, Charlie thought; his distrust deepened when he realized there wasn't any real art on the walls, only posters.

Some he recognized: Brueghel's *The Tower of Babel;* a van Gogh, *The Potato Eaters;* Bosch, *The Garden of Earthly Delights*. Others he recognized without knowing the titles or the painters, but they were all just posters. There was a white desk without a scrap of anything on it, and two yellow director's chairs before it, a high-backed carved chair behind it. On a platform, Charlie bet himself. When they were all seated, he could have transferred money from one pocket to the other, paying up. Smith Duncan Symington was now higher than he was in the low-slung director's chair.

Continuing to ignore Charlie, the little man gazed at Constance with a faint smile. "You said on the phone that you believe you have located a van Gogh. Please, tell me more."

Charlie got up from his chair; it was harder to get out of than he had anticipated, and he caught the look of amusement on Symington's face, and the stern look from Constance.

"Mr. Symington," he said brusquely, "you're a lawyer, aren't you?"

"Of course."

"Before we tell you our *little* story, I have to know if this conference is privileged even if we don't retain you, or if you decide you don't want to get involved."

"Mr. Meiklejohn! My, my, you are a suspicious one, aren't you? Yes, this is a confidential preliminary procedure, the sole purpose of which is to determine if there is anything for me to become involved with. Is that satisfactory?"

Charlie walked to a window and gazed at the park twenty floors below, scowling. What he would like to do, he thought, was tie the little man to a kite string and fly him down to the ground. "Good enough," he said. He strode across the office, picked up a real chair, and carried it back close to the desk and sat in it. "Here's the story."

He told it, omitting some details, and without mentioning any names. Symington's faced changed as Charlie talked, all traces of mockery vanished, the supercilious expression deepened to one of intent concentration, and he began to frown.

"What was the palette? The colors?" he demanded impatiently when Charlie finished.

"Pretty much like those," Charlie said, pointing to the poster of *The Potato Eaters*.

"It would have been before Paris. After his theology studies, after Antwerp, before he . . . I don't believe it! Another fake! I must see it! Where is it?"

Charlie leaned back. "Do we retain you, then?"

"Yes, yes. Of course."

"If it's genuine, Mr. Symington, what would it be worth?"

Smith Duncan Symington jumped up from his chair and crossed the floor to the nearest wall of posters, where he gestured. "You looked at these prints with scorn. I saw the look, I understood. Mr. Meiklejohn, inspired art is priceless. No man should own a painting by an inspired artist, a genius whose hand is guided by God; his work belongs to the world. But there are men of wealth who bid each other to astronomical heights, millions, many millions of dollars in order to possess such art, their pitiful attempt to acquire God's grace.

"Museums can't compete with their gold, but such inspired art belongs in a museum, where the world can gaze at it in wonder and awe. And we should keep only these reminders, echoes of God's voice guiding the hands of genius, shadows of greatness."

A buzzer sounded from his desk and he hurried back to it, opened a drawer, and snapped, "Don't interrupt us." Then he turned back to Charlie. "Mr. Meiklejohn, I must tell you that it would be an incredible find if it is genuine. I also must tell you that I sincerely doubt that it is. With that understanding, how can I be of service?"

They talked for a long time without interruption, and finally Charlie said, "It's not enough to authenticate the painting. Stop there and, no doubt, Eric will come up with his own story and put it on the market to the highest bidder. We also need to prove that it belongs to Franz Gruber, and for that we need either Eric Wall or his sister, Greta, to admit the truth about their flight from Germany. Admit their names are really Erik and Gerde Waldman."

"How can you possibly make them do such a thing?" He sounded anguished.

"We're working on it," Charlie said.

They left soon after that, and out on the street again, Constance asked. "What do you think?"

"I think the little bastard's okay," he said.

A week later they returned to Smith Duncan Symington's Central Park South office. This time they were admitted by a very large blond man. "Ray Bromleigh," he said, stepping aside for them to enter. "Smith will be out in just a second."

Charlie raised his eyebrows. Smith? Bromleigh was in his forties and he looked as if he belonged in a football uniform, six feet two, over two hundred pounds, all muscles.

Just then a second door opened and Symington came into the room, almost dancing, it appeared. "Oh, good, you've met Ray. We have all the translations printed out for you. Mr. Meiklejohn, if I doubted your story before, and I certainly did, I no longer doubt. Listening to that wretched man's voice, his misery, it broke my heart. It still remains to be determined if the painting is an original van Gogh, of course, but that man told the truth exactly as he understands it."

Charlie cast an uneasy glance at Ray Bromleigh, and Symington smiled. "Ray's my right hand. He knows everything I know. He assists me in everything I do; he guards my person, and he will assist us in whatever plan you have devised. Now, please let us get comfortable and you tell me your plan."

"I'll let Constance fill you in while I go see a few people," Charlie said. "I'll be back in a couple of hours."

Actually he had only one person to see, Brian Posner, a Manhattan private investigator he used now and then, and as usual Brian had come through for him.

"Okay," Brian said, slouched in a booth at Tilley's Deli. They both had steins of beer and were waiting for sandwiches. "I got all the kids' license numbers, and the grandkids', those old enough to drive." He proceeded to tell Charlie everything he had found out about the Wall family during the past week. "One or another, or even a bunch of them, drop in over the weekends. Seems like they're a close family, keep in touch. One son, Roger, is out there a couple of days most weeks, Monday and Tuesday, then puts in time in his office at the Trade Tower. The old man is seventy-three, in good health, mostly retired, but not all the way, chairman of the board of umpteen foundations and such; they do business from the house, trading, meetings, whatever CEO types find to do. He's called a major philanthropist; funny thing is, the more he gives away, foundations, trusts, all kinds of things, the more money rolls in. Magic touch, I guess. There's a wife, Corinne, the sister, Greta, and a lot of help, don't know how many. They entertain a lot, but Greta doesn't show up much in company. She has something wrong, a speech impediment or something that embarrasses her. That's the word, anyway."

He stopped to drink his beer. "And that's all I could dig up. If anyone in that crew ever did anything illegal, underhanded, even shadowy, I can't find a trace of it. Maybe with more time . . ."

Charlie waved that away. "That's more than enough. It's about an hour, hour-and-a-half drive up there. Can you get out before dark? Check the cars in and check them out. If there's a procession of limos, for instance, I'd like to know, especially if they don't all vamoose before about two on Monday. We're paying a call on Monday, and I'd rather not walk in on royalty, or the secretary of state, someone like that."

Their pastrami on rye sandwiches came and they talked about mutual friends, old times, football. . . . Brian didn't offer any information about how he would stake out the Wall residence, and Charlie didn't ask for any. That was Brian's business.

He took his time returning to Smith Duncan Symington's apartment. When he arrived there, Constance gave him a thumbs-up sign.

"Smith knows exactly what to do," she said. "We're all set."

"We agreed you should both call me Smith," the little man said, not quite giggling. "Ray is the one people see, of course, when we deliver material. I try to keep a very low profile—"

Ray Bromleigh laughed boisterously, and Smith did giggle then.

"But the point is that even if Mr. Wall doesn't recognize me, he might be familiar with my name," Smith said. "I'm somewhat famous in my own circles," he added modestly.

After they reclaimed their car from the parking garage and were on their way out of the city, Charlie asked, "Are you sure about him, that he'll work out?"

"Yes, I'm sorry you don't like him. I think he's a dear."

"He's as giddy as a girl primping for her first date. He's having a big adventure."

"He's drunk with the idea that he might actually hold an original van Gogh, that he might be the one to prove that it's authentic," she said quietly.

On Monday at one forty-five, Charlie turned onto the narrow road that led to the Wall estate. A black limousine with darkened windows was on the shoulder, its hood raised, a man leaning over the engine block. Charlie stopped at the side of the limousine; the side door opened and Smith got out and quickly moved into the backseat of the Volvo. My God, Charlie marveled, the little man had cut his flowing silver hair; it was beautifully styled in soft waves, and it was reasonably short. He started to drive slowly, and after a few seconds the limo followed.

When he turned into the driveway of the Wall mansion, the limo pulled off the road once more, this time blocking the driveway, and the driver got out to peer under the hood again.

Charlie drove on to the gate, opened his window to reach out and push the call button on a box mounted on a concrete block. A security camera was mounted on an identical block on the other side of the fence. No one in the car moved or made a sound as they waited for a response.

Then a tinny voice said, "Please identify yourself."

"My name is Meiklejohn. I have urgent business to discuss with Mr. Eric Wall. Tell him it concerns Hanover."

"I'm sorry, sir. Mr. Wall is not receiving visitors," the voice said.

"Give him my message. Inform him that if he doesn't see me in private, then I will have a press conference this afternoon that will bring grief to him, his sister, and his entire family. I'll wait," Charlie said.

He glanced at Smith in the rearview mirror. Today the little man was not giddy; he was pale and nervous. He looked as if he had not slept enough over the weekend; his eyes were sunken, with deep shadows beneath them.

A different voice from the speaker broke the silence. "I don't know who you are, or what you want, but if you don't leave now, I'll call the sheriff."

Son Roger, Charlie thought, the voice of authority. "I want half an hour in private with Eric Wall and his sister. It's extremely important that I see them now. I suggest that you convey that message to him directly. It's about Hanover, and I either speak to him now or I go public. Tell him that and get back to me. I'm still waiting."

Smith was chewing his lip. They waited a minute, another minute. No one in the car spoke. The problem was that Charlie had meant what he said, he would go public, and he really didn't want to do that. He had nothing personally against the Wall family, and there was still the possibility that he and Constance were wrong on this one. In that case Wall probably would sue the pants off them. Maybe charge them with attempted extortion. He glanced at Constance, who looked serene and unconcerned, as if she didn't have a thought in her mind about lawsuits, civil actions, possible criminal charges. Another minute.

"Drive straight to the entrance," the voice of authority said then. "Don't stop on the way or open your car doors. Guard dogs are on the property and they will attack you if you attempt to leave your car before you arrive at the front entrance."

The gate swung open silently. In the backseat Smith made a strange keening noise and leaned back with his eyes closed. Constance put her hand on Charlie's thigh and squeezed gently, and he could feel the tension draining from him like water from a sieve. He drove forward.

They passed trees, then a wide velvet lawn, flanked on one far side by a tennis court, and a garden on the other. The smooth concrete drive gave way to a cobbled one, the cobblestones gently rounded, and then to a tiled entrance drive and finally a covered section in front of the entrance to the building. And it had been lifted, apparently, stone by stone from its site fronting the Grand Canal in Venice. Pale blue and pink marble, wide tall windows, marble pillars on both sides of several broad steps to the front double doors.

Two men stood on the top step watching their approach. The taller of the two was dressed in a short-sleeved T-shirt and chino pants, the other wore a black suit.

"Please stop there," the taller man said when they were out of the car. "Mr. Hoskins will look through your bags, if you don't mind."

Charlie shrugged, and they waited for Mr. Hoskins to make a feeble attempt at a search. It was very clear that he would prefer to be inside polishing the silver or something. He glanced inside Constance's purse; then, with an apologetic little smile, handed it back to her. His glance inside the slim case Smith had brought along was just as cursory and embarrassing to him. He approached Charlie and touched his pockets with a light and reluctant pat that was embarrassing to both him and Charlie.

Hastily he retreated back up the stairs, and the taller man waved him inside the house.

"I'm Meiklejohn, and these are my associates, Leidl and," Charlie paused for a beat, then said, "Smith. As I said, my business is with Mr. Eric Wall and his sister."

Constance inclined her head fractionally when he mentioned her name, but to his surprise, Smith made a deep, old-world bow of a sort that Charlie had seen only in movies.

"I'm Roger Wall. Come in. Half an hour, then security will arrive. My father will see you in his study." He was a tall lean man with sharp features, a long thin nose, clearly defined cheekbones, a rather jutting chin. He looked as if he had spent a lot of time out on the tennis court. Charlie had studied pictures of his father and he thought that was exactly what Roger Wall would look like in his seventies.

Roger stepped aside for them to enter a mammoth foyer with a black-and-white marble floor, black marble stairs on both sides curving upward, held in place by black marble caryatids of nymphs who became taller but no broader as the stairs ascended. Anorexic nymphs. There were many closed doors, and a hallway that continued back through the mansion. Charlie gazed about the foyer, then started to walk toward the left. He had studied the old floor plan, and although they might have installed heating and electricity, air-conditioning, new everything, he was pretty certain they had not moved a ten-foot-wide green marble fireplace.

"Not the study," he said easily. "No hidden cameras, tape recorders, buttons to bring in the dogs. Over here somewhere. This room." He opened a door, and to his relief, there was the fireplace, and even more to his relief, the painting on the wall next to it. "Tell Mr. Wall we'd like to talk to him and Ms. Wall in here." He motioned to Constance and Smith to follow him, and entered the room.

Smith was very good, he had to admit; he saw the painting

instantly, and his every instinct must have been spurring him toward it, but he merely stood clasping his black case with both hands and gazed at the floor. One tiny jerk of his body gave him away, not a sound, not another motion, just that one little start of excitement.

They remained near the open doorway, but Charlie took in the furnishings of the room with a swift glance. At one end there was a love seat and two chairs, all dainty-looking with carved spindly legs and rose velvet upholstery. On the opposite wall, thirty feet away, backed by a tall, wide window, there was another grouping, several carved chairs at a table that gleamed with inlay of some sort. Constance nodded slightly. There was other furniture, but those were the two sites they had chosen from studying the video.

At the approach of footsteps, they turned to see Eric Wall and his sister approaching. He was a senior version of Roger, tall, lean, upright, gray-haired, dressed in a sports coat and casual slacks, shirt opened at the throat; she had inherited some peasant genes: stockier, broader-looking although not plump, just heavier bones, a wider face, bigger eyes. She was wearing blue jeans and a T-shirt, boots. Roger was behind them.

Now Constance and Smith moved to one side, and Charlie stepped forward as the Walls entered the room. "Mr. Wall, I'm Meiklejohn, and these are my associates, Leidl and Smith. I am relieved that you agreed to talk to us."

No one offered to shake hands. Eric Wall inclined his head fractionally and Greta Wall looked almost panic-stricken.

Constance nodded and Smith made his deep courtly bow to Eric Wall, and then stepped up to Greta, lifted her hand, and pressed it to his lips. He stepped back and made another bow.

"Ms. Wall," he said, "I am honored to meet you."

Charlie was amazed; Smith had assumed a heavy German accent. He sounded like Henry Kissinger.

Roger had stopped at the doorway. "I'll be right outside," he said and pulled the door closed.

"Now you tell me what the devil this is all about," Eric Wall said.

Charlie glanced at Greta as if trying to make a decision, then he looked around the room. "Mr. Wall, I'm a private investigator and my inquiries into a certain matter have unearthed some pretty surprising facts." He looked at Greta again, and said in a lower voice, "Could we just step over there for a minute or two, let me give you a quick summary, before we get to the paperwork Smith has brought?" He started to walk toward the window, and Eric Wall followed.

"Ms. Wall," Constance said brightly then, "the gardens are so lovely. You have irises blooming! In late September!" She was on one side of Greta, Smith on the other. When they both began to walk toward the love seat across the room, Greta seemed helpless. She moved with them. "Are those special irises, or planted late, or what? Mine just bloom in May and June."

"Th-th-th-ey are reb-b-b-b-bloomers," Greta said. Her stammer was very bad. She looked past Constance in agonized embarrassment. Constance pretended not to notice.

"Rebloomers? I never even heard of them. Oh, I have to make a note, remind myself to look them up in a catalogue, or at a nursery." She and Smith maneuvered Greta to the love seat and seated themselves in the chairs at the sides of it. Constance groped in her bag for a notebook, and turned on her tape recorder; she brought out the notebook, made the note, slipped it back in her bag, and placed it on the floor between her and Greta. "Of course," she said, "growing up in Europe, you must have been familiar with many flowers we simply don't know about. I imagine childhood in Europe is quite different from childhood here in the States."

Smith leaned forward. "Bah! No child should have to grow up in America!" He looked at Greta with a grimace. "They feed their children cold cereal made from sawdust, and Tinkies." His accent was lovely, just thick enough.

Greta looked bewildered, and Constance said disdainfully, "I don't know what you're talking about. Tinkies?" She smiled. "Oh, you mean Twinkies, the little cakes? There's nothing wrong with them now and then. Children love them."

"Ach! They don't know. When I was a child, we went out in June and picked the little wild strawberries. One taste, like a little kiss from heaven in your mouth. Cook mashed them, not too much, just enough, and added a touch of sugar, not like here, not like Tinkies, just a touch. While they drank in the sugar, Cook made little pancakes, just so." He held up his hands to indicate the size. "Just so. Cook rolled the strawberries in the little pancakes while they were still warm, and we ate them. Heaven!"

"With b-b-b-butter," Greta said.

"Ach, the butter! Almost white, and so sweet! Like honey!"

Charlie and Eric Wall were seated at the inlaid table, Charlie leaning forward speaking earnestly, too softly to be heard across the room, telling Eric the cock-and-bull story he and Constance had made up over the weekend. Neither Charlie nor Constance had any idea how long he could stall Eric.

She said indifferently, "I'm sure they were very nice."

"Nice! Nice! She doesn't know," he said to Greta sadly.

"I remember the apple fritters!" he cried. "Ach, the cold wet fall, walking home in the rain, and the steamy kitchen with the apple fritters ready. So round and golden, hot, with honey poured on top."

"N-n-no, n-n-no," Greta said. "N-n-not honey. Sugar with cinnamon! Powdered sugar with cinnamon."

"Honey," he insisted. "I licked it from my fingers."

"The cinnamon and sugar melted together, like syrup," Greta said dreamily. "Always cinnamon and sugar."

Smith hit his forehead with the palm of his hand. "Dummkopf! Fräulein, you are correct. Honey on the *liebkuchen!* Warm honey on the hot *liebkuchen*. We would tell the girls to beg for a taste, just a little taste of the cookie dough, and Cook would turn away just long enough for us to put a finger in the bowl and have a taste, just so long. Citron and mace, cinnamon and . . . and . . . How do you say it?" He muttered a word in German.

Constance knew very well that the word he wanted was *nutmeg*; they had written this script together, using phrases and memories provided by the tape recording of Franz Gruber's voice.

"Nutmeg," Greta said softly, her eyes large and luminous, and very distant, gazing into a childhood from more than sixty years in her past. "He said raw dough would give us worms. Of course, it never did. Sometimes he let me grind the nutmeg."

"And when the sheets of *liebkuchen* came out of the oven, golden brown, puffed up just a little, then he poured on the honey. Always warm, from a little warming pot on the back of the stove." Most of this he said in his accented English, but some was in German.

Greta nodded. She said something in German.

"When she recognizes a single German word," Constance had told Smith, "sprinkle more of them in whatever you're saying, just now and then, a few. Don't overdo it." He was doing that now, lapsing into an infrequent word or a phrase in German, as if it was easier to recall the past in his native tongue. If Constance hadn't known the script, she would have been at a loss to follow the conversation now. Both Smith and Greta ignored her, leading one another through the maze of a lost childhood.

From across the room she heard Eric Wall's voice, harsh and cold, "This is preposterous! I tell you we had no relations by that name!" He looked ready to jump up, end the ridiculous farce. Charlie caught his arm and said something in an inaudible voice. He cast a glance toward Constance and she spread her fingers, meaning five minutes. Stall him for five more minutes. Here, at this end of the room, Smith and Greta were engaged in an animated dialogue, part German, part English. Greta was smiling, correcting him again. Constance reached down into her bag for a tissue, the signal for Smith to go into the next phase. If this was going to work, it had to be now. Eric Wall wouldn't grant them much more time.

Smith stopped speaking in the middle of something. He ducked his head, and his voice became mournful as he spoke in German. The phone call in the middle of the night, the hurried preparations, the flight. Constance caught the words *das boot*.

"*Das boot*," Greta repeated, nodding. Then, "*Das boot!*" A torrent of German followed, she began to rock back and forth, staring sightlessly. "Hulga! Hulga! Herr Gruber! *Nein,* Papa! *Nein!* Herr Gruber!"

Eric Wall leaped up from his chair; Charlie caught his arm and held him back. Eric struggled, opened his mouth to yell out.

"Don't call your son unless you want to tell him the truth, Mr. Waldman," Charlie said.

Ashen-faced, Waldman sank into his chair and watched his

sister fight with the devils from the past. She was crying out, speaking incoherently, calling for Papa, for Mama. Calling Hulga. Suddenly she clamped one hand on her cheek and the other one over her mouth, and she stopped making a sound, stopped all movement. She looked catatonic: wide-eyed and paralyzed.

Constance knelt before the older woman and very gently took her hands from her face and held them both. "It's all right, Gerde. You're safe. You're safe now. It's all over." She spoke quietly, then, when Gerde remained frozen, she said to Smith, "Tell her. She's safe now, it's all over. That was a long time ago."

He leaned in to Gerde and stroked her cheek and talked to her in German. A shudder convulsed her, and her eyes shifted, another shudder, and she started to weep. Constance put her arms around her and held her while she wept.

Charlie released his grip on Erik Waldman's arm, and together they crossed the room, where Erik stood helplessly by Constance and Gerde. Gradually her sobs lessened, and at last she said in a choked voice, "I want to go to my room now. Please, I want to go to my room."

Constance helped her rise, and walked with her to the door. Gerde didn't look at any of them.

"Do you want help? Can I come with you?" Constance said.

"No. No. I need to be alone now. To think. I . . . I need to think."

"Greta—Gerde, I'll come up and we'll talk. Rest now and then we'll talk," Erik said huskily. His sister nodded and opened the door.

Roger was in the foyer. "It's all right," Erik said to him. "She's had a shock and she needs to rest. I'll be out directly." He closed the door and faced Charlie. "What do you want from us? Franz sent you, didn't he? What does he want? Money? Retribution? Revenge?"

Before Charlie could speak, Smith blurted, "She said, Gerde said your father killed that little girl, he killed Hulga. He pushed her face into the mud and killed her!" The German accent was gone, his voice shrill, and he was deathly pale.

"She isn't the only one he killed that night," Charlie said bleakly. "He killed everyone who survived the shooting, didn't he? Killed them and stripped them of everything they had, papers, money, gems, everything. He became a wealthy man off those dead bodies. If he had been able to, he would have killed Franz Gruber, or did he think he had killed him?"

Erik Waldman closed his eyes hard for a moment, then he groped for the nearest chair and sat down. He had turned into a very old man. "He was mad with fear," he said after a moment. "He said shut up, shut up or they'll hear you. Shut up. But Hulga and Gerde were hysterical, Herr Gruber's blood was all over them. They couldn't stop crying; Hulga kept calling for her mother and father, for Franz, and he pushed her face down. I don't think he meant to kill her, but she couldn't stop screaming. Her mother saw, she was crawling through the mud, trying to get to Hulga, and she was crying. She was sick. They had to carry her, but she kept crying for Hulga, crawling in the mud, and he hit her. He said we couldn't leave any papers, nothing for the Nazis to find, because they would track us all down, our friends, relatives, everyone who knew us. They would find them all and torture them, put them in the labor camps and they would all die. He said when the tide ran out, between the tides, they would come in their boats and they would take anyone they found and kill them. They kept shooting up and down the shore, into the water. . . . Searchlights, flares . . . The old man tried to pull himself up from the water, and he kept slipping back, and he collapsed. I don't know if he was dead. I don't know if his wife was dead, but he said we had to take their clothes, their papers, everything, leave nothing for the Nazis to find. And then Franz was dragging himself out of the water, clinging to rushes, to reeds, whatever he could grasp, and my father pulled him up. His head was bleeding. It was raining, so slippery, deep mud, steep. My father said Franz was dying and help get his clothes off. And he let him slide back into the water."

He had spoken in a monotone, staring at his hands on his knees. Abruptly he stood up and went to the window, with his back to them. "Gerde couldn't stop screaming, and he slapped her hard and said, Shut up, shut up, don't make a sound or they'll kill you. We gathered up everything and we ran until we could not run, and then we walked until daylight, as far away from there as we could get. He said we were no longer Germans, we were Dutch now, and German must never be spoken in our house."

He became silent.

"When Franz Gruber wrote to you, you turned him away. You kept up the pretense, didn't let the ugly past interfere with the good times," Charlie said brutally.

Waldman turned to face him, his own face now shadowed with the light behind him. "Mr. Meiklejohn, ever since that night there have been no good times. My mother was broken that night, she never recovered. Her death was a blessing to her. Gerde was silent for nearly fifteen years, terrified of our father, terrified of making a sound, and when she regained her voice, he despised her because she stammered. She never spoke to him unless he demanded a response. I determined that my own children would never have cause to hate or fear me, that they would never have cause to feel shame on my account, and then Franz wrote. I knew it would all crumble to nothing again, my children and theirs would live with the nightmare Gerde and I have shared ever since that night in the Wester Ems. I kept up the pretense."

"Mr. Waldman," Constance said, in what Charlie recognized as her professional voice, not cool exactly, but a voice that carried conviction firmly, "you were twelve, your sister just eight, children, powerless, caught in a timeless moment of absolute terror. You could do nothing to affect the events taking place, and afterward you could not undo them. Later, when you had a choice, you chose your family, a decision no one who has not had to make such a decision can either condemn or condone. Today, you have nothing to fear from Franz Gruber. He intends no harm to you or your family. What you tell your children only you will determine. If you tell them nothing about this visit, no one else ever will either. Please believe me, Charlie said at the outset that this is a private matter. It is."

He stared hard at her, then said, "What does he want from me? Why did you come?"

Charlie answered. "He wants what is his. The painting." He pointed to it.

Waldman turned his gaze to the painting. "Take it."

They watched Smith take down the painting and carry it reverently to the inlaid table, where he carefully removed the frame. Moving with the deft precision of a surgeon, he took off the brown paper from the back; the crackle of the brittle paper was the only sound in the room. In a hushed voice he read the inscription, first in Dutch, the way it was written, and then he translated it: ". . . this imperfect gift."

"I never saw the back," Waldman whispered. "I never even saw it." His voice broke. He turned away and walked stiffly to the door. "Perhaps you will leave now."

Charlie turned off the television in the small room they called their joint office, the room that held household records, odds and ends, and the TV. Constance had left minutes before, tired of the endless weather reports he kept tuning into. It was February, she had said reasonably; they could expect snowstorms in February. Blizzard, he had snarled, and now the wind was starting. He could feel it in every bone, a rising wind. He returned to the living room, where the fire burned hot and steady, and he regarded the poster that had arrived early that day. It was propped up on the couch: *A Country Inn,* identical to the one that hung in the newly renovated Gruberhaus.

The first week in October, Constance had received a gift from Gerde. Charlie had gawked when she opened it. "Roots and dirt," he had said in disbelief.

"Rhizomes!" She read the accompanying note: "We divided the rebloomers, and I would like to express my gratitude with this small token. It isn't too late to plant them, I think." She had wandered out to the back garden to find the perfect place for them, happy as a child at Christmas.

And now, today, another gift for both of them, the poster from Smith. He had called a week earlier. "We just got home, Charlie. Ray and I. From Amsterdam. It's beautiful in its proper home, The van Gogh Museum. Lovely!" He had babbled on and on, more giddy than ever, telling Charlie that Gerde had taken an apartment in Manhattan and divided her time between it and the mansion on the Hudson. She and Franz Gruber had renewed their friendship; he even cooked for her now and then. He, Smith, representing the Grubers, had negotiated the sale and they had been compensated adequately, he said, adequately. Charlie held the phone away from his ear and grimaced as the little man ran on; he already knew all this, but he had

3-11

listened patiently. "I'm sending you a little present, Charlie, for you and your lovely Constance." He giggled, and Charlie held the phone farther away from his ear. "An imperfect gift," Smith said. "No more than a token." And today it had arrived, another imperfect gift they would have to find a proper place for.

The wind gusted; a geyser of sparks flared briefly, and he shivered. What would make for a perfect gift, he wondered. Just then Constance came into the living room carrying two steaming mugs of Irish coffee. He grinned. *"Mit schlag?"*

She laughed and nodded. She knew how much he hated it when the wind rose. And she knew a few cures. *"Mit schlag,"* she said, setting the mugs down on the table between their chairs.

Watching her, he had his answer to the question what would make a perfect gift, and it wasn't coffee.